PENGUIN BOOKS

NEROPOLIS

A former professor of history, Hubert Monteilhet has achieved
considerable success in France as the author of highly intelligent
detective works, several of which have been filmed. He is also the
author of *Les Derniers feux*, which broke new ground for him in
the field of theology. In *Neropolis* he unites this interest with his
other passion, the history of the Graeco-Roman world.

HUBERT MONTEILHET

 # NEROPOLIS

A NOVEL OF LIFE IN NERO'S ROME

TRANSLATED
FROM THE FRENCH BY
CHRISTOPHER
ROBINSON

PENGUIN BOOKS

PENGUIN BOOKS

Published by the Penguin Group
27 Wrights Lane, London w8 5tz, England
Viking Penguin Inc., 40 West 23rd Street, New York, New York 10010, USA
Penguin Books Australia Ltd, Ringwood, Victoria, Australia
Penguin Books Canada Ltd, 2801 John Street, Markham, Ontario, Canada l3r 1b4
Penguin Books (NZ) Ltd, 182–190 Wairau Road, Auckland 10, New Zealand

Penguin Books Ltd, Registered Offices: Harmondsworth, Middlesex, England

First published in France by Editions Julliard 1984
This translation first published in Great Britain by Viking 1988
Published in Penguin Books 1990
1 3 5 7 9 10 8 6 4 2

Original copyright © Editions Julliard, 1984
This English translation copyright © Christopher Robinson, 1988
All rights reserved

Printed and bound in Great Britain by
Richard Clay Ltd, Bungay, Suffolk

❧ CONTENTS ❧

MAPS
ROME IN THE TIME OF NERO
ITALY IN THE TIME OF NERO
THE ROMAN EMPIRE IN THE TIME OF NERO

THE JULIO-CLAUDIANS

PART ONE   7
PART TWO   145
PART THREE   305
PART FOUR   461
PART FIVE   631

GLOSSARY   752

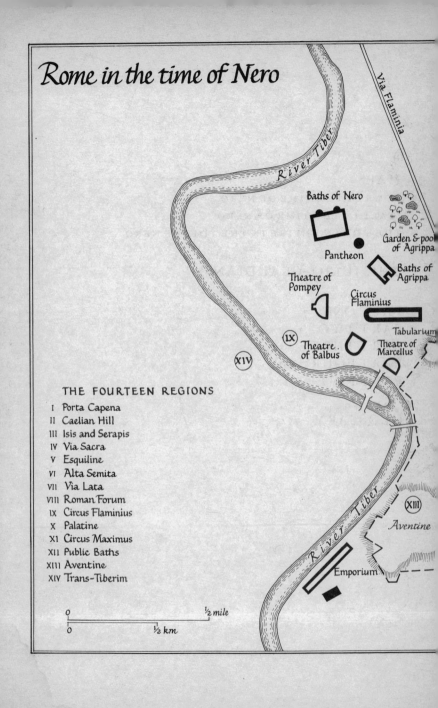

Rome in the time of Nero

Via Flaminia

River Tiber

Baths of Nero

Garden & pool of Agrippa

Pantheon

Baths of Agrippa

Theatre of Pompey

Circus Flaminius

IX

Theatre of Balbus

Tabularium

Theatre of Marcellus

XIV

THE FOURTEEN REGIONS

I Porta Capena
II Caelian Hill
III Isis and Serapis
IV Via Sacra
V Esquiline
VI Alta Semita
VII Via Lata
VIII Roman Forum
IX Circus Flaminius
X Palatine
XI Circus Maximus
XII Public Baths
XIII Aventine
XIV Trans-Tiberim

River Tiber

XIII

Aventine

Emporium

0   ½ mile
0   ½ km

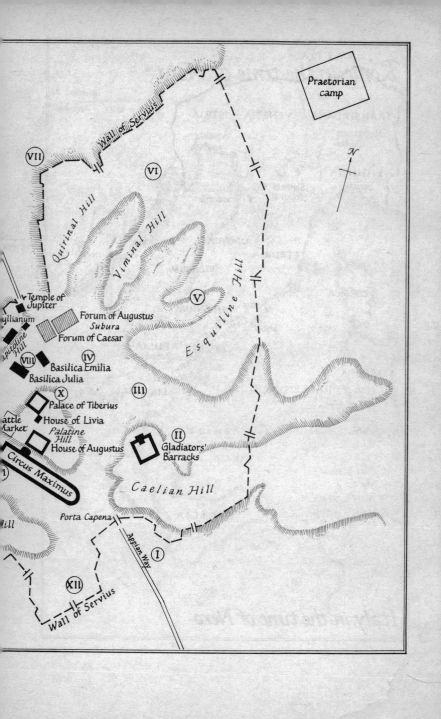

Praetorian
camp

N

Wall of Servius

VII

VI

Quirinal Hill

Viminal Hill

Esquiline Hill

Temple of
Jupiter

ullianum

Forum of Augustus
Subura
Forum of Caesar

V

apitoline Hill

VII

Basilica Emilia

IV

Basilica Julia

X

III

Palace of Tiberius

House of Livia

attle
Market

Palatine
Hill

House of Augustus

II

Gladiators'
Barracks

Circus Maximus

Caelian Hill

ill

Porta Capena

Appian Way

I

XII

Wall of Servius

Italy in the time of Nero

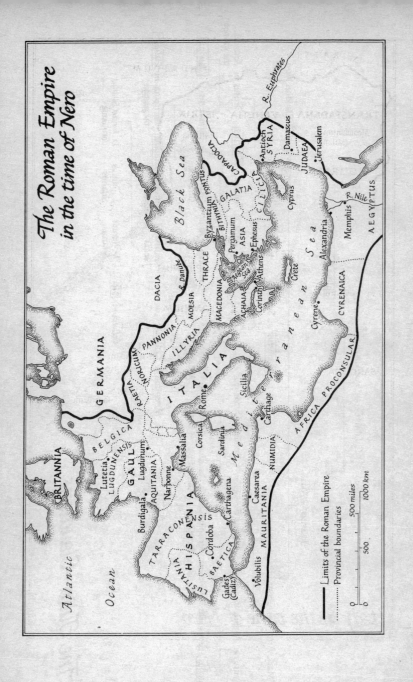

The Roman Empire
in the time of Nero

Atlantic

Ocean

BRITANNIA

GERMANIA

Lutetia
BELGICA
GAUL
LUGDUNENSIS
Lugdunum
Burdigala
AQUITANIA
Narbonne
Massalia
TARRACONENSIS
LUSITANIA
HISPANIA
Córdoba
BAETICA
Carthagena
Gades
(Cádiz)
Volubilis
MAURITANIA
Caesarea

RAETIA
NORICUM
PANNONIA
ILLYRIA
ITALIA
Rome
Corsica
Sardinia
Sicilia
Carthage
NUMIDIA
AFRICA PROCONSULAR.

DACIA

R. Danube

MOESIA
THRACE
MACEDONIA
Byzantium PONTUS
BITHYNIA
GALATIA
CAPPADOCIA
ASIA
Pergamum
Ephesus
ACHAIA
Corinth *Athens*
Aegean
Sea
Crete

Black Sea

Mediterranean Sea

CILICIA
Cyprus
Antioch SYRIA
Damascus
JUDAEA
Jerusalem
R. Euphrates

Alexandria
Memphis
AEGYPTUS
R. Nile

CYRENAICA
Gyrene

— Limits of the Roman Empire
······ Provincial boundaries

500 miles
1000 km
500
0

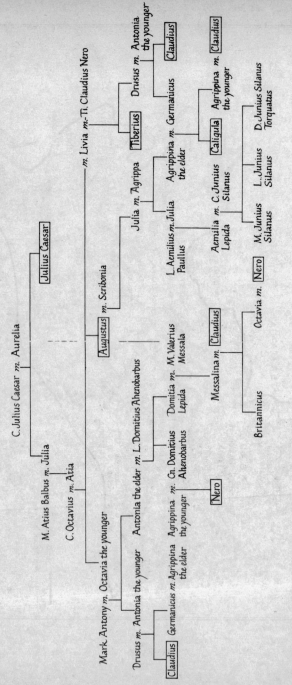

The Julio-Claudians

❧ PART ONE ❧

❈ CHAPTER ❈

I

Aponius' dresser was still busy draping his master's toga about him. He kept tightening and then loosening the belt around his waist; he gave a graceful flowing fall to the fold of material that served as the senator's pocket; he kept a careful watch to see that the broad band of deep purple along the straight edge of the semicircular piece of cloth was still in its right place – the rich colour stood out against the flat whiteness of the newly pressed wool. Ceremonial togas had recently become absurdly vast; it was out of the question to think of putting them on without professional help. And, thanks to the irritating little attentions of his barber, Aponius was already late, even though he had risen with the autumn sun.

Pomponia, who at this time of day should still have been sacrificing at the altars of sleep or entrusting her mature charms to the aesthetic care of her maids, appeared in a dressing-gown, with her hair loose. There was an air of disquiet about her. She had had a bad dream, the same bad dream which had haunted her in the first days of her remarriage, a dozen years earlier, when Aponius had almost been implicated in the fall of Sejanus, the over-ambitious favourite of the emperor Tiberius. Her husband, changed into an eagle, had circled majestically over the city a few times and suddenly fallen out of the skies into one of the yards at the back of the palace. There the servants had swooped upon him, plucked him and speared him on a spit. The dream was all the more remarkable in that there was nothing eagle-like about Aponius.

Aponius shrugged his shoulders. One was covered by his toga, the other was left free so that he could gesticulate while delivering important speeches – though he was unlikely ever to make any. He was not, of course, a man to dabble in free-thinking, and would never have been so rash or impious as to ignore dreams and portents on principle. Had Caesar listened to his fourth wife, Calpurnia, he would have survived the Ides of March. But after all, within living memory no one had come to any harm at an auction of gladiators.

'But it's not an ordinary auction, Marcus. The whole thing is very peculiar.'

'However extraordinary or peculiar it may be, I shall come back in one piece!'

'But why should Caius put so many "Juliani" up for sale?'

These imperial gladiators were very highly thought of in Rome, as in many cities in Italy and the conquered provinces. They took pride in their title, which recalled the fact that they belonged to the imperial house itself.

The reply was obvious: 'Our dear emperor has run through all the money he inherited from Tiberius. Now he must make the most of what he's got. He's been laying on public shows ever since he came to the throne: so he's capitalizing on the left-overs.'

'But up to now he's bought gladiators, not sold them.'

'Precisely. In his obsession with gladiatorial games, he increased his manpower far beyond reasonable limits. So he's getting rid of the surplus today.'

'But a sale of this sort is normally of interest only to Italian or provincial promoters who are specialists in the trade. Why should Caius invite senators – and so many of them? Why should *they* need gladiators?'

'It's true that nowadays the emperor is the only man who can still stage a public Games in Rome, whether he does it in his own name or indirectly through some favourite he wants to honour. But you're forgetting that lots of senators have substantial groups of "clients" outside Rome – friends or protégés rich enough to put on a spectacular entertainment to dazzle a town council and swing an election. People like that are always more than happy to have a few gladiators put at their disposal.'

'But that doesn't apply to you. You've only got a small number of "clients", and they're all in Rome.'

'All the more reason not to spend any money. I can't lose.'

'It's the first time an emperor will ever have been seen at an auction of gladiators. And he won't even be there in the honourable role of buyer, as a *munerarius* looking to his own popularity. He'll be selling off his own gladiatorial *familia*. That's not a very respectable job. I thought the imperial freedmen in charge of the barracks or their subordinate *lanistae* were usually supposed to do that sort of thing.'

It was a relevant point. The professional traffic in gladiators was not much higher in public esteem than the provision of bodies for sexual pleasure. There was not much to choose between the ill-repute of the pimp, trading in prostitutes of both sexes, and that of the *lanista* who kept the amphitheatres supplied. The name, moreover, was said to be appropriately derived from *lanius*, a meat-merchant.

Admittedly, those *lanistae* who were responsible for training the élite Juliani were not as utterly despised as the rest. Their role was too important, and besides, they were attached to the royal household. But no gladiatorial promoter, any more than any pimp, ever left on his tombstone a flattering inscription revealing his profession. This state of affairs suited the emperor who employed them, the public which required their services, and the gladiators whose bravery washed away the stain of their ill-repute. The stain of the *lanista* and the pimp, like that of tart and fancy-boy, lacked the mitigation of courage. They could only be cleansed by the public baths. Such is the inconsistency of public opinion.

Pomponia had a point ... But since illness had unhinged Caius (or Caligula, as he was more familiarly known), one more bit of odd behaviour on his part was neither here nor there. Aponius could have told his wife a tale or two, if his dresser hadn't been taking so active an interest in their conversation.

He sat down to have his shoes put on – dazzling, red leather, calf-length boots with the gold crescent moons on them, showing that he had held a curule magistracy – and remarked euphemistically that Caligula was a whimsical man who was capable of anything. And that was the crux of the matter. Rome had had plenty of time to form an opinion of other forms of cruelty, debauchery and dishonour. What discomfited serious men in particular about Caius' aberrations was their very unpredictability. That and an element of humour in which a zany logic played a part. At one point he had fed the wild beasts intended for the Games on convicts normally reserved for the same occasion. It was good for the beasts, he said, to get a foretaste of the diet of live flesh, because it would remind them of the happy days of their lost freedom. No zoologist could have proved him wrong. It was a whim in the worst possible taste!

But Aponius was neither eagle nor lion. What atrocity was there to fear at an auction of gladiators? While his boots were being laced up, Pomponia, who was far from convinced, made a last effort to persuade him. She argued that she could sense a trap – without, it's true, being able to give any rational explanation. And what use is intuition without reason? Aponius did his best to reassure her in a light-hearted way. He finished by saying:

'Look, Caius has invited me, along with a lot of others. If I claim to be unwell, you know him well enough to see that he'll assume I distrust him and take it as an insult. And that would be the surest way of getting myself into trouble.'

The litter-bearers were waiting under the outer portico of the entrance hall; with them was the crowd of clients Aponius had assembled to accompany him on his way to and from the auction. It would look very odd if he sent them away now.

He disengaged himself from Pomponia's embraces with characteristic Roman coolness and went out of the private apartments. Between them his barber, his dresser and his wife had made him lose precious time, and the sale would already have started. Would late arrival put him in bad odour with the emperor?

As he was crossing the *atrium*, the great clock struck half-past the third hour. Before getting into his litter, he drew his miniature sundial out of the fold of his toga and checked the time by the sun, which had risen some way into the cloudless blue sky. Mercifully the *atrium* clock appeared to be fast. As the litter swung to and fro in its precipitate descent of the aristocratic Caelian Hill and in the slow climb up the Palatine which immediately followed it, Aponius was struck, as so many others have been, by the unfathomable difficulty of calculating the exact time in Rome. One began to wonder whether they were going the right way about it . . .

Both day and night were divided into twelve hours. Accordingly, as the solstice changed, daytime and night-time hours expanded or shrank by half an hour either way. The equinoxes were the only days in the year when the hours were kind enough to be all the same length. And to make things even more confusing, the twenty-four hours of the ordinary day were calculated from midnight to midnight, each new day beginning as the sixth hour of the night became the seventh, i.e. at a point when the sun was no longer present to offer any precision to a sleeping world. Midday was obvious, midnight was anything but clear. The Greeks – and the Jews, apparently – were perhaps more sensible in starting their astronomical day at sunset, and the Babylonians theirs at sunrise.

The popularization of the concave sundial with its little pointer, the Greek *gnomon*, had been a great step forward. The way the sun lit the instrument showed, by one dimension of the shadow projected, the length of the daylight hours, and by the other the height of the sun at any given season. But every *gnomon* had to be constructed with great precision to suit the latitude of the place where it was to be used, and had to be orientated with the utmost care. Aponius thought with amusement of the famous story of M. Valerius Messala, who at the start of the First Punic

War had proudly presented the electoral assembly with a *gnomon* taken as booty at Catania. As a result the official time in Rome had been wrong for three whole generations!

Then water-clocks had become popular. They had the advantage of telling the time at night too. The water dripped out of a cylindrical glass receptacle, whose surface was divided vertically into months and horizontally into hours. Aponius even had a rotating clock, which always presented those consulting it with a view of the relationship between the column of water as it dripped out and the calibrations for the hours of the current month. So, in theory at least, the clock could cope with the fluctuating length of the hours on a monthly basis, variations within each month being negligible. But in practice it was necessary to adjust every clock according to a nearby sundial, the only source of solar precision. And the fatal flaws in the sundials, when added to those in the clocks, made for total chaos. However much ingenious chiming mechanisms activated by floats might set off little peals of silvery bells or cause feathered mechanical dolls to whistle, the Roman hour was a hit-and-miss affair. There was a great deal of truth in the old saying: 'Sooner agreement between two philosophers than two clocks!'

As the litter passed through the cosmopolitan riff-raff thronging the streets, Aponius was lulled by the surging hubbub around him. When the noise suddenly stopped, he knew that he had just entered the calm haven surrounding the newly-built palace of the late Tiberius.

The huge room was crowded with people – though the imperial throne was still unoccupied. The auctioneer was quietly disposing of a group of slaves who were only bit-parts on the gladiatorial stage – assistant referees, trumpet or horn players who specialized in the musical punctuation of the butchery, heralds and flash-board holders who ensured communication between the president of the Games, the gladiators and the public, seconds, masseurs, medical attendants, bone-setters, men who watered and raked the arena, track attendants, stretcher-bearers, undertakers' men who dressed up as Charon or Pluto to carry off the remains of the slaughtered gladiators, even a Mercury, messenger of the gods, who gave the signal for public rejoicing when the president gave him the nod. It was a whole little world of nonentities. Aponius made his way through the crowd towards the semicircle of ringside seats reserved for members of the Senate.

The walls of the room had been decorated with fresh green palm-branches and garlands of red roses, a symbolic allusion to the customary rewards for victory, and the slightly-raised stage where the lots were being paraded had been liberally sanded to look like the arena. Behind this dais someone with a nice eye for the appropriate religious detail had set up statues of the gods and goddesses to whom gladiators were particularly devoted: Hercules and Mars, Venus, to whom the lucky winners dedicated their weapons as votive offerings, and Nemesis, daughter of Necessity and avenger of crimes, the ruling deity of the bloodier forms of athletic contest. At the entrance to the room a full-length statue of Hermes gave its blessing to the commercial aspects of the occasion.

As well as the senators, there to oblige the emperor, the room was full of all the potential buyers from the tight little world of the gladiator. There were the few surviving great Capuan *lanistae* who had lived through the last years of the Republic. (In that unforgettable period of frenetic ostentation, aristocrats eaten up with political ambition had competed for the votes of the Roman populace by spilling the blood of countless gladiators.) There were the remaining small independent *lanistae* who had contrived to survive in Rome despite the crushing competition of the imperial establishments. There were *lanistae* from all over Italy and from most of the provinces, for gladiatorial games had become a universal aspect of civilization and a mark of community of spirit with the exemplar of all values, Rome. In addition a number of noble *munerarii* who wanted to offer a Games in an Italian or provincial town without going through the normal channel of the *lanistae* had made the journey. And there were even some Eastern priests of the imperial cult who made any fine spectacle the occasion for a very public display of allegiance. Arrangements for the auction had been announced in the spring.

The rest of the audience was made up of people curious to see Caligula at close quarters. In the box in the Circus Maximus, from which he looked down upon the tumultuous enthusiasm of the crowd as the chariots swept by in their clouds of dust, Caius was inaccessible. And in the other circuses, amphitheatres and theatres he was screened from the ordinary people (the *plebs*) by impenetrable rows of guards.

Aponius eventually found a seat between fat Cornelius Cordus, who at the end of his period as quaestor had wisely renounced all interest in politics and had devoted himself to eating, and lean Carvilius Ruga, an ex-consul who prided himself on his Stoicism and despised public displays of any kind. Out of the 600 members of the Senate Aponius could have put names to only 150.

Through the open windows the Forums of Caesar and Augustus could be seen down below, some way beyond the steep Victory Way, which climbed up to the Palatine. Dominating them was the Capitol, like a great stone ship at anchor, with its valley, known as the *Inter duos lucos*, between its monumental prow and poop. In the warm autumnal light it was the image of stability, tradition, and safety.

Feeling reassured, Aponius started to chat with his neighbours, while the sale took its course.

At that moment they were dealing with the lots containing *tirones*. The word *tiro* meant a raw recruit to the legions, but it had also come to be used for the gladiatorial beginners, youngsters still awaiting their first fight, whose very inexperience could be the death of them. Many of these novices were slaves, willing to try and find, in the world of armed combat, the dignity denied them by their servile status. But there was also a substantial minority of free – or freed – men who had, for cash, signed the curious *auctoratio* contract, by which a man put his liberty in the hands of a promoter for a defined period or a specified number of bouts. These gladiators under contract were often sons of good family who were totally broke, and who, having sold all their possessions, had been forced, out of desperation, to sell themselves. Their fathers had told them: 'If you go on like that, you'll end up a gladiator!' And daddy had been right.

Lanistae and *munerarii* were buying slaves body and soul, and snapping up the contracts of *auctoratio*, which livened up the bidding. Free men were always a hit with spectators at the Games, who were naturally flattered that such people were prepared to run risks for their entertainment.

Cordus told Aponius how he had just topped the bidding in a much more interesting sale: 'You'll never believe this. The day before yesterday, at dawn, down at the fish-market in the Trans Tiberim – nobody who knows what they're doing goes to the fish-market in the Velabrum – I managed to beat off a fanatical band of enthusiasts, and for just 8,000 sesterces I got a sea-perch as long as your arm. Sea-perch? What am I saying! It wasn't just any old sea-perch, it was the special *Roman* variety. What fishermen call a *catillo*, the refuse-eating parasite that lives in the Tiber just where the sewage comes out. It's also called a "between the bridges" perch. A real *catillo*, especially one that size, is absolutely priceless. You should have seen it madly lashing out with its tail in the fish tank. It was as fat as a priest of Isis or one of Cybele's eunuchs. I had it cooked alive, to make sure that it was as fresh as possible, in an elaborate spiced stock, and I ate it stuffed with a mixture of surmullet livers, sea-urchins' hearts and quenelle of lobster, with a sublime sauce thickened with Indian rice. There's something absolutely sensational about the sheer smell of *catillo*.'

15

Aponius, who was not known for the elaborateness of his domestic cuisine, made polite noises of assent, and swiftly turned to the Stoic on his other side, who put a question to him: 'There's one thing about this business which I don't understand – it's true that it isn't the sort of thing I know much about . . . I thought that the *lanistae* arranged sale-or-return contracts with the *munerarii*, who paid a hiring fee for the winners and the full price for the dead and injured. So why are the *munerarii* here paying cash for slaves and for free men's contracts?'

'You can hardly suppose I know any more about these matters than you,' replied Aponius somewhat haughtily. 'On the very rare occasions I put in an appearance at the amphitheatre, I only go for the quality of the fighting. However, I do know that anyone staging an event is wise to pay cash for his fighters when prices are rising. And as, under the present emperor, gladiatorial combat is all the rage, prices are soaring. You're bound to be able to sell them for more after the Games.'

'You seem to know rather more about it than you're willing to admit.'

Aponius demurred, uncertain whether or not the suggestion was a flattering one.

The auctioneer was trying to whip up interest in teams of *bestiarii* (animal keepers), whose price was sticking rather low. They were the menials of the arena, and – with a few notable exceptions – their reputation suffered somewhat from the fact that it was a part of their job to feed condemned criminals to the animals. Accordingly, they also had the unpleasant task of finishing them off, if the beasts had failed to do it for them by the time they had eaten their fill.

The gourmet who liked his *catillo* from the Cloaca Maxima cooked live started up again: 'I overheard what Ruga said just now about gladiatorial combat. What a sign of the decline of the aristocracy! During the Republic officials like the curule and plebeian aediles or the praetors used to lay on magnificent Games for the people, and everyone with any ambition was well up in the subject. Even Cicero dealt in gladiators on the quiet. Whereas since Augustus the whole college of praetors pick a mere two of their number by lot to put on a show which the emperor insists should not rival his own. Tiberius even went so far as to do away with the whole thing most of the time. So that these days you can become a consul without having a clue what goes on in the arena.'

It was only too true. The aristocracy were not what they used to be. They had lost the monopoly of staging Games. And at Rome the Games and the exercise of power were intimately linked.

But what on earth was the emperor up to? Had he even got up yet?

The auctioneer was polishing off some lots containing gladiators of no particular interest. Having come up against someone less skilled than themselves in their first fight they had become 'veterans', but had subsequently had undistinguished careers. Their victory palms were few and far between and their garlands fewer still.

By way of a change some female gladiators and 'huntresses' were put up for sale. The crowd was not particularly taken with them, though it showed a certain unhealthy curiosity. There was a brief surge of interest in a pair of women who had both lost the same eye, and whom the crowd consequently found very funny. The Romans always had a taste for the offbeat. A collection of midgets, two of them black, were also paraded. Midgets were often matched against female gladiators: the result was quite amusing.

The morning wore on. Caligula's arrival was still awaited, and it was impossible for the stars of the day, champions whose names were household words, to be put under the hammer in his absence. Some were slaves, most were under contract, and they came not only from the great Roman training school on the Caelian, which was the heart of gladiatorial activity in the Empire, but also from Capua, Ravenna and even Burdigala, Narbo, Corduba, Gades, Alexandria and Pergamum. It was worth paying the travelling costs for specialists like this, for whom success was a way of life. They had long given up keeping a tally of their victories. Some of them were said to have taken the palm forty, sixty, eighty, even a hundred or more times. Such achievements were all the more extraordinary because they required a combination of consummate skill and experience and exceptional powers of physical and mental control. For years now men of this quality had been pitted only against their equals; on each occasion their survival depended on more skill, more courage, more dash, and more self-control – and, for good measure, on that element of luck which the gods grant to their equals and which sets the common herd a-dreaming.

Some of them had won their *rudis*, the wooden sword which was symbolically bestowed on slaves who had won their liberty by fine performances in the arena or on men who had finished their contracts. But these *rudiarii*, overcome by a mad lust for wealth and with the last stale scent of fame still lingering in their nostrils, had heroically signed up again. Once more they had accepted the discipline of the *ludus*. (This was the name given to their barracks – appropriately, in that it signifies both game and school.) Once more their Spartan little rooms were full of tarts or society women hypnotized by their rippling muscles.

To keep the audience quiet, the stars were brought up on to the stage; the plebs at the back of the room promptly started clapping and cheering, and the rest followed suit. There were Italians, Gauls, Spaniards, Germans, Illyrians, Dalmatians, Africans, Syrians, Jews and Greeks. It was the known world in miniature, friends, enemies, neutrals all ready to kill each other for the entertainment of the man in the street.

Then the public was admitted to a display, in one corner of the room, of mementoes dedicated to the most famous gladiators, those whose loss had been virtually the occasion for public mourning. Lots of fans collected lamps, glassware and medallions bearing the portraits of the 'happy few', with exciting inscriptions.

It was almost midday, the sacred hour when most work and business finished for the day and people had a snack before taking a siesta or going to the baths. Preceded by an uproar sufficient to plunge the room into instant silence, Caligula at last made his entry. He was accompanied by his wife Caesonia, an old hag with plenty of experience of the worst excesses of the flesh, and by a group of heavily-beringed friends whose appearance made it easy to guess which way round he used them. Caius was of the opinion that a wife's finest adornment was experience, because it is so rare a quality and increases with age, whereas fresh young bodies are two a penny. Hard on the heels of this charming set came the famous Sabinus, the well-known 'Thracian' gladiator, in whose hands Caius had placed the command of his German Guard. The Praetorian Guard would have been most put out at being under the thumb of a gladiator. But the German mercenaries weren't so fussy. They shared with the pillars of the arena a reputation for unthinking loyalty to their master, whereas the Praetorians were notorious for their intrigues. Sabinus, in armour, was followed by a selection of tall, broad-shouldered, blond-haired soldiers with a look of astonishment in their blue eyes and the air of just having emerged from the forests of their homeland. The men of the German Guard never let the emperor out of their sight.

Caius' own garb caused a sensation. It was an extravagant mixture of the male, the female, the martial and the divine, the final touch being a fine powdering of gold dust on his short manly beard. The little trident, made of electrum, which he was nervily waving to and fro, suggested the god Neptune. The imperial cape, which for some indefinable reason was covered in silver stars, was out of keeping with the delicate tunic with its excessively long sleeves, for the latter betrayed to the practised eye a hint of effeminate tastes. This was confirmed by the feminine sandals, their thongs winding like vine tendrils around the thin hairy calves. What had happened to the young boy of yesteryear who had derived his nickname, Caligula (meaning little boot), from the army boots he had worn briefly to win the hearts of the legions? Since his illness and the death of his sister Drusilla, for whom he had had such a close and passionate attachment, Caius had visibly declined mentally – but how far had the decline gone?

Aponius felt a sudden shudder of irrational fear; he shrank down between his neighbours.

Caius waved to the senators to take their seats again and jumped up on to the stage. He walked briefly up and down in front of the motionless gladiators as if reviewing his troops. Every now and then he would swing abruptly round, turning his pale, closed face to the audience.

As the stage was fairly low in relation to the marble paving of the floor, the senators in the front rows could see that the prince's footsteps left letters imprinted in the sand, a fact which caused a muted whispering in their ranks. Only prostitutes of a certain class, who were afraid that potential customers might be put off by their apparently respectable appearance, were in the habit of having a pattern of nails put into their sandals. This made their walk doubly attractive by leaving a risqué message behind them as they walked. People leant forward to get a clearer view and were eventually able to read, in the sand of the narrow arena, not the notice which porters usually have inscribed over their lodges, BEWARE OF THE DOG, but: BEWARE OF THE MAN. They were shoes to be worn on his bad days. The news flew from mouth to mouth. It left Aponius with an uneasy feeling.

Having created the desired effect, Caius, to general astonishment, continued his performance by taking over as auctioneer and putting himself personally in charge of the progress of the sale. In his strident voice he started to cry up the wares with all the eloquent, self-mocking patter of a professional comedian. Soon he began to ignore the ordinary *lanistae* and *munerarii* and to concentrate his efforts on the group of senators. At first they felt obliged to go along with his game. The *patres conscripti* were perfectly well aware that the invitation had had a purpose, and they expected to be made to stump up some cash. Some of them, in their desire to keep on the right side of Caius, were even willing to burden themselves with a few gladiators, for whom they would doubtless have to pay a prohibitive price.

But things got out of hand. Caius was insatiable. He picked on them one after another, making them the target of jokes which were sometimes lighthearted, friendly or ingratiating, but sometimes pointed, vicious, cynical or obscene. He called them by their first names, invoked ties of friendship or kinship, made unsubtle references to their wealth, which was only too well-known. As their meanness was tempered by fear, he wore down their resistance systematically. Under such a hammering the victims all finished by cracking, and Caius triumphantly extracted totally disproportionate bids from them. Lots worth hundreds of thousands went for millions and tens of millions. The only limit was the emperor's whim. After all, the best part of the empire's wealth was in the hands of the senatorial aristocracy, wasn't it?

Caius was still in full swing: his relentless progress was reminiscent of a blind, ill-tempered miller's ass turning the mill wheel to grind the flour. The wretched senators, having fallen into this vicious trap and finding themselves obliged to suffer Caius' impudence on top of everything else, tried to raise a laugh at their tormentor's jokes, however out of place they were. 'In the good old days,' he said to Lepidus, 'your ancestors won over the people with gladiators who were worth a few profitable proconsulships to them. Now it's time for the Aemilia family to cough up.' And Lepidus gave a stupid smile. The crazy Caligula had an unfortunate way of hitting the nail on the head.

No senator had the courage to leave or to stand his ground. But the more sensitive of them were afflicted by a burning sense of shame at their dishonour as much as by the fear of being ruined or banished. The Roman Senate, conqueror of the world, had been reduced to bootlicking by a handful of army officers sprung from its own ranks.

The prime common characteristic of the victims was their wealth. Evidently Caius' agents had carefully preselected them.

The professional buyers and *munerarii* stood to lose nothing by the affair except a good opportunity for making or spending money. The gladiators, whom Caius flattered and praised to the skies, feeling their muscles, pawing them, groping them, and making them strike poses, thought the whole thing a big joke and had difficulty keeping straight faces. In the background, near the doors, the plebeians in their sombre clothes were enjoying the discomfiture of the senators: after all, out of the spoils of so many conquests they had left the common people nothing but the skin and the bones, a bit of black bread and a circus tune.

The senators were sharply and bitterly aware of Caius' deep-felt hatred and contempt, of the gladiators' ironic amusement as they took turns to parade up and down the stage, and of the suppressed satisfaction of the poor, behind whom stood the indistinct mass of the slaves, sighing and grinding their teeth as they waited for the day when they could devour the rich. The senators were alone in the world, isolated in the fortress of their own earthly wealth. They had been obliged, long ago, to hand over the command of the legions to adventurers of genius. Next to the emperor they were the prime beneficiaries of the social order, and there was now no one they could count on to maintain it but the successors of those self-same adventurers. Caius was therefore free to do what he liked . . . until such time as someone contrived to split him off from his bodyguard in a quiet corridor of the palace. There was nothing for it but to wait patiently.

A group of *tunicati* had been overlooked. These were the effeminate gladiators with a taste for decadent long tunics. Their fellow gladiators, who despised them, relegated them to an obscure corner of the barracks. As a joke, at the open prompting of Caesonia, Caius knocked them down for 3 million sesterces to a notorious pansy.

Then, tired out by all his frenetic activity and rhetorical outpouring, he handed command of the occasion back to the official auctioneer. The spell of madness had blown over. Things seemed to be resuming their normal course.

M. Aponius had been in a state of acute terror. He had sat there trembling with the fear of being caught in the net along with the big fish. Though his own fortune did not amount to 20 million sesterces, it had always seemed ample enough. But the insane way the bids were going up and up in this monstrous auction made it look smaller and smaller. When Caius' hateful voice died away, Aponius closed his eyes with a feeling of relief, as though emerging from the paralytic state to which a snake reduces a rabbit. And by a stroke of the most incalculable misfortune he began to rock mechanically backwards and forwards.

It was past midday and the auction was drawing to a close. The auctioneer put up the final lot: thirteen gladiators with plenty of victories to their credit. These consisted of an Armenian slave and the repurchased contracts of seven Greeks, two Gauls, a Jew, a Batavian, and a Sicilian *bestiarius* of some renown from the *ludus matutinus* in Rome. The 'morning game' was so-called because at a complete 'performance' of the Games the animals were normally put on in the morning and the gladiators in the afternoon. The animal trainer's contract contained a clause requiring him to take part in chariot displays, where fights took place on war chariots which were manoeuvred by a separate driver. He was a man of more than one talent, ambitious to make an even greater reputation for himself in the field of charioteering.

The emperor noticed Aponius. 'You see that ex-praetor over there nodding his head,' he whispered to the auctioneer. 'Take it as a bid. He's good for 9 million sesterces.'

By the time Aponius opened his eyes with a jerk, he was the owner of thirteen gladiators and their gleaming equipment, a war chariot and two stallions, not to mention the driver, who was apparently thrown in for free. Aponius looked like a chicken which has just found a carving-knife. It was all too much for him: he passed out.

He came to only as he was tottering down the palace steps, helped by fat Cornelius Cordus, in the general rush for the exit which followed the departure of the divine and maleficent Caius, on his way back to his pleasures. Most people were in a hurry to get out of a place where it seemed that anything might happen. In the narrow streets running down from the Palatine towards the Via Sacra and the Forums there was a great crush of litters, sedan chairs and mules, all about to cause a traffic jam in the area around the Senate Houses.

As many of Caius' victims, with no thought for spies or informers, were openly bewailing the emperor's high-handed behaviour, Cordus drew Aponius away from the compromising crowd as soon as he could. All Marcus could do was mutter over and over, '9 million! Where am I going to find 9 million!'

Cordus was good-natured – like many of the very fat, who often show more consideration than those who live by more austere philosophies. But he was also in a hurry to get down to a really good meal. He said, with some impatience: 'From the same place as anybody else. The "knights" have the cash. They don't know anything about how to ride a horse any more, but they're very skilled at tax-farming. Nine million is nothing to them.'

'They'll know they've got me at their mercy – they'll charge me an exorbitant rate of interest!'

'You'll pay them off by selling up.'

'But if I sell during a crash like this, I'll only get half the value. And if I wait, the interest will eat into the profit.'

'You'll still have enough to live on.'

'A million, with a bit of luck . . .'

'Well, that's exactly the property qualification for becoming – and remaining – a member of the Senate.'

Cordus, who had not yet got through more than 50 of his 100 million, said this with a totally straight face. Surely he knew that in Rome a senator needed 15 million to live comfortably and 30 to be moderately well off? And there were plenty of them who could count their millions by the hundred. How could he live decently on the income from one miserable million? Senators were morally obliged to have estates in Italy, and these did not bring in the 5 per cent you could get on liquid investments. If Aponius managed to rescue a million from the disaster, he would be left with the income of a chief centurion! If he wanted to hang on to his place in the Senate, he would have to cheesepare on every detail of his household budget just to be able to have a decent toga. It would be utter misery.

He suppressed a grim smile and said to Cordus: 'For a man who has just eaten a sea-perch worth the price of four slaves you talk about my property qualification with a fine old optimism!'

'Actually my slaves are worth more than 2,000 sesterces each. But you must be needing to rest after the shock. I can see your bearers looking for you, and your clients getting anxious . . . Good luck. Keep me informed of how things are!'

Aponius, who was still feeling completely shattered, collapsed into his litter and demanded that the two curtains be tightly shut. The greatest luxury in Rome was to live away from the crowd and the noise. How much longer would he be able to afford it?

He was only too familiar with the hard-up fringe of the Senate, and a very dubious lot they were too. Men who were always broke, men who were always trying to touch you for a loan, string-pullers who pulled the wrong strings, unsuccessful informers, misguided men who had thought they could win respect by flaunting their property qualification and their purple, and who relied on business deals which somehow always turned sour. But whatever happened they all hung on to their grimy purple like limpets to a rock. For, one way or another, if you were really going to make it in the world it had to be through the Senate, even in its present degenerate state.

He was racked by the fear of having to become one of such an un- desirable group. Struggling to keep up appearances on no money was a cross hard to bear for a man of dignity. The slave on his way to cruci- fixion suffered less: he at least was used to it.

Under Tiberius Aponius had suffered a setback to his career as a result of the fall of Sejanus – the man who had helped him to get a praetorship before the statutory age. He had hoped to recoup his losses when Caligula came to the throne, and there had been a honeymoon period between the Roman people and the son of their darling Germanicus. A consulship, or at least an appointment as *consul suffectus*, had seemed to be just round the corner. And now the passing whim of a lunatic had been enough to . . .! By all the gods of Olympus, what an unparalleled tyranny it was!

It did not occur to Aponius that the whims of the despotic ruler only made themselves felt in the Senate and at court – that is, on a few thousand privileged persons. The rest of the 60 million citizens and subjects of the Roman empire lived perfectly peaceful lives, quite indiffer- ent to Caius' fantasies, when they did not actually applaud them. Each man consults the sundial at his own door.

Aponius was stifling in his litter. He half-opened one of the curtains. The procession had arrived at a little square high on the Caelian, so small that a huge plane tree overshadowed almost the whole of it. The sun, which was declining but not yet much past the zenith, cast a shower of flecks of gold on to the ground. An offshoot of the Julian aqueduct piped cool water to the square, where it cascaded in a fountain from the mouth of a simply carved dolphin. The place was not far from Aponius' house. Unable to face going straight back to see his wife, he stopped the litter, got out, sent the bearers away and dismissed his clients with thanks for their attendance.

Soon he was alone. In the square the air was less oppressive than in the lower quarters of the city. It was siesta time, the time when the squares and streets of a city which a moment earlier had been so vibrant emptied in a flash: the time which lovers chose for their illicit meetings because there was no one about to see them slipping along the deserted footpaths.

Aponius sat down beside the fountain, plunged his hands into the water and brought them up to his face. His body seemed to have been pierced through by the arrows of the Absurd, and he felt ill-prepared to recover from their effect. Certain Sceptic philosophers delighted in the concept of the Absurd, even though they would have been frightened out of their wits if their cat had suddenly turned into a mouse or started declaiming lines of Virgil. But what had a senator to do with the Absurd? And yet it had become a method of government in the hands of the emperor, the *princeps* or 'first' among the senators. The world seemed to have been turned upside-down.

The fountain was near a quiet *popina*, which Aponius looked at with a critical gaze. The rather unattractive name *popina* was a reminder that the women who ran these 'taverns', eating and drinking places for people of the lowest class, liked to get their provisions from the *popa*, the priest in charge of sacrifices: he kept for himself and his associates the best of the meat offered to the gods – who in any case were usually palmed off with the offal. The masculine noun for the priest had, by a substantial shift of meaning, finished up as the feminine noun for the woman in charge of a tavern. The standard fare of the *popinae* also included haunches of wild animals and cuts of wild boar, deer and oryx which were sold off cheap after the massacres in the amphitheatre. The *popa* would drown these chunks of leathery meat in violently spiced sauces so as to disguise the off-putting smell. Otherwise you would have thought that you could detect, not just the flavour of this or that wild beast, but the anguished sweat of the condemned man which it had just devoured. But the choicest bits – the bears' paws for example – never got as far as the *popinae*.

Beneath a trellis from which the grapes had already been harvested, the façade of the tavern was spangled with white-washed spaces where sign-writers had painted eye-catching advertisements for coming shows: races in the Circus Maximus or the Circus Flaminius, plays at the theatres of

Pompey, Marcellus or Balbus, gladiatorial shows in the old amphitheatre of Taurus or in the electoral enclosure of the 'Saepta' on the Campus Martius, where the republican voting of former times had given way to an applause which was more reassuring for those in power.

Aponius succumbed to the temptation to get himself tipsy on a full glass of neat wine, the way alcoholics drank it. In the litter which he had carelessly thrown himself into, his handsome senatorial 'uniform', the *toga praetexta*, had come undone. The purse and the knick-knacks which had been merely tucked into its fold had then spilled out onto the feather cushions without his noticing the fact. But in any case it would not have been appropriate to sport a senatorial toga in a *popina*. Aponius accordingly rid himself of the heavy garment, which was making him sweaty. He even folded the material on his forearm in such a way as to put the purple border out of sight. He only wore his tunic with the broad vertical purple stripe when he went out without a toga.

Because of the midday heat the establishment had emptied. But an overpowering mixture of smells still assailed one's nostrils.

In the holes in the wooden shelves or in the uneven tiled floor grew a forest of *amphorae* which, when uncorked, smelled of rough wine, rancid oil, the brine used for pickling cheap fish, the grape spirit used for the more expensive process of preserving goat, stag or ox, and the *hallex*, that half-decomposed fish whose total decomposition gave a poor quality liquid *garum*. By the oven, whose fire was now out, an amphora of this crude *garum* was standing next to another of date honey, whose only certain quality was that it was five times cheaper than the *garum*. The *popa* presumably drew on these two stores to spice her stews with the contrasting flavours, as had long been the fashion.

Aponius went up to the right-angled inside counter, which was longer and better equipped than the brick and timber projection which formed a serving area for passers-by. As his eyes grew accustomed to the relative darkness, he could make out various earthenware jars and receptacles containing dried vegetables which had merely been boiled in water or reduced to a pulp: butter beans, lentils, lupins, haricot beans, chick peas ... There were also pickled rape, parsnips, marrows, lettuces, turnips, purslane and cucumbers. And black-puddings made from pork or goat's meat – what the peasants called *hircia* – and dishes of tripe, various types of sausage and minced beef, together with hard-boiled eggs, bunches of grapes, cheeses and coarse peasant bread full of bran and of dust from the gradual wearing away of the grinding stones.

Aponius surveyed this display of products with a sigh: their nature and quality were for the most part outside his experience. How long had it been since he last ate lupins? It was to places like this that his litter-bearers or his chair-bearers or the worst off among his clients went for a moment's relaxation while he was dining in town.

He woke up the fat Syrian who was snoozing behind her counter, and asked for an aperitif flavoured with aniseed, roses or violets to blot out a stench in which there was more than a hint of filth and sweat. The woman, doubtless a recent immigrant, spoke a brand of broken lower-class Latin which Aponius found incomprehensible. They immediately switched into Greek.

'You'll only get that sort of thing in the smart *thermopolia* around the Forums, sir. But I've a good Cos wine which I've set to cool in water taken from the fountain.'

'That's as close to the water as it needs to get! Wash this tumbler and fill it up.'

Under a wreath of onions and garlic hanging from the ceiling Aponius took a long drink of the wine, which made him feel better for all its mediocre quality. Though it had been stabilized with sea-water like all the fine wines of Cos, Clazomene or Rhodes, it was only a pale Italian imitation.

Two labourers came in, their day's work done. They sat in a corner and started to play *latrunculi* (the 'brigands' game' – a sort of chess). The board made Aponius think of the mental and material discomfort of the situation in which a quirk of ill-luck had placed him. In Rome, as in *latrunculi*, everyone had his own place – his own square on the board – his own rights, duties and prerogatives. Each man was defined by the laws and relationships of his milieu, in a society which was structured and hierarchical in the extreme. But as long as the strict requirements of certain rules were fulfilled, it was possible for anyone to progress from one square to another. Yet now the emperor, the master of the universe, the father of his people, the divine incarnation of all justice, by descending to the level of an irresponsible marionette blowing in the wind, had broken all the rules. Aponius was now out of the game. As a ruined senator he no longer had, in the *latrunculi* of life, a specific square on the board where he could rub shoulders with his peers and think of ways to win.

It would have taken the temperament of a Cynic philosopher, proud of living in a barrel, to weather a storm of this kind. But Aponius was in the habit of judging himself through the eyes of others and philosophy was, for him, no more than an elegant way of passing the time. To the Greeks, what counted was the concept of the individual. They had already discovered all the resources and riches of a Ulysses shipwrecked on a desert isle, merrily picking up seashells and jerking himself off, with a garland of flowers round his head, under the rays of the brilliant Apollonian sun. To the Romans the philosophy of the individual was a mystery: they had stayed on the periphery of the one true form of wisdom. It was only the possession of his own place in the State that gave a Roman substance and edge.

The characteristic smells of *hallex* and *garum* brought back to Aponius a whole shameful genealogy which he had been at pains to put out of both his own mind and other people's. For, like two thirds of the citizens of Rome, and despite the purple which every parvenu purchases in the honours market, he was only the typical product of a system of upwardly-mobile slavery which had cast up many another toward distant heights.

Aponius' great-great-grandfather had, in early youth, been carried off by Sulla, after his famous siege of Athens. A Roman master with a Philhellenic cast of mind had given him the Greek nickname 'Aponios', to show that he had a tendency to be dozy and phlegmatic. Stirred out of his apathy by the bitter rivalry rife among the slave masses, Aponios had wasted no time in realizing every slave's first ambition: to win the right to have some slaves of his own who would be held on a particularly tight rein because their master had been through the system himself. Freed after twenty years of loyal and intelligent service, Aponios had, according to custom, taken the first name of his patron and benefactor Tiberius and Junius, the name of his *gens*. To these he had added, in the place of the surname or names which helped to identify an individual citizen more closely, his single slave-name Aponios. Ti. Junius Aponios had therefore earned the Latin 'three names', but in such a form that the first two only served to bring to mind the servile origin of the bearer. Both as a slave and as a freedman remaining closely linked to his patron by bonds of close clientship, he had distinguished himself by his fruitful administration of the Junius fortune.

Aponios' first-born son had, still according to custom, his father's personal name, Aponios, a name which betrayed the blemish of slavery both by its sound and by its place as the third of the *tria nomina*. Ti. Junius Aponios junior had dedicated his native freedom to making a fortune in pickled fish, and especially in *garum*, a sauce of which the Mediterranean world consumed a prodigious quantity. Following the example of his freedman father he remained a client of the influential Junii, took a certain pride in (and derived a certain advantage from) publicly displaying the first and family names of the patron who had freed his father, but felt that Aponius sounded better than Aponios.

The only son of Ti. Junius Aponius, the exact homonym of his father, had – in order to distinguish son from father – added the surname Saturnianus to his *tria nomina*, either because of a special devotion to Saturn, an old Italian divinity, or because his escapades during the Saturnalia had been a source of much gossip. The market in surnames was a free one and you could adopt as many as you liked. Ti. Junius Aponius Saturnianus had long dreamt of getting out of fish and investing in land, the apogee of all commercial success and a precondition for any honourable political success. In this ambitious man's declining days the change was made, and there were grounds for seeing the presages as good for the future of the two sons of the house, the elder Ti. Junius Aponius and the younger Ti. Junius Aponius Rufus, so-called because his hair was of a reddish colour.

Old Saturnianus, with sly ingratitude, had gradually succeeded in loosening his bonds of clientship with the Junii as the amphoras and earthenware jars gradually changed into thousands of broad acres. (Piquantly enough, the Roman unit of land, the *jugerum*, was rectangular, to perpetuate the memory of ploughing and furrows.) He had done something even worse. In return for favours done on the quiet he was allowed to rig the boys out with Roman first names, and all mention of Ti. Junius was blotted out. A Marcus and an Aulus were born. A Marcus Aponius Saturninus and an Aulus Aponius Saturninus Rufus had even made their public appearance, for the opportunity had been taken to change Saturnianus into Saturninus, a name honourably borne by many figures distinguished in Roman history.

At last each child had a first name – and even a surname – that was all his own. For true Romans the first name – given that there were only eighteen in all – was not very important, and they called each other by their original surnames. But for outsiders of slave blood or dubious origin it was the possession of one of these much-envied first names which gave them the feeling of having finally penetrated into the intimacy of the goddess Roma. And not only had the children acquired a first name each but at the same moment the name of the *gens* to which they were subordinated had disappeared from the official records. If your name was Cn. Pompeius Trogus – like the Gallic historian – or C. Julius something or other, you might be descended from a freedman of Pompey or Caesar; but you might also be the heir of a freeborn provincial who had had recourse to their patronage to obtain his naturalization. Whereas the Ti. Juniuses, more than likely born of the same slave origins, fooled nobody.

And now all that effort had been wiped out in a flash.

By now Marcus was on his fourth tumbler of unmixed wine. Suddenly he let himself go and started talking about his father and his grandfather in a tearful voice. The Syrian owner of the *popina* had heard plenty in her time, and knew how to keep a conversation going by encouraging noises and exclamations. Gradually the taverna filled up with a crowd of low mocking types, who plainly preferred drinking to the baths. Through the haze of the first stage of drunkenness Marcus glimpsed comic faces which seemed to come straight out of the old Atellan farces.

'Do you know how the best *garum* is made?' he asked. 'I've seen it made, I have, in Baetica, in the south of Spain, when I was still young enough to wear a child's *toga praetexta* . . .'

He threw his senatorial *toga praetexta* on to a stool, seized hold of an empty earthenware jar, and filled it with aimless gestures and hollow words: 'At the bottom of the jar goes a layer of sweet-smelling herbs, fennel, coriander, celery, savory, mint, rue, lovage, pennyroyal, thyme, oregano, betony . . . I've left one out. Oh yes! agrimony. Very important, I'm told, the agrimony. Then a layer of plump fish, freshwater or sea fish it doesn't matter: eels, salmon, shad, mackerel or sardines . . . Then a layer of salt two fingers deep. And so on up to the top. You close the jar and wait seven days, the astrologers' week in honour of the seven planets which rule the universe. Then you beat the mixture thoroughly every day for twenty days. The sublime liquid which then comes flowing from the jar like oil is pure *garum*, the first juice. That's 'society *garum*'. My father had it brought from Carthage. My cook used to buy his *garum* at 6,000 sesterces for a little one- and-a-half gallon amphora. It was quite different from the stuff I can see down there . . .'

He was already talking about his household *garum* in the past tense.

The purple border on the toga which he had let drop upon the stool was visible. A gladiator from the nearby *ludus* called out: 'Look at his *toga praetexta*! He's still a child!' – a joke which aroused endless laughter. The sight of a gladiator was like a knife blow to Marcus. Somewhat sobered, he went and sat on the brick bench set against the foot of the wall. Though he did not know it, the surface against which he leant back was scratched all over with graffiti in honour of champions of the arena.

What was to become of him? Would he have to leave the Senate, where everyone derived their income from land, and take up pickling food? His childhood had been lulled by the smell of preserved fish. But he would have to start more or less from scratch in a trade whose secrets his father had not passed on to him, fighting with sharks to get his fish on the market . . . He had neither the courage nor the will to run the risks involved. At nearly forty he had thought that he had arrived, had got used to a comfy, contemplative life with his last wife, the customary little love affairs on the side, good dinners, a few choice shows, the Senate meetings which were happily few and far between: it was too late to go risking himself at sea or counting amphoras.

Worse, going back into the fish trade would deprive him of a pleasure which he found keener as each year passed, and which would in future have the great advantage of not being expensive: the pleasure of study. His father had already, in the course of business, taken an interest in law and jurisprudence and had set up an admirable library. The leisure afforded by an excessively long period of disgrace had allowed Marcus to spend some happy moments there. He had even polished up his knowledge of Greek and read a little philosophy, a branch of knowledge which he had previously touched upon only superficially. Was this damned Caius going to deprive him of his mental pleasures too?

He could not, unfortunately, think of anyone who could possibly be of help to him in his misfortune. His brother Aulus – whom he persisted in calling Rufus (Redhead), even though he was now as bald as Julius Caesar – was as leaky as a sieve when it came to money. He had run through two thirds of the money left to him by their father, and after four previous marriages had just married a seventeen-year-old beauty who had already been married at thirteen and divorced at sixteen. He wouldn't be able to do anything for him, and he wouldn't if he could. Rufus' favourite dictum was: 'Gather ye rosebuds while ye may.'

It was equally unthinkable to go and cry poverty to the Junii after shedding their distinguished patronymic, not to mention the venerable first name which went with it. The Junii would turn their backs, and with good reason. Despite their immense clientele they would even be within their rights to be angry at his impertinence and to land him in still worse trouble. The Junius Silanus branch of the family, whose dependants the Aponii had been, was very influential: they descended directly from Augustus by his wife Scribonia, whereas the emperor Caius himself only had Livia, Augustus' second wife, for ancestor. In his position it was dangerous territory to encroach upon.

As for his own clients, by the very nature of things they were people of no substance. They would gradually fade away as the cash handouts and the little presents became rarer.

What a lonely position to find himself in all of a sudden! He had to face up to a very unpleasant truth. In Roman society it was normal for every citizen – except the emperor – to have a patron who was your natural protector, on the one hand, and on the other, once you reached a certain level of income, your own clients. He would be one of the rare beings to be deprived of any support. Even slaves had a master to defend them! How difficult it would be, too, for a man whose father had unwisely broken off relations with his patron, to find a replacement. The new one, when sounded out, would be suspicious and make inquiries, being anxious not to fall out with someone powerful because of taking a family of deserters under his wing. The upper crust were terribly touchy about their clients.

Marcus consoled himself a little with the thought that the Junius Silanus family could just as well have suddenly dismissed a Ti. Junius Aponios with nothing but fair words. It was the first comforting idea he had had since the catastrophe, and it was a negative one.

Marcus went tottering back to the counter and ordered a fifth glass of Cos, which went to his head in a new flush of intoxication. He was no longer in a condition to notice that his toga had disappeared – to the advantage of some father of a family perhaps, who would have it dyed and three or four cloaks made out of it.

Tears of despair welled in Marcus' eyes, but the sound of his dead father's voice dried them abruptly: 'A Roman never cries!' he used to say to his son, as they stood watching the rolling lines of his vines. He had naturally given his sons the purest of traditional Roman educations. He had even gone further without fearing to seem ridiculous. While the upper ranks of the aristocracy had become decidedly sceptical in their beliefs, those recently assimilated adopted the most antiquated form of Roman patriotism in their anxiety that there should be no doubt about the impeccable Roman-ness of their ideas, their manners and their ancestors. So the heroes of Roman history appeared suddenly and dried Marcus' tear-stained face. But this sense of pride, which brought the senator to his feet beneath the garlands of onions and garlic, was marred by the appalling further thought that it was of such a true Roman as himself that Caius had made fun!

If this revelation cut into his courage like a whiplash and encouraged him to accept the situation with patience, the scandalous implications of it were no less upsetting. Totally overcome, he broke down and cried. Through his tears the image of his wife's face offered a new source of stimulus to his grief. He felt weak at the prospect of going back to a fine house that no longer belonged to him, to find a wife whom he had prudently chosen for the modesty of her charms, her relative stupidity and her lack of education, in the hope of finishing his days beside a faithful heart, after being deceived by a succession of expensive hussies. But what could a faithful heart do to fill a gap of 9 million sesterces – 2,250,000 *denarii* of silver, 90,000 gold *aurei*! – which had to be paid up as soon as possible? It was more gold than a dozen legionaries could carry under an autumn sun! Pomponia would be of no help to him either. She would be twice as upset as he was.

'Next time,' he said to the Syrian woman in a dull voice, 'I'll believe in my wife's premonitions. Particularly when she dreams of me with wings and feathers . . .' The effect of this announcement reminded him that he had an audience. He looked around and found himself staring stupidly at a *triclinium* whose incongruous outline he could see in a back room. What were those three dining couches doing in a place where it was surprising enough to find a few rough wooden tables and stools? Where would the absurd snobbery of the lower classes end?

The patronne explained to Marcus that the *popina* had a lot of trade in the afternoons when people came out of the baths, and she had a fine group of gladiators among her clients who liked to have couches so that they could banquet at their ease. The reference to gladiators caused him to pull a frightful face, but the scowl was misinterpreted. To arouse his interest in the other possibilities of the establishment he was shown a notice, very approximately spelled, offering three girls who were described as 'fillies', as an indication of the youthful freshness of their bodies and the warmth of their temperament. And indeed there was a wooden staircase going up to the next floor, where some recesses could be glimpsed. Marcus was deeply impressed by the extreme modesty of the prices. A half-litre of wine and a piece of bread cost one *as*. The stew was two *asses*. And a girl was eight *asses*, or two sesterces.

Marcus' first teacher had taught him to count on his fingers in the old Greek system, by which with two hands you could represent all the integers from one to a million. Unable to solve the problem in his head he started to juggle with his fingers after a fashion, and after a few mistakes which could be put down to his fuddled state, he reached this indubitable conclusion: with the 9 million sesterces which he had lost he could have drunk 18 million litres of wine, eaten 18 million stews or enjoyed 4½ million girls! Rome was certainly a cheap place if you kept your sights low. At last he had some good news for his wife. He decided to go home.

That was the moment when things started to go wrong. His purse had gone off with his litter; his toga had gone off on its own. The cries of Marcus and the *popa*, and the shouts of the audience fired by the performance of these two, finally attracted the attention of a patrol of the city guard, whose captain had, unfortunately, a very conventional notion of senators. Only the glittering boots spoke in the suspect's favour. But a man who hired out mules at the Porta Capena had the bad taste to suggest that Marcus must be an actor who had been sacked from a theatre, an idea which Marcus himself would have found unexpectedly profound if he had been in a position to reflect on it. But he was too busy trying to prove his good faith.

Everybody crowded round to look at his footwear and opinions were profusely offered. None of them had ever seen senatorial boots before, and they found Marcus' boots peculiar, with their high legs, slit on the inner side, and the tongue inside (protecting the skin from the criss-crossed laces) with its end flopping freely over the fastener. They didn't look like tragic actors' *cothurni*, but they did have the look of comedians' boots.

To be classified as a comedian put Marcus in a rage, which made his situation worse. The captain of the guard had to call him to order. An undertaker from the district around the Esquiline declared that a senator's boots were black and not red. Marcus had to agree but pointed out that this was only for those *patres conscripti* who had not held a curule magistracy. He affirmed more than once that he had been praetor and that he lived in the neighbourhood, but he was well aware that his drunken voice sounded phoney. When he added: 'I have 200,000 sesterces in my chest at home,' it wasn't remotely plausible.

The captain of the patrol reasonably decided to escort Marcus to his supposed residence to see if he would be recognized.

During the short journey Marcus reflected that if there was one thing worse than eating and drinking for an *as*, it was not having an *as* in your pocket at all.

When the *familia* of Marcus and Pomponia came running out and saw, in the Corinthian atrium, a Marcus Aponius Saturninus surrounded by soldiers, every heart went cold with fear. Caligula had struck again.

'It's just a little misunderstanding,' said Marcus. But Pomponia had already fainted.

Financial wounds are not fatal. At least, not instantly so.

✤ CHAPTER ✤
3

The eccentric Caligula didn't last five years. He passed like a comet with a blood-red tail, harbinger of new upheavals. Claudius, the family idiot, a knight without any money, who had been found trembling behind a hanging by Praetorian guardsmen unsure what to do after the murder of his nephew Caius, had bought the Empire from the soldiers with the State's money, a precedent which could only give them bad ideas and bad habits. Being descended from Julius Caesar by blood or by adoption was henceforth only a sufficient qualification for the purple if the Praetorian guard agreed. The Senate had no say in the matter once an emperor had been acclaimed by the interested parties in the permanent camp at the Porta Viminalis.

Claudius was then at the height of his physical powers . . . if that is at all an appropriate expression for a man whose legs were uncertain and his tongue still more so. After all, he was a heavy drinker and gambler, miserly, greedy and timid, with a mind which was indeed cultivated but muddled, quirky and inclined to be facetious. People wondered whether, by continually playing the imbecile so as to survive in a climate of endless plots and counterplots, he hadn't really and truly become one. A relatively attractive aspect of his character was that the cruelty which is inherent in human nature limited itself in him to an enthusiasm for the pleasures of the arena and a childish delight in the sight of the ultimate punishment of someone who had in principle deserved it. At bottom it wasn't the inner man who was bloodthirsty but the spectator. The connection between the eye and the mind was less obvious than it might have seemed.

Seven years later, after the joyous harvests of the year 801 from the founding of the city (48 A D) A. Vitellius and L. Vipsanius Agricola being eponymous consuls, the freedman Narcissus had obtained from the wavering prince, while he was half-cut, the condemnation of Messalina, the mother of his two children Britannicus and Octavia. It was true that she had overdone things. Having deceived Claudius in the grand manner with all-comers, she had remarried, during the lifetime of her imperial husband, the consul designate Silius, who had had no qualms about furnishing his house with treasures taken from the Palace. A sexual peccadillo which could have been overlooked suddenly took on disquieting political overtones.

As early as January of the following year, on the advice of the freedman Pallas, the emperor remarried. This time his bride was his close relative Agrippina the Younger. Claudius was a man easily influenced, and who was in any case worn out. He now fell under the sway of a tough, unscrupulous and ambitious woman, who already had a child of nearly twelve, the young L. Domitius Ahenobarbus. Claudius was soon to adopt this Lucius – to the great detriment of the legitimate interests of Britannicus. For the first time in Roman history a member of the fair sex could hope to enjoy the exercise of supreme power under the cover of a docile son.

M. Aponius Saturninus would never have supposed that the remarriage of Claudius would turn his own dreary existence upside down. The rebuffs which he had suffered over the previous dozen or so years had gradually led him to the conclusion that Palace intrigues took place on another planet.

On that particular January morning the lower quarters of the city were in the grip of a spell of damp cold. Marcus was abruptly roused from his slumbers by the terrible cries of a new-born child which some ruthless harridan had deposited on the dung-heap at the end of the cul-de-sac behind the apartment block where he lived. It was particularly irritating because he usually had great difficulty in getting to sleep, and the moments which preceded the dawn were the only time, apart from siesta, when the habitual Roman din died down.

An edict of Julius Caesar had made it absolutely illegal to drive carts within the city during the day – except as was necessary for the construction or repair of buildings. So it was at night that all the warehouses and markets of the city were restocked with supplies. Before the sun had disappeared behind the Janiculum an impatient swarm of vehicles, carts and wagons were outside the seventeen gates of Rome, waiting for the signal to attack. And as soon as the sun had set, carters, wagoners and draymen were whipping their horses and mules towards that vast, dark labyrinth which, under the flickering light of a myriad lanterns and torches, would be rent and shaken by cries and neighing, by rattling and trampling, until the approach of dawn.

This was the way in which supplies were brought to the great papyrus and parchment depot in the Forum, the delicatessen market at the top of the Via Sacra, the fresh vegetable market near the Busta Gallica, the oil and fish markets in the Velabrum Minus, the 'bean portico' and the bread and cake market on the Aventine, the vegetable market in the Circus Maximus, 'Livia's meat-market' on the Esquiline, where the best meat and poultry were to be found – and many other distribution and sales points. And the same time of day was used to supply the vegetable market situated in fact just outside the Porta Carmentalis, between the theatre of Marcellus and the Tarpeian rock, by the Columna Lactaria, the meeting-place of nursemaids for sale or hire. When all this was completed, the army of the night, whose rear-guard included the cesspit emptiers and the drainsmen, feverishly hurried out of the city, for any vehicle found inside after daybreak would be immobilized.

Marcus' social downfall had brought him to a tottering apartment building in the heart of the old city. His dreams were peopled with dancing vegetables and sneering horses, and through his poorly fitting shutters he could smell horse-dung, fish and human excrement. Even the resinous smell of the torches was there to remind him in his torpid state of the constant danger of fire. Together with floods and plague, fire was the great source of terror to a Roman.

But when day broke, a wave of noise broke with it. There was a pervasive dull drone punctuated with more sonorous and aggressive sounds. Shopkeepers of every sort, from barbers to slave dealers (Rome, out of a certain sense of propriety, had no real slave market worthy of the name), were taking down the wooden shutters in front of their shops and putting up their flat trays or trestles on the pavement. The tools of the coppersmiths, blacksmiths, locksmiths, gold and silver smiths rang and clanged. The foodstall owners bawled the praises of their steaming sausages or their freshly made black-puddings. The schoolmasters and their pupils shouted to one another under the porticoes. The pedlars from the Trans Tiberim barked out the merits of their packets of sulphurated firelighters, and the beggars intoned their continuous singsong plaints. There was no question of getting any more sleep before siesta time.

The abandoned baby was crying more lustily now. It was usually girls who were exposed. They put up more resistance than boys and took longer to fall silent. The begging organizations had agents who toured the dumps, legal and illicit, looking for likely strong subjects who could be mutilated and brought up, and they preferred boys to girls. The infirmities and wounds of the former usually aroused a keener sense of compassion in older women, whose emotional sensibility matched their sterility. But most pimps preferred girls.

In the next room Kaeso started to cry too, and Marcus' heart was stirred. Marcus junior, who was five years old, slept soundly, but Kaeso, who was a year younger, had a more sensitive and highly-strung temperament. The least breath was enough to disturb him. It was as if he had never recovered from Pomponia's death in childbirth, as a result of a Caesarean operation which had turned into butchery. That was why the child had been given the relatively rare first name Kaeso, indicating the tragic circumstances of his birth.

Marcus, who had piled on the tunics to protect himself from the cold, extricated himself from his covers and groped around for his slippers on the threadbare bedside rug. He found his *lucubrum*, a tiny nightlight whose small bright flame was the companion of his bouts of insomnia, and, stumbling over his earthenware chamber-pot, went to calm Kaeso down.

The boy was lying beside his sleeping brother, and the cries of the little girl below his window were still upsetting him. Marcus explained to Kaeso that the little girl was being naughty but that she would soon be punished. His paternal sensitivity helped him to find other, tender words to reassure his son and lull him back to sleep.

Marcus went back to bed for a moment, and, by the light of his *lucubrum*, familiar morose reflections repossessed his battered soul.

His downfall had had a literally vertical quality which everything in his new lifestyle constantly brought to mind. He had immediately had to give up his house on the Caelian, which he had had completely rebuilt by some well-known Greek architects only ten years or so after the highly suspicious death of Tiberius: it had burnt down in the terrible fire which had destroyed the whole area, leaving nothing standing but a statue of the emperor in the palace of the Junii. His misfortune had thus obliged him to leave one of those prestigious hills where for generations the rich strove to live away from all the bustle and noise, separated from the intolerable masses by the thickness of their walls and the breadth of their parks, in a healthier atmosphere and a climate less torrid in summer and less damp in the bad season. He had gone tumbling back down the hill, a hundred feet lower, into the populous and ill-famed Subura, a sort of melting-pot of all nations between the Esquiline, Viminal and Quirinal Hills: it was open only to the south-west, towards the Via Sacra and the Roman Forums, where the 'Argiletum', the lively street full of bookshops, ran. But Marcus' fall had been a double one, for he had equally been forced to sell his calm and prosperous villa on the 'Hill of Gardens', the Pincian, to the north of the Campus Martius, whose southern slopes had such a pleasant view over the heights, valleys and plains of a city which was the most wonderful city in the whole world – providing you were looking down on it from on high.

Now Marcus was buried beneath a mezzanine floor with six other floors above it, and squashed between two apartment blocks of the same type. From his ground-floor flat, his only views were an alley in front and a cul-de-sac behind. All the lower area of Rome had grown up towards the heavens like this, piling floors on top of one another for lack of space to expand sideways. The result was a tangle of narrow streets, which often lacked the pavements and paving which legislation had long prescribed. In summer the labyrinthine Subura was overwhelmingly dark and stuffy; in winter it was gloomy and utterly sordid.

But this vertical decline was aggravated by another form of loss which was still more everyday and intimate, for it was hidden in the heart of the house. The lowest of Latin peasants had his modest *atrium*, his piece of sky within the home. Its central light allowed him to protect his family life behind opaque walls. The rich had added peristyles in the Greek fashion, but their houses were still turned inwards. They had only opened porticoes on to nature where the view was theirs alone. But Marcus' disparate rooms, formed by bringing together four ordinary apartments, framed a courtyard which was more like the bottom of a well, a dizzying hole. And from time to time the most incongruous and revolting things would tumble down the cascade of upper floors, whose patched-up balconies were full of grubby washing and unstable flowerpots. Marcus had, after many alarms, contrived to remain the owner of the entire building. To ensure sole possession of this derisory *atrium*, he had walled up both the back of the main entrance, which gave on to the alley in front, and the back of the rear entrance, which gave on to the cul-de-sac. But despite his attempts to maintain pale pergolas in his hole or to erect makeshift awnings, he was never able to escape being overlooked. For a man who saw himself as a true Roman, such a situation, which was so hostile to the sensibilities of the region and indeed of the Mediterranean area as a whole, was quite simply monstrous.

The tenants, for their part, cordially detested Marcus: they could not forgive him for having helped himself to the hole from the moment he so high-handedly installed himself in the building. And since, to save himself the expense and the peculations of an agent, the proprietor had taken it upon himself to collect the modest rents from the countless down-at-heel tenants in person, there were endless humiliating discussions with poor devils who had overdone the subdivision of their filthy little rooms, to which, by definition, the water from the aqueducts, available everywhere at ground level, never quite reached. Such disputes bred in Marcus a mistrust of, and contempt for, all these poor wretches who had no proper family home, being predominantly migrants and foreigners. He, at any rate, still had his family altar, his *lares* and *penates*, and even his household genius, traditionally represented by a snake.

The noise of the city had exploded with daybreak. Through the thin ceilings you could already hear the tenants walking about on the mezzanine, where three little rooms had been cut off from the normal means of access to the building and had been linked by ladders with three little shops which Marcus had opened and rented out to increase his meagre income – though, alas, it meant that the inhabitable area of his own apartment was reduced accordingly. At the front of the house there was a tiny *popina*, entrusted to a Cretan woman whom Marcus himself had freed and who had been Kaeso's nurse before she was widowed, and a barber's shop, run by a Carthaginian who made some extra income by giving carving lessons to kitchen servants , using wooden animals which could be taken to pieces. On the cul-de-sac a sinister Spaniard put his energies into selling a choice of whips and instruments for punishing slaves.

Marcus was relatively happy with the *popina* and the barber's shop. As he had found himself obliged to sell his expert barber, he was pleased to be able to get himself shaved for nothing. (The time had long gone when Agrippa, to celebrate his aedileship in 720, had made a present of a year's barbering and hairdressing to every Roman man and woman!) And as his female slaves were no longer worth fucking, when business was slack Marcus sometimes slipped secretly into the curtained-off section of the *popina* with the 'little filly' of the establishment for a quick ride or a bit of relaxing masturbation. In response to their assiduous prayers Venus had granted the Romans freedom from the more serious illnesses which accompanied her cult.

On the January dungheap the little girl was already growing weaker. Perhaps it was a boy after all.

Marcus hauled himself up, half opened the shutter to let a little light in, and went to rouse the lazy slaves. There was to be a grand cleaning session that morning in honour of the unexpected visit of his niece Marcia. From a very average *familia* of some 200 slaves Marcus had been able to keep only a dozen worthless ones, whose lack of skills was made all the more evident by the fact that the tasks required of them were now more varied and incompatible. They compounded carelessness with ill-will, while promises or threats ran up against a limp obedience tempered with cunning. A slave's work was supposed to be only half as productive as a free man's: Marcus' twelve slaves achieved the work of three. Probably, despite their outstanding mediocrity, they felt they were irreplaceable.

So, under the master's personal supervision, the team of workers of both sexes set to with a great bustle of buckets, rags, cloths and sponges, feather dusters, ladders and brooms. They spread wood shavings on the still damp tiled floors to catch the dust and rubbish. Then they lit fresh charcoal in both the fixed and the movable braziers, which had been extinguished at bedtime for fear of asphyxiation, and wearily polished up two or three pieces of furniture which were still presentable and a set of cheap silver. In the old days Marcus had habitually offered five or six pounds of such stuff to his most devoted clients as New Year presents.

But cleaning and polishing could not disguise the fact that the apartment was merely a ground floor flat in a second rate *insula*.

Marcus reflected bitterly that *insula* (the word for a block of flats) meant 'island', and that he was vegetating on this island like a shipwrecked mariner, deprived of his worldly goods and with no hope of rescue.

It occurred to Marcus that he ought to sweep out the porches. On each side of the two arches was a stairwell, and the four corresponding doors on the ground floor naturally gave on to the proprietor's apartment. Marcus had told Marcia to come in by the main entrance and knock at the door on the left – the slaves had been installed the other side. But women are scatter-brained, and Marcia, not knowing the place, might come in by the entrance on the cul-de-sac. So it was important to sweep at both front and back.

As he suspected, the porches were indeed cluttered up with rubbish as usual. Still worse, the *dolia*, those huge urns where the tenants emptied their chamber-pots or night stools, were full to overflowing under the four stairwells. Yet again the cesspit emptiers had neglected this block. Despite the biting cold, the smell was becoming intolerable. But the dunghill in the cul-de-sac did not conform with police regulations. They could not possibly add the contents of four *dolia* to it. (Moreover, there was a child there who might still be breathing . . .) Nothing could be done.

In disgust Marcus went back into his apartment. In passing he gave instructions that the four door knockers should be given a good polishing – a feeble consolation.

The sky was cloudy. It was impossible to know what time it was.

Marcia, who had announced the time of her visit for about the fifth hour, was likely to arrive soon.

In the kitchen on the master's side Marcus washed his hands, face and mouth in running water, all the time thinking that he hadn't paid his water bill. This precious water, which wasn't distributed to the layabouts on the upper floors, kept all those flat-dwellers who could afford to install it firmly fixed on the ground floor. By way of breakfast Marcus drank a few mouthfuls of icy water, then changed into a clean tunic, slipped his bare feet into town shoes and ran a comb through his hair.

From the bedroom you now had to listen hard to catch the baby's dying sobs. The previous time stray dogs had dealt with the matter. It wasn't healthy for either Marcus junior or Kaeso to have such sights so close at hand. Really, the family would have been better off in the slaves' quarters. They were farther from the end of the cul-de-sac.

Once back in the reception rooms Marcus checked that the braziers were not smoking too much and were ensuring a minimum room temperature despite the open shutters. However, the atmosphere was so gloomy that the master requested that some of the lamps should be lit, on condition that they be kept well out of draughts.

An old toothless female slave brought in the young Marcus and Kaeso, who had been playing out of the way until it was time for them to be tidied up for presentation to their cousin.

These two sons, born in quick succession late in their father's life, were the only treasures that Marcus still possessed, now that he had been reduced by events to the state of a 'proletarian' – or at least saw himself as such, though his assessment was strongly marked by pessimism. In any case, his affection for the children was all the stronger because Pomponia had died in childbirth while Marcus junior was learning to take his first steps, and he had more or less had to rear them himself, since his domestic help was so little and so incompetent. The handsome pair had been born at a time when the population of Italy was falling, despite public disquiet over the fact and despite the dismayed warnings of the emperors and their attempts to provide incentives to increase the birth rate. Marcus had wanted the boys, in an instinctive reaction against the unparalleled damage done to him by fate. But the comfort offered to him by their presence brought its own fresh sources of worry. At the rate at which the remnants of the family fortune were disappearing, what money or influence would there be left to set the two youngsters up in life when the time came?

On the edge of tears Marcus abruptly dismissed his sons. His thoughts

42

returned to his niece, the sole fruit of the first marriage of his brother Rufus, who had just died. In his will, Rufus had devoted the final crumbs of his patrimony to providing himself with a grand funeral: he was evidently inconsequential, egotistical and vain to the very last. Marcia herself had, at the age of eighteen, divorced a knight who was some sort of bootlicker in the administration of the vast imperial estates, and had swiftly remarried a certain Mancinus Largus, some rustic Umbrian minor noble who owned an ocean of vines somewhere in the region of Perugia. Marcus had once dandled Marcia upon his knee, but his downfall had caused relations between the two brothers to become even more distant, and he had only seen the young woman on rare occasions, the last of which had been the funeral ceremony at which the frivolous Rufus had been reduced to smoke and ashes. He was surprised to learn that she was in Rome again and wanting to see him about 'serious matters'. Perhaps it was something to do with guardianship? He would have preferred to receive his niece in a place more worthy of her charms.

Marcus ran his hand over his face: his two-day-old beard was still very presentable. He cast a quick final glance over the room, which had been called the sitting room on the strength of the few seats which it possessed. At least it was clean.

But the important thing was that the white marble family altar and the *lararium* in precious exotic lemon-wood, which together had adorned the *atrium* of the house on the Caelian, were set up there. The little flame of sacred fire burning night and day on the altar, and the silver Minerva which looked down from the niche in the cupboard above the carved panel which hid the box of sacrificial instruments, were an attractive and comforting sight, a memento of better times and a permanent invocation to protective powers. Marcus was particularly attached to Minerva. He had chosen her as one of his *penates* in imitation of Cicero: he had always felt an almost unqualified admiration for Cicero's speeches and his career in public life.

Suddenly Marcia was announced. She was infinitely graceful and surrounded by a cloud of spicy perfume. Marcus had not been able to get a proper impression of her under her mourning veils. He was dazzled to find her so seductive at twenty.

Marcia was wearing a long red dress trimmed with gold braid, with a pleated train, pulled in at the waist by a broad flat belt and under the breasts by another slimmer belt.

Probably because she was in mourning, this *stola* was covered with a large silky shawl in shiny black, with silver embroidery representing the triumph of Aphrodite. Her torque, bracelets and ankle rings were in artfully worked gold, but the striking fineness of her hands, which, like her forehead, had been whitened with ceruse, was set off by the absence of any jewellery. The light touch of ochre on her cheeks and the darker ochre on her lips had been applied by the hand of an expert make-up artist, who had shown due regard for the triumphant youthfulness of this stunning brunette with the big brown eyes of a fawn.

Pomponia had never had any dress sense and used to overload herself with jewellery like an ass going to market.

They greeted each other. Marcia insisted on immediately dedicating a libation of pure wine to the Minerva of the *lararium*. It was a custom fast going out of fashion. Marcus was touched by her thoughtfulness.

They sat down and talked naturally of Rufus' death, which left Marcia, who had already lost her mother, an orphan with no relative but Marcus on her father's side. They felt all the more willing to talk about the funeral in that the ceremony had been very picturesque. Rufus had himself chosen the expert mime who was to lead the obsequies and had had the courage, shortly before he died, to give him his instructions personally.

The funeral processions of the upper classes were always led by mimes, who wore the death mask of the dead man, adopted his gait, and emphasized through gesture and even voice the faults and absurdities of the departed. A critique of this kind was a counterbalance to the eulogy which a relative then had to pronounce at the foot of the *rostra* in the Forum. Thus Claudius' contemporaries would be able to be present at the funeral of the tight-fisted Vespasian, where a quip by the chief mime had a prodigious success. While the august procession was going along the bank of the Tiber, the actor who was miming the prince on his way to heaven asked the cost of the ceremony and cried out: 'Then give me the money and throw my corpse in the river!' Custom similarly decreed that the soldiers following the triumphal chariot of the emperor were briefly relieved of all obligation to be respectful to their general. Caesar himself had had jokes about the absurd fringes on his tunic and about his personal habits thrown at him. 'Romans,' the legionaries bawled, 'keep your wives and your sons under lock and key! We're bringing you back that bald lecher, the depilated catamite of the king of Bithynia!' And Caesar had to grin and bear it under his laurel wreath. The Romans had a taste for contrasts of this sort. They reminded them of the vanity of things human and the ephemeral nature of all glory.

Nonetheless Marcus and Marcia wondered whether the mime hadn't overdone it a little. His portrait of a drunken, dissipated Rufus harrying the girls along the way had been a striking one. You had the impression that from beyond the great divide an impenitent Rufus was persisting in putting forward his deplorable opinions. The customary pleasantries had been accompanied by a certain gnashing of teeth.

'Fortunately,' said Marcia, 'your panegyric was first-class. What elevated thought, what elegant diction! And how right the tone was! My father's freedmen and clients were weeping like lambs going to the slaughter.'

Rufus had been more generous to his clients than to his brother or his daughter. Marcus had had to sweat blood to come up with any good qualities in the departed at all. It had been easier to praise his non-existent ancestors and feather-brained widow!

Once filial and fraternal piety had been satisfied, conversation turned to an exchange of their latest news. Marcus, who was trying to make a good impression, did not have much to say, but Marcia had not come to make polite conversation.

'The Fates have really got it in for me at the moment: first I lost my father, now Largus.'

'Good heavens! So suddenly? He was still alive at Rufus' cremation.'

'He was the victim of an *alligator*.'

'Murdered?'

'You could put it like that.'

Marcia proceeded to recount the story as though it were drawing-room gossip:

'At some time in the past Largus' family planted some groves of poplars to grow their vines up. My husband was very proud of his trees; they were loaded with vines and every autumn they were bowed down under the weight of countless bunches of little black grapes. Did you know that this method of supporting the vines is supposed to produce much higher yields than the normal method of stringing them along poles? But there are considerable difficulties involved in *alligatio* – tying up the young shoots – and in pruning both the vine stems and the poplar branches. Slaves cannot do this sort of work, you have to use specialists. They're not easy to find, and before they go up the trees they insist that the employers agree to cover the cost of their funeral expenses. The poor (and not just the poor!) have an obsession with dazzling their friends by the lavishness of their funerals. To cut matters short, Largus had an argument with one of his binder-pruners about the size and conditions of his insurance. He was a short-tempered man, who saw red whenever he was contradicted. To shame the worker out of his greed he rushed up the first poplar he found, despite the bitterly cold weather, and started binding and pruning at random . . . until he fell out of the tree like a sack of bran and broke his neck.

A witness assured me that at the moment he fell a crow flew out of the top of the tree, towards the right. As if Largus' death could be a favourable omen! And apparently it was definitely a large crow, put on a diet by the frost after stuffing itself with grain and grapes all autumn, and not a rook, which of course could only be a bird of good omen if it flew towards the left.'

It was indeed very peculiar. Marcia drew a square of yellow silk from her sleeve and dabbed her eyes with it, as propriety demanded. But it was easy to see that the highly favourable character of the omen was an effective consolation for her loss.

'Poor child,' murmured Marcus, hastening to practicalities, 'did you at least get something in his will?'

'Not an *as*, not a *nummus*! Largus had dozens of nephews and cousins, and even quite a lot of children: no less than three children by his first wife, who used to cut me dead. In any case we were no longer on good terms. He wasn't merely unfaithful to me with the servants – I could put up with that – but with all the women friends I managed to make in that backwoods place. I was a sort of introduction agency for him! And on top of that he was chronically jealous. "Nobody dips their finger in my oil but me" was his favourite saying.'

'I assume that at least you have your original dowry. Largus didn't pinch it off you to enrich his poplars or his olives?'

'He would like to have done, but papa – who was my guardian– opposed it. So I've kept the dowry which went with me after my divorce. The law is more favourable than ever to women these days. Whether the divorce is by mutual agreement or not, we have the right to get our guardian to reclaim our dowries even in cases where the original marriage contract didn't provide for its restitution if the marriage broke down. I should've been a real fool if I'd lost my dowry as well as Largus!'

'I seem to remember that my brother wasn't very open-handed in his financial arrangements for you?'

'Papa was only open-handed in his own pleasures. I had to marry at fourteen with a dowry of 300,000 sesterces. What can you do with an income of 15,000 a year? Any suitable little dress . . . But I haven't come here to grumble or to bother you about money matters . . .'

'Tell me some more about yourself.'

Marcus was delighted that Marcia did not need any immediate financial help. It would have upset him to have found himself obliged to refuse her a loan. However, he made an indirect reference to his own difficulties, and his niece cut him short:

'I'm surprised that you didn't remarry after Pomponia's unexpected death. It would only have been your fourth marriage, and you're still very spry. How can you cope with two young children on your own?'

The real answer was quite simple. Having no money Marcus could only have made a ridiculous match well below his rank. He couldn't even afford a permanent concubine.

Caught off-balance, Marcus took refuge evasively in popular generalities:

'You know how the world is . . . Marriage these days isn't what it was. For 200 years now people have been getting married to divorce and divorced to remarry. Augustus made divorce easier in the naïve hope that couples who were better matched would have more children. But if the pitcher goes to the well too often, it gets broken. Nowadays, as Seneca put it so well (he's due back from exile this spring), "Women of the highest rank have adopted the habit of counting the years not by the names of the consuls but by those of their husbands"; and to spare themselves the bother and expense of marriage, men who want at all cost to avoid having an heir of their own blood adopt the son of a friend and set up house with some quiet freedwoman or even a carefully selected slave. It's more and more fashionable. I'm very attracted by a wise course of this kind, given that I have more children to set up than I need. Yes, when all's said and done, remarriage can wait a while.'

'It can't wait at all. I've come here to marry you.'

✵ CHAPTER ✵
4

Marcus' astonishment was total. For a moment he thought that his niece had gone out of her mind. But his visitor's regular features radiated self-control, reflection and calculation, and the thoughtful head, with the glittering jewelled band which held her braids of black hair in place, inclined slightly forward to emphasize that the proposition was conceivable and the decision taken after careful consideration.

Not knowing what to say, Marcus improvised a heavy-handed joke which didn't commit him to anything and left Marcia free to contrive whatever explanation she wished:

'At first sight it looks as though you've come to the wrong address! Since the rape of the Sabine women, Roman matrons have gained the privilege of not setting foot in their own kitchens, and they even refuse to do the shopping. I need a good cook more than I need a Sabine!'

Marcia skirted round the issue:

'Like many country landowners Largus had a subscription to the Roman *Diurna*. The account of the proceedings of the Senate has long been dropped from that newspaper, but the day before my husband died I read in it some detailed adulatory references to Vitellius' speech in favour of Claudius' immediate remarriage with Agrippina.'

'References evidently inspired by Agrippina's supporters and intended for the edification of the provinces and distant garrisons. In Rome we scarcely need the *Diurna* : word of mouth is enough.'

'Since you managed to keep your place in the Senate despite your misfortunes, you must have been present on that memorable occasion?'

'How could anyone get out of it? I had to follow the trend. The enthusiastic applause had barely finished before the keenest and most unscrupulous sycophants were rushing through the city crying out that if Caesar had the least scruple about marrying his niece, they would do him violence.'

'They had the excuse that Vitellius had been very eloquent. So would you have done. Customs do change, you know, and marriages between close relatives are becoming more and more accepted. The Julii and the

Claudii are all cousins – some of them even the offspring of first cousins. Not to mention the tangled web of adoptions which strengthen blood ties that are already very close. The pharaohs regularly married their own sisters . . .'

'Yes, and Caligula honoured two of his three sisters with his attentions. I wouldn't be surprised if he had Agrippina as well! But such things shouldn't happen. Scandals of this sort bring bad luck on a state whose basis has to be its religion. The gods take vengeance in their wrath.'

'The gods have seen – and done – plenty of the same sort of thing before! In any case this so-called scandal is now legal since the Senate of which you are a member swiftly and unanimously authorized marriage between uncles and their nieces. (But not between aunts and their nephews: women's rights are still not firmly established).'

'We had no choice. That intriguer Vitellius would have shouted himself hoarse, and his son Aulus, who follows in his father's footsteps and has the same paunch and jowls . . .'

Marcus broke off. After mechanically stringing together a few sentences in a state of shock and confusion he had belatedly seen the connection between the very recent remarriage of the prince and Marcia's strange ambitions. But the fact that a union of this kind would in future, for the first time, be legally possible only accentuated its unreal and extravagant character as far as he was concerned.

Eventually he said: 'In the name of Minerva, goddess of clear thinking, and of Venus, whose whims enflame men's hearts, tell me what there is about me that you find attractive?'

Marcia gave a little smile and appproached the subject indirectly again:

'Minerva tells me that you're a man of intelligence, cultivation and character. Papa, who was deep down more fond of you than you think, used to say to me: "Marcus doesn't have the temperament to be a great man, still less the temperament to be a scoundrel. When it comes to character he is Horace's 'golden mean'." Don't you think a quality of that sort is reassuring for a woman in these times?'

'I suppose that great men and scoundrels must be difficult to live with, especially when they're one and the same person.'

'And Venus, who has to rest sometimes, whispers in my ear that you urgently need a well-born woman of good reputation to run your household. Leaving aside my dowry . . .'

'I feel that at your age, despite the relative modesty of that dowry, you could aspire to something better than a disillusioned fifty-year-old.'

Marcia smiled again, revealing sharp teeth polished with powdered horn which made a curious contrast with her languorous eyes.

'But Marcus, you're a unique catch for me.'

'I'm not so convinced of that. I still find the bride too attractive. Haven't you simply been thrown into confusion by the brutal shock of losing both your father and your husband so suddenly? Like a fledgling falling out of a nest, you're grasping on to the first branch that comes to hand. You look so young!'

The orphaned widow's smile turned into a peal of laughter.

'Since my first wedding-night I've given up crying. What's the point? Men and women won't change.'

After a short silence she went on:

'It seems to me that under a façade of amiable false modesty you're hiding a feeling of repugnance which is really based on religious scruples. Am I right?'

'I think one would have to be emperor and Pontifex Maximus not to feel it.'

'Well, your repugnance is only another reason for me to think well of you. I share it myself up to a point. Incest is like *garum*: a good cook uses it in moderation. So, of course, I'm only offering you a marriage of convenience: a father–daughter or brother–sister relationship which would preserve a certain discreet freedom for both parties. A man has to pay nature her dues, and a woman with a certain freedom can do a lot for her husband's career.'

The project was becoming decidedly more plausible as Marcia's ideas became clearer. Disappointed in her first two husbands, she was now looking for an old fogey who would have the best possible reasons for leaving her alone and whom she could cuckold at her leisure for entirely practical ends. Really, the girl's nerve was terrifying. So this was what had become of Roman womanhood since the end of the Republic!

'I can understand,' said Marcus, caught between two stools, 'that you want to get yourself set up once and for all and that any senator is better than none. But while you're doing me the kindness of offering me a small dowry and a number of possibilities for the future which are difficult to quantify, you're also proposing to expose me to the torture of Tantalus. Have you thought of that?'

'My dear uncle, I know you have enough respect for the customs of our ancestors to put up with that without flinching. And as nowadays husbands and wives have separate bedrooms, you can enjoy a Scipio-style chastity behind closed doors. Publicly you'll be an honourable husband in the terms of the new law, following in the wake of his prince with the warm approval of the Senate. Privately you'll be a chaste devotee of the old customs. You'll win both ways, in the eyes of men and of the gods. The priests have discovered thirty thousand gods. One of them is bound to be sympathetic to you. For a start there's Minerva, your favourite of the penates, a goddess so intelligent that she never got married.

But, from what I know of marriage, your torture will be short-lived. No woman can stay attractive for more than a month to a man whose daily existence she shares. Cupid feeds on mystery and variety. That's why Fortuna Virilis, the goddess who is supposed to hide women's little faults from their husbands, has so much to do in marriage. She has to watch over so many creams and lotions, so much rouge and pumice stone, draw a pleasant veil over so many disagreeable indispositions . . . At the end of three weeks you won't even notice me any more.'

Marcus made a feeble protest. He was at something of a loss as to how to hit on the right conversational tone in a situation as false and, when it came to it, as outrageous as the present one. He found the prospect of private continence no more flattering than that of public incest.

'You're arranging my life in an extraordinarily light-hearted way, my dear. If I agreed to this little arrangement, I'd instantly earn myself the contempt of every honest man – and get very little in return.'

'One of Papa's favourite sayings was: "Gather ye rosebuds while ye may." Another was: "The contempt of honest men is all the easier to bear since they can be counted on the fingers of one hand." You'll accept this marriage.'

'I strongly doubt it.'

'You'll accept it because a freedman, a centurion captain, and even a knight by the name of Alledius Severus have already hurriedly married their nieces.'

'So what?'

With a trace of impatience Marcia went straight to the heart of the matter:

'Open your eyes. Claudius is under Agrippina's thumb but he's very attentive to all the outmoded ideas of Roman religion. He suffers from scruples. So far, only Vitellius' eloquence, the Senate's unanimous enthusiasm and the sympathetic attitude of the ordinary people, who are faithful to the memory of Germanicus and Agrippina the elder, have managed to allay those scruples. Agrippina herself, full of pride as she is, only lowered herself to this expedient because she was driven to it by the demons of her insatiable ambition. Speeches are not enough to lend an air of moral justification to such a union: it needs personal sacrifice. Every marriage between an uncle and his niece is, as far as the imperial couple are concerned, the deepest, most opportune, subtle and reassuring form of flattery. Incest becomes a sweeter pill to swallow when it's shared.

Claudius and Agrippina are so anxious for their example to be promptly followed, and so sensible of the delicacy of feeling of those few devoted enough to do so, that they immediately shower their favour on all those men and women of good will who put their devotion to their prince before considerations of natural feelings.

The freedman has been made manager of a vast estate in Africa. The knight has been rewarded with a headship of department at the Central Post Office in the Campus Martius. And the emperor in person, accompanied by Agrippina, attended the wedding of the centurion captain. Imagine your prospects if you're the first senator to seize the opportunity. How else are you going to restore the fortune which was so unjustly destroyed by one of Caligula's mad whims? Don't you want to get out of your troubles? As an affectionate niece, I'm showing you the way.

And if the prince's well-known avarice frustrates our hopes, we shan't have anything to lose. One more divorce won't make any difference to either of us. The important thing is to hurry. Plenty of senators will be crying their eyes out at this moment because they haven't got an available niece. The most recently married will be the worst off.

What can your touchy conscience reproach you with? Surely not the fact that I have the praiseworthy modesty not to require you to satisfy me in all the ways of which you would be capable?'

Set out like this by a convincing ambassadress, the whole proposal suddenly seemed more reasonable and decent. Even a man of honour could be tempted by something like this. In spite of appearances to the contrary, perhaps there was a sympathetic deity looking down from on high. Who can know for certain the will of the gods and the wondrous ways in which their minds work?

The longer Marcus discussed the matter, the more he felt himself giving way: soon, the cup of shame duly swallowed, he was only arguing for form's sake.

'There's one last point which does upset me. While Messalina was alive, Claudius betrothed his daughter Octavia to L. Junius Silanus, and marked him out for public favour by conferring the ornaments of a "triumph" on him and staging a superb gladiatorial show in his honour. Once Messalina was in the vale of shadows, Agrippina hurriedly had

Silanus disgraced, probably with the ulterior motive of keeping Octavia for her own son Nero. Not only was the engagement broken off in an insulting fashion, but Silanus found himself threatened with prosecution on a trumped-up charge of committing incest with his sister Calvina. In despair the young man committed suicide on the very day that Claudius and Agrippina were married. His funeral pyre is still smoking. You must have heard about it? It's common knowledge.'

'What has Lucius' death got to do with us?'

'You know perfectly well what close links of clientship there used to be between us and the Silani. It's infinitely unpleasant to get married for the purpose of currying favour with Agrippina when she has just forced into suicide – in the most deplorable circumstances – one of the most delightful members of the *gens* who protected and helped us for so long.'

'That coincidence is nothing to do with you. In any case, if I'm not mistaken, the Silanus to whom the Aponius Saturninus family are theoretically answerable wasn't the unlucky Lucius but one of his two brothers, Marcus and Decimus, who are alive and well.'

'In principle Decimus, the eldest, should be my patron.'

'Well, perhaps our marriage will bring you a more effective patron. Where else are you going to find one, seeing that you missed your mark with Sejanus?'

Marcia had an answer to everything. Pomponia's only response to Marcus's troubles had been endless lamentations. Now he had the impression of being taken by the hand and led towards a better future by this stunning apparition who gave no sign of being evil. As the young woman had undoubtedly proved to him, he had nothing to lose and plenty to gain. He would have thought of it himself, if his failures and disillusionment had not cut him off from court intrigues and the realities of the Forum. What a lesson to him!

Anxious to strike while the iron was hot, Marcia steered the conversation on to the topic of the projected wedding. The question of the guardian's permission was a tricky one.

Women in Rome were considered as permanent minors. They always had to be 'in the hands' of a man who was legally responsible for them.

In early times marriage transferred a woman from her father's jurisdiction to her husband's. This was true whether it was a case of aristocratic marriage by *confarreatio*, where the couple offered up a cake of spelt to Jupiter Capitolinus in the presence of the Pontifex Maximus and the High Priest of Jupiter: or of plebeian marriage by *coemptio*, where the father went through the fiction of selling his daughter to her husband: or of marriage by *usus*, where after a year of uninterrupted cohabitation the girl was held to be a legitimate spouse.

But as a result of the early and considerable intermingling of aristocracy and plebeians, out of which a new nobility was to rise over a socially immobile *plebs*, a uniform form of marriage gradually developed which had reduced the three earlier forms to merely antiquarian interest. It was a revolutionary form of marriage in that the authority of guardianship over the woman was no longer given to her husband but remained the privilege of the woman's closest male relative on her father's side. In this way each woman was provided with a guardian who was a member of her own family, whose job it was to keep an eye on her dowry, to defend her interests in the event of a divorce, and to see to it that she made the best possible remarriage. The rights of the Roman husband were reduced to the right to sleep with his wife when she would let him and to advise her on her toilette the rest of the time. This highly original system was only the application to married women of the standard system, which required that a child who had lost his father be legally protected by a guardian from his father's side of the family during his minority, since in the eyes of the law the mother was incapable.

As a result of being physically subject to their husbands while remaining under the guardianship of a father, uncle or appropriate substitute, Roman women, in principle subject to a dual authority, swiftly reached the point of being in practice subject to none. It is nature's rule that contradictory forces cancel each other out. This lack of subjection was all the more remarkable in that, having gained the upper hand over their husbands, they had worked hard to undermine the authority of their guardians in any respect which might be at all restrictive. To do so they had hypocritically put forward the argument that freedom to remarry according to their fancy would inevitably lead to a substantial rise in the birth-rate. The magistrates had taken their part and granted them the right to dismiss and replace a guardian as soon as he showed signs of opposing their whims.

It was the triumph of weakness and guile over the crushing forces of husbands and fathers.

In the case of Marcus and Marcia the authorization which the guardian had to give posed a problem for one good reason: since Rufus' death it was Marcus who had inherited the guardianship of Marcia.

'You certainly can't be both my husband and my guardian,' she said. 'I should risk slavery. It would be a barbarous throw-back to the old ways. We aren't in the reign of the Tarquins any more!'

'Don't get worked up about it,' he replied. 'It would indeed be a legal scandal. Marriage *cum manu* is well and truly dead, and no one has any intention of reviving it. Clearly I shall marry you *sine manu*, like anybody else, which means you'll be in the hands of a guardian who will by definition be someone other than myself.'

'But *you* are my tutor. And I can't think of any other possible relative on my father's side.'

'The case is certainly an extraordinary one, and Claudius' legislative whim is primarily responsible for it. But after all there's always some relative 'n' times removed who'll do. It's really only a formality. In cases where an entire line has died out, it's the praetor's job to appoint a stranger of good reputation and morals who is prepared to act. A woman, married or single, must have a guardian: she can't even make a will without his express authority.'

'Couldn't I take advantage of the peculiar circumstances to get out of having a guardian at all?'

'What would be the point? Even fathers are no longer an embarrassment once the woman has been set free, in practice, by her first marriage, and other guardians interfere still less. Anyway, as far as I know, with the exception of Vestal Virgins the only Roman women exempted from guardianship, as a result of a decree of Augustus, are mothers of three children. I trust that my praiseworthy self-restraint will leave little likelihood of your having three children.'

'Rest assured. Men may not give any thought to such things but women take precautions. My mother taught me all I need to know on that topic when I married my first husband.'

'Your mother was an admirable woman. To come back to what's worrying you, I'll go and speak to Vitellius. He'll be delighted with our plans, which accord with his own interests. He'll make arrangements for us and speed things up.'

'He could even put in a word on our behalf.'

'That would be natural. And he enjoys Claudius' confidence as well as Agrippina's favour . . .'

The need to economize, rather than any sense of discretion, dictated that there should be a lightning engagement and a very simple wedding – unless any people of distinction had to be invited. Fortunately changes in custom had reduced the essential part of the ceremony to so little that any sort of celebration, from the massively lavish to the most Spartanly frugal, was conceivable.

Marcia felt that they should imitate the well-known restraint of a

Republican heroine of the same name as herself who had privately married Cato – the one who was to finish up at Utica.

'There was only one person at the wedding, their friend Brutus, who set his seal as witness to the contract. Then the witness became augur. He slit the throat of a piglet in the *atrium*, cut open its stomach, and declared with a straight face that the entrails looked fine and the auspices were favourable. Then he became witness again and the bride and groom finally exchanged vows. It's the formula "Where you are Gaius I shall be Gaia", the exchange of free consent, which is the essential part of the marriage ceremony, isn't it? All the rest is merely ornamental.'

'The contract itself isn't obligatory, but tradition requires there to be a minimum of one witness present and that the auspices be taken by a family *auspex* who's not a priest and has no official position. In Rome the religious aspect of the marriage is part of the private cult observed by each separate *gens*. The augur is always someone connected with the household. It's only the potential consequences of the ceremony that concern the State.'

'As the *auspex* is an amateur, the auspices are always favourable. I should like to see an *auspex* quibble and insist that the marriage be postponed until better times! Taking the auspices has become a pure formality. Why not drop the practice altogether?'

'That's a blasphemous suggestion!'

'On the contrary, I'm showing more respect for religion than you are. Aren't you afraid that the gods will get angry at seeing their good will invoked in the context of incest?'

'But we shall be permanently sleeping apart!'

'Let's hope you'll stick to that.'

Marcus steered the conversation into a nostalgic review of past events awakened by the reference to Cato.

'Did you know that the virtuous Cato gave up Marcia to his friend the great orator Hortensius at the pressing request of the latter? Hortensius wasn't exactly in love with her, but he passionately wanted to be bound to his revered Cato by the most intimate and prolific of bonds. Hortensius first asked for the hand of Cato's daughter, but eventually he was refused on the grounds that she was already married and pregnant for good measure. But they couldn't just reject him or his feelings would have been terribly hurt, since he was so devoted to Cato. So he was given the wife instead of the daughter, and was at last able to embrace the master's treasured relics at leisure.

And Brutus, having practised on pigs at weddings, was to end up slitting Caesar's throat in the Senate. Caesar, who knew everybody, happened to have slept with the young hero's mother at just the right time to put it into his head that Brutus looked like him. Well-informed historians think that the "*Tu quoque fili*" (which was actually said in Greek) was in fact an accusation of parricide. If Brutus didn't know about the family relationship, he found out about it in a very dramatic fashion. It would have been a scene worthy of Euripides if the young man, in the middle of his murderous frenzy, had held back his arm at the "You too, my son!" and cried "Hold on a moment. It's my dad we're bumping off!"'

Marcus, who thought it smart to entertain pro-Republican sentiments – though in a suitably discreet form – admired Stoics of the sort who would have killed both their parents to insure the survival of some dubious idea and who found a way to combine sublime friendship and sexual satisfaction in the same bed.

'Alas,' he sighed in conclusion 'there's not much chance of any man seeking you out because he wants to be able to adore what I've held in my arms, and still less likelihood of you coming back to me, like that long-ago Marcia, whom Cato remarried after the death of the pious Hortensius. That breed of superior men and devoted women has died out.'

The Republican legend, invented by the defenders of a Freedom which profited only themselves, left Marcia completely cold. In her opinion Cato of Utica was a dreamer and a blunderer, who had even managed to make his clients ill by following the archaic custom of feeding them on rape. Women of sense always join the winning camp. What can you get out of losers?

There was an uproar in the corridor outside, and suddenly a *retiarius* pursued by a *secutor* burst in across the sitting-room. Marcus junior and Kaeso, escaping from the old slave who was in charge of them, had snatched up their gladiators' gear. Rich children had expensive copies of the real thing, with uniforms cut to fit them and swords with walnut blades, gilded hilts and ebony handles. Marcus' sons were wearing cardboard uniforms and had plywood weapons but in their enthusiasm they were completely unworried by such details.

Their father, outraged by the interruption, shouted at them, and the two miscreants came over to greet their cousin, who lavishly compli-mented Marcus on their looks and health and embraced them affection-ately. Marcus junior looked sweet with his trident with its safety guard and his little net. And on the crest of Kaeso's helmet you could read the words *Sabinus victor*. (In fact the commander of the German guard under

Caligula had gone back to the arena in the reign of Claudius and had bitten the dust in defeat. He had been rescued only by the pressing intervention of Messalina: he was one of the chief studs at her orgies.)

When the children had been sent out again, Marcia asked Marcus whether he still had his little suburban gladiatorial school.

'I'm quite pleased with it . . .'

'I never understood what made you set yourself up in a trade of such ill repute after that frightful auction.'

'I've often asked myself the same question . . . Of course Caius sent someone round to offer me a derisory sum for the lot which I'd been landed with. But I was exasperated by the man's nerve, and I jibbed. When I thought it over, I told myself that after all I had an asset and I should make something out of it. Of course it wasn't easy, because I was a complete beginner. But I was fortunate enough to find an efficient trainer who took over the running of the business: obviously there was no question of a senator attending to the running of a gladiatorial *ludus* in person. Eurypylus, who is a Greek from Tarentum, pays me a fixed sum, which is quite small, and a percentage of the takings. Sometimes, when they're short, the imperial *lanistae* hire some of our gladiators for a Roman show, but most of the time we work in the cities of Italy, where they like anything that comes from the capital. My men go from Verona to Brindisi via Pompeii or Beneventum. They do their best. It's not the team it was when I first got it: I don't have the funds to preserve and renew my stock. But Eurypylus' *ludus* has a good reputation. I prefer quality to quantity: there are no slaves. We even deal with travelling *lanistae*.'

'You used to have a chariot, didn't you?'

'I still do. With two new prancing steeds! My driver, a Sicilian who also acts as *bestiarius* occasionally, is still the one that Caius maliciously landed me with. This Tyrannus – I can't remember his real name – is beginning to get on a bit, but he's indestructible and a genius with horses. The horses are more important to me than the chariot: I've a mount when I need one at no extra cost, and the children have the best possible conditions for learning to ride.'

'You're a very attentive father, Marcus. I'll make you a promise – you deserve it. Since you're putting the restitution of the fortunes of your house in my hands, I shall treat your children as if they were my own. A woman would be very stupid to have children of her own when the gods have entrusted her with such fine ones.'

The sincerest promises are the emptiest ones. When someone devotes themselves totally to a cause, they put the worst of themselves in as well as the best.

Confidently Marcus accompanied Marcia back to the stinking entrance-porch, where her chair was waiting for her, with its twin poles leaning vertically against the wall like two brothers or a husband and wife.

'Marcus and Marcia,' said the happy fiancé 'It's as though we were meant to go together.'

'Except that Marcus is a first name. Marcia is my mother's name; my maternal grandfather was a Marcius. It's in memory of mama that I prefer to be called Marcia rather than Aponia, which is what I would normally be called.'

'In fact you'll be an Aponia, daughter of Aponius and wife of Aponius. That's the sort of tangle that should please Agrippina!'

Upper-class Roman women did not in fact have a 'first name'. They used the name of their father's *gens* in the feminine, and had different surnames to distinguish them from their sisters. They retained their clan name throughout all their marriages – a very convenient arrangement. A Roman husband gave his name to his children but not to his wife.

As for any illegitimate children who might be born, they took their mother's clan name in the masculine, the irregularity being smoothed out by the addition of the phrase 'son of Spurius'. This fictitious Spurius whose sexual activity was apparently infinite was thus the father of all the bastards in Rome. The adjective *spurius* in fact means 'illegitimate', for the noun *spurium* was one of the many ways of designating the female sexual organs. Roman bastards, officially registered under the title 'son of Cunt', did not attend their mother's wedding and usually received a poor education.

Marcia set off at a trot with her four Libyan chair-bearers. From outside in the alley Marcus looked up at the vines and shrubs which the tenants had grown on the balconies of the tenement block. Was he finally going to go up in the world again? Would he get his ground-floor back on to a smart level of the city, where all he would have over his head would be birds of good omen?

※ CHAPTER ※
5

Marcus nibbled thoughtfully at some olives wrapped in a hunk of dry bread soaked in olive oil, took a few bites from a winter pear and drank a finger of rough wine mixed with water. Then, not being in a mood to take a siesta, he went and sat in his library to write a request for an audience with Vitellius *père*.

His hand hesitated between the double tablets available. If he used ordinary wooden tablets he might wound the parvenu's vanity. On the other hand the ivory tablets seemed to be saying, 'Send these precious objects back to me with your reply.' Marcus settled for the boxwood tablets, wrote a ridiculous text with the sharp edge of his stylus and promptly rubbed it out again with the flat end. The difficulty of his task reflected the awkward nature of his situation.

Finally, after numerous attempts, he decided on the following text, which he carefully engraved very legibly in the pale wax, in such a way that the uncial letters would stand out well against the background of dark wood uncovered by the point of the stylus. He even separated out certain words and expressions which he judged particularly important.

MAPONIUSSATURNINUSLVITELLIOSUOS SPLENDIDA ORATIOQUAMIN
SENATUHABUISTI VEHEMENTER ANIMUMMEUMCOMMOVITETPRINCIPI
NOSTROLAETITIAMDEDISTIETMIHIDABISNAMJAMPRIDEMMORTUIFRA-
TRISFILIAMOCCULTEAMABAMQUAMNUNCINMATRIMONIUMDUCERE
ARDENTER CUPIOQUANDOTEADSPICIAMQUANDOQUELICEBITSIVALESBE-
NEESTEGOAUTEMVALEO

It was short and sweet and perfectly clear. Only one adjective, but it was well placed. He had avoided the pitfall of letting himself go and giving himself away, thereby exposing an extra weak spot where the ill-disposed might attack him.

Latin-speakers did not usually divide up words or sentences in hand-written documents and resolutely took no account of accents or punctuation. For those few readers who would find it difficult to decipher this writing perhaps a more modern version should be given:

'M. Aponius Saturninus L. Vitellio suo s. (alutem dicit). Splendida oratio quam in senatu habuisti vehementer animum meum commovit. Et principi nostro laetitiam dedisti, et mihi dabis. Nam jampridem mortui fratris filiam occulte amabam, quam nunc in matrimonium ducere ardenter cupio. Quando te adspiciam, quandoque licebit? Si vales, bene est; ego autem valeo.'

Which in late Germanic dialect means:

'M. Aponius Saturninus presents his compliments to his friend L. Vitellius. The magnificent speech which you delivered to the Senate moved me very deeply. You have brought happiness to our prince. You could bring happiness to me too. I have for some time been secretly in love with the daughter of my dead brother. Now I passionately desire to marry her. When may I come to see you? I hope you are in good health, as I myself am.'

Marcus checked that the wax on the second flap of the double tablet was properly smooth and even, and firm enough in its bed not to mix with the wax on the other side where the letter had been written. He closed the two sides together and sealed them with his ring, a finely engraved intaglio of the wolf feeding Romulus and Remus. The number and arrangement of the lines representing the animal's coat had been designed to discourage forgery.

The suspicious Romans preferred to use seals for their day-to-day business, rather than signatures, which were always open to doubt.

The tablets came back before sunset, fixing a meeting with Marcus for the following morning, after Vitellius had seen his clients: he would then have a free moment before he had to go down to the Forum. The promptness of the reply was encouraging.

Vitellius had a large villa on the Quirinal, near a temple of Fortuna Primigenia, where there was a charming view over the Roman Forums and the temple of Jupiter Capitolinus on the side overlooking the Vicus Fori Martis. He received Marcus very graciously. But the slight edge of ironic contempt visible beneath his compliments should have put the petitioner on his guard.

For Vitellius, who had only recently achieved high social rank, and whose susceptibilities were all the more delicate, incest was pardonable in a prince, who was above the law, and was of no importance in the common herd. But as one of the most influential members of the Senate he would have preferred the *patres conscripti* to limit their expressions of approval to applause. He owed it to his career however to support Aponius' proposal – even if only feebly – since the supposed lovematch of this vulgar social climber would provide opportune support for that of Claudius and Agrippina.

The absence of potential guardians was solved with disconcerting ease: Vitellius' son would personally deal with that formality and would be happy to attend the wedding.

The prospect of this distinguished guest posed a disquieting financial problem for Marcus. If the younger Vitellius were present, they could not avoid a minimum of display. Indeed they would have to provide an exceptionally expensive feast. At thirty-four Aulus Vitellius was already enormously fat and had the well-founded triple reputation of eating all the time, eating fantastic quantities and only eating the best. His morals matched his physique. With the vigorous encouragement of his father Aulus put all his energies night and day into devouring whatever he could get his hands on: his taste for juicy bits of flesh included not merely a good steak but women oozing with ambition and courtesans dried out by overwork. Aulus would equally swallow down honorary magistracies and prospective priesthoods. He was notoriously irreligious, an ogre, and nobody could predict the limits of his monstrous appetite.

When Marcus declared that he would be absolutely delighted . . . and was anxious to organize a memorable occasion despite the limited nature of his financial resources, Vitellius laughed and said: 'Don't worry about that. You can have 500,000 sesterces for your little feast . . .'

That meant that it wouldn't be possible to put anything aside from the sum provided, since Aulus would get through a third of it on his own and nine-tenths of it with his cronies. He adored monstrous fish, extraordinary shellfish, bellyfuls of plump ortolans, fine liver pâtés of poultry or pork, dormice that had been fattened up and preserved in honey and poppyseeds, vulvas of trout *ejectitiae* cut out of the mother towards the end of pregnancy, the whole meal being copiously washed down with the best *garum* and wines of vintages normally unobtainable. His trips to the *vomitorium* and the latrines only roused his incredible appetites still further. Truffles and flap-mushrooms were mere *hors d'oeuvre* to him. His greatest triumph was a pot-pourri of his own invention, an unheard-of mixture of flamingo tongues, muraena roes, peacock brains and parrot-fish livers. He was a difficult guest to satisfy.

Marcus had to withdraw without any other precise promise, but he had the impression that, when all was said and done, things hadn't got off to too bad a start. Before plunging himself back into the shadows of the Subura he looked out over the tempting panorama and filled his lungs with fresh air.

The marriage was celebrated in the pleasant little house which the late Rufus had fitted out in the heart of a beautiful park on the Esquiline. The house, gardens and staff were mortgaged to the hilt and on the point of being sold up, but that wasn't plastered all over the walls, and appearances were saved.

Towards the middle of the afternoon Marcia came out of her apartments to receive her fiancé and Aulus Vitellius in the atrium. Vitellius' ceremonial toga did wonders for his shapeless figure. Most of Marcus' relatives had refused the invitation, and Marcia had invited only a small number of women friends, but Aulus was surrounded by a band of hard-drinking gluttons accustomed to carousing in their captain's wake.

Marcia's appearance was greeted by a shower of compliments. The traditional bridal dress suited her: a loose saffron-yellow pleated over-dress, worn over an unhemmed tunic pulled in at the waist by a 'Hercules belt' in wool with a double knot; her hair piled up, in six bandeaux separated by ribbons, the same style that the Vestal Virgins have throughout their office; and on her head a dazzling veil into which was woven a garland of myrtle and orange blossom which at that time of year must have come out of a hothouse. Perhaps she was rather overdoing it for a third marriage, but her freshness – for once she was wearing no make-up – and her modesty made one ready to forgive her anything.

Vitellius finally took his mind off food for a moment, but contrived to begin less than tactfully. 'You're a fortunate man,' he said to Marcus, 'to be marrying such an exquisite niece. She's more than a match for Agrippina. But there's no need to follow the example of Oedipus, who stupidly put his eyes out when he found out that he happened to have slept with his mother. There would be plenty of other eyes ready to take advantage of this wonderful sight . . .'

In Marcia's case her beauty excused any possible lapse of taste. Her guardian had to be excused for his highly inappropriate jokes because of his position. So everybody hastened to laugh.

When the ten witnesses had put their seals on the contract, Vitellius devoted himself to examining the palpitating entrails of a sheep, which Marcus had chosen in preference to the customary pig. The late lamented Rufus' family *auspex* had slipped away after the funeral and had not been seen since.

'Oh dear,' said the benevolent augur after messing around for a while, 'what's this I see? The left lung has a fissure, the liver is distorted, the heart is stunted and bleeding the wrong way. Moreover the animal hasn't been slaughtered in the prescribed fashion. The knife should point up for sacrifices to the heavenly deities and down for sacrifices to the gods of the underworld. Now, the man who cut this animal's throat held the knife horizontally, as if addressing himself to a god as yet unknown who lives between the clouds and the abyss. And wasn't that the cry of a mouse which I heard? Do the gods look on us with disfavour? Has some aspect of the ceremony upset them? Should we begin again? In the days when our ancestors still had some respect for the tutelary deities, auspices had to be taken again as many as thirty times because of a mistake in the ritual or a negative result . . .'

The joke was in the worst possible taste. Vitellius had gone much too far. Despite the general scepticism in such matters, there was a hint of discomfort mixed with the stifled laughter. Superstition, which flourished on the ruins of the ancestral beliefs, required that those ruins should remain standing, as an eternal testimony to the grandeur of Rome for the ruling classes and an irreplaceable source of moral instruction for the credulous lower orders. After all, if any gods did exist somewhere, a marriage such as this might surely bring bad luck?

'Don't worry,' said Marcia, 'I'm already under the protection of my guardian, the illustrious Vitellius, and our friend here is only quibbling because he wants to spoil your appetites so he can have more for himself.'

There was a burst of genuine laughter at this neat riposte. Vitellius, doubly flattered, stood up and announced as he washed his hands: 'As far as the mouse goes I'm not at all sure. When I think about it, it might have been a field-mouse. As for the rest . . . we'll discuss it when we leave the *triclinium*. For the meantime I declare the omens favourable. May the gods protect this exemplary couple in their devotion to our prince, and may the great and good Jupiter swiftly provide us with the libation of Falernian which will piously mark the beginning of our celebrations!'

Amid relieved applause Marcus and Marcia came together to exchange vows with all the gravity necessary, and the company went in to eat.

The chef, who had recently had some practice at his master's funeral banquet, had ruled out entertaining more than forty people for 500,000 sesterces with Aulus Vitellius presiding. Fortunately the winter dining-room, which faced south, contained a *sigma* with twelve places, a large crescent-shaped sofa in the curve of which the servers placed the trolleys containing each new course. The summer dining-room next door, which could be opened on to the gardens in fine weather, had three U-shaped *triclinia* which, at three people to each couch, made space for a further twenty-seven guests. That made a total of thirty-nine. The number ought not to be exceeded, for the guests had been asked not to encumber themselves with the hangers-on, so picturesquely called 'shadows', who were commonly tolerated on these occasions.

The guests took their shoes off; the men abandoned their togas, and the women their capes and coats, and they all put on a *synthesis*. This was a long tunic of fine cloth which hosts gave their dinner guests to protect their clothes. Men, women and even girls used to eat lying down, leaning on their left elbows. This involved a certain risk of accidents; when the courses were numerous it was not unusual to change one's *synthesis* during the meal.

First of all the guests stretched out more or less on their backs, to facilitate the ritual of washing the feet; this was absolutely necessary because they wore neither socks nor stockings to protect them from the dust or mud. Then they took up an eating position, stretching themselves lazily out on the fresh linen covers which protected the soft cushions. Thus only their right arm was free for eating. All Roman cuisine had long had to adapt itself to this habit of using only one hand to take refreshment.

The bridal pair and the most important guests were spread out across the *sigma*, with the two places of honour at the ends. Vitellius, the bride's guardian, was at one end, with the bride 'below' him, and the groom was at the other, with a close friend of Marcia's 'above' him. These expressions had nothing whatsoever to do with height, they were borrowed from the *triclinia*. where the main place was in principle at the centre of each couch.

Marcus hastily asked Vitellius to preside over the banquet, and the latter ordered a fairly strong mixture of wine and water in the aperitif jugs. The libation to Jupiter had been omitted, but nobody seemed put out. Using little ladles, the servers poured into each cup the number of measures decreed by the presider, a toast was drunk to the health of the emperor and his consort, and another to the valiant Roman armies, who no longer had much to do. Then, while the slaves were handing out napkins and towels, the first course, an avalanche of *hors d'oeuvre*, made its appearance, on superb silver dishes. (Marcia was hoping to save a few pieces from the rapacity of the creditors lying in wait for her.) There were to be nine courses instead of the usual four. It would be the middle of the night before they finished . . .

All banquets are alike. There seemed to be nothing original about this one except Vitellius' boundless appetite and the omission, necessitated by considerations of economy, of the tragic, comic or erotic dramatic enter-tainments between courses which had become customary. The chasteness of the bridal pair was not evident in their faces – perhaps because it was questionable.

As the courses came and went, Marcus talked to his neighbour, a woman who had abundant experience of divorce and who seemed light-weight in every sense of the expression. It was an excellent opportunity for him to find out more about his young wife. By offering all manner of lies in order to elicit the truth Marcus eventually discovered what everyone else knew already, and he himself suspected: Marcia had endowed her first husband with horns long enough to frighten even his horse. 'But I'm sure,' his neighbour said 'that she'll behave properly in future. She's clearly a sensible woman who wants to settle down. To judge from my own experience all men are pretty much the same. It's doing them too much honour to go round collecting them!' An ordinary husband would have found food for belated thought in the conversation. Fortunately Marcus was no ordinary husband.

From time to time Marcia switched her attention from Vitellius to the gold engagement ring on her third finger. In the process of disembowel-ling and chopping up their pharaohs, before taking them off and hiding them somewhere everyone could find them, the subtle priests of Egypt had discovered that an extraordinarily fine nerve runs from the third finger straight to the innermost region of the heart. The anonymous third finger thereby gained its name of 'ring-finger'. It was now all the rage to wear a ring there, but the fashion would probably fade, like all fashions.

Then Marcia's eyes sought out her uncle, to indicate to him that he was not forgotten.

Vitellius, for his part, only paused in stuffing himself in order to make a pass at the bride. She laughed as he whispered into her pink shell-like ears suggestions which everyone guessed were improper.

The sun began to set. As they drank cup upon cup of wine the guests began to lose some of their discretion and found a temporary outlet for their desires in fondling the pretty little girlish slaveboys who were hand-ing round the finger bowls. As early as the third course Vitellius reduced the proportion of water to wine in the punchbowls.

Slaves lit the hanging lamps, the adjustable candelabra and the bronze bracket-lamps with their multiple wicks, in such a way as to procure a gentle flattering light. Then they stoked up the braziers, whose toxic fumes were channelled away through concealed pipes. Outside the window panes of coloured glass and thin translucent stone it was now completely dark. The heady odour of spices mingled with that of the oil burning at the point of the wicks and with the perfumes thrown from time to time on to the glowing charcoal in the braziers.

Marcus had not been at a feast of this sort for years. All these pleasures reminded him of a long-gone period of his life. They made him less critical of the somewhat out-of-place inscriptions which Rufus, a man with a dry sense of humour, had had engraved in the marble frieze opposite the *sigma*, where nobody could fail to notice them. Exhortations to virtue of this kind were normally only seen in the houses of the absurd petit-bourgeois of Italian country towns. The former owner had evidently intended them not merely to poke malicious fun at the gentility of the lower classes but rather to encourage tendencies that the closeness of shared couches might not of itself be sufficient to awaken.

LASCIVOS VULTUS ET BLANDOS AUFER OCELLOS
CONIUGE AB ALTERIUS SIT TIBI IN ORE PUDOR

LET NOT YOUR LUSTFUL SENSUAL GAZE
UPON YOUR NEIGHBOUR'S WIFE ALIGHT
AND MAY THE WORDS UPON YOUR LIPS
BE MODEST AND POLITE

Or:

MATRONAE VENERABILIS FER PUERILITATEM QUANTO MAGIS
FUGIT IRREPARABILE TEMPUS TANTO ANUS CAUTIONES PETIT

ENDURE THE CHILDISHNESS OF THE RESPECTABLE MATRON
THE MORE THE IRRECOVERABLE YEARS FLY PAST THE MORE
THE OLD LADY NEEDS CAREFUL TREATMENT

Anus in Latin means 'old lady' or 'anus', according to the gender and the length of the first syllable, a distinction which an inscription in the nominative cannot make. One had therefore to be illiterate to miss the unnatural obscenity concealed in this piece of advice. But timid old ladies were doubtless few and far between at the amiable Rufus' little dinner parties . . .

Towards the sixth course Marcus, who had been distracted by his neighbour's chitchat, suddenly noticed that the bride was no longer in the room and that Vitellius' imposing mass was no longer looming over her frail body. He felt an absurd pang of jealousy, which he tried to put down to discontent at their contempt for the proprieties. Their absence was prolonged.

'If I know her,' his neighbour whispered in his ear, as though divining his thoughts, 'she's seized the opportunity to plead your cause with him. By the time we get to the dessert Vitellius won't be able to see straight or hear what's said to him. By that time it won't be any use flashing him a smile as he comes out of the lavatory.'

'Do you think he's likely to settle for a smile, given the state he's in already?'

'Don't worry. He's so overweight he needs sugar-tongs to get his cock out of the rolls of fat.'

She really knew how to reassure a chap!

Something odd must have happened. What could Marcia do if caught by Vitellius? Four hundred pounds to a hundred and forty! The monster didn't need sugar tongs for a sexual assault.

His neighbour went on: 'Caligula used to rape his guests' wives for the fun of seeing the expression on their husband's face. Vitellius hasn't got to that stage yet. Do taste this sultan hen . . . The only interesting thing about the ostrich pâté is the feathers.'

The reference to Caligula was the final straw for Marcus. He started to get to his feet, to go and find out what was up. But his neighbour held him down. She showed remarkable strength of wrist.

At long last Marcia came back to her place. As she passed, she threw her husband a look of satisfied complicity. She did not seem to have suffered. Vitellius came back soon afterwards. His stomach had burst through his *synthesis*, which was too tight, and his little piggy eyes had a contented look in them which was both lubricious and nasty. Instead of going back to his place beside the bride he came and sat by Marcus, squashing his feet with a lordly buttock.

'Your wife was just bathing my temples with vervain after I came out of the *vomitorium*. I think my father will look favourably on you. I should like to do something for you myself. Capito has just died and the Arval Brethren will be electing his replacement on the third day of the festival of Dia. Agrippina and I will see to it that they pick you.'

Marcus thought he was dreaming. Romulus himself had assembled the eleven sons of his adoptive mother Acca Larentia to sacrifice to Ceres, goddess of the fruits of the earth and patron deity of farmworkers. Since then Acca Larentia had been honoured by the Arval Brethren under the name of Dia. It was the oldest, most exclusive and most aristocratic of the colleges of priests in Rome, and election to it marked its members indelibly for life. Even the augurs were insignificant in comparison with the Arval Brethren.

'But,' Marcus stammered, 'the college is only open to aristocrats or to senators' sons of noble rank, like the Grand Master Vipstanius Apronianus, or Sextius Africanus, Memmius Regulus, Valerius Messala Corvinus, Faustus Cornelius Sulla Felix and the two Pisos . . . As you'll have suspected, my family is far from being an old-established one.'

'Are you trying to be offensive? I'm the Vice-master of the Order, and my grandfather was a mere knight from Nuceria. Since I haven't any ancestors to provide me with a string of surnames and have no desire for any of the common surnames, I simply use the name Vitellius. One day it'll be worth all the rest.'

The boastful Vitellius leant over Marcus and put a delicate hand on his shoulder. It was like a miniature emerging from a ham . . .

'My dear fellow, do you know how I became Vice-master? When I was twenty, like your wife, I was poncing prettily around on Capri at the feet of old Tiberius, waiting for Caius – so they say – to stifle him with a cushion. Then I drove chariots with Caligula and played dice with Claudius. So don't talk to me about "old families" when a word from the Emperor can achieve anything!'

'But Claudius, with his mania for things antiquarian, is very attached to the rules of the cult. Isn't he likely to make objections?'

'We'll say a few kind words about you to Agrippina, who isn't interested in any cult but her own. Claudius puts his seal on more decrees than he has time to read. Don't fuss. I'll look after your interests, and for the best of possible reasons: with you and L. Otho (whose distinguished relatives are confined to his mother's side) I'll feel less isolated in the Brethren, among all those figureheads. It's time for them to give way to Rome's eternal youth – to people whose ancestors are still to come!'

Vitellius' astonishing cynicism inspired an equal mixture of repulsion and attraction. But where could Marcus find enough money to cut the right sort of figure among the Brethren?

'My father,' said Marcus, 'finished his days in the equestrian order. He could have become a member earlier. A property qualification of 400,000 sesterces was hardly a barrier to him. But after holding the praetorship I had the little setback of which you will have heard . . .'

'Enough said. The little expenses involved will all be charged to the Exchequer until you've recovered your fortunes. I'll personally supervise the details of the banquet to mark your reception into the Order. It will take place on the XVI of the Kalends of January after your election.'

'I've heard it said that the College holds large numbers of feasts?'

Vitellius hooted with laughter at such naivety.

'My dear chap, we don't do anything else! It's our only reason for existing! Apart, that is, from the celebration of the spring festival of Dia, which is only an *hors d'oeuvre*, with its cow and its two young sows. And you mustn't forget that we're also chaplains of a sort to the imperial family and make sacrifices all year round on any appropriate occasion, for the happiness of the emperor, his consort and their children. The official records of the college list the sacrifices offered on all important occasions. In fact we keep the annals of the State in so far as the State is identifiable with the emperor and his household.

Naturally, as our piety is exemplary the animals sacrificed are top quality, which is more than can be said for plenty of other sacrifices, public or private. The sort of well-fattened beef with good red meat and yellow fat which the Homeric heroes are supposed to have grilled for their suppers is so impossible to find normally that you wouldn't dare serve beef on a special occasion. But you can eat it till you're weary of it at our dinners. The animals are specially raised for the Brethren on the green grassy banks of the Clitumnus: the waters of the river are said to have the property of bleaching the animals which bathe there. And there's no danger of the gods making off with your share: Prometheus got Jupiter's agreement that they'd be satisfied with the smell. An entirely logical form of self-restraint: the gods don't eat, they sniff. Of all the various priestly orders who spend their time eating, our food is the best – especially since I took over responsibility for it. All you have to do is to dig your own grave with your jaws before some other starving fellow does it for you.'

Marcus could only thank Vitellius effusively. Not only would he no longer be deprived of good food, but this honour, which was being bestowed on him as an act of charity, would introduce him into a club where the aristocracy rubbed shoulders with the favourites of the moment. It might give him the means to set his ship to rights within a few years.

On an impulse he suddenly kissed Vitellius' hand, a hand smelling of food, a hand which had caressed Tiberius in his decline, had held the reins for Caligula and thrown dice with Claudius. 'Keep your embraces for your wife,' said his benefactor gaily, 'she's worth it.' Marcus realized that even if his marriage to Marcia had been a straightforward one, he would probably have closed his eyes to the familiarities which the ogre had been able to indulge in without scruple against some corridor wall. Isn't a tyrant's greatest excuse the way in which his victims rush to demean themselves?

Vitellius, who was evidently in an amiable mood, asked 'Can I lend you a few of my escort to protect your little wedding procession against any undesirables you may run into? Where do you live?'

When it got dark, Rome was a prey to muggers and murderers, and the seven companies of the Watch were insufficient to cover the 265 quarters into which the fourteen districts of the city were divided. The tangles of little alleys were only lit by chance fires, and the seven companies of firemen could not cope with those either. The Via Sacra and the Via Nova were the only roads wide enough for two chariots to pass, and there were far more footpaths for pedestrians than roads for wheeled traffic. Every now and then the Prefect of the city had a grand cleaning-up operation. But afterwards he let things slide again. Everyone who was anyone had masses of clients and slaves to protect themselves and their belongings, didn't they? The poor murdered and robbed each other, but that wasn't much of a loss. The government was much more concerned about political crimes.

'I live . . . in the centre,' Marcus eventually replied.

'Over by the Subura?'

'In that direction, yes.'

'I adore the Subura. It's such a picturesque quarter. You shouldn't be embarrassed about living there. Even Caesar moved in there for a short while, as part of his campaign to win popular favour. And Pompey spent most of his life in the Carinae, which was hardly better.'

With these consolatory thoughts Vitellius went back to his place. He was probably hungry.

The stomachs of most of the guests were, however, beginning to cry for mercy. It was the moment to leave aside the solid food and move on to straight drinking. No one is ever too full to find room for a little neat wine.

Marcus waited patiently until the last course but one, then took his leave of Vitellius and led Marcia off towards the Subura, through the influx of night traffic. The newlyweds' procession consisted exclusively of a few slaves from the two households and a handful of men lent by Vitellius to escort them. There were no hawthorn torches to light the way, and no distaff or spindle. But under her cloak Marcia was clutching two silver dishes which she had contrived to save from her mortgaged inheritance.

They lost themselves three times before reaching the main road through the Subura off which Marcus' alley ran. Along this road they could almost have put out their lanterns and found their way by the light of the lamps which marked the prostitutes' houses. In summer the women

71

perched on high stools outside their front doors. In winter the passer-by could tell their trade only by the burning lanterns.

Marcia shivered. 'It's absurd,' she said, 'but I'm always terrified of finishing up like that.'

Marcus lifted his niece and carried her over the threshold into the house without her feet touching the ground. As he did so, the silver dishes fell out. Was it a bad omen?

They were informed that Kaeso had a high fever. Marcia spent her honeymoon night with the child. Marcus spent his wondering if he had really made a profitable deal. Claudius was notoriously miserly, and Agrippina had other fish to fry. They would leave a very minor matter such as his own to their trusted freedmen or to senators who were in favour. And the Senate had to be thrown a bone to chew over . . . Perhaps Vitellius' clique, who orchestrated the propaganda in favour of Claudius' marriage to Agrippina, might limit its support to an election to a priesthood which was highly honorific but something of a dead-end for the beneficiary. Marrying one's niece was clearly not the best qualification for landing a consulship and the governorship of a rich province. On the other hand there must be something to be gained from the new friendships which Marcus could make among the Arval Brethren . . .

❊ CHAPTER ❊
6

Kaeso's first and happiest memories dated from the marvellous time when Marcia used to take him and his brother Marcus to the baths, after siesta. Winter and summer the two children would slip their little hands into their stepmother's firm grip, and she would see to it they were not jostled as they walked via the Via Suburana and the Argiletum to the women's baths which Marcia frequented. Situated at the entry to the Forum, between the rectangular temple of Marital Harmony and the little round temple of Diana, these baths were a reputable establishment built for the benefit of her sister-citizens by a generous widow. It was not of course in the same class as the Baths of Agrippa in the Campus Martius, whose various facilities, including libraries and art galleries, spread over sixteen Roman acres, but the benefactress, whose marble bust with its calm features dominated the rest room, had not stinted.

The women-only baths were twice as expensive as the mixed baths, which only cost a quarter of an *as*, but almost the only women who went there were women of low morals who wanted to pick up a man, or tarts who on the contrary wanted to clean themselves up after a quick session with a customer in the entrance. But the baths were free for children – they had even been free for everybody during the unforgettable aedileship of Agrippa, in the days when there were nearly two hundred baths already!

The unchanging, peaceful, well-ordered ritual followed its course . . . They went in and walked through the outside *palaestra* towards the cloak-rooms, followed by a slave carrying the *endromides* (short towelling wraps), the phial of scented oil, the scrapers, the *gausapae* (fluffy scarlet bathrobes), some large towels and all the necessary toiletries and cosmetics.

They undressed in the changing rooms, and, according to the temperature and the weather, had the choice of the large outside *palaestra* and the two inside ones, one of which was covered, the other not.

In good weather it was usual to work up a sweat in the outside *palaestra*. Marcia would play catch with other bathers, using balls stuffed with sand, pummelled huge sausages filled with flour and hanging from stakes, lifted weights or dumb-bells, or trotted behind a hoop which she guided with a forked stick ... The children played with inflated pigs' bladders or with balls decorated with feathers.

If the weather was changeable or unpleasant, they would go straight into the two interconnecting indoor *palaestrae*. These were reserved for gymnastics and wrestling. Here the women stripped completely naked to get up a sweat, having first covered themselves in an ointment made of wax and oil and then sprinkled themselves with dust so that it was easier to get a 'hold' for wrestling.

When you were hot enough, you went through into one of the *sudatoria* which surrounded the central *caldarium*. In the *sudatorium* the dry heat of the hypocaust running underneath came out through the thin tiled floor and through the hollow tiles with which the dividing walls were covered. Wooden clogs were provided so that people would not burn the soles of their feet, but they had the disadvantage of spreading an unpleasant fungus called 'athlete's foot'.

When they had sweated for long enough, they went on to the *caldarium*, a steamy room containing a huge basin of very hot water and a bath with room for a dozen people, at the bottom of which the warm water became a little cooler before it was returned towards the wood-fired boiler in the hypocaust. From there the action of the heat itself caused the water to flow back to the bath. You got rid of the dirt on your body at the basin by scraping yourself down with a strigil, then lowered yourself for a brief splash-about in the vast steaming bath.

The *tepidarium*, which was less hot, provided a much appreciated transition between the *caldarium* and the *frigidarium*, where you could take a plunge in one or other of the cold baths, covered or open, according to the season.

Last came the moment for the massage, which cost extra and was sometimes omitted. Then, wrapped in comfy *gausapae*, you went and stretched out in the rest room.

Throughout the whole cycle of activity the slave stayed on guard over the belongings they had left in a niche in the changing room. The official attendant tended to be inattentive.

The Aponius children loved to play ball or play at pretend wrestling with other boys who were still young enough to be brought to the women's baths by their mother, nurse, older sister or other female relative. They found the rooms in this modest bathing establishment enormous compared with the rather meagre rooms of their apartment in the Subura, and were fascinated by the echoes which rang through them and the mysterious beam of light which came through the translucent square of selenite in the *caldarium* roof, spreading a pleasant half-light into the room. Marcus and Kaeso were reduced to silence every afternoon by the strange majesty of the place, but they swiftly lost their sense of awe and enjoyed themselves.

Kaeso, being more observant and sharper than his older brother, asked Marcia why the body-hair of such and such a woman was brown when the hair on her head was blond, why another had a fat stomach or had shaved off her pubic hair, why Marcia herself kept her dark triangle clipped very short like a mole's skin or the down on a pigeon. His stepmother would silence him with a hug and a laugh. But Kaeso did not ask why the breasts of careless slaves were studded with pinpricks and their backs striped with whip scars. He had seen Marcia punishing her slaves when she grew impatient with them at her toilette. Nor did he ask something which in his innocence he thought he knew the answer to. To him any woman with huge hanging breasts was obviously a wetnurse full of milk.

The two children had a vague and confused awareness of how highly Marcia's great beauty was prized, for women with a weakness for their own sex frequently came to pay her discreet court on the offchance. These little attentions would be paid even in the lavatories, where the women sat round in a semi-circle, gossiping, while Kaeso teased them by pretending to hide the sponges.

It was equally interesting to watch Marcia getting dressed again, the expert way in which she wound her *strophium* around her breasts or her knack of adjusting her transparent loin-cloth. The boys took turns to hold her mirror for her, like little Cupids at the feet of an Aphrodite, while she re-did her make-up with an artist's attention to detail.

The time came for Marcus and Kaeso to go back to the house for supper before the sun set. As soon as night fell, everyone barricaded themselves in, and the only people abroad were carters, revellers who were well-guarded, bandits, watchmen or firemen. As the day ended, the children would be eating their simple meals sitting on low stools in front of their parents' couch.

From time to time – particularly on nights when there was a full moon – their father drank more wine with his dinner than usual, and instead of going to sleep the two children would lie awake and listen, dreading what was about to happen . . .

Marcia's room was near theirs, so that she could keep a closer eye on them during the long and disquieting hours of darkness. First of all they would hear scratches and whispers at her door. Then there would be loud knocking, even an attempt to shake the door open, and they could hear their father's voice ringing out in the corridor in tones of pent-up emotion and entreaty. Sometimes the door eventually opened and calm was restored. Usually it remained shut and the suppliant was forced to withdraw after a volley of drunken threats and sobs.

'Why does papa want to go into mama's room at night?' Marcus whispered to his younger brother.

'Perhaps he wants to see her with no clothes on,' suggested Kaeso. 'Papa isn't allowed in the baths.'

In the morning, whether the door had opened or stayed closed, Marcus looked awful, and Marcia would cuddle the children, particularly Kaeso, even closer than usual.

Kaeso, who was very upset by the bizarre little episodes, one day said to Marcia 'You don't want to leave us, do you?' And she answered, 'I shall never leave you. I love you too much.'

As the children grew up, Marcus abandoned these pathetic efforts to get his own way, and order was restored.

One autumn, about the middle of October, when Marcus was nearly seven and Kaeso just over six, their childish pleasures came to an abrupt end. A Greek slave by the name of Diogenes took them to the mixed baths and escorted them wherever else they went, to protect them from the manifold dangers of the street, on their way to school or home. He also acted as their 'coach' for extra lessons.

The children of wealthy families were educated exclusively by private tutors, and in such establishments even the little slaves were taught at home. But for those of more modest means the only solution was the private schools with which the city abounded and which charged the very reasonable fee of two sesterces per child per month. Not only were the teachers despised because they earned a wage, but the wage was pitifully low. It was the least respectable of professions and tended to be taken up by dubious types with suspect morals.

Accompanied by their *paedagogus* the children would set off for school at dawn, quickly come out by the Forums, go along the short side of the Basilica Aemilia and down the long side of the Basilica Julia, and at last reach their 'prison'. It was virtually in the open air, being separated by a mere curtain from one of the porticos of the old (southern) Roman Forum. They were penned up in this room, which was freezing or stifling according to the season, until midday, sitting on stools and working on their knees. Only the teacher had a chair with a back. The school functioned eight days out of nine without a break, and pupils of both sexes waited impatiently for the *nundinae*, the market days when the peasants came into Rome from the surrounding countryside on business or for pleasure. Such days had come to be taken as holidays for everyone. Apart from the *nundinae* the classes hardly had a day off except during the great Quinquatria in March, in honour of Minerva, and of course the long summer vacation from the end of July until the autumn.

The traditional method of educating absolute beginners was the total antithesis of a global approach to problems. Instead it was tremendously analytical.

Before revealing the shapes of the twenty-four letters of the Latin alphabet, the teacher made his class learn the alphabet by heart from A to X and back again. Then each letter was put up on the blackboard, and the pupils tried to find the hidden character which had been engraved on the wooden backing to their tablet and trace it through the smooth, flat wax. When you knew your letters you were one of the elite *abecedarii*.

You then joined the *syllabarii*, who practised constructing imaginary syllables before going on to the real thing.

Finally the *nominarii* had the honour of spelling and writing whole words. This exercise led on to the highest literary activity to which the school aspired: declaiming short lapidary sentences in chorus and writing them on reject papyrus with a reed pen whittled with a knife and dipped in ink made on the spot by dissolving a substance in water in the ink-wells. So passers-by could hear cries of 'Idleness is the mother of all vices' or maxims and jokes in more dubious taste, such as 'For a woman to give advice to another is like one viper buying venom from another' or 'When I came across a negro shitting, his arse looked like a cauldron with a split in it.' But the fare was rarely so entertaining.

Mathematical aspirations were even more limited. You learnt the list of whole numbers, cardinal and ordinal, with their names and symbols. You manipulated the abacus and started to do elementary calculations with small counters on the surface of the counting-table. Fractions were particularly important, because they were so useful in retail trading. Five twelfths was called a quincunx, for example, a quantity redolent of its weight in lettuces or asparagus. The heights of mathematical theory were reached via dizzying calculations on the fingers which only a very small number of pupils could achieve.

To go any further in arithmetic you had to attend a technical school of the sort which trained calligraphers or stenographers.

Boys stagnated like this until they were fourteen or fifteen. Girls were there only until twelve or thirteen, since at the first signs of the onset of puberty they were kept at home.

Marcus had difficulty following the lessons but Kaeso was bored to tears because he was always years ahead of the laborious system.

For Marcus, trying to learn the Roman calendar was absolute torture. He found himself getting the whip even more often than usual, bent over the back of a crouching fellow-pupil who performed the dual function of gibbet and scoreboard. Marcus regularly became confused about the Kalends and even muddled up the months. It is true that the calendar was full of traps . . .

Two hundred years earlier they had decided to begin the year in January, instead of March, although the latter would have been more logical for the country people given that their year began with the revival of nature. Because of this change Quintilis, Sextilis, September, October, November and December were no longer, as their names seemed to indicate, the fifth, sixth, seventh, eighth, ninth and tenth months of the year but the seventh, eighth, ninth, tenth, eleventh and twelfth. Quintilis had been renamed Julius and Sextilis Augustus, in honour of Caesar and his imperial great-nephew, but the other months had kept their deceptive names.

February had twenty-eight or twenty-nine days, the other months thirty or thirty-one.

The first day of each month was known as the Kalends of the month in question. Next was the period of the Nones, from the 2nd to the 7th inclusive for March, May, July and October, or the 2nd to the 5th inclusive for the other eight months. Then came the period of the Ides, from the 8th to the 15th inclusive for March, May, July and October, but the 6th to the 13th for the other eight months. And last came the period of the Kalends.

The last day of the Nones was the Nones proper and the last day of the Ides was the Ides proper. But the last day of the Kalends was only the eve of the Kalends of the following month, a bizarre incoherence in the system which was all the more troublesome for the fact that you had in any case to count backwards to calculate the date. You specified a date in the period of the Nones by counting backwards from the Nones, and you specified a date in the period of the Ides by counting backwards from the Ides. But you specified a date in the period of the Kalends by counting backwards from the Kalends, which was the first day of the following month. So, after the Ides the days of one month bore the name of another, the end of December, for example, always being calculated from the first of January.

However, the day before the eve of the Ides of March was not counted as the second day before the Ides but the third, because the Romans had got into the habit of including the day from which they were calculating. And to round off the confusion you didn't say 'the third day before the Ides' but used the standard abbreviation 'the third day of the Ides'.

Finally, every four years in February you repeated the '6th day of the Kalends of March', so as to get a 'bissextile year'.

It was enough to send you round the bend if you were not particularly bright or were one of the 'children of Spurius' chafing at the bit at the back of the class. And you could see why Roman historians gave so few dates in their works: they would have got them wrong.

After two years at the school Marcus and Kaeso lost their teacher. The day after a miserable nocturnal funeral all the class trooped off to the tomb which the poor man had had built, scraping the cost together penny by penny with the little extra sums which he gleaned from drawing up wills. On it they could read a laudatory epitaph in which the departed congratulated himself on having shown

SUMMA CASTITATE IN DISCIPULOS SUOS

(a rigorous moral purity towards his pupils). This inscription, which was less than flattering to his colleagues in the profession, gave some hope that the parents' choice had been an enlightened one.

The teacher was replaced by a certain Psittacius, whose qualities seemed entirely reassuring. The fellow had suffered various misfortunes. There was even a rumour – entirely implausible – that he had been captured by pirates and made a eunuch by specialists from Delos. His high fluting voice when he lost his temper made his pupils laugh.

That year Marcus and Kaeso went every other morning, or one morning in three, to another teacher who had opened an elementary Greek school in a little room in the 'Argiletum' in between two book-shops. A suitable education at that period had to be bilingual, and the boys had learnt a little basic Greek at home. Their father was fluent in the language and Marcia had a pretty good knowledge of it. The new teacher used exactly the same methods as the Latin master, for the simple reason that the Romans had scrupulously copied Greek customs in everything except gymnastics.

Time passed, but the children found their lives frightfully monotonous. The emperor Claudius greedily devoured a poisonous mushroom specially picked for him by Agrippina: the children were unaware of it. Nero (probably) had his half-brother Britannicus poisoned: nobody mentioned it to them.

But their parents spent a whole dinner discussing the death of M. Junius Silanus, one of the Arval Brethren. Agrippina's first act after her son came to power had been to have Silanus assassinated in Asia Minor, where he was proconsul. He was as lazy as he was rich – Caligula had called him a 'gilded sheep' – and gave offence to nobody. Had Agrippina been afraid that he might take revenge on her for having pushed his brother Lucius to commit suicide? Or had she been motivated by the close relationship between the Silani and Augustus? Agrippina had moreover pulled off a double coup by getting rid of the freedman Narcissus, who had been Claudius' closest confidant but had been unable to prevent his murder.

At the age of thirteen in the case of Kaeso – and fifteen in the case of Marcus – the boys were sent to two 'grammarians', one Greek, one Latin, under whom they began a secondary education which would permit the best of the pupils to study rhetoric and philosophy. Some well-known grammarians made a lot of money. The men who taught the young Aponii were of barely higher standing than school teachers, and their premises in the Carinae at the top of the Via Sacra were hardly more presentable.

There too the Romans had copied the Greeks. Both courses aimed at familiarizing the pupils with the finest texts, and both relied on the same procedures and expedients.

The main object of study, in accordance with major aesthetic preoccupations, was poetry – epic, lyric or dramatic. They only skimmed at prose writers (historians or orators) so as not to impinge on the territory of the masters of rhetoric who would take the majority of the students at a later stage, philosophy being a minority interest. So Kaeso and Marcus attacked the *Iliad* (much less the *Odyssey* which has no really exemplary hero), and Virgil of course. They nitpicked their way through the tragedies of Euripides, the comedies of Menander and Terence, the light lyrics of Horace. Demosthenes and Thucydides, Cicero and Sallust were all granted a few comments.

It was terribly, terribly boring.

After exercises in diction, it was important to prepare the text for reading aloud. Only a trained reader could make sense of sentences which, in both Greek and Latin, were written without separating the words. So the text was annotated with special signs for joining or separating the syllables and for marking the accents, the quantities and the pauses . . .

Then the master would declaim. After him it would be the turn of one of the pupils. Passages were learnt by heart and declaimed from memory. After the *praelectio* there would be a short erudite introduction and then they proceeded to the minute analysis of the text. The most eminent 'grammarians' were capable of devoting an entire treatise to two lines of the *Aeneid*, and, as the generations went by, the stock of glosses grew bigger and bigger: analyses at all levels, subtle reflections on words or rhetorical 'figures' (examples of metaphor, metonymy, catachresis, litotes and syllepsis), or on aspects of history, geography, astronomy, mythology or legend . . . . It was academic fatuity run wild. Throughout their lives the victims of these dreary little pedants would have on their lips a classical quotation to fit every situation.

The Greek grammarian was a champion of the *Iliad*. One spring evening Marcus and Marcia were talking, over dinner, about the incompetence of Anicetus, the commander of the fleet at Misenum who had been incapable of sabotaging the boat which was supposed to have taken Agrippina to the bottom with it. Marcus junior, who with the passing of time had graduated from a stool to the couch, as had his younger brother, said to Kaeso: 'Let's hear Eupithes' latest piece about the failures of the heroes. It's a virtuoso exercise, the master's pride and joy, and you know it by heart.'

Kaeso had to be persuaded, but in the end he launched into his exposition:

'On the Achean side:

The son of Tydeus misses Hector with his javelin and kills the charioteer Eniopeus, son of the fiery Thebaios (Book VIII).

Teucer draws an arrow against Hector and pierces the breast of Gorgytion, son of Priam (Book VIII).

The same Teucer misses Hector again and shoots his charioteer Archeptolemos (Book VIII).

Ajax aims at Polydamas and kills Archelochos, son of Antenor (Book XIV).

Patroclus aims at Hector with a stone and kills the charioteer Cebriones, an illustrious illegitimate son of Priam, "And his two eyes dropped to the ground in the dust at the driver's feet" (Book XVI).

On the Trojan side:

Antiphos, son of Priam, misses Ajax with his javelin and kills Leucos, companion of Ulysses (Book IV).

Hector aims at Teucer and kills Amphimachos, son of Cteatos, of the blood of Actor (Book XIII).

Deiphobos aims at Idomeneus, but his spear kills Hypsenor, son of Hippaos (Book XIII).

The same Deiphobos aims at Idomeneus but his spear kills Ascalphos, son of Enyalos (Book XIII).

Hector aims at Ajax but hits Lycophron, son of Mastor and servant of Ajax (Book XV).

Meges aims at Polydamas but his lance kills Croismos (Book XV).

Sarpedon misses Patroclus but hits the horse Pedasos on the right shoulder (Book XVI).

Hector aims at Ajax and his spear kills Schedios, son of Iphitos (Book XVII).

Hector aims at Idomeneus, but his lance kills the charioteer Coiranos (Book XVII).

Thus the Acheans miss their target five times and the Trojans nine. The Achean heroes accordingly appear more skilful. But if you take into consideration the fact that all the heroes hit something when they miss their original target, the Trojan heroes, while missing nine times as against five, actually cause their enemies heavier losses, including a horse. The most maladroit and yet the most effective is Hector, who misses four times.'

Marcia glowed with pride at this masterpiece of literary criticism sustained by a brilliant memory. Kaeso's father, who had himself spent years exercising his memory on the *Iliad*, made a profound comment: 'The most skilful of all the heroes is the one your Eupithes has forgotten: in Book X Diomedes deliberately tries to miss the Trojan Dolon . . . and does so.'

Kaeso received his tribute of well-deserved applause modestly. And after dinner, by the light of the oil lamp, Marcus kept a stricter eye than usual on the work which Kaeso had been set to do at home. This was always the same. He had to take a text and put it through all the grammatical variations possible:

'Cato the Censor said: The roots of literacy are bitter but its fruits are very sweet, etc.

Cato said that the roots of literacy were bitter . . .

Cato was fond of describing the roots of literacy as . . .

Cato is reported to have called the roots of literacy . . .

O Cato, wast it not thou who saidst that . . .

And in the plural: "The Catos were fond of saying . . ."'

The fact that Kaeso, who was not yet fifteen, found such problems very easy filled his father with satisfaction and was some consolation for the failures of Marcus junior. There was every sign that Kaeso would be brilliant at rhetoric.

The change from primary to secondary education had been a source of indescribable relief to the boys. They were gradually allowed to go to school without their *paedagogus* and to take unsupervised walks in the city streets, along the paths of the Campus Martius or through the numerous magnificent gardens which formed a belt of fresh greenery around the centre of Rome. Even the fact that there were no girls – and no whips – at the 'grammar' lessons reinforced their sense of growing up.

In the summer before their painful admission to primary school their parents had taken them to a very special show which was to leave an indelible mark on their memories. It was a naval battle on the great Fucine lake in the Marsian hills. The other gladiatorial shows which they had later been able to watch from the seats reserved for children (accompanied by their *paedagogus*), at the top of the amphitheatres, had not captivated them in the same way. But now they were older, they were allowed to venture on their own into seats closer to the ringside, and catch a closer whiff of the blood of the brave and the anguished sweat of the cowards. They were equally excited by the superb chariot-races, and enjoyed the productions of comedies, which taught them in crude terms about the realities of life.

Kaeso had even learnt enough to wonder why his father no longer ever went into his mother's bedroom . . .

Apparently unaffected by the passage of time, Marcia tried hard to disguise the extent of her preference for Kaeso, but she failed. She was fond of Marcus junior, but she fell in love with Kaeso, whose good looks were, it is true, staggering. He possessed the additional charm, common in adolescents, of remaining, in his total innocence, sublimely unaware of the power he possessed to disquiet others. When Kaeso tilted his head to the side as he listened to a compliment or a rebuke, he looked like Alexander the Great on the eve of his conquests.

And naturally Kaeso, whose relationship with his father was a little chilly and constrained, harboured a devotion to Marcia which was an essential part of his happiness and served to dispel any disquiet which his keen sense of observation might otherwise have awakened. His confidence in Marcia was total.

Marcus and his wife, for their part, had carefully concealed their degree of kinship from the children, who were left in ignorance of the precise genealogical details of their father's family. According to Marcus the name Aponius came from the warm spring Aponus in the district around Padua, where the family must have owned land once upon a time . . .

So when Marcia came home at impossible hours or disappeared for a few days, Kaeso accepted at face value the explanations which she carelessly proffered, ostensibly to her husband but in fact for the benefit of the boys.

Nor was Kaeso surprised to see the house gradually improve over the years. Sometimes quite luxurious furniture arrived: at others rooms were prettily redecorated. There were even more substantial alterations. Marcus had dug an *impluvium* in the newly re-paved courtyard, surrounded it with a colonnade and added a sloping openwork roof, thus reconstituting, in the very heart of the tenement block, the *atrium* whose loss he had not ceased to bemoan. Baths had been fitted, the family had taken over the slaves' quarters, and the slaves, who were now more numerous and better fed, had been moved upstairs. The business of running the rented part of the property had been put in the hands of an agent. Marcus still talked about re-installing himself in accommodation worthier of his ancestors. But rents, in a city where the possibility of living off the State attracted vast masses of people, kept soaring so high that the question of moving house was constantly being deferred. So they had to be patient, in relative comfort.

Kaeso attributed these influxes of cash to his father's talents as a lawyer. Marcia had persuaded Marcus to set up as a legal adviser and to plead cases when the opportunity presented itself. But there was no shortage of talented lawyers and barristers in Rome, and it was not easy to make a name for oneself.

Financially the profession was particularly disappointing because members of the Bar were theoretically forbidden to accept any sort of fee at all. All they could hope for was to be included in the wills of grateful clients whose cases they had won for them. The leading barristers were paid millions in backhanders, but they were in danger of having actions brought against them, of being blackmailed and of facing trials which could go against them if their backers withdrew their support. And the lower the illicit fees they charged, the more difficult it was to screw the money out of the clients. Claudius tried to clean up a situation which had long been corrupt by setting a modest ceiling of 10,000 sesterces for honoraria which could legally be charged, but the law had been as ineffective as a sword-thrust in water.

Marcus, despairing of ever getting any business, had specialized in chamber-pots, which were always falling out of windows and had already produced a considerable body of complex case-history. Unfortunately victims could not claim any compensation for aesthetic damage suffered. As the Civil Code so nobly put it: 'As regards the scars and other forms of disfigurement which may result from such wounds, these cannot be taken into account, because no price can be put upon the body of a free man.' It was the only area of Roman law in which slaves were at an advantage relative to freemen.

Marcus junior, who was not blinded by his emotions, was not as credulous as his younger brother. But he was by nature apathetic, peace-loving and discreet, and had a wise tendency to say no more than he had to and to keep to himself anything which could upset or disturb anyone else. He was heavily-built and awkward, and his talents were physical rather than intellectual, but the gods had endowed him with one eminently desirable quality so rare in brothers: he was disarmingly incapable of jealousy. He was perfectly well aware that Kaeso was quick-witted, good-natured, handsome, charming, and irresistible whenever he put his mind to it. He loved him all the same, and found him as irresistible as everyone else.

Like Marcia, Marcus tried to distribute his affections equally between the two boys, but he couldn't prevent himself from placing a father's fondest hopes in Kaeso. He wanted the boy to succeed in everything at which he himself had failed.

This fine house of lies, paved with good intentions, might have stood firm for a long time, if the gods had not taken offence. Perhaps they were put out to hear Marcus constantly quoting, for the edification of his sons, examples of devotion, modesty and piety from the legendary history of Rome. A veneer of blatant hypocrisy is all the more irritating when it covers a solid foundation of sincere virtue.

While waiting for the gods' displeasure to strike, Marcus and Kaeso finished their years of 'grammar' without a care in their heads. The elder Marcus, who looked back to a past richly embellished with gold and silver, spent his time turning over in his mind his life's disap-pointments and rancours – and developing a pot belly. The boys' class-mates were of very modest backgrounds, few among them being even the sons of knights, but Marcus and Kaeso, despite the modesty of their finances, gave the impression of being sprung from the thigh of Jupiter, and had little difficulty in obtaining a certain respect, tinged with self-interest, from starving or impecunious teachers. To the boys the tenement block with its bastard *atrium* seemed a palace. And the Subura quarter, full of colour and life, was all the more attractive because hordes of tarts plied their profession there – and the boys had grown up.

In principle Kaeso was strictly forbidden to go into the *popina*. But at sixteen he persuaded his old Cretan nurse to let him have a free go behind the curtain with the 'little filly', who was unoccupied during slack times, and he eagerly shared his good luck with his brother. The girl, who already had to put up with the boys' father from time to time, was not well-disposed to the arrangement, but at least, under instruction from the Cretan, she held her tongue. When Kaeso came out from behind the curtain and thanked his nurse with a kiss, the leathery face of the dried-up old Greek had a strange smile. Perhaps she was thinking that it's what people don't know that gives life its spice.

In the afternoons Marcus and Kaeso spent more and more time at their father's little gladiatorial *ludus* a few miles outside Rome. The building was set well back from the Appian Way between a dovecot and some wayside tombs. The great *ludus* on the Caelian could take seven or eight hundred combatants; this one never had more than a dozen. The ruins of a farm building lurking among the cemeteries had been summarily done up to look like a typical gladiators' barracks. Ordinarily these were on only two floors, with the ground floor rooms giving on to a portico which ran round the training ground. In Aponius' *ludus* the building itself was limited to a right-angle, framing two sides of a square.

On the first floor were the living quarters of the trainer Eurypylus and of those of the gladiators who had women – and the odd child – living with them. The rooms which the other men shared in twos or threes were also on this floor. Downstairs were the dining-room, where they usually sat to eat, the kitchen, the armoury and the sick-bay. The gladiators looked after their weapons and breast-plates themselves, and Eurypylus acted as medical orderly when necessary, with the help of the two slaves who worked in the kitchen.

One end of the wing of the house had been sacrificed to form stables, coach house, barn and hayloft, and the charioteer and *bestiarius*, Tyrannus, slept there, with his driver. The entrance to the stables and coach-house was at the back, in front of the well, which was equipped with a drinking trough for the animals.

The atmosphere of the place was evidently very easy-going, and Eurypylus made every effort not to stage fights between men who had had the opportunity to get to know each other only too well.

The gladiators appreciated Marcus' strength and Kaeso's engaging manner and instinctive sense of how to adapt to his surroundings. Their lives depended on their powers of instantaneous analysis, and they were swift judges of qualities and defects. When they were fighting the two youngsters, they would constantly be saying to Marcus: 'Use your head when you fight!', and to Kaeso: 'Don't lose your cool! Don't get out of breath! When you and your opponent are equally matched in skill, it's the one who keeps calm and keeps going who'll survive.'

Sometimes amateurs from the suburbs or the area south-west of Rome came for lessons in the training ground, and the Aponius boys would take advantage of them too.

Occasionally the brothers would stay for the communal evening meal. The menu always included a large dish of barley porridge, which was supposed to be a cheap way of putting on muscle. It was still to be the diet prescribed in the following century by the great Galen, who began his career as doctor-in-chief to the imperial gladiators of five successive high priests of Pergamum. On such evenings the Aponius boys would bring an amphora of respectable wine with them, and the dinner would linger on under the flickering light of the clay lamps.

It was the moment to talk about the good old days of gladiatorial combat and the part that gladiators had played in the brawls which took place in the Forum at the end of the Republic. Nostalgia for the 'good old days' still persisted. People would recall the heroism of Mark Antony's gladiatorial *familia*, and their fidelity to their master. What a trek they had accomplished after the battle of Actium to rejoin Antony in Egypt! What an odyssey! It was a 'retreat of the ten thousand' to match Xenophon's! Admiration was also expressed for the very recent success of the *mirmillo* Spiculus, whom Nero had showered with houses and estates. But nobody had a good word for the old team of Spartacus, that deserter from the legions who had been condemned to the lower ranks of the gladiators for banditry.

Sooner or later, however, the moans would start. Nero was a softy who only made a show of liking the gladiators to please the plebs. His heart wasn't really in it. What the emperor liked, it was plain, was not the beauty of skilled feats of arms but the purely aesthetic, decorative side. Which was why people were constantly trying to fill the games with ceremonial and extravagant display. They were interested only in anything new, strange or incredible.

Three years after he came to the throne Nero had had a great wooden amphitheatre built in the Campus Martius. And what for? After a little 'naval engagement' full of sea-monsters, the arena had been dried out and 400 senators and 600 knights disguised as gladiators had fought a battle with buttoned foils! And in the mid-day entr'acte, instead of dispatching those criminals awaiting execution, the part of the programme that Claudius had always particularly enjoyed, Nero had pardoned them all. What could be more deathly than a deathless Games!

In response to the evident public disappointment Nero had made some amends. The funeral games he had put on in memory of Agrippina had been quite good, and so had the games staged by Lucan and his colleagues on the occasion of their quaestorship. But a certain frivolousness, coquetry you might say, was still evident. The same was true of the *venationes*, the great hunts put on in the mornings in the amphitheatres – or, less and less frequently, in the Circuses, where there would be a massacre after every fifth race. Instead of producing hundreds of lions and bears – the sound, classical approach – Nero liked to exterminate extravagant mixtures of wild boar, white hares, zebu, elands, aurochs, hippopotami and seals. It wasn't a dangerous and exciting *venatio*, it was a natural history lesson. And though sometimes at the end of a show they did disembowel a few elephants, who would gradually leave their guts trailing around the arena, there was a growing fashion for rodeos, where a group of Thessalian horsemen would play at rounding up a handful of bulls in an arena scattered with ridiculous quantities of Baltic amber.

It was understandable for long-standing gladiators and *bestiarii* to show disquiet at such developments. Claudius had wanted lots of blood as cheaply as possible. Nero was spending lots to keep the bloodshed down. What was going to happen to their trade?

It was not only fencing that Marcus and Kaeso learnt in the company of these men, with their instinctive uneducated shrewdness. The Aponius boys learnt that, in an uncertain and cruel world, they had only themselves to rely on. They learnt that they should be careful to keep a balance between body and mind, since everything might depend on that balance at the moment of truth which life reserves for all of us. And they should have learnt the limits of the marriage of friendship and sensibility, for it was not done to cry over those who had gone never to return. Happily, losses were rare among these experienced gladiators, each of whom had between ten and twenty victories to his credit, if not more.

Kaeso was none the less particularly fond of Capreolus, a Jew from Meninx, a southern peninsula on the eastern coast of the proconsular province of Africa. Through long practice, between sabbaths, at casting his sweep-net over fish in the depths, the 'young roebuck' Capreolus had become an excellent *retiarius*, whose elusive leaps and twirls, sudden casts of the net and unforeseen trident blows had already claimed a dozen victims. When he went to fight at Ravenna or Naples, Ancona or Clusium, Kaeso would be waiting impatiently and worriedly for his return. But the slim brown boy always came back, and would say with a laugh: 'I caught another big fish!'

Kaeso got on much less well with Amaranthus, a dissipated and corrupt youth of respectable family whose improvidence had brought him straight down to the bread-and-scrape of the *ludus*. A few years earlier a show in Pompeii had turned into a punch-up, and the overexcited *populus* of the town had massacred the rival citizens of Nuceria who had come over for the games. Amaranthus had distinguished himself by murdering everyone in sight to his heart's content, had almost been condemned to death, and had got off by the skin of his teeth. Pompeii had been forbidden to hold any games for ten years, but Nero's official mistress Poppaea, who was said to come from the town, had contrived to settle things, and grateful inscriptions in praise of the Emperor had appeared all over the walls of that bloody metropolis. The gods would punish the place sooner or later . . .

The *ludus* also provided Marcus and Kaeso with excellent opportunities to learn to ride, and later to improve their horsemanship, a skill held by Romans and Greeks alike to be the indispensable final touch to an elegant aristocratic education. Both Greeks and Romans, being Mediterranean peoples from mountainous regions, had little natural affinity with horses, unlike certain peoples from the steppes who spent their whole lives in the saddle. So these semi-mythological animals tended to frighten them.

Tyrannus' two stallions (horses were not castrated), Bucephalus and Formosus, came from the Lucanian stud-farms of Tigellinus, an ambitious fellow from Agrigentum who had become Prefect of the Watch after Agrippina's death, while waiting for something better. They were little swan-necked creatures, of Arab blood, as quick as silver and with black coats that shone in the sun. Tyrannus looked after his horses with great care, because his existence as *essedarius* depended on the swiftness and ease of their graceful turns. The whole art consisted in getting the chariot in just the right position to strike, and success was the combined product of the quality of the team, the control of the driver, and the skill of the *essedarius* in his Breton warrior's costume.

Bucephalus and Formosus each had a stall where they were free to paw with their hooves at the small, dry squares of the paved floor. In season they ate good green forage, they had hay when the the cold weather came, and all year round their rations included winter barley or two-row barley, with a pinch of salt in winter – but never oats, that dangerous weed which makes stallions capricious and crazy. On the eve of a Games some asphodel bulbs, poor man's food, would be mixed in with their barley, because the sugar content enhanced their performance without affecting their nerves.

'A horse is as good as its hooves,' Tyrannus liked to say, and in consequence paid great attention to his horses' feet. Behind the well and the drinking trough he had had a small floor made from round stones, as big as two fists together, held in by a square framework of planks. There the two animals, with their nose-bags on, could trample around and harden their hooves as much as they liked.

Kaeso and Marcus' first riding lessons had been devoted to learning the correct shoes for the horses to wear in different circumstances. The establishment had a plentiful supply. There were shoes for highroads, shoes for general terrain, shoes for rain. There were even shoes for hard frost, which was rare as far south as Rome but occurred in the Apennines in the north, and in the Abruzzi. Tyrannus, to give him his stage-name, never went out into the countryside without a variety of horseshoes, ready for every eventuality. For on the sandy surface of the Circus or the arenas the horses went unshod, but most of the time it was necessary to protect their hooves, an essential and fragile part of the body, against the rough surfaces of the roads and paths.

They had heard travellers tell that distant barbarians sometimes fixed their horseshoes on with nails, a clumsy and stupid solution, because if the front of the hoof is not free to move, the foot comes down on the horny part, and the pad on the inner part of the bottom of the foot is crushed at each contact with the ground, pushing open the two parts of the supple heel of the hoof. Any nailed-on shoe would quickly come off if it had only been fixed at the front, and if you nailed it all over, the back of the hoof would have none of the normal play and the animal would be discomforted in the same way as a man wearing shoes which are too narrow and prevent the normal elastic movement of the ball of the foot. Another disadvantage would be that since horn grows quickly, a nailed shoe, which is already poorly adapted to the hoof to start with, would fit less and less well as time passed.

In civilized regions the shoes covered only the front of the hoof, that is the toe, front of the sole and the two sides encasing the toe, thus protecting the foot horizontally as well as vertically and leaving free the part which needed to be so. These horse-sandals were simply fastened at the back to the pastern, in the indentation between the hoof and the fetlock-joint. You could take them off, put them back or change them with the greatest of ease, to ensure that the shoe – when it seemed necessary to wear one at all – would be constantly in harmony with the conditions of the road. They were taken off every night to allow the hoof to 'breathe' while in the dry.

Then Marcus and Kaeso learned how to open a horse's mouth and slip in a supple and flexible bit, how to mount the animal bare-back while holding on to its long mane with the left hand, and how to get on from the right – since for a rider attacked by bandits, every moment could be vital. Finally, how to mount the lazy way, using one of the posts for the purpose which are scattered along the major *viae*, or with the aid of a leg-up in the cupped hands of an obliging helper. It was a sacred principle of Roman education, in horse-riding as in literature, that you always began with the most difficult thing.

Then they acquired a good seat, with the flanks of their mount firmly grasped between the thighs and the legs free and relaxed. A horse was controlled and directed in the first instance by the muscles of the upper inside thigh. The rider had literally to become one with the body of his conquered steed.

When, after countless falls, they could more or less control these high-spirited stallions, which would prance about at the slightest whiff of a mare, Tyrannus allowed them to tie a cloth round the girths to protect their leather trousers. But a cloth diminished the precision of the rider's contact with the horse, and it was plain that the taciturn purist, with his dark hair and gloomy face, regarded such things as decadent expedients.

Finally, after a few demonstrations for the benefit of their delighted father – Marcia was too scared to come – the two young riders were able to caracole up the Appian Way on those fine afternoons when it was the meeting-place of everyone who was anyone in Rome, surrounded by the healthy smell of the pines and moving along between the familiar rows of melancholy tombs which were a dual invitation to pleasure and peace.

✧ CHAPTER ✧
7

In the spring of the ninth year of the reign of Nero, Burrus, the eminent Praetorian Prefect, died. He was a friend of Seneca, whose moderating influence declined accordingly. The office of Praetorian Prefect, an important post because it controlled the Praetorian guard, was then divided between the efficient Tigellinus and the pale Gaul, Faenius Rufus, a former protégé of Agrippina, who had made a name for himself as the *Praefectus annonae* (in charge of the corn supply). The previous year Flavius Sabinus (brother of the future emperor Vespasian) had been appointed Prefect of the City.

That summer Nero, who had divorced Octavia and remarried Poppaea, had his ex-wife, Britannicus' sister, put to death after eleven years of marriage. But, as the emperor liked to put it in his jocular way: 'All Octavia ever got from our marriage was the fringe benefits.'

There followed a number of trials for *lèse-majesté*. A group of senators came under suspicion, and among those put to death were Rubellius Plautus and L. Faustus Cornelius Sulla Felix, a colleague of Aponius Saturninus in the Arval Brethren. Rubellius Plautus was a descendant of Livia, the second wife of Augustus, via Tiberius. The unfortunate Felix (belying his name) was the son of Domitia Lepida, one of Nero's aunts, who had herself been one of Agrippina's victims at the end of Claudius' reign. The honeymoon between emperor and Senate was definitely over.

Now that Kaeso and Marcus had reached the end of their studies in 'grammar' and were adequately provided with quotations from Homer and Virgil, the problem of setting the two young men up in careers was becoming acute. The difficulties were opposite ones in the two cases. One of them was too dull, the other too brilliant. Marcus' talents barely extended beyond being able to stay on a horse and use a sword, while occasionally confusing Aeneas and Achilles. Kaeso had a talent for everything.

One evening towards the end of September, when Poppaea was five months pregnant and Nero happy, Lucan feverishly finishing his *Pharsalia* and Persius struggling in the final throes of his fatal illness, Marcus and

Marcia, sitting in their would-be *atrium*, came back yet again to the topic which was their main preoccupation. Everyone in the tenement block was asleep; a moonbeam from the full moon filled the place with soft light; the jolly Priapus thrust his enormous member into the air, the retracted foreskin looking like a woman's lips around the rustic glans; and the sound of the fountain gurgling in its basin made a fresh and pleasant rival to the usual dull hum of nocturnal activity.

'What we clearly need is a protector,' said Marcia. 'But who? Agrippina and her friends more or less dropped us despite what we did for them. In any case, they fell into disgrace shortly after the start of the reign, and the last murder that Nero's mother was involved in, four years ago, turned out to be her own . . .'

'How about Vitellius?' Marcus suggested. 'You know him well enough, don't you? – and he's still your guardian.'

'I know him only too well. We're virtually not on speaking terms. He's an intolerable man – he'd eat a hedgehog off your stomach! I had some hopes of poor Sulla Felix, but he's gone the way of Agrippina. Vipstanius Apronianus is as old as the hills and hardly leaves his little carriage. Salvius Otho, who succeeded his father as a member of the Brethren, is obliging enough and likes a good time, but as you know, Nero sent him off to be governor of Lusitania, and he's been mouldering there for the last five years. After moving heaven and earth to get Nero to take his wife Poppaea as his mistress, Otho was still claiming the right to sleep with her. A cuckold shouldn't push his luck.'

'What about the rest? Africanus? Regulus? Messala Corvinus? The two Pisos?'

'Africanus paid for repaving the terrace. Regulus – who's ill anyway – built the *atrium*. Corvinus dealt with the central heating system and had the boiler lined with fireproof volcanic stone from Etna. The Pisos paid for the renovation of the lavatories and competed with each other to provide the new furniture. It would be difficult to go back cap in hand to any of them. Every woman has her price, and when a man has paid up , the love he bought doesn't dispose him to friendship. Anyway I'm now over thirty . . .'

It was the first time they had talked about Marcia's lovers in such a frank way. The children's future was at stake, and the niece had no sense of embarrassment before her uncle where Kaeso's interests were involved.

By a natural process, as Marcia moved on from Vitellius to others, the Arval Brethren had adopted her as their own Egeria, the tailor-made nymph whom king Numa had long ago pretended to consult so as to keep those about him in the dark. She had even contributed to the happiness of other colleges of pious gourmets. Between banquets of superb cuts of meat whose aroma delighted the nostrils of the gods, such men appreciated an even more delicate form of flesh whose perfume was reserved exclusively for them. They had each, in their time, contributed to the expenses of the household and had left charming trinkets in the young woman's jewel case.

Marcus had been in agonies over the situation, his relationship with Marcia had been poisoned by it, then he had resigned himself to it. How could he divorce a stepmother whom the children adored? How could he deprive himself of a wife who had such gifts for running a household? He had consequently shut his eyes firmly to what was going on and had taken some consolation in the thought that his pathetic repeated attempts to get into his niece's room at night would doubtless have left no mark on the memories of the boys, who were too young at the time to notice or remember anything. If by mischance either of the boys found out about the blood relationship between their parents, he could, in tones of perfect good faith, defend the proposition that their marriage had been as pure and spotless as Nero's bizarre gladiatorial display by senators and knights had been bloodless.

That evening, however, Marcia's frankness, though he had virtually invited it, shocked Marcus. Too crude a light had finally penetrated the smoke-screen set up to protect his comfortable sense of resignation.

'Given the reputation you must have gained for yourself since the age of fourteen for bestowing your favours on all the priestly gourmets in Rome – not to mention anybody else – I'm no longer surprised that I haven't been able to get much out of my colleagues in the Brethren myself, despite my very reasonable expectations. They would have been justified in saying: "Pass the hat to someone else, my good fellow, I've already contributed!"'

'Did you manage to strike up any profitable relationships on your own after you lost your fortune? When I married you, you had no friend left but yourself – a friend who didn't spare you his sarcasm! Am I really supposed to have stopped you from obtaining the recommendations and favours of all those millionaires and court favourites in the Brethren when they were in a good mood at the end of every sacrificial feast, after stuffing themselves on veal escalopes and getting high on the best vintage wines? You became the proud owner of thirteen gladiators in your sleep. I've noticed that there are certain misfortunes which attract sympathy, and others which make people laugh and give you a reputation for being unlucky. When the injustice of Fate has made you the laughing-stock of the city, your ridiculous image follows you around for a long time.'

'Would you have preferred me to have improved my reputation by opening my veins like some of the others did after that auction? And was it my idea to marry my niece?'

'You could have done a lot worse.'

'I'm not so sure . . . In return for having my name bandied about by gossip as an incestuous cuckold who connives in his wife's infidelities, I have neither wife nor money.'

'I might point out to you that I only put up with your attentions for a time to avoid exposing Kaeso, who's such a sensitive child, to appalling scenes. It was you who gave up pestering me as soon as Kaeso was older. And as far as the money goes, you've constantly refused all the loans I've offered you.'

'The only trace of dignity I've still got is my refusal to beg for the crumbs left over from your orgies.'

'A very dreary and excessively discreet form of dignity.'

'The gods will reward me for it.'

'I hope so for your sake.'

'To hear you talk one would think that women only wanted freedom so as to have the opportunity to prostitute themselves.'

'Were you so naïve as to suppose that we wanted the freedom to work? Anyway, prostitution isn't something any woman can do just because she fancies the idea. You need charm; you need the ability to look at the ceiling or the sky and think of something else; and as far as possible you need the ability never to disgrace yourself except for love. It's the only point on which a tart can retain her self-respect. That's why all the whores in the Subura have a lover who beats them and steals their money.'

'If you're in love with anyone you keep the fact well hidden!'

'It's a secret between me and my heart.'

Getting up from the bench, Marcia went and sat on the edge of the fountain. She hung her scarf over Priapus' erection as if the unexpected allusion to an ideal lover was incompatible with the obscene tumescence, even if it did belong to a god. Then she went on:

'The more I think about it the clearer it is that there's only one way open to us if we're to launch Kaeso . . .'

'And Marcus . . .'

'Naturally. And he needs twice as much push to launch him! To go back to what I was saying – the only thing left for us is to renew relations with the Silani, which in practice means with Decimus, the head of the *gens*, who is the only one of the three brothers still alive. As Agrippina never showed you much public patronage, and the old snake is dead now anyway, Decimus has no reason to hold anything against you. You can't be held responsible for your father's ingratitude after all these years . . .'

'It will be a very difficult approach to make.'

'What have we got to lose?'

Marcia led her reluctant husband into the library and lit the new lamps. After discussions and false starts, she finally dictated the following, while he wrote it down on a pair of beautiful ivory tablets:

'M. Aponius Saturninus to D. Junius Silanus Torquatus, respectful greetings.

You will be able to place me better if I present myself under the name of T. Junius Aponius, which was my late father's name. It is not my place to criticize him for having deprived me of so illustrious a patronym, but it is with some emotion that I find myself writing it again today, for it bound us to your family for some one hundred and forty years and carries with it a host of grateful memories. I have more than sixty years of life behind me now, and in that time I have become disillusioned with many things, but I am moved by a sudden strong desire to come and pay my respects to you. I should not like to end my days under the cloud of a suspicion of ingratitude. My position in society will make it plain to you that my approach is not that of a suppliant. As a member of the Arval Brethren and a former praetor I am rich enough to be happy, and to supply the needs of a young wife whose beauty causes me as much concern as pride. She is impatient to accompany me on my visit, for you know what curiosity and sympathy your life and career arouse. Your merit matches your rank, a concurrence which is rare in our day and age, is it not? May we perhaps slip in one morning among your clients and thus renew old customs long dear to us? What other patron could I greet by that title without blushing? May the gods at all events keep you in good health.

P.S. I live in a large house off the Via Suburana, level with the little olive market – not to mention the large brothel run by the Themistocles brothers, which gives our aediles a lot of trouble. If your messenger is keen on olives or women, he will find my door easily. I have some reputation in the quarter for my modest talents as a lawyer, which occasionally profit the rich as well as the poor.'

It was certainly not customary for a client – of whatever rank – to take his wife with him on a formal visit. It would have been considered indiscreet or out-of-place. On the other hand, this was not an ordinary visit, and the out-of-the-ordinary nature of the respects to be paid might excuse the anomaly.

Three days later the tablets came back, bearing the message:

'D. Junius to T. Junius Aponius, greetings.

I have already heard of you, your difficulties with the emperor Caius and the consolations of your remarriage. I have even had report of the successes of your gladiators in the arenas of our country towns and of your wife in our great arena, Rome. Vitellius and Otho have both happened to mention to me how charming she is. I too am getting on in years, I have lost my prejudices, and I have never rebuffed a client. Being as curious to meet you, especially in such good company, as you are to meet me, I have instructed my secretary to inform you that you may visit me early tomorrow, among my privileged clients. You will find yourself, a former praetor, coming after a former consul. I wish you good health.

P.S. Your letter followed me from our old palace on the Caelian to a little house on the Palatine which I have recently acquired. It formerly belonged to Crassus, Cicero, Censorinus, and most recently to T. Statilius Sisenna, who was consul with Scribonius Libo in the third year of the reign of Tiberius. Sisenna's heirs sold it to me for less than Cicero paid for it. Strange, isn't it?'

The letter was not particularly flattering, but there was no point in asking for the impossible.

In the afternoon, between taking a siesta and bathing, Marcus, who had nothing to do and was in a reflective mood, withdrew into his little study, a room opening off the library, to work on the Libanius case. Perhaps Decimus would bring him in some more interesting work.

The Libanius case was a wretched business. Libanius himself was the son of a freedman who had made a fortune in cereals. In his will he had included the requirement that the seven beauties who made up his seraglio should kill each other over his tomb in homage to his departed spirit. It was an extremely old-fashioned instruction, apparently blending an excessively nice piety with morbid jealousy. Libanius' son, shocked by the prospect of such waste, had tried to have the will annulled on these grounds, but his sister, who was represented by her guardian, had gone to the defence of her father's last wishes. Doubtless the seven common-law stepmothers, as it were, had occupied an excessive place in the household in the eyes of a sensitive young woman. While waiting for the decision of the courts, the goods in question had been sequestrated, and the seven slaves, whose beauty was gradually fading, had been patiently waiting for twelve years to learn their fate. Marcus, who happened to be pleading the case for the daughter, had the law on his side, but against him he had the ill-will of successive praetors, none of whom wanted to be held responsible in such a disagreeable affair. Since Nero's accession to the throne a breath of humane sentiment favourable to the lower classes and even to slaves had been blowing through the legal system.

When the Prefect of the city, Pedanius Secundus – predecessor of Flavius Sabinus and a friend of Seneca – was assassinated by a slave in a quarrel over a mutual boyfriend, it was only the insistence of the hard core of very traditionalist senators which had persuaded the emperor to apply the full rigour of the law. The victim's four hundred household slaves, in an atmosphere of popular unrest hostile to the Senate, had been sent to crucifixion with their crosses on their backs. But the emperor had resisted a proposal by an ultra-conservative that the freedmen present at Pedanius' house at the moment of the crime should be deported.

Early the following morning, while they were waiting for the hired litter which was to come from the rank in the Trans Tiberim, Marcus went in person to demand the back rents owed by the Spaniard in the cul-de-sac. Whips and iron collars for slaves were not selling well. In most big houses relations between masters and servants were good, or tolerable, sometimes even excellent, and the lower classes usually punished their slaves with the flat of their hands. You could still castrate a slave or sell him/her to a pimp, but such cases were getting more and more rare and were controversial. Since Augustus' Lex Petronia, you needed a legal judgement in your favour before you could have an intolerable slave thrown to the lions, and Nero had charged the Prefect of the City with the task of receiving and investigating complaints brought by slaves against the supposed injustice of their masters. Imperial demagogy was flouting the whole principle of the right of property.

Moreover, some hazy philosophical creed had spread the idea that slaves might have a soul of sorts, and the logic of deplorable facts had added grist to the mill: when a freed slave such as the millionaire Pallas, lover and tool of the late Agrippina, and an *arriviste* whom Nero had recently put to death, could wriggle his way up to the rank of minister of state, it was difficult to deny him, if not a soul as such, at least a modicum of spirit.

Furious at the Spaniard's truculence, Marcus gave instructions that the ladder which linked his shop to his apartment on the mezzanine should be taken away. This means of bringing pressure to bear on recalcitrant tenants had become classic and had passed into the proverbial expression 'pulling up the ladder'.

The litter finally arrived. For this important visit Marcia had created for herself the image of sober, refined beauty appropriate to a virtuous noblewoman. She had avoided colours that were too gaudy and jewellery which was too bright. And she had personally helped Marcus to drape his best toga.

In the shabby litter the couple went over all there was to be known about Decimus – probably a waste of time, in that the margin between reality and gossip could be wide. A sister of the three Silanus brothers, Julia Lepida, had married C. Cassius Longinus, a well-known lawyer and descendant of the Cassius who murdered Caesar. He was the man who had argued brilliantly in the Senate for the crucifixion of the four hundred slaves of Pedanius Secundus. The couple had brought up their nephew Lucius, son of the unfortunate Marcus who had been sacrificed by Agrippina eight years earlier, to cultivate the Stoic virtues. But Decimus, a highly cultivated aesthete and dilettante, was said to be less rigid in his Stoicism. He must have been influenced by the remarkably flexible credo of Seneca. As for politics, Decimus was very proud of his relationship to Augustus, but the danger that it presented for him after the tragic end of his two brothers had turned him away from all political ambition. It was even said that, despairing of the uncertainty of life, he had belatedly thrown himself into a frenzy of elegant pleasures, lavishing his fortune on frivolous luxury. In short he was a Stoic of the worldly and sceptical variety, more concerned with embellishing his declining years than with rigorous philosophizing. Such tendencies offered Marcia practical openings which it would have been a shame to let slip.

Before the light September morning mist melted away, the house of D. Junius Silanus Torquatus was already beseiged by clients. Some of them, who had come on foot in their skimpy togas and shapeless clogs, had gathered in compact bunches along the flights of steps which climbed up the south-east slope of the Palatine from the Triumphal Way towards the front of the house. Others, in more ample togas and with better shoes, had made a flanking movement via the Clivus Victoriae and the narrow streets prolonging it.

The doors were not yet open. Marcus and Marcia joined the relatively small group of clients of the first rank and waited. Gradually the mist drifted away.

99

Cicero's 'little house', to which Silanus had referred in his letter, was only little to a Silanus. Even so, Cicero had paid 3,500,000 sesterces for it and had added a garden. Looking southward from the entrance you could see the fine panorama of countryside described by Cicero in his *Pro Domo*: the slopes of Aesula, the hilltops of Tibur, Tusculum and Alba. The branch of the Julian aqueduct which served the Palatine after refreshing the Caelian separated Cicero's house from that of Clodius, a much larger house, for which the tribune had paid 14,800,000 sesterces. It was amusing to think that the residences of Cicero and Clodius, those arch-enemies, had been separated only by the great arches of an aqueduct. Farther away to the north was a house which had once belonged to Scaurus. The site had been in great demand for a long time.

A small door opened, and the most important clients were admitted as far as the *atrium*. From there they were to be introduced in order of rank into the *tablinum*, where the family archives were kept. Here the master was waiting to grant them a brief audience.

Then the main door would be opened for the second entrée. These would be the clients who were attached to only one patron and were consequently very assiduous in their attentions. When the vast *atrium* was full, Silanus would glance through a slit in the thick hanging which separated the *tablinum* from the *atrium* to check that there were no undesirables present, then he would go out into the *atrium* and his visitors would pay him their respects. It was from among the privileged members of this category of client that the patron recruited his 'companions' every morning to escort him to the Forum, and the 'preceders', who only had time to lead the way very briefly on so short a journey.

Finally there would be the half-starved rabble of the third entrée, who put their energies into gleaning a few sesterces from a variety of patrons and who limited themselves to a humble greeting. The *nomenclator* had difficulty remembering the name of each individual to present him to Silanus and often gave a made-up name, but the wretched client dared not protest. There were huge crowds at the third entrée, and the financial returns were uncertain, because to get in at all you had to grease palms all the way from the porter at the first barrier. The times had gone when the ordinary clients arrived with all sorts of receptacles to take away gifts of food. The fashion now was for small gifts of money distributed at the end of a visit by a *dispensator*, with a very low scale of gifts which was tending to become uniform from house to house.

For patrons who were advised to keep out of politics, clients had lost their significance. They were hardly more than an expense sustained somewhat nostalgically out of vanity.

After the former consul had been received, the door-curtain of the *tablinum* was raised to admit Marcus and Marcia, who penetrated into the holy of holies.

Decimus was tall and svelte, with an aquiline nose, pale eyes and snow-white hair. He was wearing a fine amethyst-coloured cotton tunic, ornamented with elegant pleats, and his sandals were gilded. While he was speaking to them in a relaxed and fluent manner, he was mechanically playing with his rings, as though to imprint his own seal on his thoughts . . .

'It's always a genuine pleasure, Marcus, to renew acquaintance with a client one thought one had lost, especially when one finds him an honorary curule magistrate and a current member of the Arval Brethren. Most freedmen behave with total ingratitude when they come face to face with those who gave them their liberty. And these days a man who has had honours heaped upon his head is all the more liable to forget his benefactors very swiftly, as if the honours would have been possible without the liberty which brought them in its train. Your approach has touched me closely precisely because it's so rare an act. I shall see to it that it brings you as much good fortune as you merit.'

Marcia slipped aside the shawl which was half-veiling her face and said:

'My husband was saying to me only just now that his modest successes in life were merely a by-product of all the glorious deeds which have brought honour to your family since the days of Torquatus, that the greatest merit of glory is to inspire a taste for its own acquisition, and that it behoved him to pay tribute to you for what he has been able to achieve in life by the good use of the freedom which his great-great-grandfather already enjoyed under the aegis of T. Junius. If it takes four generations to make a gentleman, it's in fact to Tiberius himself that he owes all his merits. Some men would indeed have been ungrateful enough to forget their debt. Marcus is proud of it. It's not every man who has the honour of deriving his freedom from so illustrious and exemplary a source.'

Decimus had spoken absent-mindedly, and he listened in the same fashion. He asked Marcia to readjust her veil, then to let it fall open a little, then a little more, then a little less . . .

With an ecstatic expression he explained to Marcus:

'When you're in the Cattle Market, between the Arch of Janus Quadrifons and the Bronze Bull brought back from Aegina, with your back to the Basilica Sempronia and facing the small circular temple of Hercules the Conqueror, to the right of the latter building you can see the temple of Virgin Fortune, and on the left the temple of Patrician Modesty. Livy refers to it, among others, in Book X of his History. These three temples are among the oldest and most venerable in Rome. The temple of Hercules is attributed to a certain M. Octavius Hersennus; that of Virgin Fortune was built by king Servius; the temple of Patrician Modesty was founded by one of my ancestors. It's the temple of my *gens* and the priest-in-charge is always a member of our *familia*.

Long ago a fire damaged the bronze statue of Patrician Modesty, which lost its face. For years I've been planning to have the statue replaced by another in white marble, but none of the proposed designs have pleased me. There must be five or six rejected Patrician Modesties sitting around in the workshops of the greatest sculptors, which are technically perfect but neither modest nor patrician. It must be the times which are out of joint . . .

Well, here's the model I need. I was struck by the thought when your wife graciously let her veil slip. She is Patrician Modesty personified, just as I have always dreamt of it, without being able to express my vision in words.

You told me that you weren't coming to me to beg favours. The nobility of your attitude encourages me to ask you to do *me* a great service. Would you let your wife pose briefly for Polyeuctes, who's working with Zenodorus and others on the giant statue of Nero and the 120-foot sundial planned for the Domus Transitoria? The change of work will give him a rest.'

Marcus was enthusiastic, Marcia much less so . . .

'It would be very flattering for me, Decimus, to have my modesty eternalized in marble at last. But I know how sculptors of the class of Polyeuctes work in cases like this where gracefulness is of the essence. The great painters do the same. They draw the model in the nude first, and clothe it afterwards, so that the drapery will seem moulded to the contours of the living body and not merely draped over it. You know what artists' studios are like and what modesty – even of the plebeian variety! – would have to suffer there.'

Decimus hastened to assure them that every precaution would be taken to satisfy Marcia's keen sense of propriety, and Marcus bravely spoke up in support. Marcia sighed deeply and gave in.

Delighted, Decimus called one of his stewards and gave orders for Polyeuctes to be sent for immediately and for the rest of his clients to be dismissed on the pretext that he had suddenly been taken ill – though not before the appropriate sums of money had been distributed.

While they were waiting for Polyeuctes, they went into the adjacent peristyle which ran around a rose garden in full bloom. They walked along in front of galleries which turned the place into an astonishing museum, the fruit of the extensive pillaging of Greece, the Aegean islands, Alexandria and Asia Minor. There were works there by Scopas, Leochares, Lysippus, Cephisodotus, Timarchus, Tisicrates, Timotheus, Bryaxis, Doidalses and the two Boethi. The most recent statues were 150 years old and were signed Dionysos and Timarchides.

As the sun was getting higher, Decimus took his guests into the exedra where paintings by the greatest Greek masters were hung: Silanion, Nicias, Athenion, Apelles, Protogenes, Philoxenus and Euboulides.

Marcus plunged into calculations of the combined value of the statues and paintings present. The result was frightening.

'My finest works of art, the oldest, absolutely unique items, are all in my villas at Tibur, Antium and Baiae,' said Decimus casually. 'I don't think the air at Rome is favourable to conservation – too many philistines breathe it.'

'And yet,' Marcia observed, 'like everyone else I have seen pictures by Antiphilus, Artemon or Polygnotus hung practically in the open air in the porticos of Octavia, Philip and Pompey. Not to mention the galleries in the Baths of Agrippa or the new Baths of Nero ... Rome is stuffed with pictures which seem to be in a perfectly good condition.'

'They do in fact last surprisingly well. In the first place, the most important ones are painted on to a backing made from the inner honey-coloured wood of the larch, which the Greeks call *oegida*. Larches grow in the Alps and in the forests of Macedonia, and their wood stands up to sharp changes of temperature better than any other. Small pictures tend to be done on ivory or box-wood, whose resistance is equally good. Then, the larch-planks are specially treated with a coating of blue. And lastly, the painters use only four very stable colours: white, yellow, red and black. These colours, or blends of them, are used in a molten state, ground up in hot wax beside the painter's easel by his little slaves. Three hundred years later the pictures look as if they have just come out of the studio.'

'Wouldn't it be simpler just to paint on, say, a piece of canvas?'

'That's already done for women's dresses, and they rarely survive for the benefit of posterity!'

Marcia blushed at her stupidity in a charmingly confused way, and turned her attention to a round three-legged table which decorated the middle of the room. The legs were in gilded bronze and the top in an unfamiliar precious wood. Here and there the graining was astonishingly like the eyes on a peacock's tail.

'That once belonged to Cicero,' said Decimus. 'It was the first table made of citrus-wood ever seen in Rome.'

'He's supposed to have paid a million sesterces for it,' said Marcus. 'That's still the highest price for top quality citrus-wood today.'

'Why are such tables so expensive?' Marcia asked Decimus. 'What's so rare about them?'

'The citrus is a sort of cypress which grows in the distant forests of Mauretania and Arabia Petraea. For high-quality cabinet-work only the grained loops from the base of the tree are used, and it rarely grows to a sufficient thickness for one to be able to make a fine table-top from a transverse section. The difficulties are enormous.'

Decimus stroked the polished surface of the table reflectively and went on:

'Since you're a lawyer, Marcus, you can give me some advice. I bought this table and house for a derisory sum and I think I've finally discovered why. Yesterday evening, after night-fall, I was looking at these pictures before going to bed. By lamplight they take on a certain warmth of colour which I happen to like. As I was going from one picture to another, between *Embarcation for Cythera* and *The Cask of the Danaids*, I happened to glance at the black marble bust of Cicero which you can see over there . . . when suddenly there was a ghastly groaning behind me. I turned round. Cicero's head was on the table, staring at me. I had plenty of time to take in what it was before it vanished.'

After a horrified silence Marcia asked:

'Was the head black or white?'

'What difference does it make?'

'Haven't you noticed, Decimus, that an image can impress itself on our eyes in such a way that we can still see it for a moment if we direct our gaze elsewhere? If I shut my eyes, for example, I can still see you.'

Decimus was much struck by the suggestion, considered it, then said sadly:

'No, I'm afraid that, if anything, the head was a ghastly white. Just as it must have been when Cicero stretched his neck out of the litter on the shores of Gaeta, where he'd been delayed by sea-sickness, and the centurion Antonius cut it off.'

'Cicero is surely the most distinguished victim ever claimed by sea-sickness! Antonius also cut off his hands, the very hands which wrote the *Philippics*. Were they on the table too?'

'No.'

'When you lose your head, it's easy to forget your hands.'

Decimus was somewhat taken aback, but he laughed . . .

'You don't seem to be the sort of person who loses her head easily!'

As Marcus was devoted to Cicero, he objected to the turn which the conversation had taken and interrupted:

'If it's well known that the house is haunted, as plenty are, your lawyers can enter an action against the previous owner for annulment of sale on grounds of concealed defect. The case of haunting is specifically provided for in the code, and there's a rich case-history on the subject.'

'But it's an exquisite little house and I've fallen in love with the view. I have no intention of giving it up. Couldn't I just ask for a reduction in the price?'

'Since you bought it for a song, the reduction has already been made. It would be more expedient to get rid of the ghost. Perhaps all you need do is sell the table?'

'A table which once belonged to Cicero!'

'It would be better,' said Marcia, 'to do table turning, like the Chaldean magicians do, make contact with Cicero, and persuade him by flattery to go and haunt another piece of furniture in some other house. You're not short of properties, Decimus, you ought to be able to pull the wool over his eyes . . .'

Scenting money in the offing, Polyeuctes arrived in haste. He was deformed and ugly like Homer's Thersites, but his hands were strong and his wit sharp . . .

'I am unworthy, *domine*, to appear in your presence, and yet, as soon as your summons arrived, I came tumbling down from the head of Nero's statue and ran all the way here, like the famous bearer of the news of victory at the battle of Marathon. What triumph do you require of me?'

The term *dominus*, which implied a right of ownership, was never used between citizens. Slaves addressed their masters so, flatterers used the term to the emperors, who tolerated the practice, lesser clients also used it as an affectation of humility, and lovers talked about their *domina*, their 'mistress', as soon as they thought they had mastered her affections.

Decimus explained to Polyeuctes what he wanted, and the sculptor had to agree that Marcia, for the first time, gave him an idea of how to portray modesty. As he said this, he undressed her with his eyes, but at the back of his mind he was, with characteristic professionalism, already re-clothing her in the most chaste of fashions.

As they chatted, they walked up to the belvedere in the gardens. From there the entire house and the greater part of Rome could be seen stretching below them in the sun.

Experience had shown Decimus that it was impossible to get perfect service from 500 or 600 slaves divided into more or less anonymous groups of ten. 'Here I have only ninety-seven of them, and they're run by a few freedmen in whom I have the highest confidence. I could name almost every one of them, and they know it. Would you believe it, I'm better served like this than in my palace on the Caelian or my huge villa on the Pincian. The secret of real luxury is knowing the art of restraint. A select *familia* is like a permanent extension of the master's mind and body.'

There was no reply to this. On the subject of slaves, as on modesty, a man like Decimus was always right. Only the emperor would have been in a position to contradict him.

Things moved fast . . .

In the year 815 after the founding of the city, during the consulship of P. Marius Celsus and L. Asinius Gallus, one morning in mid- October, on a day marked N P in the calendar (indicating a public holiday), towards the sixth hour, at the end of a posing session, Decimus, who had come along to offer friendly advice, made love to Marcia, while Polyeuctes philosophically went on modelling some clay in a corner of the room. And since Decimus was trying very hard, the *domina* might well have derived some pleasure from it, if her mind had not been on other things.

Marcia was playing for high stakes, but her reputation made it impossible for her to play hard to get. She could only exploit the eternal theme: 'You are the paragon in a long list of mistakes', something even the most sceptical of men like to be told.

Senators' sons who decided to go into the army received a commission immediately. Marcia was soon able to announce to Marcus junior that he would be given the rank of tribune and attached to the General Staff in Vetera, on the Rhine, with a personal recommendation from D. Junius Silanus. Marcus junior had the good taste not to ask for the details. Kaeso was merely delighted with the news.

The elder Marcus joined the legion of Silanus' lawyers. Since Decimus had lands and possessions all over the place, he was permanently involved in twenty or more lawsuits, which he was in the habit of winning, Justice not being *that* blind. His new post gave Marcus the opportunity to collect some interesting back-handers and to enjoy a quantity of goods in kind which were a nice addition to the gastronomic tithes of the Arval Brethren.

On one occasion three young wild boar and some strings of thrushes found their way into his kitchen: on another, twenty-four *amphorae* of wine from Rhegium and Sorrentum, which had been maturing for some time in the *fumarium* of storerooms specially adapted so that the smoke from the hearth would pass through them. And there were some wonderful raisins which the smoke from the smithies of Africa – accorded the highest reputation among gourmets – had been responsible for slowly drying out. Marcus was also given spices. The famous *silphium* of Cyrenaica, a victim of overintensive cropping, had just died out, and it had only just been possible to find one specimen to satisfy Nero's curiosity, but black and white pepper, Indian *costum*, ginger, *malobathrum*, Syrian *sumac*, African pellitory, cinnamon, cloves, cardamom, and Indian nard, whose spikes cost 400 sesterces a pound, were gifts as welcome as the jars of scented honey which were used for preserving quinces. The master, who had never been good-looking, put on more and more weight. His attempts not to over-indulge in the best vintage wines were all too often a failure.

One fine afternoon in late December Marcia pressed Marcus to get out of the bath so that Kaeso could have his turn – sons did not bathe in their father's presence. When Kaeso was properly clean, Marcia herself gave the finishing touches to the arrangement of his short adolescent *toga praetexta* and left the house with him for a mysterious rendezvous.

They left the city by the Porta Ratumena, which owed its name to a charioteer from the neighbouring Circus Flaminius who had died when his runaway horses had dragged him there. Then they took the Via Lata across the Campus Martius towards the little Porticus Polae, named after Agrippa's sister. This monument was less crowded with passers-by than the great porticos, and lent itself better to quiet conversation. As they went, Marcia said to Kaeso, who was very intrigued: 'I'm going to present you to Decimus, of the *gens* Junia, a perfect gentleman and a relative of the Caesars. He's the patron with whom your father has recently renewed relations – to such good effect, as you know.'

Marcia insisted on the patronage relationship because in principle it was an unthinkable abuse for a patron to lay hands on the wife of one of his clients. Kaeso must be spared the least suspicion.

'Decimus is immensely rich and kind,' she went on. 'A word from him can do anything for you. You know what he's already done for your brother, who'll be leaving us in the spring in circumstances far superior to anything we could otherwise have hoped for. You know what he's done for your father, who now handles profitable cases. You know what, in an indirect sense, he has done for me, in so flatteringly asking me to lend my half-veiled face to the goddess of his *gens*, Patrician Modesty. It's essential that you make the best possible impression on him.'

Kaeso was delighted to oblige, but asked for more specific advice on how he should behave.

'Oh,' said Marcia, 'My only advice to you is to be yourself. Just be as the gods and the careful education we've given you have formed and defined you. Be pleasant and natural. Don't be timid without a reason, and don't boast either. Decimus is a very intelligent, very courteous man who'll put you at your ease very quickly. All he wants is to be able to like you. Treat him as a second father and everything will be fine.'

They were coming up to the great Virgo aqueduct, which over-shadowed the Portico of Pola and fed the baths of Agrippa. On both sides of the Via Flaminia, which is the extension of the Via Lata, could be glimpsed stretches of greenery, thinned out by the cold season. At this period the greater part of the 500 acres of the Campus Martius was still parkland.

Decimus' presence was obvious from the white litter set down in front of the portico. By it the athletic black bearers were standing frozen to attention, as if they had just heard the military command *Legio expedita* – Legion at the ready – which was the instruction to all soldiers to drop everything and be on the alert.

Decimus himself, the absolute picture of high distinction, was standing under the portico looking at a map of the universe which Augustus had had engraved there in marble. It gave the comforting impression that outside the Roman world the universe boiled down to a collection of shapeless odds and ends. The gods were on the Roman side even on maps.

The nobleman's face lit up at the sight of Marcia. You had to be as imperceptive as Kaeso not to realize quite what the smile expressed.

Marcia presented her stepson, and Decimus said to the boy: 'I'm delighted to make your acquaintance. Your mother has spoken of you to me in very high terms, and at first glance I'd say that she hasn't exaggerated. What are your aspirations in life and how can I be of help to you?'

Kaeso thought briefly and replied. 'My mother has been reminding me that you are a perfect gentleman and an exemplary patron. My only wish is that you should help me to become, and remain, a man with the same qualities.'

It was the one answer that Decimus had not foreseen. The suspicion crossed his mind that Kaeso was a nasty little bit of work who knew more than he should and was sending him up. But Kaeso's air of candour could not be an assumed one, and demanded equal candour in return.

'Well,' he finally said, 'you're asking me for the most difficult thing possible. If Destiny grants you a long life, you'll discover that it's easier to preach virtue than to live up to what one preaches in all circumstances. Nonetheless I'll do my best to match your own excellent parents.'

'If I'm fortunate enough to have three such virtuous people watching over me, I shall run the risk of becoming too good and getting bored,' said Kaeso.

His words made them laugh.

'Decimus' concept of virtue leaves room, I assume, for honourable forms of amusement,' Marcia said gaily. 'In future, Kaeso, you'll have two virtuous people to bore you and a third to entertain you.'

Decimus warmly approved of this programme, and the conversation took a more light-hearted and relaxed turn. Kaeso talked modestly about his successes at school and on horseback. He said rather less about his friendship with the gladiators, being well aware that it would not be thought to his credit.

'It seems that you've mastered Formosus and Bucephalus,' said Decimus abruptly. 'Are you as successful with girls?'

It was hardly the moment to let such a distinguished man into the secrets of his father's *popina*.

'Oh,' said Kaeso, 'girls of good family will look at me when I'm in a position to marry them. And the kind of girl one doesn't marry would have emptied my purse before I got my tunic off.'

'You've acquired a sound philosophy of life with very little effort, my boy.'

Decimus seemed enchanted.

The evening chill was falling on the Campus Martius. They separated amicably, after Decimus had whispered in Marcia's ear: 'He's perfect. So refreshing. I wish I'd been like that at his age.'

Marcia could not think of a higher compliment.

From the XVI of the Kalends of January – the 17th of December if you count like some simplistic barbarians – the Saturnalia would be unleashed on Rome. The city would be in the hands of frenzied slaves, who would make fun of all legitimate authority, with the complicity of the populace. In the Forums they would organize parodies of trials in mockery of the consuls, praetors and judges. At home, they would sprawl at their master's table, obliging the family to feast with them or serve them their drink. The king of these slave banquets, who was chosen by a throw of the dice, would take a malicious pleasure in imitating his *dominus* and dreaming up practical jokes which were not always funny. It was the world turned upside down. The female slaves, to the torture of their mistresses, would have their turn on the Ides of March and the III of the Nones of July. Republicans had often commented on the fact that Caesar, a demagogic womanizer, who, between the sheets, had been known to play the submissive girl as well, had been stabbed to death at the very moment when the city was in the hands of the humblest class of women.

During the seven days of the Saturnalia, owners afflicted with a very large *familia* would hurriedly escape to the countryside or join up with friends in discreet little bachelor apartments, where they lugubriously ate preserves and did their own washing-up, while waiting for the storm to pass. The emperor himself left the royal palace, for total chaos would break out there in a trice.

Decimus took no pleasure at all in the high-jinks of slaves. On the eve of the XVI he took refuge in a comfortable little villa which one of his freedmen regularly put at his disposal out in the direction of Antium, so that he could escape from the general frenzy.

Marcia left for the country the same day. But as she had become exceptionally careful about her reputation since she had started to model for the statue of Patrician Modesty, she took her husband with her. (The two boys, who found the Saturnalia entertaining, stayed at home.) This holiday together was supposed to allay any suspicion in Kaeso. At Antium Marcus had to put up at an inn where the service was in a state of total disorganization, while Marcia went on to Decimus' villa. Marcus was a good father, as well as a complacent husband.

When the Saturnalia were over, Marcia came back one morning and found Marcus in a little room which had not been swept for days and where he had been able to sleep only in a drunken stupor. She was the bearer of some astounding and wonderful news:

'Decimus is going to adopt Kaeso!'

Marcus staggered out of bed and asked her to say it again.

'Yes, it's all decided.'

'How did you do it?'

The remnants of his hangover prevented Marcus from noticing that his choice of words was unfortunate.

'I did . . . everything I could, but the gods did the rest. Decimus is divorced. He has no children by his previous wife. And with Cicero's head haunting that table he's living in an atmosphere of fear. The same dynastic considerations which led Agrippina to have his brothers assassinated may one day lead Nero to murder *him*. The life of his only nephew, Lucius, is hanging by a thread. If Decimus adopts Kaeso, a boy of entirely fresh blood, he'll probably be assured of some heirs to sustain the family cult and look after the temple in the Cattle Market, including my statue, which is nearly finished. He'll also have a more realistic chance of saving the major part of his fortune from the ever-watchful rapacity of the emperor and his myrmidons.'

'What exactly do you mean?'

'Well, you know what's been going on for generations now. At the slightest sign of disgrace the condemned man doesn't wait for his tortured body to be dragged to the Gemoniae and his belongings to be confiscated. He organizes a farewell gathering, has his arteries opened at his wrists – not the veins, as historians who've never tried to commit suicide are always telling us . . .'

'What difference does it make whether it's a vein or an artery?'

'One's large and the other small. Anyway, while the blood is flowing out, the victim comes up with some noble words which will stick in people's memories, leaves a few precious objects to the emperor, thanks him for his care and attention, leaves rather more to the Praetorian Prefect and a few other vampires, and offers a drink to a centurion who, by complete accident, has surrounded the house to make sure that the victim can only get out feet first.

As a result of these thoughtful provisions the emperor would look like an evil tyrant if he confiscated the goods of a man who hadn't yet been charged with anything, let alone condemned. So the terms of the will are usually respected.

Moreover, the emperor will say, in a good-humoured voice: 'What a shame! What can have come over him? I can't have frowned at him that severely, can I? Why didn't he count on my clemency? I would have had one more man in my debt . . .' Then a courtier suggests that the dead man wouldn't have sent for a surgeon if he hadn't felt more guilty than people think. And the emperor will nod his head sadly and doubtfully.

That way everybody is happy. The Praetorian Prefect will have made a little more on the side, the centurion will have had a better drink than usual, the emperor will get the Corinthian bronze he had his eye on without anyone saying he was in the wrong, and the condemned man will have rescued most of his fortune from pillaging and put it to more useful ends.

But the whole scenario depends for its smooth functioning on there being an heir, a very close heir, who is himself completely un-compromised. If a suicide has no heir who's above suspicion, it looks awkward for him to leave the bulk of his estate to friends or his nurse or a charitable foundation of some sort. By adopting someone like Kaeso, he acquires two precious advantages in one – the most direct form of heir and an heir who is absolutely innocent, because he cannot have it held against him that he is of the same stock as the victim. Now do you understand?'

'Absolutely. But to make provision for playing this neat trick on Nero and Tigellinus, Decimus could adopt someone else. He's of an age to adopt anyone he likes.'

'Who? Kaeso's birth is sufficiently obscure socially not to inspire fear or jealousy in anyone. He's legally adoptable because he has an elder brother who can maintain the family cult, and Decimus is fond of him for the same reasons that everyone else is fond of him and for the additional good reason that he is particularly fond of me too.'

'Yes, paradoxically enough, when it comes down to it, it's Kaeso's very obscurity which speaks in his favour in this instance.'

'I should point out that I too have spoken in his favour, and it wasn't easy. The rich are terribly mistrustful. I had to infiltrate all sorts of points into Decimus' head in such a way that he'd imagine he'd thought of them for himself. One wrong note and the whole thing would have been ruined. And I had to do the pleading on my feet. A suspicious millionaire is twice as suspicious in bed: the more semen you pump out of him the more he thinks you're trying to get at his heart. Still, it was for Kaeso's sake . . .'

'You were working in your own interest too. Where do you fit into the arrangement? I don't like to ask about myself . . .'

'A man like Decimus thinks he is above laws and customs. If his position were threatened, he'd be capable of simply giving himself the final pleasure of marrying me on the quiet. But has he any intention of doing so? I have to admit that I don't have the slightest idea. And I haven't made any attempt to find out.'

'I don't follow you . . .'

'Kaeso's adoption was already a large mouthful to get him to swallow without noticing it, but at least my position in the matter was completely disinterested, or relatively so. If I'd complicated the exercise by angling for a remarriage at the same time, I'd have risked losing both. There's a time and place for everything. The remarriage is another instance where Decimus will have to come up with my ideas for himself, as it were. In the meantime, he's been pressing me since the beginning of our liaison to go and live with him. It could be a good start. It was his wishes on that point which precisely gave me the chance to point out to him that my presence in his house would be more natural if it were also my son's house. Up to a certain point the adoption would be a cover for the adultery . . .'

'What an advocate for Kaeso you are!'

'When I married you I promised to devote myself to the interests of your children.'

'You're almost overdoing it.'

'When you love someone, nothing's impossible.'

'The greatest difficulty now will be breaking all this news to Kaeso.'

'It is indeed a tricky situation. But I think I've found the least unacceptable solution. We must send Kaeso away for a year, ostensibly so that he can pursue a course of higher studies in rhetoric or philosophy. There is Apollonia in Illyria – which seems too near home to me – or of course Athens or Rhodes. Decimus will be only too pleased to pay the costs.'

'It's an excellent idea. There are things that can be more easily written than said. When you're told of something at a distance by letter, the paper in your hands provides you with enough food for thought. You don't go looking elsewhere. Does Decimus know that you're my wife in name alone?'

'It's the first thing I told him, so that I would fit the image of my statue better. He roared with laughter.'

'Let's hope he keeps laughing.'

As soon as he got back to Rome, where the tenement block looked as if it had been hit by a hurricane, Marcus hastily wrote the following note to Decimus:

'T. Junius Aponius to D. Junius Silanus, friendly greetings.

My niece has just informed me of your desire to adopt my son Kaeso so as to assure yourself of an heir worthy to continue your family cult. The thought of being separated from so exceptional a boy breaks my heart. But the honour you have done us outweighs my personal sorrow. Words will never be enough to tell you how moved by that honour we all are.

Marcia has explained to you how we came to marry. I hoped to be able to replace her father after the irreparable loss she had suffered. Given the uncompromisingly chaste nature of your relationship, I am grateful for the opportunity to entrust my niece to you as well as my son. I feel that this should happen as soon as possible after Kaeso's adoption. The presence of the young woman in your house will help to mitigate the effects of a separation which so sensitive a boy will, despite everything, inevitably find cruel for a time. If Marcia's stay were to be prolonged, naturally a divorce would probably be better from the point of view of all three of us.

Marcia will have told you that Kaeso is unaware of the close kinship between myself and my official spouse and of the restricted nature of the relationship which that kinship has necessitated. In this way the child has been able to enjoy a more normal form of upbringing. I know that his adoptive father will be as discreet in the matter as his natural one. However, this legitimate precaution now presents us with a difficulty. Since he thinks of Marcia as a real wife rather than a niece, Kaeso may well be shocked by her departure from my house and her installation in the house of his adoptive father who is also the family patron.

Marcia and I feel that the most expedient course in these delicate circumstances is to send Kaeso to Athens to study. We can take advantage of his absence to prepare him by letter for both the adoption and Marcia's departure.

You will be reluctant to be deprived of Kaeso for more than a year. If he were admitted as a foreign observer into the Athenian *ephebia*, the aristocratic and athletic club where the young are given a proper polish in rhetoric and even in philosophy, Kaeso would not waste his time there and would come back to us "healthy in mind and body alike". But foreigners have to book their places several years in advance . . . I assume you have the necessary contacts to get a passage for him as soon as the start of the fine weather permits sailing again.

I am busy on your cases. Long may you remain in good health for the sake of my younger son and my beloved niece. My elder son also thanks you for the kindness shown to him.'

Marcia was happy with this euphemistic piece of prose.

Decimus soon went off to spend the winter in his villa at Tarentum. From there he dictated long letters to Marcia, which always finished with a few more intimate lines in his own hand. To Kaeso he sent occasional fatherly notes. It had been decided to say nothing to the young man about the Athens project until it was certain that there would be a place free for him in the spring in the group of foreigners admitted to the *ephebia*.

In winter, communications between Rome and Athens were like trying to square a circle. Even in summer the rounded sailing ships which made good speed from west to east had great difficulty tacking against the prevailing winds in the opposite direction. It was particularly slow and difficult to get up from Syracuse to Ostia. The Egyptian corn which constituted a third of the grain consumed in Rome was sometimes so long arriving that there were serious riots. And in the bad season merchant seamen, who were more afraid of cloudy weather than of storms, refused to go to sea at all. They needed a good starry sky to reassure them. As for the long war-galleys, whose oars were not dependent on the wind, they did not care for cloudy weather either, and their fragility turned them into canoes if Neptune was at all bad-tempered. So, during the winter, for weeks at a time the shortest sea-route between Southern Italy and Southern Illyria, from Brindisi to Dyrrachium, was out of use. But if the postal service – be it imperial or private – had to go right the way round by road, down the Dalmatian coast, where hardened pirates still lurked in the nooks and crannies, the risks were even greater.

So the winter of 815-16 went slowly by, and there was nothing to do but wait. Decimus, Marcia and her chaste cuckold were waiting for the reply from Athens, by whatever route it came. Marcus was also waiting for disaster to strike. Kaeso's adoption seemed to him too good to be true, and Marcia's fruitful remarriage more hypothetical still. Marcia herself was disturbed by her lover's sybaritic stay in the country. Decimus' absence suggested that his passion for her was less than all-embracing. She was waiting for some lying, debauched, greedy woman to get her hooks into him, and persuaded Kaeso to write him pleasant, endearing letters. Marcus junior was impatient to get into uniform and go and dazzle the Germans. Only Kaeso was not waiting for anything. He had been born with a soul which, though Roman, was pure and innocent.

In January the empress Poppaea gave birth to a little Claudia Augusta, who provided the Arval Brethren with an occasion for sumptuous sacrifices and festivities. Nero was radiantly happy. There might be a son to assure the line. The ranks of the Julio-Claudians were getting rather thin after so many assassinations.

Towards the end of February a favourable response at last arrived from Athens, and was forwarded by Decimus to the Aponii. Marcus informed Kaeso of this new act of kindness on his patron's part, and the youth, who was over the moon, rushed to his papyrus to thank Decimus effusively. Not only was his patron paying for the trip but he had offered to add a very decent sum for general expenses which would be paid to the boy in Athens as a monthly allowance.

As the sea-routes would be open again on the Ides of March, Kaeso just had time to pack his bags and travel across Latium to the large harbour at Pozzuoli in Campania. From there numerous commercial lines left for Spain, Africa and the East.

The *paedagogus* Diogenes, who had been freed and was now an assistant teacher at a school in the populous Trans Tiberim district, was invited to accompany Kaeso on the trip. He did not have to be asked twice.

On the evening before he left, Kaeso said goodbye to his teachers, his schoolfellows, his gladiator friends and his horses, and obediently listened to the advice of his parents and his elder brother. The main recommendation was to mistrust the Greeks, who were said to be even bigger tricksters at home than abroad.

In principle, Kaeso was equipped to face the world.

✤ CHAPTER ✤
8

On the very Ides of March when Kaeso and Diogenes were setting off for Athens, Paul and Luke were on board a ship bound for New Carthage, in Spain. The wind was not as favourable to them as to Kaeso and his mentor.

Paul was terrified of the sea, and yet he was constantly crossing it. Three years previously, in the autumn, he had even been shipwrecked while on his way under guard from Caesarea to Rome to be tried, and he had been stuck in Malta all winter. Then in spring the sails had bellied out again, and Paul had tacked up from Syracuse to Rhegium and from Rhegium to Pozzuoli, where there was already a Christian community. Some co-religionaries from Rome, learning of the captive's arrival, had come as far down the Appian Way as Tres Tabernae and even to Forum Appii, a small place at the mouth of the Pontine marshes, to meet him. As the Christians enlisted their supporters mainly in coastal regions, boats were a more practical method of spreading the gospel than roads.

For two years Paul had awaited trial, under relatively relaxed conditions of preventative military custody. He had had his right wrist permanently chained to the left wrist of the soldier guarding him, but could move freely within the house where he had been authorized to live and could receive whatever visitors he wished. Paul had found refuge with a Christianized Jew who lived near the Porta Capena. The Jews were numerous in this quarter. Travellers from Pozzuoli arrived down the Appian Way and through this gate, and the Chosen People were great travellers. A still larger community had set itself up on the other bank of the river in the slums of the Trans Tiberim quarter: most of the Jews were poor.

In the end the plaintiffs from Caesarea had failed to appear within the legal time-limit, and Paul had been freed. He had rediscovered the pleasure of pissing in private without some oaf passing comments on his circumcised cock. However, attempts to convert the Roman Jews had been rewarded with scant success. In his disappointment Paul hastened to leave the city with his inseparable companion Luke, and set off for Spain, a trip which he had long been planning. The sight of the erotic dancers of

Cadiz, whose castanets – which they called *crotala* – enlivened feasts everywhere, had made it plain to the Christians of the Empire that there must be souls to instruct and redeem in the region of Spain where this lewd music originated.

The unfortunate accident of the trial had set Paul back five years. Now, as he leant on the ship's rail, mechanically rubbing his right wrist with his left, he was mentally reviewing the sudden changes of fortune which had made it such a gripping adventure. Gradually the land was fading into the distance. With it went the Christians of Pozzuoli, still exposed to the traps of demons and the sophistries of false prophets. Devils and heretics, whipped into a frenzy by the apostle's rare virtues, grew in Paul's footsteps like mushrooms after the rain.

Five years earlier, after his Pentecostal speech to the Jews in Jerusalem, he had almost got himself torn to pieces yet again. Following the dictates of his customary sense of self-preservation., he had thrown himself into the arms of the Roman peace-keeping force. The Jews were summarily clubbing and stoning everyone in sight. The Romans only cut off distinguished heads after due form had been observed. The respite was always worth having.

But it was only under torture, to which he was being subjected in the hope of throwing more light on the affair, at the moment when the lead whip was already being raised, that he had shrewdly allowed himself the pleasure of admitting his precious rank of Roman citizen. He had immediately provided as proof the *praenomen* and the *nomen* of the patron responsible for his naturalization. Saul was only his Roman 'surname'. A citizen could not be whipped. In contrast, the word of an unknown man or a slave had no value in law unless it had been verified by force.

He had consequently been untied and made to appear before the Sanhedrin, the highest Jewish legal authority. There he had skilfully contrived to stir up a terrible argument among its members by speculating on the fact that the Pharisees present believed in the resurrection of the flesh while the Sadducees, who currently held internal political power, were scrupulously faithful to the oldest biblical texts in not believing in resurrection, in angels or even in punishment in the next world.

Paul – who had admittedly been trained as a Pharisee – had posed as a Pharisee persecuted for his faith in the distant resurrection of all men, although he could not prevent himself from thinking of the only valid Resurrection, the recent one of Christ, which was the model for, and harbinger of, those to come. But the trick hadn't entirely got him out of trouble.

He had been charged with complicity in an assassination plot and sent off under cover of darkness, with a sizeable Roman escort, to Felix, the governor of Judaea, whose headquarters were at Caesarea.

Antonius Felix, the brother of the freedman Pallas, was brutal, dissolute and greedy. He had married a Jew, Drusilla, daughter of Herod-Agrippa I and sister of Agrippa II and Berenice: Drusilla had abandoned her first husband Aziz, the king of Emesus. Felix had refused to hand Paul over to the Jews in Jerusalem, had arranged a comfortable captivity for him and had often come to visit him with his wife. Paul had worn himself out trying to communicate his beliefs to persons of such high rank, but Drusilla had come only out of curiosity and Felix was merely after money. There was no point of communication between him and them.

Two years had gone by. Felix had been replaced by Festus. Threatened once more with being handed over to the Jews, Paul appealed to the emperor and Festus agreed that the accused should appear before the court in Rome. Shortly after that King Agrippa II and his sister Berenice had come to greet the new governor. By way of entertainment he had suggested that they should listen to the famous Paul.

This Berenice had, at the age of thirteen, married a certain Marcus, the nephew of Philo the famous Alexandrian Jewish philosopher. Having lost her first husband very young, she married her paternal uncle Herod, king of Chalcis, by whom she had two sons, Berenicianus and Hyrcanius. Finding herself a widow for the second time at the age of twenty she had caused a scandal by becoming the concubine of her brother Agrippa II. To stop the gossip Agrippa had given Berenice in marriage to Polemon, the king of Cilicia, who in return for the honour of marrying a Jew of such rank had agreed to an eleventh-hour circumcision. Perhaps his performance had suffered as a result of it. At all events Berenice had given him the cold shoulder and gone back to the bed of her obliging brother. It was in the presence of this abominable creature (who was to be the delight of Titus at the age of forty!) and of her fraternal bedmate that Paul had been invited to deliver a pious discourse.

With his eyes fixed on Pozzuoli as it faded into a blur – Pozzuoli where the Cross had been planted – Paul murmured the words which had risen to his lips:

'Did Jesus dazzle me with lightning on the road to Damascus so that I could cast pearls before swine and other filthy creatures? Keep back, you bitch on heat, already twice married before you gave yourself up to sterile sensuality with your brother! Keep back, incestuous little king! ! You both bring shame upon the Jews and shame upon mankind, and God's eternal fires await you!'

That's what John the Baptist would have said: he had got himself decapitated simply for reproaching Herod the Tetrarch for marrying his brother's wife.

But the vile Agrippa had said to Paul: 'You may plead your cause.' And the apostle stretched out his hand in a gesture of innocence and began elegantly: 'I account myself fortunate indeed, King Agrippa, that it is before you that today I have to exculpate myself of all the crimes of which the Jews accuse me, and all the more fortunate because you are better acquainted than anyone with all the customs and controversies of the Jewish people. Therefore, I pray, listen patiently to my words. Since my youth my life . . .'

Festus, who knew nothing about the Jews, had interrupted the speaker and called him a lunatic when he alluded to the Resurrection of Christ. Berenice had giggled, while Agrippa had laughingly said: 'A bit more and you'll persuade me to turn Christian!'

'A bit more' . . .! When a man preaches about Christ rising from the dead as a show of civility to unspeakable people, he's already gone too far. What an example he had set for future missionaries! They would make up to those in power and wheedle money and security out of them, on the pretext of preserving an inspired speaker for the edification of the masses!

How patient God was with him. But the day would come when He would let his anger burst forth!

Luke came and leant beside Paul and asked him:

'What are you thinking about? Are you feeling sea-sick as usual?'

'I'm thinking that Stephen got himself stoned, and that I'm travelling with a biographer whose indulgence overwhelms me, and who, as a doctor, ministers to my body after putting my soul to shame. I'm thinking that I shan't be crucified, since I'm a Roman citizen, but that my head will fall beneath the sword sooner or later and that I shall have got a better deal than I deserve.'

Luke was quite used to these depressive self-denigrations.

'You can always drown yourself,' he said with a smile. 'It's a form of death that links citizens and slaves in the same shroud. It's probably because you're tired that you're a prey to black thoughts of this kind . . .'

'Our results so far aren't brilliant. The Jews reject us, the Greeks are sceptical and the Romans are impenetrable. Each time I found a community I have to spend hours dictating letters to its members to keep them on the right path. Despite the Holy Spirit, I feel that in the long run there's a sort of wall between our souls and our words. I'm struck by all the wrong ideas the Gentiles have about us despite our constant efforts . . .'

Eleven years earlier the 'wrong ideas' were already in circulation. And what was particularly disquieting was that they were circulating among intelligent people, as can be seen in retrospect from this correspondence between Gallio and his brother Seneca.

'L. Junius Annaeanus Gallio to L. Annaeus Seneca, brotherly greetings.

My dear younger brother, in my newly assumed position as proconsul of Achaea, a post which I owe more to your pressing interventions on my behalf than to my own merits, I find myself faced with an unpleasant affair about which I feel I need your advice.

The Corinthian Jews have dragged before me a certain Cn. Pompeius Paulus, the son of Cn. Pompeius Simeon, grandson of Cn. Pompeius Elizer, who, as his Latin *nomen* and *praenomen* indicate, was raised to Roman citizenship under the patronage of Pompey the Great. Pompey rid the Jews once and for all of the detested tutelage of the Seleucids, and substituted our protectorate. He then helped himself to a lot of money, and in return showed himself very free-handed with rights of citizenship: the gift did not cost him much. So this Paulus – or Saul in Hebrew – belongs to a Jewish family known for several generations for its attachment to Rome and rewarded for it at a period when Roman citizenship was not, after all, debased the way it is now. The accused is a tent-maker, which for a descendant of a nomadic nation suggests a neat piece of predestination.

The plaintiffs accuse this Saul of trying to persuade people to worship the Jewish god according to new formulae which are contrary to their ancestral laws. At first I thought I had misheard them. A Roman proconsul is there to apply Roman law, not to get mixed up in theological quarrels which have nothing to do with any crime defined in our universal code.

Noting my reservations, the prosecution made the most of the argument that Saul was not only a promoter of heretical doctrines and a professional blasphemer, but also a redoubtable agitator who had been sowing trouble wherever he went for the past seven years. Apparently he always proceeds in the same way. He is well received in the synagogues of Asia or Greece, where they are always curious to hear an address by any rabbi travelling through. He starts his speech off by gaining his audience's confidence with a long introduction which reveals a brilliant knowledge of the Septuagint and of Pharisaic law. Then he tells them how he met the Messiah.

You once spent many years in Alexandria, where there are plenty of Jews. While there, you mixed in the pro-Jewish, pro-Greek circles of the famous Israelite Philo. So you must have some vague notion of this Messiah of theirs, who, according to their holy scripture, will come one fine day to restore the glory of Israel ... after the fall of the Roman Empire, one assumes! Waiting for this Messiah is a fine exercise in patience for the Jews.

At this stage in the proceedings the audience becomes excited and fidgets like a child which has been given a glimpse of a bag of sweets. It's all too wonderful, but can it really be true?

Remember that to the Jews there is nothing intrinsically blasphemous in claiming to have met the Messiah or even claiming to *be* the Messiah. The Messiah is supposed to be a member of the human race and the last in a long line of prophets. Someone who makes such claims may be wrong out of sheer conceit or he may be trying to get into the public eye for personal profit, but he is not automatically guilty of impiety. It is up to the public to examine his claim.

Saul then specifies that the aforementioned Messiah is none other than a certain Jesus of Nazareth, who was crucified at Jerusalem under the procurator Pontius Pilate on the eve of the Jewish Passover, seven years before the death of Tiberius, in the year when M. Vicinius and L. Cassius Longinus were consuls and Tiberius himself was consul for the fifth time.

A wave of disappointment sweeps through the synagogue. If the Jewish Messiah died on a cross, he clearly was not the Messiah. And if he had been, what use is a crucified Messiah?

Unruffled by the sudden chill in the atmosphere, Saul fearlessly adds that his crucified Jesus is an incarnate emanation of the god Yahwe and was resurrected from his tomb shortly after the Passover. A large number of Jews are supposed to have witnessed the phenomenon in the flesh. Then Jesus rose into the heavens to be restored to the bosom of Yahwe. Moreover Saul himself has seen Jesus since his ascension: a Jesus who spoke to him and entrusted him with secrets. And what is even more difficult to take is that it now turns out that Yahwe is not one god, as previously thought, or even two, but three. A mysterious Holy Spirit, which speaks through the mouth of Saul, was responsible for the pregnancy of Jesus' virgin mother twenty years or so before the apotheosis of Augustus.

The pious and learned Jews, who have been listening sympathetically to their visiting speaker, are absolutely dumbfounded. When they begin to come to, a few timid voices are raised to ask Saul which passages of the Scriptures allude to an incarnate Yahwe who is one in three. You know as well as I do that, while one can argue about the characteristics of the Messiah to one's heart's content, the Oneness of God is the fundamental dogma of the Jewish faith. Consequently it is impossible for their god to take on human form the way our Greek and Roman gods can. I have never read the Septuagint, the Greek version of their bible – as, given your universal curiosity, you will doubtless have done – but it seems to me that if there had been the slightest reference to a trinity or to divine incarnation in it, someone would have noticed it by now.

Finding himself with his back to the wall, Saul calmly declares that if Jesus is god – of which there is no doubt – he is entitled to add a little something to the bible.

The mere idea of a postscript of this sort evidently puts the Jews in a bad temper. Various murmurings begin to be heard. Saul then becomes furious, dances with rage, declares that the blood of unbelievers will be upon their own heads, and vows that henceforth he will bear the treasures of Israel to the Gentiles. After this last charming thrust he is shown the door, and the promise of riots is in the air.

With my customary impartiality I took Saul aside and asked him if there was any truth in the charges levelled against him. As he admitted them very honestly and openly, I said to him with admirable tact: "You realize that these stories which you are putting about – I'm not in a position to judge whether they are true or false – appear to be deliberately designed to throw your fellow Jews into a state of insane fury? You know perfectly well how touchy these people are, rightly or wrongly, on certain points. So why do you go on? It's sheer provocation. You yourself admit that you recently declared that in future you would take your good news to the Gentiles. Why don't you keep your word instead of upsetting the Jews and causing trouble for the proconsul?"

To this perfectly reasonable proposal Saul replied: "The various philosophical sects in Athens laughed at me when I talked about resurrection . . ."

I told him that at first glance, in my capacity as proconsul, I would prefer ridicule to trouble. He then took up the position that he had a duty to deliver his message to the Jews first. And he added: "Since Judaism is a recognized religion at Rome, and even a privileged one since we are the only people dispensed from worshipping Caesar, the interpretations that this or that rabbi may put on it do not fall within the jurisdiction of the Roman courts. They are an internal Jewish matter. Rome's task is merely to keep public order. Who is upsetting it? Me by my words, or the Jews by their actions?" An attitude which one could define as being right in theory and wrong in practice.

This is the point we have reached in this bizarre business here in Corinth. I feel as if I were walking on my head. And that impression is heightened by the strangest of contrasts. From time to time this Saul talks like a complete lunatic. The rest of the time he speaks with sweet reason. He is a typical rhetorician, all the more convincing because he devotes all his talents to promoting an obsession.

According to my information, the accused and his companions were first expelled from Antioch in Pisidia. At Iconium they were threatened with stoning and fled the city. At Lystra in Lycaonia Saul *was* stoned and left for dead. At Philippi in Macedonia Saul was beaten up by some efficient thugs who did not know he was a Roman citizen. In Thessalonica there was a riot and they left in a hurry by night. They left Berea in a hurry too. That brings us to the present disturbances in Corinth.

I have certainly got an oddball on my hands. Wherever he goes with words of peace on his lips, there is trouble.

On digging further into the matter I have come to a disturbing conclusion. Saul is not the only one busy at this game. He would even seem to be the thirteenth in line. Before him, twelve propagandists who call themselves apostles dispersed in all directions to do the same job as he, and with equally tiresome results. I discovered with some surprise that the Jewish riots in Rome three years ago, which forced Claudius to expel a number of people, were the result of violent clashes between orthodox Jews and followers of this Jesus, who is dead according to the former and alive according to the latter. You probably remember that the uprising was attributed to the actions of a certain Chrestos, whom the police were unable to lay their hands on. Well, Saul's Jesus is also called Christ. Whether he is dead or alive there was not much chance of arresting him! And it's reasonable to ask oneself if a lot of other troubles of the same kind in many other places might not have the same origin. There are always bumpkins around to believe the silliest tales when inspired eloquence spreads them.

You will admit that relations between Rome and the Jews are quite bad enough without this Chrestos. The time is long past when Caesar himself was beseiged in Alexandria with Cleopatra for a whole winter and finally rescued by a Jewish army under the command of the ethnarch Antipater.

Do you suppose this ungrateful race really thinks that we came and chased out Alexander's successors so as to guarantee them unfettered independence? As long ago as Augustus' great census 6,000 Pharisees had the nerve to refuse the oath of allegiance to the Emperor. It was about that time that Saul's Holy Spirit must have been getting the virgin-mother pregnant. A dozen years later, after the death of Herod, there was uprising after uprising. Then we had the revolt of Judas of Galilee and the Pharisee Saddoq. Before Quintilius Varus got himself and his legions killed in the forests of Germany, he had to bring all the troops in Syria together to crush that revolt, and afterwards 2,000 rebels were crucified. When Jesus, according to Saul, spoke of bearing his cross, he knew what he was talking about. It is public knowledge what trouble the procurator Pontius Pilate had with the Jews. Two years before the death of Tiberius, on the eve of retiring and preparing for death himself, he had the Samaritans massacred at Garizim. Then, when Caligula gave the crazy order that his own statue should be put up in the Temple at Jerusalem, there was nearly a major disaster. If the legate of Syria, P. Petronius, had not contrived to drag out the arrangements, there would have been a general bloodbath. And since then, despite Claudius' efforts at appeasement – he left the priests of the Temple in charge of the care of their special robes – Judaea is in a permanent state of complaint and agitation.

But the intolerable character of the Jews, which has got nothing to do with this Christ business, does not only show itself in Judaea. The Jewish community in Rome, which a grateful Caesar helped to adapt to its new surroundings and showed great favour to, had become so turbulent by five years after the death of Augustus that Tiberius deported 4,000 Jews to the mines in Sardinia. And what about the continual outbursts of violence between Jews and Greeks which pit quarter against quarter – and no quarter given – in all the major seaports of the East as far as Cyrenaica?

The followers of Saul's sect can only fan the existing flames. Just at the moment the Corinthian Jews are particularly nervous because a large number of Jews recently expelled by Claudius have sought refuge here. If I have grasped the situation aright, those for and against Chrestos are going to continue their quarrel here, and this is how Saul has ended up in my courtroom. Curse the man! What am I to do with him?

The right of *coercitio* is indeed essential to my powers as proconsul. I can arbitrarily take rigorous measures, resulting if necessary in death, against any man who foments riot. But the rank of Roman citizen protects the culprit from this very practical *coercitio*. In the case of a citizen I can only exercise the right of *cognitio*, of recognizing the jurisdiction of the court over the case and bringing a formal charge within the provisions of Roman law. Now clearly a man cannot be said to have broken the law by thinking that he saw the ghost of Christ, still less by believing the word of others who purport to have seen it. Saul is well aware of the fact, and accordingly feels safer in my hands than in the hands of the Jews. He even claims to have had a vision in which his master assured him that he would suffer no harm in Corinth. This sedulous association with emanations of the Great Beyond is accompanied by a neat grasp of procedural skills. When I took exception to his claims to communicate with ghosts he had the audacity to say: "But to the best of my knowledge the existence of ghosts is recognized in Roman law. Correct me if I'm wrong, but aren't you allowed to bring a case for annulment of contract on grounds of hidden defect if it is established that a house you have purchased is well known to be haunted? My ghost is as good as yours!" My mouth simply dropped open. The way he's going, Saul will be taking Rome to court on a charge of hidden defect, complaining that we let his Jesus run around loose!

So I have two choices, and neither of them is entirely satisfactory.

I could release the accused and tell him to go and get himself strung up somewhere else. But Judaea, which is an overpopulated country with two million Jews crammed into it, is a volcano threatening eruption. And in every large port in the Mediterranean, even in Rome itself, the colonies of captious Jews have withdrawn into fortress-like ghettoes, where they live a life apart. Estimates put the total number of these emigrants at four million. Though in one sense they are scattered, in another they are only too concentrated. Rome is terrified at the prospect of a general uprising in Judaea which would lead to local uprisings in the hearts of so many more or less unarmed cities. How could our thirty legions, which are kept busy on the frontiers, cope with a rebellion on that scale?

Of course there has been a long tradition of Jews in whom Rome has been able to arouse affection and who have worked with and for Rome in an exemplary manner. Saul's own family tree is proof positive of the fact. Greek and Roman ideas and manners have rubbed off on many Jews, and substantial numbers have even given up their own religion. But everyone agrees that the effect has been to make the fanatics and the intransigents, whose numbers remain alarming, take an even harder line.

If the worst happens and the Jews set the Roman world on fire, and if Saul's sect has something to do with it, people in high places would surely have some justification for reproaching me with having shown uncritical tolerance to this agitator. Religious sects, even the oddest ones, are like fires in Rome: you know where they start, it's harder to predict where they will stop. If I let the matter drop and neglect the opportunity to make a salutary example of Saul, where will these "Christians" stop?

The alternative is to take a hard line. But that entails ignoring the laws of which I am supposed to be the custodian. The Jews in Judaea or Alexandria might rebel, but they might not. Perhaps my fears are exaggerated. In the meantime, if I take any illegal action against Saul, I would be exposed to the possibility of denunciation, which could put me in an awkward situation. There are a host of informers just watching every governor for the slightest *faux pas*, and you will not be Agrippina's friend and Nero's tutor for ever. In any case if I brought a case against Saul on such dubious grounds, he would immediately appeal to the Emperor, and the irregularity of my procedure would come to light.

Our friend Burrus has just become Praetorian Prefect. That makes him responsible for security and all its many problems. His honesty and administrative competence are exceptional. Have a word with him about my little difficulty. You are certain to agree with him, and that will make three of us.

I cannot prevent myself from reflecting that the Jews and their affairs bring bad luck on all who get too closely involved with them. Varus was killed in Germany and Pontius Pilate met a violent death. "But," you'll point out, "Caesar, who was a friend to the Jews, came to the same end." Perhaps they bring misfortune on everybody?

With every possible scruple I'm trying to make my pile while at the same time leaving a reputation for honesty considerably better than my predecessor's. Fortunately that is not difficult. What happened to the good old days when you could make a hundred million out of a province? The major defect of our Empire is that you can't plunder it twice.

While I am on the subject of money, I am reliably informed that it is beginning to play a significant role in Christian communities. That gives an alarming idea of the scale of their development. On the other hand, a rich sect comes more into the public eye precisely because it is rich. When a secret society becomes a financial body, the State can keep a check on it and bring pressure to bear. The Christians aim to pool their worldly goods, the old "golden age" dream which is always a godsend for a few scoundrels. When men pool their women as well, the strongest get the lion's share and the eunuchs go hungry. The Christians are also much enamoured of collecting for charity, though it is not clear what happens to the money afterwards.

Give me some detailed news of what is going on in Rome. You will appreciate how useful such information is sooner or later in one's career.

I hope that you are well. How is your asthma? Thanks be to Aesculapius, I am fine.'

'L. Annaeus Seneca to L. Junius Annaeanus Gallio, brotherly greetings.

My dear elder brother, I gave Burrus a brief account of the contents of your letter, and his advice on the matter is the same as mine. We feel that the tiresome company of this fellow Saul has finally affected your brain. You are "seeing Jews up every mews" as the saying goes. If the Jews in Judaea make a move, they will be dealt with. As for those of the *diaspora*, the Greek, not to mention the Roman, population will keep them under control until our reinforcements arrive. Your ghost story is too vague and too silly to stir people up for long. Ghosts disappear the way they appear, with the greatest of ease. Burrus' advice is to send this Saul packing. These Christians are so insignificant that he has never heard of them before, and neither have I. He commends you, nonetheless, for the seriousness with which you have treated the incident. You have shown remarkable conscientiousness. Thorough administration is in fact a matter of attention to detail, and a good proconsul should not neglect anything out of hand.

I offer you my personal congratulations on the honest moderation you are showing in the traditional shearing of your lambs. There are still fortunes to be made elsewhere. It would be particularly awkward for me if, at the end of your term of office, you were to face a charge of peculation. Someone who envies your success can easily stir up that sort of thing in a Senate meeting. It was I who vouched for your honesty to the eminent friends who arranged this lavish little trip for you. It's a case of *Non cuivis homini contingit adire Corinthum*! (Not every man gets a chance to go to Corinth.)

As you reminded me, I spent several years in Egypt during the reign of Tiberius, in the days when Galerius, our uncle by marriage, achieved the rare feat of being Prefect there for fourteen years. Because I was related to the Prefect, all doors were open to me. I found this particularly valuable because I was passionately interested in every aspect of that stupendous country, including its history. It's no wonder that the Caesars made such an extraordinary place their personal property. In those days Philo's reputation was just beginning to flower, and I was only a young man. This man of powerful intellect did me the honour of singling me out and instructing me in his system of ideas. I saw Philo again at Rome shortly before Caligula was murdered. He had been sent on an embassy by the Jewish community in Alexandria to request the privilege of being absolved from worshipping the Emperor's statue. He was trembling at the thought of having to appear before Caius and deliver such a message, and he asked me to help him. I was already a successful lawyer.

More than ten years have passed, but my memories of that extraordinary audience are as vivid as ever. Your letter brought them back to me, because the affair was a perfect illustration of all the difficulties which the Romans and Jews have in understanding one another. (Most Romans, even the educated ones, are utterly ignorant when it comes to the Jews. Such ignorance is deplorable, if one remembers that the Jews largely live within the Empire and not in unknown parts.) Among his other fancies Caligula had put on that famous breastplate which he had had taken from the tomb of Alexander the Great and polished up. Luckily he was having a good day . . . or perhaps one should say, he was momentarily in a good mood, for his mood swung like a weathercock. Philo and I took it in turns to explain, as eloquently as possible, what it was all about. I shall never know whether Caius hadn't understood a word we said, or whether his reply should be put down to his deplorable sense of humour. What he said was: "The solution is quite simple. All it needs is an exchange of civilities. The Jews can sacrifice to the statue of Augustus and the Jewish god will be received with full pomp into the Roman Pantheon. That way, the Jews will become Romans and the Romans Jews." Philo threw me a look of absolute despair.

A few weeks later Caligula was murdered, his wife Caesonia run through with a sword and his daughter smashed against the wall. The god of the Jews could breathe again.

As you guessed, while I was in Egypt I did in fact get to know the Septuagint, which was closely analysed in Philo's circle, just as I visited plenty of Egyptian priests, who are the repositories of such astonishing traditions. It is even the case that during the eight interminable months when I was mouldering in exile in the Corsican *maquis* as a punishment for having become too well acquainted with Germanicus' daughters, I had a copy of that little bible in my library. It is certainly a very interesting work, said to have been translated from Hebrew into Greek by seventy-two translators during the reign of Ptolemy II Philadelphus, at his command – he was the Ptolemy who had the great lighthouse at Alexandria built. Three hundred years ago the Egyptian Jews were already beginning to forget their Hebrew. (But I suspect that many passages were translated much more recently.) Yes, it is an interesting work, but not a convincing one. There is an essential dimension missing. With a lot of attendant nonsense and naïvety the book gives us an account of the relationship between a people and their national deity. I feel that that sort of religious concept is now hopelessly old-fashioned.

In my youth I followed the teachings of the dissident Stoic sect of the Sextii. They preached vegetarianism and the examination of one's own conscience. In particular they believed in the immortality of the soul, and the necessity of making one's thoughts and actions conform to an immutable order of nature and the objective world. I am still a vegetarian and I have never for a moment doubted that either truth is universal or it does not exist. A god who attaches himself to a nation instead of to humanity as a whole is a mutilated god. The exclusive prison in which he confines himself limits his influence: he deserves no more for himself than the oblivion to which he has consigned the majority of mankind.

My dear Novatus – I like to call you by your childhood name, even though adoption has deprived you of it – you will understand why Philo and his friends were so anxious to interpret their bible in neo-Platonic, or even Pythagorean or Stoic, terms. They were aware that their brainchild was beginning to smell a little musty, and they devoted all the resources of their exegetical and allegorical virtuosity to exposing it to the fresh air of more or less fashionable Greek philosophy.

I should mention that in places the translators of the Septuagint had manipulated the original Hebrew to make the text harmonize better with Greek sensibilities. At least, distinguished Hebrew scholars have told me so. The famous formula in Exodus where Yahwe defines his transcendent nature: "I am that I am", in Greek becomes – more Platonically and prosaically – "I am what is". Philo, who only knows the rudiments of Hebrew, admitted these distortions, but thought them relatively unimportant and, if anything, helpful in his studies.

So the most common form of the bible today is a Greek translation with a Greek commentary.

To come back to your Cn. Pompeius Paulus. It is remarkable to see this visionary offering the Gentiles an interpretation of the Septuagint which is, to say the least of it, original. The idea of liberating the truth from its Jewish prison is evidently at work.

But I am very sceptical as to the likelihood of such attempts succeeding, whether in the hands of eminent philosophers or passing adventurers. The bible is too shot through with Jewishness to adapt itself to other nations or other ways of thinking. Either, despite Philo's efforts, the bible is not acceptable to a foreigner because its text is too faithful to

Jewish history and ideas. Or someone like Saul has to distort the fundamental nature of the text to disseminate it among other races. And then it is not the bible any more.

I can in any case assure you that real Jews, who know the text by heart, will never accept this fairy story about a triple god, incarnate, crucified and resurrected. To them, it would have a nasty taste of Egyptian or Greco-Roman mythology about it. I find it extraordinary that a Jew could even come up with such a tale. It is so contrary to the very core of the Jewish nature. For Jews to believe in this Jesus, he would have to be resurrected under their very noses!

In the meantime, there is a passage in the Septuagint which I thoroughly appreciate – the story of the flood. I myself was recently nearly drowned, and I was not the only one. The story is worth telling.

High on Claudius' list of grand public works, to which Rome owes its beautiful aqueducts, was the draining of Lake Fucinus – a lake in the hills to the east of the city. Under the supervision of Narcissus, work was done over a long period with the aim of breaking through the rock barrier which separates this lake from the Liri, whose turbulent waters flow southwards towards the gulf of Minturnae. It was a Cyclopean task, which recently reached its final stage. A few more pick-axe blows and the vast mass of water in one of the most beautiful lakes in Italy was going to hurl itself into the Liri and sweep down towards the Tyrrhenian Sea. Around what was left of the lake vast expanses of excellent land would be available for farming, thus providing precious new resources for the hill-folk of the region.

At that point Claudius had the bright idea of celebrating the event by a grand naval battle on the lake, at the end of which the waters would be released. This would crown eleven years of determined work by thirty thousand navvies and be a fitting tribute to the energy of the Emperor and his freedman. Claudius' taste for blood-drenched spectaculars outstrips his taste for history and literature.

The Roman passion for these mock naval battles is all the stronger because they are so rare. The first, as you know, was the fruit of the genius of Julius Caesar himself, when he celebrated his four triumphs, over Gaul, Pontus, Egypt and Africa. Caesar had a lake dug out in the Campus Codetanus on the right bank of the Tiber, a little further down stream than the Vatican bridge. The site allowed the liquid arena to be easily reached from the river, so that it could take large galleys designed for the high seas, and not just light-weight constructions knocked together quickly near the proposed scene of action. A "Tyrian" fleet fought an

"Egyptian" fleet, in front of an enormous throng of spectators. Rome had not forgotten that she had opened up her way to world domination by her naval victories against Carthage, which had cost her the loss of seven hundred ships and huge numbers of rowers and legionaries. The peasant farmers had willingly become sailors and had cut furrows through the waters with as much energy as they had previously ploughed their ancestral fields.

Less well known is the fact that the second naval battle of this type took place during the period of our unhappy civil wars. Sex. Pompey captured a squadron of Agrippa's men and compelled the prisoners to fight each other in the Straits of Messina for the entertainment of his supporters. It was the first sea engagement where the few survivors on the winning side were promptly massacred as a reward for their brief triumph.

The third naval battle was held to mark the dedication of the new Forum and of the Temple of Mars Ultor. Augustus had a new lake 600 metres by 400 metres dug in the wood of Lucius and Caius Caesar, on the right bank of the Tiber again but between the Tiber island and the Janiculum. The "lake" was provided with water from the Alsietina aqueduct which had just been opened. More than thirty "Athenian" and "Persian" ships, with 3,000 rowers and fighting men aboard, tried to give the right impression. But in the nature of things the boats were rather small.

Haunted by the memory of Julius Caesar, Claudius wanted a really grandiose spectacle. He was excited by the possibilities afforded by a lake the size of Fucinus and by the convenient proximity of the forests as a source of wood for constructing the galleys.

When the day came, the weather was wonderful, and enthusiastic crowds were massed on the sloping shores around the lake as though in a natural amphitheatre. The Marsian peasants from the surrounding countryside had taken up their places at dawn. Then hordes of people came flocking in from nearby districts and from Rome itself, which is only fifty miles from Lake Fucinus. Finally the whole court arrived and sat on platforms close to the water's edge.

As Nero's tutor I naturally had to be close to the royal party. Since my pupil was educated in the Greek style and, under my careful tuition, has come to accept progressive views, he does not care for massacres. But young Britannicus, who is eleven years old, shared the general impatience as the sun grew higher.

Gradually the 6,000 condemned men reached the twelve "Sicilian" triremes and the twelve "Rhodian" ones, where their oars and weapons were awaiting them, while the Praetorian cohorts lined up on the rafts surrounding the battle area and closed off all possible escape routes. To prevent a revolt and discourage hostile manoeuvres, behind the enclosing fences the ballistas and catapults of the imperial guard were trained on the twenty-four vessels which were lined up facing each other. It was a superb sight: a riot of colour, breastplates shining, plumes waving, and sails rippling in the breeze.

Suddenly an ingenious device made a silver Triton with a trumpet to his lips burst up out of the depths of the lake and give the signal to attack. There followed another striking innovation – the 6,000 men, in concert, shouted: "Hail, Caesar! We who are about to die bid you farewell." Claudius likes a joke. Spurred on by some evil demon he was moved to reply: "Time will tell." The peculiarity of an intervention by the emperor at this stage of the ceremony, and the nature of the intervention, unleashed a misunderstanding which rapidly took on staggering proportions. The rumour spread among the sacrificial victims that the emperor had reprieved them. The good news sped by word of mouth and gesture among the ordinary criminals and prisoners of war who had converged on this peaceful lake from Brittany, Armenia, Germany and the deserts of Africa. After a great cry of gratitude and joy, the whole lot of them crossed their arms. Claudius' unfortunate intervention had brought about the first ever gladiators' strike. It took a long time to correct their misapprehension, for there's none so deaf as those that will not hear. Claudius had to go limping around the lake in person, threatening or exhorting the refractory ones to make them fight. His speeches were somewhat less than audible because our emperor, though capable of reading a text in the most delightful way, stammers as soon as he has to improvise. Old Augustus was always amazed by the contrast.

At last everything was ready. The condemned men wiped each other out as arranged, with such enthusiasm that those left at the end really were pardoned.

Up to this point, then, everything had gone off wonderfully well, with the exception of the utterly ridiculous incident at the beginning. I myself do not much care for Circus Games, although I accept that they are politically necessary. But even I had begun to catch the thrill of popular enthusiasm at certain moments of particularly picturesque combat. Even philosophers are not immune from human failings.

Now I am getting to the crux of the story. Once the galleys had been anchored, and the survivors and the Praetorian Guard evacuated, they started to work to break through the tiny tongue of land preventing the waters of Fucinus from pouring out into the Liri down a monstrous canal nearly three miles long. As the sun began to slip down behind the hills, the spectators held their breath ... until finally they saw a light current begin to move down the canal, then stop.

The general disappointment was overwhelming. Narcissus explained that he had been over-cautious for fear of a dangerous waterfall forming if the ground was dug out too deeply at the critical point. But it was easy to remedy. Agrippina advised Narcissus in the crispest terms not to spare his efforts, and the court went back to Rome feeling rather frustrated, despite the beautiful day. The blood had made its due appearance but the water was missing.

Some days later a new crowd – smaller but still of considerable size – was gathered around Fucinus. In the absence of a naval battle to pull in the crowds some gladiatorial combat had been arranged, using the rafts on which the Praetorian Guard had previously stood. It was easy to break up the circle to provide a single jetty appropriate to the new use. Despite the perpetual attempts to come up with something bigger and better, all these massacres are the same, and I shan't waste any ink describing them. Besides, Claudius, being economical, tends to go for quantity rather than quality.

In the middle of the afternoon the court was called to a feast. Couches had been set out on the grass, looking like so many huge mushrooms in a field, right near the mouth of the canal, so that when the moment came, the guests could enjoy the liberation of the waters from the front row of the stalls. The increased depth of the channel and the height of the piece of rock blocking it suggested that we were in for an exceptional experience.

While I was still nibbling a few grated roots amid all the smell and smoke of grilled meats and sauces, the approach works had already effected a certain seepage through the slim barrier which remained. Towards the close of the afternoon, while we were on the last course, in that climate of euphoria which always reigns at the end of a banquet, this obstacle suddenly gave way with a dull rumbling sound and the swirling waters of Fucinus poured out into the new channel with a violence which excited universal admiration.

But the extreme difficulty of using theoretical calculations to control works of this kind had caused an appalling error. In the first place, the unforeseen strength of the current broke the ropes mooring the huge raft, which bore down on the noble assembly at an ever-increasing speed, threatening to crush everything beneath its bulk. We all thought our last hour had come, when by a sort of miracle the waters of the lake, and with them the raft, became still for a brief moment. Then the considerable difference in ground levels and relative narrowness of the channel temporarily reversed the direction of flow of the water. The phenomenon was so violent, given the forces unleashed, that a tidal-wave came sweeping back over what a moment earlier had been a scene of joyful feasting.

However, as the monstrous wave was flowing upstream and Fucinus is not very deep at the western end, we got off with no more than a terrible fright.

But, by all the gods in Hades, what a sight there was after the muddy waters had resumed their normal course and were beginning to lose velocity! As Roman clothing, unlike that of barbarians, is not close-fitting, the first effect of the impact had been to reduce the court to a state of nature. Just picture for yourself a shore covered in half-drowned plucked chickens totally bemused by the whim of fate which had thrown them up there and abandoned them in the strangest of postures, while the emperor's purple cloak, Agrippina's cloth-of-gold chlamys, the light muslin overalls worn by the men and women to protect their clothes while eating, the light-coloured togas and embroidered capes left "in the cloakroom" as it were, the women's multicoloured dresses, seductive underwear, blond German wigs and all their most deceptive false beauty-aids, were disappearing pell-mell downstream towards the distant realms of Neptune. Matrons on all fours, their thick make-up washed away by the flood, were looking through the heaps of debris on the shore-line for their jewellery or their false teeth. Few of the men's tunics had survived the disaster and many a senator found himself all the more naked for having come with only a loin-cloth on under his toga because of the heat.

Only the Praetorian guards in their tightly fastened breastplates had retained a modicum of decency, and they were granted the stupefying sight of their masters as naked as when they emerged from their mothers' wombs.

One cannot help wondering what would have happened to Rome if the emperor, his wife, relatives and friends, the influential members of his Councils and government and a large proportion of the Senate had all been drowned like rats in the course of this affair. It certainly gives one pause for thought. Even a philosopher is struck dumb at the prospect!

No sooner had Agrippina been rescued from the waters, like Philo's Moses, and got over her fear, than in a sudden fit of blind rage she started shouting at Narcissus in the most aggressive tone. She levelled an incoherent list of accusations against him: that he was incapable of organizing major public works, that his administration was venal, that his greed was insatiable, and all this in front of Claudius, who was standing there still dazed by the catastrophe . . . and doubtless the wine as well! At that point we heard and saw something absolutely unbelievable. Narcissus is a freedman, a slave's son who has himself spent many years in servitude, who has been accustomed from birth to grovelling and dissimulation, who has learnt prudence and intrigue under the iron rule of capricious masters, who has risen to the highest ranks solely through the trust and favour of Claudius (an extremely precarious position to find oneself in). Yet he now lost his self-control completely and denounced the high-handed character and insatiable ambition of the "empress"! An oriental freedman daring to raise his voice to the elder daughter of Germanicus, a grand-daughter of Augustus' consort and eldest daughter of another Agrippina who was a granddaughter of Augustus himself! This individual, risen from nowhere, with his tail between his legs but his tongue unbridled, was insulting Agrippina the Younger, a woman born into the purple – though for the time being dressed exclusively in an indigo G-string, as dear Petronius would have noted in one of his racy novels. Narcissus barely refrained from accusing the empress of responsibility for certain perhaps unnecessary gory incidents and from making a wounding allusion to her intimate relationship with that other upstart freedman, Pallas. But he clearly meant every word. What would old Cato have said?

You asked me, my dear Novatus, for news from Rome which will help you in your career. Well, Narcissus had obviously ruined himself. Agrippina was already discreetly hostile to him, but she'll never forget the mud-slinging at the Fucine. Narcissus' life is now entirely dependent on that of Claudius, who appreciates the fellow's incontestable fidelity to his master's real interests.

We all trooped off to camp as best we could at Cerfennia, and the following day we made our way back down the Via Valeria. A sorry sight we were, too!

Among other little irritations I had almost lost Nero. I just managed to grab hold of his hand at the fatal moment, and next moment found myself lying dazed and choking in the grass with the boy beside me. As we came in through the Esquiline Gate, just as I was going to take my leave of him, the lad thanked me again for my foresight.

Throughout all the troubles of life my pupil is a great consolation to me. I do not despair of one day making him my disciple. He is, I might remind you, coming up for fifteen, his birthday being the XVIII of the

Kalends of January, nine months to the day from the death of Tiberius. So young Lucius came into the world in mid-December, two days before the Saturnalia, on the very day we sacrifice to Consus, the god of horses, on the altar in the Circus Maximus. Nero was much struck by the coincidence, and I wonder whether his growing passion for horses does not have some connection with this divine accident. But he was already almost twelve when Agrippina hauled me out of my Corsican exile and entrusted him to me. The two of us have found the going pretty stiff.

The child had experienced much unhappiness and fear in his life, and his misfortunes had had a bad influence on his character. Lucius was only two when his mother was implicated in the conspiracy of my poor friend Gaetulicus against Caligula, in which I almost perished myself. Lucius was then brought up by his paternal aunt Domitia Lepida. Then his father Domitius Ahenobarbus, Germanicus' cousin, died. When Claudius came to the throne, Agrippina recovered her fortune and most of her credit at court: she promptly married Crispus Passienus, who had just divorced the second Domitia, another of Lucius' paternal aunts. Passienus, who was related to the imperial family, was able to protect Agrippina from Messalina's intrigues for several years, but he had no more than what one might call moral authority over Lucius, who, in accordance with custom, had been provided with a tutor, Asconeus Labeo – an entirely admirable man as it happened. Lucius was not quite seven when Passienus died. So the boy lost his mother early and his father soon after, was tossed to and fro between a stepfather and a tutor, went from his two oriental wet-nurses into the hands of a dancer and a barber, and from them to two freedmen, Anicetus and Beryllus, with whom he remained until I took him in hand. Anicetus and Beryllus were capable of teaching him basic Latin and Greek, but not of instructing him in virtue. Chaeremon, an Egyptian priest with whom I had been friendly in Alexandria in the old days, exerted a better influence on him. He was a Stoic, a very cultured man with a considerable talent as a teacher, and it was he who started to acquaint Lucius with good books. But it was a little late in the day for a man of his quality, and he had the failing of encouraging Lucius to see himself as a little Pharaoh. It was high time he acquired a Roman teacher with a better philosophy.

I found him a young creature with the sensitivity of a man who has been flayed alive. He had been deprived of all tenderness, and wanted to put his trust in someone but didn't dare. He was nervous and sly; the absence of a mother figure disturbed him but he was crushed by the – fortunately rare – presence of a frighteningly authoritarian woman.

Gradually I won Lucius' heart the way one tames a turtle dove. I eradicated his few faults and brought out all the qualities which merely needed room to blossom. Today Nero is a handsome, lively, subtle boy, lazy at learning anything which doesn't interest him and passionately keen to study what does. I almost have to moderate his enthusiasm for Greek plays and epic poetry, frescoes and paintings, the best Greek sculpture and chariot races in the Circus Maximus – which in fact take place right under the noses of the fortunate inhabitants of the Palatine. And I've had to put up with his learning the cithara, the sound of which moves him to tears.

You may say that all this aesthetic enthusiasm is misplaced in a Roman and that our traditionalists would find fault with it. But, after some thought, I decided not to put up very strong opposition to it. I could not help reflecting what a blessing it would be for the world and for society if one day, for the first time in the history of Rome, a man with a fine artistic sensibility were to share the responsibilities of power fraternally with his *alter ego*, a thoughtful administrator like Britannicus. Since he adopted Lucius two years ago Claudius has been constantly fretting over the question of the succession to the throne, and that might perhaps be a solution . . .

One fact is certain in any case, and it's a comforting point. Artists have difficulty, it is true, in avoiding a sort of sacred egoism, which is a basic ingredient of their talent; on the other hand their very temperament distances them from acts of cruelty and keeps them from unnecessary bloodshed. Nero is very gentle and finds the butchery in the amphitheatres vulgar. That augurs well.

I am doing my best, following in the footsteps of Chaeremon, to complete my pupil's education by inculcating in him a little serious Stoicism, though not with any very evident success. He appears naturally inclined to a greed and a sensuality that do not go well with an austere philosophy. But the natural pleasures of youth are not really to be condemned unless taken to excess and distorted.

It is a pity that I am not more strongly backed up in my efforts by Agrippina. Art leaves her cold and Stoicism even colder.

Nevertheless I sometimes find myself dreaming . . . If Destiny were to arrange for Britannicus to scratch from the race, it would be the first and most memorable example of a great ruler being carefully trained by a philosopher since Aristotle tutored Alexander the Great. Posterity – which is often over-flattering – will be the judge of my achievements. What glory for me and what a triumph for the things of the mind if I were to be midwife to the birth of a new Golden Age.

The prospect is not inconceivable. The only blot on the horizon is the feeling of insecurity which young Nero cannot manage to rid himself of. I myself find it difficult to combat because the Roman upper classes have been brought up in an atmosphere of fear for generations. Fear of this sort, which is such a bad counsellor, does not disappear overnight. It is up to me to make the boy feel that, if the gods invest him with the weightiest of responsibilities, the only way to break the evil spell is to be a moderate ruler who safeguards a desirable balance of power between emperor and Senate.

My asthma is still torturing me. It's a noteworthy characteristic of the illness that every attack makes you think you're going to die. The experience is so salutary for a philosopher that I have nicknamed the disease *meditatio mortis*. When a little air dilates one's lungs again after a long period of agony, it feels like coming back to life. Above all one feels more detached than ever from the vanities of the world. Basically it is an excellent training.

I have lost all my confidence in doctors, except the great Asclepias, who treated Pompey and Caesar among others. Asclepias' merit derived from having originally been a teacher of rhetoric and having deliberately remained completely ignorant of medicine throughout his profitable career. This absence of medical training led him to a form of common-sense preventative medicine which at least could do no harm. He was physician to the healthy, who fortunately outnumber the sick. He was responsible, with the aid of a little persuasive rhetoric, for a fashion for diets, abstinence, for body-rubs and massage after cold baths, followed by jogging. For the less energetic, Asclepias discovered that the swinging motion of litters is good for the humours. He used to explain to anyone who would listen – playing on the double meaning of the word *gestatio* (both "a ride in a litter" and "pregnancy") – that the rhythmic movement of this means of transport had a calming and reassuring effect on the patient, by making him slip back into childhood. Asclepias made a bet that he would never fall ill, and died at a ripe old age as a result of falling down a flight of stairs – having never consulted a doctor in his life. When you need a doctor, it's too late, isn't it?

I have even less confidence in insensitive surgeons, ever since they adopted the sinister habit of practising leisurely vivisection on condemned criminals in the hope of perfecting their charitable art. It is said that Hierophilus, copied by Erasistratus, used to be very proud of having dissected 600 of them, a total which clearly demonstrated outstanding scientific zeal. It is more pleasant to reflect upon the fact that Nero, who put on the *toga virilis* last year, is next year to marry his adoptive sister, relative and fiancée, Octavia. She will be twelve.

Before sealing this letter I have re-read it, if only to correct a few mistakes made by my secretary, and it occurred to me that an aspect of the Jewish problem – admittedly a philosophical one – had escaped you. In practice the Jews are as attractive as they are irritating. A small portion of this unprecedented people undoubtedly only tolerates our occasionally tactless administration with a degree of impatience which might seem disquieting. On the other hand the entirely new concept of a single, transcendent god who is creator and protector of all things is worthy of consideration. The Jews have egoistically helped themselves to this lucky find. A number of Greeks and Romans concerned about the ideal and enamoured with the concept of moral progress have nonetheless discovered the potential riches of this important idea. So, outside the Temple in Jerusalem and the synagogues of the diaspora, there is a lively current of interest and sympathy among many non-Jews who are as impressed by the essential ideas as they are hostile to Jewish customs. This Jewish religion is more accessible to the outside world than might be supposed at first sight. If this single god really existed, passing customs would be of no significance. This Jewish god could have the future on his side, if he survives for long enough, provided that the Jews, who have made a national attribute of him, are dispossessed of their proprietorial rights. He has the stature to absorb all religions and even all systems of thought. But to make the development easier the Jews need to end up by going along with it and not causing too much trouble. They need quietly to forget their still barbarous customs and prejudices and become civilized. Then we shall doubtless find that Yahwe can be written in Latin as well as Greek and Hebrew. Perhaps one day I am destined to give up my pantheistic dreams?

I am very sorry that events – my Egyptian trip, my exile, the necessities of your career – have kept us apart so long and persist in placing so much land and sea between us. The opportunity to correspond with you by a trustworthy courier seems all the more precious for being so rare. Our brother Mela is well and I am applying myself to the advancement of his career. Thanks largely to the favour shown me by Agrippina my fortune is now more than one hundred and thirty million sesterces. But what is that compared to the *meditatio mortis* which I experience sometimes daily? Money frequently accrues in the hands of the sage who despises it.

I wish you good health. I am as well as can be expected.'

*

Marcus junior left for Vetera the day after Kaeso sailed. In the meantime Decimus came back and, to the intense relief of Marcus Senior and his niece, at once took Marcia into his own house, where the elegant life style for which she had so evidently been fashioned duly awaited her. The nobleman's southern holiday did not seem to have modified his plans in any respect.

A few hours after Marcia's installation Decimus confided to her: 'In every Stoic there's a slumbering Epicurean. Epicurus teaches us to regulate our smallest pleasures carefully and if necessary to defer them so as to make the ultimate enjoyment of them all the more satisfying. At my age a pleasure like you has to be earned by a delicious withdrawal. But I shan't leave you again now that I've well and truly earned you. I realized I must love you more than I thought, because I love you just as you are and not as I might imagine you if I were younger.

It's the privilege of experience to be lucid and to find the ultimate source of satisfaction in that lucidity. For a woman who has lived life to the full, before being turned into marble in a sanctuary, the first quality necessary in a lover is enlightened indulgence.'

During siesta time, while Decimus was delivering this charming little speech, a slave presented herself at Aponius' tenement block, bearing a whole accordion of sealed tablets to be put into the hands of the master himself.

Marcus was woken up and received the girl in the pseudo-*atrium*. He recognized Decimus' seal, broke it, and read with increasing delight:

'Decimus to his dear friend Marcus, greetings.

During the autumn you suggested to me that I should take your niece into my house after Kaeso's adoption. I have done so a little earlier than you had foreseen. Please pardon this precipitate action in a man whose years must be more strictly counted than other men's. The action will tell you how dear Marcia is to me, as are all those who rightly hold her in esteem and affection. She is a woman who has an extraordinary fire of life within her, a concealed and passionate soul capable of bringing warmth to an old cynic like myself.

The impropriety of the action I have taken deserves some reparation both for your sake and to mollify Kaeso, whom I am more than ever determined to adopt on his return. It is impossible, in any case, to imagine Marcia separated from Kaeso, and my middle-aged charms are no match for those of such an accomplished son. I should not like her ever to be faced with the choice between us.

I shall therefore marry Marcia as soon as the divorce goes through. So, when Kaeso gets back, he will find an entirely proper situation suited to his tender sensibilities.

You will be the only person whose absence from the intimate little ceremony I shall regret, but otherwise there would be one husband too many for the scandalmongers – though hitherto I have always proudly ignored gossip.

Your present loneliness distresses me, especially since I am responsible for it. I have looked for the most perfect gift I could find to fill the gap. I have selected the bearer of these tablets from the ranks of all the slaves brought to me by the best dealers. She will be honoured to be the plaything of a senator.

Selene must be about twenty-two or three years old. She originally came from Alexandria and her measurements correspond exactly to those which the most exacting of Greek sculptors demand. Her face pleads too eloquently in its own favour for me to linger over its description. I merely observe that her chestnut-coloured hair is admirable and her eyes are of a rare shade of grey. Afranius, who sold her to me, guaranteed her health, even temper, wealth of experience and the range of her repertoire. She is adequately educated, reads and writes Greek fluently, has a competent command of household Latin, and is very quick-witted. I never buy an expensive slave without inquiring into her past. The dealers know it and don't bother to offer me any but those whose *curriculum vitae* is free of important blanks. Most of these girls are like horses. If they are difficult to handle, there is always a good reason. Their memories are better than their reasoning powers.

Fortunately Selene's life has been fairly banal. Her parents apparently ran a little business in *garum castimoniale*, the variety of garum which uses only fish with scales and is intended for the Jewish market. After one of those riots which are only too frequent in Alexandria their business was ruined. Consequently the girl was reduced to slavery when she was almost fifteen and became the property of a priest of some Egyptian god. At sixteen she had a child which was immediately exposed and therefore did not ruin the shape of her breasts. Then she spent a brief period in a brothel with a good reputation, before being picked out by various sculptors and painters to serve as their model. Finally a procurator of the imperial estates helped himself to her, and sold her to Afranius when he got bored with her.

I now arrive at a delicate matter, which, though trivial, none the less continues to rankle with me. When Afranius undressed Selene so that I would be in a position to see whether her beauty conformed to his description of it, Marcia was present. I thought her advice was important given that the present was intended for you. As the girl was exquisitely graceful and beyond comparison with anything I had seen so far, the sale was swiftly concluded and my steward paid out the required sum on the spot.

While Selene was getting dressed again, I started to ask her about her life in Alexandria. (I never trust what the dealers tell one.) But the slave's account tallied more or less exactly with Afranius'.

The girl's beauty was such that Marcia was sorry to see her put her clothes back on. Ever thoughtful for my pleasure and sincerely curious to know how close her own measurements came to those of the model, Marcia ordered Selene to strip again, and undressed herself. Well, after the most detailed verification the differences were almost imperceptible. Which, given the difference in their ages, is all to the credit of your niece.

It is astonishing to think that we take so much trouble over the bodily perfection of our female slaves, but are reduced to relying on vague and deceptive impressions when it comes to selecting our wives! Now I know who I am marrying.

As one might have expected, the amiable and flattering comparison was accompanied by playful teasing, delicate touching and caresses as purposeful as they were affectionate, the sort of thing which becomes pure art when the couple are painted. All that was missing was a third Grace, a role I was, alas, far from being able to fulfil.

Suddenly we had to accept what was only too clear. The girl had suffered that mutilatory operation which has been traditional for I do not know how many thousands of years among the Egyptians, but which is not normal among Greeks or Jews.

In the face of this deception over the merchandise Marcia was even more outraged than I. When you purchase slaves, you also buy their total capacity for pleasure and even pain.

Selene wept as she told us that the Egyptian priest – who was in fact a eunuch – had had it cut out on principle as soon as she was in his hands. But the surgeon had left the inner membranes and limited himself to cutting off the projecting head of the organ.

We asked the girl why she had misled us about her quality, and she could only stammer and assure us that Afranius was not in the know. But what trust can you put in the word of a slave, especially when she has just been caught out in a lie?

There was no question of overlooking such deplorable concealment of the true state of affairs. Marcia immediately whipped the girl while I sent my servants to scour the town for Afranius.

The pimp naturally put on a show of being flabbergasted, but we made him put his finger on the evidence, and he had to admit negligence at the very least. His first defence was to minimize the defect by jokingly invoking the favourite proverb of those who accuse others of seeing difficulties where there are none: "You're looking for knots in a bulrush!" I became angry, threatened him with a court case which would have damaged his business, and he finished by offering a reduction in the price. After some hesitation, with Marcia's agreement, I accepted a reimbursement of 20,000 sesterces on the original price of 60,000, hoping that this slight and well-concealed mutilation would perhaps not matter to you. If Selene suits you just as she is, I'll have the balance of the price sent on to you. If not, do not hesitate to send her back and I'll see to it that you don't lose on the exchange.

At all events, I wish you good health.'

For the first time since the auction which had plunged him into such distress, Marcus had the feeling that the lunatic wheel of Fortune was in the process of turning in his favour. A clouded sky was clearing in all directions at once. His shameful marriage was finally being dissolved, and the outcome was an extraordinary social success. As if by a miracle careers had been found for his two sons. And he himself had a niece and a friend worth all the treasures of the world to give security to his old age.

Decimus' refined elegance and delicacy of forethought touched him deeply. What a charming way of making a present of 20,000 *nummi* to a man in need!

Marcus' gaze lingered on the wonderful apparition. Her face had a perfectly neutral expression. She reminded her new owner of those Egyptian sphinxes which keep their secrets just as well despite emerging from the sands.

He smiled good-naturedly at Selene and said: 'Go and get undressed in the room at the back, dear, and may my house bring you good fortune.'

Selene smiled back at the fat man, who would always be a little vulgar, and turned away with hatred in her eyes. Horses are never difficult to handle without a reason.

❧ PART TWO ❧

❧ CHAPTER ❧
I

In that spring of the year 861 after the foundation of Rome, during the consulship of Memmius Regulus and Virginius Rufus, Marcus received a letter from his elder son which he read and then forwarded to Marcia at Silanus' house. It was the first time that Marcus junior had occasion to write to his parents. He must have found it a real struggle to fill the slim roll of papyrus with the prosaic thoughts and ink blots which reflected the simplicity of his nature.

'M. Aponius Saturninus to his dear father and mother, greetings.

I think you'll get this note quite quickly, as I'm sending it by the imperial post, which keeps moving day and night. It covers up to 100 miles in twenty-four hours, at least double what the private postal service manages. Money is no object when you urgently need to get good – or bad – news to Rome.

My journey here was fine, but the countryside got more and more cold and bleak. We can't have lost much by the fact that Julius Caesar stopped at the Loire. It's only in the south of Gaul that life is pleasant.

Vetera, on the left bank of the Rhine, is sixty miles downstream from Cologne. The fortified camp, which has recently been surrounded by a thick, brick rampart, contains two of the four legions which are stationed in Lower Germany, the 5th Alauda and the 15th Primigenia, not to mention the auxiliary footsoldiers and cavalry. So it's a sort of city. The Praetorium is built of solid material, the soldiers' tents have turned into houses, and suburbs of a sort have grown up outside the ramparts and towers, where you'll find merchants, craftsmen and girls to suit every taste. During the winter, which is long and bitterly cold, the troops make themselves snug in Vetera. Then, when the weather improves, they show the flag on the frontier along the Rhine and relieve the isolated garrisons in the little forts which keep watch over the course of the river. Our German war fleet shares in this surveillance and protects the merchant ships which go upstream as far as Cologne and even further.

The Rhine is an enormous river, virtually a sea. There's no point of comparison with the Tiber, and the legions are reluctant to cross it. On the left bank there are occasional cultivated areas, but on the other bank of the Rhine there are only barren heaths, impenetrable marshes and deep forests. Our policy is resolutely defensive and deterrent. All the barbarian tribes who roam the immense wastes of Germany would like to cross the Rhine and find better land to cultivate. They want to give up their nomadic existence and live like us. But we keep good guard. It would be impossible to assimilate immigrant populations on such a large scale. We've already got our work cut out with the 10,000 Batavians who were unwisely permitted to settle inside the Empire, in the Rhine delta.

On the strength of Silanus' recommendations I have received an excellent welcome, but the legate said: "Pray to the gods that the noble Silanus lives a long life. If he shared the fate of his two brothers, there'd be nothing I could do for you." That sort of remark makes you think.

In the meantime I've been allotted to the *frumentarii*, or to be more precise, to the tiny and prestigious part of the administration which deals with information. A young tribune has much more freedom there than in an ordinary army corps, and you don't have to find a solution to the delicate problem of giving orders to an elderly centurion who knows much more about the job than you do.

In this capacity I've already had occasion to run up against the Germans, about whom we hear so much and know so little.

I think it was the Greek philosopher Posidonius of Apamea, who died more than a century ago, who first used the word "Germanii". But it was definitely Caesar who incorrectly extended to all the Germanic tribes this use of the ancient name of the present-day Tungri. (They were called Germanii in the days when they made themselves famous by being the first to cross the Rhine.) The Germans, in the general sense of the word, thus owe their name to Rome. But each of their tribes lives a life apart and is only linked to its neighbours by a close similarity of manners and customs. Today the main tribes settled on the right bank of the Rhine both upstream and down are the Batavians – part of whom emigrated from our side, as I said – the Tencteri, the Usipetes, and the Nemetes. The Ubii, the Tribocci, the Treviri and the Vangiones, who crossed the Rhine in the old days, no longer exist as independent tribes. To the east of the Batavians and their more southerly relatives are to be found, going from north to south, the Frisii, Bructeri, Marsi and Chatti. Further off still are the Chauchi, Angrivarii, Cherusci and Hermunduri, the last two being beyond the river Weser. Our intelligence services have heard tell of other tribes to the east of the Elbe, such as the Angles, Saxons and

Semnones. Still less is known about the Varini, Rugii, Suebi, Burgundiones and Goths. The *frumentarii* on the Danube are quite well informed about the Marcomani and the Quadi, but they have no information on the Bastarnae and the Skirians. The huge number of these different tribes, of which I have only quoted the main ones, rules out any prospect of conquering and civilizing them.

The Germans are large, strong and stupid. They live in enormous long communal huts which are held up by wooden pillars. A reed roof comes down very low and the walls are made of plaited reed blended with clay. In the centre of the communal hall there is a fire whose smoke goes out through a hole in the roof. Otherwise the hut is divided into cubicles which open on to a central corridor. This is where both the people and their pitiful animals sleep. Germans smell like animals. The first time I went into one of these huts I was almost suffocated.

There are isolated farms. As for built-up areas, the biggest of them never contain more than fifty huts, scattered higgledy-piggledy over an open space.

The German peasants scratch up the soil with primitive ploughs to get their meagre harvests. When the soil is exhausted, after a certain amount of alternating between cultivating plots and leaving them fallow, they carry their household gods off somewhere else. So abandoned cabins are common. The goats, sheep, cows and horses in these regions are small in stature. When a hulking German gets on a horse, his feet trail on the ground. Their habit of keeping geese and chickens is taken from the Gauls. The local breed of dog, called *torfspitz* is a really fierce brute.

The Germans know how to extract and work iron, how to weave and dye, and they have some knowledge of carpentry and woodwork. But it's all very crude stuff.

The men wear trousers and an overall. The women have long dresses fastened at the shoulder with a brooch. The woven materials are complemented by animal skins, and in winter by furs.

The warriors fight on foot, bare-headed and stripped to the waist. Only the chieftains wear helmets. Their standard tactic is to form up in a wedge shape and hurl themselves on the enemy uttering frightful cries from behind their shields. Swords and spears are their favourite weapons.

Trade with Germany is restricted for obvious reasons. It's the women's blond hair, which makes such pretty wigs for Roman women, which is principally of interest to us. The Germans are mad about blonds. Anyone dark bleaches their hair.

But they can't count, read or write. For some time now we've been finding examples of a strange alphabet, like Etruscan. It's only used for engraving on metal or carving in wood. I had an inscription on a spearhead translated into the Latin alphabet for me. It means: "I belong to Eruler, companion of Ansgisl. I bring luck, I dedicate this spearhead to glorious slaughter," which in German dialect comes out as: "Elk erilaz asugisalas muha aita ga ga ga gihu gahelija wiju big g." What hope is there for anyone afflicted with a language like that?

From what I've told you, you'll be wondering why the Romans need seven legions to cope with the Germans on the Rhine – not to mention those on the Danube. You'll also be wondering how the Cimbri and the Teutones managed to massacre three of our armies before Marius defeated them. And how Arminius wiped out Varus' legions before Germanicus taught him a lesson.

Because they are uncivilized, the Germans get very bored. They have no chariot races, theatre or gladiatorial shows. So they've devoted themselves to destruction and pillaging. The only thing they know how to do well is fight, and they make up for what they lack in tactical skill and weaponry by their undoubted courage. Their religion, which is fed on constant human sacrifice, is utterly brutal and wallows in the worship of blood-thirsty heroes. At Rome a man is a hero because he sacrifices himself for the sake of the State. In Germany a hero is the man who kills the largest number of the enemy.

Tendencies of this sort wouldn't be dangerous if the Germans confined themselves to family feuds, as they usually do. But from time to time a scratch collection of tribes team up to undertake an expedition in search of excitement abroad. Then it takes a Caesar to defeat an Ariovistus on the plains of Alsace.

Our nightmare is that a large number of Germans might mass together and come tumbling down on the Empire. That's why we put all our energies into keeping them divided. When, by a successful bit of manoeuvring, we contrive to organize a nice little war between tribes, it's one more victory for Rome, and a cheap one at that.

A fair number of Romanized Germans help us as far as possible, but they are a double-edged weapon. If they desert our cause, they're in a position to teach their compatriots how to fight even better. The German national hero, Arminius, who was a Cheruscan by birth, was a Roman citizen and achieved the rank of knight. Before he went over to the other side he had distinguished himself under our colours. A new Arminius would be even more of a nuisance, given that the Armenian question is still not settled – will it ever be? – and that the revolt of the Britones is running its course.

That's what I say to myself in my fireside nook – we're still having to keep ourselves warm up here in Vetera – and when I say "nook", I mean it. In proper houses the fireplace is tucked into a corner of the room with an ingenious pipe to channel the smoke out through the roof. It's more healthy and more practical than the braziers used in sunny climes, and you can have a really raging fire. But the risk of the house burning down is very high. If we had pipes like this in our Roman tenement blocks, given their scamped construction they'd be up in flames even more often than they are already.

When I'm not busy plotting to encourage the extermination of the filthy Germans, I've almost no means of entertaining myself. I have a pretty girl of the Chatti tribe to do my cooking, but her conversation's limited. The arenas provide the main source of distraction. Every permanent camp of any importance has its own. But there's no money to bring professional gladiators up here. You have to make do with German prisoners, and they're pretty disappointing. Most of them refuse to fight except against members of another tribe, and a lot of them, rather than appear in the arena, will strangle themselves with their belts or choke themselves to death with the lavatory sponges. This last-mentioned method of suicide gives you some idea of their sense of delicacy!

At Rome you hear that the Germans have preserved virtues which we're supposed to have lost. They're said to be capable of stimulating our regeneration if we were prepared to learn from them. The idiots who spread that sort of rumour have never seen a German in his natural state – drunk and stupid; sometimes the drink makes them melancholy dreamers, sometimes they go berserk. There's one thing that gives away how limited they are. The Germans are the only barbarians who can't cope with slavery. In towns they're intolerable, and if you try to use them for farming you have to keep them chained together, for fear of the worst happening. How can a barbarian hope to become civilized if he doesn't know how to become a good slave? In the meantime, the Germans make excellent mercenaries, though you can't expect any finesse from them. When Caligula was murdered by his Praetorian Guard, his faithful German troops cut down any senator who got in their path, though most of them had nothing to do with the plot. Everyone was struck by this mindless passion.

The *frumentarii* also have to keep in touch with the state of our troops' morale, which is none too wonderful. If soldiers get lazy they go downhill. If you send them off to get killed for the sake of it, they get furious. To get the most out of a professional army you need outstanding leaders. But mediocre recruitment and ambitions aren't the only black point. With a professional army you're maintaining a relatively small standing force at a prohibitive cost. And patriotism is replaced by an *esprit de corps* which is by no means entirely a good thing. There are of course some Gauls in the army in Germany, but the majority of the auxiliaries are German. As a result the Rhine legions despise the Gauls, and the local Gauls are afraid of the soldiers who are there to protect them. While the Germans are unconquered and the Spaniards resisted us for generations, it only took Caesar a few years to overcome the Gauls. Gaul has a soft underbelly: the Gauls are incapable of defending themselves on their own.

Send me some good news from Rome. Last week I put on the *toga virilis* and cut and consecrated my beard: the double occasion was an excuse for a pleasantly drunken celebration which has put me into the red for a bit. But I gained in authority from it.

I'm worried about Kaeso. I know that, like me, you feel that he doesn't see the world as it really is. Sooner or later the world will insist on imposing its laws on him, and then the fur will fly. When that happens, you'll have to be understanding with him. I couldn't ask for a better brother.

Fare well. Please thank Silanus for his protection again.'

A couple of weeks later the courier from Athens brought Marcus two letters from Kaeso, one addressed to him and the other to Marcia. Marcus was very intrigued and a trifle annoyed. What could Kaeso possibly have to say to his stepmother that he didn't want his father to read? Marcus wondered for a moment whether he could break the seal of Marcia's letter, decided against it, and opened his own letter with a sigh.

'K. Aponius Saturninus to his beloved father, greetings.

I had a wonderful journey and learnt a lot of things.

I verified, for example, that, as certain philosophers claim, the earth is indeed round, for on the vast expanse of the ocean you see the mast of a ship appear first over the horizon, and then the boat as a whole gradually becomes visible as it gets nearer to you. Astonishing, is it not?

I have got to know all sorts of boats, especially as the "ephebes" hold a regatta during the festival of the Panathenaea. So I have paid particular attention to rowing.

Vase paintings and bas-reliefs are deceptive. They are too often done by people who have never been anywhere near a boat.

The way the rowers are arranged depends on the width of the boat.

There are only four possible arrangements, given that whatever happens the men have to keep their backs to the bows.

I. In a narrow boat each oarsman has two oars.

II. In a wider boat there is a row of oarsmen on each side. That's how the Homeric pirate ships were arranged. The stern was rounded, because that was the part that used to be pulled up on to the beach, in such a way that it could be launched quickly in case of danger.

III. On ships such as triremes, the benches are set out in a fishbone pattern in relation to the bows, with three men to a bench, each of them having an oar. That way there's hardly more than a foot between the oars on each bench, and no more than three feet between the central oar in one bank of oars and the central oar in another. With this oblique lay-out you can get the maximum possible number of oars into the space available. The classic trireme, though small in size, has 174 rowers. On the outside are the *thalamitae*, in the middle a little higher up are the *zeugitae*, and on the inside a little higher still are the *thranitae*. They have the back-breaking position, and they get paid more, because their oar is the longest and heaviest.

When it comes to warships real sailors have a passion for triremes, which they think are ideal for this purpose. The extraordinary number of oars in proportion to the tonnage does actually allow the boat to be manoeuvred very easily and quickly. The *biremis*, with two oars per bench, is not as responsive as the trireme, and it is not possible to get four rowers on one bench using the same principle, because the innermost rower wouldn't have the strength to manipulate his oar. But to get the crew of a trireme to synchronize their oarstrokes perfectly requires long intensive training.

IV. The increase in tonnage and the rarity of expert crews made up of patriotic citizens has led to the adoption, on the largest ships, of the only practical system: to increase the number of rowers per oar on a bench. A *quinquereme*, for example, has only thirty oars on each side, but five rowers per oar, which gives a total of three hundred men for sixty oars. But a *quinquereme* is more colloquially known as a "5". In the same way one talks about a "6" a "7" or an "8", referring in each case to the number of rowers per oar. The most powerful warship ever built was a "40" with 4,000 rowers, made for Ptolemy Philopator . . . but it never actually put to sea. In fact the longer the ship's oars, the shorter the distance it can cover, because the displacement required of the highest placed rower obviously increases in proportion to the length of the instrument he wields.

I am giving you all these details because landlubbers, particularly painters and sculptors, are very confused about the differences between triremes, "5"s and "6"s. Some have even imagined that the ships have several floors, with rows of oars one above the other, which makes any sailor hoot with laughter.

The Roman naval victory over Carthage, which gave us control of the Mediterranean, was a victory of our "5"s and "6"s over the light Carthaginian triremes, which are heavily laden with rowers but short on soldiers. There's no point in a boat being able to manoeuvre exceptionally well if it has no weight when it comes to boarding. It was in fact our incompetence as sailors which pushed us into constructing larger vessels, and so led to our success. Nowadays things have swung back again. Recently the Prefect gave the thumbs down to proposals for building a great "6" at Misenum. Policing the seas, to keep down pirates, is now carried out by fast-moving *liburnae*.

You know how essential control of the high seas is to life in the Roman world. Provisioning Rome itself, the most important part of all trade, depends on it. Boats are a hundred times more important than roads, which are of mainly military significance.

I was very moved as I came ashore in Greece, a place so vibrant with history and intellect, and I felt deeply grateful to both of you and to dear Silanus. The barracks where the "ephebes" live, and the stadium and palaestra which are attached to it, are in the Piraeus, the great port of Athens, which has benefited in the past from a remarkable piece of urban planning.

What first struck me, and disconcerted me, about Athens was the way in which all the principal monuments are gaudily painted in all the colours of the rainbow. Much of this decoration is in a poor condition and no one appears to be in a hurry to restore it. However, the city has a very engaging charm: everything about it seems purer and more elegant than in Rome, despite the modesty of the houses and the untidy way in which building is presently going on.

As for the Athenian *ephebia*, it's the most droll thing you ever saw.

After the disaster at Chaeronea, where the combined forces of the Athenians and Thebans were crushed by Philip of Macedon, the far-sighted democracy decided that it was time to set up a solid land-army. They drew their inspiration from the institutions of Sparta and gave the *ephebia* its definitive form. All young citizens who had reached the age of majority, which is eighteen, were called upon to do two years' military service, which was also to be a moral and religious preparation for the exercise of their full rights. There were in any case only 500 or 600 conscripts a year.

This *ephebia*, the purpose of which was already completely out of date by the time it came into being, was nonetheless carefully preserved under the authority of the kings of Macedon, and then of the Romans, but the period of service was reduced to one year and only aristocrats were admitted to it. A little more than 150 years ago the Athenian *ephebia* even began to open its ranks to young foreigners who came from Rome or from Greek-speaking countries. As there are not many aristocrats in Attica, and Athens is a very pleasant place to stay, there are often more foreign ephebes than local ones. Our year has 53 Athenians and 124 foreigners in it. So the army of the country which invented democracy is reduced to a band of young nobles from all over the world!

And what do we do in our gilded cage?

The military instruction properly speaking is limited to a few pleasant fencing lessons and some picnics which are supposed to be "field exercises". The bulk of the programme is made up of physical education and lessons in rhetoric and philosophy which are designed to give a sufficient smattering of culture to allow one to shine socially. The fathers of all these ephebes are filthy rich and can't see the point in their little darlings doing too much in the way of higher studies. I shall come back no wiser than I went – though I shall probably talk twice as much.

Our *ephebia* is best known as a college of advanced athletic studies for gifted amateurs, a halfway house between the professional sports training which currently plays such an important role in Greek-speaking areas, and the ordinary training provided by the obscurest local authorities. In a word, it is just what our emperor Nero dreams of for Roman youth but has such difficulty getting put into practice.

Despite the Greek saying: "He can't read or swim", which is the definition of an idiot, swimming and rowing are of secondary importance here, as is riding. Our athletics teacher, the *paidotribes*, who is the most important person in the school, concentrates on the sports which are included in the Olympic Games and many other similar competitions: running, long jump, discus and javelin throwing, and wrestling.

Running races normally take place in a *stadion* or stadium – the word itself means the place, the track and the distance, which is about 600 Roman feet. (The value of the Greek foot as a measure varies from city to city, so there is a corresponding variation in the *stadion*.) We also run the "double *stadion*" and sometimes the "quadruple *stadion*", not to mention distances of seven, twelve, twenty or twenty-four laps. Running in armour is here done over two circuits of the stadium.

The long jump with a run-up is made more difficult by the fact that we jump with dumb-bells. We throw a fairly heavy bronze discus, which is rubbed in fine sand to make one's grip on it more secure. Throwing a lightweight javelin is made easier by the use of a sling, the thin leather strap we call an *amentum* and the Greeks an *ankule*. In wrestling the aim is to make one's opponent touch the ground without falling down oneself. It is not enough to bring him to his knees, the upper part of the body has to touch.

Those are the five classic events in the pentathlon which are found in all competitions.

In addition we have lessons in boxing, but our fists are wrapped in the soft bandages which were used in the old days, and not the hard leather which has been standard for some time. The ephebes are proud of their looks and do not want them spoiled. All the more reason, then, why our initiation into the art of *pankration* has also been very cautious. Naturally our training for events of this sort has been accompanied by a preparatory gymnastic training which the Greeks have got worked out to the last detail.

So we spend hours every day stark naked in the sun, covered in oil and dust – didn't Philostratus distinguish five categories of dust, each with its own properties? And we wait impatiently for the moment when we can bathe and scrape ourselves down.

The baths next to the *palaestra* are very basic compared to our Roman baths. Here, the baths are an annexe to the sports facilities, whereas at Rome it is the baths which are far and away the more important. The new Baths of Nero were the first to provide sports facilities on a large scale, and, as you know, the masses are far from sharing the Greek point of view on these matters, and mostly confine themselves to watching.

Our *palaestra* is also attached to a well-proportioned lecture theatre, a sort of little theatre with tiered rows of seats. So we do not waste any time between sport and study.

Eminent scholars give us supplementary lectures in Greek "grammar" at a high level, on Homer and the tragedians; they also deal with the great prose authors, although more superficially. But the main thrust of the teaching is directed to rhetoric and philosophy.

As a result of the changes in the nature of Greek politics, political rhetoric, which teaches one how to convince an assembly of anything at all, is rather neglected. Our legions carry more weight than any orator. Forensic rhetoric is scarcely any more brilliant, because there aren't any big cases any more. It is "epideictic", or occasional, oratory – the art of putting together a neat little lecture – which is getting all the attention.

And since the first quality required in a public speaker, who has nothing to protect him but his voice, is prudence, people concentrate on the innocent genre of funeral orations – a pretty practical discipline, it is true, since all of us will, alas, one day have the task of delivering an encomium on someone dear to us. The typical speech has forty points divided into six parts. With schemas of that sort one is ready for any eventuality.

In Athens the intelligentsia prides itself on its Atticism, using only words, expressions and turns of phrase that would have been familiar to Demosthenes or Xenophon. As you know, archaizing tendencies of this sort are equally fashionable in Rome. But there the comparison stops. I was surprised to see how closely popular Greek resembles classical Greek. The language moves very slowly. Whereas our literary Latin is now like a foreign tongue compared with the Latin that is spoken in the streets. As early as Plautus, whose humour was of course primarily addressed to the *plebs*, you find letters dropping out completely at the ends of words. He writes "*viden*" instead of "*videsne*". He drops "e"s and runs different words together. So, for example, "*copia est*" becomes "*copiast*", "*certum est*" "*certumst*", "*ornati est*" "*ornatist*", "*facto est*" "*factost*", etc. And syncope is habitual: "*tabernaculo*" becomes "*tabernaclo*", "*periculum*" "*periclum*"; similarly in verbs "*amisisti*" is transformed into "*amisti*", "*paravisti*" into "*parasti*". "*Si*" also occasions contractions: "*si vis*" ends up as "*sis*" and "*si vultis*" as "*sultis*". Since those days spoken Latin has been enriched by a host of words judged too vulgar for use in literary Latin, and the grammar of the spoken language has fallen apart. The man in the street barely uses more cases than the nominative and the accusative; he simply multiplies the prepositional uses around the latter case. And Plautus' shortened forms have invaded everywhere. What slave talks about her "*domina*"? Isn't "*domna*" easier? At the same time the massacre of the short and long syllables has pursued its course, and a tonic accent has arrived to punctuate ordinary speech. The student of Latin is obliged to write an artificial language, and it takes an effort to find an appropriate way of declaiming it.

I have questioned well-informed people about the reasons for this astonishing difference between the evolution of Greek and Latin, but I couldn't get much out of them. What is certain is that the rapid development of our language cannot be entirely blamed on our conquests, because spoken Latin is as sloppy and as different from written Latin in Rome and Italy as in the provinces.

One may regret the phenomenon. One may also regret that spoken Latin has no other written outlet than the obscene graffiti of lavatories and slums. But it is a source of consolation to reflect that Virgil is currently known from Tangier to Damascus and from Carthage to Cologne, while a single legal and administrative language is used to govern so many diverse peoples.

Unlike most of my comrades here, I prefer philosophy to rhetoric. Of course it is impossible to think well without being able to speak well, but there are advantages in having something in your head before you open your mouth.

And yet most philosophers present their ideas in a thoroughly off-putting fashion, because of the way they split hairs, and invent new words or give new meanings to old ones, as if the lofty nature of their thought made it impossible for them to talk like everyone else. Moreover, they spend even more time criticizing their fellow philosophers than praising their own ideas.

But if you take a closer look, you find that the sum effort of philosophy has been expended on discoursing in a complicated way on a small number of permanent problems which are very simple to list. Is the world inert matter and our own consciousness a temporary and paradoxical emanation of the afore-mentioned matter? Epicurus – or in our case Lucretius – has popularized this sort of materialism. Or is the solution more or less pantheist, as Platonic and Stoic philosophers think? This fashionable solution has the advantage that it is difficult for an intelligent person to imagine that the gods could exist outside time and space. Alternatively one can be a Sceptic. The Greeks, who created philosophy, have pursued the study of it so thoroughly that in Athens today schools which cultivate every possible doctrinal nuance grow like weeds. It seems difficult to come up with an idea that the Greeks have not already thought of. This multiplicity of schools is dizzying, but also an encouragement to concentrate on the essential. In such a climate our Roman gods seem like pictures for children. I tell myself that if we have conquered the entire earth it is not because our gods were good but because we thought they were. Man's propensity for firmly believing in things that cannot be proven is very strange. Something on which almost all philosophers agree is the existence of a crushing fate. Whether from good sense or ignorance we Romans do not share that prejudice. We instinctively think that the world is what man has made it. That is the doctrine of the victor.

To complete my description I ought to tell you about the lectures on music, but they are madly theoretical.

To start with we study the numerical ratios which define the various intervals in the scale: 2/1 for the octave, 3/2 for the fifth, 4/3 for the fourth, 5/4 and 6/5 for the major and minor thirds, etc., while 9/8, the value obtained by expressing the difference between the fifth and the fourth, is the measure of major tonality. By this means you can arrive at a value for a twelfth of a tone. The Greeks have not discovered a way of taking direct measurements of the frequency of sound vibrations, but they calculate them indirectly by measuring the length of the vibrating string on a monochordal instrument or the length of the resonating section on a pipe. The lengths are then in inverse proportion to the frequency of the vibrations.

This discovery is the pride and joy of the Pythagoreans, who have taken advantage of it to philosophize intemperately. But it hasn't occurred to them to apply their treatises on acoustics to the construction of theatres and concert halls. Being by nature lazy, in order to make a theatre the Greeks content themselves with digging out a hillside, and it turns out accidentally that the acoustics are good. Here in Greece there is no more cooperation than in Rome between the sciences and the techniques of the craftsmen: the latter have been abandoned to empiricism.

Then we study the theory of rhythm. Instead of dividing and sub-dividing an initial value, the Greeks add up the indivisible units of value starting from Aristoxenos' "basic time". This gives them a very flexible system which can describe the richest and most complex rhythms.

And instead of giving us instruments they lecture us on the different virtues of the Dorian, Hypodorian, Phrygian, Lydian and Hypolydian modes . . .

Mathematics proper is only a rather thin appendix to philosophy.

You can see how busy we are, but we are free in the evenings and the Attic nights are splendid. Since all the young men are well off, the tolerable but rather basic food in the barracks is often neglected in favour of banquets which turn into interesting discussions. The elegance of these perfectly organized little dinner parties is beyond my powers of description.

In fact the gladiatorial shows are the only thing here to remind me of my native city. The Greeks have reached the point of being as passionate about this form of entertainment as we are ourselves, and in this respect Athens has become the true rival to Corinth. But wood is too rare and too expensive to build the huge sloping amphitheatres you find in the west, and there is not sufficient money to build in stone, as at Pompeii, the first amphitheatre of its kind and one of the rare ones so built to this day. So the Greeks give their shows in the public squares, or in open spaces near the cities, or even simply in their theatres. At Athens fine *munera* take place at the foot of the Acropolis, on the stage of the theatre of Dionysius, and there are philosophers who see in that a lapse of taste, if not even a hint of impiety. But it is all idle chatter. As at Rome, bloodshed and the prospect of money to be made attracts the crowds. Apparently shows of this sort also make women more amenable, and as Ovid so neatly puts it: "He who has come to gaze on wounds finds himself wounded by the arrows of love."

My *paedagogus* Diogenes, having been rescued from the hell of his classroom, finds life here an absolute dream. He has nothing to do but accompany me as a mark of esteem when I go out into the town with my little round hat and my black cloak, which are the school uniform.

I am very grateful to you for this unusual experience. I shall probably benefit a lot from it. I am taking this opportunity to thank you also for the education which you have given me, despite so many difficulties. The gods have granted me exceptional parents.

I am writing separately to Marcia to ask her advice on a little problem which is worrying me. I think that it is a subject on which a woman will be more perceptive than a man, being less immediately involved. I will give her permission to tell you as much about it as, with her customary sense of tact, she thinks proper.

I hope you are in good health. While playing hockey I got a clout with a stick which has temporarily absolved me from physical education. That is how I have found the time to write. I shall be fit again soon.'

Marcus showed Selene the end of Kaeso's letter, and asked her opinion, which he had become accustomed to taking seriously. When it came to it, Marcus always needed an intelligent woman to tell him what to think.

'I'm surprised,' the slave said, 'that the Athenians should be getting excited about women during the butchery in the Theatre of Dionysius. They must have changed.'

'What do you mean?'

'Either your son needs his eyes tested or he's pretending. Athenians are only really interested in boys.'

'Then you think that Kaeso's little problem . . .?'

'Didn't you tell me that Kaeso was as handsome as a young god? If you let a young god loose in Athens, he can't turn his back without something happening to him. Being upset about it, the young god is consulting his mother, who is for him an ambiguous symbol of chastity and experience. As the young man so neatly puts it, fathers are disqualified from judging the issue by their very competence in it.'

Selene's disillusioned cynicism frequently led her to make shocking

160

statements for which she had to be forgiven because they were so perceptive. There was no point, moreover, in being annoyed by the superiority of her intelligence, because she was after all her master's property. It was the intelligence of emancipated wives which was annoying.

Marcus felt gloomy and worried. He dismissed Selene with a flicker of ill-humour.

❧ CHAPTER ❧

2

Kaeso's letter to Marcia caused her considerable emotional upheaval:

'K. Aponius Saturninus to his dear mother, greetings.

I am writing to my father by the same courier and you can read good news of your affectionate son in that letter. The reason that I am also writing to you is to take advantage of your wisdom and virtue to get advice on a question which is causing me considerable heart-searching. I know that it is not usual for children to dare to be so open with their parents, but to me you are not an ordinary mother. You are less than a mother, because there is no blood relationship between us, and I have the impression that that fact relieves me of a sense of embarrassment as I pen these lines. You are more than a mother, when I think of how you treated your two stepsons with a devotion and enlightened tenderness of which most mothers would be incapable. The first reward for all your kindness is the boundless confidence which you have inspired in me, and the freedom with which I am submitting my worries to you. It is as though I were holding a conversation with an *alter ego*.

In Rome we praise the self-control of Scipio, who refrained from touching a young Spanish female hostage for reasons of political expediency. But did you know that the equivalent Greek example of continence is the Spartan king Agesilaos, who had fallen in love with Megabates, the son of Spithridates, as violently "as a man of very ardent temperament can love a very beautiful object", in the words of his friend Xenophon, the model of Attic elegance? Clearly to both the narrator and his reading public there would not have been any great merit in leaving a woman untouched, but the very beautiful Megabates was a different matter. Xenophon elsewhere writes: "Now I must speak to you of pederasty, since it is a part of education."

So the word is out, and very bizarre we Romans find it. In Rome relations of this sort are mentioned without comment, in those cases where they do not rouse the wrath of some moralizers or the amused contempt of the majority. But they are an integral part of the educational ideals of the Greek world.

In the circle of Socrates the opinion was put forward that the most invincible army would be made up of pairs of lovers. The troop of heroes created by Gorgias was exactly that, and from it Pelopidas raised the famous "Sacred Battalion". Only the Theban pederasts could beat the Spartan pederasts. You know that those brave men now rest beneath the monument which commemorates the battle of Chaeronea: it was raised as a memorial to both their courage and the passion which united them. The Macedonians who took them apart at that battle were not all pederasts, but there were more of them and their spears were longer. Being a pederast is not a guarantee of victory, but you do share a pleasanter death.

In the Cretan *ephebia* it was traditional for a lover to abduct his beloved and take him off to the aristocratic club to present him there. Then the two young men, accompanied by their male "bridesmaids", as it were, would go off into the countryside for a two-month honeymoon, feasting and hunting together. When their honeymoon trip was over, the lover gave his beloved a suit of armour and took him as his squire. It is all very well Strabo claiming that in relationships of this kind beauty was of less importance than valour and good education; there is still something startling about it to a Westerner. Strabo must have died during the reign of Tiberius, if my memory serves me aright. So these honeymoons were still current recently.

With the disappearance of the Greek armies, military pederasty, with a certain amount of nostalgia, has found refuge in the institutions for ephebes in the various cities. If the Greeks, from force of circumstances, have laid down their arms, it has been to surrender, not to the toga, but to love.

It is not only the military exploits which pederasty has inspired which have led to a prejudice in its favour. Greece is indebted to a cohort of pederasts for getting rid of its tyrants. At Athens the Pisistratid Hipparchus was assassinated by the aptly named Aristogeiton because the tyrant kept making unwelcome passes at the handsome Harmodios. Similarly Antileon assassinated the tyrant of Metapontum, who was his rival for Hipparinos. And for the same reason Chariton and Melanippos conspired together to free themselves from the tyrant of Agrigentum. The list could go on for ever. It was not the taste for freedom which led to the tyrants being driven out, it was "crimes of passion". Which is understandable, given that the nicest part about being a tyrant in Greece was that you could rape everyone else's boyfriends with impunity. Sooner or later something had to snap.

Nowadays, given the decline in opportunity for pederasty in a military or political context, it flourishes in the philosophical schools, where it is the done thing for the pupils to have intimate relations with their masters. It is the triumph of oral education. First pure ideas are passed from mouth to mouth, then erections. Socrates, when he was not knocking up plots for Euripides' plays, was knocking off all the bright young things of Athens. Plato was the lover of Dion and Alexis, among others. Just within the Academy, Xenocrates was the lover of Polemon, Polemon of Crates, and Crantor of Archesilaos. Their successor Bion also slept with his pupils. So the members of the Academy contrived to reproduce themselves from generation to generation through this sterile coupling, thus obtaining immortality on the cheap. Aristotle was also the lover of his pupil Hermias, tyrant of Atarnea, to whom he dedicated a hymn worthy of the pederastic elegies of Theognis of Megara. And if we leave philosophy for the moment, Euripides, after getting his instruction in the art from Socrates, was the lover of the tragic poet Agathon, Phidias was the lover of his pupil Agoracrites of Paros, and the doctor Theomedon was the lover of the astronomer Eudoxos of Cnidos. As for Sophocles, there is a famous funny story about him. He had given in to the attractions of a boy who was on the make under the ramparts of Athens and the lad made off with his fine cloak. So the poetic genius had to walk through the Ceramicus on a brisk autumn day, wearing the boy's cloak, which came halfway up his thighs. The braver, more intelligent and talented a Greek is, the greater his passion for boys.

I have talked very frankly about the issue to my Athenian comrades, and even, in the relaxed circumstances of a banquet, to the father of one of them, who said to me:

"Here we love beauty, and a man is beautiful as such. Clearly a woman is only beautiful in so far as she's made into an instrument for reproduction or pleasure. Here we love intelligence, and women are deficient in it, not for educational reasons but by nature. There has never been a woman philosopher, and I doubt that there ever will be. Here we love all the arts whose charms give a physical expression to beauty. There's never been a great woman sculptor, painter or musician. They've come up with one great poet, Sappho. Consequently, if you love all that's best in the world, you'll look for those qualities in another man, with a view to making them your own. And when they're yours, you'll be sufficiently altruistic to want others to profit from them, so that the chain of knowledge and art is well oiled by love."

This reference to oil which turned up so appositely in his little speech made everybody laugh, because in this country there are more uses than one for stadium oil. The father of another ephebe, encouraged by the *double-entendre*, lowered the tone of the conversation a little farther still:

"Anaximenes," he said, "is talking about gold, but perhaps I should say a few words about silver and bronze to complete the instruction of this young conqueror of the universe. Woman also suffers from the latent defect of not being constructed for prolonged liaisons with anyone of a sex other than her own. Either she finds no pleasure in marriage, as often happens and is very tiresome for both parties, or she enjoys it much more than her husband, who cuts a sorry figure while waiting to be cuckolded. A harmonious physical match between a man and a woman is rare and fleeting. Sometimes the plectrum is too small, at others too big, to get the best out of the lyre that it's plucking.

So a rational man will have a better and more satisfying physical relationship with a youth of his own sex. From piety to his city he'll go through some disappointing sex with a wife until she's pregnant – the danger being to unleash her appetites by too much sex and too much inventive eroticism. He can enjoy that sort of thing in the company of concubines and hetaeras, who've only got to pretend.

That's the trilogy which has assured the happiness of Athenians for centuries. It represents the only conceivable balance of interests."

"So the gods formed women only for reproduction or the brothel?" I asked.

All the middle-aged guests agreed that this was so, shedding a tear into their glass over the fate of the few women they had made pregnant and the numerous prostitutes who had pretended pleasure for them. It was hardly the time or place to quote the perfect dignity of my dear parents' lives as a counter-example.

But I find it disturbing that the Greeks, who have taught us everything except a military pederasty which was not enough to save them, should feel that experience justifies such sentiments? I cannot make out how far there is any truth in their ideas.

While waiting to learn the answer I have noted that Greek male love, as one might expect, does not remain platonic. It is even crudely said in Athens that a man who has it off with another man, instead of with imperfect womankind, concentrates in himself all the possibilities, all the sensations and all the pleasures: while playing a passive role in his early youth and old age, he can distinguish himself by his active propensities from the flower of youth to the autumn of his days.

We have just come back from an excursion to Thera, a strange island in the Cyclades about 130 Roman miles from the Piraeus, where Vulcan is supposed to have once had his forges. Plato, in his *Critias*, situates Atlantis to the west of the Pillars of Hercules, but old legends suggest that this flooded continent could be around Thera. Close to the sanctuary of Apollo Carneios the rocks are covered with obscene graffiti, such as: "By Apollo, it was right here that Krimon fucked his boyfriend, Bathycles' brother," etc. Roman tourists, here for sight-seeing, have joined in in Latin: "I came, I saw, I fucked" for example, and "Here I screwed Greece" – and one can bet that "Greece" was male. In our country homosexual graffiti are in a minority. In Greece it is the other way round: people hardly ever bother to boast about having a woman.

What is more, religious myths canonize Greek love. Zeus and Ganymede, Herakles and Hylas, Apollo and Hyacinthus, the rape of young Chrysippos by Laios in Menander's noble epic ... And from Alcaeus to Pindar the great lyric poets vie in the celebration of pederasty.

The point of all this chat about the past and the present is that I am under some pressure to take a lover so as to conform to the customs of the school and the city which have given me such a warm welcome. My restraint in this respect has brought me the nickname "Agesilaos", and it is always wiser not to make oneself conspicuous. But before giving in to the fashion I want your advice, because it is my greatest ambition never to deceive you over anything.

I am also held back by a vague fear. I have noticed that some Greeks, doubtless from force of habit in submitting to shameful sexual practices, have become more or less incapable of servicing a woman. Even in Athens they are held in a certain amount of contempt for failing to sustain the sacred trilogy, the desirable balance between what goes up them and what they go up.

I shall await your reply with impatience. In the *palaestra* baths I am the recipient of homage from a host of erections, "unwearied by the rigours of the chase". The reason why Greeks can run so fast is that there's always a boy in front of them!

Most beautiful and exquisite of women, most attentive of mothers and best of friends, I cannot even reproach you with responsibility for my beauty and sensitivity. Where will your perfection end?

I hope you are well. Assure Silanus once again of all my most grateful and respectful friendship. The allowance which he has so generously

166

made me is adequate in principle. But in Athens you can have a boy for free; hetaeras cost money. If you order me to, I will do my utmost to seduce one for nothing. Venus, goddess of success, will help me.

Love me as I love you.'

Thrown into a greater state of confusion than she would have thought possible, Marcia eventually asked Silanus for his advice. She had just married him on the quiet, with omens which were all the more favourable because her spouse was the head of the distinguished dining-club of augurs.

Marcia wailed: 'People complain that children don't confide in their parents. When one of them does confide in you, what sort of relevant advice can you give? In Rome, under the new regime, homosexuality is on the offensive. In the woods next to the site of Augustus' naval battle on the other bank of the Tiber Nero has had a permanent sex-fair set up, where tarts toss off male prostitutes for the entertainment of the passers-by. In the close-knit group of long-haired *augustiani* who serve as the emperor's cheer-leaders, every boy is just waiting for the prince to drop his handkerchief. Life in this city has become a perpetual party where everything is mixed up in a frightful way. We had thought that in Athens Kaeso would at least find an elegant, discreet form of pederasty, sweetened by the passage of time and favouring things of the mind, which he would naturally look down on. But I can see that the Greeks are as randy as ever. They use athleticism as a pretext for chasing after the biggest in-nocents on earth, brandishing their weapons at the ready. What are we to say to Kaeso? Are hetaeras actually preferable?'

For Silanus, who had, quite recently even, found a pleasant diversion from his ennui and his worries in the refined practice of Greek love, it was difficult to take the situation too seriously. He hastened to reassure his young wife with moderate views which he considered good sense. The newly-wed couple went over and over the topic until Silanus was weary of it. Marcus was given a vague idea of what was going on, so that it could not be said he had been left in the dark.

Finally, after a last round of discussions, Silanus, to his credit, put pen to paper to settle matters as best he could – in an elegantly Atticizing Greek.

'D. Junius Silanus to his dear Kaeso, greetings.

With your father's permission your mother confided to me the fears which your letter had aroused and which had upset her sense of propriety. Your parents probably felt that a friend with so much experience of life was still better qualified than they are to give you prudent advice on the right course to take in a delicate matter of this kind. So your reply comes from me, a person particularly qualified to comment because I am myself no stranger to the situation which is worrying you.

From your letter it seems as if you have already intuitively realized what you should think and do, when you admit that you are under pressure to give in to customs which are more or less the norm there. What difference does it make whether or not other people want you to drink resinated Greek wine? What counts is surely whether you like it or not?

It is certainly wise to respect the majority of the customs of the milieu in which you find yourself. There is almost always a good reason for them, and there would be no point in setting out on your own to change daily habits which are well ingrained. But this unassertive wisdom only applies to customs of secondary significance. You can follow such customs without involving your whole self and without affecting your happiness or self-esteem. Love relationships between the sexes are something so important that a great goddess has made them her sole subject of interest. But you should take note of the fact that while our forefathers dedicated a temple to Venus Erycine, goddess of passion, they also dedicated another to Venus Verticordia, who turns our hearts from immoral pleasures and wards off the debauches which accompany them. Whatever you do, then, you will have a goddess at your service, though that is not meant to encourage you to do any old thing. On the contrary you should act as a free agent. You should do what you really want to, and not worry about local customs and passing fads. You are of an age to be seduced by the pleasure principle. Well then, be rigorous about your own principles and follow your own natural, innermost inclination to pleasure. Nobody else can experience it for you.

If you had announced a genuine passion for a young man, we would have made a sacrifice for you to Venus Erycine. But if you encumbered yourself with a boy merely out of politeness to your hosts, it would be fair neither to the boy nor to yourself. Venus Erycine would veil her face in sorrow just as much as Venus Verticordia, and all the more so the statue of Patrician Modesty, which looks so like your mother, in the heart of the little temple in the Cattle Market. And both I and your parents would also regret it.

I happened to re-read the passage in Cicero where he records that he sent his son 66,000 sesterces a month when he was studying at Athens. Given the fall in the value of money I ought to do better than that. I have taken it on myself to triple your allowance, so that you can pay for love if your beauty is not sufficient argument. Zeus himself had to send a shower of gold upon Danae's breast in order to open up the way to her heart.

Your parents send you their love, and thank you for your exemplary approach to them, which they found very touching.

You can always count on my friendship and advice. Fare well, and may all the Venuses keep you in their protection!

P.S. The little Claudia Augusta, despite the sacrifices made by the Arval Brethren, has just died quite suddenly, and the imperial couple are deeply upset. Your father, who is overwhelmed with funeral feasting, can barely digest his sorrow.

Nero abruptly left a public reading of the *Pharsalia* by Lucan, Mela's son and Seneca's nephew. Seneca has chosen to turn his back on the court. Lucan is going to be obliged to do so whether he likes it or not. It has to be said that he had done everything to bring this disgrace on himself. It is to be hoped for his sake that the matter will not go any farther.

To start with, Lucan was the apple of the emperor's eye. Three years ago, when the Greek-style quinquennial Games were organized by the emperor, he was awarded a laurel wreath for an unqualified eulogy of Nero. But it seems that his Stoicism and his talent both went to his head, and he started to take himself very seriously. His *Pharsalia* reflect that dangerous evolution. The beginning of the poem contains nothing to upset the emperor, who is even compared to Phoebus Apollo. However, as the work proceeds, the criticisms of the regime become more obvious and acerbic. Cato of Utica, Caesar's mortal enemy, takes on the air of a demi-god. The rapid hellenization of all aspects of Roman life, so dear to Nero, is treated with increasing contempt. Even the principle of absolutism is put in question. And all this not in the name of some Virgilian optimism: the author's despairing pessimism is deep-seated and contrasts strongly with the atmosphere of permanent fiesta which Nero has made a principle of government. If I know Lucan, instead of keeping a low profile, he will accentuate his rashly expressed attitudes still more strongly in the books to come.

I am telling you all this to prevent you launching on any unconsidered eulogies of Lucan, should the fancy take you. Even at Athens walls have ears.

We live on an Atlantis which may go down at any moment, temples, obscene graffiti and all. Be prudent, for my sake as well as your own.'

This slightly embarrassed note from Silanus was an illumination to Kaeso.

So all true morality depended on ignoring other people's opinions. When he thought about it, it was not particularly surprising if this lesson in morality was delivered in the name of the morality of pleasure, for that is the most personal and intimate form of morality, the one which requires the greatest restraint, caution and asceticism if it is to be practised with full aristocratic rigour. As Silanus so felicitously expressed it '. . . nobody else can experience pleasure for you'. Nor was it so surprising that the lesson had been given by a Roman noble well-versed in Greek culture to a young Roman visiting Athens. While the Romans had on the whole remained very gregarious, the self-same Greeks who were importuning Kaeso had developed the seeds of an uncontrolled individualism amid the ruins of their conquered cities. The remedy, like the danger, lay in Greece.

Freed from the burden of his non-problem Kaeso thanked Silanus with all his heart, and instead of going in for boys like everyone else, marked himself out by the quality of his hetaeras and the elegance of his dinner parties.

The year went on and finished with some more innocuous summer and autumn correspondence. After worrying about Kaeso and boys, Marcia began worrying about Kaeso and girls. For the first time in his life Kaeso told her less than the truth, though the sudden rise in his expenditure made his lies entirely transparent. Top class hetaeras were fabulously expensive. At least Kaeso enriched his vocabulary. The wealth of amusing obscenities in Greek was even greater than in Latin.

Corbulo had pulled things together again on the Armenian front, and the Romans were as sick and tired of the eternal conflict as the Parthians. Nero, who could take it no longer, got them to accept a reasonable compromise: Armenia, the apple of discord, would have Tiridates, the candidate whom the Arsacids wanted to impose, on the throne, but he would receive his crown from the hands of the Roman emperor. In this way the Roman protectorate over Armenia would be maintained in principle. In the mean time the revolt of the Britones was put down once and for all. The winter looked as though it would be peaceful.

With Marcus divorced and Marcia and Silanus re-married, the letter which was to inform Kaeso of these events and of the plans for his adoption had been constantly deferred. It was up to Marcus to write it, but the right words went straight out of his head as soon as he started to sharpen a quill.

At last, during January 817, he took himself in hand and forced himself to do the task imposed on him. The habit of lying inspired him with some pretty turns of phrase. Moreover he knew that the art of lying consists in being clear without being too precise, concise without being summary, with that varnish of fine sentiments and dignity which always makes an impression on the young. It was in any case only a question of white lies told to protect the boy's sensibilities.

'M. Aponius Saturninus to his dear son Kaeso, greetings.

I have been rather slow to tell you some important news which I alone have the right to communicate to you. It was difficult for me to find the right words. The news is sad in one sense and happy in another, and a mixture of that sort is always difficult to express. But the spring of your return is coming nearer, and needs must when the devil drives.

I am writing to tell you that Silanus fell deeply in love with Marcia, that I agreed to a divorce and that they have married.

Yes, after all these years of happily married life Marcia and I made this sacrifice. I had difficulty in persuading her to it. Naturally she holds Silanus in great esteem as a man of the highest merit. But she had hoped that after me there would be no other. You know how close we have always been, and will appreciate what a wrench it was to part.

What finally decided Marcia was the same very powerful reason which helped me to overcome her reluctance to marry me. The task of parents is not finished while they are in a position to pluck a piece from their very hearts to help their children.

Not only can Silanus do anything for my two dear sons, but he has decided to adopt you. As you can imagine, the remarriage and this brilliant adoption are not unconnected.

Please keep your gratitude for Marcia. My sacrifice is a natural one. Hers is extraordinary, for it is after all only by chance that she is your mother.

I can now confess to you that on many occasions in the past she could have left me for a new marriage more worthy of her charms and deserts. But her love for both of you – I do not dare speak for myself – was doubtless enough to keep her in my house. The gods were holding in reserve an opportunity for her to launch you in the world which it would have been impious to refuse. This is the crowning point of all the motherly attention which she has heaped on you day after day.

Your instinctive good sense has normally spared me the trouble of giving you orders. You will forgive me for exercising my authority in the present circumstances. Since the deed is done an instinctive reaction on your part to reject the fruits of our devotion would plunge both Marcia and me into the most bitter despair and would be an insult to Silanus, who has done nothing which could be held against him. Everything has been done in the most honourable fashion. So I am bringing all my authority as a father to bear on you to require you to accept the exceptional good fortune which awaits you and which will be the consolation of my closing years.

This good fortune will require a certain amount of effort on your part. Silanus, as head of his *gens* and already very rich by right of that fact, has also inherited part of the fortune of his brother Lucius, who died without issue, having committed suicide before he could be condemned to death. And the will of his murdered brother Marcus, who left a young son – Lucius – also contained a clause in his favour. So that your future adoptive father possesses one of the largest fortunes in Rome. He has long been one of those extremely rare and privileged people whose fortune is so large he could not calculate its precise size. As Silanus has prudently kept out of politics, he has had plenty of time to spend his money, but also plenty of time to supervise the management of both his estates and his liquid assets. He must be a billionaire. You will understand what "effort" on your part I was referring to.

There is something frightening about making you the heir to such a gold mine at your age. I found it equally difficult to convince Marcia that you would be able to prove yourself worthy of the ever-ambiguous smile of the gods. I pledged in your name that you would not behave like a wastrel. I guaranteed that you would not dissipate on sterile pleasures the vast wealth which it has taken centuries to amass. No, your duty will be to maintain it, and, if only in memory of me, to exercise control over your mind, heart and senses, in a moderate and sober fashion, so as to leave intact the untarnished reputation which I bequeath you. I have nothing else – and nothing more precious – to give you at this moment of separation. The difficulty you will experience in controlling both your fortune and yourself will be all the greater, because the temptations will be enormous and constant. Luckily there are more examples than mine in Roman history to inspire you.

As you will soon be travelling from east to west against the prevailing winds, I assume you will come back by the land route, which involves only a brief sea-crossing between Dyrrhachium and Brindisi. Silanus and Marcia are currently spending the winter months in their villa at Tarentum. When the good weather comes back they will return to Rome. On the way Silanus will spend a few weeks in his magnificent Campanian villa near Baiae, so as to be with his beloved fish, while Marcia, who has little interest in fish-ponds, will continue north. Decimus is crazy about fish, they have him absolutely hooked. As Campania is on your way, your future adoptive father would be very happy if you were to take the opportunity to make contact with him again. You would then be able to finish your journey in his company and enjoy the best possible travelling arrangements. Silanus would not be satisfied with the facilities available in common inns, and he does not like to put his friends out, so he has private stopping places, with every possible comfort laid on, all the way from Baiae to Rome.

You will be able to talk to him about the proposed adoption. Silanus has been kind enough to express the hope that it will take place soon. But before that – it will only make the adoption an even more solemn event – you can take the *toga virilis* and consecrate your beard as well, as your brother Marcus has done in Vetera. That way I shall have your child's *bulla* and the clippings of your young beard to cherish after you change *lares* and *penates*. Silanus has offered to pay for the traditional banquet, which will ease my financial situation. It will be a very moving and very memorable moment.

Marcia hugs you to her heart. She will have the inestimable advantage of having you at her side as in the past, a pleasure which fate has denied me. Naturally, after this banquet, I could not be a frequent guest of the newly married couple. It would be indiscreet.

My painful solitude has been somewhat lightened by the presence of a Greek slave who has a certain charm . . . But to judge from your expenses, I am preaching to the converted and you will forgive me this human weakness. Old age must have its fling.

Fare well. Be a credit to me!'

When his father's letter arrived, Kaeso was sweating over an exercise in rhetoric whose unreality was quite remarkable even in the imperial climate of the times: 'A philosopher persuades a tyrant to kill himself. Compose the speech made by the philosopher in support of his claim for the reward promised by the law on tyrannicide.' This subject, which was as unflattering to the intelligence of tyrants as to the disinterestedness of philosophers, was to contain an *exordium, narratio, digressio* and *peroratio*, each part, according to its place in the speech, being treated in the humble, moderate or sublime style. A whole detailed system of mnemonics based on the association of visual images had been perfected to help the memory, for orators had no prompters. Similarly the language of accompanying gestures had been worked out to the last detail. After such an elaborate intellectual preparation one could at last proceed to the development of the quality which pre-eminently distinguishes a good speaker from a mediocre one – improvisation. And that was a matter of talent: it could not be reduced to a set of rules.

Marcus' letter plunged Kaeso into unplumbed depths of shame. He felt he could die of it. While he was in Athens, playing at 'Chase me Charlie' with a jolly band of gays, embellishing his mind with metaphysical ratiocinations and rhetorical trivia, and favouring high-class tarts with his custom, back in Rome, which was a country of good, solid old-fashioned morality, even if there were a few imperfections, they were thinking only of him and making sacrifices just for him. A mother more sublime than the highest oratory was leaving her loving husband to go with an outsider in order to secure a career for her prodigal son. 'It's all for my sake,' Kaeso kept saying to himself, 'that my mother has gone off to sleep with that old Stoic with his sybaritic airs and graces.' The crowning shame was that he couldn't refuse. What had he done to deserve to be loved so much? The greater physical knowledge of women which the young man was beginning to acquire aroused in him images which were cruel because they were so precise. Marcia, sustained by the thought of Kaeso, going along with the most outlandish whims of a cold-blooded fish-lover, as compliantly as any tart. It was not only Marcia who emerged sullied from this loveless coupling, it was Kaeso. How could Marcia, even when blinded by an excessive sense of duty and led astray by misguided maternal tenderness, have inflicted such an ordeal on him?

Fresh images brought back to him the Marcia of yesteryear at the women's baths near the Forum, in all the grace of her youth and chaste nudity, like Diana rising from the waves. But another picture came into Kaeso's mind: a woman the spitting image of Marcia whom he had by chance seen at the new mixed baths built by Nero, when he was just sixteen and the little 'filly' in his father's *popina* had recently begun to put up with his hasty copulation. As though he were sleep-walking Kaeso had gone slowly up to the woman who was chatting coquettishly with two naked middle-aged men, both of whom had enough expensive rings on their fingers to indicate a good position in society. One of these old goats was stroking the nipple of her right breast with his index finger and the other was examining her left breast, as though they had decided to save money by dividing the goods equally into two. The youth had found himself in a very confused state. He was trembling with desire and yet the extraordinary resemblance made his legs feel as heavy as lead. He had stopped, speechless, a few feet away from the group. The woman had suddenly seen him, had seemed to lose her balance for a moment, then pulled herself together: and Kaeso had heard her say to him, in a flat voice: 'Go and play somewhere else, little boy. Can't you see I'm with the grown-ups?' Her two suitors had laughed, and Kaeso had turned away in confusion.

When Kaeso had told Marcia about the incident that evening, she had joked about it and declared: 'The mistake is a flattering one. You must have recognized the woman I was a decade ago!' And the next day, his father had dropped into the conversation a reference to the fact that at the critical time Marcia was at home.

But in future there would be two Marcias. The *domina* of the apartment block in the Subura, who on fine days would sweep haughtily past the prostitutes of the locality as they perched on stools outside their houses, and the woman who took her cue from the prostitute at the new baths. Yet how could he hold against them a disgrace which had been brought about by pure altruism?

During that winter night Kaeso was haunted in his dreams by Marcia's triangle of short black pubic hair which for years had been at the height of his lips in the women's baths and which would have been enough on its own for him to recognize his mother amid the constant to-ing and fro-ing of all those naked women. Long before Aristophanes had served the image up in every shape and size the Greeks had given that triangle the name of 'garden'. It was no accident, in a dry sunlit country where good grass was rare, that the word 'garden' was so commonly applied to the only little patch of vegetation which the gods seemed to make grow with no effort.

When Kaeso awoke, with his mouth sour and his mind fuzzy, the song which had mutedly accompanied his dream was still ringing gently in his ears. The couplets, which had naturally originally been intended for a boy, had been laboriously adapted for those who preferred girls. Kaeso's young Ionian hetaera put plenty of feeling into singing the verses, whose *leitmotiv* still carried what any Greek would recognize as an obscene allusion . . .

> If I were gardener of love
> And passion made me lose my way
> I'd hesitate which road to take
> Through the dark grove where lovers play
>
> If I were gardener of love
> I'd often travel to and fro

Twixt the two wells of tenderness,
Bedewing all that there doth grow.

If I were gardener of love
I'd gaily plough by day and night,
In the dark furrow of your arse,
The double ring of your delight.

The pederastic origins of this fashionable ditty, which was being hummed in the backstreets of the Piraeus and the *agora* of the capital alike, were easily detectable in its word-play. But Greek women were well aware that you must bait your hook with something tasty, and that if you want to keep men with such deplorable tastes, you cannot afford to be fussy.

The vision of Decimus 'ploughing' Marcia Greek-style while the poor woman read the newspaper suddenly flashed into Kaeso's feverish imagination, and he bit his pillow in despair.

Not for a moment had Kaeso given any thought to the billion sesterces which were to come his way. The lofty indifference of the young to questions of money is so scandalous to persons of mature judgement that they find it barely credible. As a consequence they can be guilty of serious errors of perspective.

❖ CHAPTER ❖

3

On the Ides of March in that fateful year 817, Kaeso and his *paedagogus* were on the quay at Dyrrachium, looking out for the first boat bound for Brindisi. They were lucky enough not to have to wait more than a few days. The north wind, which had been blowing in fierce squalls as far south as Ragusa, had tempered its worst excesses, leaving a fresh breeze blowing in the right direction. All the boats set sail together, to make good use of the opportunity.

Kaeso had written a dignified and tactful letter to Silanus, in which he expressed an entirely appropriate mixture of pleasure and sorrow. Rhetoric had its uses after all. In consequence Silanus had sent off a flood of letters of recommendation to all those of his wealthy friends who happened to have houses on Kaeso's route. Their stewards would make a point of being as welcoming as their masters, should the latter – as was highly probable – not be in residence. Kaeso and Diogenes hired a little two-horse gig and set off up the Appian Way, which runs up from Brindisi to Rome. Their first stop was to be the villa near Tarentum which Silanus and Marcia had only recently left.

The Appian Way, which is the main route to the Orient, was absolutely packed now that the shipping routes were beginning to function again. There were couriers of the imperial postal service – always in a hurry – students, civil servants, tax-collectors, merchants, soldiers, and tourists on their way to or from the countries of the Greek east. It was very pleasant to be able to avoid the dubious and overcrowded inns and stay in heavenly places where they put the central heating on as soon as they knew that important guests were expected. In Rome even the very rich had space problems. But in the astonishing villas which were built on all the most beautiful lakeside, riverside or seaside sites in central or southern Italy – the Romans, being peasants at heart, adored water provided that they could, as far as possible, avoid drinking it or sailing on it – money had had the freedom to spread itself in every direction. Suddenly the whole scale of things changed, and the most beautiful houses in Athens were mere hovels compared to these princely villas. Only Roman palaces could withstand comparison with them.

Silanus' Tarentine estate, which ran along a considerable stretch of the coast, was enchanting. The villa stood amid gardens and parks, its façade looking straight out over the sea. From the terraces you could see a small private harbour, where a yacht and a miniature galley (for those days when there was a flat calm) were riding gently on the swell. Inside, the villa was a veritable museum: people like Silanus positively collected museums!

Kaeso and Diogenes arrived during the afternoon. They were struck dumb with admiration. Kaeso was even more silent than his companion, because to a slave who had only recently been freed it was only natural that there should be very rich people all over the world. But for a freeborn boy with honest ambitions such sights were a tangible representation of the immeasurable distance which always existed between average life-styles and the luxurious lot of the happy few. You pay all the more attention to a mountain peak if you are likely to be climbing it – and Kaeso had soared there by accident, borne on a woman's beating wings.

When they had taken a bath the guests were shown over the whole house, from the 4,000 pounds of fine silver displayed in the atrium to the bedroom which the master and his wife had occupied, a room notable for its bawdy paintings, lamps representing erotic subjects, and huge mirrors in which Kaeso felt he saw Marcia's reflection lingering sadly.

Kaeso preferred to have dinner with his *paedagogus* in a little summerhouse surrounded by aviaries and a little zoo.

On his profitable estates around Rome, Silanus' staff raised a variety of birds on a huge scale, for purchase by gourmets. There were doves, thrushes, quail, partridge, teal, coots, wild duck, ptarmigan (who would not sing in captivity), storks and cranes (over whose merits the *cognoscenti* disagreed), peacocks, pheasant, clouds of buntings, a few ostriches from Mesopotamia or the Libyan border, and even swans, fattened up with their eyelids sewn up – their flesh was thought indigestible but doctors valued the grease to be got from it. Since Apicius had discovered that the brains, and in particular the tongues, of flamingoes were delicious, huge flocks of them had been added to the poultry-yards. Similarly, there were immense enclosures where they raised wild boar, stags, roe-deer, fallow-deer, antelope and hare, which were caught and fattened up until they reached the right age. The steward explained that commercial snail-farms were now a thing of the past but there was over-production of dormice, now that every peasant had taken up the habit of feeding his own animals full to bursting at the bottom of a dark barrel.

In the aviaries which the travellers had before them the birds had been chosen purely for their decorative looks or their pretty singing – pheasants, nightingales and parrots. The peacocks were wandering free, as were the sultan hens, who killed mice, small reptiles and a variety of insects. In the animal cages there were exotic animals strolling about, most of them unknown to the average man.

As the chef had only two people to cater for, dinner was particularly delicious. Towards the end of it, while the sun was going down behind the trees, Kaeso said to Diogenes, who was stretched out beside him:

'You have been a devoted servant to us. When you took me to school, you always held my hand or gave me a pick-a-back, no matter how wet or windy it was. And you taught me all sorts of little things which I can now see are the basis of everything, the first rungs on the ladder of knowledge. Yet I often made you absolutely furious. The older one gets, the more paradoxical it is to have a slave as one's tutor. My father was kind enough to free you as a reward for your years of loyal service. But a poor freedman is often in a worse position than a slave, who is at least sure of his board and lodging. It's my turn to do something for you. Towards the end of my stay in Athens I no longer felt like the company of hetaeras, and I managed to save some money. I'll give you what you need to set yourself up, get married perhaps . . . or buy yourself a handsome little male slave who'll remind you of what I was like as a boy.'

Diogenes was incoherent with emotion, and the tears flowed down his deeply lined face, with its air of dog-like devotion.

Like many *paedagogi* Diogenes had unnatural tendencies. In Rome his conduct had been so proper, prudent and perfect that it had been a long time before the Aponii had suspected the truth. In Athens, however, the old man had let himself go, and Kaeso had caught him off his guard one day talking to a young male prostitute in a side road close to the *agora*.

Kaeso, who was also very moved, went on:

'I should thank you for never having made a gesture or uttered a word capable of corrupting me. I now know that your self-control must have cost you all the more, because your feelings for me were deep and sincere. Rather like the feelings of a wet-nurse, but she at least has the satisfaction of suckling the child she loves. What could I have got from the nipples of an old stick like you?'

Diogenes smiled through his tears, kissed his master's hand and admitted candidly:

'You're overpoweringly handsome. It took no small effort on my part to be so virtuous, since I would cheerfully have been whipped to death if I could have had a kiss from you first.'

Feeling more and more touched Kaeso asked Diogenes:

'Would 50,000 sesterces be enough? Would you like more?'

The freedman nodded his head vigorously, to his benefactor's great surprise. Then they both burst out laughing as they realized the confusion. The Greeks, unlike other peoples, shake their heads forwards and backwards to say 'no'. The case of Ulysses in the *Odyssey* is an early example. You have to be very used to the custom not to make a mistake. One of the first things Roman tourist guides always did was to draw attention to this bewildering characteristic, since ignorance of it led travellers into difficulties and did not make relations between the sexes any easier. Diogenes had been brought up in the slums of Corinth and had come to Rome at the age of twenty. The habit of acquiescing or refusing in the Greek manner, which he had gradually lost during his years in Italy, had come back to him in Athens.

'Since you're so adamant that 50,000 will do, you shall have 100,000,' said Kaeso. 'And I shall give you something better still, since you're so tender-hearted . . .'

Matching the deed to the word, the young man threw his arms around his elderly *paedagogus*, kissed him full on his toothless mouth without any sign of repugnance and added: 'While I live no one shall cause trouble for you ever again.'

At a bend in the path a young Spanish slave, who was bringing a basket of fruit ripened in the greenhouse, and a young Gaulish slave, who was carrying the finger-bowls, stopped short in amazement at this charming sight. And in an abominable Latin, worse even than Silanus' when he was not thinking about it, a Latin with no short or long vowels, with no genitives, datives or absolutes, a Latin which was slurred and swallowed and hacked to pieces, stuffed full of misused prepositions and fantastical tonic accents, coated in barbarisms and solecisms, but which, for all that, was a rather beautiful Latin because it allowed all members of the human race who would think of themselves as such to understand each other in conversation, the elder said to the apprentice:

'There's another example of what them Greek fags get up to. Your Romans send a young nobleman, still in 'is *toga praetexta*, off to Athens, as innocent as a new-born babe. 'E's only there a few months, and when 'e comes back, 'e's so randy for it 'e's 'ardly off the boat before he's trying to 'ave it off with 'is old teacher.'

Diogenes clutched at his chest. He was choking for breath, and the nostrils of his marrow-like nose contracted and began to turn purple. The emotion had been too much for him. Suddenly, overwhelmed by the excess of happiness, he breathed his last and collapsed into Kaeso's arms. A heart attack in the full sense of the word.

Kaeso left the steward enough money to put up a decent tomb for Diogenes' ashes in a shady corner of the park, by a murmuring brook, and requested that the epitaph should include the words which had already honoured his first school teacher:

SUMMA CASTITATE IN DISCIPULOS SUOS

A RIGOROUS MORAL PURITY TOWARDS HIS PUPILS

As the two indiscreet young slaves had chattered to all and sundry about what they had seen, this epitaph was an inexhaustible source of merriment for the entire staff of the estate. Life is paved with mis-understandings.

Two days later Kaeso continued his journey to Baiae alone. The funeral pyre had consumed a whole part of his youth. He had the impression that he had suddenly grown much older.

The journey from Brindisi to Rome normally took only eight or nine days, travelling at a smart pace. In four luxurious stages, flitting from country house to country house like a butterfly from flower to flower, Kaeso reached Baiae. In summer those nobles to whom money was no object would spend a refreshing holiday on the slopes of Mount Albanus or the hills around Tibur. In addition to the villas in these picturesque sites there were others on the coast quite close to Latium. In winter really elegant aristocrats flocked to the Tarentine riviera. But at all seasons there were devotees of the hot springs and varied scenery of the Cam-panian coast, and in particular of the resorts which lay along the shores of the gulfs of Pozzuoli and Naples, between Cape Misenum and Sorrento, with Vesuvius and a blue sky behind them.

It was to Baiae, a place renowned for its frenetic decadence, that even the bigoted old puritan Augustus had come to relieve his sciatica. It was on Capri that Tiberius had installed his main residence, having worked out a quite effective way of postponing his assassination for as long as possible: keeping out of Rome and changing beds at frequent intervals. It was on this gulf, blessed by the gods, that large numbers of the most magnificent villas had been built. The *crème de la crème* of the Roman upper classes, everyone who was anyone in the capital, armed to the teeth with money and taste (sometimes bad), had fought each other for every acre of the shoreline.

As the first signs of warm weather had drawn increased numbers of visitors and spring travellers towards Baiae and Pozzuoli, the road from the Baiae spa itself was as crowded as the Appian Way just outside Rome. In both directions there were mules and horses, litters and vehicles of every kind, including some fitted out like apartments, in which you could spend the night. Kaeso's gig had to weave its way between the two lines of traffic.

After travelling along the embankment separating lakes Lucrinus and Avernus from the sea, Kaeso crossed Baiae, where the hustle and bustle was enormous. By following the southern shore of the little gulf, he reached the promontory covered in dense vegetation where, as was well known, Silanus' villa lurked.

The steward, learning of his arrival, came and told Kaeso that Silanus was down by the sea, at the fish ponds. When he had changed his clothes the boy hurried down to find his future adoptive father. A slave showed him the way.

From the villa there was a view to the north over Baiae and its gulf, and to the south over Bauli and Misenum. The front of the villa looked towards the gulf of Pozzuoli, with the island of Nesis and the large promontory of Mount Pausilippus cutting off the view to the east. It was a splendid position. But the fish ponds in which Silanus was so passionately interested were on the coast to the north, and well sheltered by the indentations of the gulf. The sun was going down, and the shadows were growing longer along the slopes colonized by the rich.

Decimus, dressed in a studiedly negligent fashion and barefooted like a fisherman, was occupied in the supervision of major works. He turned away for just long enough to greet Kaeso with all the outward appearance of gracious affection. Before going back to Rome Marcia had drummed into him what things he must not say and what he should hint at to keep the young man in the state of innocence that suited him so well. He had promised to do his best. Since the days when everyone had been trying to put one over on him, his knowledge of human nature had considerably increased. In any case he liked Kaeso a lot, and was only too happy to show him affection for as long as he enjoyed doing so.

After embracing him Decimus addressed Kaeso in the most friendly, but ordinary, of tones, as if he had seen him only the day before, and talked to him at once about his own preoccupations. This was the surest way to get the young man to relax and to take his mind off things . . .

'You see, I'm going to put this vaulted roof up over this new summer pond so that my precious surmullets can get out of the sun and into the shade when the weather is very hot. The surmullet is one of the most difficult fish to raise. My gilt bream, sea-perch, burbot, turbot, even the sole, though very delicate, don't cause me as much trouble. On the other hand the *murenae* give me no difficulty at all. Since you're going to inherit all this one day, you must learn all about fish, so that my "tenants" will be in good hands.'

There followed a technical lecture which left Kaeso in a state of some confusion and with his ears ringing . . .

People had been successful in acclimatizing some sea fish to fresh water, in particular gilt bream in the Etruscan lakes. But the upper ranks of the aristocracy had above all devoted themselves to breeding sea fish, and the Campanian coast was the leading area for the activity. Such fish ponds were very expensive to construct, stock and maintain, and the return on investment was rather dubious because some enthusiasts did not have the heart to sell or eat their finest products.

The depth of the ponds and the quality of the water in them needed to be carefully adapted to the various species. There were also difficult problems of diet and general care to be resolved. But the hardest thing of all, in the case of ponds which communicated with the sea, was to establish a blending and renewal of water which would be favourable to re-production and growth. Along almost 1,800 feet of rocky coastline – in an area where land with access to the sea was priceless – Silanus had had dykes built, with a system of sluice gates, to capture substantial sections of salt water. These were the winter ponds. For the summer ponds, deep pools had been cut out of the heart of the volcanic rock, every time that it had been possible to harness the effects of a favourable tide. But as this was not always possible in a sea where tides are of restricted size, there were also sections sheltered by wide vaulted brick roofs, with currents of fresh air blowing through them. The work being carried out was Cyc-lopean, and the workmen were still hard at it in the late afternoon, at a period when everyone protested violently at the idea of so much as lifting their little finger after lunch. However, summer was approaching, and of course noble surmullets could not be expected to wait.

'I spend a lot of money on my fish ponds,' Silanus admitted. 'But it's a source of pleasure like no other. People are right when they say that plebeian swimming pools may be refreshing, but they lack the kick of our aristocratic salt-water ponds.'

Silanus took Kaeso round each of the ponds. Some of them were thick with fish, others seemed empty. You had to look hard to make out the sole hiding in the sand; and most of the rock fish, such as the wrasse, were lurking in artificial caves which had been specially devised for them.

Silanus left it to other less ambitious or less well-off breeders to keep such common fish as *dentex*, sea-bream, mullet, plaice, sea carp, and grayling.

While they were walking along, Silanus talked about the most famous of the fish farms in the region. They still bore the names of their illustrious founders, although most of them had changed hands, often ending up as part of the enormous imperial estates. Sergius, nicknamed 'Gilt Bream', and Licinius, nicknamed 'Murena', had been pioneers. Sergius Orata (or Aurata) had in fact specialized in the 'orata' or gilt bream and Murena in the *murena*, Hirrius had been able to supply Caesar with 6,000 *murenae* at one go for one of his popular banquets where the best vintages flowed liberally. The fish farm of Philippus, and that of Hortensius at Bauli, had equally good reputations. One of the Lucullus brothers had set himself up at Misenum and the other on the little island of Nesis opposite Mount Pausilippus. At the foot of Pausilippus the famous Pollio had had his rival establishment.

'It was the same Pollio,' said Decimus carelessly, 'whom Augustus, who must have been in an unusually soft-hearted mood that day, made fill in one of his ponds because he was punishing slaves for their misdeeds by feeding them to his *murenae*. It was an act of tyranny which totally ignored rights of ownership and foreshadowed black times to come. The rule of law falls into disrepute if you claim to override a law on the pretext of possible misuses of it.'

Decimus was particularly proud of one pond, which was reserved for parrot-fish. Parrot-fish, whose liver was highly prized by Vitellius (the guardian who had both neglected and misused Marcia) could not normally be found in the Mediterranean farther west than Sicily, and attempts to acclimatize them had, for a long time, failed. But under Claudius, Lucius Optatus, the prefect of the fleet at Misenum, had had large quantities caught in the eastern Mediterranean. The shoals had been transported in floating fish tanks and put back into the sea between Ostia and Sorrento, with a ban on fishing the species for five years. Silanus' fry had come from this source and gave promise of developing successfully.

In front of an apparently empty pond Decimus clapped his hands and a shoal of *murenae* soon came undulating out of their den towards him. The largest one, which had ear-rings, even came and rubbed itself against his hand like a cat . . .

'I call her Agrippina. Like our late unlamented empress she adores human flesh. She prefers blacks – they must have a better flavour – and they're dearer too, given their rarity. But she doesn't seem to make any distinction between boys, girls and eunuchs. I've taught Marcia to stroke her.'

Kaeso had just heard so many astonishing details that his capacity for surprise was somewhat dulled. What struck him unpleasantly was the thought that Marcia, whom he knew detested *murenae*, with their monstrous heads and sharp teeth, had been able to overcome her dislike sufficiently to touch the savage creature. It was for his sake, yet again, that she had run the risk, with a smile on her lips. He began to understand how she could be capable of sleeping with Silanus. It was probably a question of pure self-control.

Here and there at the bottom of the water could be seen pieces of children's skeletons and little skulls which the marine vegetation had more or less turned green. But one of the skeletons was still gleaming white.

Kaeso found it difficult to believe the evidence of his own eyes. While Silanus was stroking his Agrippina and whispering affectionately to her, the boy discreetly asked the servant who was guiding them:

'How many little slaves do these *murenae* eat every month?'

'I couldn't say. There are so many of us, it's difficult to tell the difference . . .'

'Are you pulling my leg by any chance?'

'The joke is the master's.'

Decimus took the thoroughly confused Kaeso into a grotto facing the pool. Comfortable furniture had been set up around a small fountain fed by water seeping through the rock. They sat down in the gentle, refreshing shadow of the place, and were served a spiced aperitif wine, chilled with splinters of ice which winter had formed in the mountains for the benefit of the rich.

After enjoying Kaeso's embarrassment for some time, Decimus said: 'The myth about Pollio is hard to kill, and one has to cater for pretty and naïve women visitors. As you can imagine, there haven't been many women in my life prepared to say "no" to me, but it's sometimes necessary to bring a little pressure to bear on a woman who is playing hard to get. A girl will already be emotionally disturbed by what I've told her, and as soon as she sees the silver skeletons in the pool, she'll come over faint. This grotto is then here to receive her. The most effective twin gods aren't Castor and Pollux, beloved of the Spartans, but Eros and Thanatos!'

This miniature set and props for a millionaire's theatrical seductions offered food for thought.

'The presence of a skeleton,' added Decimus, 'also enlivens a number of our feasts. Some find it a stimulus to pleasure, others are discouraged by it. We go by appearances, and these very appearances are susceptible of contradictory interpretations. The illusion which I have given tangible form to here makes one think of Plato's myth of the cave, doesn't it ? But do keep the secret of the macabre little swooning love affairs which this grotto has harboured, won't you. Marcia, as you will have understood, means more to me than just appearances: she's the quintessence of woman-hood.'

Silanus had learned that sharing a personal secret, especially between an older and a younger man, was a surer way of taming men than even a *murena*.

As night fell, and the lights began to twinkle across the bay at Baiae, they went back up to the villa in a litter. Silanus had had the path hewn out of the rock especially so that he could be carried down to see his fish. The Romans hated walking, probably because, from Spain to the Parthian frontier, laden with arms and baggage, they had in the past done far too much of it.

They took a relaxed bathe. Then, as it was a warm evening, they dined together by lamplight on a terrace looking out over the lights of Baiae. Kaeso was astonished by the sight, for in those days the night imposed its rule on cities and countryside alike. Sometimes, when there was a great festival, the heart of Rome was lit up, but because of the terror of setting the whole place on fire, such disconcerting experiences were rare.

'Baiae is as alive by night as by day. It burns the candle at both ends. And, as you can see, the sea itself is lit up by the lights of the pleasure boats. If we were nearer, you'd be able to hear the noise of the merrymaking, as all those "travellers set sail to Aphrodite's isle".'

The food, though not abundant in quantity, was absolutely exquisite. Now that Decimus had completed his future son's education in pisci-culture, he set about instructing him in gastronomy.

'The first concern and absolute duty of the real gourmet – there's no shortage of imitations – is to know all the characteristics of the raw materials. Everything is at its best in a given place at a given season. I have to admit to my shame, for example, that the burbots from the fish-farms at Clupea, an African port on the Promuntorium Mercurii, are even better than mine. That's why it's important to be able to produce everything oneself: you know what you're eating.

Sometimes nature does her job perfectly and it would be pointless to try to add anything to her efforts. But sometimes it's absolutely indispensable to give nature a hand, and that can only be done if you know and respect her laws. That's why wild game is always more tasty than the same animal when bred in a game-preserve, whereas our horticulturalists have produced more than sixty varieties of pear, from little winter pears to *pira libralia*, so-called because they are now supposed to weigh a pound a piece.

You might almost say that, compared to these considerations, which gluttons might consider merely preliminary, the art of the chef is of secondary importance. At any rate his principal task is to see that all the original quality of the product is evident. And of course the gourmet eats and drinks in moderation. In fact I'd say that a gourmet doesn't so much eat, as *taste*.'

Kaeso asked Decimus why he was passionately keen on fish . . .

'That's a very relevant question, and one I've often asked myself. In the old days I used to take part in vast hunts. A crowd of beaters would drive a crowd of animals into the nets. At the amphitheatre, like everybody else, I've seen a *retiarius* catching a man in his net. But when one thinks about it, isn't it a little too easy, a trifle vulgar even, to kill something trapped in a net? My fish ponds are like a huge net, but in them I can watch the *life* of everything I've caught, instead of merely its death.

I find the problems of raising fish in captivity much more interesting than the equivalent problems posed by game, or even by human beings. Birds, animals and men are always to some degree spoiled by the bars of their cage or the irons which restrain them. The art of the piscophile consists in recreating down to the last detail the natural environment in which the creature should live, so that it will be as succulent as possible. Fish are such delicate things it would be presumptuous and pointless to imagine producing any better than those raised by Neptune. However correctly you feed game, lack of exercise will deprive its flesh of flavour. You can improve a goose by stuffing it with figs. But sea fish, which never change their nature in any significant way, will only be born and grow in a fish pond if you have penetrated the secrets of the gods and copied them in every detail. It's a very exciting creative activity.'

Towards the end of the meal Decimus turned the conversation to religion. Despite the efforts of the elder Marcus to inspire a measure of respect for Roman religion in his sons, Kaeso shared the negative prejudices that were in the air, and his stay in the land of philosophers and sophists had not increased his piety. Since the day when Cicero had said that two soothsayers could not look each other in the eye without laughing, the famous phrase had become a sort of dogma among the aristocracy. Even the common people were in a fair way to making a joke out of what once had terrified them. As Silanus was actually an augur himself, Kaeso listened to what he had to say with particular interest.

He began with a long and minute account of the special form of religion specific to his *gens*. Kaeso needed to be well informed about many old customs and requirements if he were to take over responsibility on his adoptive father's death, give instructions to the sexton whose job it was to tend the *lararium* set up by Silanus in a chapel specially built for that purpose, and also keep a check on the family soothsayer and the minor priests of the temple of Patrician Modesty.

The importance the speaker seemed to attach to these trifles inevitably surprised Kaeso. Silanus noticed this surprise, although it was barely perceptible, because he was expecting it. Somewhat piqued nonetheless, he reacted vigorously:

'I'm an augur, Kaeso, and I can assure you that what I've just been telling you is no laughing matter. Roman religion is the wisest form of religion in the world, and when it disappears, people will regret the fact.'

As Kaeso had difficulty in perceiving quite what its qualities were, Decimus gave him a clear explanation:

'The first virtue of our national religion – which it shares with that of the Greeks – is that it's a religion without priests. By that I mean that in some countries, of which the Pharaohs' Egypt was a prime example, a doctrinaire and authoritarian closed priestly caste, which had a finger in every pie and was possessive, indiscreet, secretive and guilty of all manner of abuses, had the State in its grip. While here, in the service of an accommodating and vaguely-defined Pantheon, we have only functionaries whose role is confined to seeing that certain rules are respected, so that harmony between the Roman world and the heavens which look down upon it can be maintained. Our priests, whether elected or co-opted, temporary or permanent, have duties and responsibilities which are never merely ritual. At Rome anyone may one day be a priest, just as they might be procurator or consul. Better still, plurality of office is now very common. So the State can breathe freely. Since everyone is potentially a priest, priests are everywhere and nowhere. The priesthood and the people are the same thing, thus ensuring that the priesthood is an integral part of the genius of the nation.

The second virtue of our religion is that the priest is under no obligation to anyone when carrying out his office. When he offers up sacrifices to seek the favour of the gods, you can't ask more of him than that he should make sure that the traditional rites are strictly observed. If the sacrifice doesn't lead to the desired conclusion, it's taken for granted that it's through no fault of the priest. When he formally consults the omens to know whether the gods look kindly on a given enterprise, he's still not responsible for any errors of interpretation which he might be led to commit in such a delicate matter. "To err is human" and our priests are men, like anyone else. Generals have been sacked for refusing to consult the sacred chickens on the eve of a battle when invested with the special authority to do so. Generals have been sacked for joining battle despite the evident lack of appetite of the sacred chickens. But when a general gets himself wiped out after the chickens have eaten everything in sight, we merely observe sadly that General X has no luck with his chickens. Such a system has nothing but advantages. The most sceptical of men are always delighted to learn that the gods seem favourably disposed to their actions, and their courage merely gets a fillip from the fact. But if the results are disastrous, what does it matter ? Isn't the priest's mistake what anyone else would have done in his position? Who could flatter themselves they could have done better? Even in disaster everything is in order, because the finest quality of our religion is its humanity.

Its third virtue places it even higher than the religion of the Greeks. A Greek supposes that the gods are sufficiently powerful to impose their will on him. If you'll excuse the expression in this exclusively male company, a Greek lets himself be buggered about by his gods all day long. Whereas Rome was built by the will of a few men, who knew from experience that human will power is unlimited, because the obligations and the forms of freedom which man invents for himself are unlimited. The ill-will of the gods is not a limitation in our eyes. We're prepared simply to wait for a benevolent rift in the clouds of their anger, before we do whatever it is we wanted to do in the first place. And we're patient. So we always get the last word in the end. Do you understand?'

Kaeso thought for a moment, and then said:

'You mean that at bottom the strength of Roman religion is that it teaches us to manage without the help of the gods just as we manage without the help of the priests? That our gods are definitely not our masters?'

Silanus smiled and remarked:

'With a subtlety remarkable in one so young you've gone straight to the heart of my meaning.'

'Then the strength of our religion on that score is also its weakness. Many people want more from a religion than an encouraging ritual at the service of their own interests. By instinct man would rather show heaven his arse than his face. Don't we run the danger that one day a band of interfering priests will muscle in and start to lay down the law to us?'

'While there are true Romans, there's no danger of that. And that's exactly why I've spent so long talking to you about my family's private cult.'

Kaeso finally made an effort to get Silanus to talk about politics, but his host proved very guarded and limited himself to a few generalities:

'Things are going badly. The worm is in the bud, and has been for a long time. Roman civilization is myself and a handful of distinguished people who do their best to imitate me. I owe the possibility of leading this inimitable lifestyle of mine to the fact that the Roman peasantry lost its roots in the land while fighting abroad. So they came to the big city to beg scraps from my table, or they turned themselves into a few legions of mercenaries hungry for money. How long do you think such a situation can last?

Currently elevation to the imperial throne is in the gift of the Praetorian Guard. Sooner or later the provincial armies will want to share the privilege. Then we shall have new civil wars compared with which the old ones will look like a picnic. And the first thing which will occur to all these lovely people is to help themselves to what's going. So they'll share out among themselves my lands and those who cultivate them, my villas and my 3,000 slaves in town, and they'll grill my fish on the red-hot ashes of Baiae.

There's no longer any serious obstacle to such a threat. The whole notion of the *civis romanus* himself is in the process of becoming a figure of speech. There are already perhaps five or six million of them, and emancipation and naturalization are constantly increasing the number. In a few generations this collection of people with second-degree privileges, who could have served as a barrier to social disorder if their numbers had been kept within reasonable limits, will have grown to include all free men within the empire. The day of the citizen will be over because everyone will have the right to call himself citizen. And then the weary back of the Empire will break. But such an evolution is inevitable. In the first phase you rob every foreigner you can get your hands on: in the second and final phase when there is nothing left to pillage anywhere, you give the conquered races the title of citizen to keep them quiet. Mercenaries bring military disorder. The vulgarization of the rank of citizen brings general dishonour and civil disorder.

What is worse, the more we trade, the more we ruin ourselves. The gold from the eastern part of the empire goes off into the coffers of the Parthians, the Arabs, the Hindus, even the Chinese. And the gold from the western part of the empire goes the same way. By some strange curse of fate all precious goods go from east to west and all merchandise of little value from west to east. The Gauls smoke hams and the Phoenicians make purple dyes. In consequence the more purple the emperor wears, the less ham he can eat. The day will come when the west will no longer even be able to pay its mercenaries in ready cash, though that is the only way to maintain a modicum of discipline. Our frontiers will be wide open, our cities sacked, and the last traces of civilization will be wiped out, given that, as things stand at present, the definition of civilization is spending in town the money one has got from one's estates in the country. When it comes to it, if there is one thing worse than the criminal insolence of the mercenaries and the urban lower classes, it is the complete disappearance of both categories of people.

But perhaps I'm being too pessimistic. It's a frequent fault of those who own a lot of property.'

It was difficult to imagine such disasters when you were looking out over the glittering prospect of Baiae by night.

'You forget one thing,' said Kaeso. 'Everyone acknowledges the right of Caesar's descendants to command the armies. That sort of legitimacy carries some weight.'

'Yes,' said Decimus. 'The last time I dined with Nero I noticed that he'd put on weight ... I myself am also one of Augustus' heirs, but I seem to be getting slimmer. Marriage, perhaps?'

Kaeso should not have mentioned the emperor, who was certainly the most immediate source of danger to Silanus. Nero was in a position to get Decimus' weight down faster even than Marcia.

Decimus rose from his couch and bade Kaeso good night. The young man passed a restless night, filled with nightmares of *murenae*, skeletons, berserk mercenaries and *plebs* bent on arson. His initiation into the true form of Roman civilization of which Silanus claimed to be the epitome was decidedly perturbing.

❧ Chapter ❧
4

Silanus lingered for another two weeks at Baiae, for, despite the high rates of pay, he had considerable difficulty in getting Campanian builders prepared to work from morning to evening. The afternoon team was constantly plagued by absence and by inadequate work. And there were stormy discussions with the union representatives. The workers were organized into *collegia*, where the same interests and a sense of solidarity united free men and slaves for the purpose of worshipping a god or making sure that one of their members had a decent funeral. These dubious associations, which were constantly being banned, were equally constantly being re-formed without the authorities daring to take severe measures for fear of stirring up unnecessary trouble. Religious and funerary motives provided a good cover for defending professional privileges. Anyway, these people were necessary. A round arch of wide span needs a specialist to build it, doesn't it?

While the roof over the surmullets was very gradually going up, Kaeso was familiarizing himself with the exquisite lifestyle of the cream of the aristocracy. It formed an interesting complement to his education hitherto. They watched a respectable *munus* from one of the best boxes in the amphitheatre close to Pompeii, which had a good reputation and brought together all the fans from several days' walking distance in all directions. They listened politely to the public recital of a boring tragedy, whose verse would have put off an ordinary audience. They slummed it at the theatre, where the bloody violence and vulgar obscenities found favour with the *plebs*. There were also sea trips on one of the yachts or galleys in the marina at Baiae, and litter rides in the surrounding countryside. Silanus had shares in the company running the famous oyster beds of Lake Lucrinus, and was happy to go and see his succulent flat shell-fish, with their smooth shells, the celebrated *leiostreia*. People preferred the more delicate flavour of fresh-water oysters: there were oyster beds everywhere from Tarentum to Brittany, and they were eaten as far inland as the Swiss mountains or even the German frontier. They were however twice as dear as sea-urchins, which were equally in demand. There were also farms raising cockles, mussels, clams and scallops. You did not give a formal dinner party of a certain smartness without serving shell-fish.

Excellent dinner followed excellent dinner, at Silanus' house or elsewhere, and the chefs tried to outdo each other in imagination and expense.

When Silanus had guests at sunset for parties which went on under a great blaze of lights, his first care was to select a pretty young woman and say to her, with a wink to Kaeso:

'If your husband (or your companion) will permit it, my future son will show you my *murenae* before the sun goes down.'

If he did not like the look of the husband or companion, Kaeso would give in to the temptation, although he felt a strange distaste for love-making since Marcia's remarriage. Silanus' little trick was more or less infallible. Kaeso had only one failure: a silly woman who was absolutely determined to see a child eaten raw on the spot.

On such evenings the conversation was exceptionally brilliant, for Silanus knew how to pick his guests. On one occasion Petronius was invited, after a public reading of a long excerpt from his almost-completed *Satyricon*. The discussion at the end of the reading had been particularly animated and had continued over supper. For the first time educated people had been presented with a work which was not only a pastiche of a popular novel, but contained many episodes written up in a Latin close to the spoken form of the language. The innovation had aroused more shock than interest. Petronius seemed to set little store by his experiment, although it had amused the emperor. But he was clearly disappointed that his message should have run up against so much prejudice.

Petronius had arrived with a stunningly beautiful girl, and Kaeso was surprised by Decimus' silence when Petronius said to him: 'I promised Popillia that you would show her the pond where you keep your *murenae* – and of course the grotto where Venus is supposed to have repaired her make-up after rising from the waves. You will grant me the favour, won't you?' Since Petronius was in the secret, it would have been churlish to disappoint him.

This *dolce vita* had so many delightful aspects that the suspicion crossed Kaeso's mind that Marcia's sacrifice was possibly less painful than he had supposed. But he was all the more pleased for her sake, since she would thus have compensations of which clearly she would have been unaware. It took a long time for his eyes to be properly opened.

Well aware that he would be on thin ice, Silanus made little reference to his wife and less still to her previous husband. The evening before they were due to leave, however, he screwed himself up to speak to Kaeso:

'I've detected in you a trace of chilliness towards me which can no longer be put down to timidity, now that you know me somewhat better after your two-week stay here. It's not in your character to be able to conceal this coldness completely – a piece of honesty which only confirms me in my high opinion of you. It's something which I understand and forgive in so far as it's a reflection of an entirely natural prejudice. The standing of stepfathers is no higher than that of stepmothers. Since I'm vain enough to think that it's a question of prejudice rather than impartial judgement, I should like to help you be rational about it, on the basis of such experience as I may have.

You know the story of the unfortunate fate of Actaeon, the young huntsman of insatiable curiosity who was changed into a deer because he came across Diana while she was bathing, and was then devoured by his own hounds. The facts of the story are indeed exact, but a deeper understanding of the events throws a new light on them. Contrary to what one imagines, Diana was not a virgin at all. During the daytime she pretended to be one for the sake of her reputation, but by moonlight Eros would come and find her on the grass. From their embraces was born the handsome Actaeon, a naïve boy, who had less excuse than other men, given that he was her son, for believing her to be a virgin. It's true that he was even more virgin than his mother. On the evening when, pursued by vague misgivings, he surprised Diana in her bath, the virgin was not alone. Eros was riding her *more ferarum* while beating his wings. Diana hastily turned Actaeon into a stag, not as a punishment but to spare him the shock which innocent children always feel on these occasions. Some time later Actaeon was mounting a complacent hind when he suddenly remembered the scene which Diana had tried to banish from his memory. He was so upset by it that he left the hind in the lurch and hadn't the heart to run away the first time he met his own hounds.

The fact is that children forgive their mother for having made love once – but not twice. The deep resentment which they nurture against their father knows no holding when it comes to a stepfather, because the necessities of procreation cannot be invoked as a cloak for pleasures from which children are excluded. But intelligent children, once they hear the true story of Diana and Actaeon, learn it by heart so as to rid themselves of their illusions.'

Kaeso was very struck by the fable and eventually said to its author: 'If I'd known this story earlier, I would have drawn the right lesson from it for my own benefit and for yours. I'll try not to think about you and my mother any more when I'm mounting a hind.'

'That's the best way to ensure that you do think of us. Think about it as much as you like, but remember that Marcia and I have as much right as you to do what we like with our own bodies.'

Silanus' broadmindedness and perceptivity gradually overcame Kaeso's resistance despite his instinctive feeling of repugnance.

On the morning they were due to leave, a crowd of people assembled to say goodbye to Silanus. There were various friends, clients attached to his Campanian vine-yards, and the president and vice-president of the local builders' funeral association, who wanted to assure him that the building work would continue to make good progress . . .

The caravan only got under way relatively late. Past Capua they took the Appian Way rather than the Via Latina, because on this route lay the two stop-overs, with baths and kitchens, which Silanus kept up so that he could spend two or three nights a year in them while travelling. To break the monotony of the journey and prevent his muscles from stiffening into a curved position the nobleman kept changing method of transport, moving from his litter to a four-horse chariot, and from the chariot to horseback, and from the horse to a luxurious travelling-carriage. Behind him, drawn by mules, came a kitchen-wagon to provide food for picnics on the journey and a dozen baggage-carts, including one which contained the sumptuous wardrobe of clothes which Decimus had presented to Kaeso. The front and rear of the column were protected by tight-knit bands of slaves.

The forests of Campania were infested with brigands, called *grassatores* or *sicarii*. They set up their ambushes right up to the entry of the Pontine marshes, which were crossed by a causeway some eighteen Roman miles long. This seemed to have been built expressly for the benefit of the bandits. Once travellers had entered the trap, their assailants could catch up with them, mount an attack and then escape into the labyrinth of the marshes. The second danger zone was the area immediately around Rome, where the *sicarii* had established themselves at a respectful distance from the city police. On the Appian Way their favourite point of attack was the place known as the 'Tomb of Basilius', near a sinister wood.

A show of force being the most successful form of dissuasion, the journey proceeded without incident or accident. People along the route admired at their leisure a procession which could have been described as imperial if the current emperor had been a man of more modest tastes. On the afternoon of the third day they approached the area of the tombs along the Appian Way.

For twelve to fifteen miles outside Rome all the major roads were bordered by tombs. The more frequently used the road was, and the closer the area was to Rome, the more continuous the line of tombs became. The Appian Way, the Flaminian Way and the Via Latina were particularly spoiled by their frieze of the dead. The grandest monuments were closest to the road and had a special place for private cremation. The further one went from the road, the poorer the tombs became. Set-pieces in which imagination had been given free rein imperceptibly gave way to the humblest of tombstones. Every now and then there was an open space for public cremation, attached to an inn where the lower middle classes would hold their funeral celebrations.

Silanus, who had taken the reins of his chariot, occasionally held the horses in for long enough to read an epitaph which he did not yet know and comment on it to Kaeso.

Well-off Romans rarely had themselves buried in their own grounds. It was their aim that when they died they should join the very masses they had spent their lives avoiding, ask them to remember them kindly, and bequeath them an improving message. And where better than a fine road to establish and maintain permanent contact between the dead and the living? This thirst for continual dialogue made the epitaphs extremely varied and freed from the least hint of convention when it came to the essence of the text. Every virtue and every vice were thus expressed in this eternal prose. The vain heaped up a dozen surnames as an introduction to a ridiculous *curriculum vitae*. Famous men – some of them only too well known – went in for sobriety. The thoughts and feelings aired were utterly disparate, some very profound, some utterly trivial. The Romans suddenly turned out to be much more original when dead than they had been alive.

Kaeso in his turn drew Decimus' attention to this or that extract which had struck him for one reason or another . . .

'Here lies Similis, a former Praetorian Prefect: he put up with life for fifty years, but only really lived for seven of them.'

'Virtue is open to all. Neither rank nor riches are prerequisites; the man alone is enough.'

'While I lived, I had a good time. My play is over, yours will be soon. Farewell and applaud my exit.'

'During my life I said no ill of anyone. In death I curse the gods of Hell.'

'T. Lollius has been placed close to this road so that passers-by may say "Dear Lollius, farewell!"'

'Here lies Amymone, wife of Marcus, an excellent and very beautiful woman who span wool, was pious, modest, honourable and chaste, and stayed at home.'

'To the dearest of wives: the only pain she ever caused me was by her death.'

'I beseech you, most holy spirits of the Nether World, to look after my very dear husband and to grant me the favour of seeing him during the hours of the night.'

'The only thing I am taking with me is what I ate and drank.'

'Pious, valiant, faithful, risen from nowhere, he left thirty million sesterces and always refused to pay any attention to philosophers. Follow his example and may your health be good.'

'Young man, however much you may be in a hurry, this stone requires that you lift your head and read it. Here lies the poet M. Pacuvius. That is all I wished to tell you. Farewell.'

'Earth, lie not heavy on this child, who never was a burden to you.'

'Good health to him who greets me as he passes!'

There was even an anonymous tomb:

'My name, my father, my place of birth and my deeds in life I shall conceal. Dumb for eternity I am no more than a pile of bones and ashes, thrice nothing. Sprung from nothing I am returned to nothing and never shall exist again. Do not reproach me for my lack of faith, for my fate awaits you too.'

Kaeso asked Decimus:

'Do you believe our souls are immortal?'

'It's not worth spending time pondering on questions to which there are no answers. What's certain is that we ought to live our lives as though we were immortal.'

Silanus stopped the chariot again and got out. They were in front of a broad tower of ashlar. The base was of white marble, as was the frieze at the top: the latter was decorated with carvings of ox-heads, garlands of leaves and libation-bowls, which were emblems of sacrifice. It was the family tomb of the Silani.

The guardian of the tomb opened up the funeral chamber for the master, and Kaeso was surprised that in the half-light he could make out rows of marble sarcophagi on different levels. It was not the number of sarcophagi which surprised him: illustrious families could afford such reunions. But he would have expected to see the usual funerary urns.

Decimus explained that the oldest of the Roman *gentes* were not in the habit of cremating their dead. 'Sulla, for example, was the first of the *gens* Cornelia to finish on the funeral pyre. Having had Marius' corpse disinterred he was anxious to protect himself against suffering the same fate. His fear is indicative of the general motives behind the change in our customs which has led to the prevalence of cremation. It's a practical habit adopted by nomadic peoples. This way they can carry their dead around with them easily and cheaply, and ensure that their ashes don't fall into enemy hands. It's probable that invading tribes imposed the custom on us in times now lost in the mists of legend. But the Romans were all the more happy to adopt it because they were likely to die while serving in distant parts with the legions, and the repatriation of their remains then presented no difficulties. Even today sarcophagi are standard in our family, to remind us of the antiquity of our origins.'

However, Decimus went up to a wall containing several niches in which urns had been placed.

'These are the ashes of ancestors of mine who fell in battle in foreign parts. This last urn contains my poor brother Marcus, who was assassinated while proconsul in Asia Minor. That sarcophagus there belongs to my younger brother Lucius who was obliged to commit suicide in Rome.'

Decimus turned away to brush the tears from his eyes and discreetly blow his nose. Then he told Kaeso what victim should be sacrificed to appease the Manes of the dead on the IX of the Kalends of March, during the festival of the Parentalia, and what religious formalities were standard to appease them again and keep them away from dwelling-places during the festival of the Lemuria on the II, V, and VII of the Ides of May. The Romans, who were afraid of no man alive, went in fear of the dissatisfaction of the dead.

Kaeso took note of everything down to the last detail with exemplary seriousness. It was not, in any case, a place in which one felt like laughing.

Satisfied by this display of good will Decimus thought fit to add:

'I've already explained to you why we should see to it that our religion survives. The essential Roman virtues are bound up with it. What finer religion is there than one which doesn't seek to prevent man from doing everything he wants to and everything he's able to? On that point the greatest and the least of Roman politicians would all agree with me. The most sceptical of those in power will defend our national religion to the last against any influence, creed or system which risked destroying it. The risk is fortunately very slight, for among the Romans religion is simply and solely a question of ritual, and it's difficult to see why anybody should be upset by it. The greatest danger is that the Romans themselves might abandon old practices because they find them more and more absurd. Make fun of religion as much as you like in the company of a Petronius, Kaeso, but never do so in the presence of the poor and the ignorant. And, if only for their sake, keep up every tradition which deserves to survive, and keep them up with a straight face. If they died out, what would we have to put in their place?

In my private life I'm inclined to accept the Stoic position. On that point gossip is correct. While you were in Athens you must have attended plenty of lectures on the currently fashionable Stoicism, so I won't bore you with another. I'll just briefly say this: Stoicism teaches us not to preoccupy ourselves with what doesn't depend on ourselves, so that we can be divinely free in the things which depend on our own will. The better we understand the nature of the universe, to which wisdom requires that we should make our thoughts and aspirations conform, the easier it is to tell the two categories apart.'

'Isn't this freedom in matters which are dependent on ourselves a permanent force for disorder in most people?'

'That is indeed the crux of the problem. Some people apply their freedom to the creation of order, others to disorder. But when a blind freedom has unleashed irremediable disorder a Stoic still has the freedom to withdraw from public affairs, as both Seneca and I have done. And as a last resort he still has the ultimate freedom to withdraw from life.'

Among the epitaphs decorating the burial chamber were the usual curses against any sacrilegious man who dared to disturb the slumbers of the dead: 'Let him lie unburied!' 'Let his line die out with him!'

'My nephew Lucius, the son of my poor brother Marcus. is under the same threat as I,' said Decimus, 'but thanks to you I shall perhaps not be the last of my line ... .'

They went back out into the fresh air. Along the Via Appia – the Romans' favourite place for taking a stroll – the crowds were getting thicker. At some points traffic was brought to a standstill, particularly the tradesmen's carts on their way to the Porta Capena, where they would pile up outside until permitted to enter the city at nightfall. By special dispensation parts of the Campus Martius, the other favourite place for walks, had also taken on the air of a cemetery. The Romans lived with their dead all around them.

They gave one last look at the imposing monument. Because it was intended for communal use, it had no epitaphs on the outside. There was only the standard, already weather-worn, lettering: H. M. H. N. S. meaning 'This monument is not the property of the heir.'

Under Roman law, by an extraordinary exception to all the rules, the dead were in effect the owners of their own tombs. Their permission was needed before tombs could be touched, and needless to say such permission was not often forthcoming even from dead foreigners . . . At the foot of the Esquiline, where the Sacred Way begins, you could still see the place where four hundred years earlier Brennus' Gauls had cremated their dead during their seven-month siege of the Capitol.

They soon found themselves in front of the pretentious little sepulchre where Uncle Rufus' ashes were kept. Kaeso pointed out to Decimus the curious inscription: 'He died as he lived – unintentionally.' It was one of the inscriptions which found particular favour with sightseers.

Then Decimus took a sideroad. They passed by the huge *columbaria* containing the ashes of the imperial *familia* and also of those freedmen unable or unwilling to pay for a private monument. Finally they went into a vast *columbarium* belonging to the Silani. There were thousands of niches, each containing an urn with an inscription done in red lead, recording the name, rank, and often the function, of the freedman or slave.

Decimus was obviously proud of the size of this collection. 'This host of slaves preferred the indignity of their condition to Stoic suicide, thus proving that they deserved their lot. But think how many free men are slaves to their passions, prejudices and errors. Doesn't such a sight encourage one to free oneself from all forms of external slavery, however anodyne? Especially from the most dangerous forms, which come from within ourselves.'

Marcia had, among other things, insisted to Decimus that Kaeso should be kept in ignorance of the origins of his family. But Decimus thought it an appropriate place to be unfaithful to Marcia in a matter which he saw as trivial. He pointed out an inscription to Kaeso:

'T. Junius Aponios, treasurer.'

'Your great-great-grandfather greets you from that urn,' he said.

Seeing the young man's surprise and confusion, he went on:

'That's the origin of the affectionate and grateful clientship which your worthy father observes towards me. An entirely forgivable sense of pride encourages me to tell you the truth. You're rather like my fish – the product of a process of rearing which has taken generations of care.

The oldest of my fishponds was created by my grandfather. Perhaps your great-grandfather was in charge of the finance for it and kept the accounts. By adopting you I am reaping where we sowed. It's no stranger I'm adopting. But my slaves had some difficulty locating this inscription; there are so many of them in here . . .

Don't get upset. Most Roman citizens alive today are descendants of the hordes of prisoners taken captive by our legionaries. Rome took those slaves and made men of them – sometimes even made consuls of them. You're in pretty good company. In any case many of the slaves were much more talented than their masters, particularly the Greeks like your great-grandfather. The worst I can wish you is not to spare me the benefit of the good lessons you've learnt. Would you like me to put up a suitable sepulchre for our Aponios here, with a fine epitaph: HE SOWED THE SEEDS OF LIBERTY AND FREEDOM?'

'No thank you. He's all right where he is.'

Decimus smiled at Kaeso's reaction. 'There's a trace of his father's snobbery about him,' he thought. But what was upsetting Kaeso was not the fact of his humble origins so much as the treacherous path which this new vista had revealed to him. How could they have been so petty-minded as to hide such a thing from him? Even Marcia . . . But it must have been his father who had obliged his wife to keep silent on the point.

In the litter in which they rode up to the Porta Capena Decimus broached the subject of his assumption of the *toga virilis* and of the formalities of the adoption. When he launched into a lecture on the merits of the Roman system of adoption, not the least of which was the fact that it allowed the adoptive father to choose an adult who had proved himself, or an adolescent who gave promise, to guarantee the continuation of the family cult, Kaeso said, somewhat impatiently: '*Domine*, I am not worthy to enter your house.' But Decimus replied: 'I'm the unworthy one. I'm not worthy to adopt you since I haven't been able to produce a boy as handsome as you myself.' Decimus had grown accustomed to having the last word.

After all this Kaeso found his father's house very mediocre and his father more mediocre still, despite his loyal efforts to think of him in the same way as before. Children are trained by the nature of their own understandable requirements to learn to despise their parents either by imperceptible degrees or accidentally and abruptly. Decimus' tactlessness, occasioned by his vanity, had precipitated matters. But it was possible that Kaeso had already, without realizing it, climbed a few steps of the secret stairway of contempt. It was time that by the grace of the gods and with the blessing of the law, he changed fathers.

Confidence is a solid block: it cannot be reduced without destroying it. Kaeso wondered what else might have been hidden from him, and his curiosity matched his fear of finding out. The fable of Actaeon was not enough to hold him back on this perilous path and set his mind at ease.

If there was one thing which his father was flaunting, it was Selene. Marcus, who had previously been so discreet and respectful in front of Marcia and the children, looked at the slave so lustfully and treated her so familiarly that there could be no doubt about the nature of the relationship between them.

For a long time now men had had nothing to gain from marriage, since they were deprived by law of any authority over their wives. They were even prevented from getting their hands on the dowry if their unfaithful spouse took flight. Living with a freedwoman or a slave was therefore more and more common. No one raised an eyebrow at it, least of all Kaeso. But in this particular case he could not prevent himself from contrasting the previous moral propriety, of which a great show had been made, and the overt moral laxity which he could hardly have avoided noticing. He found the situation particularly embarrassing and upsetting because Selene was stunningly beautiful and matched Marcus' unpleasant vulgarity with imperturbable poise and good manners. Kaeso was embarrassed for his father's sake, because Marcus presented an image of such degradation, and he was upset for Selene's sake, on aesthetic grounds. He felt that in a well-run society, the enjoyment of perfect beauty should be reserved for young people of taste and discretion who were in the right physical condition to appreciate it. The idea even flashed across his mind – though he banished it as indecent – that once he was sufficiently well ensconced in Silanus' favour, he would be in a position to buy the slave from his father for a sum which would overcome any scruples.

Despite only too frequent bouts of over-eating and drinking Marcus had retained sufficient sensitivity to perceive what Kaeso was feeling. One evening, while the three of them were dining, encouraged by the effect of a wine from Clazomenae, he said with a touch of impatience:

'Everyone has to take what they can get. Fate deprived me of a pretty wife: good fortune provided me with another, who has everything – well, almost everything – necessary to a man's happiness. It's natural that I should look admiringly at this treasure, as and when I feel like it. I'm in my own house, and she's a slave.'

Kaeso, who was stretched out opposite the couple, said nothing and gazed at his feet. Marcus took the opportunity to give his concubine a little pat on the rump – she was of course sitting 'below' him on the couch – and went on:

'You'll shortly assume the *toga virilis*, Kaeso; it's time for you to become thoroughly steeped in the old Roman morality which I have been trying to teach you since you were a little child. As far as women are concerned it comes down to one principle: respect your own wife and other people's, respect young virgins who are still subject to their father's authority – marriage when it comes will give them only too free a rein. Keep your wild oats for whores and the slaves which a tolerant law puts at our disposal. That way you won't hurt anyone. That was old Cato's opinion: he married a young girl when he was seventy.'

Faced with Kaeso's impenetrable silence he added, weighing his words carefully:

'Marcia mentioned your problems with the Greek pederasts. All the men over there are that way inclined to a greater or lesser degree – it's a country which is easy-going to the point of decadence. What is shameful among the Greeks is their pretension, supposedly on honourable grounds, to corrupt young men of good family. Our Roman laws, which are, alas, not applied, continue to hold that such relationships between citizens are shameful and subject to punishment, because the passive partner is irremediably sullied by the experience. But the law turns a blind eye to what one may do with a pretty slave-boy. As far as both men and women go, when it comes to sex, slavery is there to preserve the citizens' honour. Even if that was all slaves were used for, they would still be indispensable.'

The way in which Marcus, the descendant of a Greek slave who must have had to pander to all his master's whims, talked about Greeks and slaves was so lacking in awareness that, however typical of basic human nature, it was nonetheless very remarkable. Kaeso could only copy Selene and remain silent. There was too much he could have said.

For many Romans of modest means one of the biggest attractions of concubinage with a slave or a freedwoman was that she could also automatically be made to work in the kitchen, whereas Roman wives, since the mythical rape of the Sabines, had sworn never even to pass the threshold. Since Marcus' financial situation had improved a little he had, for 10,000 sesterces, bought a Syrian chef who was reasonably competent but had no talent for making cakes and pastries. In a household of a certain standing the kitchen would have had a minimum staff of two – chef and pastry-cook – but as there could be no question of Marcus purchasing a pastry-cook, Selene had offered to fill that office in her free moments, which were numerous, since age had dimmed Marcus' ardour to the point where 'his once-bright torch now burned with feeble flame'. His bouts of copulation were brief and rare, generally occurring when the moon was full and requiring elaborate preparation to get him going. The rest of the time he only roused from his dozing or his legal work to require of his slave little favours of no consequence, which merely brought a glint to her eye and sweat to her palms. When the moon was full Selene would often become obsessed with cooking and be up till all hours in the kitchen making cakes. On those evenings Marcus had to choose between his lunar lubriciousness and his permanent greed.

Selene was expert at making *liba*, the ritual cakes offered to the gods in such vast quantities that the priests' slaves became sick of them and preferred a decent loaf. But she was equally skilled at other things – crunchy *crustula*: *globuli*, little doughnuts dipped in honey and fried in oil: crescent-shaped *hamus*: the different sorts of *lagana*, made of thin pastry cut into long strips, fried and eaten hot with pepper and *garum* (now more and more commonly called *liquamen*): *lucunculi*, a sort of crisp fritter: *perlucida*, like pancakes but rolled out so thin that you could see through them: wheel-shaped *summanalia* which were in principle an offering to Jupiter: Greek *thrion*, made with grated cheese: thick Roman *placenta* which was rather like *thrion* but more indigestible: and all sorts of custards and sweet omelettes, bread pudding, and dates stuffed with nuts and pepper, then salted and baked in honey . . . The list, in which fruit and aperitif wines held an important place, was interminable.

But butter, a barbarian product which was used as a diet food, was never used. The heat in southern countries made its production, conservation and transport difficult. Selene worked with fresh lard and 'summer oil' from Venafrum, in Samnium. This was the oil with the best reputation: the first pressing was made in September with olives which were not yet green.

Sometimes when Kaeso had nothing to do he would keep Selene company in the kitchen. By the soft light of the oil lamps he could see the outline of her body, as perfect as though it had been carved by Praxiteles.

This kitchen, in which Kaeso had previously hardly ever set foot – still less Marcia – had had the benefit of all sorts of improvements as money gradually became more plentiful. The oven, where the cakes browned, the casseroles stewed and even the meat, after preliminary boiling, was roasted on spits, had been rebuilt. The number of grills and cooking-rings had been increased. The place was overflowing with every sort of saucepan, frying-pan and stew-pot. When the Syrian chef, who took himself and his job very seriously, took over, all sorts of dishes of varying degrees of flatness had appeared, most of them smart enough to warrant Greek names – the *artocreas* or *artolaganon*, *epityrum*, *tyropatina* or *tyrotarichum*. Not to mention a sheet of metal with hemispherical indentations so that the fried eggs shouldn't run into one another while cooking. The shelf of seasonings and spices from Italy and overseas – some of them very exotic – which were indispensable to the numerous sauces made had become very imposing in its range. Among sixty-odd different products pride of place was given to the best honey and the best *garum*, the finest pepper and the precious kernels of certain kinds of pine which were often only grown for the benefit of gourmets. The Syrian also kept to hand a whole library of cookery books, most of which were Greek – it was the Greeks who taught the Romans how to cook – but which also contained the three treatises by C. Matius, a friend of Caesar's (though the latter had paid no attention to what he ate) and of course the complete works of Gavius Apicius, the gourmet with an insatiable appetite for tasty recipes and pretty kitchen-boys. Apicius, whose school of *cordon bleu* cookery had flourished during the reign of Tiberius, had committed suicide, after eating his way through a fortune, when he realized that he only had ten million sesterces left. A martyr to the cult of exquisite sensation, he had preferred an exemplary death to a reduction in his culinary lifestyle.

On that particular evening Selene was at work on an Egyptian *canopicum* As she put down *The Art of Bakery* by Chrysippus of Tyana, Kaeso suddenly asked her:

'The other day when my father said that you had "almost everything" necessary to a man's happiness I happened to notice your knuckles whiten on your snail-fork. It was rather a strong reaction to a pretty banal joke, wasn't it? What was the matter?'

'Silanus gave your father my body. Do you want to own my mind as well?'

'Silanus?'

'Don't tell anyone I told you. Silanus and your father agreed that nothing would be said in front of you. I was a gift from the nobleman to my master as recompense for the departure of your stepmother. The gesture was flattering to me, given what amazing charms – so I'm told – Marcia possesses, but I'm not pleased with the exchange. I've known men less actively unpleasant than your father – though I can't say many men are actually pleasant.'

Kaeso finally understood how his father had been able to afford such an expensive slave.

In a dream he went on, in Greek now, since it was Selene's mother tongue and therefore the one in which she was perhaps more likely to confide in him:

'You didn't answer my question.'

'I've already told you one secret. You're nosy. And you've no right to press me. I don't belong to you.'

Kaeso's curiosity was now thoroughly aroused and he could not refrain from endless speculation. Selene was very reticent by nature, but the boy's charm was not merely ordinary male sexual attractiveness, to which the young woman was barely susceptible. He gave off an easy air of human sympathy – and the heart has reasons of its own in which sexuality plays no part.

Her resistance finally overcome, Selene wept and said:

'In sex, as you must know, some men delight in the pleasure experienced by their partners, but others get the most enjoyment from the total passivity of their victim. Young boys who have barely reached puberty are castrated to serve in homosexual brothels and certain arch-perverts even have their boyfriends gelded, as Nero is supposed to have done to his poor Sporus. Women aren't spared such whims. In Egypt an ancient custom requires that girls be circumcised at an early age. The sacrificial knife cuts out what the Greeks call their *kleitoris* the "little key" to pleasure, the *myrton* or bay of myrtle, or the "maggot" – there are lots of other names for it. You should know, if you went with hetaeras in Athens. The Romans call it "the little column", "the charm of Venus", "myrtle" or "little priapus". I know less Latin than Greek. I went under the knife quite late in life, when my "little key" had already opened fresh horizons of pleasure to me. Your father is very cruel to joke about it, given that . . .'

'That it was him . . .?'

Kaeso's mistake tempted Selene, and she gave in to the temptation. She was so pleased with the idea of getting her own back on Marcus that she gave no thought to the feelings of her interlocutor.

She lowered her eyes and murmured: 'Please don't tell the master that I gave away his perversion to you. Though he's not the only man in Rome to enjoy that particular little fantasy, which the Egyptians were responsible for spreading, he would have me whipped.'

In his horror Kaeso was prepared to swear anything.

The more you embroider a lie, the more pleasure you get from it.

Selene, in floods of tears, described in gory detail the scene of the sacrifice, in which Marcus' vicious cruelty took on epic tones. Because Selene's imagination was feeding on a sorrow which was ineradicable, real and bitterly felt, she wove her tale all the more brilliantly. But the filth became too foul, and Kaeso cried out in disbelief.

It was no moment for half-measures. Gently but firmly Selene took Kaeso's right hand and forced it up under her dress towards the scene of the crime. His fumbling inspection was made easier by the fact that the young woman's pubes were kept freshly shaved to emphasize her purity of line. Kaeso found the right place and felt it. He believed her.

He was overcome with a sudden desire to vomit. He broke away from her and turned round. His gaze fell on a stewpot in which half a dozen roast suckling puppies were floating in a thick sauce. Eating dog had gone out of fashion long ago. But suckling puppies were still a ritual element at certain election banquets given by the religious colleges. They were sacrificed to gods or goddesses, notably Genita Mana, the patron goddess of menstruation. Marcus had evidently brought back the recipe for this particular delicacy from one of his evenings-out undertaken in the name of piety.

Feeling utterly nauseated, Kaeso vomited the entire contents of his stomach into the pot and fled.

CHAPTER
5

Usually young Romans ceremonially laid down their *toga praetexta* and put on the *toga virilis* between the ages of fourteen and twenty, on the XIIth of the Kalends of April, that is on March 17th – one of the days marked NP in the calendar, when the Liberalia, the feast of Bacchus, was celebrated.

On *dies fasti* the courts were in session, on *dies nefasti* they were not, because on those days the gods ceased to assume any responsibility for what might happen. A day marked NP in the calendar was a *dies nefastus* which coincided with a feast day. A *dies intercisus* was *nefastus* morning and evening and *fastus* in between. On *dies funesti*, days of mourning when the anniversary of some catastrophe was celebrated, no business, public or private, was conducted. On *dies comitiales*, there had in the old days been meetings of the various electoral assemblies, the *comitia curiata*, the *comitia centuriata* and the *comitia tributa*, but these assemblies had gradually been reduced to nothing.

On the morning of this particular feast of Bacchus the young man who was to lay down his *praetexta* went and hung his good-luck charm, the *bulla*, on the neck of one of the household gods, then, wrapped in his new *toga virilis* and surrounded by family and friends, he climbed up to the Capitol to make a sacrifice, and then came down to the Forums, to take a stroll and make known to the world that Rome had acquired one more citizen. The day naturally ended with a banquet, since the Romans never missed a good opportunity to stretch out and tuck in to a good meal. During the Liberalia the city was criss-crossed with processions making their way between the Capitol, the Forums and the banqueting rooms.

Of necessity you could assume the *toga virilis* on some other day of the year. Marcus junior, on receiving his posting abroad, had had to leave on the eve of the Liberalia the year before, and Kaeso had left on the day before that, the Ides of March, and had only come back in April. Marcus was adamant that Kaeso should take the *toga virilis* before his adoption, so that the ceremony would take place under the good auspices of the family religion of the Aponii, and the young man's *bulla* would be kept in the *lararium* of the house in the Subura and not in that of the Silani. So they decided to perform the ritual on the XIth of the Kalends of May (i.e. the 21st of April), which coincided with another great public festival, the Palilia, the anniversary of the founding of the city of Rome. That was the day when the Game of Troy took place, and everyone who was anyone among the gilded youth of Rome took part in the horseback manoeuvres and races. The noble gravity of the Palilia was entirely suited to the assumption of the *toga virilis*.

A week after the Palilia, as April gave way to May, began the Floral Games, when it would have been indecent to put on the *toga virilis* for the first time. These Floralia, in honour of Flora, goddess of fecundity and more particularly of pleasure, were in fact the great nocturnal festival of the prostitutes. They came out from under every stone. Those of the best class, who worked the porticoes of the Campus Martius and the area around the nearby temple of Isis, goddess of pimps: those of the second rank, who hung around in the roofed-in parts of the Circuses, theatres and amphitheatres, or at the entrance to public baths: those of the third rank, who cluttered up the Sublician bridge, down by the docks, and the gates into the city: and lots of girls from brothels – the reasonably elegant establishments on the Aventine, the brothels of the Velabrum and Subura, which were patronized by the lowest classes and those enthusiasts who liked violent sensations and strong smells, and the specialized hell of the Summoenium, where the girls lurked in narrow cells behind filthy curtains. They came in their thousands and formed long processions which threaded their way slowly across the city towards the theatres. It was a spectacle unique in the Roman year and doubtless unique in the entire civilized world: at the pressing invitation of the crowds of spectators each girl would start to undress, reciting as she did so her address and her price, which ranged from two *asses* to thousands of *nummi*. An army of naked women suddenly took possession of the Eternal City.

The young *castrati* from the male brothels did not join in the festival. Indecency is a matter of degree.

Between the Palilia and the Floralia the only festival was the *Vinalia*, in honour of the tasting of the wines of the previous harvest. However, the Bacchic element in the festival had allowed the prostitutes to turn it into a sort of *hors-d'oeuvre* to the Floralia. As soon as dawn broke, they would hurry to the temple of Venus at the Porta Collina to make offerings to the goddess. Afterwards, outside the temple, there was a great prostitutes' fair, for the delight of pimps, customers and sightseers.

If they wanted to associate Kaeso's change of toga with a suitable festival without putting it off to the Greek Kalends, there was no other solution but the Palilia.

As the day approached Marcus grew more and more grave and moralizing. He even kept his hands off Selene . . .

'The great day is approaching, Kaeso. The fact that the *toga praetexta* is decorated with the same purple band as you'll find on my senatorial toga has a profound and uplifting significance to it. It's the symbol of the special value of childhood, which has the right to all honour and protection. You are now about to enter the adult world and make your choice of career: the bar, the army, the Senate, where I have a certain influence . . . Silanus will crown my efforts to ensure that you become a man worthy of the name and a true Roman. Marcia will also give you good advice . . .'

Selene was impassively enjoying the growing disgust which Marcus inspired in his son. She felt less isolated.

On several occasions Marcia had sent the boy a note asking him to drop in and see her, but he had postponed his visit from day to day, and had finally decided not to see her until the last possible moment, when he took the new toga and offered up his first beard.

Kaeso was now in a permanent state of unease. First he had been shocked by Marcia's re-marriage, then, since Selene's revolting revelation, he had been even more shocked by the idea that his stepmother could have lived for so long with such a hypocritical and cruel man as his father. Before sacrificing herself for his sake in Silanus' bed, had she already sacrificed herself for the same cause in his father's bed? From somewhere in the depths of his subconscious the memory of Marcus weeping outside his wife's bedroom door came back to Kaeso and suddenly acquired a horrific meaning. But there was something incredible about the idea that she could have made quite so many sacrifices.

Then Kaeso remembered how kind his father had been to him. Perhaps he was only cruel to slaves? Or perhaps, since Marcia's departure, his character had turned sour and become insanely vicious? Kaeso did not know what to think. He lacked the courage to find himself alone with Marcia in such an unwholesome atmosphere. He was afraid of new chasms opening up before him.

Selene posed a further problem for him. When he first came back, he had paid no more attention to her than to the exquisite marble women who inhabited Silanus' villa at Baiae. But since he had had to put his hand into the hollow of the statue to find out how smooth it was, he was haunted by the strange warmth he had found there, which never ceased to have a disturbing effect on him. The veil of pity was pierced by a shaft of incestuous desire.

On the eve of the Palilia Kaeso received a note from Silanus asking him to call in after siesta, and a short letter from his brother:

'M. Aponius Saturninus to his dear brother Kaeso, greetings.

I'd love to have been in Rome when you put on the toga but the legate won't release me. At this time of the year we restart military activity, to make an impression on the Germans. At the end of winter the Germans do the same. They're full of a renewed hunger for battle, like bears waking up after their long sleep and going out to steal honey. Our intelligence service is worn out, because you have to catch these brutes while they're in the right mood and make sure they fight each other and not the legions. Our troops have made one or two forays on to the other bank of the river, reconnoitring and cleaning up a few suspect areas. Sometimes when you chase a German and cut him off, he'll hide up in a tree to get away from our hunting dogs, and our archers and slingsmen have to bring him tumbling down like ripe fruit. But as an entertainment it doesn't stand comparison with a banquet to celebrate the assumption of the toga, held in the house of a member of the imperial family!

I've heard about your coming adoption. It's a piece of luck which seems almost miraculous. You must show yourself worthy of it by being very prudent and diplomatic. As happens to all of us, sooner or later you're going to find out things which you won't like. That'll be the moment to keep your thoughts to yourself and put a good face on it. There's a lot of difference between the world as one would like it to be and the real world where the gods play with our hopes and feelings. I've always felt very fond of Marcia, for example, although when it comes to it she's quite indifferent to me. But she has a real passion for you. You're worthy of it, but it could be a source of embarrassment. Be careful that Silanus doesn't take offence at your relationship. A man who's getting on in years easily gets jealous, and the occasions for misunderstandings in every day life are numerous. I'd advise you to get away as soon as you decently can.

I still have hopes of being able to take leave in the next few weeks, so I can hop back to Rome and have a bit of fun. Here in February even the oil froze! That shows you what a god-forsaken place this is.

I'm fine. Look after yourself.'

Kaeso appreciated his brother's good sense, a quality which intelligence and education cannot develop in someone who lacks it. He made a mental note that one day he must put Marcia on her guard, as tactfully as possible, against the danger which Marcus junior had nosed out from afar. Though perhaps his good sense had led him to exaggerate the danger?

Silanus greeted Kaeso in the *atrium* of Cicero's house on the Palatine. Marcia was nowhere to be seen. But all around the vast room the cupboards in which the death masks of the ancestors of the *gens* Junia were kept had been opened wide. These very realistic wax masks were very striking. They were painted the pale colours of dying flesh but fixed in the act of breathing the last breath which a son felt from his father's mouth. At a funeral the freshly-made mask of the dead man was carried by the professional mime employed to criticize him. The other masks were borne by silent people who had put on the costume of the relevant period and the insignia of the offices the various ancestors had held. The dead man humorously conducted his own funeral before a procession of his ancestors who were only entitled to praise.

Silanus took Kaeso on a tour of the funerary cupboards, giving him an historical, and where possible a moral, commentary on each mask. They went the rounds of consuls, proconsuls, dictators, tribunes, generals, men who had been distinguished at the bar or in the field of letters (or who had at least helped themselves to the relevant titles), aesthetes and fish-breeding enthusiasts, and ended up with the master of the house's two unfortunate brothers. Then Silanus showed Kaeso a genealogical tree of some complexity, and tried to sum up for him what he saw as the essentials of it:

'Now listen carefully . . .

C. Julius Caesar – one of whose sisters married Marius – had three children by his wife Aurelia: the great Julius Caesar and his two sisters, who were both called Julia.

Julius Caesar married four times. His first wife was Cossuta, who had a fine dowry. His second wife was Cornelia, the daughter of Cinna, who was leader of the popular party after Marius' death. His third wife was Pompeia and his fourth Calpurnia, the daughter of one of the Pisos. Out of all those marriages he only had one child, a daughter Julia, by Cornelia. She married Pompey and died without offspring.

But one of the Caesar's two sisters married M. Atius Balbus. The daughter of that marriage, Atia, married C. Octavius and had two children, Octavia the younger and the future emperor Augustus. (By a previous marriage with Ancharia, C. Octavius had had Octavia the elder, who was therefore not related by blood to Caesar, so I've left her out . . .)

Caesar's other sister married Q. Pedius, one of the executors of Augustus' will, but that branch soon died out.

Augustus is therefore a descendant of one of Caesar's sisters, *faute de mieux*.

By his first marriage with Scribonia, Augustus had only one daughter, another Julia, who married M. Claudius Marcellus, Agrippa and Tiberius in that order. By Agrippa, Augustus' only daughter had Caius and Lucius Caesar, Agrippa Postumus, Agrippina the elder – the wife of Germanicus – and yet another Julia, who married L. Aemilius Paullus. This last Julia had a daughter by Paullus called Aemilia Lepida, who married C. Junius Silvanus, my father.

So I'm a direct descendant of Augustus by the two Julias, his daughter and granddaughter, and Agrippa is my great-grandfather. Are you with me?'

'Completely.'

'Augustus had no children by his second marriage with Livia, but Livia had two sons by her previous marriage to Ti. Claudius Nero, Tiberius and Drusus. The line of descent from Tiberius' marriage to Vipsania Agrippina has died out, with a little assistance. However, Drusus married Antonia the younger – she and her sister Antonia the elder were the daughters of Mark Antony and Augustus' sister, Octavia the younger. Antonia the younger and Drusus had a daughter Claudia Livilla, but the line of descent from her has now been brutally wiped out. They also had two sons, Claudius and Germanicus.

Germanicus and Agrippina the elder, Augustus' granddaughter, had seven children, including Caligula and Agrippina the younger, the dead mother of our present prince. Death has worked its ravages there too. Claudius married Urgulanilla, Paetina and Messina before choosing his niece Agrippina the younger. His descendants have also disappeared in tragic circumstances.

Antonia the elder – the other daughter of Mark Antony and Augustus' sister Octavia the younger – married L. Domitius Ahenobarbus. They had two daughters, both called Domitia. and a son, Cn. Domitius Ahenobarbus, who was the first husband of Agrippina the younger. Cneius and Agrippina were the parents of our Nero.

Consequently the line of Livia, Augustus' second wife, joined the line of Caesar via the marriage of Drusus to Antonia, the daughter of Mark Antony and Augustus' sister Octavia.

On this family tree, as you can see, some names are marked in black. Those are the names of those men and women who have suffered violent deaths. The legend of the Atrides is small beer compared with the realities of the Julio-Claudian family. You'll find more than thirty distinguished victims here. You will also notice that the present emperor, my nephew Lucius and myself are among the very last to be able to boast of being of Caesar's blood.

Rather than tremble for the fate of a son of my own making, I think it is more reasonable to adopt a boy whom the happy accident of the obscurity of his line will protect from assassination attempts.'

Silanus' reassurance came not a moment too soon. Kaeso had no desire whatsoever to find himself in the middle of the snake-pit of these new Atrides.

To take Silanus' mind off these gloomy obsessions, he said:

'If one is being purely logical, it's difficult to see why people attach so much importance to these genealogical exercises. Given how little virtue women in general seem to possess, isn't the tree simply falsified by cuckoldry from one end to the other?'

Silanus, who had never thought of his tree in this light, had to admit the pertinence of the remark: 'You've put your finger on the crux of the problem. Only a matrilinear system, such as one finds among some distant barbarian peoples, could be guaranteed foolproof. But if the theory behind our system is dubious, the reality of the inheritances which depend on it is tangible.'

After some reflection he added, as he stared at the tree:

'It's almost a pity that there aren't more cuckolds in there. The blood of the *gens*, which has been tainted by all those marriages between close relatives, might perhaps be better. All those people are related to each other in "n" different ways. Augustus married his daughter to his sister's son, then to his stepson. Messala, Octavia's grandson, married one of Octavia's granddaughters. The second Drusus married Claudia Livilla, his uncle's daughter. Tiberius' granddaughter married his great nephew. Cn. Domitius Ahenobarbus, the son of the elder Antonia, married Agrippina the younger, the granddaughter of the younger Antonia. Claudius, before marrying his niece, married Messalina, Octavia's great-granddaughter: he himself was of course a grandson of Octavia. Nero is the great-grandson of Antonia the younger and the grandson of Antonia the elder. Perhaps it's the blood of Mark Antony which puts all those oriental mirages into his head? And I haven't mentioned Caligula's incest with his sisters.

All the great noble families are inextricably interrelated: the Domitii, the Calpurnius Pisos, the Cornelius Sullas, the Anii, the Valerius Messalas, the Manlii, the Quinctii – and the Silani are just like the rest. It was high time for some fresh blood, like yours, to be brought into this tightknit little group of back-stabbers. And as I'm adopting you, I'm sure of one thing at least. Whatever might make me a cuckold, it isn't the fact of your birth!'

Marcia, fresh from a bath and the skilful hands of her masseuses, found the two of them laughing together. She had never been more radiant than she was that fine April afternoon.

She began by scolding Kaeso.

'I asked you to come and see me several times – a visit which only seems natural after such a long separation – but it takes a note from my husband before you actually give us the pleasure of your company. That's not very nice of you.'

'Perhaps he's in love,' said Decimus. 'At Baiae he was terribly sought after. Even my *murenae* welcomed him with open fins.'

Kaeso leapt at the suggestion. The first lie which came to his lips was a quite amusing one. 'I have to admit that I've come across a girl of rare beauty. I stay at home gazing at her. I don't dare to confess my feelings to her, she seems to be made of marble. My father says she's a Greek slave he bought to make his cakes. She's called Selene, and doesn't seem to have a lover as far as I can tell. When the cakes arrive on the table father smiles through his tears. It's the only thing that consoles him.'

Marcia and Silanus were visibly embarrassed, the nobleman looking slightly amused and Marcia somewhat irritated. She reacted first:

'A slave! What a fine prospective conquest! And a marble slave at that. In any case it's quite likely that your father, despite his tears and his greed, has bought her to act as more than a pastry-cook. Take my advice. Do your statue-gazing elsewhere.'

Decimus thought it appropriate to suggest that they go and look at a few statues there and then. They went through to the peristyle, where the rose-garden looked as though it would be lovely when the flowers opened.

Despite his stay in Greece Kaeso could not tell the difference between a masterpiece and the innumerable copies. Though his aesthetic responses were sometimes strong, they were still rather confused. Sensitivity to works of art was widespread among the Greeks, but most Romans, despite the progressive metamorphosis of Rome into a museum-city, had no interest in official art, or only affected an interest in it out of snobbery. This absence of good taste made Nero despair.

Silanus showed Kaeso over the historic house. He was particularly struck by the quantity and quality of the furnishings, which were normally sparse to the point of deficiency even in the houses of the rich. Here there were heaps of fine silver, oil-lamps in solid gold, vases and Greek bronzes of the best period, glass and precious ornaments, beds, cupboards, tables, chests. Every item was worth commenting upon. There were ornamented braziers, armchairs and upright chairs, benches and sofas upholstered in fine leather. There were sumptuous hangings and rare carpets. As they stood in front of a glass case full of cameos Silanus drew his attention to one of those carpets which the Greeks call 'white Persian carpets': it was 600 years old and was made with more than 1,500,000 knots. It apparently took three years' work to complete an intricate piece of work of this kind on the plains of Scythia.

In this respect the house was even more beautiful than the villas at Tarentum and Baiae. Admittedly Cicero's house had become Silanus' permanent residence.

Every now and then, behind her husband's back, Marcia slipped Kaeso an affectionate glance which clearly meant 'Thanks to my hard work and devotion all this will one day be yours.' Kaeso was embarrassed and looked the other way.

At the end of the tour they admired the picture gallery, where Cicero's citrus wood table seemed entirely harmless at that hour of the day. 'I shall also leave you a ghost,' Decimus said, and explained that the sensational apparitions had continued to occur. There had been about a dozen of them, all in the evenings and also involving people other than Silanus. Marcia herself had experienced them.

'Yes,' she said, 'twice. These picturesque visitations help to prove how harmless ghosts are. The dead can't touch or bite. For a tender-hearted, nervous woman that's an essential point. It's of no importance if they impose on you visually or utter a few groans. You can always look elsewhere or shout louder than they do. They're beaten before they start. The last time Cicero came and troubled me I put this bronze bust on his head and he went away. I can't understand why Decimus gets so upset . . .'

Silanus protested. 'I am delighted that you can take the whole thing so coolly. But there's always the possibility that the dead visit us with the intention of communicating some useful message to us. If that's the case, I should like to know what it is. You'll hardly get Cicero to speak more clearly by hitting him on the head with a bronze bust.'

Marcia ran her fingers over the polished citrus-wood surface and sighed.

'I shan't do it again,' she said. 'But I'm not at all certain that it's in your interest to get messages, whether good or bad, from that old chatterbox. In the first place there's no reason to suppose that he can see any more clearly in the infernal regions than we can up here. After all, he has to go round with his head under one arm and his hands under the other. A dead man who wants to make conversation might say anything, just to make himself seem interesting. There's no reason why his wits should be any sharper dead than alive. During his lifetime Cicero made political error after political error, and died as a result of it. That's hardly a good reference for the quality of the information he might be bringing up from Hades for you. And more to the point, you know very well that Rome is full of magicians, astrologers and cheiromancers who use all manner of tricks to make the dead talk. According to the law, that is "illicit super-stition" and a punishable offence. In practice the government doesn't give a damn about such superstition among the *plebs* or its own supporters. But nothing rounds off an accusation of *lèse-majesté* so neatly as a charge of magical practices, thrown in for good measure. The suspect is accused of getting into communication with the spirits of the dead in order to find out the date of the emperor's death or to put a curse on him. In your situation, Decimus, you really don't need to lay yourself open to trouble of that sort. And if you won't take my advice, then at least don't ask too many visitors round!'

Kaeso agreed with Marcia, and Silanus acknowledged that she was right.

As he accompanied Kaeso back, Decimus amiably suggested that for his celebratory banquet, which was to take place in the gardens of his villa on the Pincian, Kaeso might like him to lay on, as a diversion, a fight by a pair of gladiators who could be hired from Marcus' *ludus*. Such a thoughtful suggestion could not be turned down.

Kaeso hurried off to speak to his father about the proposal, and Marcus asked him to go to the *ludus* and make the appropriate arrangements. Since his recent return from Greece, the honorary ephebe had been in such a state of disillusionment and confusion that he had not been back to see his old friends.

The sun was going down. The waiting carts were so numerous until well beyond the Porta Capena that Kaeso took a short cut to reach the *ludus*.

His route lay through anonymous cemeteries reserved for the poor, which were kept even further back from the main road than the most modest of individual tombs. Most of the cemeteries of this kind were just outside the Esquiline Gate, but there were others near all the gates of the city. People did not want to walk a long way just to bury a nobody. All the communal tombs worked on the same principle: there were brick cellars, covered with sealed flagstones which were unsealed and raised so as to throw in the corpses of the poor wretches brought in by night on stretchers. Daytime funerals were forbidden by law, but the rich and the comfortably-off had for a long time been allowed to ignore the fact. Whereas, in the case of the poor, the obscurity of the night matched the obscurity of the dead. It was the lowest class of slaves, the *vespillones* – so-called because they operated at night – whose job it was to feed the cellars. They also called them 'corpse-robbers', because if the families were in the least negligent, they had no scruples about robbing the dead of their shrouds, if they had one, and of the bronze coin which was put into their mouths as payment to Charon, the boatman of Hell, for ferrying them across the Styx. In cases of abnormal death the city reluctantly paid for cremation. The *vespillones* piled the corpses of the dead on great pyres, mixing the bodies of the women in among those of the men because the fair sex had a reputation for burning more easily. When you went through such cemeteries, it became easier to understand why the lower classes and slaves whose masters were poorly off were so concerned about what would happen to their bodies after death, and why they formed themselves into colleges with the stated aim of organizing decent funerals for their members. Often the frightful *vespillones*, left to their own devices, sexually abused the bodies of women and young boys before putting them into the ground.

In the thickening dusk, amid the penetrating smell of death, the *vespillones* were already at work. Kaeso, who was feeling more and more uneasy, was thankful that he had hidden a short sword under his hooded Gaulish cloak and had taken a slave to accompany him.

The *vespillones* were not the only people to be found prowling around the various necropolises. The famished came there to steal the food left out for the souls of the dead. Bands of thieves, who sometimes set up their lairs in the 'sacred woods' around the city where armed police were not allowed to go, were also fond of the cemeteries, where they were confident of not being disturbed, because of the fear which others felt at the proximity of the dead. During the day prostitutes disguised themselves as tearful widows so as to entice anyone naïve enough to offer them consolation into the shadow of a tomb. In the evenings tarts in red wigs appeared all along the Appian Way.

There were also foul witches, looking for bones and magic herbs to make love potions – or brews for evil purposes, if the classic voodoo of sticking pins in a wax model of the victim failed. And among the tombs people hid lead tablets engraved with imprecations of hate against a gladiator, or a rival or competitor of some kind.

The silhouettes of the *ludus* and the neighbouring *columbarium* could already be seen in the distance when, suddenly, four hideous *vespillones* leapt out on Kaeso and his Illyrian slave, who was killed instantly. Kaeso just had time to rid himself of his cloak, make a shield of it with his left arm and seize hold of his sword. He faced the long knives which his would-be killers were handling expertly, holding them up at an angle and pointing them at his stomach. A sword offered only a very slight superiority in these conditions. Kaeso had to keep whirling round anxiously to prevent himself from being taken from behind. He was naturally trying to manoeuvre so that he could open up a way of escape to the nearby *ludus*, but the *vespillones* skilfully blocked off that direction. He did not dare cry out: he was more likely to attract reinforcements for the murderers than assistance for himself.

A very brief space of time passed, though it seemed an age to Kaeso. To his physical fear there was now added a shocking metaphysical fear – fear of finishing his life in the most unexpected and absurd fashion, stabbed by undertakers' men and secretly thrust into a common grave just at the moment in his life when the vista of an existence of quiet reflection and elegant delights was opening before him. So much for the monumental tomb which would have honoured his death! Despite his schoolboy scepticism he offered prayers and promises of sacrifices to all the known gods and even to the unknown god whom the prudent priests had added to the pantheon for fear of leaving anyone out.

This momentary elevation of the soul to the heavens had the same effect on Kaeso as the taking of favourable auspices had on a credulous legionary. He remembered the advice which his father's gladiators had given him when they were teaching him to fence: 'Keep your cool!'

One of the *vespillones*, who was an old man, was limping. Kaeso concentrated on him and eventually succeeded in cutting off his nose with a backward stroke of his sword. The shrieks of the mutilated man distracted his neighbour, and Kaeso ran him through the throat with a thrust as he momentarily turned his head. Courage was not the foremost quality of a *vespillo*, since they were not brought up Roman-style. Accordingly, the three who were still on their feet ran off into the night, and the conqueror hastened on to the *ludus* in a cold sweat and with his heart beating wildly.

At the door of the establishment Kaeso felt faint and had to lean against a wall to recover. He was suddenly aware what an astonishing quantity of heroism and inexhaustible nervous strength the top gladiators possessed. Whether they were slaves or free men they voluntarily exposed themselves day after day, year after year, to this deadly anguish, and thereby set all men the finest example of self-control. Only permanent physical exercise, hard training and an appropriate diet could ensure that the fundamental qualities triumphed in the arena. A drunken, greedy or lazy gladiator did not live long, and such a man's epitaph would list few victories.

Aponius' men were finishing dinner. Kaeso was struck on entering by the acrid smell of the cheap lamp-oil, something he had not smelled since he embarked at Brindisi. He was beginning to lose contact with ordinary people.

But his father's little family of gladiators were worth visiting, precisely because their courage put them a cut above the ordinary, cowardly, cruel *plebs*, of whom the *vespillo*, desecrator of corpses, was almost a symbol. Many Romans found it inexplicable that as a result of watching so many gladiatorial fights the masses did not become more virtuous. Doubtless they were destined to a debasement from which nothing could save them.

Kaeso found his old friends again and met some new ones. He felt a particular pride and joy at having emerged with honour from the horrible experience which he had just undergone. He had now been initiated into danger, and the ordeal had taught him something which the soul of a brave man could never forget. He was relieved to find that Capreolus was still alive.

The *lanista* Eurypylus and his little band were delighted to learn that Silanus wanted a pair of the best gladiators to honour Kaeso on such a solemn occasion. There would probably be a good fee. Everybody knew that the nobleman was anything but stingy. This extra job was particularly welcome, as under-employment was a frequent problem for the men of a relatively obscure private *ludus*. Nero did not even use his own resources to the full, and gladiators were too expensive for most private entertainments.

Silanus – perhaps because of his penchant for fish – had asked for a good *retiarius* if there was one. The best Eurypylus had was Capreolus, who had just won his seventeenth fight. A *retiarius* was usually matched against a specialist fighter called a *secutor* (or follower), because this kind of combat required a very particular technique from both of them. The ludus had two *secutores*, Armentarius ('the cowboy'), a strapping Sardinian freedman, and Dardanus, a free man from Antioch and a very lithe fellow. The two men were of equally high repute – each had won twenty or so victories – but the Sardinian had been with them for two years, whereas the Greek was a newcomer. Capreolus was given the choice between a comrade whose faults and virtues he knew intimately – and vice versa - and an unknown, who might have good or bad surprises in store for him, but whom he would not be tempted to treat gently. After long hesitation Capreolus chose Dardanus.

'The temptation to spare a friend,' he said wisely, 'is all the more dangerous because he may not feel quite the same about you. And we owe it to our patron to stage a fight to remember.'

Since the company of the police was always something to be avoided, Kaeso asked the assembled company to help him bury the dead *vespillo* and the Illyrian who had died in his service. They would have to put them into one of the communal graves. He would have preferred to treat the slave more elegantly, but after all, he was doing him no harm which philosophers would not have found disputable. In practice, however, the *vespillones* had already done what was necessary. Where better to murder people than in the midst of the frightful common graves? It was the perfect setting for the perfect crime.

There was no question of going to stroke the stallions, as it would frighten them at such an hour. Kaeso set out for home, escorted by Capreolus and Dardanus at their insistence.

As they were about to set off for the Appian Way, Kaeso suddenly wondered whether they might not have looked for the two bodies in the wrong place. He was overcome by a desire to check for himself. He found the scene of the attack easily, but the corpses had indeed disappeared. By the pale light of the moon they could just make out a tomb, about 150 feet away, one of whose flagstones had been disarranged. The three men walked silently in that direction and soon caught the sound of stifled moans. Redoubling their care they finally managed to make out Kaeso's *vespillones* in the shadow of the tomb wall. Two of them were trying to dress the face-wounds of the third, having already thrown the two corpses into the underground chamber below.

Without a word Kaeso and the two gladiators drew their swords, leapt upon the three wretches and massacred them before they could even draw their knives. It was just as well the tomb was open that evening!

'That makes two men you've killed tonight. You're becoming quite a professional,' said Capreolus jokingly to Kaeso.

But could they really be called men?

They reached the Appian Way by the shortest route and walked swiftly into Rome. The night was fresh. As they approached the Subura, they made a detour to avoid a band of drunks who were very noisily destroying some shops, when they were not giving the bumps, in a huge cloak, to any odd burghers or tarts they could lay their hands on. Layabouts of this kind were all the more dangerous because Nero, in the first flush of youth, had enjoyed taking part in expeditions of this kind, the proceeds being auctioned for the benefit of charitable works in a room at the palace. One evening the emperor had even been given a black eye by a senator with a bad memory for faces, whose wife he had groped. His imperial despair had been so great that the insolent fellow had felt obliged to cut his wrists as a result. Even Nero could not go singing in public with an eye all the colours of the rainbow. The risk of mistaking the emperor for a thug had reduced victims of nocturnal assaults to a deplorable passivity and discouraged the Watch from taking action.

All three of them reached the entrance to the apartment block without further incident. Kaeso had not dined, so he invited the two gladiators to have a snack in the kitchen while he was eating. Everyone seemed to have gone to bed. While they were crossing the hall, the nightingale on the clock which Marcia had given Marcus for one of his birthdays sounded the fourth hour of the night.

In the kitchen Selene was gloomily waiting for a cake to cook. Capreolus and Dardanus were struck with deep admiration for the slave as she busied herself serving them. The sight of her made them forget to eat and drink.

Kaeso, despite everything, thought of his growing desire for Selene as something shameful, since, until circumstances changed, the hind belonged in his father's private hunting-ground. Suddenly he felt a puritanical need to punish himself by pleasing everyone else. While Selene was whipping up an omelette, Kaeso whispered to Capreolus, who was sitting beside him:

'Do you fancy her?'

'Sure! Especially as she's a Jew like me.'

'A Jew? How can you tell?'

'A Jew can't always tell another male Jew, but he can always spot a Jewess – it's a question of intuition.'

'If you like the idea, my room's over there on the right.'

'What about Dardanus?'

'He's a Greek.'

'So?'

'Doesn't he prefer boys?'

222

'I don't know. He's new. Anyway, he's eating her up with his eyes.'

'With Greeks that doesn't mean a thing. Silanus assured me that all the most beautiful statues of women have been carved by confirmed pederasts.'

'That makes them twice as good! If you'll allow me, I'll just ask the interested party for his views . . .'

After a discreet consultation Capreolus murmured to Kaeso: 'He says he's not a ped. tonight!'

'As the omelette, lavishly peppered and sprinkled with honey and garum, arrived on the table, Kaeso said graciously to Selene:

'I feel that your tireless devotion to my father merits a reward, given the little gratitude he shows you for it. These two magnificent young men have been struck with an overpowering sudden passion for you. Look and see whether the master is sleeping properly, and make the most of the occasion, if Flora and Venus prompt you to it.'

Selene remained bizarrely silent. Some masters did everything they could to prevent their slaves copulating. Others closed their eyes to the most brutal profligacy as long as the household was properly run. Still others mated their slaves against their will so as to rear the products. And others allowed them to live in pairs if they wanted to. But such liberalism was uncommon, and to be given an opportunity for a little sexual pleasure, even if it were a fleeting one night stand, was usually a treat much appreciated by slaves.

Selene's silence grew more and more oppressive. Kaeso had fully understood that the operation inflicted on the girl had reduced her physical sensations, but he assumed that she had enough left to enjoy a Capreolus and a Dardanus. Weren't all girls crazy about gladiators? Even married women . . .

Kaeso's diagnosis, though crass, was physiologically correct. His serious mistake was a psychological one.

Selene took her cake out of the oven and said: 'I'll make love with all three of you together, or not at all. You can see I'm a pastry-cook. I like a juicy little something in my mouth as well.'

It was the turn of Kaeso and his friends to maintain an embarrassed silence. Kaeso's recent allusion to his father had made it plain that he himself could not be included in the party. Selene's obscene joke sounded like an excuse.

Capreolus and Dardanus rapidly withdrew and Selene went on with her act:

'Don't you fancy me?'

'That's not the point and you know it!'

'Do you think I'd have gone back on my word if you'd agreed to the proposal?'

'It wasn't much of a risk, was it! But if I'd given in, you'd have certainly been capable of sticking to your word. You'd have made love with my two friends for the pleasure of being able to make a fool of my father by having sex with me!'

'In either case, then, I get complete satisfaction.'

'I'm not here for you to use for your own ends.'

'And I'm only here to be used by those who paid for me.'

'Suppose that one day I had the money to buy you off my father?'

'Then you wouldn't have to ask my permission before you offer me round your friends.'

'I thought that you might at least fancy Capreolus . . .'

'Why?'

'You don't know what his nationality is?'

'Not a clue, and I don't care either.'

Jews might always be able to spot a Jewess but the reverse clearly did not apply. Perhaps her operation had deprived Selene of more instincts than one . . .

Anything involving Jews was so complicated.

✤ CHAPTER ✤
6

On the great day when he was to put on the *toga virilis* for the first time, a day that every Roman youth awaited with impatience, Kaeso awoke at cock-crow – the tenants on the floor above had a formidable bird on their balcony. He was in a very bad frame of mind. His father was not the man he had thought him. Marcia was perhaps not the woman he had thought her. Selene was not yet what he would have liked her to be. And Silanus was clearly adopting him half to please Marcia and half to protect his lineage – or more precisely his belongings – from the blow he could sense was coming. At least Silanus was a model of honesty and openness compared to the other three. One could only be grateful to him for the fact. Although when you're sitting on a pile worth countless millions, there's less merit in being honest than when you're poor. The occasions when a lie is indispensable are a good deal rarer.

At first light Kaeso went down to the Carthaginian barber to have his hair trimmed and be shaved for the first time. The process was long and boring, and gave him a sinister foretaste of the servitude to which adulthood was subject.

Nero had had his beard shaved off on the day of a great Greek-style gymnastic competition, complete with a grand sacrificial offering of white bulls, and had placed the divine hair in a golden casket decorated with enormous pearls, which he had then dedicated to Jupiter Capitolinus. The emperor had a flair for public display. Kaeso's beard was not going any farther than the Aponius family *lararium*, which was also to receive his *bulla*.

Marcia unexpectedly came round early to see him, so that she could help him wrap himself in the toga which his father, obviously very moved, had just presented to him. The *toga praetexta* worn by adolescents was shorter and narrower than the toga worn by citizens, and was much easier to put on. As she busied herself arranging the cumbersome *toga virilis* with the minute care and attention of an experienced dresser, Marcia was the very picture of happiness and pride.

The reception rooms of the apartment gradually began to fill up. The number of visitors might have seemed surprising if a rumour had not already gone the rounds of the city that Kaeso was shortly to be adopted by one of the most important members of the nobility. People notorious for borrowing money were already there to prepare the ground. So were those who specialized in getting legacies left to them. This was an indefatigable group whose vampiric manoeuvres would go on patiently for years. Some had been known to work for twenty years to inherit a tenth-rate slave or an old stool. They had the details of every fortune in Rome filed away in their cupboards or their heads. There was no household of any importance where they did not try to get a foot in the door. They hung around with the clients, they attended the assumptions of togas, they were present for births, marriages and deaths, and all for the purpose of weaving their intrigues and hatching their plots. The sight of them was the surest indication of social success.

In the old days, Marcus had failed miserably at this particular activity. He felt a certain pleasurable revenge at the sight of the sly, slimy faces of this rabble, who were pretending to go into ecstasies over his furniture.

Exhausted by the crowds, Kaeso withdrew to a bench in the makeshift *atrium*, where most of the visitors did not dare to set foot without a specific invitation. The presence of the altar and the *lararium* gave the reception-room the air of an extremely theoretical *atrium*, making the would-be *atrium* at the centre into a peristyle, a room always regarded as private in a Roman house.

Then a middle-aged woman, dressed to kill, came and sat right beside Kaeso, as though she were trying to share the same ray of sun. Her filmy dress half-revealed a body which was slim to the point of skinniness. Even allowing for the fact that current fashion demanded that breasts be tightly pulled in, he wondered whether the bands of her *strophium* had anything much to flatten. But her hair was artfully dressed and her face well preserved. Too well preserved, perhaps, because beneath her perfume you could detect the clinging smell of make-up made from lanolin (the natural grease of sheeps' wool), a substance which Roman matrons anxious to keep their looks put on their faces at night. The best type of lanolin came from Athens, and Kaeso had become familiar with its smell there, on hetaeras who were starting to go over the hill.

'How handsome you are!' the woman said, rapturously. 'Let me introduce myself. I'm a great friend of Marcia's.'

Though his first, wicked instinct was to baa like a ram, Kaeso pricked up his ears at this piece of information. He had never been allowed to have much contact with Marcia's friends, and as he grew up he had seen gradually less and less of them, as though they were infected with some shameful and contagious disease.

So he replied, very gracefully:

'You could only be a friend of Marcia's. Each one of her friends is even prettier than the next.'

The woman cooed, purred, and poured out her heart to him:

'Do you know, when I was much younger, I sat next to your father at dinner, when Marcia was remarried? What a moving day that was! Your father and Marcia were so well matched: nobility and beauty. Vitellius himself, for all that he's so hard-bitten, was touched by it . . .'

'Had Marcia been married before then?'

'Well now, I wonder . . . perhaps I've got that wrong . . . In her yellow dress and with her bright veil she looked such a slip of a girl. And her father's recent death gave her an unaccustomedly serious air . . .'

Realizing that she had dropped a brick in talking about remarriage, the woman had got herself out of the frying pan only to jump straight into the fire.

Kaeso went on, reflectively:

'Oh yes, her father . . . She did tell me that she lost her father shortly before her marriage. Of course, I hardly knew him . . .'

'Well, you were so young. And of course your father and your uncle Rufus didn't really get on. But let's not talk about that, it's too sad.'

Kaeso could hardly believe his ears. He had to make a superhuman effort to stay cool, as if he were fighting four *vespillones* at once. To make sure that he had understood properly, he said in an offhand way:

'Uncle Rufus can't have been a very attentive father.'

'Oh, he spent money like water. And he didn't make any more provision for his daughter than for himself.'

'But why isn't Marcia called Aponia, from Rufus' patronymic?'

'Even before she remarried she preferred to use her mother's name . . . Before she married, I mean.'

'You must excuse me for leaving you. I have a feeling the procession is getting ready to leave for the Capitol.'

So, after a first marriage of which no one had ever breathed a word to Kaeso, Marcia had married her father's brother. Since she was her husband's niece, that made her not only stepmother to the boys but also first cousin. The news came as a real shock to him. The veil of mystery surrounding Marcia was getting thicker. Why should a young, pretty, brilliant woman have disregarded all the conventions and taken as her second husband a senator who was already middle-aged and had no

227

fortune at all? And having done so, why hadn't she left this lecherous uncle, who was capable of torturing a beautiful slave for his own perverted pleasure? In the key letter which Kaeso had received in Athens, Marcus had modestly suggested that Marcia had only stayed with him because of her attachment to Kaeso and Marcus junior. But would an intelligent woman, with ideas of her own, who found she had made a mistake, sacrifice the rest of her life to her step-maternal affections? Without doubting the quality of the motherly love Marcia bore him, Kaeso became aware for the first time in his life that such a sacrifice would be out of character.

What else had they hidden from him? In the space of a few days he had discovered that he was the descendant of a Greek slave and that his stepmother's marriage was incestuous – not to mention the fact that his father was a lying scoundrel. Was the list of revelations now closed?

Plunged in thought, Kaeso mechanically took his place in the procession and went through the motions of existence as though walking through a fog, until the banquet. He was so abstracted and inattentive that when Silanus was kind enough to join the celebratory party at the altar on the Capitoline, he gave a completely irrelevant answer to something he asked. His abstraction was put down to emotion.

The vast villa on the Pincian was particularly notable for its magnificent gardens, which rivalled the nearby gardens of Lucullus, those of Sallust, between the Pincius and the Quirinal, those of Asinius Pollio and of Cicero's son-in-law Crasipes beyond the Porta Capena, those of Maecenas on the Esquiline, those of Lucius and Gaius on the lower slopes of the Janiculum, those of Caesar and Pompey, also on the right bank of the river opposite the Aventine and the granaries of Sulpicius Galba, those of Scapula and Nero near the Vatican, those of Agrippina which overlooked the Tiber upstream of the Vatican, those of Agrippa himself in the heart of the Campus Martius, those of Drusus and Cusinius and Trebonius and Clodia and many others. To these had recently been added the superb gardens landscaped for the freedmen who were favourites of the emperor. The gardens of the Junius palace on the Caelian, although smaller, were considered equally good.

For generations now every rich and famous Roman had considered himself honour bound to lay out a garden. Many of these masterpieces, where nothing had been spared in the attempt to delight and surprise the visitor, had become part of the imperial estates and were more or less open to the public. Together with the open spaces of the Campus Martius and the many large baths, these gardens provided a much-appreciated compensation for the overcrowded conditions in the multi-storey lodging-houses. In Nero's Rome, with close on one and a half million inhabitants, there were fewer than two thousand private houses as opposed to fifty thousand tenement blocks. No wonder people felt a need to get out into the fresh air.

Silanus and Marcus had invited two hundred people to the banquet to celebrate Kaeso's assumption of the *toga virilis*, as it was also to be the occasion on which the nobleman's intention to adopt Kaeso, now a Roman citizen, would be formally made public. The boy's expensive stay in Athens as an ephebe had given him an aura of well-bred distinction in things sporting, military and intellectual. Four hundred guests turned up. In the end, a quarter of them were turned away.

After a rather cool night a breath of warmth heralding the onset of summer had blown through the city during the day. It was clear that the banquet would take place in the pleasant atmosphere of a warm evening, and the couches had been set up in the gardens in a semi-circle around a sizeable arena, with all Rome as the backdrop.

While the April sun was going down, Kaeso was introduced to all sorts of distinguished people, friends of Silanus or Arval Brethren. Vitellius, who had contrived to worm his way well into Nero's good graces, had consented to put in an appearance, attracted no doubt by the reputation of Silanus' head chef, whose services had only been obtained at phenomenal expense.

'Your stepmother is an absolute treasure, young man,' the enormous Vitellius said to Kaeso. 'Take good care of her, and you may be emperor one day . . . if Nero adopts you, of course.'

Vitellius' jokes always had the same edge to them.

At last, under canopies or in leafy pergolas, the feast began. First there were the usual pious libations, followed by sea-food *hors d'oeuvres* – sea-urchins, oysters, mussels, cockles, limpets, black and white sea-acorns, scallops, jellyfish, and two sorts of purple-fish, accompanied by breast of chicken in a sauce and thrushes on a bed of asparagus. Meanwhile the wine-waiters and servants went round with the aperitif wines.

Kaeso was in the place of honour at one of the *triclinia* with Marcia below him. She had become aware of a change in his attitude which disturbed her deeply, and was making a sterling effort to rouse him from his visible preoccupations. She had no idea what could have caused the change and thought it best to behave as naturally as possible and wait for enlightenment, which the near future would surely bring. Silanus was at a nearby *triclinium*, with Vitellius and Marcus. The conversation between three such different men must have been rather hard going.

Since her 'n'th marriage Marcia was taking propriety very seriously. Accordingly – and with the possible incidental purpose of removing any unnecessary temptations from Kaeso's way – she had made vast cuts in the number of homosexuals in Silanus' service. The squads of young, graceful boys trained up to serve at the *triclinia* had been screened according to criteria which, for want of any better, had had to be based on appearance rather than morals. Inspection of faces had prevailed over inspection of arses, and all those who looked 'the type' had been got rid of. Silanus had not even been able to save a fifteen-year-old called Epictetus, whose intelligence he valued: the boy had been sold to Epaphroditus, one of Nero's most debauched freedmen. Nonetheless the service had retained its remarkable quality. The master's policy, all carrot and stick, was based on the principle that one should be exacting and implacable in everything connected with work, and accommodating in a distant and disdainful fashion about anything else. The important thing for slaves was to know where they stood. So Silanus was better thought of by his *familia* than many other masters who alternated between indulgence and fury in an unpredictable fashion over quite different issues. Admittedly the division and specialization of jobs was such that the work was far from being back-breaking. The situation of urban slaves was in general an absolute dream compared to that of slaves in the countryside. They were even better off than many citizens, whose only capital was a threadbare toga.

Between the *gustatio* of sea-food and the *prima cena*, which was composed entirely of hot entrées, the guests were entertained with poetic intermezzi. An orator gave a declamation in Greek of extracts from the ninth book of the *Iliad*, where Homer instructs his readers how to roast meat properly:

'Then Achilles, by the light of the fire, set up the great table on which to cut the meat. He placed on it a saddle of mutton and a meaty saddle of goat and a good fat chine of appetizing pork. Automedon presented the meats and the divine Achilles sliced them, then cut them into little pieces, which he spiked on skewers. The son of Menoetios, the equal of the gods, stirred up a great fire. Then, when the fire had burned and the flame had died away, he flattened out the hot embers and arranged the skewers on them. Later, lifting the skewers from the fire-dogs, he sprinkled the meat with divine salt. When Patroclus had finished roasting them . . .'

Vitellius, who was now even more partial to the very rare sort of beef which was exclusive to those who shared the tables of the gods, applauded the extract and observed how accurate the advice was. Only roast over the embers, since the slightest flame gives a burnt taste, and salt towards the end of the roasting, after cauterizing the surface of the joint with the heat. But at the same table Petronius was pulling a face over what seemed to him, despite the apparent guarantee offered by the poet's distinction, very primitive culinary habits.

Another orator, this time in Latin, set off on Virgil's second *Eclogue*:

'For the fair Alexis, beloved of his master, the shepherd Corydon burned with a hopeless passion . . .'

The audience knew by heart the passionate laments of the unhappy Corydon, disdained by an Alexis accustomed to the luxury of city life and in no hurry to set up house in a cabin in the country for the pleasure of being screwed by an uncouth yokel. At every *triclinium* the elaborate love-plaints of the naïve Corydon were taken up *sotto voce* by men or women who had experienced similar pangs of unrequited love.

Marcia herself murmured, in time with the artist's warm, subtly-cadenced voice:

'Come to me, handsome child: for you, see how the Nymphs bring full baskets of lilies; for you the white-skinned Naiad, gathering pale gilly-flowers and poppies, brings narcissus and the flower of sweet-smelling fennel; then interweaving them with spurge olive and other scented herbs, she matches the tender whortleberry blossom with the yellow marigold . . .'

And shortly afterwards she murmured more loudly, with her gaze fixed on a Rome set on fire by the dying rays of the sun: '. . . the sun as it goes down makes the shadows longer; yet I am still consumed by love; can love then have an ending?'

Kaeso wondered who Marcia could have loved. In fact her love had never been more immediate than it was at present.

Silanus caught Kaeso's eye and signalled to him that this moving declaration was offered as a homage to his studies. He gave him a little wink as well to show that, where Corydons were concerned, he would perhaps not be as severe as Marcia.

The *prima cena* consisted of pigeon, guinea-fowl and a further selection of sea-foods, this time hot, including octopus and a choice of expensive fish – turbot, hake, gilt bream, sterlet, sea-perch, surmullet and sole, parrot-fish, salmon and John Dory, and even those huge sturgeon from the Po, called *attili*, which were served on vast platters surrounded by salmon trout. All these fish were freshly caught. It was the constant preoccupation of gourmets to relate the excellence of the ingredients to their precise origin, a given creature needing to come from a specific coast, river or lake. So chefs with unlimited funds had no other way of obtaining certain ingredients in a state of perfect freshness than by purchasing them from special suppliers, who had them sent by boat, or overland by cart, in tanks of sea-water lined with lead. Fortunately the enormous increase in fish-farming was reducing the distances involved.

'There are no *murenae*,' Marcia said to Kaeso. 'Silanus is too fond of the monsters to see them devoured under his very nose.'

'Decimus told me that you stroked Agrippina.'

'It's important for a woman to train herself to accept unpleasant physical contact.'

It would have been indiscreet to ask her for more details.

Between these entrées and the *pièce de résistance* of the *altera cena* the guests' appetites were stimulated with a performance by some dancers from Cadiz, wearing virtually nothing but their castanets, who performed among the *triclinia*, the sand of the arena not being suited to their erotic contortions. Only the declining light lent them a little modesty.

The *altera cena* continued by the light of torches and candelabra, which flickered in the evening breeze. Now was the time for sow's vulva and udders, boar's head, pheasant and peacock, hare and wild duck, all served in the most diverse ways imaginable. In honour of Vitellius, Silanus had even managed to get hold, at an extortionate price, of a fatted sacrificial bull worthy of the Arval Brethren. Each guest received a piece roasted in the archaic method prescribed by Homer. The unusual dish caused a sensation.

Towards the end of the third course a troupe of performing dogs appeared in the arena. During their training sessions their feet had been burned with red hot iron. And yet these animals, devoid of all sense of dignity, still came of their own accord and licked their master's hand between tricks. What could be done for creatures like that? They were to the world of quadrupeds what slaves were to the world of bipeds.

The Romans had little sympathy for dogs since the dogs guarding the Capitol had impiously fallen asleep and had nearly let the fortress fall into the hands of the Gauls. Only the cackling of the geese had saved it. In commemoration of the fact, every year on the III of the Nones of August, while the white geese of the temple of Juno, dressed in purple and gold, were borne along in a procession of litters, the same procession carried crucified dogs to the field of execution, near the Palatine bridge, between the Temple of Youth and the Temple of Summanus. The priests of Juno bred dogs specially for the ceremony, a fine patriotic example of grudge-bearing.

After this entertaining display the master and his pupils withdrew to the side of the arena. The master of ceremonies, whose staff had admitted, announced and placed the guests, then informed the audience that the mime artist Terpander, with three colleagues, was going to present an improvisation on a mythological subject, 'The imprudence and punishment of the unfortunate Actaeon' – a surprise guaranteed to disconcert Kaeso.

Terpander was one of the most popular mimes of the moment. His scandals and whims were the talk of the town, but he was forgiven everything because of his talent. It was also whispered abroad that Nero had at one time been fond of his precious person. It was traditional for famous mimes to enjoy the intimate favours of the less virtuous emperors.

In the role of Diana – female roles could not be entrusted to superficial, prattling women – Terpander was indeed quite remarkable. His merit was increased by the fact that the story had been strangely reworked by Silanus to offer the opposite meaning to the traditional version. Thus Terpander lost his virginity in the arms of Cupid, and, quite astonished to see himself visibly swelling up, finally gave birth to a fully-grown, indiscreet Actaeon. The despair of Diana caught in the act, the movement of divine modesty which caused her to transform Actaeon into a stag, his loss of memory and awakening during his mating with the hind, everything was clearly conveyed in perfect detail. A great silence had fallen over the assembled company. People held their breath before a quality of expression which the very absence of speech seemed to push to the ultimate. The only sound to be heard was sweet, plaintive music which accompanied the scenes in the woodland grove. At the end the performing dogs devoured Actaeon.

The charm of the ballet was broken by frenetic applause. A subject of that kind, which no one ever mentioned, was surely exceptionally serious, exceptionally fraught with the most significant consequences for the education and development of us all?

Decimus looked pointedly at Kaeso again and the look was as expressive as one of Terpander's. 'Look out!' it said. 'I'm telling you again, through the medium of a talent far greater than my own, that a woman's and a mother's secrets are for her husbands and her lovers and are none of her son's business. Don't try to lift the veil.'

Silanus could not have been more perceptive, thoughtful or fatherly in the best sense of the word. It was unfortunate that circumstances were against him.

Now the *mensae secundae* or dessert arrived, with a range of cakes, custards, exotic fruit and original *pièces montées* (cakes and puddings shaped to resemble other objects), while the aperitif wines gave way to the finest vintage wines.

Rather than make an impression by the number of courses or the extravagance of the dishes, Silanus preferred to stick to the four standard courses and solidly classical recipes at his receptions. But the succulence and variety of the food was absolutely top-class. Every guest, with such a wide choice before him, could work within the limits of his own appetite and compose the menu which he himself wanted. A Seneca could have dined on three sea-urchins, a little asparagus and a pear, washed down with pure water.

Extra lights were being set up around the arena in preparation for the fight. Marcia, who had been unmoved by the art of Terpander, became more animated, her eyes sparkling. She adored gladiators. Her excitement reminded Kaeso of the women at Baiae when they were faced with the sharp mouths of Silanus' *murenae*. All the comparison needed, to be complete, was for the excitement to be resolved in sexual submission. It was not thought proper for respectable Roman women to go to the theatre, where the pornographic plays were too crude, but attendance in the amphitheatre was considered compatible with their virtue and their desires. Although cruelty was in principle a bracing spectacle for the strong, in practice women, children and slaves, all those humbled in life by nature, rank or accident of fate, found in it a recompense for their own misfortune. Women, who shed their own blood to the cyclic rhythm of the moon, enjoyed the sight of male blood being spilled.

Gladiatorial combat was always accompanied by music, and a small orchestra had taken up its position on the right of the arena. There were horns and trumpets, which were military instruments, but there were also a few flutes, which normally accompanied boxing bouts, and a hydraulic organ, a novelty which had carved itself pride of place at *munera*. Once the heavy instrument was installed, the virtuoso who was to play it tried out a few chords to ensure that everything was in order. She was a frail, ethereal young girl, who made a pleasant contrast with the violence about to be unleashed.

The musical accompaniment to a *munus* required plenty of experience and talent. There were set pieces, such as the overture and the music for the dead, but the accompaniment to the fighting itself involved a certain amount of improvisation, related to the type of weapons used and the incidents occurring. Good orchestras even knew how to use anguished silence and pregnant pauses at the most effective moments. It was no longer a question of Orpheus charming the wild beasts. He encouraged them to unleash their most savage instincts.

At last the fanfare rang out, sustained by the powerful voice of the organ and accompanied by the shrill song of the flutes. Capreolus and Dardanus made a prompt appearance, coming into the arena side by side, as on the evening when they had brought Kaeso back to his house. In front of them came a well-known referee with his baton. The leading referees were always freed men, members of grandiose 'colleges', who felt themselves untouched by the supposed dishonourable status of gladiatorial combat.

As the occasion was a private one and the combatants relatively unknown, the referee chose to give a brief introduction, stressing the number of victories each had won. Then the adversaries saluted Silanus, who was 'presiding' over the occasion, one using his trident and the other his sword. At a signal from the referee's baton they took up battle stations.

To increase the interest of such confrontations the rules laid down that the combatants should each use a different sort of weapon. A fight between a *secutor* and a *retiarius* was the perfect illustration of the point. Stripped to the waist, bare-legged and bare-headed, the *retiarius* had no protection but a piece of jointed armour around his left arm, topped with a broad epaulette which formed a small shield. He was armed only with a trident and a net – the knife at his waist was simply there so that he could dispatch his victim promptly. The *secutor* wore a helmet covering his whole face, very simple in design, and its absence of ornament made a great contrast with the fantastic filigree work on other armour. He could see the *retiarius* only through two round holes pierced in his lowered visor, which looked like the hypnotic gaze of a huge and deadly beast of prey. He had a supple guard on his right arm and a round shield to defend his left side, and in his hand he carried a short sword. Some of these swords had a sharpened hook at their tip, which was supposed to allow the *secutor*, when caught in the net, to cut his way out with the blade more easily – if he had the time. But the advantage was extremely theoretical, and a hook made stabbing thrusts less effective. Dardanus preferred straight blades. A *secutor* wore no shin guards on his legs, to leave them unhampered as he ran, but this also left them exposed to cunning blows from the long trident.

The net was even more of a danger to him than the prongs of the trident. So, by pretending to open himself up unwisely, the *secutor* had to incite the *retiarius* to a bad throw, then profit from the fact that the net was for a brief space of time unusable to seize a decisive advantage. The *retiarius*' tactic, in contrast, was only to throw the net when he was absolutely sure of finding his mark, so that he could massacre the *secutor* while he was caught up in its links. Otherwise he had to rely on the swiftness of his running to find time to get the net back into his hand in such a way that he could stage a counter-attack. These reciprocal attacks and feints, as carried out by trained specialists, were irresistibly interesting. Many people who made a show of philosophical disdain for gladiatorial combat found that they were captivated, as though in a tragic net, by the bloodstained grace of the spectacle. Even old Seneca went to the amphitheatre just often enough to be able to disparage it elegantly.

At each *triclinium* bets had been laid. Most people backed the *secutor* to win, because the arena was thought to be too small to guarantee the *retiarius* the necessary breathing space. Capreolus was perfectly well aware of the fact, and could win only by exceptional skill and prudence.

The trumpets and horns fell silent while the flutes and organ played a discreet, dancing tune: the combatants were observing one another. Capreolus shortened the reach of his trident to encourage Dardanus to come in too close, but the Greek was circling him at a respectful distance. The crowd finally began to get impatient with all these precautions. 'Are you trying to catch him alive?' Marcia called out to Capreolus, amid a burst of laughter. Dardanus made a sudden attack but was repulsed by a brutal trident-blow on his helmet, which rang like a bell. Changing direction in a flash the trident suddenly pinned the Greek's left foot to the ground, where the light garden soil had been covered for the occasion with a very thin layer of sand. It was only then that the net closed over the whimpering Dardanus. Everybody applauded the pretty manoeuvre. With remarkable coolness Capreolus had kept his net back until he was absolutely sure to find his target. A little luck had come to the aid of consummate skill.

Without losing his self-control the Jew allowed himself a moment to think. Being unable to raise his hand to ask for mercy, Dardanus could have dropped his sword and shield as a sign of his intentions. But with Stoic determination he remained fully armed, pinned to the ground under the net and holding in his cries of pain. To finish the Greek off Capreolus needed to take his trident out, since his knife would not be enough in the present situation. However, by a piece of bad luck, two of the prongs of the trident had gone round Dardanus' heel, and his foot was only superficially wounded.

During this immensely touching moment of tense expectation, the trumpets and horns joined in again and the little organist really let herself go with the special effects. It was even more moving than Virgil's pederastic poetry.

Capreolus finally decided to take his trident out. But capricious fate turned against him. As he withdrew it, the trident caught on the net, the Greek twisted himself neatly out of it, and despite his wounded foot, hurled himself at the *retiarius*. Capreolus found himself with his trident tangled up in his net, and fled, trailing both behind him. In the chase Dardanus' good foot stumbled on the net by accident. and instead of the net coming off the trident, it was the trident which fell out of the Jew's sweaty grasp. All resistance was now impossible. Capreolus immediately knelt on the sand and raised his hand, trying to look proud and dignified, while his eyes desperately sought Kaeso's.

The referee had put his baton between the two opponents and the orchestra had fallen silent. It was the moment which Romans of both sexes awaited with the greatest pleasure.

Out of politeness the well-bred audience was looking to see what Silanus' decision was before expressing its own. An equal politesse inclined the giver of the *munus* towards the death of the loser, to show that one more financial sacrifice for the good of his guests was neither here nor there. A corpse was much more expensive than the hiring fee. After a moment's hesitation Silanus decided to hand over his authority to Kaeso. The boy made a pretence of hesitating himself, for form's sake, then gave the thumbs up to indicate mercy. Most of the spectators followed his example. There were some who protested that the fight had been too short, but loud applause covered the muttering. The orchestra burst into a swift jolly march instead of the lugubrious strains of the death-call. Dardanus limped out of the arena leaning on Capreolus' shoulder, an image of brotherhood-at-arms which, paradoxically, was only belied at the moment when the weapons themselves gave testimony.

All the lights around the arena were put out and a new spectacle caught their attention for a moment. Rome on a clear spring night. Beyond the shadowy spaces of the Campus Martius they could see, directly opposite, the silhouette of the fortress on the Janiculum, and to the left the outlines of the Capitol and the Quirinal. The old city was shot through, at this hour, with lights from the torches and lanterns of nocturnal travellers, and in such of the lowest parts of the city as could be seen from high up on the Pincian a few apartment blocks on fire added their red and smoky glow. A rather larger blaze was ravaging part of the Trans Tiberim. But Silanus' guests were only heedful of the pleasure of the vast panorama.

They gave no thought to incidents as common and insignificant as a fire. They lived in houses isolated by their gardens and defended against fire by the Watch and by the ever-vigilant private fire-brigades. Only fires on an unusually large scale would be a cause of any concern to them.

Silanus had fresh wines served and the young slaves snuffed out a number of lamps and torches around the *triclinia*. After such a successful feast it was very pleasant to turn one's back on general conversation and get into more intimate chat with the man or woman beside one. The wine made them even more charming in the gentle half-light.

'I'd like to make you a present of the whole of Rome,' said Marcia to Kaeso.

'If that's our house burning down there in the Subura, the whole of Rome would suit me nicely.'

'From now on the Subura doesn't matter any more.'

As she lay there in her spotless, filmy *synthesis*, flushed with excitement from the fight – and possibly from one or two drinks over the odds as well – Marcia had never been more beautiful. Like many high-class whores she was as particular about her personal cleanliness as a cat. Her intense joy at Kaeso's success gave her charming face a special and touching radiance. Her eyes were lifted to her son in adoration.

Suddenly, Kaeso felt as if Capreolus had planted his trident in his heart. That humble, affectionate look, so full of admiration, devotion, abandon and promise – he knew it, he recognized it. He had seen it on the face of Hegesippos, a graceless ephebe who had pressed him, pestered him and stuck to him until his suicide by drowning, which had been passed off as an accident, had freed Kaeso of his attentions. It was a look of passionate love, a love all the more serious and irremediable because desire was ultimately no more than a small though ineradicable part of it.

Marcia's eyes had already concealed the truth again, but it was too late. Now Kaeso knew. He was terrified. All the secrets from which Marcia had protected and cradled him, all the secrets of the past, present and future, were nothing compared to this, the secret which had bred all the rest and which would soon engender new lies. He had just found Diana sporting with Cupid, and Cupid was none other than himself!

Marcia took his trembling hand and said:

'What's made you tremble like this, so suddenly, on such a fine evening? If a shadow's pursuing you, at least try to describe it to me. Then I can dispel it, as I used to do when you were little.'

'I suddenly had the feeling that you . . . loved me too much.'

'Well, it's the first time a man has ever reproached me for that,' retorted Marcia, laughing.

It was probably the first time, too, that she had ever told the truth.

The situation was intolerable. Kaeso swiftly found a pretext to take leave of his stepmother, and went to thank Silanus and bid him goodnight. Decimus was in conversation with his nephew Lucius and Petronius: Vitellius and Marcus were exchanging noisy pleasantries. Before leaving Kaeso spontaneously whispered to a somewhat startled Decimus: 'Well, *I'll* never betray you.' Recovering from his surprise, Decimus simply said: 'Betray me for a good cause instead, and we can stay friends.'

Kaeso could not get to sleep all night. Sometimes he felt that it was all a nightmare; at others implacable reality took its place, every doubt vanished and he saw himself trapped.

By dawn he was still caught between the certainty of lightning intuition and reasonable doubt.

CHAPTER
7

Such a crucial doubt, once planted, developed like a fever. It urged him to set all modesty aside and demanded to be clarified as soon as possible. The date of the miraculous adoption depended on the solution to the problem. It had been fixed for the Kalends of May, and there were only ten days left till then. Silanus was determined to celebrate the adoption then, because it was the date of the spring Laralia, dedicated to honouring the *lares* who protected the city of Rome. They had a shrine locally. Silanus' entirely political piety never wavered.

But how was he to find out the truth? If he put Marcia to the test by declaring a sudden passion for her, and if she was pure of any concealed incestuous attentions, he would find himself in an impossible situation, in which odium and ridicule would be finely balanced. If Marcia was in love with him, she would have been jealously guarding her secret for so many years that she would not give it away without unpleasant manoeuvres in which Kaeso ran a grave risk of losing face before she did.

However much he racked his brains to devise a way out of the impasse, Kaeso had to admit that the wall was still up and that he was likely to run out of ideas long before there was any probability of his undermining it. He needed advice from a new source. But who could he turn to in a matter where the slightest indiscretion might have incalculable, unforeseen consequences? Given the circumstances the only person he could rely on was his brother Marcus, but he was a thousand miles away.

In his distress it suddenly occurred to him that Selene was a solitary type, who seemed to despise men and trust nobody. And being a Jewish Greek (or a Greek Jewess?) she was not short of perception, finesse, and an eye for the relevant detail. She was a slave, it was true. Female slaves were supposed to be less reliable than males. but as they were slaves you had a hold over them through fear or personal advantage, and as they were women you had an emotional hold on them too. And Kaeso's relationship with the young woman had taken on a certain intimacy, which, however strange it was, ought to make an exchange of confidence and advice easier. And then again, he had put his hand between her legs and had tried to arrange a little pleasure by proxy for her. That sort of thing brings people together despite everything.

Despairing as to what he should do, as the dawn light filtered into his room, Kaeso tossed a bronze coin. He had decided that if fate brought the coin down showing the double face of Janus, he would make no approach. But the coin was showing its obverse, decorated with the prow of a ship in memory of the arrival of Saturn in Latium. The gods had declined ambiguity and granted the advantage to action, under the aegis of the most Roman god of them all.

Selene was not in her room. He asked a slave, who pointed to Marcus' room as he passed. Through the door he could hear Marcus' loud snores. He must still be in a drunken stupor. Only the four outer doors were protected by locks – very complicated ones at that – not to mention their bolts. Kaeso gently eased the door open a crack. His father was lying on his bed asleep. Selene, wrapped in a blanket, had taken refuge on the bedside rug, where she was sleeping peacefully with her head on a cushion. The noises in the street outside, which were beginning to break out, seemed not to trouble her slumbers. Her master had probably prevented her from sleeping for a good part of the night.

Kaeso was disconcerted by the sight of the half-naked girl, but at that moment Selene, disturbed by the cries of a cheese-merchant who was coming up the alley with his goats, stretched, uncovered herself completely, and observed without surprise the head of the young man who was staring at her round the half-opened door. Kaeso signalled to her to come and join him. She got up nonchalantly and put on her housecoat and slippers. She seemed quite unconcerned by her nudity.

When the door was shut again she said to Kaeso:

'Last time you wanted me to make love with two gladiators. Now you want to watch me sleeping with your father. What are you, a virgin or a pervert? You don't suppose you can get that sort of thing for nothing nowadays, do you?'

The conversation blessed by Saturn which Kaeso had been promising himself was starting badly. He hurriedly corrected her unfortunate mis-apprehension and led her into the rooms opposite. When the slaves were moved to an upper floor of the building, they had been converted into a rest-room for Marcia and a bathroom. At this time of day they were empty.

They sat down in a sort of boudoir which lay between Marcia's former bedroom and the would-be *atrium*.

'What did you want to talk to me about?' asked Selene. 'You look like a child who has seen a spook in his sleep.'

'The spook is real flesh-and-blood and it's eating my heart out.'

Kaeso expatiated on the situation at some length in fluent Greek, with full details. The confession made him feel better. Selene listened to him with an attention which seemed largely sympathetic. He finished: 'You confided some sad facts to me the other day. I'm doing the same to you today. Like you I'm subject to a cruel fate which leaves me little room for manoeuvre. Inside I'm completely convinced that my stepmother's feelings towards me aren't what they should be, but I have to admit that I have absolutely no proof. I've got to be absolutely sure one way or the other in the next few days, because the date for my adoption is fast approaching. I have a duty towards Silanus, who has never been anything but kindness itself towards me. I can't repay that kindness by bringing down scandal on his house. In the name of all the gods how am I to find out the answer to something which matters so much to me?'

After a moment's reflection Selene declared:

'It's quite simple. You must use the kind of device a playwright uses to get the action moving when it's stuck. A phoney letter, for example. That works every time.'

Very doubtfully Kaeso asked Selene to explain. She did so with the utmost clarity.

'Have you ever written to Marcia in Greek?'

'Never. She doesn't know the language perfectly, although she's made a lot of progress in it. She finds it difficult to write a correct letter in it.'

'She wouldn't recognize your Greek handwriting, however individual it may be?'

'Absolutely not. But what's the point of the question?'

'Suppose that I give some messenger or other – someone that Silanus' slaves won't recognize – some tablets sealed with your seal, to be left with their gateman. And suppose I've filled these tablets with a declaration of love in Greek, in my handwriting. Two things can happen. Either Marcia is possessed by Eros, in which case she'll leap on your neck. Or her feelings are purely maternal, in which case she'll make indignant protests. In both cases you pretend that you don't know what she's on about. Once she has explained, you affirm that the note isn't in your handwriting. You maintain that someone with a grudge against you must have borrowed your seal while you were asleep, with a view to playing an unpleasant practical joke on you. Whatever happens, you come out of the terrible interview with your hands clean. Marcia has to give herself away. She has

242

no reason to suspect a trick, and even if she has the slightest suspicion about you afterwards, I'll always be there to dispel it. Can you think of a better solution?'

Kaeso was dumbstruck at the swift and effective simplicity of the ploy, which was like something straight out of a play. Clearly it was just what he needed. Feeling as though a huge burden had been lifted from him he kissed Selene. 'The use of your seal,' she went on, 'and the fact that I'm the only person in the house apart from the master who can write fluent Greek, will point the finger of suspicion at me immediately and expose me to Marcia's hatred. I'd bet that when Marcia's angry, she'd go to any lengths to get her revenge. Will you be able to protect me?'

Kaeso had been asking himself the same question. It was a very embarrassing point.

Selene went on: 'Naturally Marcia's revenge would have nothing, ostensibly, to do with the writing-tablets. In either of the circumstances envisaged. She wouldn't say a word about them to anyone, for her own sake and for the sake of plenty of others. But she could harm me in some roundabout fashion on some trumped-up pretext, as soon as she had the opportunity. My only protection would be in your hands.'

'Why?'

'Whether she's innocent or guilty Marcia won't move a step if – out of affection for me – you threaten to divulge the whole business to Silanus. If she *is* in love with you, the revelation of her depravity would be a catastrophe for her. If she's innocent, the whole story is calculated to put unnecessary ideas into her husband's head. And you're in a position to carry the threat out whether Silanus adopts you or not.'

Kaeso thought the plan over, then remarked:

'If Marcia is in love with me, I should feel I had a good excuse to defend you. But if she's innocent, I wouldn't have any valid excuse in her eyes. Even if one accepts the first hypothesis – let alone the second – by defending you I shall make myself look like your accomplice.'

'That's a risk you'll have to take if you want to get to the bottom of things and protect my interests at the same time. But your Marcia's as guilty as hell in any case.'

Kaeso started: 'What makes you say that?'

'I'll say it in Latin. *In vino veritas*. When the master's drunk, he sometimes lets slip significant remarks. He's suspected something for ages, and it makes him jealous. But since he's no more proof than you have, he pushes the whole thing to the back of his mind. The fact that you and he should come up with the same suspicion is too much of a coincidence. It's a thousand to one against innocence. My money's on love. And what's more, in this little episode it's love and the secrecy it imposes which offer me the greatest protection – for as long, at least, as you're willing to play your part.'

Kaeso thought hard, then, desperate to find out the truth once and for all, swore by all the gods to protect Selene as if she were the apple of his own eye.

Following her idea through, the young woman went a step further: 'The day when Silanus loses interest in Marcia my life won't be worth an *as*. I only have one life, and I'm not keen to lose it.'

However hard Kaeso maintained that Marcia's charms could perform miracles, he could not guarantee that they would work for ever.

'I'll just have to take my chance,' said Selene. 'Rumour has it that it won't be long before Silanus joins his brothers, and when noblemen cut their wrists it's the done thing for their wives to follow suit. But I can't absolutely rely on Nero, and there's still a risk that you can't guarantee to protect me from. In case of trouble it would be very useful to have some money put aside . . .'

Kaeso had managed to save about 120,000 sesterces from his allowance and his travelling costs. Diogenes' 100,000 sesterces ended up in Selene's pocket.

'You're a good businesswoman,' Kaeso acknowledged. 'But as you're a slave, how are you going to go about safe-keeping a sum of that size? I doubt whether any honest temple would accept responsibility for it if you tried to deposit it.'

'I shall leave it with a holy man of my own religion.'

'Are you sure you can trust him? Priests are such thieves.'

'Not ours. Anyway, I trust you.'

'What makes you think I'll protect you as promised?'

'My knowledge of men, and my physical charms . . . Bring me the writing-tablets and a stylus.'

Selene felt a warm thrill of satisfaction at the thought of getting her revenge on Marcia, who had whipped her and sexually abused her. At each blow of the lash she had prayed to Yahwe for vengeance. The day had arrived sooner than expected. It was worth running a few risks for such a pleasure – not to mention the 100,000 sesterces.

Kaeso and Selene briefly discussed the language of the letter. Selene could clearly only allude to ideas and facts which she could have picked up from an over-confiding Kaeso. The false letter had to have a basis in credibility.

Kaeso willingly furnished all the necessary information. Selene wrote accordingly:

'K. Aponius Saturninus to his beloved Marcia, greetings.

Now that I am about to come and live with you for ever, I must confess to you why none of the boys in Athens took my fancy, why I never spent more than one night with any hetaera, why I find all Roman prostitutes devoid of attraction and all Roman girls insipid. I am in the grip of a more powerful passion, and have been since my childhood. For a long time it was a 'love that dared not speak its name', but since I returned from Greece, it has taken on your face and your voice, saying to me 'Kaeso, you and I are inseparable.' This confession has obliged me to look clearly at myself. If there is a woman in the world worth all the rest put together, a woman in whom the qualities of all women are summed up, a woman without whom life would not be worth living, that woman is you, the model of grace and generosity. Everything I have came from your hands. My hands are here to cherish you and to give you back everything I ever took from yours. But how can I ever discharge my debt to you? Be indulgent to my youthful clumsiness. Oh, why have my eyes taken so long to open? How joyfully I would have stayed faithful to you while I was in Athens, if only I had understood. Write to me at once and tell me where and when I can belong to you entirely. My love for you is a wound, a whip and a well of delight. I wish long life to your beauty and peace to your heart.'

Kaeso found all this talk of wounds and whips excessive, but Selene swore to him that lovers habitually talked that way. He was so anxious to find out the truth that the dishonourable nature of the trick caused him only a slight feeling of embarrassment.

On reflection Kaeso told himself that, all the same, Marcia had never admitted anything. However much she were in love with him, there was no guarantee that she had any intention of changing her tactics. On the other hand, even if she were impatient to reveal the truth, she would certainly wait for the adoption to be completed, so as to have Kaeso to hand and under her spell. This last consideration was sufficient to mitigate a natural feeling of shame.

By mid-afternoon there had been no reply. Kaeso, who was becoming very anxious, decided to pay a visit to Marcia's supposedly bosom friend, to whom he already owed such momentous revelations. If he could make her talk more, he would be in a much better position when he had to turn up at his critical confrontation with Marcia. He found out that the woman, whose name was Arria, lived alone, with a few slaves, in a small house on the Viminal, in the heart of the VIth district, Alta Semita, between the place where the third company of the Watch was posted and the former ramparts of Servius. Time was short and Kaeso set off for the house on the offchance of finding her at home.

It was hot along the shaded rocky paths of the old quarter of the Viminal, and Kaeso was glad that he had come out just in his tunic. A passer-by finally pointed the house out to him. It was a modest little villa, half hidden amid the greenery of an equally modest and rather poorly kept up garden. Kaeso opened the garden gate, went up to the door and knocked. He was just coming to the conclusion that the house was empty when he heard a whining male voice, apparently coming from the rear, calling: 'Lady, lady! They're goin' t' be frozen off!' And Arria's voice calling back: 'Just a little longer, Arsenus.'

Intrigued, Kaeso went round the house to the right, crossed a kitchen which opened straight onto a hen-house, and found himself face to face with the afore-mentioned Arsenus. If you can call it 'face to face' when their necks were at such different heights. The slave was stark naked and up to his neck in the cold bath of a rudimentary set of baths whose boiler was in any case not lit. From the look of the flushed face of the big red-headed Gaul, it looked as though the bath was part of some medical treatment or other. At the sight of Kaeso Arsenus hurriedly called out: 'Lady, a noble visitor for you!' Kaeso called out his name and Arria asked him to wait a moment. Shortly, with an air of delight, she opened the door herself and showed him into a room cluttered up with sofas and cushions and smelling strongly of sweat and musk. In the half-light Arria's loose-cut dress looked like a sack hanging on a stake.

Kaeso knew that he wouldn't get anywhere if he just baldly stated the object of his visit. He realized that if he wanted to get anything out of her, he had no option but to pretend that he had come to flirt with her. But it was rapidly made clear that his hostess wanted something more than flirtation. As she would have been terribly put out if he refused to go the whole way, all Kaeso could do was give in. The lady was really extremely slim, and her sexual athleticism was not sufficient compensation for the lack of tangible physical attractions. Her bony pubes and breasts like fried eggs positively turned him off. Despite his natural courtesy and good will Kaeso made a bad job of it, and although Arria was not exactly cross with him, she was disappointed, to say the least.

Consequently Kaeso could get nothing interesting out of Marcia's great friend. Though she had been ready to open her legs to him, she was as closed as an oyster when it came to opening up her heart. It was as if she wanted to pay him back for the lack of pleasure which he had brought her by keeping silent or making inconsequential chitchat.

As she was seeing him out, Arria gave him a sort of motherly look and said:

'They say a great destiny awaits you, but Fortune is capricious. One day, perhaps, all you'll have to help you on in life is your charm and beauty. That day, everything will depend on your ability to inspire a lasting passion for you in some woman. You appreciate that if you don't perform better with her than you did with me, you can't expect to hope for much.'

'Forgive me, please. Despite appearances I have a lot on my mind at the moment.'

'But it's precisely the men who are thinking of something else who give one the most satisfaction.'

'That's a strange paradox!'

'What a child you are! You need some advice. Won't you let me fill in the gaps in your education? A man doesn't hook a woman by giving her a bit of acute but superficial pleasure. What really gets women going is a deep, indescribable pleasure, something so strong it makes them positively pass out. Not every woman achieves that degree of pleasure, and for those that do, it's usually a very lengthy process. Once a woman has experienced it, all she wants to do is experience it again, because her pleasure outstrips her partner's by miles. So it's absolutely essential that if a man can't get it up again quickly, and often, he should be able to hold off his climax for a long time. Do you understand?'

'Oh yes, absolutely. But how?'

'While you're making love, never think of the woman you're with. Count sheep or goats. Hold back as long as you can. And when you think you're coming, go and jump in a cold bath.'

The image of Arsenus in his bath flashed into Kaeso's mind and he could not stop himself from bursting out laughing.

'Well,' said Arria, 'that Gaul is much better at it than you are. And just as well too. I can only afford one slave suitable for the job, and I have to squeeze him absolutely dry. Arsenus thinks of Caesar's siege of Alesia, and a bath or two to relax his tension and keep him on form doesn't do him any harm. He's a very devoted boy.'

Thanks to Arsenus Kaeso finally withdrew in a relatively good mood, but his mood soon darkened again. On reflection it was scandalous and disturbing that only well-trained slaves could bring a woman real and repeated pleasure. What free man would happily submit himself to such ridiculous, degrading gymnastics? Perhaps the Greeks were right, and sexual relations in marriage could only be disappointing.

Another point for gloomy reflection also struck him. Marcia had some pretty odd fish among her friends. Probably there were plenty of married women in Rome who slept with their slaves: the laws designed to combat the offence had little effect. Often enough in the leafy heart of the Campus Martius or of some garden you'd see a huge closed litter, surrounded by an odd number of muscular litter-bearers standing with their arms folded, while their invisible missing comrade, enfolded in his mistress's arms, was screwing away behind the closed curtains. Each of them would take turns to pleasure their mistress, before they had to go and take their master off to work. Admittedly excesses of that kind inevitably stained a reputation. An honest woman would refuse to be seen in the company of anyone so utterly shameless.

When Kaeso got back to the house, he found that the tablets had got back before him. Marcia had prudently erased Kaeso's compromising text with the flat end of the stylus and had written in its place:

'Marcia to Kaeso, greetings.

Tomorrow morning I shall be at the house of my friend Arria on the Viminal. Going up from the Subura you will find it just beyond the place where the third company of the Watch is stationed. There is a large poplar in the garden. Fare well.'

Selene was triumphant, but Kaeso, who was in such a state of turmoil he had had difficulty breaking the seal, was overcome with distress. His intuition had been right.

The following day was the festival of the Vinalia. While the great procession of prostitutes was in full swing in front of the temple of Venus at the Porta Collina, Kaeso was standing outside Arria's house at the appointed time. He had never thought that he would see Arria again, and certainly not so soon. He found it very disagreeable that the rendezvous should have been fixed for a place whose claim to fame was the exploits of an Arsenus, not to mention his own fiasco. But, for the purpose Marcia had in mind, the spot was certainly well chosen and Arria's discretion reassuring. To give the encounter a more dignified tone Kaeso had put on his new toga, which he thought would also provide him with a degree of physical protection. It would be difficult for a woman to commit an effective sexual assault on a boy in a toga who clung determinedly to the symbol of his manhood.

Marcia herself opened the door to him. 'The slaves are at the market and Arria is out visiting,' she said, in a completely natural voice. And with no more ado she led Kaeso through to the little room with which he was already familiar. Gentle April light was filtering through the half-opened shutters. She sat down and said tenderly: 'You have taken enough time to realize that you're the only man in my life, that I only breathe through you and for you. Come and sit down, and let me touch you the way you've given me the right to . . .'

Now was the time to play dumb. Kaeso did his best. The mis-understanding was dispelled in a few words, Selene implicated, and Kaeso found himself standing there, staring bemusedly at a woman in a cruel state of shock who had just revealed her true feelings to him by accident.

'Well,' she finally said, after a long silence, 'now at least we both know where we stand. Selene is a perceptive go-between who has seen through me in a bizarre fashion. But was she wrong about you?'

Kaeso said that the revelation was so abrupt, so unexpected, that he needed time to get used to it and decide how he should behave.

'If you need time to know whether you love me or not, your love is a very timid thing compared with mine.'

Kaeso found that he was tying himself in knots every time he tried to speak. He took the easy way out and started to ask Marcia questions. His legitimate curiosity was, moreover, insatiable.

'You've been living with this passion for years, but I've only just found out about it. It would be rather frivolous of me to enter into a very serious relationship with someone dear to me when I'm only just re-covering from my surprise at the revelation. But there's more to it than that. We're not on an equal footing. You know everything about me, whereas I know next to nothing about you. A stepson can reasonably be expected not to know a lot of things about his father's wife. A future lover ought to know all about everything, oughtn't he? You wouldn't want me to make love to a stranger.'

'I admit that would be presumptuous on my part. What do you want to know?'

'Silanus told me the story of the slave Aponios, which doesn't directly concern you, of course. Selene admitted that she was a present from Silanus to my father to compensate for your departure, which concerns you even less. But Arria accidentally revealed, without any malice afore-thought, that your marriage to my father wasn't your first, and that you were his niece. You have to admit that that's all rather disconcerting.'

'I agree entirely. You're old enough now to understand that there are white lies which for a long time are to the advantage of both parents and children.'

'Of course. The lies were all told for my own good. But now it's not my stepmother talking to me; it's a woman who has a rather different kind of relationship in view.'

'From now on I shan't hide anything from you. I swear by all I hold dear that I'll answer all your questions perfectly frankly. But I think you've already been told the essential points of what we've tried to keep from you for as long as possible.'

'How can I be sure?'

Marcia took off her shawl and leaned back on the cushions, with her dress pulled up a little and her breasts half-revealed, in the languorous, patient pose of a woman preparing to satisfy an indiscreet questioner at great length.

'How many times have you been married?'

'Four, including Silanus. I married a knight, a rather boring man, when I was still very young. Women are still deprived of one freedom, perhaps the one that means the most to them, the freedom to choose their first husband for themselves. A wretched unmarried girl is as hemmed in as a married, divorced, remarried or widowed woman is free. I know that up-to-date fathers pay more and more attention to their daughters' feelings about the matter, but it's a fashion which is taking a long time to become the rule.'

'My first time was with the little 'filly' in my father's *popina*. That wasn't an ideal way to begin either.'

'For a boy the first time is less important.'

'Were you unfaithful to this knight?'

'Oh, over and over again. He was a brute. I only married him to get away from home.'

'It was pleasure you were after?'

'In the sense that I wanted to know what it was. But any woman who undertakes that particular quest is likely to be disappointed. Men think only of themselves.'

'What advice would you give me if the chance presented itself?'

'Take your time. A woman is like a musical instrument. You have to pluck all the chords for hours if you want the music to ring out the way it should. Anyway, I divorced my knight and married a country gentleman, who promptly got himself accidentally killed.'

'Were you in love with him?'

'A bit – for a few weeks.'

'Then why remarry?'

'I couldn't live decently on my dowry, and women of rank can't undertake paid employment – unless they happen to be doctors. A pretty woman without a fortune has no choice but to marry. And if there isn't an eligible match available, she has to settle for the least ineligible.'

'Were you unfaithful to your second husband?'

'Not as often as to the first. I liked my position.'

'Were you still pursuing this famous overwhelming pleasure which is supposed to be so powerful that some women even faint from it?'

'I've never experienced it. But just to be with you is enough to make me faint with happiness, Kaeso.'

Now he was coming to the tricky bit . . .

'I don't understand why you married my father, especially given that he's your uncle.'

'Claudius had just married his niece Agrippina, and we leapt at the chance of getting into the emperor's good books. It was a partial failure. All Marcus got out of it was election to the Arval Brethren, and he was incapable of making any capital out of his contacts there.'

'Did you never make love with my father? Ever?'

Marcia shook her head.

Kaeso sat down abruptly. Marcia's feelings suddenly took on a completely different aspect. The paralysing idea of incest was gradually fading.

Capitalizing on this sudden advantage, Marcia sat up and took hold of Kaeso's hand. But he quickly withdrew it.

'You're not being completely honest with me. Marcus and I can remember when our father used to kick up a din outside your bedroom door, and we know that sometimes you used to let him in.'

'Your memory is better than mine. Yes, if I think about it, I suppose I gave in five or six times, for the sake of you and your brother.'

'What do you mean?'

'When we were first married, as you both noticed, your father used to get in a frantic state, despite his constant promises. The scenes he made used to terrify you. At the cost of giving in briefly a few times I made sure that you had some peace and sleep. Do you suppose I enjoyed it?'

'How much you must have loved us even when we were little!'

'Thank you for appreciating the fact. I've always loved children. I can't go past a rubbish dump and hear babies bawling without getting a lump in my throat. But I didn't want any children by my first husband because I didn't love him. I didn't want any by my second husband because I didn't love him enough. My marriage to Marcus had to be sterile for obvious reasons. And I don't want children by Silanus either – in the unlikely event of his being able to provide me with any. So your rights of inheritance won't be affected. While I was with Marcus, I was able to look after the children I'd have liked to have. Naturally I was very fond of them.'

'When did your feelings for me turn into something stronger?'

'When I began to get jealous of the poor little prostitute in our *popina*, I think. There's nothing like jealousy for opening one's eyes.'

Kaeso thought, then went on carefully:

'During this marriage of convenience . . . or at least relative convenience . . . to my father, I suppose you didn't give up having lovers?'

'You suppose right.'

'A few superficial affairs?'

'A few.'

'And apart from that?'

'I used my body for the advantage of you and your brother yet again.'

'Again?'

'For years Marcus and I were short of money. Sometimes it ran out completely. Several times I nearly walked out of that impossible household, but you looked at me so trustingly that I hadn't the heart to go. There were even times when we didn't have anything to feed the slaves on. One day we had to put a sick slave and a crippled one out on the streets. Some edict of Claudius had decided that in such cases the man automatically became a freedman, but I'm afraid those two freedmen probably died of hunger fairly quickly. When the money ran out, the slaves would look beseechingly at me. Marcus just turned his head away. I knew then what I had to do.'

'Admirable conduct. But the family finances eventually improved and that didn't discourage you from taking more lovers. It was you I accidentally ran into at the baths of Nero that day, wasn't it?'

'Women find it difficult to tell the difference between a necessity and a luxury. Whether you open your legs for 100 sesterces, or 1,000 – or in the case of Silanus, 1,000,000 – what's the difference?'

'It's certainly a difference of money rather than position . . . You seem to have recruited your clients in very varied milieux.'

'True. Discreet liaisons with rich men are often very disappointing. You have to spend a lot of time, pander to a lot of sexual whims, and be content with presents which are difficult to turn into hard cash. A certain level of elegance is incompatible with really fruitful prostitution, except in rare cases. So when we were really short of cash, I would go and find myself a saviour at the new Baths of Nero, or under a portico in the Campus Martius, though I was always afraid of being spotted and beaten up by pimps jealous of their prerogatives. You can see how much I've loved you, Kaeso!'

'Have all the little luxuries in my life been paid for like that, then?'

'Two-thirds of them, perhaps even four-fifths . . .'

'Does Silanus know all this?'

'He suspects it and doesn't give a damn.'

'How very wise!'

'You could be just as wise.'

Kaeso pondered briefly on how very frank Marcia had been. Realizing that it was doubtful whether she could keep anything else secret for long, she had taken a heroic decision to hide nothing at all. Her unhesitating self-abasement gave Kaeso a moving reason to set her on her feet again as affectionately as possible.

'I ought to thank you,' he said. 'You've already done more for me than I knew – or could have wished. But I feel a little overwhelmed at the thought of becoming the successor to such a long line of husbands, lovers and mere customers . . .'

'All trace of those men has run off me like water off a duck's back. I've forgotten them. I never loved them. You're the only man I've ever loved and ever will love.'

'There's one of them that I for one can't forget, because he's supposed to be adopting me shortly.'

'Silanus is broad-minded. He's had heaps of wives and mistresses and fancy-boys.'

'He isn't adopting me so I can sleep with his wife.'

'If, one day, he found out, he'd probably close his eyes to the whole thing. Men of distinction are remarkably good at playing the role of cuckold with dignity.'

'I challenge you to tell him of your intentions before he adopts me.'

'Why run the slightest risk when one of the largest fortunes in Rome is at stake?'

Kaeso thought again and said:

'Everyone is made differently. There are some things one can do and some one can't. I can't allow myself to be adopted by Silanus in such circumstances. And when I say that, I'm thinking of myself rather than Silanus.'

'Well then, let's pretend nothing has happened. Let's pretend that

Selene never wrote me that pretty declaration of love. As my own admission was the result of an abuse of trust, I think I have the right to withdraw it. Let yourself be adopted as arranged, and have no fear that I'll give you any trouble. One sacrifice more, to ensure you get your fine fortune, won't cost me anything. I'm used to it, aren't I?'

'Unfortunately Selene did write that letter, and I now know as much about you as you have always known about me. That passionately possessive way you sometimes look at me – how long do you think you're going to be able to hide that, when we're facing each other over dinner day after day in Cicero's house, or at Tarentum, or Baiae, or anywhere else? And now that I know you were never really my father's wife, how long do you suppose I should be able to resist your intelligence and charm?'

'If you refused to be adopted, would you still have scruples about deceiving Silanus?'

The question caught Kaeso off-balance, and his hesitation to give an answer spoke volumes.

'I think,' he said in the end, 'I'd still have scruples. Silanus has been so good to me . . .'

'Because I have been so good to him . . .'

'That doesn't deprive him of all merit.'

Marcia said brightly: 'If it'll dispel your least scruples, how about the opposite solution. You are adopted, but I divorce Silanus, and we fall into each other's arms. What do you think of that as a suggestion ?'

'I think . . . an arrangement of that sort would still stir up a number of scruples in me. In particular, I could never allow you to give up such a brilliant social position just for love.'

'I'll give it up anyway. And to dispel your last scruple I'll make you one last honourable proposal. I'll divorce him and you turn down the adoption. What moral objection can there possibly be to that?'

After a painful silence Marcia burst into tears. 'The real problem,' she sobbed, 'is that you don't love me, and that you're the only man alive who doesn't want to sleep with me'.

When the first torrent of tears was over, Kaeso said:

'That's not true. On the contrary I want you physically so much that the vision of your divine body frequently haunts me at night. But you played the part of an exemplary mother to me for so many years that my desire comes up against an invisible barrier. For me you are two quite different women. Since one of them is a person I cannot have sexual relations with, I'd better make love with someone else altogether. It's not your fault and it's not mine either. And despite everything I'm so unsure of myself that I'm genuinely afraid that if I became Silanus' son I might give in to you.'

'What are you going to do, then?'

'How do I know!' Kaeso said, despairingly. 'I feel as though I'm at the bottom of a well . . .'

It was midday, as the gradual fading of the noise rising from the city testified. Work had come to a halt, and everyone had downed tools as siesta took its hold on the inhabitants. Kaeso was at the end of his tether. When he made to go, Marcia clung to his toga, her physical and verbal self-possession falling apart, and begged him to make love to her just once, as a reward for all her devotion to him. The request was made more moving by the fact that it was not the product of a mere desire for physical satisfaction. This woman, to whom no husband or lover had ever managed to bring sexual fulfilment, knew only too well that such a moment as this could never bring her that ultimate pleasure which would turn her whole being inside out. She only wanted to hear her heart beating as it had never beaten before.

But all Kaeso could do was repeat over and over again: 'Leave me alone, leave me alone. Can't you see the state I'm in? Another time . . . perhaps . . .'

In the end he got away from her and fled, leaving his toga in her hands as a derisive symbol of how little he could offer her.

As he was going down towards the Subura, Kaeso ran into Arria at a corner in a flight of steps. She was on the way back up to her house, and gave him a conspiratorial and quizzical look. But his haggard look promptly disabused her.

'Your house brings nothing but bad luck,' Kaeso said to her. 'Cupid can only drown there.'

All around the Subura brothels of every sort were already beginning to stir as they got themselves ready for the ninth hour, the legal opening time. In future, the sight of every tart would make Kaeso think of his mother. As the streets of Rome were full of them, he would have plenty of occasion to think of Marcia.

❧ CHAPTER ❧
8

As he went along Kaeso suddenly saw the situation in all its appalling clarity.

If he were adopted by Silanus, he would be at the mercy of all Marcia's most seductive attentions. It wasn't at all sure that he could escape them simply by flight. You cannot just run away without a good pretext. If he resisted the temptation, Marcia would be reduced to despair, and capable of causing a frightful scandal. If he gave in to her, he would never be able to look Silanus in the face, and would risk being caught sooner or later. The more slaves a Roman matron had around her, the more difficult it was for her to deceive her husband without his finding out. In high society many husbands and wives lived independent lives based on mutual tolerance and indifference. But it was obvious that Silanus was still in love with Marcia and likely to remain so for a long time. Augustus' laws punishing adultery by exile were still in force. However theoretical they may have seemed when promulgated, and however much they had fallen into disuse, an unlucky lover and an adulterous woman were still exposed to the vengeance of a husband who wanted to claim his dues.

Even if Silanus, for fear of looking ridiculous, was not prepared to go that far, the outraged husband would not be short of ways of punishing such an infamous betrayal. His own son, the guardian of the family cult, would have brought dishonour on his house.

There were, also, black marks on Silanus' family tree which showed that, when it came to it, such an adoption was not entirely without its risks. When the Julio-Claudians started massacring one another, the social obscurity of their friends and relations did not automatically protect them from suffering the same fate as their master. Freedmen and slaves were tortured to provide 'evidence' and nobody was spared the worst kinds of suspicion.

As for saying no to Silanus so that he could live a life of bliss with a thrice-divorced ex-stepmother, Kaeso was not very keen on the idea. He naturally wanted to be free to enjoy life. Life under the thumb of a possessive and jealous Marcia would hardly be a bed of roses. A woman like that, who used a keen mind to further her designs and her passions, exercised a strange dominion over all those she set out to conquer. She had barely raised her little finger and Silanus had fallen. How many men had she forced to give her what she wanted – marriage, a little pleasure, affection, money? Given that he was in the habit of obeying her, of letting himself be influenced by her, in his role as a loving, trusting, submissive son, if Kaeso got into Marcia's bed he would be squeezed dry drop by drop, like a lemon in a lemon squeezer. What she would want from him were the ultimate pleasures that no man yet had ever given her. Like Arria, she would have him in the bath for more reasons than a good wash. Kaeso did not feel ready for slavery of that sort.

Besides, you couldn't live a life of bliss if you were broke. Marcia was accustomed to a certain level of luxury. Not only was it close to her heart, it was becoming more and more necessary to the preservation of her looks. As Kaeso's motherly mistress, she would soon find herself serving his interests under some portico again. The bitter bread of shame was something of which he had eaten quite enough already!

And given the difference in their ages, how long could a passionate liaison of that kind last any way? Kaeso had seen men who were stuck with ageing, shrewish mistresses . . . It was only human nature for such relationships to come adrift.

The only thing to be done was to break off relations with her. He would have to inflict a wound on his own heart to survive. And yet he needed Marcia. The thought of never seeing her again was torture to him. She had watched over him for so many years with a rare constancy and attentiveness. Who would he be able to go to in the future for advice and enlightenment? He felt more and more like an orphan.

To crown his troubles there was a purely practical difficulty which at first sight looked insurmountable. He absolutely had to get out of the adoption. But how could he find a totally convincing excuse for doing so? One doesn't pass up a billion sesterces on an obscure or trivial pretext. If Kaeso did not put forward a reason, or if the reason he gave were not credible, Silanus, who would be annoyed and mistrustful, would start thinking. And given his sharp wits, he was highly liable to arrive at the truth – a truth which could ruin Marcia.

As Kaeso reached a little ruined temple, close to his family home and set back a little from the alley leading to it, he had a miraculous surprise. There, like a gift from the gods, was his brother Marcus. As he went past Kaeso recognized his brother's broad back. Marcus was temporarily occupied watering the wall of the building below a somewhat peremptory notice:

DUODECIM DEOS ET DIANAM ET JOVEM OPTIMUM MAXIMUM
HABEAT IRATOS QUISQUIS HIC MINXERIT AUT CACAVERIT

(May the twelve gods and Diana and Jupiter the Good and Great vent their anger on any man who urinates or defecates here.)

Marcus, all dusty from the journey, was still in his armour. In a typically free-and-easy military way he couldn't be bothered to go on as far as the half-barrels or broken amphorae set up at crossroads for this purpose.

Kaeso tapped him on the shoulder and they embraced. Marcus had been given unexpected leave. He had been sent with particularly important messages for the headquarters of the *frumentarii*, and had permission to spend eight days in Rome. The young tribune seemed uneasy. He had been hoping to catch Kaeso so as to ask him for news while their father was not there.

The two young men went and sat at a table in the garden of a small *popina*, under a leafy trellis. The elder brother ordered some chilled wine and Kaeso revealed to him in detail how far the presentiments of disaster which he had felt in exile had been justified. Kaeso kept nothing from him – apart from Marcia's prostitution. Not that there was anything for him to tell Marcus junior on that score that his brother was not already fully aware of.

'I rather thought that Marcia had designs on you,' said Marcus. Everyone was more or less aware of it at home. You were the only person who didn't seem to notice. A woman who's deeply in love can't hide her feelings indefinitely. Even if she says nothing, everything about her speaks for her. Oh yes, Marcia's crazy about you. But so what? You've just told me that our stepmother was the daughter of our Uncle Rufus and therefore our first cousin, but that she never actually shared our father's bed give or take the odd occasion. So there was practically no incest between them. From which it can be deduced that there wouldn't be any incest if Marcia became your mistress. So you could reasonably look at such a liaison in a new light, if you found the prospect of it attractive and to your advantage. I'm speaking to you as a friend rather than a brother . . .'

'If you were in my place, wouldn't you be inclined to hesitate? Wouldn't you feel a certain instinctive repugnance?'

'We were already quite big when Marcia admitted to us she was our mother by choice and not by nature, and she presented the situation in such a way that it appealed to our feelings as sons. It's certainly not easy to go straight from seeing her as a mother to seeing her as a lover. But all it needs is a little time. One thing is certain. Marcia is very attractive, she likes you, and she's shown that her love can provide you with incidental benefits. If you drive her to desperation, I'm afraid that something awful will happen. Hell hath no fury like a woman scorned.'

'And if I steel myself and give her everything she wants, how do you suppose Silanus might react?'

'He hasn't yet been cuckolded, he hasn't yet found out that he has been cuckolded, and it isn't even certain that the news would have a particularly bad effect on him. If rumour is to be believed, it wouldn't be the first time that Silanus experienced that particular misfortune, and he's proved accommodating up to now.'

'He didn't adopt the lovers of his other wives and make them responsible for safeguarding the family cult of his *gens*.'

'Silanus' religion is just a front. In families like his, as far as piety is concerned, what isn't public doesn't exist.'

'Silanus loves Marcia.'

'Only in the way a man surfeited with pleasure *can* love a woman. Just suppose that out of a sense of honour you pass up this extraordinary fortune which, out of the blue, the gods are offering you on a plate. And suppose that in five or ten years' time you meet Silanus in the Forum and tell him about your noble conduct. And then suppose that Silanus says: "What a fool you were! I would have been only too happy to share Marcia with you. At my age one develops a taste for *ménages à trois*." . . . You've been trained as a sophist – what would you say in your defence?'

'You're not trying to tell me that for the sake of a few sesterces you'd be prepared to fool around in bed in a threesome with Marcia and that elderly idiot?'

'For the hundreds of millions of sesterces we're talking about, I'm afraid I certainly would.'

Marcus emptied his cup and continued, with all the seriousness in the world:

'I may not be much of a philosopher, Kaeso, but there's one thing I do know. None of us knows where we'll end up when we're dead, or even whether we'll end up anywhere. So there's only one reasonable basis for morality in my eyes, and that's success. You can be successful at the expense of the State or at the expense of other people, which I don't recommend, because the general good, the good of all of us, is damaged by that sort of conduct. But what harm can there be in having a bit of fun and games with a generous patron and a woman who's devoted to you? It's what every young Roman dreams of these days. After all, as far as blood goes, Silanus is no more your father than Marcia is our mother. And I've noticed that sooner or later every famous man has had to pay for his success with his body in order to make it to the top.'

'Not Cato of Utica!'

'All he achieved was suicide. I don't know any more about religion than I do about philosophy, but one thing seems obvious to me. In our good old Roman religion, the gods have multiplied to the point where there's one for every human activity – soldiers, gladiators, lovers, thieves. Every virtue has a god to protect it – and so does every vice. I think there's something deeply significant about looking at the world in that way. In the *Iliad* which we read so much at school, and which you know much better than me, the gods take up human causes of the most pedestrian and contradictory sorts. What matters, for a pious man, is surely to devote himself to the interests of someone who can protect him effectively, ward off the blows and assure him of good fortune. That way, if the gods exist, you'll always find one to match your own interests. And if they don't, there's all the more reason for following your own star, isn't there?'

'Your "good sense" terrifies me. To me morality means something completely different.'

'Then you're not looking at things in a Roman way. Perhaps you've become infected by some oriental superstition or other?'

'No I haven't. I'm just following my natural inclinations, for want of a clearly visible star . . .'

'It's a direction that isn't likely to do anything for my career,' said Marcus with a forced laugh. 'I can see I shall stay a tribune for a long time.'

His laugh clearly disguised a genuine and legitimate unease.

Disappointed and hurt, Kaeso retorted: 'I can't accept the idea of Marcia sleeping with Silanus for the sake of my career. I'm not prepared to sleep with Marcia for the sake of yours, with Silanus cheering us on – if he fancied the role, which is a very doubtful hypothesis. If Silanus had decent views on marriage, both our careers would come to a sharp halt once and for all. The old morality and the path of prudence may turn out to be the same thing.'

During the light family lunch the atmosphere was decidedly uncomfortable. There was a shadow over them all, despite everyone's delight at the visit of Marcus junior. Everything in the house, from the clock to the smallest piece of furniture, now made Kaeso think of Marcia's countless discreet acts of devotion. Everything was suspect and sullied. His father's satisfied countenance took on new depths of abjection for him.

During siesta, while his brother was out assuaging his sexual appetites, Kaeso took Selene aside in the would-be *atrium* and gave her a blow-by-blow account of the dramatic success of her ruse – without mentioning Marcia's well-remunerated little lapses – and asked her once again what he should do. What good and honourable reason could he now invoke for calling off the adoption?

Selene, unlike the younger Marcus, made no attempt to persuade Kaeso to give in to his stepmother. It was as if the young man's Stoical resistance seemed perfectly normal to her under the circumstances. Eventually she took him into her own room, opened a chest and took out a large, yellow-parchment book, and gave it to him.

'I'm Jewish,' she said in explanation. 'This is the Septuagint, the holy book of my religion, in what is already a very ancient translation from the Hebrew original. Put everything else aside and immerse yourself in this text. You'll find what you need to say to Silanus to get yourself out of this tight corner in an honourable fashion and without any suspicion falling on Marcia. If you can't find anything for yourself, I'll help you.'

Considerably taken aback, Kaeso withdrew into his own room and bravely undertook to read his way through the strange book. Where the Jews were concerned, the average Roman was more or less totally ignorant. Most people knew that they were a difficult and touchy race who had spread all over the place, that they liked to live separate lives from other races and that their religion was decidedly offbeat. But people could not usually say how, or how far, it differed from other religions. Various misrepresentations and extravagant distortions had exacerbated this mistrustful and contemptuous ignorance, as always happens when a sect tries to cut itself off from a world which is not prepared to assimilate it.

Kaeso was very disconcerted by the apparently legendary history of the relations between a god and the people which he had marked out as his own. At first sight he could not imagine how a compendium of folklore of such a sort could help him. In addition he was disturbed in his reading by a baby whimpering on the rubbish heap in the cul-de-sac. In winter babies shut up pretty quickly. In spring they tended to linger.

None the less certain points caught his attention . . .

The god of the Jews presented himself as the god of all humanity, the creator of light, the sky, the earth, the seas, man and all things which existed. That was certainly a new idea, of obvious philosophical significance, and so simple, when it came down to it, that one wondered why the Greeks, who had given such matters so much thought, hadn't been capable of doing it a favour and putting it in a better form. From Gaul to India all the gods were more or less caught up in matter, prisoners of space and time in the same way that Silanus' fish were prisoners in their ponds. Plato himself had barely gone farther than a pantheist doctrine of metempsychosis which merely disguised the fundamental problem: why should there be anything rather than nothing? Putting a mysterious Chronos or an obscure Fate in charge of families of wandering gods was not an acceptable answer. The Jewish god was coherent: if he had created matter, he had also created time and space, and could make them disappear when he liked, since man could not conceive of time and space except in the context of matter, which allowed their fragmentation. To put it in philosophical terms, 'immanent' gods were thus replaced by a 'transcendent' god. All that was entirely coherent.

The explanation of the presence of evil in the world by original sin and the Fall was interesting, and justified by the fact that mankind created in the image of god, i.e. sovereignly free, must be free to commit evil without god being held responsible for it. Moreover it was not individual sin which was transmitted from generation to generation but an inclination towards evil, which was itself the result of the moral damage inflicted on humanity by its assiduous practice of all the sins possible. Yes, it was an extremely ingenious idea.

Unfortunately it was tied up in a web of contradictions.

Abraham, who was just an ordinary chap and not even a Jew by birth, was suddenly chosen to found the prolific Jewish race, which the god of all mankind then, for reasons unknown, took under his special protection. Having made a good start, the god of all mankind had curiously restricted his field of activity. But the Jews did not all derive from Abraham. Indeed Abraham had only been circumcised, with all his people, when he was nearly 100. And on that occasion even slaves bought from foreigners had been circumcised. So from the outset it was very difficult to define a Jew. Or at least, the only possible definition had to be based on religion. A Jew was a circumcised individual who believed in Yahwe. The definition of his race was extremely doubtful. Moreover, Kaeso later read that the Jews had hastened to fill their harems with women and slave-girls from every race and clime. The idea of 'descendants of Abraham' was a myth. Circumcised outsiders were clearly far more numerous than the actual progeny of the patriarch. In any case, by an ultimate paradox, he must have begotten his own children before undergoing circumcision.

Reading on, Kaeso found a torrent of rules and regulations which were a mixture of good and bad. The two Decalogues, Exodus and Deuteronomy, had a certain style – although it was odd to ban painting and sculpture. But the distinction between pure and impure animals was absolutely ridiculous. Why ban the camel, the precious pig, the delicious hare, the innocent snail, all fish without fins and scales, ostriches, herons and storks? Yahwe was an eccentric chef!

There were lots of other pointless or extravagant rules, such as those on not touching the mother bird when capturing fledglings, on not mixing linen and wool, and on attaching four tassels to the fringe of clothing.

And when you got to punishments, the whole thing became the most primitive form of total madness . . .

The death penalty was prescribed for:

(1) Jews who abandoned Yahwe for a foreign god (fortunately a tolerant Rome was there to protect those unwise enough to transgress this particular commandment).

(2) Bulls who gored anyone.

(3) Adulterous married women and their lovers.

(4) An engaged girl and her lover if the lover were anyone other than her fiancé.

(5) Any girl who lost her virginity before marriage and any daughter of a priest who prostituted herself.

(6) Active and passive homosexuals and witches.

(7) Men or women who fooled around with animals (the animals also got it in the neck).

(8) Improper relations between a man and his mother, his daughter, his stepmother, his stepsister, his sister or his aunt.

(9) Anyone who married two sisters or a mother and daughter at the same time.

(10) Anyone who made love to a woman while she was having a period.

The second Decalogue, in which these bans were imposed, was less successful than the first, but unfortunately it only seemed to bring to the surface certain tendencies virtual in it.

Though Yahwe was so obsessed with pretty bizarre sexual prohibitions, he appeared to have neglected a few points, such as relations between uncles and nieces, first cousins and lesbians. It was also unclear whether it was permissible to bugger a woman, whether or not she was having a period at the time. If Yahwe did not know, who did?

Somewhat discouraged, Kaeso hurriedly read on. The story of the Jews' troubled relationship with their god was rather boring in the long run, like a play in which the same effects are repeated over and over again. Kaeso began to flick rapidly through the centuries, psalms and prophets, and the book finally fell out of his hands . . .

The baby on the night soil heap had finally lost heart as well. It had had less luck than Job. Did the commandment in the Decalogue 'Thou shalt not kill' include little creatures like that? Doubtless they had something of the animal about them, but if you let them live, they grew up into human beings. The biblical god recommended that when towns were captured and sacked by bands of wild Jews – who entertained themselves by cooking their prisoners alive in bakers' ovens – all male children should be exterminated and only female children preserved. But this same god must nonetheless be opposed to the killing of Jewish children, since his all-seeing eyes condemned Onan's use of the good old contraceptive method of coitus interruptus, at which the Romans tried to outshine one another with great joy and vigour. If Rome had had to be subjected to Jewish laws of morality there would not have been a dozen non-Jews left alive amid the ashes of the funeral pyres and the corpses of those stoned to death.

While his father was frolicking with Selene in the house baths, Kaeso received a surprise visit from Capreolus, who was anxious to speak to him privately. For greater security Kaeso asked him to join him for a cool drink in the garden of the same *popina* where he had had his long conversation with his brother before lunch. There Capreolus said to him:

'Towards the eighth hour your stepmother Marcia sent for me urgently, and I went to her house. She told me that your slave Selene had committed the most abominable of crimes against her but that she could not go through the legal procedure of having her crucified or thrown to the wild animals, and would therefore be obliged if I would cut her throat at the first possible opportunity. She offered me a very large sum of money to do so – a sum appropriate to that wonderful house on the Palatine. I told her that I would have been delighted to oblige, but that I'm a Jew, like the slave in question, that Jews don't kill each other except for a very good reason, and that I'd be awfully relieved if she would get someone else to do the job. She didn't press me and paid me 12,000 *nummi* to keep my mouth shut. But after all, she's your slave, and you saved my life the evening you put on the toga. I thought that my promise to keep quiet didn't apply where you're concerned.'

Kaeso was appalled by Marcia's cruelty and by the speed with which she had moved. He at once took Capreolus back to the house, gave him twelve thousand of his remaining fifteen thousand sesterces, and wrote a quick note, of which he read the first four sentences to the gladiator before he sealed it:

'Kaeso to Marcia, greetings.

Honesty requires that Capreolus bring your money back to you, since on reflection he came to the conclusion that your business with him concerned me too. You make me love Selene all the more, and I will not allow anyone to touch her. Capreolus is equally under my protection. He has spoken to no one but me and will not gossip. If through your agency either Selene or this boy come to any harm, I shall cease to love you and to have anything to do with you. Just because you are so upset, you must not let yourself get carried away with ideas of this sort. Don't you know that I feel the same as you?

I hope you keep well. Keep all your affection for me.'

Kaeso had written the note in his own room. While he was doing so, Capreolus had been gazing at the Bible with curiosity. When he had thanked Kaeso for his generosity and protection, he took the liberty of opening the book and making a flattering remark on the clarity of the copyists' handwriting. The Jewish scribes who copied Holy Scripture were very well trained.

Kaeso explained that he had borrowed it from Selene. He added that he had read a large part of the work and observed:

'Your god takes a very hard line on anything connected with sex. You Jews stone and burn people for next to nothing.'

'Oh yes, we're the most virtuous race on earth,' said Capreolus modestly. 'And the Jews from the little African island where I was born, which is flat and dotted with palm-trees, are the most pious of the lot.'

'How can they tolerate all these moral requirements and all the terrible punishments you incur if you're guilty of failure?'

'In the first place, every little slip isn't punished with death. A Jew can have a good wank without anything awful happening, providing he does it on his own and doesn't ask any gossipy friends to enjoy it with him.'

'Oh, yes, that's magnificently liberal! It's almost disturbing. A severe and just god, who is himself the source of every detail of legislation, ought not to let anyone get away with anything.'

'Our God is also a God of goodness. But there are other loopholes. The penalties on adultery only apply to married or engaged women and their lovers. There's no law against going with prostitutes. When we beseiged the city of Jericho, whose walls eventually crumbled at the sound of our trumpets, Joshua's spies took refuge with a brave tart, and she and her family were well rewarded for her assistance.'

'Yahwe even performed a special miracle for her. When I read the story, I was struck by the fact that Rahab's house was against the city wall, and had rooms built into the wall itself. So that, by the grace of Yahwe, everything fell down except the brothel.'

'You could teach our rabbis a thing or two already! Yes, we give prostitutes the freedom of the city. What's more, though polygamy has rather fallen out of fashion, men retain the privilege of repudiating their wives and changing them when they feel like it.'

'That's just linear polygamy!'

'How else could we live? And of course the laws are tolerant about sexual relations with one's servants, as they are everywhere.'

'I see. So the theory is that, with prostitutes, servants and wives who can be swapped, the Jews would have to be very perverted to try unnatural forms of copulation as well.'

'That's exactly what we think. I should also point out that it isn't every man that's capable of understanding all the finer points of the Law. For the Jews, the deepest piety is the product of education, and many ordinary people sin through ignorance. I'm a bit like that. May God forgive me.'

Selene was just coming out of the bathroom as Kaeso was seeing Capreolus out, so the latter was able to say to her before he left: 'My name is Isaac, and you can give thanks to our Creator for the fact.'

When Capreolus had gone, Selene asked Kaeso what the gladiator had meant. But, as he was anxious not to alarm her pointlessly, he wouldn't give her a straight answer. The idea that all that beauty, all that freshness had so nearly been turned to dust at the whim of an unbalanced woman brought a lump to his throat.

The elder Marcus came out of the bathroom in his turn, his eyes still gleaming at the thought of Selene's naked body, and beckoned to the slave to follow him.

It was only after dinner, while Marcus junior was still out, that Kaeso was at last able to talk to Selene about what he had on his mind. As night fell, they went and sat on a stone bench in front of the little ruined temple nearby, with the racket from the Subura all around them.

'I have to admit,' said Kaeso, 'that I couldn't find anything in your Bible which I could use. Telling Silanus that I'm impressed by Jewish ideas wouldn't provide me with a good motive for calling off the adoption. What do the Jews matter to a Silanus?'

'You seemed to have missed the essential point. Didn't you read that our god is a jealous God, jealous of his status as the sole God?'

'Yes, he's what Greek philosophers call a "transcendent metaphysical entity". Their opinion, if my memory serves me right, is that one cannot make any practical use of a principle which is unknowable in nature. For them that's the philosophical impasse. I'm still waiting for you to prove the opposite.'

'The opposite has already been proved, since this entity spoke to Moses and six million people follow his laws.'

'But what use is that to me . . .?'

'Since there is only one God, jealous of his status, "transcendent" to use your intellectual terminology, all the other gods, who wander about the material world as though it were an idolatrous prison, no longer have any conceivable interest or reason for existing. The Jewish God can't be thought of as an *extra* god. He suppresses and replaces all the others. You ought to be able to explain all that to Silanus, who is cultured and intelligent. You should even be able to explain it in the language of the Greek philosophers, which you know better than I do.'

'Of course. That's simple. But what happens next?'

'Consequently, a Jew cannot sacrifice to any god but Yahwe. The Jews have been so firm on that point that Rome has granted them dispensation from sacrificing to the gods of the city, or to Rome, or to Augustus. They are allowed to substitute prayers for sacrifices, and they are the only people in the world who enjoy that dispensation. They pray, without much conviction, for the prosperity of the Emperor and the Empire, but they only sacrifice to their own national god. So if you look like taking up Judaism, you couldn't possibly be adopted by a Roman, because you would no longer be capable of maintaining the family cult. Now as far as I have understood it, Silanus is especially keen on that particular angle of the adoption: it's largely the reason why he's adopting you at all. As a Jew you would have a very good, watertight reason for backing out, and the pretext would be entirely honourable. It would be a matter of conscience. For the Romans sacrifices are only a formality, but it's precisely because that's all they are that they are so keen they should go on from generation to generation. What would they have left if even the formalities were to disappear?'

It was like a blinding flash of light to Kaeso. Selene's idea was inspired. There was however one difficulty . . .

'It's a very clever ruse. It's precisely because a matter of conscience is something astonishing and metaphysical that it's impossible to argue about it. And no other religion could offer me a comparable way out. But if I want my perfect good faith not to be suspect, I can't limit myself to vague sympathies with Judaism. I should have to pretend to be a real Jew. And how can I pretend to be circumcised without taking bad faith to unpleasant extremes?'

'Circumcision isn't much of a business . . .'

'At my age . . .'

'Abraham was ninety-nine . . .'

'When you're past it, you're less likely to notice the drawbacks.'

'It's a very quick operation and your convalescence would provide you with an excellent reason for putting off the adoption. And you'll find it an advantage afterwards.'

'From what point of view?'

'Women with big sexual appetites dream of treating themselves to a Jewish slave. Cutting off the foreskin slightly reduces the sensations during coitus and therefore holds back the moment of the man's orgasm. In bed a Jew can keep it up longer than anyone. Then if one day you do sleep with your Marcia, she'll thank you for it.'

It was not a very attractive prospect. All women, first Arria and now Selene, were trying to turn Kaeso into an indefatigable sex-machine. A Jewish slave, plunged into a cold bath at regular intervals so as to keep his strength up, was evidently the *ne plus ultra*!

Kaeso hummed and hawed for some time, but ended up by bowing to the inevitable. He owed it to Marcia, despite all her faults, to do everything he could to deflect Silanus' suspicions from her.

Selene went on: 'Time is pressing. I'll write you a note of introduction to the priest in the Trans Tiberim who I've entrusted my 100,000 sesterces to. He's a Pharisee. All the most pious Jews are. They know the Law best, and they love twisting it inside out and round about to suit their interests and their pleasure. Every day they add subtle developments to it which provide them with a new opportunity for cheating. But our Law is so strong and all-pervading that it resists their attacks with admirable constancy. A Pharisee will always follow his conscience when he can't see any way out, and it's hard to ask more of a man than that. You can trust Rabbi Samuel completely. Go and see him tomorrow morning. He'll complete your education in things

Jewish. He may even be prepared to recommend a pious surgeon himself.'

'Why "may be"?'

'It's submission to God which makes one worthy of becoming a Jew. Your submission is highly dubious, and you won't fool Samuel. But I'll try to give my letter the right sort of flavour . . .'

They went back to the house, and, in the intimacy of her room, Selene penned the following lines in Greek and showed them to Kaeso:

'Selene to Rabbi Samuel, very respectful greetings.

I warmly recommend to you young Kaeso, the younger son of my master Marcus, a senator and Arval Brother. Kaeso's stepmother has divorced Marcus and married D. Junius Silvanus, a member of the imperial family. He is therefore a boy with a great future. Partly as a result of my chaste and modest influence, Kaeso, like some other Romans, has studied our Bible with increasing sympathy. The hand of Him whose name one dares not speak has had such an effect on him that it is now his ambition to do more than simply stay on the fringes of our community. To be precise he has told me that, after mature reflection, he would like to become a Jew and is prepared to be circumcised. With your customary wisdom you will be able to judge the relative parts played in his decision by youthful enthusiasm and genuine predisposition.

Could you not find a totally secure investment for my money at 6 per cent rather than 5?

I wish you good health and hope you will pray for the same for me.'

It was a perfect letter. The high regard in which Kaeso already held Selene rose even higher as a result. Marcia had deserted him, but he had found another strong-willed and intelligent woman to guide him. She possessed the additional advantage that, having been circumcised, she would never have ulterior motives for helping him. He embraced Selene very affectionately, and could not help squinting at her admirable breasts as he did so, forgetting his father's rights. Selene gently disengaged herself from his arms and sent him away.

❋ CHAPTER ❋
9

The Jewish ghetto in the Trans Tiberim, by far the most important in Rome, was really a city apart. The idea of confining a community to one district would never have occurred to Roman lawyers. If all over the world pious, practising Jews – then the great majority – lived in separate communities, it was not because Roman law imposed it on them but because their own Law did. A strict Jew was obsessed with the idea of impurity and could never feel at ease in a non-Jewish milieu. He found everything shocking, and his social context continually posed insoluble problems for him. The food, dress, manners and morals of the race were extraordinary, and provided a constant challenge to the civilization around them.

The poorest and most hard-working quarter of Rome sprawled higgledy-piggledy across the XIVth district of the Trans Tiberim, to the north of the Janiculum fortress. Recent immigrants of all nationalities concentrated there in the hope of one day moving to the slums on the left bank and eventually storming one of the six famous hills (the Capitol, being stuffed full of grand monuments, was no longer inhabited except by a few priests and night-watchmen). In the Trans Tiberim the Jewish ghetto was particularly mysterious, particularly densely packed, and remarkably filthy.

The Jews did not in fact go to the Roman baths, which they held in abomination. Their idea of cleanliness, though obsessive, tended to the metaphysical. Whenever they came into contact with 'impurity' they had to wash themselves. Men washed themselves after this or that illness, after an attack of gonorrhoea or lice, after a spontaneous ejaculation or even simply after having sex with their wives. And women had to have a bath at the end of their period. But though every synagogue was provided with modest baths for the monthly purification of female Jews, men's ablutions were localized, furtive and heavily symbolic. Jews, being children of the desert, were nowhere near as passionate about water as the Romans.

The sun was already high when Kaeso reached the wretched hovel where Rabbi Samuel lived. It was in an area where there were far more flimsily built individual constructions than apartment blocks. What could all these Jews be doing with the money they were supposed to make hand over fist?

The Rabbi's servant took the message to her master, leaving Kaeso, whom Selene had draped in another toga, to wait as patiently as he could in a dark corridor.

Then the Rabbi came in person to find him. He was elderly, tall, gaunt and bent, with grey hair and a thick black beard, and was wearing a curious tasselled coat of the sort which Kaeso had already noticed in the alleys off the 'Vicus Judaicus'.

The Pharisee seemed very taken aback and rather embarrassed. He stared at Kaeso inquisitively, and kept stroking his beard with a shrivelled, wrinkled hand. The beard seemed to give off a strong and unpleasant smell.

Eventually he said in rather harsh Greek, but in a very amiable tone:

'You do me a great honour in troubling to come here to listen to my humble words and profit from my little store of knowledge. But it is against our customs for strangers, however distinguished and well-disposed, to cross the threshold of our houses and receive hospitality in them. They could transgress our Law out of mere ignorance. It can happen so quickly. I myself have difficulty avoiding all the tiny impurities lying in wait for us. But since we have been scattered across the wide world, our learned men have discovered a solution for everything. May I rent my house to you for one *as*? That way I shall no longer be in my own home, and will no longer be responsible for any mistakes which you might unwittingly commit. Naturally I would accept credit, without interest, since on principle we lend for nothing to our compatriots and our friends.'

Astonished by this extraordinary piece of casuistry, Kaeso hurriedly rented the house on such advantageous terms and followed the rabbi into a quiet little room, lined with scrolls and volumes. It gave on to a tiny garden, where a huge cat, a pure animal, was playing with a lizard, an impure animal.

Samuel immediately came to the point. The Jews were always absolutely delighted that noble foreigners should take an interest in their ideas, doctrines and religious and moral concepts. Moreover the Chief Rabbi of Rome was well-thought of at court. The empress Poppaea, Acte who had long been the emperor's mistress, and various other Roman notables, all looked on the Jews with a certain amount of favour. But from there to having oneself circumcised was an enormous step which was very rarely taken.

'And yet,' said Kaeso, 'as I understand it, nothing in Jewish law is against conversion. because it's precisely by conversion that the Jews were created.'

'In theory you are of course absolutely right. But circumcision is only one of the characteristics of a Jew. To be a Jew you also have to have assimilated the whole Bible, including the commentaries of the Mishna (*midrash* in Hebrew), which date from our return from exile in Babylon. That takes a considerable time, especially as to understand the texts properly it is highly advisable to learn Hebrew, and even Aramaic. There are many learned commentaries in that language. The Septuagint, though very useful given the alarming drop in the numbers who know Hebrew, is never more than a second-best. And then there's the fact that instruction in Judaism leads on to assiduous, detailed, scrupulous daily practice of the requirements of the religion. Those not born to our customs cannot even envisage such attention to detail, and the majority of them would be unable to accept or tolerate it. So you can see how much knowledge and information and how many new customs you have to acquire before even thinking of the great moment of circumcision. In the meantime your favourable attitude will be very precious and useful to us.'

'You're asking a great deal more of me than God did of Abraham.'

'Ah, but then you're not Abraham. Not of course that that lessens your outstanding merit.'

'I have the impression that plenty of Jews have barely any instruction . . .'

'That is only too true. But the question is whether you want to be a good Jew or a bad Jew. There will always be too many bad Jews as it is. Good Jews will always be rare. Why limit your ambitions, my son?'

Things seemed to be at an impasse.

Kaeso then raised a problem which his initial contact with the Bible had already brought to his attention.

'Can you explain to me why the universal god of Genesis, instead of treating all men on an equal footing, quickly concentrated his favours – and sometimes his wrath – on the Jewish people, whom he created with his own hands in such an artificial fashion? In other words, looking at the thing from a universal perspective, what part do the Jews have to play in Yahwe's scheme of things?'

'An excellent question and one which, when it comes to it, every pious and intelligent Jew ought to ask himself. I can see three answers, which are not mutually exclusive.

First, the necessary and sufficient answer: Yahwe's scheme of things is known only to Yahwe and we can only know the little of it which he chooses to reveal to us.

Secondly there is the answer based in humility. Yahwe chose Abraham and his natural and spiritual descendants because he wanted to hold the first place in men's hearts. Among ignorant nomads and those at the very dawn of any form of civilization there is no obstacle to Yahwe's orders except original sin. God is everything to him who is nothing, and the humility of the chosen few only makes the magnificence of divine grace the more resplendent. When the chosen gain in wisdom, their books will speak only of their Creator.

Thirdly, there is the answer based in pride. The Jews have been chosen by Yahwe to be the salt of the earth, to inform the whole world of His existence and His wishes, and to set the best example to all nations. That would explain to you why the Jews cannot increase their numbers at will without risking loss of quality. Do not join us, Kaeso, unless you are worthy of it.'

In the garden the large (pure) cat was devouring the (impure) lizard without a second thought. He hadn't understood the system.

As he dug farther, Kaeso came up with a disappointing discovery: the Jews limited recruitment to save themselves unnecessary trouble. Admittedly, with their character they were not short of trouble already.

'Yes,' the rabbi finally admitted, 'Rome clearly would not tolerate massive conversions to Judaism, because that would increase the numbers of those refusing to sacrifice to Rome, Augustus and all the false State gods in a way which would be very alarming to the authorities. Jews are only tolerated for their oddity, which is of a nature to discourage conversion. All that is as it should be. What would happen to the prodigious holiness of Israel if its gates were suddenly opened wide to the uneducated masses of every nation?'

This cultivated self-satisfaction and tranquil egoism got on Kaeso's nerves. 'I don't know what is at the back of Yahwe's mind any more than you do,' he said. 'But one thing seems clear to me. Gods cannot live for long in contradiction with themselves any more than men can. A transcendent god needs a universal religion; immanent gods have particular religions. A transcendent and universal god could only make himself a local god for a good reason, and the reasons you have just offered me, mysterious, humble or proud, are not entirely satisfactory. Someone ill-

273

disposed to you might think that either your god was a myth or that the Jews had helped themselves to a god intended for the whole world.'

Faced with this accusation of prevarication old Samuel was most put out, and had difficulty in keeping calm.

'Are you aware,' he said, 'that while Yahwe heaps his favour upon my people, he also makes far greater demands on us than on others? Try following our morality for a little and perhaps your reproaches will be a little less sharp. We are like the great lighthouse at Alexandria, sometimes in sunshine, sometimes in storm. But I have always seen the light shining from afar.'

'I must admit that my moral ambitions are much less elevated than yours. Rather than introduce myself with great difficulty into the eminent circles of specialists in the Law and make myself their disciple, I had hoped for a more welcoming and pleasant religion, though not necessarily a less demanding one. A religion in which requirements like circumcision might not be impossibly difficult to achieve and where your unique god, who won't tolerate the existence of other gods, might perhaps have come to my aid in my weakness. Please forgive me for having disturbed you for nothing.'

Kaeso got up and the rabbi accompanied him to the door with chilly politeness.

As Kaeso was bidding him goodbye on the doorstep, Samuel hesitated, then said abruptly:

'You won't have disturbed me for nothing. Given your ambitions I think I know where you can find what you want. A most unexpected Jewish sect has recently grown up. It recruits in large numbers and doesn't insist on circumcision. To make things even easier, these people have dropped the clearest and most precise parts of our Law and replaced them by some astounding innovations. If they could convert a real live patrician to hasten the advance of their cause, they'd be in seventh heaven. Up to now the social standing of their Roman converts hasn't been conspicuously high. They'll welcome you like the Messiah, with open arms. The extravagant symbol of this sect is the cross. Its Jewish founder breathed his last on one during the reign of Tiberius. But that accident shouldn't discourage you. A god who didn't entail the inconvenience of circumcision or the Law is just right for a young man who can't face a long period of religious study, isn't it?'

'I'm looking, as you'll appreciate, for something truly serious which would have the additional advantage of making a favourable impression on . . . a relative, for example.'

'I'm not sure whether the adjective "serious" is entirely appropriate to these "Christians", but I can tell you that their preaching, despite – or perhaps because of – their strange doctrines, has had a certain success in the East, to the point of causing the authorities some concern. One of the leaders of the sect, Cn. Pompeius Paulus, a naturalized Jew who's strangely proud of the fact, even spent two years in Rome awaiting trial, but he was released last spring. He distinguished himself at Caesarea by, among other things, delivering a propaganda speech to King Agrippa and his concubine and sister Berenice. You can see that Paul knows the right people. And as his Roman friends have declared him innocent, there's nothing to prevent you from being seen in his company. He's a rather talkative man, but he has a subtle and interesting mind. He's supposed to have had some amazing vision in the dust near Damascus, and there's nobody like him for commenting on the scriptures in a highly original fashion.'

'Is he in Rome at the moment?'

'So I recently heard. He's just back from carrying the good news to Spain, and he's staying in the city briefly before pressing on to the East. He's always on the move. If you want to catch him and get some extra information on his sect, with any luck you'll find him in the mornings at the huge public lavatories which are heated in winter, where the Forum of Augustus and the Forum of Caesar intersect. This Pompeius Paulus isn't ashamed to live like a Greek or a Roman, and your lavatories are real salons. You can meet all sorts of interesting and useful people there. It's an ideal place for an ambitious preacher to try his ideas out.'

'What proof is there that one is a Christian? They must have substituted something for circumcision.'

'Obviously.'

'A tattoo perhaps?'

'Tattooing, like transvestism, is forbidden by the Bible, because the image of Yahwe must not be disfigured. Doubtless these Christians have hastily had to authorize it, but as far as I know they don't use it as a recognition mark. Tattooing takes a long time and is extremely painful. The Christians had to have something quick and painless, suitable for groups, and which could be used anywhere, when the chance presented itself. Their solution is simply to give their converts a bath.'

(The idea crossed Kaeso's mind that Arsenus might be a Christian, but he rejected it as inherently improbable.)

'The Christians call this bathing "baptism", and where necessary a small amount of water will do. They'll be delighted to baptize you on the spot, with enthusiasm. And at the stage they're at now, their preliminary studies are miraculously brief. They claim that the entire doctrine of Christianity can be summed up in a few words. You won't have any difficulty learning it by heart. It's a religion tailor-made for young men in a hurry.'

Kaeso left in a thoughtful mood. with this last sally ringing in his ears. He was aware that he had not made a very good impression on the rabbi, and wondered why the mistrustful Pharisee had deliberately criticized the Christians in such a way as to excite his curiosity.

As soon as the door was shut, the servant, who had been standing in the shadows listening to the end of the conversation, said to her master:

'Did my ears deceive me? Why mention the Christians to that elegant young man? In his ignorance he's quite likely to go and see them, and get mixed up with them.'

She was a woman in middle age and used to speaking frankly – a mistress-cum-housekeeper who had been running the household since the rabbi's fifth wife died under the strain of her continual pregnancies.

This gave Samuel the chance to formulate his thought more precisely.

'Like the renegade Pompeius Paulus on the road to Damascus, I just had a vision, though a better one than his. Yahwe said to me: "The prerequisite for forcing the idle Romans, who pay no attention to what we tell them, to take as much interest in the Christians as they should, is that the blaspheming rabble should get a foothold in the aristocracy." Seven years ago Pomponia Graecina, the wife of the general Aulus Plautius, was accused of "illegal superstition": she was probably a Christian. But she was saved from the law by the unthinking complicity of her husband. That first blow came to nothing. We should encourage a repetition of the offence.'

'Our noble visitor runs the risk of getting into trouble all because of you.'

'The boy wanted to become a Jew with a minimum of effort. Isn't that what the Christians are there for?'

Kaeso was tired of walking. He hired a litter to take him home. The characteristics of the Christian sect sounded promising. But if it was going to be difficult to get a conversion to Judaism past Silanus, a conversion to Christianity, a sect which no one had ever heard of and would probably shortly fade out, posed even greater problems of plausibility. Baptism by bathing or sprinkling of water didn't have the same undeniable and spectacular quality as circumcision, that source of women's delight.

To get back to the centre of Rome, the bearers could go over the nearby Janiculum bridge, or cross via the Tiber island or use the Palatine bridge, which was still called the 'Senatorial bridge'. Kaeso asked to be put down for a moment on the Tiber island, beside the obelisk which stood between the temple of Vejovis and the great temple of Aesculapius. The god of medicine had been acclimatized on the island with great pomp and ceremony in the year 461 from the founding of the city. Fabricius and Cestus had equipped all the part of the island downstream from the bridges with a quay shaped like the poop of a trireme, to commemorate the ship from which the god had disembarked there in the guise of a snake (an impure creature to the Jews!).

Around the temple of Aesculapius a crowd of the sick were waiting under the porticoes for miraculous cures which were slow to materialize. Kaeso bought a cock from one of the many street-sellers who made their living by exploiting public credulity, with the connivance of the priests. On the off-chance he asked them to sacrifice the bird to safeguard his good health.

He was more and more aware, in fact, that he was not in a normal condition. All the blows which had struck him in so short a space of time had shaken and then destroyed the protective edifice which had sheltered his childhood and the happy beginnings of his adolescence. Under these accumulated ruins the ground itself seemed to be shifting. Kaeso was well aware that he would have needed a firm philosophical credo and a strong belief to be able to surmount the crisis, to show him where his duty lay and to give him the courage to carry it out without flinching. But where was he to find a truth capable of dealing with a situation like the one in which he found himself? He would have thought his situation unparalleled if Euripides' *Hippolytus* and Seneca's recent play *Phaedra* had not existed to show him that others shared his misfortunes. The Roman gods were silent or mutually contradictory, and it was very doubtful whether they could or would intervene. The Jewish god suffered from the defect of being more of a Jew than a god, and his Christian avatar did not inspire confidence. As for the various schools of philosophy, they reflected all the tendencies of human thought. Their jargon-ridden verbosity did not simplify their approach.

Cn. Pompeius Paulus had just left the magnificent lavatories which his burning desire to spread his message impelled him to frequent. A number of Romans who could afford it began the day there. Together with the barbers' shops it was a vibrant centre for the diffusion of news, true or false.

Pursuing his reflections to the swaying rhythm of the litter, Kaeso thought for a moment of all the mystical oriental cults which had gradually gained a foothold in Rome, after a preliminary stay in Greek-speaking territories where the Hellenic spirit had left its mark on them. There were the cults of Anatolia, those of Cybele and Attis in particular, which had been carefully reformed by the emperor Claudius; there were the Egyptian cults like that of Isis, which had been banished by Tiberius but publicly re-admitted by Caligula; there was the Syrian cult of Hadad and his consort Atargatis, a recent import favoured by Nero. Mithras was still waiting to be admitted . . . But such cults had a very poor reputation among Roman traditionalists. Kaeso's father, who could not be wrong all the time despite his talent for mistakes, had always been strongly against Chaldeans, Commageneans, Phrygians and Egyptians who mixed astrology and obscenity, hypnotism and music, divination and hysteria, self-maceration and dancing, prostitution and castration, while promising their initiates happy immortality, pleasure beyond the tomb or salvation through rebirth. Kaeso clearly had no interest in getting mixed up with all these charlatans who played on the sensibilities and anxieties of the simple-minded. Even in January you could see bigots immersing themselves in the Tiber to satisfy the whim of some priest who claimed it would be regenerative. In any case, though such cults were profoundly different from the old Roman religion, which was so depressing on the subject of after-lives, in that they offered you the chance, by appropriate techniques, of melting into the bosom of a divine saviour, they all shared with the official religion the simple fact of being admitted to the Roman pantheon, whose elasticity seemed limitless. The only oriental cult out of the common was Judaism, which indeed was consciously the opposite of all the others.

As for the orgiastic cults, you could not decently touch those except with a pair of long-handled tongs. The last significant manifestations of them had occurred as long ago as the distant days of the civil wars, but despite all official interdictions they still survived. Women of loose morals, men dressed up as women – the sort of thing only allowed at the Saturnalia or on the Kalends of January – a random collection of individuals who included free men, freedmen and even slaves would get together secretly at night and indulge in every possible sexual excess, in one compact mass. They were trying to find some sort of divine ecstasy and sublime communion in the dark through their intoxication, the confusion of sexes and ages, and the most extravagant erotic excitement. Divine possession and sexual possession became inseparable. Pleasure and pain, violence and abandon were thought to introduce those taking part into a world without frontiers and limits, without walls and barriers. It was liberation through group sex. But the State had eventually reacted against it, because on such occasions the most inviolable civil laws were inevitably trampled under foot. Incest, female adultery (the only sort punishable by law), and sexual relations between free women and slaves were all part and parcel of the experience.

Kaeso's problem was to liberate his mind, not his body. Time was becoming more and more pressing.

His father had gone out early to take the air in the Forum and Marcus junior was out after women again. According to the clock in the hall it was not yet the fifth hour. Kaeso saw Selene sitting motionless in the would-be *atrium*, like a sentient statue.

He greeted her and gave her a summary of his disappointing interview with rabbi Samuel. Selene had vaguely heard of the Christians. They had first appeared in Rome during the reign of Claudius and had been a thorn in the flesh of orthodox Jews for some time. How had the Jews been able to put up with competition on their own territory? The Christian heresy, by developing beyond all reasonable expectation, imperilled their precious singularity and their privileges. Their very safety was at risk, since a relatively inexperienced imperial police force had too often blamed the Jews for this or that disturbance which the presence of Christians had been entirely responsible for. The authorities, overwhelmed with complaints and evidence supplied by outraged rabbis, were barely beginning to be able to tell real Jews from false ones. What complicated the question was that some Christians were circumcised and others were not. They sensed, not without reason, the possibility of terrible muddles and were not keen to get mixed up in them. In any case, whenever the emperor was not directly concerned, the Roman police were very slow to react. They waited for a situation to degenerate dangerously before taking steps. When they did act, they did so globally, brutally and without observing fine distinctions.

'The Christians,' said Selene, 'have one characteristic you should know about. They claim in all seriousness, so I've heard, that the head of their sect, a certain Jesus, who was crucified at Jerusalem during the reign of Tiberius, was responsible for his own resurrection!'

'That's not particularly original. In lots of oriental religions, particularly

Egyptian ones, gods and goddesses spend their time dying and coming back to life. Sometimes once a year.'

'You haven't grasped my point. I'm not talking about gods or myths of spring. I'm talking about a carpenter who died on a cross and who is supposed to have later been seen walking about.'

'Then it's a spectre. Cicero's ghost haunts Silanus' house, and that doesn't mean that Cicero has been resurrected.'

'You still haven't taken my point. The Christians claim that they could touch this resuscitated Jesus. They even say that he had a good appetite.'

This was indeed an extra worry, and a really serious one.

'Just my luck!' moaned Kaeso. 'If I tell Silanus that I've become a Christian, he'll take me for a liar or a lunatic. There goes my last hope. The situation is desperate.'

'I admit that the story's a bit unsubtle. Carpenters make crosses, they occasionally die on them, but they don't often come back afterwards.'

'Was this Jesus really a carpenter? You must admit that, for a patrician, that makes a sect leader in rather dubious taste. He seems to have all the qualities necessary to be a big hit!'

'He was a carpenter to the core and so was his legal father, Joseph. His mother Mary, a randy piece, had him on some one night stand. Some rabbis claim that Joseph, to get his own back for being deceived, made the cross on which Jesus died. But that might just be slander. However, the Christians have no choice but to admit that their Jesus was illegitimate. To disguise this distressing reality, they claim that Mary was made pregnant by an angel. But Jewish angels rarely have a cock that long . . .'

'Oh wonderful! What a delightful family!'

This business of resurrection was the last straw for Kaeso. The poor boy looked so utterly wretched that Selene, moved to compassion, suddenly threw herself at his feet, embraced his knees, and said:

'It really upsets me to see you so disappointed. I'm all the more sorry for your troubles because I recently caused you unnecessary suffering by telling you a lie which I must own up to. I'm sorry I lied, and I beg you to forgive me for it. Rabbi Samuel, my director of conscience, reproached me for it in the strongest terms . . .'

Selene admitted to Kaeso that his father had nothing to do with the terrible mutilation which had brought a cloud over her life.

The repentant Selene made a very touching sight. The marble had come alive, her beautiful grey eyes were full of tears, and her throat was palpitating with little sobs.

This revelation took a weight off his mind. Kaeso drew the interview out, his downward view of Selene's charms was not something he wished to cut short.

In the end he made her stand up and asked:

'Why did you invent such a horrible lie? What devil incited you?'

'I wanted to get my own back on your father for forcing me to have unpleasant sexual relations with him. I ought also to confess that a similar feeling of revenge played a part in the love letter I wrote to Marcia for you.'

'Marcia? What had Marcia done?'

'I've already told you that Silanus bought me as a present for your father. I expect you've seen the random selection of slaves set out for sale on the platforms in the shops: prisoners of war with laurel crowns, individuals from overseas with chalk on their feet, slaves of difficult temperament or dubious character, sold without guarantee and marked by white woollen bonnets ... But high-class slaves aren't subjected to that sort of promiscuous contact. The slave-masters bring them round to prospective masters in their own homes. So Afranius, who has his sales pitch beside the temple of Castor, opposite the old Forum, brought me round and showed me off naked to Silanus and Marcia – the patrician had already taken her into his house before marrying her. The business arrangements were soon settled, and Marcia asked me to strip off again, on the pretext of checking whether her own measurements were close to mine. Consequently she also stripped off herself. But in fact what she really wanted to do was to enjoy me sexually, so that Silanus could get a thrill out of watching us. I was struck by the fact that she knew exactly what she was doing. Her knowledge could only be the fruit of long experience. She had just asked Silanus to join in our frolics ("We must just try out Marcus' present for him," she said) when she suddenly noticed that I had been circumcised. Afranius hadn't mentioned the fact because he didn't know it himself. She was furious with me for concealing it, and ordered me to be whipped on the spot. The punishment would have been even more severely administered if the noble Silanus hadn't asked his specialist not to break my skin as he shortly wanted to make a present of me to someone else. You can see why I'm not exactly fond of Marcia. She's cruel and perverted.'

Devastated, Kaeso fled into his room, threw himself on his bed and burst into tears. What was there left now of the image of Marcia which had dominated his childhood?

Silanus also took on a new and troubling dimension. If he had taken so much pleasure in Marcia's dissolute behaviour with Selene, could he one day show the same perverted taste for any sexual activity in which his wife and Kaeso might indulge? Perhaps the hypothesis put forward by Marcus junior, who had always flattered himself on his absence of illusions, was appropriate to the character of a very rich man, who was already quite old and had plenty of experience of all manner of pleasures? Was it necessary for Kaeso to sacrifice a golden future out of respect for the honour of someone who had none, or who at least had a very unusual concept of it? But the crux of the problem was elsewhere. In accepting the pleasure and shame of a threesome to secure himself a fine career, Kaeso would be entering the world of prostitution. Marcia's example had just unveiled the degrading aspect of that very world. After prostituting herself for Kaeso, was Marcia going to crown her triumph by initiating Kaeso into her own profession?

Selene tapped humbly at his door, eventually came in, and sat on the young man's bed, looking at his grief-stricken face.

'I shouldn't have talked to you about Marcia like that . . .'

'On the contrary, what you told me didn't come as much of a surprise . . .'

Kaeso told Selene what Marcia had revealed to him about the excesses of her devotion.

'So, without realizing it, you were the true love of a common tart, whom you looked on as a mother.'

'Fate could hardly play me a more ironic trick.'

'I feel all the more sympathy for you and your misfortunes because I myself have had my share of similar unhappiness. The grocery business which my parents ran was sacked by Greeks from the neighbouring quarter. Since my father couldn't pay off his creditors, at the age of fifteen I ended up as the slave of an Egyptian eunuch priest. He immediately had me circumcised, in accordance with the barbarous traditional customs of the country. I was still a virgin at the time. The male slaves of this monster promptly took advantage of my charms, and I found myself pregnant. The child was exposed on birth: it was a girl. Upset by this evidence of my wantonness, my master then sold me to one of the best brothels in Alexandria. I wasn't yet seventeen. As the different forms of penetration revolted me, I did my best to suck off as many of my customers as possible, and became an expert at it. A visiting philosopher once told me, very learnedly, that it was a perfect application of the law of least evil, the finest ethical principle yet discovered. In the brothel I came across artists who appreciated my beauty, and I changed owner to become a model. For several years I served various painters and sculptors until a rich procurator of the imperial estates spotted me. But he reproached me with a certain coldness, and sold me to Afranius, who was on a trip to Alexandria and Canopus to buy choice stock. Afranius never touched me; the kind of man who pays a lot of money for a slave would be very put out if her dealer had been screwing her. But on the boat as soon as Afranius turned his back, the sailors raped me, and I dared not complain for fear of being thrown overboard. You know the rest. As you can see, you're not the only one to suffer.'

Her distress, though it had a servile quality, was contagious. Kaeso put his hand tenderly on Selene's head, and she moved it quite naturally down towards his crutch, where her well-trained mouth was soon hard at work. 'Let me do this,' she said. 'I want to humiliate myself for a moment, so as to earn your forgiveness properly.'

The sexual morality of the Romans and the Greeks was in effect dominated by the facile and obvious distinction between giver and receiver. An active man always kept his gate-keeper's respect, whereas women and passive men emerged sullied from their experiences. The reasonable or sublime paradise of love was already a hell of prejudice.

Part of the reason why Selene really enjoyed what she was doing to Kaeso was that it gave her a pleasant feeling of scoring off Marcus at no cost to herself while increasing her power over the honourable recipient of her attentions. Kaeso for his part was thinking that the definition of incest is after all a matter of opinion.

In the promiscuity of the large households of the Roman upper classes it was not in any case unusual for disrespectful sons to have it off on the quiet with the pretty slaves of both sexes who were already providing the same service for their fathers. There were jealous wives who took a certain vengeful delight in these 'hole-and-corner' irregularities . . .

Kaeso climaxed and lay back, panting. Selene said to him, with a touch of humour: 'You've just enjoyed an exceptional moment: it'll be a long time before it happens again. In Latin an exemplary wife, who has only had one husband, is said to be *univira*. I shall be your "unifellatrix", a once-only experience.'

The meaning of this neologism, whose morphological formation was somewhat dubious, was entirely clear. Kaeso took it as read.

As he could not get Marcia's talents at lesbian love-making out of his mind, and found the idea astonishing and upsetting, he asked Selene about it, knowing that her experience would be very wide.

'Given what you've just told me about the woman,' she replied, 'such talents can be taken for granted. You must realize that in the world as men have made it – because they have more strength in their biceps than in their cocks' (here she gave Kaeso's flaccid member a little tap) '– if women are largely condemned to sleeping with males, it isn't because they choose to. They can only find affection and pleasure with members of their own sex. And as prostitutes are particularly hard done by in this respect, they're all the more likely to enjoy amorous companionship with other women. This well-known fact gives you a key to Marcia's brutal conduct towards me. Fate had deprived me of the one organ which has found favour with her up to now . . .'

Selene hurriedly added: 'For most women lesbian relations are only second-best. Deep in their hearts they are waiting for a "grand passion". When that day comes, the organ of their dreams can never be too big. If Marcia finally gets her hands on you, that's the compliment she'll pay you. And for once in her life she'll be telling the truth.'

Kaeso's father had just come home and was calling loudly for Selene. The young woman carefully wiped her mouth on the hem of her dress and ran off to greet her master with a smile.

Kaeso began to remember Marcia's rather special relationship with her maids. She liked them to be very feminine, small, plump and graceful. Her attitude towards them was a mixture of caresses – which now seemed highly suspect – and punishments. The *domina* was doubtless getting her revenge on the undesirable men who had subjected her to their degrading penetration. The blows of a cane across the buttocks and the blows of a stylus across the breasts were thus neatly matched with friendly pinches, soft caresses and little pecking kisses.

But of course it was all Kaeso's fault. If Marcia had not had to lead a wretched existence, sacrificing herself to balance the household budget and provide for the children's future, she wouldn't have found it necessary to grope her maids and beat them up. Another revealing point: Marcus seemed to leave the maids severely alone when he was on heat. Were they a strictly private hunting-ground?

Kaeso was suddenly struck by a lightning suspicion. He leapt to his feet and rushed off to his father's little *popina*. His old nurse was behind the counter. At this time of day work was just over and all sorts of working men had come in for a drink and a bite to eat.

He leant towards the bony old Cretan and whispered in her ear:

'Why didn't you tell me that my father was also enjoying the "little filly"? If you weren't my nurse you'd get what for!'

The woman started and said embarrassedly: 'It wasn't for me to tell you. It was a family secret. The only thing you can hold against me is that

I tried to provide you with a bit of fun. Are you really angry, dear?'

Kaeso gave a gloomy smile and reassured her. His nurse had persuaded him to commit incest even before his mother tried. It was in the order of things. But his own innocence was just as clear. There was something of *Phaedra* or *Oedipus* about his case. Some god had seized on him as his victim in a fit of anger.

During the frugal lunch, while Marcus junior was recounting his successes, Selene was particularly charming to the delighted Marcus *père*. But there was something about the way she sucked her thumb which spoke volumes about her capacity for malice. Despite all the rabbis' slanders, the family of Jesus the carpenter couldn't have been worse. She was to be avoided.

They had reached the fruit when Kaeso knocked over a salt cellar as he was rearranging his cushion with his left hand. Part of the spilled salt fell into an empty egg-shell which he had failed to crush after eating the egg. A glacial silence fell on the little group.

It was customary to be careful not to come into the dining room left foot first, not to touch anything on the table with your left hand, to crush all empty egg-shells, so that no sorcerer could use them whole to put a spell on whoever had eaten the egg, and above all not to spill the salt, which was thought to presage death.

Kaeso immediately broke up the shell with his right hand, a prophylactic gesture which was fairly derisory given the accumulation of ill omens.

While they were feverishly discussing other measures which could be taken to improve the situation, Kaeso suddenly felt exhausted and withdrew. Had the gods wanted to warn him that they were displeased with Selene's charming action?

Kaeso went for a brief walk in the would-be *atrium* to calm himself down. His thoughts went straight to the problem of incest, which was now more topical than ever. After Claudius' remarriage with his niece, Nero had become a source of gossip on the subject. The scandal-mongers were all agreed that he was his mother's lover, but they were divided into two camps as to which of the two, mother or son, had actually seduced the other and imposed the guilty relationship on their partner. The whole ill-starred chronicle of the Julio-Claudians was steeped in a stifling atmosphere of sexual relations between very close relatives.

It seemed to Kaeso that these caprices of the aristocracy, exacerbated by the sexual liberation currently fashionable, were only an expression of a wider and deeper malaise. Whether in the huts of the peasantry or the apartment buildings of Rome, promiscuity on a staggering scale went on non-stop. Those whom the laws favoured, because they were the strongest and most powerful, were exposed to shameful temptations. In the huge aristocratic households, for example, sons were faced with the problem of exciting young stepmothers, not to mention concubines their father had finished with or attractive boys who were temporarily out of favour.

It was a sign of the times that accusations of treason were frequently backed up by a charge of incest, as if there were no political smoke without secret, erotic fire.

Another consideration of some importance: the laws against incest by definition only concerned citizens and freedmen, because only they were legally capable of marrying and having children. Since slaves were outside the law, no one paid much attention to what they did. Their sexual activity, whether acknowledged or secret, was unclear and the government exercised no control over it. Who worries about whether flies round a lamp are committing incest? But once these slaves were freed, they contributed to the stock of the citizenry.

Further back in history, incest between stepson and stepmother, or mother and son, had been one of the great themes of Greek theatre. It was still a huge success with everyone. Seneca himself, who was always very sensitive to the moral mood of his milieu, explored the subject in one of the nine tragedies which he had written for public recitation or private performance before a cultured élite.

If one went further back still, one was struck by the importance and precision of the laws regulating sexual relations in primitive and nomadic societies. The Septuagint was eloquent testimony to this. In a small tribe isolated amid a hostile world, it was essential to know who was allowed to sleep with whom. Had the Greeks and Romans originally been so very different from these bizarre Jews?

Kaeso's troubles seemed to have their origins far back in time. That did not make them any easier to bear.

In his desperation Kaeso thought of Seneca. During siesta he wrote to Silanus:

'K. Aponius Saturninus to D. Junius Silanus Torquatus, very filial greetings.

Thank you again for the celebrations organized for my assumption of the *toga virilis*. Everything was perfect and absolutely fascinating throughout. The taste and generosity which you display on all such occasions prove that you really deserve to possess such riches. I have never seen Marcia looking prettier or happier than on that evening. I hope she may be able to give you, who apparently have everything, whatever you still lack.

I have not stopped thinking about the ideas on traditional religion which you were kind enough to expound to me. But they only concern appearances. Since in your inmost heart and mind you are a Stoic, I would naturally like to gain a deeper knowledge of that doctrine before becoming your affectionate son. But I have already strained your patience to the uttermost. You belong to the same circles as Seneca, whom you admire as I do, and as a friend of his you have the entrée to his house. I have always wanted to meet the great man, who spends his life bringing intellectual enlightenment to himself and others. I know that if you asked him to spare a little time to your future son, he would grant the request with his customary affability. The only way I can obtain the pleasure and honour of such an interview is via you. I am asking you this favour because I want to understand and love you better. And it is a fault of mine to do everything in a rush.

Fare well.'

Kaeso told the messenger to hurry. While waiting for one of Silanus' slaves to bring the tablets back, he went off to the bookshop belonging to the brothers Sosius. The bookshops were mostly concentrated in the Argiletum, but there were also some all round the Forums. The Sosii's shop was next to the temple of Vertumnus, between the Pig Market and the Cattle Market. It was a very popular shop, where the learned meetings of some literary circle or other were always being held. Kaeso used to buy his books there while he was still studying under the *grammaticus*, and in view of his interview with Seneca he wanted to acquire the latest volume of his *Letters to Lucilius*.

Since the previous summer Seneca had been using the enforced leisure of his voluntary withdrawal from court life to send beautifully polished letters to his friend Lucilius Junior, the procurator of Sicily. His lucky correspondent immediately dispatched them for collected publication. These writings were of particular interest to Kaeso because in them Seneca was trying to persuade Lucilius to reject Epicureanism and take up Stoicism. The implication was that the passage from materialism to pantheism could be a source of moral progress. In any case, though Epicureanism, whether moderate or indulgent, had long been in favour with cultivated Romans, it was no longer in tune with the times. Things were too unsettled for such a complacent creed to ring true. Kaeso had read the first of the *Letters* while he was in Athens, notably the one in Book II which could have been entitled 'Travel is not a way to cure the sickness of one's soul'.

The Sosii's shop had not changed. The frontage was still decorated with a host of books, the long list of authors and their works for sale was still posted up there, spreading out over the conveniently adjacent pillars of the portico. A quick glance showed that Seneca had published yet more of his moral dissertations for the upper classes.

Kaeso went into the room where one of the Sosius brothers was usually to be found, among the partitions fitted out with cylindrical horizontal compartments so prettily called 'nests', where the book-rolls were kept. There were also some huge 'tomes' on shelves. The younger Sosius knew about Kaeso's forthcoming adoption, and hurried to serve him and offer him credit. His behaviour had always been perfectly correct. Now he had suddenly become positively friendly.

Unfortunately the last copy of the *Letters to Lucilius* had been snapped up, but new copies were being made. Sosius offered to take Kaeso into the workshop, if that would be of any interest to him, where they could find out at once how far the work had got. The Sosii were not merely booksellers like most of their comrades in the trade, some of whom were even itinerant pedlars. They were also bookmakers and publishers. A substantial part of their production, if a work was selling well, was distributed for sale by other shops whose finances were not solid enough to support their own workshops.

First they went through a room which was full of papyri and, to a lesser extent, parchment, which came from the huge warehouse near the Forum at the foot of the Palatine. There were nine sorts of papyrus, from the rough *emporetica*, used as wrapping paper, to the costly *augustalis* for de luxe editions, which came in five different sizes. The Egyptians had been selling this paper since time immemorial, and had accidentally been responsible for the creation of parchment more than three hundred years earlier. Proud of the 700,000 scrolls in his library at Alexandria, Ptolemy had put an embargo on the export of papyrus to Pergamum, where King Eumenes was hoping to set up a library of rival proportions. The Pergamenes then dreamed up a way of replacing papyrus by sheep skins, cunningly cured and worked. Unfortunately the product was incomparably more expensive than papyrus, and editions on parchment were of necessity relatively few. Sosius showed Kaeso some skins which were naturally yellow and had the advantage of not tiring the eyes, and some whitened skins which some people found more attractive.

There were several workshops containing scribes, each of them producing a single work, for they were not copyists. They wrote on their knees to the dictation of a reader. In this way a large number of copies could be made concurrently from a single original. Kaeso watched the work curiously for a moment. The scribes dipped their pens in ink-wells containing a mixture of black ink and sepia. They had compasses for measuring the spacing and length of lines, rulers for tracing lines, and sponges and scrapers for making corrections.

But since, with such a system, the scribes inevitably made a considerable number of mistakes, it was essential to have a section of the workshop specializing exclusively in corrections. The price of a book was closely related to the quality of these corrections, and every work had to bear the name of its corrector.

Once the sheets of papyrus and parchment had been collated and corrected, they were taken to another part of the workshop for binding. Workmen glued the sheets of papyrus one to another in sequence and fixed the last to a cylindrical length of wood called an *umbilicus*, around which the scroll was rolled. These pieces of wood varied in length and thickness. On each end of the *umbilicus*, after the two flat surfaces (called *frontes*) had been smoothed and polished, was mounted a disc or crescent the same in diameter as the rolled book. Finally, the book was slipped into a bag of hide or cloth, fitted with straps for holding the contents in tight, and a label was stuck on the outside of the bag, bearing the name of the author and the work in red lead. The sheets of parchment were made into flat books. Once they had been put one above the other in the right sequence, they were sewn and stuck on the left edge and fitted with a cover in leather or wood. The final product was called a *tomus*.

The basic material from which certain expensive books were made was bleached with a special oil to protect it from worms and humidity, and the ink used was mixed with absinth to discourage mice.

Other workers were wiping or scraping papyri or parchments on unsold copies to make palimpsests, which could be used again for cheap books. The quality of the material in some unsold books did not even warrant this treatment. These were sold by weight to cut-price book-pedlars. Children learnt to read from them, practised writing on the backs of the pages, or even enjoyed the malicious pleasure of wiping their arses on the evidence of their hard work, for sponges were quite expensive because of the relative rarity of good divers. Sometimes reject books ended up in fish or grocery shops, where they were used as wrapping paper.

The elder Sosius, who was in the process of supervising corrections to an edition of Ovid, informed Kaeso that a new consignment of the *Letters to Lucilius* had just been completed. The work was displayed for his admiration. It was a scroll without an *umbilicus*, because its shortness meant that it did not require lengthy unrolling. Short works of an everyday kind on papyrus were sometimes bound in the form of a *tomus*, a form normally used only for luxury editions on parchment. If sheepskin were made into a roll, it would be very difficult to unwind once it had taken on the shape of the central spindle.

The conversation came round to Ovid. Grandfather Sosius had known him well, and the father had talked about him to his sons.

'Forty-six or seven years ago,' said the elder Sosius, 'the poor man died of despair during his distant and very strict exile. The pretext for his condemnation has remained a mystery to this very day. But the real reason, which put him beyond all hope of appeal against the sentence, is something I *can* tell you. While old Augustus, who had sown plenty of wild oats in his youth, was slaving away trying to bring the antique Roman virtues back into favour – virtues which had been bringing a smile to the lips of all our aristocracy for years – Ovid committed the capital crime of revealing, in a wonderfully talented way, what everyone knew from experience already: that if she only knew how to go about it, even the most virtuous married woman could find herself squealing with pleasure in bed. Our thoughtless author actually wrote about the sexual enjoyment to be had by women, who weren't supposed to enjoy sex ever. Augustus had terrible trouble with his daughter and granddaughter, who were absolute hussies despite their strict upbringing. Suddenly he was treated to the spectacle of the leading court poet proposing to the world at large images of the Roman male, conqueror of nations, and the Roman wife, mother of Roman heroes, which the emperor found intolerable. Ovid portrayed a lover on all fours in ecstasy as he uses his tongue not only on his neighbour's wife, but, even worse, sometimes on his own! His advice and techniques were obviously of interest to all men and women, and overthrew all barriers and prejudices. There was no longer any distinction between a Roman mother and a prostitute.'

'The difference,' interposed the younger Sosius, 'is that the girls in a brothel get a lot less pleasure out of their work than men imagine.'

'Yes,' the elder brother went on sadly, 'it's as though men feel slighted by female enjoyment. Perhaps it's because all men have mothers that they refuse to imagine them on heat, shrieking like a wolverine in the twilight.'

'It's my impression,' said Kaeso, 'that the mother of today has no inhibitions about shrieking her head off, and in broad daylight too.'

He changed the subject of a conversation which he was beginning to find unpleasant. The Sosii offered him a piece of exquisite craftsmanship: the whole of the *Iliad* on a roll of very fine paper, which fitted into a nutshell in solid gold. But Kaeso had sweated long enough already over the *Iliad*. He merely bought Seneca's latest letters.

The Cattle Market was two steps away. Kaeso went in that direction with the intention of going to see Marcia's statue. At that time of day the Forums are nowhere near as crowded as in the mornings. Lots of Romans were at the baths, in the Campus Martius, on the Appian Way or in one of the public gardens, and the beggars, both real and false, of whom there were usually large numbers in the Forums, tended to follow the crowds. As night fell, the real beggars, and large numbers of those without a roof over their heads, encouraged by the first signs of warm weather, would go and install themselves in a theatre or a Circus. The police tolerated this arrangement so as to rid the streets, porticoes and gardens of the rabble. The vast monuments also served occasionally as a place of refuge for soldiers passing through the city.

In front of the temple of Patrician Modesty there was still one blind man left, his purulent eyes covered in flies. He made Kaeso think of Oedipus. For the first time the boy wondered why it was his *eyes* that Oedipus had put out after discovering that he had married his own mother. Why not punish the hand which had stroked her, or the nose which had breathed in the scent of her body, or the prick which had done much worse things? Couldn't Oedipus still see the images which haunted him, when his eyes were closed once and for all?

The beggar had a little painting in a naïve style hanging round his neck, which showed him swimming in a wild sea, while a boat was sinking on the horizon. It was immediately obvious what was supposed to be the reason for his misery. But facetious boys had added cruel graffiti to the picture – a siren playing a *cithara*, the words 'drinking water' . . . Kaeso was touched by the man's pitiful condition, something which would previously have left him relatively cold. Since he had been so suddenly struck down by misfortune, he found he was more sensitive to other people's troubles. The beggar told him where to find the guardian of the temple, who lived nearby, and Kaeso gave him a denarius in exchange, an unusually liberal gift.

The guardian was at the baths, but his wife opened the temple for Kaeso. Temples were usually kept closed. Particular care was taken with them, as they sometimes served as banks. The sacrificial altar was always in the open space below the steps, whose number was carefully calculated so that the right foot could play its beneficial part.

In the half-shadow of the old sanctuary Marcia's statue was indeed a great success. It was easy to see why Silanus should have thought it worthy of the place. Beneath the veil the face expressed all the modesty which men like to read in the eyes of a wife or mother whom they suppose to be frigid. The cold quality of the marble itself accentuated the impression of delicacy and purity still more.

Kaeso told the woman: 'It was my mother who was the model for the statue.'

'How lucky you are.'

With a deep sigh Kaeso gave a small tip to his sycophantic guide and went home.

His father was in his library, trying to get to grips with a tricky case which had already given birth to contradictory legal judgements. One of Silanus' many protégés, a dissipated young man of good family who had run through all his money, had signed a contract as a gladiator. Then, taking fright, he had wheedled some money out of one of his married sisters and had managed to buy himself out before actually doing any fighting. The question was: did the 'infamy' officially attaching to the status of gladiator derive from the contract or from the first appearance in the arena?

Marcus was only too happy to be interrupted in his researches by Kaeso, with whom, since his return from Greece, he had hardly had a chance to talk. He felt that a shadow had grown up between himself and his son, but was far from suspecting its nature or importance.

Kaeso began by putting his father in a good humour by reminding him of happy times they had spent together. Marcus, in his anxiety to give a flattering image of himself, had often dragged the boys off to see some civil or criminal case in which he was acting. One of Kaeso's earliest memories was of the trial of a Greek on a charge of unlawfully claiming Roman citizenship. The emperor Claudius chose to preside, and his grotesque sense of humour left its mark on the occasion. As the lawyers could not agree as to whether the accused should wear a Roman toga or a Greek cloak during the trial, Claudius, with superb impartiality, had decreed that he should be dressed Roman-style while his own counsel was pleading his cause and Greek-style when the prosecution were putting their case. Marcus, despite his distant family origins, had agreed to appear for the prosecution, but his eloquence had quite deserted him in the resulting atmosphere of total farce, and the Greek had got off. Later Kaeso had sat through interminable civil cases that ran through as many as seven water-clocks (about two and a half hours): they were heard before the *centumviri* in the vast Basilica Julia, with a packed crowd of onlookers. As there were frequently four cases going on at once, it was the lawyers with the loudest voices who made themselves heard best in the cacophony, and it was the richest lawyers who got the most applause, because they could afford to pay a claque to cheer them on. Marcus, with his rather thin voice and empty pockets, was not cut out for a brilliant career in that grandiose building. Nonetheless Kaeso had been impressed by his father's eloquence. He now tried to rediscover his naïve childhood frame of mind so that he could flatter his father on a point about which he was sensitive.

All this was simply intended to work up the best possible atmosphere for the question which was suddenly preoccupying him. What had his real mother, Pomponia, been like? The young man was overcome with a keen desire to find out about her. He had rarely heard people speak of her, and had learned little when they had.

Marcus was only too happy to let himself go with information about a period when he had been rich, happy and above all proud of himself. But although Kaeso plied him with questions, his replies were terribly disappointing because they were totally devoid of original features. Marcus sounded like Livy tirelessly reciting all the classic virtues of the Roman matron of the good old days. Pomponia had been chaste, faithful, home-loving, discreet, reserved, modest, affectionate, economical, severe and just with the slaves . . . dignity personified. Kaeso understood that with a man of his father's type he would never manage to find out any more. It was like losing his mother a second time, for ever. He thanked his father and withdrew with tears in his eyes.

Selene gave Kaeso the tablets which had just come back from Silanus, and Kaeso sat in a corner of the *atrium* to examine their contents.

'D. Junius Silanus to his dear Kaeso, greetings.

Seneca has asked me to tell you that you can find "the great man who spends his life bringing intellectual enlightenment to himself and others" at the Palatine library until closing time. He will be there again tomorrow in the late afternoon. Your sudden passion for Stoicism flatters me, but I have the impression, from a little phrase which doubtless slipped in without your noticing it, that you are wanting to throw some light on your own conscience. I wonder why your honourable father, or your stepmother or I myself, do not seem more than amply competent to help you with that? Perhaps because your problem of conscience has some relationship with your prospective adoption?

I talked to Marcia about your disquiet, and I mentioned your curious remark to me on the night of the banquet for your assumption of the toga: "I shall never betray you!" You had a very odd look on your face at that moment.

I had the feeling that Marcia was concealing something from me, and I flatter myself on having been able to inspire sufficient confidence in her to get her little secret out of her in the end.

In the summer before you left for Greece you suddenly noticed that your feelings for Marcia were entering a new phase and you could not hide from her the passion which was eating you up. You felt you couldn't live, you threatened to commit suicide if the woman of your thoughts treated so deep and lasting a devotion as mere childishness.

When I was your age I had a few grand passions as well. Some of them lasted more than six months. The ones which were unrequited lasted longer than the others. The young have a tendency to mythologize the most natural and simple of acts.

In any case Marcia herself was largely responsible for this sudden passion, because she had just revealed to you that her marriage to your father had always been a pure formality. You no longer had to think of her as a real stepmother, so it is hardly surprising if you then developed a burning desire for her.

I think that, in giving in to your desires, Marcia acted very reasonably. It is good for an adolescent for his first experience to be guided by a woman markedly older than he is, whose qualities of sensibility and delicacy are equal to the task. My first mistress was over forty, and I am still grateful to her for everything she taught me. She saved me from many dangers and many mistakes.

Marcia, who knows a lot about men, had another motive which was of some importance. In the course of their amorous frolics men are pursued throughout their lives by the pure and tender image of their mothers, a contradiction which can lead to a certain lack of balance, sometimes even to peculiar behaviour. If the gods allowed it, it would certainly be in the public interest for every boy to sleep with his mother while she is still young and attractive. They would certainly be relieved of a burden afterwards. You had the marvellous good fortune to sleep with a delightful mother without the gods being able to take offence. The intoxicating perfume is incestuous but the scent-bottle itself is innocent. You should be grateful to Marcia, who has always been so devoted to you.

Your letter to your stepmother about Greek homosexuality, which I took it upon myself to answer, showed what a good turn she had done you, and testified to the new, confident nature of your relationship. The crisis was over. You were no longer afraid to be open about your emotional and moral problems to a woman who had been both mother and lover to you. And the amiable hetaeras whom you preferred to the boys were a further proof that you were happily over your difficulties.

Now, with a scrupulousness which does you credit, you wonder whether it is right for you to be adopted by the husband of this woman who initiated you into love before she knew me. I can personally assure you that you are being excessively sensitive. I think too well of myself to have ever been jealous, and the stupidest form of jealousy is jealousy of the past.

Perhaps you are not quite sure of yourself? Perhaps you are afraid of a recurrence of former temptations, if you found yourself living at close quarters with such a beautiful, attractive woman? I know that in those circumstances you would do everything possible not to give in. But I am also aware that the frigidity of old age is only round the corner for me, that all men – and it is even more true of women – are weak when pleasure beckons, and that nature, to which we must all submit without a murmur, always gives the palm to youth. If you found yourself burning with the same old passion, and Marcia were, in a maternal way, willing to yield, I should take an indulgent stance, rather than bruise my hand thumping the table. What is important to me is to be able to spend my declining years in the company of two such exquisitely beautiful people as you and Marcia.

You see, I am setting your mind at rest.

I hope you are well. I am wonderfully fit, give or take a little rheumatism.'

When Kaeso read: 'I think that Marcia, in giving in to your desires . . .', he let out, despite himself, a cry of surprise and distress which brought Selene into the *atrium* to find out the cause. When he had finished reading the letter for himself, he read it again to her. It seemed to make a considerable impression on her.

'Marcia,' she said, 'has turned the tables on you completely. Baby was trembling with lust. Mummy calmed him down with an absent-minded caress. Baby has grown up and now his mind is being "set at rest". You now have no valid reason for refusing adoption. Silanus has ceased to be an obstacle. The cleverest thing of all is that if you were so socially tactless as to tell him the whole truth, your version would sound false in comparison with the subtle lies that he seems to be so proud of himself for having "got out" of Marcia. How could you ever escape from the clutches of such a formidable woman?'

Kaeso groaned:

'I still have a good reason for getting out of this rotten situation. I really don't think I could face sleeping with Marcia.'

'Well that's the one reason you can't give, because it's the only one which women won't accept and men have difficulty believing. Anyway, aren't you supposed to have jumped the gun already?'

'Oh, don't I know it! I was a heart-throb without knowing it, and still without knowing it I became an honorary lover. I wish someone would get this vampire off me!'

'I might point out that my life is now in danger. When I helped you to throw some light on your distressing situation, you swore to protect me. Now the threat to tell Silanus about Marcia's depraved behaviour no longer has any meaning. Your future good relations with her are my only guarantee of safety.'

'Say what you mean. Am I supposed to sleep with my stepmother just to save your skin?'

'It's a matter for your conscience.'

Kaeso put his head in his hands and tore his hair. 'I'm completely surrounded by female vampires.'

'After the little favour I did you, the description is less than kind. But the other vampire could disappear.'

'Meaning?'

'Don't gladiators exist to provide a solution to conflicts of this kind? Would you like me to speak to Capreolus? He's a Jew and an understanding sort of chap. For a reasonable sum he might be persuaded to help?'

Selene had the excuse that Marcia had already attempted to have her murdered in the same way, but the excuse was merely a theoretical one since the slave knew nothing about the incident.

Kaeso was horrified. He thrust away the temptation which had just brushed across his mind.

'Marcia is still my mother. There have been quite enough matricides in Rome as it is. Don't worry. I'll manage to protect you one way or another.'

'If you don't, I shall rise from the grave and suck out your blood for good and all!'

Given Selene's exceptional talents, the perspective was terrifying. Well-trained tarts and expert homosexuals must make merciless vampires.

In this climate of mysterious and abnormal unease Seneca's personality seemed to Kaeso like a haven of peace and reason. After a few words of reassurance to Selene, the young man sped off towards the Palatine library, with his copy of the *Letters to Lucilius* under his arm.

Lucullus, the famous writer on cookery, had helped himself to all the books he could find during his brilliant campaigns in Asia. Bibliophiles had then been given the run of the rich library which he had established in his splendid villa on the Pincian. Later Asinius Pollio had founded the first public library on the Aventine, near the Atrium of Liberty. Next to the portico of Octavia, Augustus had built the Octavian library, then the Palatine library on the hill of the same name. This building opened on to the portico or *atrium* of Apollo. Everywhere readers could find an excuse to stretch their legs while thinking or chatting.

The Palatine library was the most important and the most luxurious. It was made up of three huge, majestic galleries. To the south-west it gave on to the temple of Apollo Palatine and its portico, and to the north-west on to a little cluster of temples, which were reached by the Porta Mugonia, one of the main entries to the Palatine precinct. There was the temple of Jupiter Propugnator, the temple of Fortuna Respiciens, the temple of Fides, the temple of Febris, the temple of Juno Sospita, the temple of Cybele, the temple of Bacchus, and the temple of Viriplaca, consecrated to the goddess who placated furious husbands. This overworked goddess was an elevated and sensible example of how remarkably specialized the traditional Roman gods could be, especially as the monument was very old. The continual wars of the old days had caused it to be put up. When a cuckolded legionary came home after years of campaigning, it was all too often necessary to make a sacrifice to Viriplaca. And as women no longer needed the excuse of long military campaigns to be unfaithful, the worried wives who now beseiged Viriplaca were not embarrassed to be seen there. They were the victims of hot-tempered husbands, only a small proportion of whom fail to call their wife's virtue in question. These were the most desperate cases, because the pleasures of the double bed can do nothing to remedy incompatability of temperament.

Kaeso went into the central gallery, which was more like a museum than a reading-room. It was decorated with busts of all the famous dead writers and dominated by a bronze statue of Augustus. Kaeso looked for Seneca in the adjoining rooms. There, in the bookcases of cedar-wood, whose smell of resin helped to keep worms away, lay a multitude of book-rolls, each in its pigeon-hole. Every *tomus* was laid out flat on a little table. The floor was of green marble, to prevent dazzle.

They were just calling closing time when Kaeso spotted Seneca. He recognized him from the widely-distributed marble busts of him. Seneca had probably stashed away three hundred million sesterces in legal back-handers, usury, and various back-stairs deals in the corridors of power, firstly with Agrippina's blessing, then Nero's. He was very elegant, but with the heavily lined face of an unhealthy and neurotic vegetarian.

Seneca greeted Kaeso, the flattering little work tucked under his arm, with the most urbane cordiality. After the death of Burrus, the appointment of Tigellinus as Praetorian Prefect, Nero's remarriage to Poppaea, the death of Octavia and the wave of trials for *lèse-majesté* against suspect senators, the philosopher had despaired of his pupil and withdrawn into his ivory tower on tiptoe. But his secret sympathies quite evidently lay with the opposition, some of it organized, some of it random, which, without hoping for the impossible in the form of a return to the Republic, at least wanted an enlightened monarchy on the pattern of Augustus rather than a Greek-style tyranny. Seneca was therefore on the best of terms with all sorts of aristocratic circles and pressure groups. He was as well received by the Stoic Thrasea as by the vaguely Epicurean Calpurnius Piso. And he had a high regard for the sorely tried Silani.

The *custodes* were herding the readers towards the exits: given the dangers of fire it would have been unthinkable to work in a library at night. Seneca took Kaeso into the portico of Apollo, and they strolled up and down chatting.

Kaeso thought it better not to launch himself straight into painful intimate secrets, and started the conversation with some general points, notably directed to the issue of what happens to the soul after death. As a society lecturer and talented lawyer, the distinguished philospher had no difficulty dealing with such a trifling point . . .

'I touched on the matter – you may perchance recall – in my *Consolation to Marcia*. After leaving the body, the soul spends a period in purgatory in proportion to its faults and merits, then rises to heaven. There it finds peace and joy, is delivered from evil, doubt and ignorance, and has all the secrets of the universe open to it. But as you know, to Stoics the evolution of the universe, which is conceived of as eternal, is cyclical. Sometimes the universe contracts into the general inferno of a huge "conflagration"; at others it expands and gradually reorganizes itself. Seen in this way, the immortality of the individual soul lasts only from one conflagration to the next, though they are separated by what may be called infinity. At each conflagration the soul returns to the individual elements from which it was compounded. The Stoics think that the destructive and constructive energy of the whole system is due to a sort of fire. But we are not materialists in the same sense as the Epicureans, whose interlocking atoms are governed by a sort of chance. On the contrary we believe that the universe is consubstantial with a god, Reason. What we call matter is only an emanation of that divine reason. The spirit reigns everywhere and in everything.'

'So god is a part of the world, an organizing and regulating force, like the Platonic divine craftsman, and not a creator like the Jewish god, of whom you must have heard since I gather that you knew Philo quite well?'

'You are absolutely right. I admit that the Jewish god did make me think, and even tempted me for a short while. The concept of transcendency certainly does do away with certain difficulties. But it raises others which are just as embarrassing. If god is pure spirit outside the world, as the Jews say, one wonders how he could act within it, how he can communicate with it, express his desires and his will. Their Yahwe walking on Sinai is clearly childish nonsense.'

'Do you know anything about the Christians?'

'Oh, I'd heard of them before you, I should imagine. When my brother Gallio was proconsul at Corinth, a certain Pompeius Paulus, a Jew from Tarsus who claimed to be a Christian, caused him a lot of irritation and trouble, which he wrote to me about. It seems the Christians believe not just in a Yahwe who walks on Sinai, but a god incarnate, crucified and resurrected. Forgive me if I smile! The Jews are always obsessed with this keen desire, inherent in their system, to establish direct contact with a heaven which they nonetheless see as immaterial. Despite the total implausibility of its postulates this Christian sect has spread surprisingly since then. As this fellow Paul is currently in Rome, I could not resist having him introduced to me the day before yesterday. Our discussion was, alas, a complete failure. Paul is a propagandist with a training which is rabbinical rather than philosophical. His Greek culture is very superficial. All he can do is repeat highly arguable explanations or make extravagant dogmatic assertions. He's half Jewish and half mad. But like many insane people, he can reason perfectly. He speaks with plenty of fire and conviction. He's entirely spontaneous. No one could ever find him boring, which is more than I can say for some of my philosopher friends.'

Kaeso finally came to the point which was tormenting him. He spilled everything out in a long-winded and confused way, encouraged from time to time by a pertinent question from Seneca, who eventually acquired a fairly clear grasp of what was at issue. The sage thought for a moment, and then said:

'I feel some sympathy for you, because your story is, when it comes to it, very like my own. Throughout my life destiny has constantly posed me the tragic question of how far the sage is justified in finding an accommodation with evil in order to avoid something worse. My wealth has been held against me; but for a true Stoic money is surely synonymous with independence and dignity. I have been reproached with sycophancy for writing my *Consolation to Polybius*, during my awful exile in Corsica, because it was addressed to one of Claudius' favourites, a freedman who had just lost his younger brother. It is true that it is an occasional piece of absolute platitude – and it did not even secure my recall! But cannot a Seneca do more good in Rome than in Corsica, where his only audience are the goats? After Agrippina's death I was reproached for having written the letter which Nero read to the Senate, in which the matricide was both justified and made out to be suicide. But Burrus and I were faced with a *fait accompli*, and thanks in part to my influence the preceding and the following years were the best of the reign, in harmony with the sentiments of my dialogue *On Clemency,* where I argue the merits of enlightened absolutism. What's more, think of all the assassinations for which Agrippina had been responsible. Your future adoptive father is only too familiar with some of them. But this Stoic *eukairia*, if you will allow the lapse into Greek, this reasoned opportunism has its limits. There comes a time when you have to commit yourself, to write a lampoon such as *The Apotheopumpkinificosis of the Emperor Claudius*. And there comes another time when you have to leave the field, when you cannot take the rules of the game any longer. I reached that point two years ago. And, ever since, my wife Paulina has been trying to console me for this, as it were, self-imposed second exile here in Rome itself.'

As he talked, Seneca had begun to forget the boy he was speaking to. He became aware of the fact and hurriedly came back to Kaeso's problems.

'As for your own troubles, I'll put a question to you which I put to all the young men who come to ask my advice: "What do you actually want me to say?" Men only ever follow advice that they want to hear in the first place and which they could have discovered for themselves with a little thought. A counsellor is merely a mid-wife, who draws out of someone else's heart and mind what was already there.'

'In confessing the whole story to you, and thanks to your sympathetic questions, I think I've already clarified my ideas.'

'I had the same feelings when I wrote my *Consolation* to my mother, Helvia, a very private work which I sent her from the wilds of Corsica to dry her tears.' (Seneca seemed to have offered formal consolation to an awful lot of people.)

'One thing is certain. However willing Silanus might be to turn a blind eye – and I leave it to you to judge whether such an attitude would be exemplary or shameful – I couldn't now envisage a liaison with Marcia.'

'Why?'

'Once upon a time I had an infinite regard for her and no desire. Or at least, if my desire was awakened, my fear of incest kept it in my subconscious. As I've just told you, I found out that her marriage to my father was on the whole merely a formality, but she had to admit that she had briefly shared his bed. That cut my desire off instantly, and the sense of paralysis is still with me. Incest isn't determined by the number of times you do it.'

'That is a view which can be advanced without fear of contradiction.'

'If I gave in to Marcia's charms, wouldn't the physical manifestations of my love be poisoned by that obvious fact?'

'That is very possible.'

'My affection for her still exists, but the great part of the respect I once had for her has vanished. With the best of intentions she has, like you, struck a bargain with the devil.'

'Without wishing to be offensive, I would point out that I prostituted my talents for rather higher causes!'

'I accept that I am indeed only an insignificant cause. At all events, what is love without respect?'

'It is typical of the idealism of youth to use such noble language.'

'Now, if I allow myself to be adopted, I'm lost. No one could resist the machinations of a woman who is so passionate, so enterprising and so implacable.'

'I agree that you would be a light weight to throw in the balance against her.'

'Worse still – if anything could be worse – my personality would be crushed by hers. I should be reduced to a state of slavery and cease to exist. All my time would be spent satisfying her demands.'

'That is indeed an important point to consider. But if you decline this threatening adoption, what are you going to say to Silanus, who has welcomed you with open arms? For that matter, what are you going to say to Marcia to spare her the desperation of an irremediable humiliation? Hell hath no fury like a woman scorned; my plays offer eloquent testimony to the fact.'

'I did briefly think of taking up Judaism, so as to have a good excuse for not taking responsibility for Silanus' family cult.'

Seneca stopped and smiled.

'That is a brilliant idea, if ever there was one. Why did you give up the idea?'

'The rabbi I consulted made it sound as though my circumcision could only occur in a misty and distant future.'

'Of course! If the Romans went in for mass circumcision, there would be no more Roman religion and no more Judaism. Trumpery imitation Jews would refuse to sacrifice to our gods, and that would be the end of everything . . . supposing that Caesar and the *populus* allowed it without reacting.'

'Then I thought of the Christians, but from what you yourself said . . .'

Seneca thought for a moment, and then said, choosing his words carefully:

'Where sacrifices are concerned, the Christians have naturally adopted the Jewish position. Since what you are looking for is a good excuse, Pompeius Paulus, who is desperate for conversions, will provide you with it much quicker than the rabbis.'

'But all that rubbish about incarnation and resurrection, isn't it sure to ruin the whole thing? Can you see me recounting all those fairy tales to Silanus with a straight face?'

'Given what is at stake there's nothing to prevent you, without infringing your moral code, from dressing up their crazier claims in the familiar borrowed finery of some mythology or other. Silanus will be too upset by your defection to notice the small print.'

Seneca was due to dine with Piso, and his litter had arrived. The philosopher excused himself for having to break off so interesting a conversation, and said to Kaeso by way of conclusion: 'The only solution which you will find satisfactory is to obey the voice of your conscience. I can see that it's already forearmed.'

Kaeso accompanied Seneca right to his litter and said:

'But if god and the world are the same, he is not a person. So what valid truths can he whisper to my conscience?'

Before stretching himself out on his cushions, the multi-millionaire philosopher replied:

'Pray to the gods that god is not a person capable of giving your weak mind orders which brook no disobedience. When that day comes enslavement to a woman won't be the only fate you have to fear!'

❧ PART THREE ❧

PART THREE

❋ Chapter ❋

I

Paul was staying in Rome only out of a sense of duty. He felt the most extreme repugnance at lingering there. Everything in this monstrous city got his back up. The insolence of a handful of rich people, who wasted the revenues of enormous estates, and many of whom had no over-powering reason for being in Rome except senatorial or political obliga-tions. The incurable idleness of the ordinary people, who worked less and less and demanded more and more from a state which played providence to them. The wretched condition, in moral even more than in material terms, of a huge mass of public and private slaves, most of them born into slavery, whether by accident or design, and brought to this Babel from every part of the world. The swarms of beggars, both amateur and professional. The incredible number of prostitutes of both sexes. The obscene mixed baths. The bloodthirsty violence of the *munera*. The dangerous brutality of the chariot races, where many of the drivers were killed by being dragged in the dust or crushed by the horses' hooves. The cruel pornography of the theatres. The frequent abandoning of new born children on the rubbish tips. Nero's personal programme – the emperor, partly from inner conviction and partly out of a calculated desire to pander to the people, had encouraged all the vices of Babylon and Sodom to an unprecedented degree. It was official policy – and shamelessly advertised as such – for the people to enjoy themselves to the full at both ends. They were to enjoy themselves non-stop, to be reduced to a stupor by continual pleasure: get them by the belly and the crutch and keep them emptied of thought or feeling.

As a permanent symbol of the surrounding idolatry, the city was full of statues. It was a hateful sight to someone born a Jew. They were as much the fruits of the pillage of the known world as of non-stop production by Roman sculptors. There were full-length statues, busts, groups, set up in serried rows in all the squares, at all the cross-roads, under all the por-ticoes, and every excuse to have more was a good one. Man created in the image of God had insolently reproduced himself in bronze, stone and marble, as if the atoms of Epicurus had suddenly copulated frenetically so

307

as to insult the heavens with their empty gaze. Many of the imperial statues even had detachable heads, so that they could hurriedly be changed at the dawn of a new reign. These tottering heads seemed to be a divine warning to the devilish Prince of this world. Moreover most of the statues were of very mediocre workmanship, and every now and then an army of them would be sent for breaking up. But the evil spread unceasingly, and legislation had proved powerless to stop it. It is true that Paul was incapable of distinguishing between an Aphrodite by Praxiteles and some crude piece by a village sculptor. And his exasperated disapproval was directed against all the pictures too, for he considered them as impious as the statues.

However, he had to devote some time to Rome before leaving for Greece and the East, where, essentially, the corruption was no less, just on a less grandiose scale. Even libidinous Corinth itself was no bigger than a mere district of Rome, which was a city of inhuman proportions. Paul's presence was particularly useful because Peter, who flatly detested Rome, was very rarely there. He had the excuse of not being a Roman citizen. Paul had not.

As a citizen Paul would like to have loved this impossible city. Sometimes he let himself go with the absurdest dreams: a Rome without temples, statues, pictures, race-courses, *munera*, theatres or immodest baths, a Rome where sodomites and catamites would be mercilessly stoned and crucified, where the necessary courtesans would be made to observe discretion and modesty by punctilious aediles, where women would be indissolubly married to faithful husbands, where adulterers would be pursued and subject to exemplary punishments, where people would be put to death for killing children, where slaves would lead happy lives in obedience to the beribboned canes of paternalistic masters. Sometimes he even imagined bread and wine being distributed to a rapt audience, who were neither greedy nor drunken, in a basilica purged of its legal pettifoggers and idle onlookers, or in a temple whose idol had been smashed to pieces. But he was well aware that he would never see this ideal Rome. It existed only in the mind of the Holy Trinity, as pure ideas did in the mind of Plato's god.

In the meantime the situation of Christians inside and outside Rome was none too good. In the East their preaching had had its greatest successes in the wilds of Asia Minor among uneducated people who were willing to believe anything. The Christian missionaries, who were not very interested in peasants, had especially selected the large cities as targets, but there they ran up against the unyielding animosity of the

Jews and the mordant mockery of the Greeks. In the West, Christian communities were still small and few and far between. Even in Rome the Gospel had in the main made only little oil-slicks on the surface of the vast household staffs of a few aristocrats, including the immense *familia* of the emperor. The reason why such modest progress as they had made was in such quarters was perfectly clear. On the one hand many of the slaves in aristocratic households were Greek-speaking and the preachers spoke Greek; on the other Christian *episcopi* or *presbyteri* (the terms were more or less interchangeable at the period) had evidently grasped that the conversion of Greek slaves from good households was the most rapid and certain way to obtain the conversion of cultivated masters who knew Greek as well as Latin. A Christian concubine or catamite had opportunities to insinuate the true faith into the heart of a troubled *dominus*, while the little maids could prepare ground with their mistresses. The conversion of a patrician, a member of the aristocracy, a simple knight, or even a politically influential freedman would have been extremely important. The new Christian would inevitably promote the spread of the Gospel among his peers and his own household, and *familiae* of 500 slaves were already current among Romans with very average fortunes of, say, twenty or thirty million sesterces.

In Rome Paul and his emulators were obsessed with the idea of getting in at the top. Paul was well aware that persuasion would always be insufficient to change manners as they were or overthrow existing interests. The Empire could only be converted if one day the emperor himself were converted. Then the force of arms and the lure of money and favours would come to the aid of the exhausted powers of verbal persuasion. And to prepare for the coming of that great day, it was first necessary to convince those who had money, land and manpower.

These visions of the distant future revealed in Paul increased scepticism as to the imminence of the apocalyptic upheavals which certain of Jesus' words seemed to have foretold. Whether it was the destruction of Jerusalem or the end of the world they were waiting for, life had to be lived. A generation had almost passed since Jesus died on Calvary.

Unfortunately the conversion of even the lowest of the Roman nobility was no small task. These people had assimilated enough Greek culture and smart philosophy to prove great rationalists and sceptics. To these unpromising predispositions were added, in those of really old stock, the weighty heritage of the peasant mentality: a marked preference for the concrete, a fierce attachment to the good things of this world, a distrust of novelty and of fine talk, ineradicable superstitiousness, a formal respect for the most obscure of traditions, and inveterate pride. It was almost easier to convert a rabbi than a true Roman.

The Jews at Rome, some of whom had even managed to penetrate the palace, were particularly hostile and reactionary. They could not forget the deportations they had had to endure under Claudius as a result of the first Christian preaching and the riots which had stemmed from it. At their first contact the followers of 'Chrestos' had caused trouble for them.

None of this was very encouraging. Even the Greek slaves, who were supposed to play the role of Trojan horse, but who often had far more wit than a horse, caused continual unpleasant problems. Some had a tendency to believe that the freedom brought by the Gospel ought to have broken their chains, and they had to be lectured. Some of the young ones of both sexes had worries which it was difficult to allay. 'How can I be chaste?' a maid asked. 'My master never stops raping me.' Paul answered naturally that, where there was no alternative, there was no sin. Virtue in those circumstances consists in not taking pleasure in what you are doing. 'But,' the girl went on, 'my master makes me enjoy it.' When boys came along with similar complaints, Paul, who detested homosexuals, lost his temper and referred them to Luke, whose sweetness of nature was unfailing.

Paul often thought about Nero. He was fascinated by his extraordinary personality. In his troubled sleep images of lubricious Neros were succeeded by Neros at prayer surrounded by seraphim.

Kaeso for his part spent a very restless night. Seneca, who seemed to sum up all the most traditional forms of wisdom, had not given him the help he had expected.

On the morning of the Robigalia, the day when red-haired dogs were traditionally sacrificed to the god Robigus so that he would protect the young corn from rust, Kaeso got up left foot forward, gave a start, leapt back into bed and got out again properly, right foot forward. He decided against putting on his toga. He had thought it obligatory for the rabbi and Seneca, but he had been stiflingly hot in it. A fine tunic would do for this fellow Paul.

The fourth hour had already sounded when Kaeso arrived at the great lavatories in the Forum, which were some of the finest in the city, with their central heating in winter and their white marble walls. The elegant *hemicyclium* had twenty-four seats separated by arm-rests sculpted to look like dolphins. Above the seats three niches were occupied by a goddess of Fortune, with an Aesculapius and a Bacchus on either side, while across the diameter of the room, facing the semicircle, was a reassuring line of the seven sages of Greece, who must have had to empty their bladders and intestines with philosophical and regular ease. A small cloakroom, guarded by two public slaves, adjoined the building. One of them was always free to go and fetch a drink or a snack from one of the nearby *thermopolia*, the other helped to put your cloak back on or arrange the folds of your toga.

Under the semicircle of seats there ran a strong current of water permanently carrying matter away to the drain, and linked to each horizontal hole was a vertical indentation in which there rested a soft African or Greek sponge, attached to a handle. At the foot of the seats, behind the customers' ankles, a more modest flow of water ran along a small channel, for rinsing the sponges. And in the centre a fountain gurgling in a basin was used for washing one's hands.

Because of its harmonious beauty and its position in the heart of Rome, amid the morning crowds of the Forum, this very utilitarian building had become an elegant place for men to meet. (The lavatories at the mixed baths were common to both sexes, but women did not venture into public lavatories elsewhere. And as they could not urinate in the amphorae or barrels liberally distributed around, they were obliged to contain themselves, a habit which in other respects they had lost.) So people liked to hang around, leaning on the dolphins. People exchanged gossip. Homosexuals eyed up interesting parties and offered them a sponge with a greedy look. Some people hung around hoping to pick up an invitation to dinner.

There was currently going the rounds an amusing epigram by the young Martial, a poet for hire who had recently arrived in Rome from his native region of Tarragona in Sapin. It apostrophized the parasite Vacerra as follows:

> IN OMNIBUS VACERRA QUOD CONCLAVIBUS
> CONSUMIT HORAS ET DIE TOTO SEDET
> CENATURIT VACERRA NON CACATURIT

> Vacerra in the public loos
> For hours and days on end will sit.
> He spends so long because he goes
> To cadge a dinner, not to shit!

Kaeso went into the lavatories, which were dominated by a powerful smell which had something eminently intimate and social about it. Because it is used to its own smell, an animal takes fright at the smells of others. Man, who appreciates the smells of his own well-formed turds, is usually much less enthusiastic about those of others. The smell of these latrines, which was the result of a successful blend of a number of different smells, was a sign that the Romans had learnt to put up with their neighbours and share their humblest pleasures with them.

There was no one there who looked like Kaeso's idea of a Jew. One of the slaves confirmed that Pompeius Paulus, who was already well known because of his harangues, had not yet put in an appearance.

Kaeso went on to the Basilica Julia, where justice was on holiday, it being a feast-day. He felt as though he could still hear his father's voice ringing under the vaulted roof, drowning the cries of the children playing hopscotch on the tiled floor. He came out again, and to pass the time went back up the Sacred Way to the 'gourmet market', where the strangest and most expensive rare foods could be bought. By an extraordinary paradox, given their peasant origins, well-off Romans were not only wild about fish and other sea-food, but had also insisted, with insatiable curiosity, on trying out everything edible from all over the world. The inaccessibility and extravagant cost of products counted for a lot in the fantastic amounts lavished on food by some gastromaniacs.

The crowd were admiring a consignment of parrots. Following Apicius' recipe, gourmets ate only the bird's brain and tongue.

In a corner of the market was a huge barrel, lying on its side and wedged with stones to keep it stable. It was one of those barrels which are shipped to Rome from Gaul, while at Ostia mountains of broken amphorae pile up and are treated as non-returnable packing material. The lid of the barrel, which served as a door, had been put to one side so that its occupant, who was still at home, could enjoy the fresh air. Among the down-at-heel philosophers of all schools who crowded into the city to spread their ideas and fill their stomachs, the cynic Gratus Lupus – nicknamed Leo because of his mane – had gained a certain renown for himself. Like many others of the same school he sought to do away rigorously with everything in life which he found unnecessary. He had smashed his only drinking-cup the day he saw a child drinking out of its cupped hands. But though he drank without ceremony, he had set up his household in a luxury market, where his consultations could be paid for in kind.

For the first time in his life Kaeso was struck by the immeasurable distance between Leo's concept of basic necessity and the superfluity enjoyed by opportunist Stoics like Seneca and Silanus. If you could be perfectly happy living in a barrel, why wear yourself out finding ways of having the world at your feet? And if material success was of no value in itself, what other sort of success was?

For the first time, too, Kaeso was suddenly thrown off balance by the overwhelming temptation to commit suicide – always an attractive possibility to young people who have not learned to cling to life through long years of struggle. He leant over to the solitary Leo and asked: 'What do you think of suicide?' Leo replied simply: 'There's no such thing as suicide: you commit suicide every morning.'

That was something to think about. Kaeso went and bought a parrot, and offered it to the philosopher. 'I can see you have no use for its brain or tongue,' he said, 'But teach it to speak. Then you'll always have an audience for your advice.'

Kaeso went back to the lavatories. Paul and Luke had now arrived. He found them at once, modestly dressed, on either side of a rich 'knight' who was listening to them with only half an ear.

Metaphysicians come in two sizes, fat and thin. The thin ones seek out the fat ones for their solidity, and the fat ones cling to the thin ones for their nervous energy. The relationship between Paul and Luke was of this type. Paul, lean and excitable, slighly stooping, had one of those knife-blade Semitic faces, set on a long neck. His red sleepless eyes seemed to be looking into himself, when they were not piercing others with their strange acuity. Luke, a Syrian from Antioch of Greek extraction, was tubby, and radiated a deep and simple peacefulness. When the knight withdrew, Kaeso hitched up his tunic, and sat down between the two travellers. For the time being the conversations of the other occupants were neither noisy nor intense. After carefully checking in Greek that he was talking to the right people, Kaeso went straight to the heart of the matter.

'My name is Kaeso. My father is Aponius Saturninus. He's a senator and a member of the Arval Brethren.'

Luke asked: 'Before you go on, tell us what the Arval Brethren are. We are just passing through Rome and we still don't know the city well.'

'It's one of the most aristocratic of the priestly colleges. Its function is to offer sacrifices to the goddess Dia and to keep the historical records of everything relating to the emperor.'

'We also make sacrifices,' said Paul, 'but not to statues.'

'To be brief,' Kaeso went on, 'D. Junius Silanus Torquatus, a direct descendant of Augustus and great-grandson of Agrippa, is shortly to adopt me, on the Kalends of May, so that I can later take responsibility for his family cult. I've just finished my higher education in the Athenian *ephebia*. I expect you've heard of it. Now I'm searching for the truth.'

Paul and Luke had indeed heard about that nest of quivering queers and gilded good-for-nothings. But nonetheless the reference to Silanus made Kaeso sound an absolute godsend. Here at last was a chance to carry the Gospel into the highest ranks of the aristocracy, not via the doubtfully effective agency of some insignificant slave, but through the adopted son of a leading member of the imperial family.

'Since you're in search of truth,' said Paul, without preamble, 'you couldn't have had better luck. I possess the whole truth, and I'm satisfied with it.'

'And your friend here too?'

'My friend Luke too.'

'If both of you know the truth in its entirety, give or take a few differences in what you've learned of it, you can't have arrived at it by studying – unlike the philosophers, or even the Jews, who immerse themselves in interminable holy writings.'

'You're quite right. Our truth is addressed to ignorant and learned alike, because it isn't just ours. It comes from Almighty God.'

'In philosophical, religious or scientific circles it's generally considered presumptuous to claim to possess the whole truth. What authority have you for claiming that you've been inspired with the truth by an all-powerful god?'

'Our Lord Jesus said: "I am the Truth and the Life", and He gave us proof that He knew what He was talking about.'

'Before contacting you I read Genesis, Exodus, Leviticus, Numbers and Deuteronomy quite carefully, and ran my eye quickly over the rest, which I found a bit indigestible. I noted that the reason why educated Jews claimed to possess the truth in the same way you do was that Moses had heard voices on Sinai. You must admit that accidents of that sort can't compel complete credence from rational men. How could a transcendent divine creator stoop to hocus-pocus of that kind?'

'I readily acknowledge that the revelations of Yahwe to the Jewish people are not of a kind to compel complete credence from a non-Jew. But these revelations, however dubious when subjected to the light of reason, were only the forerunners of an ultimate indisputable Revelation, addressed not just to the Jews but to all mankind.'

'What, in material terms, constitutes the difference, for you, between the dubious and the indisputable?'

'God did not limit himself to speech. He became flesh in the person of our Lord Jesus, who was both true God and true Man.'

314

'As an example of communication between the transcendent and our material world, that is incontestably a novelty. So you were able to see, hear and touch your god at your leisure. He ate like us, went to the lavatory like us and slept with tarts like us.'

'Jesus attended numerous banquets, and was perfectly well acquainted with lavatories, and He had a great influence on pious women. But in order to devote more time to his mission, he took no interest in sexual pleasures. Neither, for that matter, do I.'

'A god incarnate but virgin?'

'Precisely so.'

'What proof is there that your Jesus was god? Is the fact clearly proclaimed in Jewish writings?'

'If one interprets certain passages of the Bible correctly, one can see that they foretell the coming of a Messiah who suffers and is sacrificed, who will be Jesus. But I have to admit in all honesty that the coming of incarnate god is not foretold in so many words.'

'Don't you see any difficulty in the silence of the Scriptures on that essential point?'

'On the contrary. After original sin and banishment from Paradise, humanity fell into terrible darkness. It was Yahwe's first concern to keep the idea of his transcendent providence alive on earth, when a host of idolaters had forgotten it. The Jews were selected from among all nations and marked with the divine seal, to protect the tiny spark which should have turned into flame and fire, illuminating the whole universe. But the Jews crowded round the sublime flame so that they would be the only ones to profit by it. In their self-satisfied pride they refused to understand that they were only a provisional stage in the divine plan for the reconquest of men's souls. They persisted in being blind to God's foremost quality, his infinite love for all creatures. By means of the concept of transcendency, a God made inhuman – or rather a-human, since we are speaking Greek – was pushed out beyond the boundaries of time and space into a sort of ghetto. Whereas we should see the true God, who made man in his own image, as not only the most distant of beings but also the closest. Transcendency is a concept useless to man if love is excluded. So God decided to take on human form to remind us that the Lord is also a father and brother, servant and slave to us. Jesus' profound humility is directly proportionate to his wondrous divinity.

If you ask me why the Scriptures don't clearly foretell the Incarnation, my answer is that, in our divinely inspired Bible, there is an element sent from God, but there is also an element of stiff-necked Jewish pride. The Incarnation, which is God's triumph over Satan's pride and the marriage of God with his creatures, is still an uncomprehended scandal and fearful blasphemy to most Jews. So when Jesus, a Jew among Jews, presents himself as God incarnate, there are only two explanations which common sense can accept. Either He's God, or He's nuts. Nobody can maintain that our Messiah helped himself to a chance divinity which he came across in some obscure Biblical text. If Jesus were a charlatan who wanted to be well received by the Jews, the Incarnation would be the last thing He'd have dreamed up. On this essential point, Jesus, the product of an ultra-traditional Jewish milieu, goes totally against the trend of His environment. You'll understand why what Jews see as the greatest possible objection is for the Christians the point most in His favour. For the Jews crucifying a false Messiah was a very secondary issue. What in their blindness they claimed to be sacrificing was a false god. It's precisely because the God Jesus had *not* been foretold in their scriptures – the greatest proof of His divinity – that His Incarnation was the cause of His death.'

The subtlety of the argument was remarkable.

The latrines had filled up, and people were beginning to get impatient. Paul and Luke, who had held themselves in until now, prepared to relieve themselves. Paul farted loudly, Luke more gently. Kaeso suddenly said to himself that a Providence with an eye for detail had evidently decided that his first course of instruction in the Incarnation should be given him in the public lavatories so as to underline the scandalous nature of the idea of the humanity of a god descending from the clouds in unfathomable shit so as to cover the stiff-necked Jews in it.

After a moment's thought Kaeso said: 'I asked for proofs and all you have offered me are favourable presumptions.'

As Paul seemed reluctant to go on, Luke said: 'Jesus did not preach in the language of the prophets but like a man who has full authority. On several occasions He granted remission of sins, which only God can do.'

'That only means that a visionary Jesus thought he was god. I need more than that before I shall feel a need for your baptism.'

Paul was still hesitant. He had lost far too many sheep already by talking to them about the Resurrection too soon. It was the hardest thing of all to get people to accept. There was no foolproof formula for doing it. In despair he had drawn up a file of arguments appropriate to different places and different personalities, but he had found from experience that every case was unique. There was a further reason for hesitation. While he was only too familiar with the mentality of the Jews and the Greeks, that of the Roman nobility remained a closed book to him in many respects.

The siege was abandoned. Only when the trio were outside in the sunny, crowded Forum did Paul finally go on:

'There's only one proof of the divinity of Jesus, our anointed and consecrated Christ, and in providing that proof God laid it on thick, to say the least. At any rate I can't be suspected of having invented the facts, because if I'd wanted to make my mission easy without reference to the truth I'd have dreamed up something more plausible. When I put this proof forward, the philosophers of Athens fell about laughing. So did Gallio, Seneca's brother, so did the governor Festus. Even king Agrippa and Berenice thought it a great joke . . .'

'You pleaded your cause before the famous Berenice?'

'I'm not particularly proud of the fact.'

'They say she's very beautiful.'

'It's Satan's beauty.'

'If you didn't invent this piece of conclusive evidence, you may have naïvely swallowed a story made up by someone else.'

'If there were the slightest doubt on the subject my life would be a good deal more peaceful, I can tell you! To put the whole thing in a nutshell, Jesus who died on the cross to redeem our sins – for God loved us so much He was willing to die for us – this Jesus . . . He rose from the tomb on the third day and appeared many times to hundreds of our brethren. I've had the privilege of talking to many of those who saw Him: particularly Simon Peter, James, son of Zebedee, John, James's brother, Matthew, Andrew, Philip, and doubting Thomas who insisted on touching Him. This fantastic Resurrection was something nobody was expecting, and nobody was willing to believe in it. But He wasn't a ghost. You can't touch ghosts and they don't eat fish. Jesus spent forty days with His followers, completing His teaching, then He went up to heaven.'

'You didn't actually see the resurrected Christ yourself?'

'While I was involved in persecuting Christians, He appeared to me just outside Damascus. But as it was after His ascension to heaven, I only saw His dazzling light and heard His words. You can refuse to believe me when I tell you this. I won't hold it against you. But you've got to believe what a crowd of 500 people saw, heard and touched for forty whole days.'

'Why were you persecuting the Christians?'

'Because I'm a Pharisee of the tribe of Benjamin. To a pious Jew who hasn't been given the gift of grace the incarnation of God in the person of his Son is a sacrilege and an intolerable absurdity.'

'If a pious Jew like you needed a personal revelation to change his views, doesn't that give sceptics a cut and dried excuse for not accepting what you tell them?'

'It's for God to find excuses for them, not me. Every day I pray to the Holy Spirit to enlighten them.'

'In many oriental religions miracle-workers abound and bewitch whole peoples. Mightn't your Jesus have been something of a magician too?'

'That's not a proof of divinity. I myself cured a man crippled with rheumatism in the legs. That was at Lystra in Lykaonia. Probably men possessed by devils can hoodwink the naïve by chasing out lesser devils. Jesus certainly cured all sorts of people, but He also brought His friend Lazarus back from the dead when his corpse was already beginning to stink. The talents of the arch-deceiver Satan, who is death personified, don't stretch that far.'

Luke added: 'At Joppa Peter resuscitated Dorcas, a very holy woman whose body had already been washed for burial. And then there was young Eutychus who fell out of a third-floor window on to the pavement while you were preaching in the Troad. You brought him back to life yourself, didn't you Paul?'

Paul was irritated by this list of references, which didn't sound at all plausible. He gave Luke a reproachful look, gestured with his hands to play down the subject and said with a studiedly casual air:

'I was responsible for making the poor boy drop off with my boring sermon. The least I could do was to wake him up again. Anyway, can we be sure he was really dead?'

Kaeso was beginning to find the long list of resurrections funny. Though he tried hard to keep a straight face, he couldn't resist saying:

'Since you've got the knack of bringing people back to life, I'm surprised you don't use it more widely. What are you short of – the power or the will?'

Paul shot another look at Luke, even darker than the first one, which evidently meant 'Now see what you've gone and done, putting your foot in it like that!'

The walk across the Forums had brought them to the Cattle Market, in front of the temple of Patrician Modesty. Fearing that he might have hurt Paul by his inopportune display of incredulity, Kaeso changed the topic of conversation.

'It was the family of my future adoptive father which founded this little temple, and my ex-stepmother, Silanus' present wife, posed for the statue in the sanctuary. She makes a very successful Patrician Modesty.'

The blind man, with his little picture, was still there, looking more and more pitiful as the days passed.

Paul, who was in a fair way to losing his temper, abruptly said to Kaeso: 'We don't only perform miracles out of charity. We also do it as proof that God has just visited the world.'

He untied the blue silk scarf from around Kaeso's neck, and wiped the pus from the blind man's eyes. Suddenly the beggar began to leap about and shriek like a lunatic: 'I can see! I can see! The good goddess of Patrician Modesty has cured me!' The guardian of the temple and his wife had left the doors slightly open in order to clean the place out. The man, who was beside himself, rushed unsteadily into the building and threw himself at the feet of the statue of Marcia, while crowds of onlookers came trooping up.

Paul was outraged and tried to set matters to rights but his impious words stirred up such mutterings that Luke and Kaeso had to whisk him out of the clutches of the *plebs*, who were threatening to do him an injury.

They took refuge in one of the *thermopolia* where there were a host of drinks and tasty snacks available for their refreshment. But Paul was too downcast to take the slightest pleasure in earthly nourishment.

'It's always like this,' he said. 'When Barnabas and I cured the sick man at Lystra, people gave Zeus the credit for the miracle. The Jews soon got themselves mixed up in the affair, and all I got out of it was to be stoned and left for dead.'

Kaeso said: 'You used my scarf to cure a blind man who'd set up a permanent home in front of the temple of Patrician Modesty. At first sight there's no reason not to attribute the miracle to the good goddess, or even to my scarf. You've got to take everything into consideration.'

Paul gave Kaeso a look which was so bitter and furious that Luke hurriedly put his hand on his arm to calm him down. With a great effort Paul managed to contain himself. He would have been quite capable of ruining such a precious conversion by losing his temper at the wrong moment. After all, it was the young man's stepmother, probably a pious and modest Roman matron, who had posed for the statue. It was perfectly natural for her stepson to express certain polite reservations.

In point of fact Kaeso was not so much incredulous as thunderstruck. The company of these missionaries was anything but restful. They combined impeccable rational argument, lunatic assertions and mysterious miracle-working in a way which he found most uncomfortable. But if he wanted to be baptized as soon as possible, he needed to adopt soothing tactics and pile up convictions double-quick, while appearing to give ground only foot by foot for form's sake, so as not to arouse their suspicions. While Luke was nibbling cakes and sipping an aperitif, Kaeso prepared to calm Paul down and advance his own cause . . .

'On further reflection, your demonstration of healing inspires me with confidence. Neither the goddess of Patrician Modesty nor my scarf has ever cured anyone before, and if you were possessed by devils yourself and merely chased out devils less powerful than your own, your own devil would have given itself away by now, which is far from being the case.'

'Kind of you to say so!'

'So, I accept that the god of the Bible, for so long alone and hidden from our eyes, suddenly took on human form in the person of his son Jesus Christ, who was crucified to redeem our sins . . .'

'And original sin!'

'I was going to include that. The lesser is subsumed in the greater. Anyway, Jesus came back to life on the third day, and ascended to heaven forty days later, after appearing in the flesh to numerous disciples. During this time people could touch him, he ate fish, but he wasn't visible all the time.'

'No. And all the witnesses told me there was something different about Him. Sometimes people didn't even recognize Him straight off.'

'Oh – really?'

'But some familiar trait soon revealed who He was.'

'That's undoubtedly the surest way of identifying someone. An impostor can disguise himself, but he can't fake a familiar trait.'

'That wasn't your own idea. The Holy Spirit must have inspired you with it.'

Kaeso swaggered a little and pressed his advantage.

'Why wasn't he visible all the time during those forty days?'

'His body was celestial: it could pass through walls. He was freed from the restrictions of time and space.'

'Then how could people touch it and how could he eat?'

'Please accept that if we'd made the whole thing up, we should have got rid of the contradictions by opting for one line or the other. We're merely scrupulous witnesses to the truth.'

'And when he ate fish and then went through the wall, did the fish become part of the celestial body and follow him through?'

'I suggest you ask the fish.'

'After ascending into heaven, did Jesus keep his body? He can't have had any further use for it.'

'Oh yes, His resuscitated body prefigures the resurrection of all mankind at the Last Judgement, for better or worse. Among the Jews, the Sadducees don't believe in this resurrection but the Pharisees do.'

'So there's to be a judgement on the last day of creation?'

'People will either be sent to Heaven, where they will see God, or to Hell, where they will just see their own navels roasting.'

Luke cut in. 'Jesus said to one of the thieves crucified with Him: "From today you will be with me in Paradise." So there must be a private judgement before there is a general one.'

Paul pulled a wry face and admitted that there, too, there was a contradiction which was difficult to resolve.

Ever anxious for approval, Kaeso came to his aid.

'The solution seems entirely simple to me. It must derive from the fact that your Christ is true god and true man at the same time. When he speaks as god, who knows neither time nor space, all the events of history coexist in his mind as though in a perpetual present. He therefore has a tendency to bring everything together in a single undated event. When he speaks as a man, who is sensitive to the flow of time and the contingency of space, he naturally uses concepts such as today and tomorrow.'

Luke and Paul looked at each other with surprise and delight, and complimented the young man on his ingenious solution.

'Oh,' said Kaeso modestly, 'it's only the result of my philosophical studies in the *ephebia*. If you want your doctrine to be really solid and not at all fuzzy at the edges, you must get the Greek philosophers to go over it in detail. They're all gay, but they have wonderfully logical minds.'

Seeing the pursed mouths of his two companions Kaeso realized that he had made a serious blunder. He made a mental note to be more cautious, and changed the subject.

'Tell me some more about the human origins of this incarnate god. Who were his father and mother?'

Luke took up the conversation. 'A young girl called Mary was engaged to a carpenter of the line of David, at Nazareth in Galilee. The angel Gabriel appeared to her to tell her that she would have a son by the agency of the Holy Ghost. Another angel was swiftly dispatched to Joseph the carpenter to inform him of what was happening, and to advise him to marry Mary and serve as foster-father to Jesus. The Saviour was born in Bethlehem, in a stable, because the inns were full: there was a census on.'

'Did Mary have other children?'

'She remained a virgin.'

'That doesn't surprise me. When one has given birth to a god of that kind, self-restraint becomes a duty.'

Paul and Luke relaxed. Such delicate points were rarely accepted with such good grace, and the phrase 'self-restraint beomes a duty' was felicitously expressed.

'What about Joseph?' asked Kaeso. 'As a village notable I suppose he took a concubine to console himself?'

'Certainly not,' said Luke hurriedly.

'The poor fellow stayed a virgin too, then?'

'He did. As the example of the Essenian monasteries shows, continence in Joseph's day looked like becoming a common virtue among many pious Jews.'

'So a virgin father and a virgin mother had a child who remained a virgin, fathered by a virgin Spirit?'

'An excellent summary of the facts.'

It was getting worse and worse. A tale absolutely *not* to be told to Silanus except as a last resort, and then only dressed up in a good dose of reassuring mythology.

'I suppose Jesus' disciples have the right to make love to women?'

It was Paul who answered.

'Most of the apostles were indeed married, but a number of them had to be away from their wives for long periods for the needs of their mission. I myself thought it more practical not to get married.'

'Aren't you allowed a few pretty girls as you travel around?'

'No. Jesus revealed to us that in future Christians would only have the right to have sexual relations with a woman to whom they were lawfully wedded, and that the marriage would be indissoluble. In cases of incompatability it is forbidden to remarry while your spouse is still alive.'

That was the richest yet!

'Do you know,' said Kaeso, putting his hand on the missionary's bony shoulder, 'you've almost convinced me of the divinity of your Christ?'

'Why?'

'As far as I can see, coming back to life, sooner or later, individually or en masse, is becoming quite common among you. But to have the nerve to come up with the idea of indissoluble marriage in a world where marriage is in the process of dying out, you'd have to be a god. Where could Jesus have come across an idea like that? There's never been any question of such a thing anywhere.'

322

'Peter did indeed say to me that the apostles had been taken aback at the instruction and had asked him to repeat it several times. And they retorted to Jesus that it was better not to marry at all than to marry under such wretched conditions.'

'I share their surprise. I'm beginning to understand why you've stayed single.'

Paul merely smiled.

❧ CHAPTER ❧
2

After this disturbing first meeting Kaeso went for a walk at random, going over in his head everything he had heard and seen. His steps led him to the Campus Martius, which was comparatively empty at that time of the morning. He finished up in the gardens of Agrippa, which were next to the baths of the same name, sat down beside the pretty pool, which was rippling in a light breeze, and read the Gospel according to Mark. The narrative was becoming more generally available; Paul had lent Kaeso the shortish text, written on a roll without an umbilicus, and recommended him to take the greatest possible care of it. 'I've travelled with Mark and know him well,' Paul had said to his future convert. 'Mark, together with my friend Sylvanus, is the official interpreter of Peter, whom Jesus made pre-eminent over us all. (Peter's Greek is none too good, and his Latin's even worse.) In this little work you'll find a somewhat disordered but absolutely authentic summary of Christ's all too short stay among us, directly inspired by the memories of Peter and the Aramaic text of another apostle called Matthew.'

Kaeso was disconcerted by what he read. The story, which was written in rather inelegant Greek, was quite unlike either Greek or Roman mythological literature, or the elucubrations of the priests of those oriental religions which had invaded Rome. Still less did it resemble the usual philosophical treatises. Witnesses limited themselves to recounting without embroidery what they had seen, or thought they saw, and their memories must have been good, because in their accounts Jesus had a presence, a manner and a coherent style which were all his own. This made it all the more astounding to read: 'The man who repudiates his wife and marries another commits adultery with regard to his first wife. If a woman repudiates her husband and marries another, she too commits adultery.'

Paul hadn't been exaggerating. Jesus really had been responsible for absurd pronouncements of that kind. It only went to show that he had no concept of social realities. The Christian religion clearly didn't have much of a future.

For hundreds of years wealthy Athenians had, as a rule, had a lover, a legitimate wife, concubines to run the household, hetaeras to accompany them to banquets and give them status in the city, and the occasional catamite. The poor divided their time between their wife – if they had one – obliging boys and the cheap brothels which Solon had organized. (The continued existence of these brothels had been officially encouraged because they brought the city large sums in taxes.) The same system functioned in all the large cities of Greece and the Greek East.

In Rome the rich normally had at their disposal a lawful wife and concubines or boys, not to mention the high-society prostitutes and chance liaisons with emancipated female citizens which were an original characteristic of the Roman scene in the cities of the West. In the East a married woman was still largely restricted to her own home, where she had nothing else to amuse her but the conversation of her husband's concubines, if he had enough money to have any. In Rome a married woman went where she pleased. The poor in Rome – as in Athens and elsewhere – had largely to resort to the brothels, which in the city of Romulus were kept in order by attentive magistrates. These brothels were also much frequented by slaves who wanted to vary their menu.

Such behaviour patterns were so firmly anchored, so universal and apparently so irreversible, that a society where divorce was forbidden and conjugal fidelity was required of both parties seemed unthinkable to any one with any common sense. For a man, bringing the dead to life was indeed easier than being faithful.

Not only did the social realities escape Jesus, but he did not have the least notion of elementary psychological and physiological realities either. It was only too obvious that he had remained completely virgin! The limited experience which Kaeso had so far gained from the 'little filly' at the *popina* and expensive hetaeras had persuaded him that one thing was incontestably true. Women, who only have to open their legs, are capable of making love because they have to until kingdom come. But a man, whatever his morality and good intentions, cannot 'make a stand' on this particular point out of a sense of duty. Jesus' concept of indissoluble marriage, applied to the letter, would soon have led to the husband abstaining in disgust and the wife abstaining whether she liked it or not. Was that what the Christians wanted?

Another sign of his lack of awareness: for the first time in recorded history the same sexual law was intended to apply equally to men and women, despite their very different constitutions and the ingrained disharmony between their ways of, and capacities for, enjoyment. If Jesus had really been interested in harmony, he would have maintained polygamy for the sake of frigid women, who derived a bit of welcome rest from it, and on the other hand would have provided a tribe of husbands for women like Arria, who were reduced to the expedient of immersing their slaves in baths of cold water to prolong their use. In the meantime, worn-out husbands were continually at the mercy of hysterical wives whom a whole legion could not have satisfied.

The Gospel according to Mark ended rather abruptly at the empty tomb and the Angel's message to the three women who had come bearing ointments. Kaeso decided that for the sake of plausibility he ought to go into this resurrection business with Paul. He had given the impression of accepting it a bit quickly. Had not Paul himself declared that it was the only valid proof of Jesus' divinity?

Kaeso carefully washed his miracle-working scarf in the pond and went home to lunch. Since the improvement in his father's finances the brief midday meal, which people in Rome usually took wherever they happened to be at whatever time was convenient, had changed into a light family luncheon-party, on the pattern of wealthier households.

Paul had been delighted at the prospect of seeing Kaeso again as soon as possible so that he could get on with his instruction without delay. So he had fixed a rendezvous with him for after siesta at an address by the Porta Capena. He had moved back in with the Christian Jew in whose house he had been shut up for two years awaiting trial. The owner, who was now quite comfortably off, made tents for the army. The campaigns in Armenia and Britain had been a godsend for business.

The building was crawling with Christians and had the air of a head-quarters. Nobody made the least suggestion to Kaeso, as the rabbi had done, that he should rent the place. Paul had taken over a little room on the first floor. He presented his protégé to the tent-maker, and even to his wife, which was, again, a departure from orthodox Jewish practice.

'I'm delighted,' said Kaeso graciously, 'to meet a faithful, indissolubly married couple for the first time in my life. When you read about that sort of thing in Mark, it's like a dream. But one only has to come into your house to find the dream made flesh. Your religion is full of surprising incarnations.'

There was a trace of embarrassment in the air. The wife said: 'When my husband was converted, he got rid of two of his three concubines. He kept the third. He'd had children by her, and she was old and would have died of hunger if he'd put her out – or so he says.'

'You know very well that Daphnis is like a sister to me these days!' protested her husband.

Paul broke in before the disagreement turned into a family quarrel which would have been inopportune, to say the least. 'Regularizing certain situations sometimes poses delicate problems, but fortunately our hearts can resolve what our heads cannot.'

Kaeso hurriedly passed from the particular to the general.

'Before I had the great honour of getting to know Pompeius Paulus, I met a rabbi who said such unpleasant things about the Christians that I wanted to see some at close quarters. This rabbi accused Paulus and his followers of keeping only those parts of Jewish law which suited them. If I understood aright, the Christians have added the indissolubility of marriage to the Ten Commandments, but have dropped circumcision and all the detailed rules and regulations which the Pharisees have made such a lengthy study of?'

'You're quite right,' Paul acknowledged. 'With the proviso that the Christians haven't added or taken away anything. It was Christ himself who re-established marriage as it had been ordained by God from the beginning, and it was Christ who declared that all these details you referred to were out-of-date.'

'I read in Mark that Jesus was not afraid to eat with anybody – without washing his hands, as pious Jews, and even some impious Romans, do – that he ate everything instead of insisting on all that mumbo-jumbo about pure and impure, and that he took a very relaxed attitude to the sanctity of the sabbath. Did he leave an exhaustive list of which of the Pharisees' prescriptions he wanted kept and which got rid of?'

'He had better things to do!'

'You mean the Christians took it upon themselves to abolish a large number of Jewish customs on the basis of a few general ideas which Jesus expressed?'

'That is undoubtedly the case. The issue has caused a great deal of discussion among us.'

'Did Jesus do away with circumcision?'

Paul looked put out by the question, and finally answered:

'The decision to do that was taken at a council at Jerusalem. The intention was to make conversions easier. But if you've set your heart on being circumcised, there's nothing wrong in that!'

'How do you know Jesus approves of dropping the custom?'

'When He ascended into heaven, Jesus left us the Holy Spirit, which cannot lead us astray. It speaks through the mouths of Peter and the other apostles.'

'That's a very practical solution, but only if everyone says the same thing. The Pharisees doubtless overdo things with their endless dos and don'ts, but I wonder whether the Christians aren't taking things too far the other way? Couldn't such a policy be damaging? I find the religion attractive and I wouldn't like it to die out too quickly.'

His audience looked at him with round eyes, and the amateur theologian went on:

'I also read in Mark the predictions about the destruction of Jerusalem and the Temple there, the end of the world and the persecution of the Christians. The most likely of these is the persecution, if the movement develops beyond a certain point. The Romans wouldn't excuse the Christans from making sacrifices as they have been forced to do in the case of the Jews. Now on your own admission you're creating Christians very fast, with a very light intellectual luggage. How would most of these converts stand up to trouble with the police when they don't have the weapons which a deep knowledge of holy scripture and scrupulous daily ritual provide for pious Jews? The whole movement will fall apart. The Holy Spirit is clearly very powerful, but you need to give it a little assistance.'

The tent-maker approved this common-sense diagnosis. But Paul rejected its accuracy with a flash of bad temper. He said to Kaeso: 'I hope for your sake that your Christian instruction will allow you to make as good a martyr as any Jew!'

Kaeso laughed and said: 'It'll be the little people, as always, who suffer from the crack-down. The aristocracy, and even ordinary citizens, will escape scot-free.'

Paul gave Kaeso a deeply pained look.

'What's the meaning of that peculiar look? Are you reproaching me for calling a spade a spade? Is it my fault if Roman justice has two sets of weights and measures?'

'No, it's not that. I've just had a vision. It happens from time to time . . .'

'A vision of the future?'

'Yes. They're always right.'

'And what did you see?'

'I'll tell you later.'

'These phenomena of prescience pose a problem for our philosophers, because they seem incompatible with free will. Some philosophers maintain that visions of the future are impossible unless everything is pre-ordained. How can you reconcile your visions and your freedom?'

'I'm not a philosopher.'

'We could say that God knows in advance what we shall do of our own free will.'

'Yes, why not?'

'One more paradox either way won't make any odds to God.'

The subject was irritating Paul. Kaeso took him for a walk in the hope of getting him to take a bath. The Romans washed all the time; the Jews washed themselves rarely; the Christians had given up almost entirely, and you could smell the fact.

The two men walked towards the Campus Martius through the district around the Circus Maximus and on into the Velabrum. With the Subura these were the areas on the left bank of the Tiber which were the most densely populated, and where prostitution, which was present everywhere, was particularly active. But Paul, with his thoughts turned inward, saw nothing. He delivered an inexhaustible flow of conversation about his new God, about his Father and the Holy Ghost. Kaeso finally grasped that he was talking about three aspects of the same reality: three 'persons' equal in all respects, who were really one. Paul himself cheerfully admitted that it was a great mystery.

'Any self-respecting religion,' said Kaeso amicably, 'has to have its mysteries. The ordinary people adore them.'

'What's it got to do with ordinary people? Does the Trinity need them in order to be what it is?'

Kaeso thought it did, but elementary diplomacy warned him to be tactful.

They had arrived at the new Baths of Nero, which had been built close to the Baths of Agrippa and were fed by the Alexandrina, an offshoot of the principal aqueduct, the Virgo.

'It's bathing time,' suggested Kaeso. 'You've adopted Roman ways, haven't you?'

Paul started. 'I've adopted them where they don't involve any sin. Do you suppose I'm going to risk myself in among all those naked men and women?'

'I may be wrong, but I don't recall that the Pentateuch forbids it. The expression "Thou shalt not uncover the nudity of such and such a person" clearly means "You're not to have sex with her".'

'The letter of the law is one thing. The spirit of it – and common sense – are quite another.'

'Do you think that the sight of naked people will give you naughty thoughts?'

'It's a risk I'm not prepared to take.'

'I don't want to offend you, but if you're hoping to move in aristocratic circles in Rome, you're going to have to take a bath. We'll do a swap. You get me into a baptismal bath and I'll take you into the Baths of Nero.'

'Never!'

To get out of a tricky situation Kaeso took off his scarf and said, as if he were joking: 'With this miraculous scarf, which gave his sight back to a feeble-minded blind man, I'm going to perform a miracle myself. I shall find a way for you to bathe without exposing you to any unhealthy temptations.'

So saying, Kaeso tied the scarf firmly round Paul's eyes, then pushed and pulled him towards the door of the baths. Paul did not dare to protest too much. 'We can pretend that you're having trouble with your eyes and the slightest light upsets you,' Kaeso said.

Keeping his spirits up in adversity, Paul showed exemplary patience in allowing himself to be physically manipulated, merely giving vent to the occasional little sigh which could have been a sign of pleasure or exasperation.

While Kaeso was getting the filth off Paul with great strokes of his strigil in the *caldarium*, he found himself face to face with his brother Marcus, who was performing the same service for a giggling girl. Only people on their own used the bath-house personnel to have their backs scraped. Kaeso presented Paul to Marcus as 'an eminent pontiff of a new religion with a great future.'

Somewhat surprised, Marcus asked: 'Is it a religion where you approach the future with your eyes shut?'

Kaeso gave him the agreed explanation, but then murmured in his ear: 'In fact I'm giving a bath to a Jew who can't cope with the sight of naked men and women.'

Marcus was greatly amused by the whole thing and wished Kaeso good luck.

Paul and Kaeso sat down for a moment in a corner of the *tepidarium*, and Kaeso said to his companion: 'Since physical blindness favours contemplative withdrawal, I'd like to take the opportunity to get some more details about your story of the resurrection, which is apparently the key to your whole doctrine. Might not people suspect that the Christians had simply hidden Jesus' body?'

'That's what the Jews say, but the idea won't hold water. Despite Jesus' warnings, the disciples refused to believe in the possibility of the crucifixion, still less that, once crucified, they were to expect a resurrection. They were in a state of complete disarray. It was precisely the Resurrection and the workings of the Holy Spirit which gave them back their confidence. How could timid and quite simple-minded people like that have come up with the idea of inventing a false resurrection which no one would have believed in and which could only cause trouble for them if anyone – which is unlikely – did believe in it?'

'That seems a persuasive argument.'

'My main argument is as follows: there is no satisfactory explanation of Jesus' resurrection in purely human terms. When something is not explicable with the resources of the human critical intelligence, then the only alternative has to be that the hand of God is behind it all.'

'The most plausible secular explanation is still that the disciples *thought* that they saw, heard and touched a resurrected Jesus.'

'Agreed. But the number of witnesses, the detailed nature of their testimony, its identical and uniform content runs counter to such a hypothesis. And now that I have my eyes bandaged, I'll tell you what it was I just foresaw. You too are going to die for your faith in the Resurrection.'

'That's hardly a way to encourage me to get baptized!'

'Don't worry, you'll get your baptism.'

There was nothing reassuring in his remarks.

When they came out of the baths, Kaeso unbound Paul's eyes again and the two set off to the nearby Pantheon, which Kaeso wanted his newly-clean Christian Jew to admire.

The back of the building overlooked the Baths of Agrippa; the front gave on to the still relatively undeveloped green spaces of the Campus Martius. Agrippa had consecrated the Pantheon to Jupiter Ultor and all the gods during his third consulship, i.e. in the year 729 from the founding of the city, as the bronze inscription on the pediment recorded. It was one of the most grandiose temples in the city and undoubtedly the most original. Inventive architects had realized that, after the Parthenon at Athens, the unsurpassable model of classical perfection, they had to come up with something completely different. Taking their inspiration from Persian sources, they had constructed a circular temple, with a Corinthian peristyle added.

This peristyle had sixteen monolithic columns in red or grey granite, of impressive height and girth. At the top of the pediment, eighty-seven feet above the pavement, was a bronze chariot.

As the temple was open to the public during the day, Kaeso and Paul went in. The gigantic cupola, 147 feet in diameter, was pierced in the centre with a round opening twenty-eight feet in diameter, through which blue sky was visible.

The whole thing was lavishly luxurious. Both under the peristyle and inside, everywhere was covered in white marble. The cupola rested on yellow marble columns, and the ground was paved with squares of marble in yellow or white veined with violet, decorated with great circles of porphyry. The dome was covered in gilded bronze tiles shaped like laurel leaves, and there was more bronze, set off with touches of silver and gold, all over the decorations in the vaulted roofs of the peristyle and the sanctuary. The statue of Jupiter, facing the entrance, was a riot of ivory and precious metals.

'Extraordinary, isn't it?' said Kaeso. 'Could you imagine anything more splendid?'

Paul pulled a face.

'The day will come, God willing, when that statue of Jupiter will be destroyed and the Christians will take possession of this temple to hold their own ceremonies.'

'You forget that Agrippa is the great-grandfather of my future adoptive father! You're getting a little carried away with your predictions.'

'You must excuse me for seeing further into the future than you.'

'What are your rituals like?'

'Jesus was crucified on a Friday, the 14th day of Nisan – that's the day of the Feast of the Passover among the Jews. He was buried before nightfall, just as the Sabbath was beginning. So He celebrated Passover with His disciples a day early, on the Thursday evening. On this occasion He blessed the bread and wine, saying: "Take, eat, this is my blood, this is my body. Do this in memory of me." Our priests consequently consecrate bread and wine and distribute them to the faithful.'

'I can't see much point in that.'

'You're not the only one. The apostles told me that they hadn't been able to either.'

'Why didn't they question Jesus on the subject?'

'They rarely dared to ask Him questions, for fear of looking stupid in front of each other. But John, our most distinguished theologian, in whom Jesus confided, maintains that Jesus' words must be taken literally.'

'A sort of ritual cannibalism?'

'I can think of more felicitous ways of putting it.'

'Anyway, that's a thoroughly un-Jewish trait.'

'Jesus was God and God isn't merely a Jew.'

The idea of Eastern ritual cannibalism being carried out in the Pantheon of Agrippa by an heretical Jewish sect was so grotesque that Kaeso no longer felt he need take Paul's predictions – even the sinister one about his death – seriously. It would be quite safe to ask for baptism.

In the square in front of the Pantheon, with its inevitable altar, Paul said to Kaeso:

'In addition to the religious instruction I shall give you, which we call a catechism, I shall ask you a considerable favour. We Christians are of Greek or Jewish extraction. Many aspects of the Roman world are unfamiliar to us. The Romans and Greeks are alike but they are not the same. Would you, from time to time, talk to me about this city and its inhabitants, who have conquered the world and are supposed to be model examples?'

Kaeso was only too happy to be at Paul's disposal.

'Would you be interested in the 120 principal temples of Rome, beginning with the temple of Jupiter Capitolinus? Or the nine largest basilicas? I hardly like to mention the innumerable baths, some of which are the size of a small city . . .'

'I'm not much interested in stones. It's men I want to know about. To come straight to the point, who really counts here?'

'If I were a Christian I should say "the very poor". But you're clearly not going to get your hands on my pantheon with a band of paupers. First of all there's the emperor. He commands the armies and he's the richest of us all. Then there are the armies, and above all the permanent Praetorian Guard. It's the good-will of the soldiers which puts Caesar in power and keeps him there. The Senate and the rich are also important, although they're unarmed, because they hold all the liquid and capital assets. Freedmen and slaves are important when the emperor or the rich put them in a position of importance. That's everyone who matters in Rome, and in the provinces too. Everyone with a positive value, that is.

Others have a purely negative value, in the sense that they don't count usually, but they can become significant if they're too discontented. I'm thinking of the citizens who make up the Roman *plebs*. They're entitled to the free distribution of corn. These free handouts from the Annona are the only means of survival for 200,000 families. If, in the autumn, the corn ships from Alexandria arrive late, the whole court starts to tremble.

There's also the vast number of unemployed foreigners "of no fixed abode" who clutter up the city. They include people who've come down in the world, beggars and the criminal fringe. Absurdly, the *plebs* proper look down on them. But the two groups could make common cause, if the *plebs* were pushed into civil disorder by famine.

Then there are the numerous "clients" of the big families, who nowadays find it harder to live on their patron's reduced handouts. They no longer have a political value to their protector, as they did in the old days when votes in the Forum were still of immense importance.

And lastly there are the slaves, who could spread terror everywhere, as they have done before, if they acted in concert.

All these people live down in the city slums, at the mercy of floods, earthquakes and plagues. During the day they're kept in order by the four cohorts of city police, under the command of the prefect of the City, and at night by the seven cohorts of the Watch, under the command of the Prefect of the Watch. To the "forces of law and order" you can add the Praetorian Guard and the German Guard, under the command of the Praetorian Prefect. That's hardly more than 20,000 men altogether.'

'What about free craftsmen?'

'They are the least important people in the city. The competition from slaves reduces their number and importance. When I bought a little trinket for my stepmother's birthday from a goldsmith, he complained to me about how hard his life was. According to him, out of every 100 goldsmiths, thirty-five are slaves and fifty-eight freedmen. The proportions will be more or less the same in other crafts.'

'Who do you think are the people in such a society most likely to listen to the good news of the Resurrection?'

'The emperor, who on principle has to think of himself as a god, will obviously turn a deaf ear. The soldiers are accustomed to crucifying criminals, and won't want a crucified god. The rich won't go along with it because they're too educated. The poor are only interested in food, entertainment and the brothels. And the dazzling spectacle of spiritual liberation which you'll hold before the eyes of the slaves will never be worth as much to them as a legal liberation from their master.'

'And why do *you* listen to me?'

With perfect hypocrisy Kaeso lifted his eyes to the vault of heaven and replied: 'You must have been told that in a vision.'

They had just come back into Rome by the Porta Carmentalis, at the foot of the west front of the Capitol. Faced with the sobering perspectives which Kaeso had listed, Paul seemed rather downcast.

Kaeso asked him: 'How long does it take before one can be baptized?'

'We have often gone in for baptizing people much too soon. You yourself put a lot of emphasis on the advantages of a solid Jewish-style instruction.'

'In my particular case, if we assume I can manage it in double-quick time, will it take days or weeks?'

'Weeks rather than days. It's not your instruction which worries me, it's your soul. You don't yet talk like a Christian.'

'Tell me how I ought to talk then.'

'From the heart.'

The sun was clearly on its way down. Paul was due to dine with Luke and some others at the house of a recently converted member of the lower middle classes, a Greek freedman who was a scribe at the Public Treasury. Monetary reform on some considerable scale was in the air, but no one knew quite what form it would take. Fortunately the Greek had been able to give Paul inside information, which was of great interest to him since he was responsible for administering sizeable liquid funds, comprising gifts from generous Christians for the poor of the community.

With thoughts of evangelism at the back of his mind, Paul imparted the precious information to Kaeso, adding: 'Couldn't you, in the strictest secrecy, pass the tip on to your adoptive father and indicate to him that the Christians are responsible for doing him this favour?'

Their financial discussion was interrupted by a sound of running footsteps and cries of 'Stop thief! Stop thief!' A fleeing form came hurtling into the legs of the two men as they rounded a corner in the narrow road. As one man they automatically grabbed hold of the fugitive, who turned out to be a girl. But you could have been forgiven for not noticing the fact, because the child, who was about eleven or twelve and lithe as a cat, had the short hair which street-walkers usually hid under a special tiara or wig.

The police, the pimp who was trying to reclaim his goods and a handful of citizens of good will came hurtling round the corner in their turn and let out a cry of triumph on seeing their prey immobilized. The *leno* thanked Paul and Kaeso profusely, and, putting his hand on the lead collar round the child's neck, read aloud what was written on it to prove to everyone that there was no mistake. 'My name is Myra. If I run away, catch me and take me back to the Phoenix brothel. Good reward offered.'

Dangerous slaves or those likely to run away, when not kept under lock and key, were fitted out with a collar made of bronze or lead to make their escape more difficult.

Holding the collar with one hand the *leno* immediately started beating the living daylights out of the girl with a stick. The police and spectators discreetly withdrew: in Rome it was considered unforgivably rude for an outsider to interfere in a matter of this kind.

The fugitive was howling with despair. Kaeso and Paul exchanged concerned looks. To distract the brute's attention Kaeso asked him:

'Why did you shout "Stop thief!"? Had she robbed you?'

'By Hercules! What a stupid question! She was trying to rob me of herself.'

Paul could think of nothing that could be done for the girl, and turned away with a sigh. But Selene's misfortunes had made Kaeso sensitive to a problem which had never troubled him before. The sight was all the more pitiful because the victim was so young. The strict laws protecting minors did not of course apply to slaves. In Rome, girls were put into brothels as they approached puberty. In Athens, Corinth and Alexandria, where there were plenty of customers with a taste for tender young flesh, children of six or seven were made into prostitutes.

Kaeso finally called out: 'Stop beating her. You'll ruin her and I don't want my property spoiled.'

The *leno* stopped at once and looked at Kaeso's fine tunic with interest and Paul's Greek cloak with contempt.

'Are you intending to buy her?'

'A runaway slave of that age shouldn't cost much.'

At this the *leno* began to protest vehemently. He immediately launched into an enthusiastic account of his property's grace and talent, pinching her fresh young cheek and uncovering a developing breast. Kaeso wanted to bring the disgusting discussion to a close as soon as possible. In a nearby shop he signed a definite purchase contract, at an agreed price of 7,000 sesterces, to be paid over the next day, and got permission to take the girl at once. His father's senatorial rank and the name of Silanus had inspired confidence in the ignoble individual he was dealing with. Everybody in Rome despised the pimps, but they were nonetheless indispensable.

The child followed them along like a dog. She had come by a circuitous route from one of the islands of the Cyclades, and she innocently asked Kaeso in Greek how many girls worked in his brothel.

Paul told her to shut up. He did not seem too happy with the purchase: he was probably afraid for the fragile virtue of this somewhat strange young Roman, who inspired him with only limited confidence. Understanding this reaction, Kaeso said to him, 'Don't get in a twist. I like them a bit older than that.' But he saw at once from Paul's face that yet again he had expressed himself in a deplorable style. If you were going to speak like a true Christian, you had to watch every word.

To make amends for the brick he had dropped, Kaeso invited Paul to come in for a moment, insisting that the whole population of the apartment building, from its owner to the road sweepers, were potential converts. At the same time it had occurred to Kaeso that it wouldn't be a bad idea if his father saw Paul for a moment, or at least heard that he had dropped in. His good faith would be less suspect when the day came to break Marcus' heart. For the same reason it wouldn't be a bad idea to mention Paul to Silanus.

Marcus had gone out, but Selene, who rarely put her nose out of doors, was hanging around the house. Kaeso told her briefly about the purchase of Myra, and instructed her to give the child a bath and something to eat. Myra was very surprised, never having seen a brothel like this one before. Then they all went into the drawing-room and chatted.

At the sight of Selene's beauty Paul seemed a little put out, as though he saw in her yet another peril for Kaeso. But he appeared relieved to learn that the Jewish slave belonged to the master of the house, and was very charming to her when introduced in the most flattering of terms.

'I don't only preach about a God crucified to redeem our sins,' said Paul to Selene, 'but a God of Truth, a truth to liberate masters and slaves alike and make them equal under God's loving eye.'

'I can't imagine, venerable rabbi, that you want to encourage slaves to revolt, like the misguided Stoics who set all Asia alight and awash with blood in those already long-ago days when the Romans were helping themselves to the inheritance of the King of Pergamum?'

'Certainly not. We're against all forms of violence of that sort. The mere fact of their uselessness makes them unjust. How could one imagine a society without slaves?'

'But a minority of masters use unjust violence against their slaves. They maltreat them cruelly on the slightest pretext. They castrate young boys to make them catamites or singers. They prostitute wretched children of both sexes at an early age. Sometimes, on the other hand, they prevent slaves from copulating by putting a ring through a man's foreskin (Jews are lucky) or through the lips of the vagina. And every day lustful individuals abuse their servants, male and female. Such acts of violence seem to me neither just nor useful.'

'My heart bleeds at what you say. But as slavery is a sad necessity, the only possible improvement is the one I am offering. Slaves, touched by the gift of grace, will zealously obey every decent order their master gives them. Their masters, touched by the same gift of grace, will order only decent things, and will in future behave like attentive fathers and not tyrants. Gradually, if the Christians gain influence in this city, laws which offer genuine protection will see the light of day.'

'In the meantime what has your fine doctrine got to offer me if I'm dissatisfied with my master?'

'You'll have the satisfaction of suffering for your sins and for his. Your humiliations will take on an eternal value and Christ will console you for them in paradise.'

'Since you claim to speak for all men, and not just for the Jews as the orthodox rabbis do, you ought to re-read the Jewish Law. Everyone in the synagogues knows that you've thoughtlessly put most of it in the waste-paper basket. You'll find in Exodus that the Hebrew slave of a Hebrew master must be released, with his wife, at the end of seven years. In Leviticus you'll see that the Hebrew slaves of Hebrew masters must be released, with their wives and children, in our jubilee year, which comes once every fifty years. Instead of talking about love with a bleeding heart, why don't you incorporate the same programme into your universal mission? Why shouldn't there be rights for all slaves, as there are for the Hebrew slaves of Hebrew masters? But you won't do anything of the kind. Like all propagandists of your breed, what you're interested in is the masters. You only begin by seducing the slaves because you want them to convince their masters for you. And if you want to find yourself dining with Silanus and his like one of these days, you mustn't upset them by interfering with their human capital. So you're worth a lot less to a slave like me than a Jew would be. A Jew would promise me a better fate than you can, if he respected his own Law – a Law which you were in a hurry to forget in your desire for quick success. You're a phoney, and the God of my fathers, who has his eye on you, will punish you for your treachery and your hypocrisy one of these days.'

Paul was choking with rage and turning all the colours of the rainbow. Kaeso, amused by this argument between Jews, gave Selene a good telling-off, for form's sake. The apostle, who was overflowing with sincere, charitable sentiments, was all the more shocked because Selene's insulting remarks were, from her standpoint as a slave, irrefutable.

Paul emerged from his disarray, saying: 'I beg of you to believe that if there were any chance of the Greeks and Romans adopting those old Jewish laws we should have incorporated them into our doctrine.'

Selene replied: 'You're prepared to put lots of effort into persuading the Gentiles that your Jesus rose from the dead, and yet you feel incapable of persuading them to release a slave once every fifty years? In that case you couldn't persuade a mouse to eat cheese!'

Kaeso put on a grim face and showed Selene the door, but he winked at her as he did so. At the same time he made his excuses to Paul, adding:

'As the girl is my father's concubine, she treats the house as her own. The Christians are good at pardoning: here's an excellent opportunity to put the gospel into practice.'

'That is exactly what I am doing. The slave is visibly unhappy and unhappiness unbalances the mind.'

Kaeso accompanied Paul to the door, and they arranged to meet again the next day.

While waiting for dinner time, Kaeso took up his tablets and wrote a note to Silanus.

'K. Aponius Saturninus to D. Junius Silanus Torquatus, filial greetings.

I was deeply moved by the enlightened and generous attitude expressed in your last letter to me. What can I add, since you claim to know all and to be able to guess what you have not actually been told? You will now understand why I was not as assiduous in my attentions to you when I came back to Italy as perhaps I should have been and as you certainly deserved. A natural sense of embarrassment held me back.

I have recently met a rather interesting and highly colourful individual, a certain Cn. Pompeius Paulus, a Jew from Tarsus, who makes an eccentric Roman. He is one of the leaders of a heretical Jewish sect called the Christians, which claims to be spreading the doctrines of the Greek Bible, the Septuagint, to the whole world. You may have heard of the Septuagint from Seneca, who has read all of it. Paul has something in common with the Stoics; he insists on the freedom given us by providence to determine our own conduct, starting from what depends specifically on ourselves. He has also cut his Bible about and added to it with imagination and originality, sometimes coloured by avant-garde mythology. He's a man to follow. I must admit he has made a big impression on me.

What is bound to impress you is a piece of news which is more important than all the rest, and which Paulus kindly asked me to pass on to you. He got it from one of his followers, some scribbler whose job makes him well-up in the secrets of the Treasury. The modalities of the devaluation which everyone is talking about have been decided on and the decree will be out shortly. In future our Roman pound will have forty-five *aurei* instead of forty-two, and ninety-six *denarii* instead of eighty-four. Which comes down to saying that the weight of the silver *denarius* will be cut down by a little more than one eighth, and that of the *aureus* by only a little more than one nineteenth. But – and this is the vital piece of information – the relationship of twenty-five silver *denarii* to one *aureus* will be maintained. Everybody at court who is in the know, with Tigellinus at their head, is therefore buying up silver, so that after devaluation they can use greatly devalued *denarii* to buy up much less devalued *aurei*. The measure is designed to favour the knights and businessmen, who handle vast quantities of *denarii*, at the expense of the nobility, which is supposed to hoard gold with a jealous passion. What is more, the new *denarius* will be worth the *drachma*, which is valid throughout the East. That will make commercial exchange easier. You have everything to gain and nothing to lose by attending religiously to this Christian revelation.'

Little Myra, once bathed, fed to her heart's content and wearing a dress of Selene's which was much too long for her and made a droll sort of train, kept trailing about behind Kaeso.

Finally she dared to ask him: 'I'd like to know, if you don't mind, who I'm supposed to sleep with around here.'

Irritated, Kaeso retorted: 'With nobody. I bought you so that you can sleep all by yourself with your doll!'

The child burst into tears in her anxiety. Since the day when, at the age of eight, she had become a prostitute in a brothel in Corinth, she had had the impression that her body, which was her curse, was also her only safeguard, the only thing she had of any value in the world. How long would they go on feeding her if they weren't going to use her?

Kaeso continued his letter with a request for a loan of seven thousand sesterces, and suggested: 'The obscene nocturnal Floralia continue beyond the Kalends of May. Paulus has a Jewish sense of decency which takes fright at the slightest thing. He would prefer me to postpone my adoption until the Ides of the same month, a day traditionally sacred to Jupiter. I take the liberty of putting the same request. I need time for further thought to prepare myself better for the honour which you want to pay me.'

As Myra went on snivelling, Kaeso gave her permission to sleep in a corner of his own room.

❋ CHAPTER ❋

3

Early the next morning, on the sixth day of the Kalends of May, Silanus sent Kaeso the 7,000 sesterces with a friendly covering note and Marcia separately sent him a short note of her own.

'Marcia to Kaeso, greetings.

Decimus was annoyed that you should defer the ceremony after the noble letter in which he clarified the situation on the basis of the information he wheedled out of me. What could I have said to him which would have been more to your advantage? The news of your decision has plunged me into the most sinister torments, made worse by your absence. How hard you are on the only woman who loves you! My life is in your ungrateful hands. I could not live if you abandoned me.

I hope you are in better health than I am.'

This blackmail was terribly depressing.

From her corner Myra asked: 'Bad news?'

Without thinking Kaeso deigned to answer her. 'A woman is threatening to kill herself if I abandon her.'

The little girl's eyes shone. All prostitutes adored dramatic love stories. The mythology of 'true love' was some compensation for their work.

'That doesn't surprise me. You're as handsome as a god. What are you going to do?'

'I'd like to know the answer to that myself.'

'Me, I only know one thing. Love is a bird you can't keep when it isn't hungry any more. And if you put it in a cage, you kill its appetite.'

Out of the mouths of babes and sucklings!

'Don't you fancy me?'

Another Marcia, asking questions!

'I've just taken up a new religion. You stay a virgin till marriage, marry a virgin and while your wife is alive you're not allowed to sleep with anyone else and neither is she.'

Myra threw a pained look at Kaeso. He was making fun of her. Feeling equally pained, Kaeso looked the other way. It was really impossible to

341

grasp what the attraction of the new doctrine could be. It wouldn't even serve as a tactful pretext for chastity.

For hours on end Kaeso wallowed in gloomy reflections. He had a desultory lunch, and after siesta decided to rejoin Paul, who ought at that moment to be haranguing the passers-by in the Campus Martius in front of the Villa Publica.

All sorts of zealots liked to expound their ideas in the Forums in the mornings, to the most mixed audience on earth. The crowds in the Campus Martius in the afternoons were distinctly more elegant. There were fewer people, and distinguished Hellenophone listeners were relatively more numerous. Moreover, passers-by paid more attention because they were less busy: they were on their way to or from the Baths of Agrippa or Nero, or simply taking a stroll in the Portico of the Argonauts or looking at the luxury shops nearby.

The Villa Publica, which among other purposes was used to receive foreign embassies which the Senate did not want to allow into the city, was the centre for the major antique dealers. It was separated from the temple of Bellona, goddess of War, only by the width of the Circus Flaminius. In the immense *atrium* of this Villa Publica, Sulla had once upon a time had 4,000 outlaws massacred while he was presiding over a sitting of the Senate right next door in the temple of Bellona. When the screams of the victims disturbed the session, Sulla had laughingly said to the *patres conscripti*: 'Don't worry: it's just some naughty boys I'm having punished.' (His audience were not entirely reassured.) The proscriptions carried out by the popular party were a chaotic affair. Sulla's had been brilliantly organized and outstandingly methodical.

It was in front of this memorable monument that Paul, with an audience of some thirty people, was preparing souls to receive his message. But the disappointments he had had in Athens and elsewhere had made him cautious. He no longer risked talking about the Resurrection until he had gauged the feel of his audience.

Kaeso gave the speaker a friendly smile and joined the little group. Paul first proclaimed the existence of a god who was the creator of all things. Then he described him as a Father, who never overlooked a single detail of what went on in life, and who required each man to show his neighbour the same love that God showed to him. Just as God caused the sun to shine on good and bad alike, man should do good and even return good for evil.

The novelty of the proposition attracted some attention. A middle-aged man in a toga, who seemed very much at his ease, interrupted

342

the speaker. 'If we return good for evil, shan't we encourage others to act in a harmful fashion? For every wrong-doer that you disarm by your display of weakness, won't there be many more who pursue their activities with increased boldness? In the end won't you do a lot of harm by trying to do good? In this *atrium* Sulla had 4,000 murderers executed – men whose hands were stained with the blood of my ancestors and of the finest of the Roman nobility. If all those criminals had lived, wouldn't they have repeated their crimes at the first possible opportunity?'

Politics was slippery terrain. Paul – like Christ – preferred the more solid ground of personal morality.

'Augustus, we're told, pardoned Cinna, with fortunate results,' he replied. 'But I've never claimed that wrong-doers shouldn't be punished in accordance with just laws. Forgiving one's neighbour isn't the same as leaving him free to do harm. It's a question of loving him before, during and after his punishment. It's a question of excluding from one's heart all feelings of revenge. We are all sinners and must one day ask God to forgive us.'

Kaeso intervened, flatteringly: 'The doctrine you are preaching is a very wise and far-sighted one. Justice should bring peace and should not exclude clemency, whereas every act of vengeance demands another. All our unfortunate civil wars testify to the truth of that.'

A murmur of approval arose. Paul thanked his listeners for their attention and came up to Kaeso.

'Thanks to you I actually managed to finish a speech without getting myself stoned.'

'In theatres, and in the basilicas during a trial, the claque plays an important role. You should never start speaking without a few friends to second you and to applaud.'

'God has no need of a claque.'

'True belief is not incompatible with making the most of a situation. There's plenty of potential hired applause going to waste, and that's a pity.'

Paul sighed and seized on the opportunity to raise a topic which was tormenting him:

'While we're on the subject of the theatre, my brief stay in Rome has shown me the enormous importance which festivals and Games have for the Romans. It's quite out of proportion to what I've found in Greece or the East. All the inhabitants of the city seem to be bewitched by these continual spectacles, which are the absolute antithesis of gentleness and decency. How can one get them out of this dung-heap? What do you see as the source of such a destructive passion?'

They had arrived in front of the main entrance to the vast Circus Flaminius, which, however, looked like a model beside the enormous Circus Maximus.

Kaeso replied: 'Everything has contributed to this obsession. Shows have got bigger and more spectacular. In the last years of the Republic, those with political ambitions vied with each other to lay on Games for the *plebs*. Today Caesar is the only man with political interests left in the ring. There is a tendency for the displays of imperial largesse to get more and more lavish with every succeeding reign, because the emperor's popularity is strictly proportionate to the scale of the entertainments provided. It's easier to entertain people than to feed or house them.

That's why we have nineteen major festivals of a religious nature in our calendar, mostly involving rituals which have something to do with farming or war, apart from those intended to protect us against the baleful influences of the gods or the dead. Some of the festivals go on for several days. The Saturnalia are perhaps the most striking and best known to foreigners, because that's when slaves are allowed to play the role of masters.

We have ten main series of Public Games, running from April to December, which often coincide with the religious festival which serves as their pretext. Then in addition every four years we have the Ludi Actiaci which were instituted by Augustus to celebrate the anniversary of his victory at Actium at the beginning of September. I'll pass over the Ludi Saeculares – they only happen once every 120 years or so. At the beginning of the present month we have the Ludi Megalenses in honour of Cybele. When we come out of the Cerilia, held in honour of Ceres, we shall go into the licentious Floralia. You'd better not put your nose out of doors on the evening before the Floralia, because the city will be crawling with naked women. This month alone we shall have had twenty odd days of Games. Under the Republic there were about sixty days of ordinary Games per year, with additional extraordinary Games to mark special occasions, given by the State or private individuals. Nowadays festivals and Games normally take up almost 200 days of the year.'

Paul was aghast. 'Do you mean to say that more than one day in two is spent at the theatre, in an amphitheatre or circus, or at some other immoral activity?'

'It has to be, to keep the people happy.'

'But when do they ever do any work?'

'The Romans are renowned throughout the world for their achievements. In fact they're probably more gifted for work than any other race. But what is certain is that there's less work done in Rome than anywhere else. Rome devours the revenues of the entire universe, but all it produces is Games. That's the fruit of our victories.

You can see that you're not going to find it easy to make Christians out of the sort of people you'll find here. Basic human nature throughout the world is at odds with your magnificent doctrine, but in Rome, capital of the earth, you've got to contend with the mania for Games as well. When a people get an obsession of that sort you can't reverse the whole process. Would you like to go to a show, to see for yourself how far the Roman *plebs* has become the victim of its own institutions? As the son of a senator and a friend of Silanus I can get hold of some good seats.'

'The nobility attend these shows as well! Do you yourself go?'

'One can go to the same entertainments as the lower classes from time to time without being a prisoner of them. It's a question of taste and discretion. A man as wise as you will have no problem.'

'A Christian couldn't possibly go to these Games.'

'Why ever not?'

Kaeso felt an instinctive reluctance to deceive Paul more than was necessary, and the idea of having to promise to abstain from this particular pleasure just to secure his baptism irritated him. Paul took such an exaggerated stance on everything.

'Look,' he said, pointing to the race track in the Circus Flaminius which stretched away in a great curve in front of them. 'What excites people here is a passion for watching horses racing and betting on them. Even if one accepts that betting is an un-Christian activity, there's no harm in admiring horses.'

'You yourself used the word "passion". A passion for God should be enough for any man.'

'Would you refuse me baptism if I only agreed to promise to give up betting?'

'If you only go to the Circus occasionally, and then don't bet, you can still call yourself a Christian.'

'It'll be just as well if you show yourself a little flexible. If you refuse the faithful permission to enjoy even the least bit of entertainment of a more or less decent kind, they risk becoming utterly bored and giving in to worse temptations.'

'There's something in what you say.'

Kaeso pointed out the silhouette of the moderate-sized old amphitheatre of Taurus on the horizon, and then the great wooden amphitheatre of Nero, which had been put up seven years ago. He went on:

'Where the bloodlust which fills the amphitheatres is concerned, you need to make another distinction.'

'Just at the moment I can't see on what criteria.'

'You're not going to tell me that you'll insist that Christians refrain from hunting, are you? The great hunts in the arena are a fine sight. If you'll accept that a Christian may kill a rabbit, there's no reason why he shouldn't watch lions or bears or elephants being killed. Where on the scale of numbers of animals killed does it start to be a sin?'

With distaste Paul conceded:

'Very well, I'll accept hunts, if I absolutely must. But only hunts.'

'There's another entirely innocent amusement, although it's debatable whether it's worth watching: after the morning hunts, during the midday interval, they execute those condemned criminals who haven't been thrown to the wild beasts. Sometimes they add a few artistic effects for the benefit of the humbler members of the *plebs* – and of the children, who stay to eat their picnic lunches with their *paedagogus* on the seats at the top of the theatre. For some time now the organizers have been seriously trying – and the effort seems to me entirely praiseworthy – to get away from the monotonous butchery which used to characterize this part of the programme once upon a time, by staging morally instructive scenes which illustrate some fable or other from our abundant mythology. You might see Icarus, for example, moving his wings up and down high up on a platform. He hesitates to jump, as if suspecting that the conquest of the air needed longer preliminary experiment. He's finally firmly persuaded to make the jump, does so and crashes to his death with a cry of disillusionment. When a child has seen the story of Icarus illustrated like that, it remains engraved on his memory. It's good for education to draw upon the services of pictures. What sin could there be in watching condemned criminals, who have earned their fate a hundred times over, being executed? I would point out to you that if one reads your Bible, one has the impression that the Jews never miss a good stoning, and that people are even encouraged to enjoy taking part in them.'

Paul found this appeal to biblical authority even more embarrassing than Kaeso would have guessed.

'You're turning the knife in the wound. When the Jews stoned Stephen, the first Christian martyr, I was only too pleased to hold the cloaks of the witnesses for the prosecution, who were called on to throw the first stones.'

'There you are then. What you now regret is not the fact that you conscientiously took part in a stoning, where you acted as cloakroom attendant, but that, in your ignorance, you were an accomplice in the execution of a Christian, a judicial error from your point of view. If they had been stoning an adulterous woman, your part in it would have left you with an absolutely clear conscience.'

'According to John, Jesus intervened to save such a woman from stoning.'

'Perhaps she was pretty? In any case, despite that charitable gesture, I don't think Jesus called the law in question on that point. You yourself are probably strongly in favour of exemplary punishment for adulterous Christian wives . . . in the unlikely event of there ever being any such.'

'I'm afraid there probably already are some. Yes, of course, there must be a sanction against adultery, and one which ought to penalize both sexes equally, if the laws were truly Christian.'

'So you'll accept that a Christian can go and watch respectable executions? What's good for a Jew should be good for a Roman.'

'What I find unacceptable is the supposedly artistic and entertaining side. A Christian should not dress up necessary acts of cruelty.'

'In all probability that is a question of manners which will vary from country to country and individual to individual, rather than a moral issue.'

Kaeso, the heir to a gladiatorial *ludus*, had succeeded in manoeuvring Paul in two areas which were of very minor importance to him. But Paul turned out to be absolutely intractable over gladiatorial combat. The fact that all the combatants, whether slaves or free men under contract, had by the nature of things chosen of their own free will to be gladiators seemed to make no impression on him at all. Indeed he found something sinful in their very willingness, since in his opinion the right to kill should always derive from the legitimate need to defend oneself, whether socially or individually. To him, by a paradox which Kaeso found incomprehensible, the most thuggish soldier or the most grasping, complacent petty capitalist was morally justified in exercising his function in the normal way, whereas the most distinguished of gladiators was not.

Illogicality of such a sort did not deserve more than a false promise. Kaeso had no scruples about making one.

They walked along the outside of the Circus Flaminius and reached the Portico of Pompey. At the far end was the back wall of the stage of the theatre of the same name. There was a great deal of hustle and bustle in

347

preparation for the Floral Games which were to open two days later. Stagehands and cleaners were swarming everywhere.

The theatre of Pompey had been the first theatre in Rome to be built of stone. Its semicircular auditorium could seat 27,000 spectators comfortably. During the reign of Augustus two other theatres had been added in the same area of the city: the theatre of Marcellus, with another 14,000 places, and the theatre of Balbus with a further 7,700. The capacity was still very slight compared with that of the permanent or *ad hoc* amphitheatres, or more particularly in comparison to that of the Circus Maximus, which was continually being expanded and could now hold a quarter of a million. Despite efforts to renew the genres and the repertoire the theatre was still a poor relation in the entertainment family.

Kaeso explained to Paul that the theatre did not have as many enthusiasts as gladiatorial *munera* and horse racing. People even tried, as far as possible, to avoid putting on theatrical shows while *munera* or races were being held, because in such circumstances they had been known to lose most of their audience to the amphitheatre or the Circus, whose competition was irresistible. *Munera*, which were rarer and more expensive to stage, were even more popular than horse racing.

Paul had heard second-hand accounts of Greek provincial theatre, which had totally degenerated, and he had been told revolting tales about Roman theatre. He asked Kaeso to tell him everything and not to mince his words.

Rather than launch into an abstract discussion Kaeso asked Paul to walk around the building with him. Whereas the Greeks had dug out hills to form their theatres, the Romans were not afraid to build on the flat. The reason for this was that they had perfected effective techniques for constructing frameworks and filling them in with rubble. This gave the core of the building, which was then given a suitable outer coating. At the back the theatre was attached to a three-storey temple of Venus: the top storey was at the height of the top of the auditorium, and was fitted out with a covered walkway. Paul and Kaeso went up to it. A detachment of sailors was in the process of fixing up the fine linen curtain which was to shut off the wings of the theatre, for while, during the Floralia, prostitutes might strip off at night in the streets and in the theatres, the festival also involved more routine daytime performances.

Kaeso pointed out the impressive dimensions of Pompey's masterpiece for Paul's approval. When the stalls, which were reserved for senators, knights and other notables, the tiers, the walkway and the square in front of the temple of Venus were all full, the capacity could be raised to 40,000 spectators. From their Venusian observatory the two visitors could make out the tiny figures of the workmen on the stage.

'The very size of our first stone theatre,' said Kaeso, 'sounded the death knell for a form of entertainment which was already more or less on its last legs. Imagine the effect of concentrating seven legions in this space –and legions formed from the dregs of society at that – with all the constant noise you get from a crowd of that size: people chatting, shouting, bantering with the prostitutes, shifting around, walking about, eating, drinking, urinating in these little gutters which have a trickle of refreshing water flowing down them – an invention of Pompey's engineers which deserved more respect! How could an actor make himself heard and understood by an ignorant audience who are completely insensitive to the beauty of the text? He has noise, space and ignorance against him.

In the golden era of the Greek theatre, or of Roman theatre which was an inventive imitation of it, the problem was already a difficult one, for which there were only palliatives rather than solutions, despite the fact that audiences were smaller and more knowledgeable. For example, the stage was fitted out with a wooden board to reflect sound, and the actors had huge masks which acted as megaphones. Masks and costumes were stylized and in different colours. Female roles were played by men, because only they had the lung power even to attempt to dominate the chaotic conditions. That was, for good or ill, the state of things in the days of our old Roman tragedies and comedies, whether in the Greek or the Roman style. But they gradually became less and less comprehensible to a larger and noisier populace. Nowadays they are hardly ever performed to the general public.

Gradually a fatal evolution has taken place. The tragic chorus has left its place in the pit and gone up on to the stage to share the main action with the leading roles. Singing and music are more audible than words. Tragedy has accordingly become a repertoire of popular songs, *cantica*. At Caesar's funeral, the weeping masses were warbling a chorus from Pacuvius: "*Men' servasse ut essent qui me perderent?*" (Did I only save them to perish at their hands?)

But, for 40,000 spectators, it's an even safer bet to rely on what they can see rather than what they can hear. So not only has the text been sacrificed to singing, but singing has been sacrificed to dance and mime. Today all tragedy is first and foremost a dumbshow, backed up by this or that soloist, with a chorus behind him, and accompanied by *entrechats* and lots of oompahpah. Mimes can be almost as big celebrities as gladiators!

At the same time the subjects of tragedy have become more and more daring and vulgar. They're full of the worst aspects of mythology – Pasiphaes offering themselves to bulls in Cretan labyrinths. The art of the mime is entirely one of suggestion.

As for comedy, it has abandoned all the conventions of decency and sunk into the crudest form of realism. It's no longer a question of suggesting, but of showing. Brutality and pornography – torture, assassination, rape – are its standard fare. In comedy the mime-artists are of both sexes. King Pentheus is torn to pieces by the Bacchants, Hercules burns to death on his pyre, the brigand Laureolus is not only duly crucified but eaten by a bear to boot, tearful girls are raped by lusting donkeys before being strangled by thugs . . .'

'I don't think I've quite understood . . . We're still talking about miming, aren't we?'

'Not at all. In our Roman comedies the much decried mimes of both sexes do what they can. But, with the tacit acceptance of those in power who may soon actually legalize the arrangement, the stage has become an ideal place for dispatching condemned criminals, male or female, who are naturally substituted for the mimes at the critical moment. In this way we have a realist theatre unlike any other. Such shows succeed in holding the attention of the maximum possible audience.

As a future Christian I am fully aware that I should feel some reservations, if not about the application of aesthetic considerations to executions, at least about the rapes, which undoubtedly take place outside the sacrament of indissoluble marriage.'

'You do indeed have grounds for your reservations!'

Overcome, Paul sat down and stared at the distant stage, where magnificent scenery was going up. All the resources of stage machinery and *trompe-l'oeil* had taken on a great importance in theatrical presentation. Between scenes, a curtain went up to hide the activities of the stage crew.

Kaeso thought he should add a few details. 'It's a pious custom at Rome to rape virgins before executing them. For example, Sejanus' daughter was deflowered by her executioners. But I obviously couldn't guarantee that all the female condemned criminals who get raped on the stage are virgins. Abuses slip in everywhere . . .'

Paul put his fingers in his ears and left the theatre of Pompey without a backward glance.

For a short while Kaeso and Paul walked along the Triumphal Way, which led to the Campus Vaticanus via the bridge of the same name. Like the Appian Way at the same time of day it was a meeting-place for all sorts of smart people.

To distract Paul from his painful depression, Kaeso asked him:

'Tell me something about yourself. Where did you study?'

'Firstly at Tarsus in Asia Minor. Up to the age of twelve, like all Jewish children, I was exempt from the Law. Then I studied the Law with my father at the synagogue in Tarsus. As an adolescent I had a growing passion for the Law and studied it further at Jerusalem, under the direction of the famous rabbi Gamaliel, whom all Jews looked on as a great *nassi* –that means prince – in those days. From him I learnt a very liberal approach to the Scriptures. For example, Gamaliel considered that all beggars, non-Jews as well as Jews, should be given access to a field for gleaning.'

'Very generous of him! What language was standard at Tarsus, in Cilicia?'

'Greek. But with Gamaliel I perfected my Aramaic, the language of Jesus and his disciples.'

'Didn't Jesus speak Hebrew?'

'These days Hebrew is only a religious and liturgical language. You study it in books. It isn't spoken. And as the Jews have had the Septuagint at their disposal for a long time, the number of people who know Hebrew, particularly in Egypt, gets smaller and smaller. Jesus had spent time in the synagogues and must have known a little. Most of his disciples knew none at all. I'm not strong in it myself.'

'In any case Jesus must have known some basic Greek.'

'Why do you say that?'

'Because according to Mark he talked to Pilate without an interpreter, and I'm sure Pilate didn't speak Aramaic.'

'I hadn't thought of that. It's perfectly possible. Greek is in very widespread use as a second language in those parts. Some of the disciples, including some from the humblest backgrounds, had a smattering.'

'You don't speak Latin?'

'I can understand it reasonably well, but I still make a lot of mistakes. After Greek the absence of articles is very off-putting. But why are you so obsessed with all this business about languages?'

'With good reason.'

'Meaning?'

'Put yourself in my place. Your Jesus preached in Aramaic, an impossible *patois*, to crowds of the uneducated. I'm anxious to know whether his audiences understood him properly, whether they repeated Jesus' words exactly to people capable of translating them into Greek, and whether the translation is accurate. Even the Gospel according to Mark raises great problems of authenticity. I'm surprised that you don't seem aware of them.'

Paul and Kaeso had struck off to the right, towards the gardens of Agrippa, and were walking along the banks of a pool which was all that was left of the 'Goat's Marsh' into which Romulus was supposed to have disappeared.

After thinking for a moment, Paul answered: 'Your disquiet is natural, but there's no justification for it, for reasons which should be obvious. In the first place, Jesus expressed himself in the most simple and concrete fashion. All the versions of His words which have come down to us are exactly the same in overall tenor, even if they do present slight differences of form.

Secondly, despite what a Gentile who knows nothing of the Jewish scriptures might suppose, most of Jesus' pronouncements, given that he wasn't a moralist, are only original in the very personal way in which they're expressed. Except on the point about marriage Jesus made no innovations in practical morality. He limited himself to going back to the spirit of the Jewish law, instead of concentrating on its literal details. Even when He preaches love for God and one's neighbour, be he Jew or non-Jew, He often takes up ideas and expressions already present in the Scriptures, whether ancient or more recent, and already defended by some enlightened Pharisees. But He collects them, links them and gets their essence out of them. Of course, if that was the whole of it, we should only be dealing with another prophet in a certain Jewish tradition. The problem of authority would then be no more tricky than it is with any of the other prophets or learned men.

In the third place there is indeed a problem of authenticity, but it has much more to do with deeds than words, and can be summed up in the question: "Did Jesus come back from the dead or didn't He?" If He didn't, then His words are of no significance. If He did, then His words are still relatively unimportant, because then one can be quite certain that the Holy Spirit is watching over us closely to see that we know what we need for the government of our conduct.

When Jesus spoke to me on the road to Damascus to reproach me for persecuting Him, He spoke to me in His mother-tongue. "Saul, Saul!" he cried in Aramaic. What difference would it have made if he'd spoken in Hebrew, or in Greek as he did to Pilate?'

Kaeso was beginning to understand Paul's strange mentality better. Nonetheless he remarked to him:

'It's not the same for you. You can take a different view of things, because a god has spoken to you in his mother-tongue. But he hasn't yet said anything to me in any language whatsoever. You must forgive me for my legitimate curiosity. In the hope that you might be able to come up with a more satisfactory answer, I'd advise you to take a closer interest in Jesus' precise words. For want of a vision on the road to Damascus most Christians won't have anything else to get their teeth into.'

'We didn't need *you* to tell us that! Not just Mark but other disciples too, my friend Luke for one, are working on translating everything Jesus said or did from the Greek or Aramaic, either personally or with the help of faithful secretaries.'

'I was forgetting the secretaries.'

'When I send official letters to a community I use secretaries most of the time, and just write the last few lines in my own hand. But I've never noticed that my thought was deformed by the process.'

'Could you give me one of those letters to read? I assume that copies were kept, as with Seneca's letters to Lucilius.'

'You flatter me by comparing me with that very wealthy rhetorician. I'll get a copy to you, by this evening, of a letter to James, Jesus' "brother", whom the Jews stoned in Jerusalem while I was recently being held in captivity here in Rome. And I'll add my letters to the Thessalonians, Corinthians, Philippians, Galatians, Romans, Colossians and Ephesians – the last two were written while I was in prison. But don't expect to find a complete account of our doctrine in them. I talk about particular questions which arose here or elsewhere at a given moment. The Devil is at work behind my back sowing discord. The Resurrection has made him beside himself with rage.'

'The Devil hasn't also appeared to you, like Jesus did, and spoken to you in Garamantian or Chinese?'

Paul started to laugh. 'Christians see the Devil at close enough quarters every day.'

They were coming back towards the city, which lay tightly enclosed between the old ramparts of Servius. The paths along these ramparts were no longer used except by the night-watchmen of the seven cohorts of freedmen who were responsible for fighting fires with the help of the authorities in the region of the city affected. The sun was going down in a blaze of red.

A number of Christians were still waiting for the end of the world to take place as a sort of Stoic *conflagratio*, but Paul was becoming more and more doubtful of the imminence of the event. Surely the Gospel would have to be preached everywhere first? And the world could well be bigger than people thought. All that the Christians could hope for, apart from living indefinitely in a ghetto like the Jews, was the end of Nero's world. It would not come to an end of its own accord. Fortunately Roman civilization was very fragile: a collection of idle cities, defended by a few mercenaries of dubious loyalties. If these cities were destroyed, the insolent civilization which was opposed to Christ in every fibre of its being would cease to be an obstacle to grace. The Romans naïvely thought their empire was eternal. The Christians had already instinctively understood that they could only establish their humble domination over ruins and deserts.

Kaeso asked: 'What are you thinking about? What fine vision can you see behind that red sun?'

'I'm thinking of the end of the world.'

'What does it matter to a rational man whether he dies all alone or with a flock of sheep. Isn't death the end of the world for everyone?'

When would Kaeso learn to talk like a Christian?

While awaiting this linguistic conversion the would-be convert was for the first time struck by a suspicion which might have occurred to him sooner if he had given the matter more thought. He said to Paul:

'Your faith makes quite an impression on me. If I know one thing about you, it's that you're not a liar. You certainly believe in the story you're telling. So I'll ask you to answer as frankly as possible a very specific question which is of some importance to me. You can reproach the Romans with all the vices in creation, but they do have the virtue of not compelling you to share them. Nero freely gives you permission to stay a virgin, to keep away from his theatre, and you could even refuse to worship idols if you were still a Jew like the others. It's a quite unoppressive form of tyranny as far as you're concerned. But if Nero was a Christian, would there still be gladiators and mixed baths and divorces?'

'The first duty of a Christian Nero would certainly be to knock down all the idols and impose Christian laws on all the inhabitants of the Empire.'

'With their consent or by force?'

'It would then be right to use force in the service of the law, since the law and the will of the Almighty would be one and the same thing.'

'I'd forgotten that Jesus addressed you as Saul.'

354

'Then you'd forgotten the essential.'

Kaeso realized that you cannot discuss anything with people who are on intimate terms with a transcendent but incarnate god. When he thought about it, their position was impregnable, since such a god had the unmatchable virtue of being as terrestrial as possible while paradoxically drawing his strength from heaven.

Paul wanted to know where he could see Nero before leaving Rome, even if he only saw him for an instant at a distance. There were numerous horse-races during the Floralia. In the Circus Maximus the first day of the festival was given over to them from daybreak to nightfall. There was bound to be an occasion when Nero would be presiding, high up in his Palatine box, the *pulvinar*, from which emperors dominated the whole of the Circus. If they had seats close to the box, it would be easy to see the divine Ahenobarbus, who was destined for apotheosis.

Paul's interest in Nero's person amused Kaeso. He found it very provincial. Citizens resident at Rome thought themselves so far above all nations that the distance between themselves and the emperor seemed much less than the distance separating themselves and the indistinct mass of non-citizens elsewhere in the Empire. They had the feeling that, with the Prince, they were part of the society which exploited the vanquished. And every one knew it was only an accident of war which had pushed the Julio-Claudians into the front rank. Relations between true Romans and the emperor were marked more by envious familiarity than by any sort of respect. Wiser emperors did not even believe in their own divinity, which was the object of many a good joke in private.

Paul and Kaeso were approaching the Forums when the apostle noticed a baby abandoned next to a discarded cooking pot. To protect abandoned children from dogs – in a pretty derisory way, it is true – while awaiting their hypothetical rescue by a professional beggar or a pimp with an eye to the future, they were sometimes exposed in a receptacle of some kind. Paul put the baby in the pot and asked Kaeso:

'What are the laws on abortion in Rome?'

'In principle it's a crime if the woman has an abortion without her husband's consent. Equally in principle an exemplary wife should not refuse to have an abortion if her husband wants one. But deliberate abortion is very dangerous. The custom of exposing unwanted children exists to solve the problem without risk to health. A Christian Nero would, I imagine, condemn both abortion and exposure?'

'He would even forbid any attempt to prevent conception during conjugal relations.'

'That would provide wonderful opportunities for kinky spies!'

In his transcendent madness Paul seemed to consider such a situation entirely natural.

They made another arrangement to meet the next day. Then, despite his feeling of repugnance, Kaeso turned his steps towards Silanus' house. At this time of day Silanus would be getting ready to go out and dine in town. The richer you were, the later you tended to dine and the longer your dinners tended to last.

Kaeso was well aware that he could not put off paying a formal call any longer. It would in any case be very brief. Duty also obliged him to smile at Marcia a little, if nothing else.

Silanus' *familia* had just been thrown into disarray. The incongruous head of Cicero, not content with troubling the master and irritating the *domina*, had given hysterics to a Greek slave who was fond of paintings and had been day-dreaming in front of the pictures when night fell.

When Kaeso, guided by a servant who was still trembling all over, arrived in the peristyle, Marcia, in Silanus' presence, was in the process of making a band of shocked slaves see reason. She was shouting at them: 'It's not phantoms you need be afraid of, it's the living. Who's going to whip you if fear of the other world makes you neglect your tasks – Cicero or your master?'

Kaeso's arrival was a good excuse to cut the lecture short and send the terrified slaves back to whatever they had been doing.

Despite Cicero's deplorable whims, Silanus was in an excellent mood, and he at once told Kaeso why. 'I'm particularly happy to see you, because I must thank you profusely. The financial tips you passed on to me are first class. When I read your note, I didn't really believe it. But I made inquiries. Today Seneca and a few others are getting rid of their gold and putting everything into *denarii*. There'll be several million profit for me in this business.'

Even a multimillionaire never fails to enjoy making a few millions more with the minimum of effort.

Kaeso said that the gratitude ought to go to Paul.

'Does this Jew want a commission?'

'No, money isn't his motive.'

'I know what you mean. Philosophers and priests are never after money. It comes as an extra, as a reward for their disinterestedness, and they hang on to it like mad.'

'Yes, Paul is rather like that. But at the moment his ambition is to see

Nero before he leaves Rome. Could you get us some good seats near the *pulvinar* for the Circus the day after tomorrow?'

'You can have mine. I've had enough of horses for the moment. But if your Paul wants to see Nero at closer quarters, that's easily arranged. The prince is coming to dine here shortly. As soon as the date is fixed, I'll let you know. By inviting him here from time to time I set myself up with an excuse not to go and pay court to him as often as I ought. I can't breath in the stifling brothel-like atmosphere of the palace.'

'You actually have him here?'

'In the garden at the back, if the weather's fine.'

'It might be a good idea, that evening, to shut the doors of the picture gallery so that the ghost doesn't spoil the dinner party.'

'Excellent advice. Nero is already haunted by the ghosts of Octavia and Agrippina, and probably the ghost of Britannicus as well. He detests ghosts. But he's equally scared of assassins. You'll answer for this chap Paul, will you? I would prefer Nero to have his throat cut somewhere other than at my house.'

'Paul is gentleness personified. The very sight of gladiators sends him into a frenzy, and he pats the heads of abandoned babies as he passes the rubbish heaps. There's no danger of his proving violent until he has thirty legions under his command, and we won't have to worry about that for a while yet.'

Kaeso was very charming to Marcia, who had lost some weight and hid a sorrowful look behind her painted eyelashes. Kaeso felt a pang of remorse which almost made him give up his programme of self-preservation. He cut short his visit.

Silanus, as he showed him out, was visibly trying to control himself. He confided to him:

'Marcia needs you as a son. I absolutely need Marcia. You're too intelligent for childish scruples to restrain you for long from doing what will ensure both her happiness and mine. Perhaps you're afraid of losing your freedom? Trust in my experience. There's only one form of freedom which stands up to the accidents and deceptions of life, and that's the freedom you get from money. Everything I have is yours. You've only to stoop to pick it up.'

Kaeso had no objection to bending down. Lowering himself was another matter.

❧ CHAPTER ❧
4

Over dinner Kaeso had to admit to his father that he had deferred his adoption to the Ides of May. His inability to provide a plausible motive for doing so made Marcus deeply uneasy. He had always thought, in his heart of hearts, that despite so much apparently being in its favour, the whole thing was too good to be true. Now, on the eve of drinking in long beneficial draughts, the cup of good fortune was being torn away from his lips.

Selene came to Kaeso's aid. 'After all you've done for him, it's perfectly normal for your son to put off the moment of leaving you for a brief while.'

Marcus bad temperedly observed that it was for Kaeso, not her, to put forward a fine-sounding excuse of that sort.

'Have you never heard say that the young are naturally modest?' Selene retorted.

All Kaeso could do was to lower his gaze bashfully.

It was coming up to full moon, and Selene was encouraging Marcus to drink a lot. She intended, shortly, to go into the kitchen and make cakes. Myra was curled up at Kaeso's feet, looking at him devotedly.

Marcus suddenly asked his son: 'Why did you buy that child? You don't seem to pay any attention to her.'

'To watch her grow up in beauty and virtue.'

It was not the answer Marcus wanted. The girl's youthfulness had roused his desires.

Kaeso said: 'Myra belongs to me. If any household slave took the liberty of laying a hand on her, I'd have to reimburse you with his price, since I'd have killed him with my own hands.'

Selene, in one of her drily mischievous moods, added: 'Kaeso's thinking of having a ring inserted in her vagina to protect her from any attack. He means to sleep with her in ten years time, when her attractions are at their highest.'

Marcus rose from his couch in a very bad mood.

Early the following day Kaeso received a few lines from Silanus:

'Decimus to Kaeso, greetings.

Yesterday evening at Thrasea's house the rumour was going around that Marcia's statue had cured a blind man. The wife of the temple guardian has just told me that she heard your friend Paul lay claim to the miracle in your presence. Why did you not tell me yesterday afternoon about this strange business? What am I to believe? If Paul has talents of that kind, I would be obliged if he could do something about my rheumatism.

I hope you are as well as the blind man.'

Before going out Kaeso replied:

'Kaeso to D. Junius Silanus Torquatus, greetings.

I hesitated to talk to you about what happened because I do not know what to believe myself. I hoped that Paul's company might throw some decisive light on the matter. The facts of the case are these. The Jew, who has been banned from the synagogues, rubbed the blind man's eyes with the blue scarf which Marcia once gave me as a present, the blind man promptly recovered his sight, rushed off and threw himself at the feet of the statue in the sanctuary. That is all I know. Paul claims that he is quite an old hand at this sort of thing, and his friend Luke even affirms that he brought back to life a member of the audience who had been overcome by one of his speeches. I will speak to him about your rheumatism – it is bound to cost you a great deal less than a resurrection.

I hope your good sense will help you withstand the Christians. Mine is being sorely tried.'

Kaeso suddenly realized that if the noble Torquatus, cured of his rheumatism – or brought back to life with a flick of the wrist – had the disastrous idea of becoming a Christian, his own baptism would become perfectly pointless, since the family cult of his patrician adoptive father would fall into oblivion. Fortunately Silanus seemed an absolutely safe bet. Even if he were struck down and then brought back from the dead, he would still be a Stoic sybarite. Paul's powers of conviction had their limits.

When Kaeso arrived at the house of the Christian Jew by the Porta Capena, the faithful were gathered together in a room which he was not allowed to enter. But they let him watch what happened through the half-open door. In fact the ritual was very disappointing. The people were simply eating bread and drinking wine, distributed by Paul. Then, before splitting up, those present sang a hymn in a popular style, which seemed something to do with a lamb.

Paul, Luke and Kaeso went into the little garden behind the house and sat under a pergola in bloom. Kaeso asked Paul:

'Are all Christians authorized to hand round the bread and wine?'

'Only the pastors, who are called *presbyteri* or *episcopi*.'

'Are those the same thing?'

'There is no greater honour among us than the right to distribute the bread and wine. The *episcopi*, or bishops, merely have a supervisory role as well.'

'Do the sons of the priests and bishops become priests and bishops in their turn?'

'They couldn't do better, but the priesthood is open to all, by co-option.'

'Who's in charge?'

'Jesus Christ.'

'But you must have a leader.'

'Jesus gave the highest authority to Peter, but without specifying what it consisted in. I myself have had some uncomfortable discussions with him . . .'

'Jesus didn't entrust a particular area to Peter?'

'Not as far as I know. Peter, like the rest of us, dreams of implanting the Christian faith solidly at Rome. He has spent long periods here, and many of the faithful in the city come to us on his authority. He can't bear Rome, but he keeps coming back to it like a duck to a pond, and he would like to leave a successor here. Peter's pre-eminence can of course be passed on.'

'Will he appoint his successor?'

'The Christians will see to it.'

'Apart from preaching, co-opting colleagues, blessing bread and wine and sleeping with their wives to provide new priests, what do your elders get up to?'

'They grant remission of sins to those who repent, publicly if their sin is public and privately if it's secret. Jesus accorded them this privilege, because in reality it's he who is granting the pardon through the voice of the priest.'

'Are all the sins of those who repent pardoned?'

'Yes, all of them. But the value of the pardon is obviously proportionate to the genuineness of the repentance. You can deceive the priest but not God. The priests bring the Holy Spirit down upon the baptized faithful to enlighten them, and they rub the dying with a sacred oil which some-times restores them to life and in any case rids them of their sins – if they are in a properly penitent mood.'

'So this anointing duplicates the job of the standard remission from sins?'

Luke gave a little, embarrassed cough and Paul himself replied with a trace of hesitation:

'The late lamented James was the expert on this particular aspect. I have to admit that it's not very clear. Mark also refers to it. Isn't the essential point that it works?'

Luke confirmed that unction worked a treat most of the time.

'And what about marriage?' said Kaeso. 'Do your priests marry people?'

'They merely serve as witnesses, in the name of the Church. It's the free commitment of themselves by the two partners which really makes the marriage. In cases of absolute necessity the presence of the priest is not even essential. Other witnesses will do, preferably Christian as far as possible.'

'Is entering into the partnership of one's own free will an essential part of a Christian marriage, then?'

'Otherwise the marriage is in fact null and void in the sight of God, and our Church can therefore annul it.'

Kaeso got up, thoughtfully, and walked about for a moment. The previous evening, after dinner, a messenger had brought to the house the letter from James and those of Paul's letters which were available. The supposed candidate for baptism had read or skimmed through them for a large part of the night, by the light of his *lucubrum*. He had been interested, despite himself. After all the biblical folklore, and the bald and naïve testimony collected by John Mark, these letters brought one, by an extra-ordinary sort of acceleration of history, to the stage of personal reflection on the facts. Paul in particular, while offering his God up for the admira-tion of the masses, revealed even more of himself at the same time. Whatever the details of a reasoning process which was from time to time more rabbinical than Greek, the author was expressing himself in a genre which was much more familiar to the Greco-Roman world than the Bible or the Gospel. The personality of Seneca, for example, was responsible for the charm of many of the works on which it had left its imprint. The Bible was 'the Jews as seen by themselves'. The Gospel of Mark was 'Jesus as seen by the man in the street'. The letters of Paul were 'Jesus as seen by Paul'. And, given Kaeso's remarkable memory, which had been so long trained on Homer and Virgil, the question, which Selene had already answered from her partial viewpoint, arose. Was Paul a hypocrite?

Kaeso came back to his two companions and said:

'I haven't found anything specific in Mark or even in James about this anointing with oil. Did Jesus invent it or did the Holy Spirit?'

Paul took it on himself to answer.

'The Holy Spirit, for sure. James was a close friend of Jesus, and one can have complete trust in him. Either Jesus mentioned it to him in private, or James, under the influence of the Holy Spirit, pronounced what Jesus himself could have said.'

'Do all those who are baptized receive the inspiration of the Holy Spirit?'

'Those baptized by a priest in particular.'

'In cases where Jesus said nothing, or where his words haven't been reported, what criteria can be applied to prove whether or not the Holy Spirit is indeed inspiring the man who claims to be so inspired?'

'The Church is the final arbiter.'

Paul defended his cause very cleverly, but he had been too imprudent in his own writings not to be caught with his trousers down. Kaeso went on, smoothly:

'I noted in your letters, which I glanced through last night, an honest and attractive distinction between what you claim to come from Jesus and what you affirm on your own responsibility. The fact that you admit such a distinction commands the highest respect.

In your letter to the Romans, for example, you write this very sensible passage: "Every person must submit to the supreme authorities. There is no authority but by act of God, and the existing authorities are instituted by him; consequently anyone who rebels against authority is resisting a divine institution, and those who so resist have themselves to thank for the punishment they will receive. For government, a terror to crime, has no terrors for good behaviour . . . That is why you are obliged to submit. It is an obligation imposed not merely by fear of retribution but by conscience. That is also why you pay taxes. The authorities are in God's service and to these duties they devote their energies. Discharge your obligations to all men. Pay tax and toll, reverence and respect, to those to whom they are due."

But in your first letter to the Corinthians you write: "If one of your number has a dispute with another, has he the face to take it to pagan law-courts instead of to the community of God's people? . . . If you have such business disputes, how can you entrust jurisdiction to outsiders, men who count for nothing in our community? . . . Must brother go to law with brother – and before unbelievers?"

So, on the one hand you invite them to submit to the rulings of the civil authorities for reasons of conscience. And on the other, you claim to set up a semblance of confessional justice in competition with the established order, and call these same magistrates unjust, contemptible unbelievers. I assume the contradiction derives from you and not from Christ.'

Paul was very put out by this little attack. There was only a year separating the writing of the first letter to the Corinthians from that of the letter to the Romans. He couldn't even argue that his thought had evolved. His agile brain offered him the only possible answer. 'In the letter to the Romans I'm speaking generally. In the letter to the Corinthians I'm dealing with an exceptional case. It's naturally deplorable for Christians to go to law with one another before Gentiles. You must appreciate that, given the unusual nature of our moral code, Roman tribunals are inevitably not competent to deal with certain types of litigation.'

'Now you're speaking with the subtlety of the angels again. But why in that case, having said that the magistrates are worthy of honour, do you shower them with insults? They're only doing their duty and aren't at all responsible for the peculiar novelty of your beliefs. Is that Christ speaking, or Paul?'

'It's Paul, and I said more than I should have done.'

Luke cut in. 'Paul has written a lot, and sometimes he has had to write very fast, because of the pressure of the situation or the strength of his own feelings. It's not surprising if his pen has produced a certain amount of work of poor quality. What is surprising is that there hasn't been more.'

Paul, without noticeable warmth, thanked Luke for the compliment. Kaeso associated himself with it before going on:

'Again, in the first letter to the Corinthians, we read: "As in all congregations of God's people, women should not address the meeting. They have no licence to speak, and should keep their place as the law directs. If there is something they want to know, they can ask their own husbands at home. It is a shocking thing for a woman to address the congregation . . . If anyone claims to be inspired or a prophet, let him recognize that what I write has the Lord's authority. If he does not acknowledge this, God does not acknowledge him."

Now I note here that, though you have made such substantial excisions from the Jewish Law, often with the effect of creating more enlightenment, you have carefully preserved its instruction to make women keep silent in public. It's clear that you didn't receive this instruction from Christ, because if you had done, you would have hastened to say so. And yet in this context you have the temerity to invoke the authority of the Lord. Don't you think it's pointless and dishonest, just to ensure that women keep their mouths shut in church, to mobilize the authority of the Lord, who said nothing on the subject, and to hide behind the Jews, whose yoke you have shaken off? There again, is that Christ speaking or Paul?'

As Paul remained silent, Kaeso made this observation: 'In speaking to you like this I am taking the humble role of a brother offering advice. I'm likely to marry a Roman girl who will be in the habit of speaking as loudly, if not louder, in public as a man. And allow me to add, in the interests of the success of your propaganda in Rome, that you're going to line up all the women against you if you thoughtlessly let letters of that sort become public. If Roman women are going to be converted to your Gospel, with all the freedom they already have, they're going to want other proofs than your opinions before they keep their mouths shut. Christ was more pleasant than you towards women. You could do with modelling yourself on him.'

Eventually Paul said, in bitter tones: 'There too I have to acknowledge that it was I who spoke and not Christ.'

Luke murmured: 'I've often said to Paul that he took a rather high-handed line towards women. Even the homosexuals whom he is always fulminating against are more to be pitied than blamed.'

In exasperation Paul cried: 'I'll leave the women to you, but at least let me deal with the filthy queers!'

With increasing gentleness, Kaeso came in for the kill:

'I find it distressing and disquieting to see an apostle invoke the words of his Lord at random. Satan doesn't only work behind your back, he sometimes makes a frontal approach. But I have no desire to abuse your patience, which is in any case limited, and I'll confine myself to underlining one last substantial contradiction.

Just now you claimed that Christian marriage required free choice on the part of both partners. Now in the unfortunate first letter to the Corinthians, certain passages of which undoubtedly need rewriting, you say words to this effect: "But if a man has a virgin daughter, and feels that he is not behaving properly towards her in allowing her to pass her prime unmarried, and that things should take their normal course, he may do as he pleases; there is nothing wrong in it; let the girl be married. But if a man is steadfast in his purpose, being under no compulsion, and has complete control of his own choice, and if he has decided in his own mind to preserve his daughter in virginity, he will do well. Thus, he who gives his daughter in marriage does well, and he who does not will do better."

Consequently, for you, the only freedom in marriage, if one is to believe what you write rather than what you say, is the freedom of the father to dispose of his daughter as he wishes. That seems to me a very clumsy introduction to the indissolubility and freedom which you are so proud of. Is it Jesus or Paul who is responsible here for giving a father permission to prevent his daughter from marrying?

What I'm saying, yet again, is simply said in the interests of your doctrine. It's increasingly the custom in Rome for fathers to take their daughter's inclination into account, and once married, women will not even allow the authority of their guardians to stop them from remarrying as they will. So you're putting yourself not only at odds with contemporary Roman *mores* – which I appreciate are of no importance to you – but also with yourself, which I find rather more serious. If a father can give, or refuse to give, his daughter in marriage as he wishes, according to your barbarian view, which doubtless goes back to the era of the Flood, where does the victim's freedom of consent come in?

It's as if, out of misogyny or inconsequential frivolity, you were busily sowing the seeds for a vast harvest of what will be non-marriages in the eyes of your god, although precious few of them will be legally annulled if Christian judges are anything like you. The freedom which you're offering women is about as attractive as the freedom you offer slaves. But your blinkered attitude will work against the interests of your own morality. Unless they are utterly stupid, these Christian women, forcibly married by tyrannical fathers, will be perfectly well aware in their heart of hearts that their marriage is void from a religious point of view. From that fact they will derive the logical conclusion that their husbands are tailor-made for cuckoldry. And when you advise fathers to keep their daughters celibate, you are equally taking on yourself the responsibility for all the masturbation and sly fornication which will result from such an abnormal situation.

If Jesus pardoned an adulterous woman, it was probably because she'd been married against her will by some irresponsible person like you.

It's a pity that the Jesus you met near Damascus didn't spend a little longer in conversation with you. After reproaching you for persecuting him, he might have suggested that you give up persecuting young girls. In fact, perhaps the two persecutions come down to the same thing?'

In a flat voice Paul asked Kaeso to withdraw for a moment. He started talking to Luke in an animated way. Snatches of conversation in heated tones reached Kaeso as he stood watching some snails eating greenery at the bottom of the little garden. The snails certainly had more freedom than a Christian woman in the eyes of Paul of Tarsus.

Paul called Kaeso back and said to him:

'It's always easy to take someone apart on the strength of a few unfortunately phrased or excessive remarks. You might have recalled some of the numerous other passages in which I insist on the worthiness of woman. Though women are temporally subordinate to men, they are nonetheless their equal on a spiritual level. That equality, which for all my awkwardness and inadequacy I do predict, is one of essence. It is everlasting, because it is founded in the word of God. Whereas the liberty acquired by Roman matrons is destined for destruction. What is the good of marrying freely if it only results in divorce and sterility?

You might care to bear in mind the fact that the positive moral laws which should govern relations between men and women have long been susceptible to evolution, in contrast to the other permanent and intangible rules contained in the Commandments. The Bible itself bears witness to such a process of change. In Genesis, we see Jacob marry two sisters, a week apart, although this sort of promiscuity is later forbidden in Leviticus. At one time it was relatively acceptable to have several wives and to divorce. God tolerated it as a consequence of the hardening of our hearts after the Fall. With Jesus, the ideal marriage has at last been rediscovered and defined. But the ideal, as you are only too well aware, is in direct contrast to the current *mores* of all races. It will probably take centuries of effort for it to be incorporated into legal codes . . . if the Last Judgement doesn't intervene and make all those efforts superfluous.

In the meantime, the divide between what Christ wants and the outlook of the average man is so great that Christians – even Christians who saw Jesus at closer quarters than I can see you now – find it difficult to throw off "the old Adam". It's difficult for them not to argue and feel about women the way that they were taught to in their youth. In my letters perhaps the Jew wins out over the Christian in this tricky area. Perhaps the bad Christian gets the better of the good. Seeing Christ does not preserve us from all error and all sin: our freedom is still more important than our virtue, because the former is the source of the latter.

You have stressed contradictions in my thought which are only too real. I've just explained how they came about. I shall work at reducing and resolving them. The Church will always in principle defend freedom of consent, but priests will take a long time before they can match their actions, and even what they say, to the principle. God willing, grace will win the day and will turn even my lack of consequentiality to the benefit of myself and my neighbour.'

'You mean to say that when you speak well of women, it is god who speaks through your voice; and when you say stupid things about them, it is women who make you say them?'

'Exactly!' Paul acknowledged with a laugh. 'You're a pleasure to teach.'

'You always land on your feet, like a cat.'

'And if you persist in tormenting me like this, you'll succeed in making me hiss and scratch.'

For a man who had been in the intimate company of God, Paul had preserved a humility and a good faith which were attractive and really very much to his credit, given how difficult his character was. Once convinced by a rigorous demonstration of proof that he was wrong, he still managed to control himself and make honourable amends.

It was lunch time. As they were going to the dining-room, Luke, who was walking just behind Kaeso, said to him quietly: 'You very much upset Paul, and he didn't deserve it. Even when your perceptions are accurate, you have a very arrogant way of expressing yourself. You talk as if you were sprung from the thigh of Jupiter, whereas your tiny head once came into the world, like everyone else's, through female genitals between the urinary tract and the anal intestine.'

'You won't let anyone forget you studied medicine, will you?'

They ate lunch sitting on cushions around low serving-tables. There were a dozen or so men – the women ate elsewhere.

To re-establish a friendly atmosphere Kaeso asked Paul:

'Since Jesus celebrated Passover one day in advance, on the Thursday evening, so as to have time to be buried before the sabbath began on the following evening – remarkable forethought on his part – the bread and wine were blessed during the traditional meal. I noticed this morning that this act of blessing is no longer associated with an actual meal. Why has it become separated?'

'Because Jesus is no longer there to keep the guzzlers and the potential drunks in order with a look. Wherever I have any influence I recommend, to prevent abuse, that the sacred *Cena* be made a meal apart, preceding the actual meal. There is in any case a great difference between the *Cena* arranged by Christ and ours. Jesus changed the bread and wine into Body and Blood which were going to be sacrificed for our sins and our errors. In His hands the host was a "prototype", if you will forgive me the neologism. Whereas our host today is the Body and Blood already sacrificed, the whole reality of a Body crucified, resurrected and made transcendent. Jesus' *Cena* was a harbinger, ours is an actualization, a renewal of the sacrifice, and the number of people taking part happens to be considerably larger. So it is legitimate to move from the family atmosphere of the original *Cena* to a more formal atmosphere, where everything is designed to demonstrate the true majestic character of the event. The host which Jesus "designed" as his death approached has been brought to fulfilment through the words of our priests.'

'What happens to the hosts which are not eaten?'

'They are given to the sick and the dying.'

In an indirect fashion Kaeso passed Silanus' thanks on to Paul and told him that he would be able to see Nero at relatively close quarters the following morning, thanks to the patrician's kindness.

Feeling himself on very thin ice he went on: 'Silanus has heard via the talk of the town about the ease with which you cured the blind man outside the temple of Patrician Modesty. He'd be very glad if you could do something about his rheumatism. He's finding it particularly troublesome as he has only recently remarried.'

Paul frowned again, at a loss for words.

Kaeso pushed his point. 'It's not a question of charity, although that's never totally absent from any miracle cure. Obviously the Christians cannot cure everyone on grounds of charity: there would be no merit in being a believer and Paradise would have to be substantially expanded. But it would be a good opportunity for you to prove yet again that "God has just visited the world", to use your own magnificent expression. Silanus is a cousin of the emperor, he could give you a recommendation, and if you simply cured Nero of a cold in the head on the eve of an elegant singing competition, the fortune of the Christians would be made. If you can bring relief to the first person you come across, you can do it for my stepmother's distinguished husband. He's also pursuing the quest for truth, within his own modest limits, and he's well-disposed towards you.'

Paul finally decided on a reply. 'It's not I who do the healing. Explain to your noble relative, as tactfully as you think fit, that whereas God may reasonably be expected to take pity on the worst sufferings of the poor, it is difficult for me to trouble him over the backache of a newly married millionaire.'

'But,' said Luke, 'Jesus changed the water into wine at the wedding in Cana. It was his first miracle, according to John.'

'That was because the Virgin asked Him to.'

'Then I'll tell Silanus,' said Kaeso with a sigh, 'that the Lord is too busy with gastronomic miracles to take any interest in his rheumatism.'

'I should prefer to tell him so myself, if the opportunity presents itself. I have the impression that I might put it better than you.'

All this business about miracles was very confused.

Kaeso glanced around. Luke was impassive, but the other guests gave the impression of thinking that, in the interests of the cause, Paul might have made just a little effort to do something about the rheumatism of a cousin of the emperor.

'What do you know about the ways of God?' Paul asked them. 'Did you cure the blind man – and various others – or did I?'

There was no come-back to a remark like that from a specialist.

Kaeso asked Paul again:

'I read in Mark that illness often takes the form of possession by demons. What is your opinion on that?'

'Death and disease are indeed the result of the sin of Eve and Adam, who disobeyed God when tempted by the Devil.'

'Then how could Jesus, who by definition was not an heir to original sin, suffer and die?'

'Though exempt from sin, he accepted its consequences out of love for mankind. Satan even tried in vain to tempt him.'

'When this Satan disobeyed God, he couldn't have been tempted by the Devil, since he was the first fallen angel of his type.'

Paul and Luke looked at each other as though that particular problem had never crossed their minds before.

Kaeso went on:

'Disobedience to God without the excuse of having been tempted by the Devil indicates an incredible concentration of vice.'

'Well,' said Paul, 'an incredible concentration of vice is the best possible definition of the Devil, who invented all possible vice out of nothing. So take care. Satan excels at working behind the mask of the best possible sentiments. If he is present in vice, he is even more so in virtue.'

The best way to guarantee keeping Satan at a distance seemed to be to keep one's moral ambitions modest. A nasty suspicion crossed Kaeso's mind that he was too virtuous for the Devil not to get a good hold on him. The Christians talked about the Devil and Hell with an impressive and contagious sense of certainty, as if they had understood that man is more susceptible to fear than to love. Like a slave master the Christian god worked with both stick and carrot.

Kaeso arranged to meet Paul and Luke at the Circus Maximus the following morning and went home for siesta. After a rest he ordered his cook to take some food and an amphora of wine to the Christian Jew from the Porta Capena in thanks for his hospitality. Marcus junior was in the kitchen, eating a belated snack. He was out of the house most of the time, getting every ounce of enjoyment out of his leave. Kaeso invited him to go with him to the majestic new Baths of Nero, which offered more entertainment than the private bath installed in the house from the proceeds of Marcia's sacrifices. When you had been with Paul for a while, you felt the need for a change of intellectual air. Little Myra was told she might come too. Selene, who never went to the public baths, contented herself with wishing them a pleasant afternoon, and advised the kitchen boy not to put any pork in the hamper for the Christian Jew, because most converted Jews still kept an invincible prejudice against that useful animal.

'What about you?' asked Kaeso. 'You eat pork, don't you?'

In a blackly humorous vein Selene answered: 'If you're prepared to suck a man's cock, there's no reason to gib at a bit of pig-meat,' which was undoubtedly a logical way of looking at things. It was undoubtedly a black mark against prostitution that it encouraged a loss of respect for religious dietary prohibitions.

With their swimming bags under their arms the trio set off for the baths. There had been occasional showers during the previous few days, but fine weather seemed to be settling in, which suggested that the races on the first day of the Floralia would be superb.

The baths were surrounded by Praetorians and soldiers of the German Guard, and the cloakrooms were full of policemen. Nero had come for a bathe. From time to time, in a blatant attempt to curry popularity, the emperor would make an appearance in one of the public baths, where he would immediately find himself surrounded by huge crowds. The present initiative was doubtless connected with the fact that he would be presiding over the races the next day. The Games gave the Prince a periodic chance to test his popularity. It was not a bad idea to go more or less without a break from the public baths to the Olympian imperial box of the Circus Maximus.

There was another advantage to these contacts with the man in the street. They were the only contacts of their kind which were more or less guaranteed to be absolutely safe. A naked emperor, surrounded by strongmen and naked friends, exposed himself to the vibrant sympathy of bathers of both sexes, who could not have concealed about their persons even one of those styluses which Claudius had been so neurotic about, on the grounds that Caesar had been stabbed with one on the Ides of March. By taking a surprise bathe in the city, Nero achieved an exquisite combination of maximum publicity and maximum security, the eternal headache of the much criticized security services.

When the two Aponius brothers and little Myra got into the baths, Nero was already splashing about in the pool in the *frigidarium*, with friends all around him to prevent the circle of sightseers and flatterers from accidentally drowning the august object of their attention. From the churning waters and the edge of the pool all sorts of remarks were being shouted at the heir to the Caesars, and Nero was joking back, with his attendants occasionally adding some pleasantry of their own. The atmosphere was noisy, relaxed and good-humoured.

The most frequent question was: 'When, O divine scion of the Muses, will you agree to sing in public to your much beloved people?' Nero replied, with sincere humility: 'I practise night and day, but I'm not yet ready. Vatinius will tell you how long it takes to learn to make even a simple shoe.' Whereupon Vatinius sniggered and said: 'I'll sing with my feet before Caesar dares appear on stage. He's not afraid of you, he's afraid of himself.'

Vatinius, who had been brought up by a cobbler, was as ugly as sin and as destructive as the pox. He served as court jester and one of the leading spies. His perspicacity in matters of slander and libel even managed to make Poppaea and Tigellinus tremble. The dreadful Vatinius was quite right. Like anyone with an artistic temperament Nero was paralysed with stage fright, and kept putting off his confrontation with the general public from day to day and year to year. Up till then he had only exercised his talents as actor, charioteer, poet, singer and *cithara* player on private occasions – with most encouraging results, it is true to say. But the general public was a completely different prospect. It was an astonishing paradox. This man had the universe at his feet, but he was terrified at the prospect of making an exhibition of himself in front of people he did not know. Yet the great aim of his life was to conquer them all. It was an added spur to his determination that he flattered himself that, the day when his genius burst forth unfettered, he would establish such a rapport with the people that the foundations of his political power would be strengthened as a result. His aesthetic dream had acquired a political tinge. For the first time in history supreme material power saw itself as, and wanted to be, supreme aesthetic power. Alexander and Orpheus hand in hand.

Marcus junior and Kaeso elbowed their way through to the edge of the vast covered pool. Myra, who was perched on Marcus's shoulders, blew Nero little kisses, and he sent her great damp ones back. A naked emperor has nothing else to give.

Nero, who had celebrated his twenty-fifth birthday the previous December, had already put on weight as a result of feasting and drinking, despite the diets and occasional purgatives which were intended to maintain all his artistic abilities at their height. The generally acknowledged beauty of the adolescent with his silky red-blond hair and short-sighted blue eyes had vanished. The imperious nobility of the upper half of his face made a sharp contrast with the double chin and the leech-like mouth. On the prince's personal command, recent coinage had abandoned the traditional idealized view of its subject and portrayed a heavy brutal version of Nero's face. It was the face of a man who had put childhood behind him and who now intended to impose the full weight of his will.

The emperor, who sweated a great deal and bathed several times a day, lingered in the chilly water. His fat prevented him from feeling the cold, but the skinny Vatinius' teeth were beginning to chatter.

A little to the side of the main group another courtier seemed to be finding that time went by slowly. Marcus pointed him out to Kaeso as Flavius Vespasianus, an ex-consul and brother of Flavius Sabinus, the Prefect of the City. This Vespasian, who was of humble origins, had been in the good graces of Narcissus during the reign of Claudius, when he had triumphed over the Britons on the Isle of Wight. He had collected a fistful of distinguished offices as a result. At the outset of Nero's reign Agrippina had put him on the retired list. He had finally managed to get the administration of the province of Africa, but had come back without a penny after the Hadrumetines he was supposed to be administering had pelted him with root vegetables. The integrity of this middle-aged soldier was his finest quality, but it was a useless one in the eyes of the present regime. Since his return he had been hanging around the emperor, dying of boredom, in the hope of being given an important military command. But it was slow in coming. Nero adored spending money and was suspicious of honest men. He thought more highly of Vespasian's brother, the Prefect, whose integrity was less obvious. In order to keep up the expenditure necessary to his rank, poor Vespasian had been known to deal in horses, a fact which was not calculated to improve his standing. The fact that the emperor's aspirations as a singer bored him to death explained the surliness of his expression.

The Prince shook himself and came out of the waters, revealing his very short neck, then his pot belly, then his thin legs. The pack of attendants closed around him and the cortège swept off towards the cloakrooms amid a great buzz of chatter.

Marcus took Myra off his shoulders and said to her: 'Aren't you proud that Nero blew you kisses?'

'I think that for an emperor he's got a very little winkie.'

This piece of childish naïvety made Kaeso and Marcus laugh till they cried.

'That's because he's got fat,' Kaeso explained. 'If he was as thin as that snake Vatinius, his cock would have looked larger to you.'

' . . .Everything is relative,' he added, a favourite expression of the philosopher who had taught him Scepticism when he was in the *ephebia*.

On the way home Kaeso revealed to Marcus the salvage scheme which Selene had devised for him, and the extraordinary contacts with first the Jews and then the Christians which had resulted from it.

Marcus did not think it worth trying.

'That way,' he said, 'you may keep Silanus' esteem, and perhaps even his favour, for a while – but for how long? Marcia will never believe in your sincerity – and she'll have every reason not to! She'll be in a state of bitter despair, which may well drive her to all sorts of acts of revenge. She'll immediately do everything she can to get you into Silanus's bad books.'

'She loves me too much to try to harm me. There's much more danger of her killing herself. That's the possibility which I find worrying.'

'That's another reason for being reasonable and accommodating.'

Kaeso revealed to his brother the lies which Marcia had told and Silanus' complacent attitude.

'But Kaeso, whatever's holding you back? Our stepmother has skilfully set the whole thing up. As far as Silanus is concerned you're already her lover and he's prepared to put up with it. It's a dream situation. How I'd like to be in your place.'

It was difficult to get someone so obtuse to grasp the essential moral nuances of the situation. However, Marcus soon came up with a rather disturbing argument. 'For you to make a fool of Silanus and Marcia may not matter, but is it wise of you to make fun of this Christian god? You yourself say he isn't a god like the others in the pantheon. There you can always find another god as an antidote to balance out the anger of a god who is unfavourable to you. But when it's a question of a higher god who claims to replace all the others, where are you to turn?'

The idea suddenly struck Kaeso that Paul's god might actually exist. After all, he was no more philosophically improbable than the tens of thousands of immanent gods and their ridiculous tangled web of relationships. If this god did exist, wouldn't baptism bring bad luck on anyone who undertook it rashly? The Christian god, being a close relative of the Jewish god, didn't sound like someone who took things lightly.

After dinner Kaeso re-read the Gospel according to Mark in detail. An extraordinarily important point suddenly leapt out at him. He checked it relentlessly phrase by phrase. You could naturally argue about what Jesus was supposed to have done according to the eye-witness reports, but when it came to what the supposed god had said, there was nothing stupid and nothing contradictory. It was easy to catch Paul red-handed using intemperate language, but Jesus, whether what he was saying was extraordinary or entirely familiar, was remarkably coherent. This fact posed a new question. A man who puts himself forward as a god, and master of life and death, is necessarily either mad or dishonest. Jesus' words excluded both hypotheses. So . . .

❖ CHAPTER ❖
5

By midnight the lower classes were already queueing in front of the Circus Maximus.

Of course entry to the Games was free. But you still had to see about getting a good seat, or even about getting a seat at all. At the Circus, the amphitheatre and the theatre the senators had their own reserved rows, and Nero had given the knights the same honour. What's more, for specific shows organizers distributed *tesserae*, small thin pieces of wood, metal, bone or ivory, sometimes round, sometimes oblong, which reserved a place or places for those for whom one wanted to secure the best seats after the senators and knights. Most of this privileged group came from those citizens who, under the corn laws, already ate in part at the State's expense. But some of these would give up their opportunity to see the show and sell their *tessera* to touts. They, in turn, sold them to fans at a profit. The police preferred to turn a blind eye to this black-market dealing, which was to the advantage of all concerned and hurt nobody. The seats left free at the top of the building could themselves become the object of commercial transaction. Citizens or freedmen in financial distress, or even slaves, would occupy a place at dawn and then give it up to a fan of modest means when the place began to get crowded.

Women, and children in the company of their *paedagogus*, also enjoyed the privilege of reserved rows, to preserve their modesty and safeguard them from being pestered with unwanted attentions. This arrangement was not, however, obligatory, and many women preferred to be able to be at close quarters with men at the great moments of shared emotion.

In the golden age of Rome, the grassy Murcian valley between the Palatine and the Aventine was already used for horse and chariot races. From generation to generation this natural circus had gradually been made larger and more luxurious until it measured 2,000 feet by 700. After the smaller Circus of Flaminius Nepos had been built in the Campus Martius some 280 years earlier, the first Circus had become known as the Circus Maximus. Understandably, it had kept the name when the Circus built by Caligula, the smallest of the three, was constructed in the gardens on the Vatican.

The fifty-odd *jugera* of the Circus Maximus, stretching roughly east–west between the two hills, had seen increasing numbers of marble, stone and above all wooden seats take the Palatine and Aventine by storm, above the retaining walls which dominated the track. The capacity of 150,000 seats had almost doubled in Nero's time. Two centuries later it was to reach 385,000. It was the biggest architectural ensemble in the world.

The monumental entrance, dominated by two towers, was situated to the west, by the Velabrum, next to the temple of Ceres and the Tiber. To the right and left rose the rows of seats, joining at the back in an arc, at a point where the back retaining wall was pierced by another door, opening to the east on to the Appian Way.

The western part sheltered twelve marble *carceres*, the stalls where the chariots waited at the start of a race. Their façade formed a curve carefully designed so that the four teams competing in each race could in principle – whatever stall they started from – arrive side by side in a straight line on the track to the right, where they were to race. The first third of the arena, which was carpeted with shining sand, was empty; a longitudinal stretch of banking called a *spina* (dorsal fin) separated the rest of the arena into two separate tracks, which got gradually slightly narrower as they ran from west to east, so as to increase the difficulties of cornering and the dangers of collision at the far end of the Circus. The head and tail of this *spina*, which was 750 (Roman) feet long, were protected by two conical gilded bronze pillars thirty feet high – fruit of the munificence of Claudius. The base of each was rounded off on the side towards the arena. The pillar which faced the *carceres* was the *meta prima*; the further one was the *meta secunda*. Every race was of seven laps, over a total distance of about four kilometres. From twelve races a day under Augustus the programme had swelled to thirty-four under Caligula, was now about sixty and would peak at 100 or so in the reign of Domitian – with, it is true, a reduction from seven to five laps per race. There were thus about six hours of actual racing with which to sate the public.

The finishing line was situated in front of the Palatine *pulvinar*, level with the *meta prima*.

This process of development had forced the organizers to specialize exclusively in horses. In the old days there had been huge hunts of wild beasts in between races, and Caesar had been obliged to protect the spectators with a ditch filled with water. Now the hunts were more or less restricted to morning shows at the amphitheatre – where the retaining wall below the tiers of seats was distinctly higher. In the intervals between races only very minor items were staged, just sufficient to help people keep their patience.

When Paul, Luke and Kaeso arrived in the little box which they owed to Silanus' kindness, towards the fourth hour of the morning, the arena was temporarily full of heavyweight boxers enthusiastically beating each other up to the sound of flutes. The hands and forearms of these fine fellows were armed with *caestus*, leather bands fitted with lead studs, the whole thing weighing nine pounds. The most effective technique was of course to go for your opponent's head. If someone accidentally caught a good blow straight to the mouth, he was condemned to live off soup for the rest of his days. Under the blows from the *caestus*, which were manoeuvred by athletes built like lumberjacks, mouths and noses were crushed, smashed eyes came out of their sockets, ears came off, fragments of brain flew out of fractured skulls. The first heavy blow was decisive, and fights were accordingly short. After a few passes, a few feints, one of the two opponents would collapse, dead or disfigured. What was moving about this form of boxing – and a less blasé public would have been touched by the fact – was that at each fight every competitor risked not only his life but his physical wholeness for the sake of the spectators' pleasure. In doing so they went even further than gladiators. Most boxers were eliminated from competition quite quickly, and careers of any length were rare.

Rather than watch this massacre, for which he was unprepared, the nauseated Paul stared at the emperor's still-unoccupied box. Nero went to bed late and never got up early. But they were already bringing couches and cushions into the *pulvinar*, which confirmed that the emperor would be arriving shortly. The term *pulvinar* meant the cushion on which statues of the gods were laid out during *lectisternia*, sacred festivals where the gods banqueted alongside ordinary mortals. By extension the word had also come to mean a state bed, or a box of some kind, from which the Caesars watched a show. The *pulvinar* of the Circus Maximus, which was covered and vast, connected direct to the old palace of Augustus and the rest of the palaces on the hill.

Luke, being Greek by birth, had been to shows in the East before his conversion, and was initially surprised by the grandiose look of the place. From the high imperial *pulvinar* to the retaining wall overlooking the water-filled ditch (the *euripus*) and the tracks, there was a cascade of white togas, military dress-uniforms, brightly-coloured women's dresses.

377

On all the lower tiers of the Circus were masses of white togas, and there were others on the terrace above the *carceres*, where whoever was presiding over the Games sat with his retinue. Emperors were constantly reminding citizens that they should wear togas for the occasion, but many, including some senators, needed a lot of persuading, preferring instead to mix anonymously with the crowds of *pullati*, the lowest class of *plebs* who wore brown. There they had more chance of placing a good bet and were free to have something to eat. Everybody remembered the row between the emperor Augustus and a knight whom he reproached for drinking in public while wearing his toga. The man had rudely replied: 'When you go off for lunch there's some chance of you finding your seat still free when you get back.' Officialdom turned a blind eye when the *pullati* had a blow-out.

The enormous crowd was impatiently awaiting the next race. Kaeso pointed out to Luke the beauties of the greenery and buildings on the Aventine. But the view from the slopes of the Aventine over the Palatine, with its crown of sumptuous monuments, was even more beautiful.

The final bouts wound to an end. The dead and injured were hauled off, and the tracks were raked to get rid of the traces of blood, then watered from perforated goat-skin bottles.

Paul said to Kaeso:

'You didn't warn me that human blood was gratuitously spilled even at horse races.'

'There's no compulsion to watch. Come on, rise above it, think of your . . . think of our Christ and how he wasn't afraid to mix with the dregs of the population. How will you be able to convert the Romans if you shut yourself off in a ghetto like the Jews? Your formal presence does not imply your complicity.'

Paul thought the point over, but found it difficult to comprehend. Kaeso went on: 'You've borrowed a toga to appear here today. Think of it this way. The fact that you're a Roman citizen obliges you to give thoughtful consideration to our customs without being systematically hostile to them. Try to understand before you condemn. Otherwise you ought to give up your citizenship. Either you wear the toga or you don't. You're entitled to wear it, and you're actually wearing it, so don't spit on it!'

Kaeso had touched on a question which never ceased to preoccupy Paul. A Jew could accept Roman citizenship without qualms, to the extent that Roman law assured him a legal place in the Empire. Was the same true for a Christian, who could not plead membership of a specific nation as a reason for living on the fringes of the manners, and on occasion the laws, currently in force?

As if Kaeso had intuitively gone straight to the heart of the problem, he summed it up in a cutting and unintentionally cruel remark:

'Citizens who behave intolerably merely get their heads cut off, whereas non-citizens are crucified, thrown to wild animals, and dispatched in the most dishonourable and abject ways. Don't abuse your right to wear the toga.'

Touched on the raw, Paul answered: 'If my Roman citizenship wasn't a help in my mission to the Gentiles, I should have renounced the honour long ago.'

'I believe you. But in that case you're exploiting the toga to spread a doctrine in which the victorious toga has no part.'

'I'm not spitting on the toga. The Romans have defiled it for me. I'm trying to get it clean.'

Luke, who, in his Greek cloak, looked like the servant of the other two, gently intervened. 'You must both be right, because at first sight I can't come up with a solution. When a Christian adopts the Roman toga, even if he only inherits it, as was the case with Paul, should he, after careful thought, try to cleanse it, or should he abandon it? It would be a pity to abandon it, for Christians aspire to be good citizens, even perhaps better citizens than the rest. But in the meantime it is indeed difficult to keep one's toga clean in the midst of so much filth.'

With a shriek the last boxer, his mouth a bloody pulp, had bitten the dust, and the winner, who had been turned away from his prey by the referee, was hastening off towards the terrace above the starting boxes to receive his prize, to the accompaniment of rather thin applause. Boxers were only stop-gaps in a Circus programme. Their great ambition was to be able to run wild as bodyguard to some timid rich man who had to go out a lot at night. But most such jobs tended to go to out-of-work or retired gladiators.

People were busy over by the *carceres*. Slaves were getting in position to open the gates behind which the horses were pawing the ground. Further away others were preparing to lower the rope, attached at each end to statues of Hermes, which barred the entry to the stalls. There were also people busy around the *spina*, with its gilded statues of gods, its altars, commemorative columns and the 120-foot-high granite column which Augustus had had brought from Heliopolis. It was at the *spina* that the seven rounds of the track were counted and the count displayed. Opposite the finishing line a huge wooden egg was hoisted for each completed circuit, and at the other end of the *spina* one of the bronze dolphins dating from the days of Agrippa was lowered at every half-circuit. The boxing interlude was over. Serious matters were starting up again.

On the terrace above the starting-boxes trumpets sounded, four gates opened and four new two-horsed chariots, *bigae*, came forward to the starting line.

The races always began with these two-horse teams, the number of horses per chariot increasing as the day went by. They would go from *trigae* and *quadrigae* up to six, eight and even ten horses. But for most of the time, the majority of races were for *bigae* and *quadrigae*, in a proportion of two to one in favour of the former.

The grooms hung on to the horses' mouths and had difficulty holding them back. This crucial moment was always a long one, because it was the occasion for placing the last bets with the bookies who were moving to and fro among the rows of spectators. Before the opening of the Games the curule magistrate presiding drew lots as to which chariots in each class would race against one another. The public was informed of the result by mounted officials who called out the details, and by men with placards, but the teams waited for some time at the starting line so that the spectators could verify the information and judge the state of the horses. Their appearance at least was superb: they had plumes on their heads, their manes and tails were artistically plaited, their chests were covered in myriad small clinking metal discs and they had a supple collar around their necks. The stud-farms of Apulia, Sicily, Thessaly, Africa and, in particular, Spain, did their best to produce the fastest runners, which were put into training as three-year-olds and made their debut in the Circus as five-year-olds.

The charioteers themselves stood up in their light, narrow vehicles, with helmets on their heads, well-laced boots, and wearing the colours of their *factio*, which were also to be found in the horses' plumes. In one hand they held their whips at the alert. With the other they pulled on the reins, the long ends of which were wound around their waists. The more horses there were, the more indispensable this dangerous arrangement became, to allow the drivers full control. If they fell, they were equipped with a sharp knife, but it gave them a very slender chance of disengaging themselves from the deadly grip of the reins.

'If I know my Romans,' said Paul to Kaeso, 'the excitement now running round the Circus isn't what one might in one's naïvety suppose it to be. What they can smell isn't horses, it's blood.'

'Your toga or public gossip must have told you,' replied Kaeso with a smile. 'The risk of a disaster – we call it a shipwreck in Latin – is very high. But there are compensations. Most of the charioteers are ex-slaves. But some of them, the *miliarii*, have won more than a 1,000 races and picked up tens of millions of sesterces. Together with the élite of the gladiators and the mimes they are the darlings of all the women and the favourites of the Prince. He's so indulgent to their escapades because they lead a wild life, never knowing what tomorrow will bring. For every one who retires as a freedman having made his pile, there are many who die at twenty having gone too close to a marker-post.

You must already have noticed that their horses are almost as famous as they are. You see their names everywhere, from pottery lamps to mosaic pavements, and tombstones are raised to them with their victories engraved on them. Every animal has its family tree and its fans. On the eighteenth day of the Kalends of January, in the middle of December, which happens to be Nero's birthday, we sacrifice to Consus, god of horses, whose temple is concealed beneath the pillar at the *meta prima*. And on the Ides of October, the right-hand horse of whichever victorious *biga* runs the longest distance is sacrificed to Mars, on his altar in the Campus Martius. We call it the "October horse" festival. (The winner is drawn by lot, otherwise a charioteer who loved his horses wouldn't be in a hurry to win a race like that.) Caligula is supposed to have wanted to make his favourite horse a consul. So you can see what a fuss we make of these quadrupeds here in Rome.'

From his box on high the biped curule aedile presiding suddenly threw down a white napkin into the arena. The trumpets sounded anew, the starting rope dropped and the four *bigae* dashed forward. It was the nineteenth race of the morning, despite an inaugural ceremony of some length.

A hail of shouts of encouragement for the Blues or the Greens came raining down. Paul asked why the Whites and Reds were left out.

'Because,' explained Kaeso, 'the Blues and Reds, on one side, and the Greens and Whites on the other have ended up by making two factions, so as to make it easier to meet the considerable costs involved in training both horses and men. The prizes paid to the winners and the generous donations from the emperor don't always cover the costs. So in practice there are only two factions, the plebeian Greens, supported by Nero, and the Blues. But each of the four nominal factions keeps its own stables and training-grounds. The headquarters of the drivers, a real hive of activity, is in the Campus Martius, not far from the Janiculum bridge, the one still called the bridge of Agrippa. My future ancestor – if I can put it like that – left his name everywhere.'

The four chariots had one after the other survived the danger constituted by the first boundary post. Given the direction in which the circuit turned, and the fact that the *metae* were all to the left of the teams as they raced, the charioteers always put their best trained horses on that side. The closer the chariot ran to the boundary post, the faster you got round the course. The width of the track allowed several chariots to go round abreast, but the distance taken up in such a manoeuvre made those who were badly placed lose a lot of ground, whereas they lost less by keeping on their opponents' heels and trying to pass them on the subsequent straight. As the race went on, speeds became more frantic and the risk of bumping and 'shipwrecks' increased dramatically in the area of the *metae*.

There were charioteers who thought they could take the lead at the start and keep it for seven rounds, but others liked to stay in second place and come through at the last minute. Still others weren't afraid to hold their horses back, with the idea of exploiting the gradual tiring of the fastest teams as the rounds went by and pipping the favourite at the finishing line.

A little before the last *meta secunda* two axles collided, and the Blue charioteer was thrown, but miraculously managed to cut his reins.

Kaeso said to Paul and Luke: 'It isn't so easy to do that when the driver has the reins of a ten-horse team, the *decemjugis* – or even those of a *quadriga* – around his body. The public preference for *quadrigae* probably derives from the fact that they not only need more skilful driving, but there's also more risk involved.'

The White charioteer, by dint of plentiful use of the whip, crossed the finishing line first. So the Greens won the race.

The storm of shouts of support gave way to cries of joy or disappointment, although the heaviest betting was reserved for *quadrigae* or even bigger teams later in the programme.

The three chariots which had finished left the arena by the door which divided the two sets of starting-boxes and opened on to a large courtyard, which itself gave on to the stables and the first of the western access gates to the Circus.

The winning driver swiftly went up to get his honorific recompense from the president's hands: a palm and a garland of gold and silver laurel leaves. The money prize was given later. The solemnity of the occasion was increased by the superb dress of the presiding magistrate: purple tunic, brocade toga, a gold crown so heavy that a slave had to make sure from time to time that it was straight, and an ivory staff topped with an eagle, wings outstretched.

No sooner was he crowned than the charioteer hurriedly put his garland on the bald head of a man in the aedile's retinue.

Kaeso had to give another explanation. 'If the charioteer is a slave or a freedman, he honours his master like that, before sharing the money with him according to the established conventions – the subject of constant blackmail. The free charioteers sell themselves very dearly to one or another of the factions.'

From the porticoed walkway overlooking the tiers of seats two green pigeons suddenly flew out, a little to the right of the *pulvinar*, behind the box where Kaeso and his guests were sitting. As, in great surprise, Paul and Luke followed the strange creatures with their eyes, Kaeso laughed and said: 'That's the owner of the winning team letting his wife, or a friend, know the result. White pigeons painted blue or red look just as comic. Only white pigeons belonging to the Whites get away unpainted.'

The sun was getting quite high in the sky, and the Circus was now more or less full, particularly in the reserved areas. When some well-known personality was taking his seat there would be a wave of applause or abuse in the seats nearby. After the disappearance of elections of the sort which had been held under the Republic – and which had only ever favoured the rich of all parties – public shows had become the most effective occasions for the populace to show its sympathies and anti-pathies. The most conservative senators were in general those who came in for the most abuse.

This time the interlude consisted of a performance by *desultores*, acrobats who rode two horses at once, leaping from one to another (whence Ovid's charming expression '*desultor amoris*' to describe someone fickle in love.) Other acrobats rode bareback in every possible position, picked up handkerchiefs from the track at the gallop, or leapt over a *quadriga* in one bound. There was even an absolutely classic race between nine Arab stallions from the stud-farms of Cordova. But the public was not par-ticularly interested in this sort of event: a rider falling off a horse was much less spectacular than a really good crash involving *decemjuges*.

During these fanciful items Marcia came and sat in the box. She was wearing a dazzling *stola*, and was sheltered from the sun by a large parasol carried by a little Ethiopian boy. The pale green of the parasol, canary yellow of the *stola* and black skin of the red-clad Ethiopian formed a riot of colour which was hardly intended to pass unnoticed.

When the introductions were over Marcia sat herself firmly between Paul and her stepson, with Luke on Paul's other side. There was nothing odd about Marcia's sudden presence. Now that she was separated from Kaeso she would be taking every possible opportunity to see him and exert her charm on him.

'Ah,' said Marcia to Paul, 'so you're the famous Christian Jew who is an expert on devaluation, brings back to life audiences who have been put to sleep and competes with my statue at curing the blind?'

It was not a promising beginning. Paul would automatically excite Marcia's natural jealousy against anyone and anything likely to take Kaeso away from her, while in the eyes of a virtuous misogynist this brilliant woman summed up all the faults and dangers of her sex.

Marcia's question was so obviously rhetorical that all Paul had to do was bow in acknowledgement.

'When are you going to come and do something about my husband's rheumatism?'

'I'm afraid I'm not competent to treat rheumatism.'

'Why not? If you can manage big things, you can manage small ones.'

'Quite the opposite. The God whom I serve always brings the dead back to life, sometimes cures the sick and the badly crippled but thinks the little inconveniences of life are morally improving for us.'

'What an annoying sort of god, if you have to wait to die before you can get any service out of him.'

'Death is indeed the surest way of getting to know Him.'

'Is he the god of the Jews or of the Christians?'

'They are both one.'

'Well, that's novel.'

'The novelty of the century – maybe the novelty of all time . . .'

Marcia said to Kaeso, without lowering her voice: 'Your friend is awfully entertaining. I adore people who say the most outrageous things in a terribly prophetic tone of voice.'

Kaeso tried to calm things down: 'Paul's doctrine may seem a bit abrupt at first sight, but it's rich in interesting detail. Once you admit the unbelievable, the rest follows automatically, in the most logical and tempting fashion.'

As it was a good opportunity to give Marcia a hint that his interest in certain Christian dogmas might be sincere, Kaeso went on:

'It's difficult to be in Paul's company without becoming gradually convinced of the truth of what he puts forward. His ideas on marriage, for example, are new and sublime.'

'New ideas – on a subject as old as time?'

'Yes, men won't be allowed to divorce and remarry or to be unfaithful to their wives, or to make love outside marriage or to cheat in bed so as to avoid pregnancy.'

Marcia gave a grim look at Paul, who assumed an air of importance, and turned back to Kaeso. 'Under that system women will die like flies in childbirth, so men won't need to divorce them. You're not going to ask me to believe that you're favourably impressed by a lot of nonsense like that, are you?'

'Oh, you should hear Paul, who's as chaste as the mother of his god, making his case in accents in which you can feel a breath of heavenly air. After all, what does it matter if women drop dead in childbirth, as long as he's on hand to bring them back to life?'

Following his customary bad habit, Paul was beginning to lose his temper. Luke, who was tapping him on the arm to cool him down, took it on himself to say to Marcia:

'Above all, *clarissima*, we think that God's intention in creating Christian marriage was to make provision for procreation, and that legitimate desire itself should be subordinated to that end. Surely you, who have brought Kaeso up so well and of whom he speaks with honour, can understand that?'

'That sounds better.'

Yet another race was about to begin, when the portico on both sides of the *pulvinar* filled up with Praetorian guards, and soldiers of the German Guard came and took up position in the imperial box itself. At last Nero appeared, in the dress of a general celebrating a triumph which was standard on such occasions. He was accompanied by Poppaea, some friends and *augustiani*, and a Vestal Virgin, her rank recognizable from her white robe and the way she wore her hair up in bandeaux.

The emperor remained standing for a moment, to acknowledge the ovation of welcome. But the crowd shortly took it into its head to demand the *quadrigae* before their allotted time on the programme. As the Prince showed no sign of favouring the request, insults could soon be heard among the entreaties. Free, anonymous abuse of Caesar at public shows was the last political liberty left to citizens and the first ever acquired by slaves and freedmen. Understandably, any excuse was a good excuse.

Nero let it go on, listening as attentively as to a tune on the *cithara*, and trying to tell the true and false notes apart. The *plebs* of the Green faction were braying: 'Matricide, fratricide, murderer of your wife and relatives . . .' but these customary examples of politesse were phrased in the reassuring, sometimes amused tones of an accomplice. What they really meant was: 'Even though you're even more of a debauched scoundrel than the rest of us – and indeed because of that fact – we love you really.' Whereas for several years the tiers of the Blues, who had aristocratic pretensions, had given less and less satisfaction. A few over-excited characters were yapping in an aggressive way; most of them preserved a heavy, disagreeable silence.

Nero said to Petronius: 'Can you hear what I hear?'

Petronius listened for a moment and replied:

'I can hear the silence, and there are quite obviously too many people taking part in it. Barking dogs never bite.'

'Ah! You noticed too.'

'After you. You listen to the sound of this surge and thunder with the ear of an artist who misses nothing. The only thing which will bring about unanimity is your voice.'

The compliment was neatly matched to its recipient. Nero was intelligent, but an artist, and to a true artist no compliment can ever seem excessive.

The emperor shrugged his shoulders and sent word to the president of the games to produce the *quadrigae*. They would simply have to put what were left of the *bigae* towards the end of the programme, before the chariots with six or more horses. With an amiable circular wave of the hand, which immediately unleashed a burst of enthusiasm, Nero sat down. The 250,000 spectators who had risen at his entrance sat down too, some on stone, some on wood, others on cushions they had hired or brought with them. Some of the women, perched on cushions, even had little stools for their feet.

Paul was very surprised by the coarse insolence of the *plebs* and Nero's magnanimous tranquillity. The emperor was so close to Silanus' box that he had been able to watch his face very closely. Totally misconstruing the reaction, he wondered whether it might not be a token of remorse, and of confused Christian leanings which only needed enlightening. In the East crowds passed straight from sycophancy to riot. The last potentates of those parts, touchy clients of Rome, did not have Nero's hail-fellow-well-met side to their nature.

After the critical pause at the ropes, four *quadrigae* leapt out and the spectators' excitement went up a notch. Only the two mares in the middle were linked to the shafts by their collars. The two stallions on the outside, positioned in a very slight V formation, were called *funales* because they were only attached by ropes or *funes*. The accuracy of turns at the turning-posts depended on the left-hand *funalis*.

Marcia was watching the manoeuvres of the *quadrigae* with the frank enjoyment which she brought to all Games, but the possible influence of Paul did not cease to preoccupy her. Far too many naïve idealistic young Romans had been the victims of all manner of charlatans, who worked to gain control over people's minds via some sect or other. Frequently therapeutic pretensions were associated with sexual oddities, to disturb and disorientate their victims more easily. This Paul was a typical figure of his times.

Sometimes witches or wizards even stole young children, made them die of starvation, buried up to their necks in front of plates of food, and made love philtres out of their marrow and liver. The tragic epitaph in the Esquiline cemetery was only too well known by every parent in Rome:

JUCUNDUS, SON OF GRYPHUS AND OF VITALIS. I WAS NEARLY FOUR BUT I AM BURIED BENEATH THE GROUND INSTEAD OF BEING A JOY TO MY FATHER AND MOTHER. AN ABOMINABLE WITCH TOOK MY LIFE. SHE IS STILL ALIVE AND PRACTISING HER CRUEL TRICKS. YOU, PARENTS, GUARD YOUR CHILDREN WELL, IF YOU DO NOT WANT YOUR HEARTS TRANSFIXED WITH SORROW.

But there were things worse than wizards, who merely took your life. Propagandists such as Paul even attacked the souls of the young. By playing the ass to irritate his stepmother Kaeso might actually become one.

After a race without an accident, a Red and a Green chariot arrived at the finishing line together, causing a disputed decision, always a delicate matter, which had to be decided by the line-judges under the frenzied and contradictory pressures of the audience.

While the jury was making up its mind, two squadrons of German Guards from the barracks on the Esquiline – which was nearer to the Palace than the Praetorian camp – came into the arena at the same time through the east and west gates of the Circus Maximus, and launched into a fencing display to the martial sound of trumpets.

Nero's attention was caught by the presence of Marcia and a handsome young man in a box which he had forgotten belonged to Silanus. While Poppaea, whose hieratic beauty was the focus of all looks, was gossiping with the Vestal, who still had the freshness of youth, he scribbled a quick note on his imperial tablets and sent it to Marcia, who was sitting a little further down on the right.

After breaking the divine seal Marcia read:

'Your beauty is as great as that of the young man next to you. What are you both doing after the show?'

The messenger was waiting for a reply and offered the stylus to write it. Marcia read the two phrases to Kaeso loud enough for Paul, and indeed Luke, to hear.

Flattered, though also somewhat disturbed, Kaeso said to Paul:

'The beauty of the young man next to you – that must be you. You wanted to meet Nero, and he's already taken a fancy to you. Isn't this the moment – now or never – to submit yourself to the master's will, as you always recommend to slaves? Then you'll be able to insinuate the pure doctrine into him.'

'This is no time for jokes,' said Marcia. 'The emperor has his eye on us.'

Faced with such a proposition it would have been impolitic to reflect for too long. So Marcia wrote back, reading in an undertone to Kaeso and Paul as she wrote:

'I am the new wife of your faithful servant D. Junius Silanus Torquatus, and the young man next to me is my stepson, whom I have raised for the past fifteen years. So you can see how flattering your description is! We shall be able to tell you so in person on the evening of the IV of the Nones of May, because Decimus has just told me that you will be dining with us then.'

After Nero had read the reply, Marcia and the emperor exchanged a smile of polite regret.

Kaeso said to Paul:

'Now there's an example of old-style Roman virtue. The emperor makes a discreet pass at both myself and my stepmother, with a view to an agreeable little *tête-à-tête*, from which there might be much to be gained. But Marcia and I both send him packing. Even among Jews and Christians modesty of that order is rare.'

'I do indeed deeply admire your action,' replied Paul. 'But I'd heard that the emperors don't scruple to dishonour those of both sexes who take their fancy.'

'Every emperor,' said Marcia, 'has his own habits. Caligula would rape anyone. To increase his income, he even abducted a number of respectable women who happened to be out and about in the city, and installed them in a makeshift brothel set up in a wing of the palace. But attacks of that sort didn't bring him any luck. Claudius never touched anybody's wife and Nero has been relatively discreet on that point up to now. He knows how to behave in society.

By the way, my husband wants to thank you for the financial information you gave him. As, apparently, you're more interested in Nero than in money, Decimus asked me to tell you that you are also invited for the evening of the IV of the coming Nones. We shall put you in a place where you can follow the conversation at the imperial couch.'

'That will give me the greatest of pleasure. You are doing me a considerable honour.'

'But you must behave yourself! Don't go ticking Nero off for making love outside marriage.'

'Have no fears on that subject! I can be diplomatic when I have to.'

Kaeso specified: 'Paul is used to high society. He once expounded his beliefs in the presence of King Agrippa and the delicious Berenice, and I'm certain he didn't take the king to task for sleeping with his sister. The tactful silence he adopts in good company probably even encouraged them. I read in a little book which Paul lent me the sad story of a Jewish prophet called John the Baptist, who got his head cut off for criticizing a local ruler for having taken his brother's wife. Paul doesn't belong to the same insolent breed. For the time being at any rate the Christians are gentleness and tact personified.'

Luke was tapping Paul's arm with increasing urgency to prevent a painful outburst. Kaeso, in his innocence, had a genius for putting both feet in it.

Paul merely asked: 'On what day does the IV of the next Nones fall? I can calculate the date in the Greek and Jewish ways but the Roman calendar is a headache for people from the East.'

Marcia counted on her fingers and said: 'The IV of the Nones is also the fourth day after the Kalends, the Kalends of course being included in the count.'

'Why do the Romans count backwards, and not forwards from a given day?'

'Kaeso knows everything. Perhaps he can tell you . . .'

'This backwards counting is, I think, an indication of the deeply religious character of the Romans. The Nones, Ides and Kalends correspond to old festival days, and when you're preparing for a festival, it's natural to cross one day off the calendar each day, like a legionary waiting to be demobbed.'

Addressing himself to Paul in particular, Kaeso developed this line of thinking. 'Your new religion could do worse than to take its inspiration from the Roman religious calendar. The year would be divided into commemorative festivals: the birth, baptism, transfiguration, crucifixion, resurrection, ascension . . . whatever . . . of Jesus. The Western peoples, who are already used to calculating the days by a coming date, would in future deduce them in relation to one of these events.'

However fanciful the idea, it was a striking one and showed an enlightened interest in the implantation of Christianity in the West.

After long discussions, the jury had just given the victory to the Green *quadriga* amid a storm of protest from the Blues. The troublemakers no longer limited themselves to invoking the shades of Britannicus, Agrippina and Octavia. The insults were getting really vicious. People pointed at the Vestal installed in the *pulvinar* and accusations of sacrilege rang out. An opposition ever ready to slander had accused Nero of raping the aforementioned Vestal, one Rubria, on the principle that, since the cap clearly fitted, there was no reason why he shouldn't wear it. The emperor, to deal with these absurd rumours once and for all, had deliberately appeared in public with the Vestal at his side. But the accusation had simply changed into one of impious concubinage.

Tired of this orgy of idiocies, Nero gave the order to expel some of the more violent agitators; from the porticoed walkway which crowned the enclosure on three sides soldiers of the urban cohorts, helped here and there by Praetorians, dived into the rows of seats and grabbed the culprits, occasioning some pretty violent scuffles.

But the crowd instinctively knew how far it could go. For while the Circuses, amphitheatres and theatres favoured, by a phenomenon of contagion, the most insolent forms of verbal opposition, they were also magnificent mouse-traps, where a small number of soldiers could put to the sword an enormous number of unarmed people, with all the blows falling on to a mass of excited people packed in like sardines.

Paul asked: 'Will the insolent fellows be put to death?'

'Oh no,' said Marcia. 'The emperor is usually patience itself when it comes to personal and public abuse. The authors of satires and epigrams, and satirical actors and mimes get off lightly. After Agrippina's death a witty woman who exposed a boy in the Forum with a notice round its neck saying "I abandon you for fear that one day you may assassinate me" had a great success and didn't get into any sort of trouble at all. What Nero won't pardon are direct attacks on his power, his safety and his artistic reputation, the three things being inter-related in his mind.'

Amid relative calm the *quadrigae* took off again.

Paul had not grasped much of the Rubria incident: the girl was red in the face and was now being comforted by Poppaea. Kaeso put him in the picture and gave him a brief sketch of the famous Vestal Virgins. 'The emperor, as Pontifex Maximus – high priest – takes the girls between the ages of six and eleven from noble families which in theory go back to the earliest days of Rome. Their hair is cut short, they are novices for ten years, carry out their ministry for ten years and train novices for another ten years. At about the age of forty they have the right to go back into the world and marry, but they rarely decide to give up their privileges for this hypothetical marriage. So there are usually more than six Vestals, the number considered necessary and sufficient.

These pious ladies are free of all tutelage, they go out in a curule chariot or a litter, the magistrates lower their *fasces* before them and give way to them, they have the right to pardon criminals whom they happen to meet, many citizens leave their wills with them, and they have reserved seats at shows. They have no legal authority, but they inspire so much reverence that their discreet intercession in public or private affairs is always effective. The Vestals are said to have dissuaded Sulla from putting Julius Caesar on the proscribed lists.

They live in a circular building between the Palatine and the Capitol, which was not consecrated by the augurs, so that the Senate cannot meet there. It's not a real temple, and men aren't allowed inside after nightfall. The sacred fire which the Vestals tend is lit on the Kalends of March by the sun itself, reflected in a concave metal mirror. Any Vestal who lets the fire go out risks being whipped. And any who breaks her vow of chastity could, in theory, be buried alive.'

After the acclamations which greeted the victory of a Red chariot had quietened down, Kaeso added: 'Given the importance of virginity in your religion, it would seem entirely appropriate, and yet also within Roman tradition, for well-disposed Christian fathers to cut their daughters' hair short at an early age and shut them up in houses of prayer. At the least sin against chastity they could be crucified, as a popular entertainment . . .'

Neither Paul nor Luke seemed enthralled at the prospect, and Kaeso momentarily gave up trying to offer them good advice. He turned to Marcia and they chatted as they had done in the old days, while the races and interludes took their course.

At noon there was a break. Nero and those with reserved seats withdrew to lunch in town. The others, both *pullati* and *togati*, got up and went for a walk to stretch their legs in the covered walkway, where itinerant sellers of cold – and even hot – food had appeared. Or else they simply stayed in their seats and nibbled at bread, olives and onions.

Marcia, well aware that Kaeso was preparing to slip away from her, prolonged her chitchat.

The big handouts designed to console the losers and complete the happiness of the winners took the form of banquets and various presents, and were traditionally held back until the end of the day. But Nero was not one to stint over attentions paid to his beloved *plebs*, and slaves were already running along the rows of seats throwing handfuls of tokens among the thinned ranks of spectators. One of these tokens happened to fall on Paul's knees, and he showed it to Marcia with a questioning look.

'Each of these tokens,' she said, 'entitles one to a present of some sort. Yours is valid for a visit to the "Three Sisters".'

'But where or what is that?'

'It's a rather up-market brothel on the Aventine, opposite,' explained Kaeso. 'But there's nothing to force you to go up there. This is still a free country.'

Paul's embarrassment was comical. If he put the token in his purse, the action would be equivocal. But if he rejected it and left it as a present for someone else, he would have their sin on his conscience.

That, however, was what Kaeso advised him to do.

'Give it to me. Let one of my father's slaves have the benefit of it. In all good ethical codes there can be no sin without consciousness of wrong-doing.'

'God's knowledge of the deed is the only prerequisite for sin. You can see why neither Peter nor I care for Rome.'

'If other people's sins upset you,' said Marcia, 'there are only two solutions: stop them sinning or go and live in a desert.'

'I've only just left one, *clarissima*. I began my new Christian life with a retreat in Arabia.'

Paul got up in exasperation, with the hateful token in his hand, and the three others followed him towards the exit.

In front of her litter, which was waiting near the Tiber, close by the temple of Castor, Marcia turned on Kaeso. 'I suppose that you prefer the Arabian desert to my company nowadays?'

'But we shall be seeing each other again shortly.'

'Seven days! You call that "shortly"?'

'Six and a half – just after the Floralia.'

Kaeso lent forward to Marcia's ear and murmured: 'Although you have been my mistress – if I'm to trust your memory – I shall always love you.'

'It's high time that our memories were identical . . .'

Whereupon Marcia got back into her litter, uncovering a perfectly formed leg as she did so, and Kaeso invited his two friends to lunch.

❧ CHAPTER ❧
6

The heavily populated quarter around the Circus Maximus hummed with even more activity than usual during the races. The lowest eating houses were positively taken by storm. Kaeso took Paul and Luke into the much quieter area of the nearby Caelian. While they were walking round the eastern end of the Circus, Paul, who had just thrown his token into a drain, was astounded by the number of wooden booths and the considerable size of the stores of wooden beams necessary for the constant reconstruction of the scaffolding holding up the immense building. He commented on the fire risk.

'Indeed,' Kaeso acknowledged, 'the emperor, on the Palatine, sleeps on top of a volcano. Fortunately good care is taken to watch out for fire. The fourth company of the Watch is based on the Aventine, and the fifth on the Caelian, and from there you can keep an eye on the whole Circus area. The patrols are frequent and there's a permanent strong concentration of police here, because of the number of brothels and gambling-dens. The Praetorian spies learn plenty there, and are the first to cry fire. They don't want the pleasant little establishments where they habitually hang out destroyed by a blaze.'

'I thought that gaming was forbidden in Rome,' said Paul.

'In theory playing for money is only authorized during the Saturnalia, when everything is turned upside down. The rest of the time the only legal form of gambling is placing bets on horses and gladiators. But the Romans have a passion for every sort of game possible, and the authorities are forced to tolerate what they can't prevent. I suppose that for Christians gambling is a sin?'

'Yes, because we shouldn't put into the hands of fortune the money which Providence gives us to make decent and pious use of.'

Kaeso had automatically walked on towards the fine villa where his parents had once lived, before the emperor Caius, with a flick of the hand, had dispatched his father into outer darkness. When the children had been old enough to understand, Marcus had told them a little of the sorry business, the curse of his existence. But in his version he played the role of a fabulously rich Roman who had been a prey to the jealousy and vindictiveness of Caligula. How could he have admitted that the madman had crushed him by accident, as a lion sweeps away a fly with its tail? To understand the greatest misfortunes, children have to see them portrayed in an apparently rational form.

Kaeso pointed out the red roofs of the property, above the trees in the park and the surrounding wall, and said with some emotion in his voice: 'That's where my mother once lived before the family suffered its long-drawn-out series of misfortunes. She died in the Subura giving birth to me. That was the first and greatest of my misfortunes, and from it stem all the others. Nothing can replace a mother. Sometimes, when I walk this way, I linger in front of those roofs and try to picture it all. But I now realize that my mother has left no trace in my life other than my life itself, which she gave me at the cost of her own. Do the Christians believe that you see those who loved you in Paradise?'

Paul passed the question over to Luke:

'All good people are in Paradise, where they keep company with one another under the eye of God.'

'Seneca claims there must be a Purgatory where souls are purified before proceeding higher.'

'That's a Jewish idea too. It's mentioned in Maccabees, but many rabbis don't accept the authority of that book. For Christians today the question is neither topical nor significant. The essential thing is to be on the right side.'

'I don't like to think of my mother in some sort of Purgatory. Anyway if, when she's resurrected, she's liberated from time and space, like Jesus walking through the wall, how could she stay provisionally in one place?'

'I certainly can't tell you.'

'I can't imagine my mother in Hell either.'

Paul and Luke politely protested against such a possibility being conceivable.

'So perhaps I shall see her in Paradise? But in what form? When Paul saw Christ, how did he look?'

'I was dazzled by His light,' Paul recalled. 'All I could see was His light. I became blinded by it for a while. The apostles told me that Jesus was bearded, like all Pharisees.'

'And after his resurrection did he still have his beard?'

'I assume so . . . Why does it matter?'

'What matters is that I should know what my mother will look like so I can recognize her!'

Paul and Luke tried to explain to Kaeso that the primary quality of a resurrected body was the possession of an entirely satisfactory appearance.

Kaeso suddenly asked: 'If all people of good character go to heaven, what's the use of baptism? Won't each man be judged on the capital which God invested in him? And in that case isn't one man's capital as good as another's?'

The two theologians looked at each other inquiringly. Luke replied: 'Baptism is only necessary for salvation for those who have consciously refused that salvation. A just man who hasn't heard of the true religion can be saved. But baptism allows us to do more good in this world and to occupy a higher rank in the next. As everyone in Paradise is happy with their own status, the person who gets the most benefit from rank there is God, in his love. So it's firstly to please God and secondly in the interest of your neighbour that you should ask for baptism.'

They went back down for lunch at the nearby *popina* where, in days gone by, Marcus had taken refuge and got himself drunk, after Caligula's historic auction of gladiators.

The little square with its fountain and plane-tree was still just as quiet, and the *popina* had not changed. It was particularly empty today because the whole of the Caelian had emptied itself into the Circus Maximus. Even the 'little fillies' of the establishment had gone down to watch the races. It was the Floralia, their evening festival. Behind the counter there was only one young hostess, who seemed to be of Syrian or Palestinian origin. She had stayed behind to keep an eye on the tavern, rather than to increase the takings.

Kaeso ordered a jug of wine, but declined the offer of a quarter of pickled bear, left-overs from the last *venatio* in Nero's great wooden amphitheatre. Lions and bears were great eaters of unwashed condemned criminals and a snack of that kind might have offended Paul's delicate sensibilities. The girl offered to cook the bear, but her customers preferred a little fried fish followed by a *minutal*, a dish made from minced meat. The authorities were always harassing the taverns over what hot food they could and could not serve, with the intention of reducing their drawing power and discouraging the assembly of crowds which could easily be seen as subversive. But decrees of the sort went the way of all such proscriptions: they were despised and ignored.

While absent-mindedly eating his fish, which was in fact excellent, Paul said to Kaeso: 'You have, I hope, grasped the full difference between the Paradise we offer and the sad underground fate suffered by souls in the traditional Greek and Roman religions. As Christians we aren't afraid that the dead will come back and tweak our toes. Those who are groaning in Hell for eternity are out of harm's way, and our brothers who have won a place in Heaven by the ardour of their faith will help us with their prayers until the day when we rejoin them. The only dead man whose actions can affect us is no longer a bogeyman but an influential friend and a model to follow. Because of Christ, relations with the dead have changed.'

Kaeso asked:

'Do you cremate your dead or do you bury them?'

'We bury them like the Jews. Man should not destroy his Maker's image.'

The close proximity of the family villa made Kaeso think of his father despite himself. He asked: 'I assume that among the Christians it's forbidden to marry one's niece?'

Luke stopped eating his fish and discussed the point with Paul. It was in fact a problem. Among the Jews uncles had the right to marry their nieces, but Paul and some others were inclined to forbid this, and even to outlaw marriages between first cousins. Kaeso was more surprised at the liberal views of the Jews than at the narrow attitude of the Christians. A race who specialized in piety but thought marriage between uncles and nieces normal? Kaeso felt a wave of sympathy for the Jews, and cried:

'If the Bible allows marriages of this sort and Jesus did not abolish them, what right have you to attack them?'

The sharpness of his reaction astounded his audience. Paul inquired: 'Could you possibly, despite your age, be thinking of marrying your niece?'

'I simply noted with disquiet that you use the Holy Spirit as an excuse to bring in all sorts of innovations and suppressions which aren't formally authorized by either Jesus or Holy Scripture. If the Holy Spirit didn't exist, you would – given the intensive use you make of it – have had to invent it.'

Paul showed signs of being affronted at this remark. Luke hurriedly calmed him down and quietly explained:

'Although I'm a Greek by birth, I've thought about the Scriptures a good deal, and in my opinion the Jews permitted uncles to marry their nieces because the Levirate law already obliged a man to marry his dead brother's wife. If you can marry the wife, why not the daughter? Among the Jews themselves the Levirate is hardly ever applied nowadays, but its accidental consequences remain. Isn't it desirable for Christians to do away with the anomaly?'

'I can see another reason,' said Kaeso. 'When the sister-in-law was plain, the brother at death's door and the daughter very pretty, a wise brother made a bee-line for the girl, to get out of marrying the mother.'

Paul and Luke had never considered the question from that angle. The discussion became more heated over the *minutal*.

Kaeso cut them short impatiently. 'As far as I can see, Holy Scripture is not the word of God. You can take it or leave it.'

Paul started and said:

'Our Scriptures are inspired by God. That means that Yahwe, Jesus and the Holy Spirit are only known to us historically by human reports which are of course fallible, to a greater or lesser degree. So, in the Old Testament you can find improbabilities and large numbers of prejudices. Not all of it is of the same interest or the same value. And even in the Gospels which have appeared or are being prepared, there inevitably are, and will be, contradictions. For example, Luke has given a scholarly genealogy of Christ starting from Adam, while Matthew in his Aramaic version gives one starting from Abraham, and the two lists have only two names in common before they get to Joseph, who was in any case only his legal father.

Hence the necessity for a respected authority – the rabbis in the case of the Jews and the *presbyteri* with us – which can define a correct reading. God in some sense keeps aloof from the sacred texts, but with the intention of giving the believer more freedom to find in them what he's looking for at each stage of his life and at each stage of the development of the human race. In that way the Scriptures can live and evolve. If one day a false god, who gained a following for himself, were to give man a work written with his own hand, we should immediately see men lose their human faculties as they bowed down to its every letter. The Christian God speaks through our free mouths, and it's because He has the humility to do so that He can appeal to, and permanently move, our hearts and our reason.'

'You mean that commenting on an inspired text should be left to those who are inspired?'

'God's spirit touches everyone who asks Him, and He reads the Scriptures with us. There are often many ways of interpreting even the most trivial passage, and they're not necessarily mutually exclusive. The meaning of some statements will only be understood at the end of time.'

Luke fancied some cheese, but, given the season, the shelf of fresh cheeses had little on it, as the shepherds had not yet gone to work on the summer pastures. The Romans did not make cheeses by the gruyère method. The curds, once spiced and salted, were put under weights to press out the whey. Sometimes they were then plunged into boiling water, pressed by hand, dried and smoked. Some cheese-makers in the Velabrum, who specialized in goats' cheeses, used apple-wood for their smoking. More or less every region of Italy provided Rome with cheeses. The total of cheeses produced at Luna in Etruria weighed as much as 1,000 pounds, but there were others from Nîmes, Lozère, Gevaudan, Dalmatia, the Carnic Alps and Bithynia. When a cheese, in particular one made from sheep's milk, became too old and dry, it would be marinated in grape-must. Luke eventually allowed himself to be tempted by a cheese of this sort.

As the young hostess spoke indistinct Latin and mangled Greek, Paul and Luke ended up talking to her in her mother-tongue, which was Aramaic. Kaeso had difficulty imagining a god with pretensions to be universal expressing himself in such a language. He wondered yet again what Jesus had come down to earth *for*.

'The more I think about it,' he said, 'the more I feel that the essence of your doctrine escapes me. At any rate, I don't respond to it the way you do. I can accept that the son of a transcendent god should be incarnated to remind us of his father. But why did he need to die on the cross to redeem our sins? Couldn't he have obtained the same effect by playing the flute?'

'A divine love so great that a God who could have remained impassive was willing to suffer and sacrifice his life is indeed a great mystery,' Paul acknowledged. 'Reason can't cope with such a concept. Only our hearts can help us to approach it. Haven't your father and mother, and your stepmother too, all sacrificed themselves for you at one time or another?'

'Without wanting to sound ungrateful, such actions might seem indiscreet when taken to excess.'

For the first time the gentle Luke burst out in irritation:

'When you see Christ, complain to Him that His sacrifice was indiscreet, and see what He says to you!'

Kaeso was very sceptical of the chances of survival for a religion so irrational that its myths claimed the right to be treated as literal truths. It was an important point as far as Silanus was concerned. If Christianity were soon to disappear in a wave of ridicule, as everything encouraged him to believe, he himself would be made to look pretty stupid in front of that intelligent and perceptive patrician. So he drew Paul and Luke's attention to the necessity of coming to terms with the habits and sensibilities of the society around them, especially as the Romans, for want of firm beliefs, lived on their traditions:

'Eastern and Roman priests have characteristic modes of dress. Even the Pharisees have a special cloak which makes them immediately identifiable. But Christian priests look like anybody else. Discretion taken to that extent can only have a bad effect on the man-in-the-street. Sooner or later the police will see it as the mark of a secret society unwilling for publicity. If you want to be effective, and if you want the authorities to grant you the sort of recognition the Jews have got, you must pay careful attention to externals, particularly during the celebration of your religious rites.

From what I could judge of the rites at the house of the Christian Jew at the Porta Capena, your Communion is awfully boring. You must liven it up, to attract people. The Romans like gorgeous and solemn clothing, music and lights. Since the Romans have altars – and the Jews do too in the Temple – and god is a person who sacrifices himself for you, why don't you replace the ordinary table by a fine sculpted altar, with gilding? And what about the plates and cups? When you eat and drink an incarnate and resurrected god, surely what you need is something visibly expensive and beautiful?

Better still, the Romans are accustomed to keeping a sacred flame burning on their family altar, just as the Vestals do for the State flame. Wouldn't it have a very felicitous effect to keep a lamp permanently alight on your altar?

I also noted that the bread you use at your Eucharist is ordinary bread, presumably to distinguish yourselves yet again from the Jews who, so I've read, use unleavened bread at their annual passover. But don't forget that unleavened bread has particular religious associations for the Romans, because it takes us back to the very old days when the peasants hadn't yet learnt about using yeast. Our *flamen* of Jupiter traditionally eats unleavened bread. Roman converts would be flattered to find such bread on Christian altars. Why confuse people for no good reason?

What's indisputable is that a religion must have its own particular tangible symbol around which to rally. I think that for the Christians the cross would do nicely. Now, you talk endlessly about this famous cross, but I've never seen a representation of it. In a city devoted to blood and violence, wouldn't it, for example, have a striking effect to see, on an altar, a crucified figure expiring on his cross? But without a beard. For the contemporary Roman there's something foreign and peculiar about beards. After all, as soon as he was converted, Paul hurriedly shaved his off, to make a better impression.'

At this Paul and Luke, who had been listening to Kaeso with a rather disapproving interest, protested with one voice. Luke went so far as to say, with pained vehemence: 'You're talking to men whose friends saw Christ on the Cross. They're not in any hurry to see Him on that instrument of torture again. The Cross is in our hearts and on our backs. Spare us the sight of it before our eyes!'

It made good sense in emotional terms. Kaeso apologized for his tactlessness and led the conversation into more general areas.

'Perhaps I'm not competent in religious matters,' he said, 'but as far as organization is concerned, you could usefully learn a thing or two from the Romans. Every army needs a leader and a code of discipline. In Peter's case, Jesus oddly omitted to be precise about his powers. That seems to me a recipe for future dissension. And as far as the rank-and-file are concerned, I was struck, on reading Paul's letters, at the disorder and confusion which develops as soon as his back is turned. It's a deplorable situation which, I think, derives from two factors: first, there's no hierarchy worth the name under your rather vaguely defined leader, and second, despite the passage of time the essential truths of the faith haven't yet been summed up and defined in an authoritative book. So that instead of organizing and running the sect, you waste your time in theological debate. Personally, before I'm baptized, I'd like to know what, in your beliefs, is fundamental, and what is secondary and optional. A rabbi assured me contemptuously that your entire doctrine could be summed up in a few lines. Could I at least know what they are?'

Paul acknowledged that the Christians gave the impression of being rather chaotic, and even added, staring feverishly at Kaeso:

'The disorder is even worse than you might suppose. I'll give you a good example. After Jesus' Ascension, the Holy Spirit came down upon the Apostles in the form of tongues of fire. And suddenly, as though the unity of man lost at Babel had been restored, when these modest, timid Galileans spoke to the crowd, every man seemed to hear them speak in his own language. Peter's Aramaic became Parthian to a Parthian, Cretan to a Cretan, and Arabic to an Arab. Peter and the others have now lost that gift . . . unless it's just that the Gentiles have closed their ears. But when I'm not there to keep an eye on Communion, it's not at all unusual for individuals to disturb the ceremony by claiming that they possess the gift of tongues. On a pretext of divine inspiration they launch into a load of incomprehensible jabbering. Things have gone so far that in one of my letters I've advised that those afflicted with a hysterical condition of this kind should be provided with the assistance of perceptive interpreters.

To sum up, since the Holy Spirit enveloped the entire Church, a healthy ferment has been accompanied by aberrant phenomena. The Spirit breathes everywhere, but so does the Devil. Yet it's out of all this tumult that tomorrow's Church will rise. The Holy Spirit always keeps control of the disorder necessary to its activity.

You said just now that if the Spirit didn't exist, we should have had to invent it, given the use we make of it. You were absolutely right, even if unintentionally so. If the Spirit were not upon us, we should be prisoners of the Gospel in the same way that the Jews have become prisoners of the letter of the Old Testament. Only the Holy Spirit enables us to complete and deepen the message destined for the whole universe. That entails some incoherence and some risk, but that's how life and grace work. Order will come in time. May it be God's will that the coming of order doesn't make us regret the passing of disorder!

As for the summary which you asked for, it is indeed quite brief. You would do well to engrave the words in your heart, since you have such a good memory:

I believe in God, the Father Almighty,

And in Jesus Christ, his Only Son, Our Lord,

Who was conceived of the Holy Ghost, born of the Virgin Mary,

Suffered under Pontius Pilate, was crucified, dead, and buried,

He descended into Hell, and on the third day He rose again from the dead,

He ascended into heaven, and sitteth on the right hand of God, the Father Almighty,

Whence He shall come to judge the quick and the dead.

I believe in the Holy Ghost,

The Holy Catholic Church, the Communion of saints,

The remission of sins,

The resurrection of the body,

And the life everlasting. Amen.'

Kaeso got Paul to go through it twice. His Roman mind was receptive to its relative clarity.

After a moment's thought he ordered a new jug of wine and said:

'What's all this about a descent into Hell, between death and resurrection?'

'Jesus,' replied Paul, 'descended into what one could define as limbo, and delivered the souls of the just who were awaiting their redemption. Adam's sin had closed paradise, and Jesus' sacrifice re-opened it.'

'I can't disguise the fact that that little phrase causes me some difficulty.'

'Why?'

'It raises the same problem as the hypothesis of a Purgatory. Wasn't the resurrected Christ, on his own admission, freed from time and space? So it's possible to imagine the other world as containing joy or suffering, but not as a place where souls could be waiting to change state. These two difficulties are very reminiscent of the contradiction we've already found between general extra-temporal Judgement and individual Judgement, which is subject to the laws of time. Could I leave that particular phrase out and still be baptized?'

Paul and Luke seemed very put out by this ticklish point. They started talking in Greek, but quickly switched to Aramaic, which, though somewhat impolite, allowed them to speak more freely despite the poverty of the dialect from a theological point of view.

Luke eventually said to Kaeso: 'We haven't forgotten your remarkable reflection on the notions of time and eternity in the context of Jesus as Man and as God. It may throw some light on our problem now. We therefore give you permission to substitute "He re-opened paradise to the Just of all times" for the phrase which you dislike. As you can see, we're not giving a precise date.'

That made the dogma more presentable, and Kaeso contented himself with it. But he was surprised that many at first sight seemingly essential truths such as baptism, communion, the indissolubility of marriage and the anointing of the sick with sacred oil were absent from the Creed.

'Baptism,' said Paul, 'is part of the remission of sins, since it washes out the stain of original sin. As for the indissolubility . . .'

'You don't want to frighten away your followers?'

'Well let's say, rather, that the indissolubility of marriage is not an article of faith but a moral law.'

The pleasant wine had put them in a good mood as they went back down towards the Porta Capena. Kaeso's imagination was busily at work, and to give pleasure to the two missionaries he suggested:

'When the Christians have converted everybody – whether it's by persuasion or compulsion – wouldn't it be a superb idea to bring in a new era which would be calculated from the crucifixion? Unlike the foundation of Rome it's an event which can be dated within a year or two.'

'Why not from the birth of Christ?' Luke suggested. 'Peter told me he was born twenty-five years after Actium, about twenty years before Augustus' death.'

'At what time of the year?'

'Very probably in the summer, since it was during a census and the shepherds were out in the fields.'

'Then we should be in about the year seventy of the era of Christ. Whereas if we took the crucifixion as our point of reference . . .'

'We should be in the year 34, since it's after the Jewish Passover. Jesus was about thirty-five at the time of Calvary . . .'

In the jostling crowds around the Circus Maximus, Kaeso asked:

'What happened to Jesus' mother?'

'As Christ was dying,' said Luke, 'he entrusted his mother to the young John, a prudent lad, who hastily took her off to safety in Ephesus.'

'Jesus had provided for the martyrdom of some of his friends and their relations, but not for his own mother?'

'It's the first time I've ever heard anyone hold that against him.'

'It wasn't a reproach. I was merely noting that Jesus had a sense of family solidarity. It's perfectly natural.'

'The Virgin had suffered enough already.'

'No more than the mother of any crucified slave. Is the venerable lady still alive?'

'She'd be over eighty. Twenty years ago, in Ephesus, when she was ill, Paul and I were finally able to pay her a visit.'

Paul intervened:

'Luke is speaking for himself. My own visit was very brief. I'm not on very good terms with John, who delights in very personal theological hair-splitting. Only Luke was allowed to stay, though Mary did in fact confide some very interesting things to him. She told him about the visit of the Angel who came to her to announce Jesus' birth.'

'Mary died,' Luke went on, 'shortly after our stay in Ephesus, where she was living a very quiet life with John.'

'I assume that, given his family feeling, Jesus will have resurrected his mother straight away, so as to have her by him and be able to embrace her and hear her voice. At any rate, that's what I would have done in his place.'

As Paul and Luke looked surprised at the hypothesis, Kaeso, went on:

'I'll bet you three sesterces to a race horse that Mary's tomb is empty.'

'For the moment,' said Paul with irritation, 'Jesus' empty tomb is quite enough. Don't let's complicate matters.'

'Why is there no mention of Mary in your letters?'

'She's present in the figure of Jesus. What more can one ask of her than to have given us Christ?'

They had arrived in front of the house of the Christian Jew. Before taking his leave, Kaeso could not resist a judicious observation:

'It's a great mistake, Paul, to leave Mary out. The Romans are used to deities of both sexes, whether they're gods of the city, or eastern cults which have been gradually acclimatized. Your letters would be more effective with a trace of the female principle about them. If I were you, I'd quickly set up a cult of Mary alongside her son. Men need a mother rather than a father. If Mary read your early letters, I can see why your visit to her was a short one.'

'I doubt whether Mary could read.'

'John could have read the letters to her. She'd hardly have been flattered by them.

And another thing, while we're on this subject. You ought to give this "communion of saints" mentioned in your Creed a practical everyday role to play. The Romans are used to dealing with gods of all types, each of them specialized in some particular activity. And every man has his own Genius to watch over him, rather like your guardian angels. Give a bit of publicity to the deserving saints in your paradise, give them a reputation for being specialists in this or that, so that Christians can pray to them to intercede in their interest. Innocent men condemned to death, for example, could pray to Stephen, whom you and your old friends dispatched to the next world; Joseph, after due announcement by an angel of the honour to be done to him, could replace the goddess Viriplaca, who appeases deceived husbands; the Virgin herself, an unmarried mother by courtesy of the Holy Ghost, could, among other things, play the part of Genita Mana, who takes a close interest in the regularity of menstruation. You see what I'm getting at? You need to humanize your system. You must think of the *plebs*.'

Paul could contain himself no longer, and cried: 'I can see only too well what you're getting at. It's not the Holy Spirit speaking through your mouth either!'

'How would you know? The Holy Spirit has more than one trump up its sleeve. Since the role of the Holy Spirit is to innovate in the general interest, what criteria do we have for determining whether someone who speaks in strange tongues or who prophesies is a saint or a practical joker?'

'It's also the task of the Holy Spirit to maintain the truth, and the truths which we have taught you are quite enough to show me that I can well do without your advice.'

Paul turned away and went into the house.

Luke said gently to Kaeso: 'In a clumsy fashion, which it would be unjust to hold against you in view of how newly acquired your faith is, you have certainly said some interesting things. In the Gospel which I mean to publish I shall talk about the Virgin as far as is appropriate. In the meantime I shall go and calm Paul down, and ask him to forgive you in view of your excellent intentions.'

So saying, Luke gave Kaeso the kiss of peace, and went to rejoin his companion.

Kaeso had had enough of the Christians, but he was impatient to extort from them the baptism which he was certain would get him out of his present troubles. This desire was all the more paradoxical given the fact that quite obviously baptism was designed to throw man, a slave to himself, into the slavery of a god much more stifling than Marcia. Everything new and attractive about Christian ideas was counter-balanced by a terrifying truth: in the manner of the Jews, the Christians claimed to give the world into the hands of a pure spirit, which was creator and master. But whereas the Jews had the good taste and pru-dence to allow themselves to be tyrannized by their god in the privacy of the family, the Christian god was aiming at replacing Nero, but with powers which were infinitely wider and more probing. The Jewish god had spoken to Moses on Sinai. Christ was much more than a voice on a mountain. In flesh and blood he interrogated the whole earth from his cross, ready to condemn all those who did not give him the right answer. When it came down to it, that was where the really new aspect of Christianity lay. For the first time god was present inside the world as well as outside, with a foot in each camp, so that nothing should escape him anywhere. After the accident of original sin had infected the flock, god had come back into the sheepfold covered in blood and looking pitiful, to inspire confidence, but with a whip behind the cross.

Kaeso realized why he found it difficult to put up with Paul's conversa-tion, or even Luke's, for long. This pair of intellectual layabouts had a limited or highly specialized education and a dogmatic vocabulary and manner to go with it. The trouble was that if their Christ had really been resurrected, they were absolutely right to be so impertinently cocksure and to do their best to impose their point of view. God could not be wrong, and he could not be refused the right to complete authority everywhere, since everywhere was his.

Kaeso even wondered whether, despite every rational indication to the contrary, the Christians might not succeed in stirring things up for some generations to come. The irrational element which was their weakness was perhaps also their strength. They could never prove that their god had been incarnate. But who could prove that he hadn't? A sword of certainty lay on the soft pillow of doubt, threatening to cut any sleeper who awoke with a start.

During his siesta back at the house Kaeso was struck down with a migraine and a fever. The illness seemed to affect his brain, and towards the end of the afternoon, to the terror of little Myra, he became delirious. After a terrible night the elder Marcus became panic-stricken and sent a message to Silanus asking him to send his private Greek doctor as fast as possible. Silanus had a whole tribe of doctors to keep his herd of slaves in good health, and had reserved the one who seemed the most competent for his private use. Selene also got permission to send for a Jewish doctor. Jewish doctors had a very good reputation. It was in fact the one area in which the Jews did have a good reputation. And Marcus junior managed to winkle out Dioscorides who, like Paul, was a native of Cilicia – Marcus had thought well of him on one of his tours of office in Germany. Dioscorides was a military surgeon and had no rival when it came to preparing medicines. It was essential that an eminent expert in medicines and dosages should be there to help the doctors. There was always a danger that they would not know their stuff.

When Rome began to win a reputation for itself, all the dregs of the Greek medical profession had flooded into the city to take the ignorant Romans for a ride. The situation had barely improved with the passage of time. The school of medicine with the best reputation, the one at Alexandria, did not deign to give diplomas to its pupils, and medicine was therefore a web of lies and trickery.

Under Nero most of the practitioners still quoted Hippocrates and his maxims in support of their art. His best known maxim, famous for centuries, was: 'Deep-seated ills need far-reaching cures.' But Silanus' doctor was more of the school of the society doctor, Asclepiades, who had flourished a hundred or so years earlier and respected the neat formula: '*Cito, tute, jucunde*' (Swiftly, surely and pleasantly). The followers of Asclepiades had realized that, for a successful physician, the *jucunde* was essential, and to this bias, which they paraded with great satisfaction, they added a discreet and prudent conviction that, in the prevailing fog of ignorance, what you did not do, you could not do badly.

Both Hippocratists and Asclepiadists had in any case jointly benefited from the work of Celsus who had, in the reign of Augustus, assured himself a reputation for encyclopaedic knowledge by making a logically ordered catalogue of illnesses on the basis of the remedies appropriate to them. Dioscorides naturally had particular respect for Celsus. Dioscorides inspired particular confidence because he had been able to get practical experience at his leisure in the military hospitals, which were remarkably well equipped. In Rome there were no hospitals. There were too many sick people, and they were of no value.

So Silanus' man, Dioscorides and the Jew sat around Kaeso's bed. But whenever his delirious fever left him, he merely lapsed into a temporary coma.

The Asclepiadist, a Greek from Alexandria, limited himself to checking Kaeso's pulse with a water clock, gambling on a sudden improvement, where he would feel more confident. He was not exactly a specialist in emergency cases. Dioscorides, with his dropping-tube, administered sedatives, whose most visible effect was to accentuate the periodic comas. The Jew blamed air-borne infections in the quarter. There had been little spring rain, and in the Subura the Etruscan drains, which had been extended and converted into sewers, were already giving off the sort of stench which usually came with summer. Marcia had rushed to the boy's bedside. She did not know what to say and was in a state of collapse.

The next day but one, on the eve of the Kalends of May, the patient was unrecognizable. He already had the signs of the characteristic appearance of approaching death as defined by Hippocrates: skeletal nose, sunken eyes, hollow temples, cold sweat, greenish tinge to the face. The final moment was evidently close.

On the morning of the Kalends of May Marcia had the unconscious Kaeso transported to Cicero's house. The three doctors, faced with a patient who was patently dying, continued their impotent discussions. Silanus, who had come to take a pained look at the dying boy, summoned reinforcements of Greek doctors. Some suggested cold baths, others hot baths. Yet others opted for nourishing enemas of boiled spelt, which Celsus had introduced for desperate cases, when the sick man's stomach could not tolerate even the thinnest gruel. In the atrium Marcus *père* was crying and calling on the goddesses Febris and Mephitis.

A little before midday the pulse became too rapid to calculate by any water clock. The Greek doctors were out of their depth. They knew the description of the 147 wounds found in the *Iliad*: 106 made by spear, with a mortality rate of 80 per cent; seventeen by sword, all fatal; twelve by arrow, with a mortality rate of 42 per cent; twelve by catapult, mortality rate 66 per cent; the overall index of mortal wounds coming to 77.6 per cent. But Homer had said nothing about death without glory, and the omission was irreparable.

At noon, Kaeso died, and Marcia fell senseless into the arms of Silanus.

In her despair Marcia finally said to the Asclepiadist:

'Asclepiades is said to have resuscitated a corpse on its way to the funeral pyre. You're a follower of his, aren't you? If you could bring Kaeso back to life for us, Silanus would give you millions of sesterces.'

'It's an authenticated fact, *domina*, but it was the great Asclepiades himself who did it. I, alas, am only one of his pupils.'

Marcia turned to the Jew, to Dioscorides and to the rest of the company. They were already looking the other way and trying to slip out unnoticed.

So, despite her instinctive repugnance, Marcia wrote to Paul:

'Marcia, wife of Silanus, to Cn. Pompeius Paulus, greetings.

Kaeso fell ill on the afternoon of the first day of the Floralia, and has just died of a malignant fever. You claim to have already brought someone back to life. Actions speak louder than words. I am waiting. I hope you are better than we are.'

The note reached Paul at dinner, just as he had finished a lecture on the catechism at the house of the Christian Jew. He was profoundly shocked by it. Luke gazed in silence at the thunderbolt contained in the tablets. Paul had brought Dorcas back to life in Joppa and had resuscitated Eutychus at Troas, but he himself had never done anything of that kind. Paul was unclear what God's intentions in the matter were. Bringing people back to life was child's play but it depended on God's taking charge of the matter. After withdrawing into himself in search of inspiration Paul finally said: 'It's the will of God. Let's go.'

As night was falling, Paul and Luke, accompanied by Marcia, Silanus, and the two Marcuses, were introduced into the dimly-lit room where Kaeso lay. The body, which had been washed, was cold, and rigor mortis seemed to have set in.

Marcia asked Paul whether there was anything he needed, to help him carry out the resuscitation. Paul sat down beside Kaeso, took his hand, seemed to be taking his pulse and said: 'There's still some sign of life. He should be back with us soon.'

Whereupon Kaeso opened his eyes, looked at Paul for a moment without any apparent surprise, and suddenly addressed him in Aramaic:

'Wretched Saul, why are you wasting your time among the rich when the wide countryside of the whole Empire is still in sorrow and anguish because it has not yet heard the Good News? Jesus walked the roads of Galilee and Judaea to preach the truth to the humblest of people. Fetch your stick and your sandals, and leave this city of perdition. Go off and eat the gruel of the peasants who are awaiting your coming. The cross must be planted on the roads, in the fields, even in the forests – but not in the towns.'

Having well and truly delivered this message, Kaeso closed his eyes and fell into a refreshing sleep.

Their experience of the Holy Spirit had taught Paul and Luke not to be surprised by anything much. They lived in a world of essences, beyond appearances. They were therefore more impressed by the tenor of the message than by the strangeness of the events and the form they took. It was difficult not to see the paradoxical inspiration of the Holy Spirit at work.

Paul got up and said, simply: 'There, just as I said: he's fine. He'll be up for the banquet for Nero.'

The two missionaries discreetly withdrew, leaving Marcia, Silanus and the two Marcuses dumbstruck with stupefaction.

Silanus eventually said: 'By Zeus, that fellow's even better at it than Asclepiades. He'll make a fortune, and his books will sell like hot cakes.'

Marcia and the others said nothing, which is the wisest course for those who have understood nothing.

As could be expected, Kaeso's convalescence was remarkably rapid. People soon began to doubt whether he had really been dead for a few hours. It was like a bad dream. Moreover Kaeso himself could hardly remember his brain fever, let alone his departure, return and the speech he had addressed to Paul in an incomprehensible language. As curious as ever, Silanus asked Kaeso about the next world, but to no avail. All he got were confused statements or little jokes.

'If Paul really brought me back from the dead, we must ask him what his god did with my soul during the afternoon when I was apparently dead. The Christians imagine a Hell and a Paradise which offer no escape for those who find them boring. The Stoics and some Jews envisage a Purgatory, a point on which the Christians have not made up their minds.

But the way out of Purgatory only leads to Heaven, so I can't have been there. The Christian Creed makes reference to a rather shadowy spot where the souls of the Just who died unbaptized before Christ's coming are supposed to have been vegetating while they waited for the death of Jesus to open Paradise for them. But in that case too the exit only led in one direction. Yes, I shall have to ask Paul, even if it means that I put him in a temper again. He's better at bringing people back to life than at philosophy.'

'The Christian god,' suggested Silanus, 'must have popped you into a specially designed waiting-room for a moment.'

The day after the Kalends, the evening of the sixth of the Nones of May, Kaeso good-naturedly wrote to Paul the sort of letter he knew he would like:

'Kaeso to his dear Paul, greetings.

Why have you not already been back so that we could thank you? After all, you have restored me to good health, and even to life, if I am to believe those who saw you do it. Thanks to you, everyone here is beside himself with joy. Marcia, most of all, wants to kneel before you and kiss your hand. She would anoint your feet with perfume if you did not run so fast.

My relatives are more fortunate than I. They did not experience as I did, even if only for an instant, the delights from which I was called back and which almost make me regret the astonishing efficacy of your cure.

I have in any case good news for your guidance. You are always talking about Paradise, but you must occasionally have some doubts about it, for the Devil sometimes creeps into the souls of even the purest and most confident believers. Well, this Paradise of yours really does exist. If I were a spinner of fairy tales, I should tell you that I saw God the Father with a long beard like Jupiter. But since the Father was not incarnate I saw only his light, which still warms my heart. On the other hand I saw Christ in glory complete with beard, the very man who blinded you to bring you to a better frame of mind. And I also saw the Holy Spirit. It too had taken on animate form, in the shape of a dove, during Jesus' baptism, before it winged its way back up to God the Father. You'll find the story in Mark's gospel. The man who has not looked upon Christ, in the light emanating from the Holy Father, with the dove winging its way across, cannot know what true happiness is.

My mother, who seemed adorably young, sends you her best wishes. I was infinitely pleased to establish that, as Luke has declared, baptism is not the only talisman which opens the gates of Paradise. I found an immense crowd of people there, and naturally you could still count those who had been baptized on the fingers of your hands.

Nonetheless I must once again ask you for baptism, not so that I can get back into Paradise, but to help me defend the interests of my neighbours here on this earth.

It goes without saying that I shall be discreet about my trip. A Christian should be modest enough not to draw attention to himself.

I am told that on re-awakening I spoke to you in a strange language. I wonder what I could have said. Did I "speak in tongues" as Christians have got into the habit of doing? Or did I use the language of Paradise, which I had just learnt but am in the process of forgetting?

Fare well. Please do not bring me back to life again the next time I die!'

This letter threw Paul and Luke into a great state of puzzlement.

It would of course have been possible to see in it a manifestation of that misplaced sense of humour in which Kaeso specialized. But was it conceivable that a boy newly risen from the dead could joke about such subjects?

And then again, nothing which Kaeso wrote was frankly implausible. The point about the incarnation and ascent of the Dove gave scope for discussions of some delicacy. There were already enough bizarre things in the new faith . . .

'Our friend's letter,' said Luke, 'in any case poses a question which our theology owes it to itself to find an answer to. Where do the souls of the dead which we and Jesus have brought back to life go in the meantime? With Lazarus, the daughter of Jairus, the widow's son at Nain, Dorcas, Eutychus and Kaeso, that makes six to date. People will begin to wonder. Kaeso is the first to have said where he went, but since his revelation may not be serious, it hardly helps us resolve the question. Suppose that a seventh person rises from the dead and tells a different story. The contradiction would make a very unfortunate impression. In the Gospel which I am projecting, I should do well, if you see no objection, to leave the resurrection of this disturbing Roman out of account. And wouldn't it be preferable, when all is said and done, to give up resuscitating these dead people who touch our emotions? Basically, in all fairness, you have to ask yourself the question? "Why them and not someone else?" In the long run, even if God were kind enough to go on helping us, it could be a source of jealousy and trouble.'

'God told me that Kaeso would be the last,' Paul assured him. 'Perhaps the Holy Spirit wanted to use him to deliver that disturbing message in Aramaic to me. But there's something else. In one way or another that boy is at the heart of a divine plan – I know it, I can feel it – a vast plan which concerns us all. That's why he had to live a little longer.'

On the morning of the V of the Nones of May, while they were discussing his destiny in such sybilline terms, Kaeso was saying goodbye to his brother, who had had permission to prolong his leave by a few days.

Kaeso was still far from well. He was lying stretched out in the belvedere garden where Nero was to dine on the following evening. Marcus junior wracked his brains for the ideas and phrases which would have the most effect on Kaeso and seem the most convincing. Then he declared:

'You see how difficult it is to judge even the most basic things. We don't even know if you were really dead or alive on the afternoon of the Kalends of May. And you, the person most closely involved, can't even tell us yourself. Judging by the corpses of Germans I've seen at close quarters, I'd have said you were dead for sure. Yet now you look as though you're recovering from a bad cold.

Please, let the fact that it's so difficult to form a judgement make you modest and prudent, wise and reasonable in your behaviour towards Silanus and Marcia. Although we've avoided discussing the matter, we've both guessed, me first, then you, what Marcia, for the past fifteen years, has been doing for the two of us and for the household in general. But what she did, she did for *you*. You were her favourite, the one with all the qualities that attracted her. Don't sacrifices on that scale give her some right to expect your gratitude?'

Kaeso broke in wearily:

'Paul's Christ also gave his body for sinners who hadn't asked him for anything. I'm fed up to the back teeth with these Christs and Marcias who martyr themselves to touch people's emotions and bring them help. How restful life is going to be when I'm no longer exposed to that sort of excessive devotion!'

'But Marcia isn't like Christ. She's asking for virtually nothing. She simply wants to breathe the same air as you do, enjoy having you around, see you get up in the morning . . .'

'Provided I'm getting out of her bed.'

'I have more experience of women than you . . .'

'Yes, and what women!'

'Women are all the same. "*Tota mulier est in utero*" (the womb is the key to woman). I can say from experience that that adage doesn't have the obscene meaning which most people attribute to it. Women are probably more visceral than cerebral, but of the organs that rule their lives, the heart and the womb are the most important. Sleeping with you is important to Marcia, but not essential. She would prefer to live in your company without your touching her than to lose you altogether. When we were waiting for Paul to come, she seemed to age ten years, and your recovery took fifteen years off again. If you refuse to be adopted, you'll drive her mad. She'll be quite capable of committing suicide. I should find it hard to forgive you if she came to such a sad end, when she's given you so much and asks for so little.'

'All she's asking for is my body!'

'Well, it isn't so precious that you can't let her have it without troubling your conscience.'

'It's easy for you to talk.'

'Promise me to go easy on Marcia.'

'I'll do what I can.'

Marcus embraced his brother sadly and withdrew.

Marcus took his leave of Silanus and thanked him. Then, as he was saying goodbye to Marcia in the atrium, he added: 'I've made Kaeso promise to honour his debt to you. I hope he'll keep his word. He told me how things stand and I must admit that I'm very worried for both of you – and very tangentially for myself. Why shouldn't love be blind, as people always say it is? I shouldn't have waited to be asked to love you. I already feel so much affection towards you, going back so many years. If Kaeso's lack of gratitude one day drives you to despair, before you do anything stupid please think of me. You have a big faithful bear out in Germany who would like to keep you for a long time yet.'

Marcia was deeply touched. She held him tight in her arms and murmured: 'If love weren't blind, I'd have chosen you, and not that young dreamer. He'll lead me to destruction.'

When Marcus had gone, a slave brought in Myra, with a note for Kaeso. In a fit of quite natural curiosity Marcia accompanied the girl to where the convalescent lay. Kaeso gave a brief explanation of the circumstances in which he had acquired Myra, and asked Marcia to read the message, which turned out to be from Selene:

'Selene to Kaeso, greetings.

Your father is so pleased about your recovery that I'm having difficulty protecting Myra from his advances. Though I should be up to the job! So

I have advised the child to take refuge with you. She's still worried that nobody suitable is taking any notice of her charms. Try to reassure her one way or another. Why not in the most natural way? I hope you are continuing to get better.'

Marcia dropped the tablets irritably. 'It's always such a pleasure to read a letter from Selene!'

Kaeso tried to calm her down with a few humorous remarks, but for Marcia Selene was no laughing matter.

'If I'd died,' he asked her, 'you'd have had her killed, wouldn't you?'

'You did die. Heaps of doctors certified the fact and there was every reason to have confidence in their judgement. Your Paul gave life back to two people for the price of one. On that ghastly afternoon, on the Kalends, while I was waiting for him, I sent for Dardanus and arranged for him to deal with Selene. But you needn't worry. I cancelled the instruction the same evening.'

'How you hate the poor girl.'

'I'm in danger of losing my life because of her.'

'If you die, it'll be your own fault. Spare me that sort of blackmail. And promise me not to touch Selene, even if something happens to me.'

'You knew about that phoney love-letter, didn't you.'

'Even if I told you I didn't, you wouldn't believe me. I absolutely had to find out what your real feelings were before I let myself be adopted. It wasn't entirely out of the question that your love for me was purely maternal. How else could I have found out your secret?'

'But I assume the idea of the letter came from Selene?'

'From what she told me afterwards, she had plenty of excuses for getting her own back. One could justify your pleasure at caressing her or at having her beaten – but not both.'

'I had her whipped for telling a lie.'

'So she told me. I concluded from her story that you would have me whipped if my cock wasn't long enough to satisfy you.'

Marcia, who had sat down beside Kaeso, got up with a nervous laugh. 'An inch either way is irrelevant where love is concerned.'

As she was turning to go, Kaeso called her back.

'Will you promise me not to touch Selene?'

'Are you by any chance in love with her?'

'What I'm interested in is justice.'

'Why should my promise inspire any confidence in you? The only god

I acknowledge is you. If I lose you, what does it matter if the world falls apart?'

'As a god or gods may or may not exist, it's advisable to take both possibilities into account in our actions. I speak as one recently returned from the dead.'

Marcia shrugged her shoulders and went out.

Kaeso called Myra, who was playing with an improvised top on one of the garden paths, and said to her:

'Sometimes, in the evenings, a ghost appears in the picture-gallery in the peristyle. I wouldn't hang around there at that time of night. But in case your curiosity gets the better of you, you might as well know that the ghost won't do you any harm and there's no need to be frightened of it.'

'Whose ghost is it?'

'An old lawyer, who lost his head because he backed the wrong horse.'

'You're making fun of me.'

'No I'm not. I'm giving you a very brief summary. How can I explain to you who Cicero was? You know so little about life.'

'When you've slept with as many women as I have men, you can start making comparisons about our experience of life.' The child stormed crossly off to go on with her game.

Kaeso reflected that Paul's doctrine of marriage was perhaps justifiable in so far as all women, as his brother claimed, were alike. That was what all great womanizers ended up by saying, though that did not stop them from continuing their chase with a passion which was as illogical as it was tireless. If it was true, wouldn't one find out more about women by examining a single example at leisure?

At that point the tablets which Kaeso had sent to Paul came back. Paul expressed himself as follows:

'Paul of Tarsus to his dear friend Kaeso.

We are delighted that your health is keeping up after the trip which you have described to us so picturesquely. You are the sixth person to have had this brief experience, seven counting Jesus, who came back from the dead under his own steam. Great truths always go in threes, sevens or nines. But the five ordinary people who preceded you had a great deal less to say than you about what happened to them. Perhaps your soul stayed close to your body while waiting for me to come, and had a dream?

When you woke up, you called me Saul and spoke to me in Aramaic, which caused me something of a shock. Since you know so much about the next world, you must know what you said to me.

You keep asking me to baptize you, and yet I feel that your faith does not match up to ours. There is a mystery there, but the solution to it escapes me. I shall baptize you nevertheless, since I am not competent to "search men's hearts and thoughts". Baptism isn't simply something between you and me, it's between you and God.

At dusk tomorrow evening, while I'm dining at Silanus' house so that I can get a closer view of Nero, the Jewish Sabbath will be beginning, and it will finish the following evening. The Christians have given up the Jewish custom on this point. Their Lord's day starts just as the Jewish Sabbath finishes. So our Sunday goes from Saturday evening to the following evening. On Saturday evenings we have our main Communion, so that we can begin the week in as holy a state as possible. This is when we have the biggest attendance. On the evening of the day after tomorrow there will be a Communion at the villa of Eunomos, outside the Porta Viminalis, beyond the Praetorian camp and training ground. Eunomos is a rich slave of the imperial *familia*, whose job, against his will, is to pander to Nero's pleasures. This would provide an immediate opportunity for your baptism, if you are willing. Afterwards, when I have left Rome, absolutely trustworthy people will complete your education and you will eventually receive the Holy Spirit.

To come back to the subject of your faith, which still seems very confused and insecure, despite your loyal efforts at conveying information: I shall merely recount the end of a parable of Jesus' which Luke told me. A rich sinner, being tortured by the flames of Hell – Jesus told the story, so the details must be correct – asked Abraham to let one of the elect come back to the world for a moment to warn those of his friends and relatives in great danger of perdition. Abraham replied: 'If they won't listen to Moses or the Prophets, even if someone comes back from the dead they won't be convinced.' Since then Jesus has come back from the dead, and so have you. What else do you need to be convinced? What excuse would you have for not being so?

I hope your soul is well.'

Kaeso replied at once, on the same tablets:

'Kaeso to Paul, greetings.

But I do believe. Of course I do. I mean that I already accept the incredible as possible. Isn't that a good start? Doesn't it give every hope for the future and qualify me for immediate baptism? You yourself describe your belief as "a scandal for a Jew and madness for a Gentile". Be a little patient and try to understand that grace does not work upon all souls in the same way. Some are struck blind outside Damascus. Others open their eyes cautiously and their progress is slower. Sometimes the dam gives way all at once. In other cases the waters slowly wear away the rock. I feel more Christian with every passing day.

But I am surprised that you should invoke Abraham in upbraiding me for the lukewarm nature of my faith. If one is to believe Genesis, which I read very carefully, his reputation seems to me particularly dubious. A chap who passes off his wife as his sister so that he can live off her charms! And who is quite happy to leave Egypt with the product of this shameful and dishonest activity! If your Abraham, patron saint of pimps, got into Paradise by accident, he might have the goodness to refrain from lecturing the rest of us from up there, since we would all be absolutely justified in shouting "Up yours too" at him.

I must also tell you frankly that I am not attracted by the prospect of being baptized at the house of Eunomos. He is supposed to play precisely the same role in relation to Nero that Abraham did for Pharaoh, with the difference, perhaps, that he does not prostitute his own concubine to the emperor.

Please understand me. I do not hold it against Eunomos that he is a slave. The Stoics have taught us that all men are equal if not in merit at least in worth. And for many years now free men have associated with slaves in many religious colleges. Nor do I hold it against him that he is a sinner, since only God is in a position to make a proper comparison of our sins by comparing the contexts in which we committed them. On the contrary, where Eunomos is concerned I feel a pious envy. In your letters there is a gaping hole into which men like Eunomos have fallen, without your appearing to notice the cross which they have to bear. Every time you address yourself to slaves, you recommend them to accept their unhappy lot patiently, not to change their condition, and to respect and love their master. So if a Christian slave is compelled by his master to be a partner in all his vices, what is he expected to do? You forbid him to commit suicide, which is the elegant solution proposed by the Stoics as a way out of hopeless situations. You forbid him to rebel. You forbid him to run away. In fact you oblige him to share in his master's sins, and his only consolation is that he will not be held responsible, provided that it is plain that he had no choice.

Can't you see for yourself where this wretched contradiction in terms leads? Are there to be two categories of Christians, one lot dedicated to chastity and all the virtues, the other condemned by a harsh Providence to suffer their master's erotic caprices in body and soul? It is merely hypocritical verbiage to say that there is no taint of sin for the victims in such cases. Human nature is such that abuses of that kind, even if they leave the soul untouched, inevitably leave their mark on body and mind, both through the humiliation experienced and the pleasure which, despite everything, the victims are bound to feel from time to time.

Eunomos is touched by the grace of God, but at the same time he purveys little boys and girls to Nero. Whatever he has to undergo, he is thus the beneficiary of a strange degree of tolerance at the heart of your otherwise very straightlaced morality. I have to content myself with just one woman. Yet he has the right to say to me: "I'm a Christian and here's my wings to prove it; I'm a pimp and a tart and here's my arse to prove it."

If we take the point a little further . . . couldn't your fine theory of a sin which melts away if committed under constraint be extended to free men who are caught in the toils of harsh necessity? Where does slavery begin and end? Couldn't everyone be said to run the risk of falling into the quasi-slavery of someone else's domination sooner or later, in a world as violent and arbitrary as ours? If Nero had me kidnapped so that he could enjoy my charms, would you be as indulgent to me when I gave in as you are to Eunomos and his compromising conduct? I have every reason to be jealous of Eunomos, and I shall have myself baptized elsewhere.

I pray to Heaven that the emperor never takes too close an interest in your own person.

Fare well, and may Abraham's blessing be upon you.'

The sun had reached its highest point in the sky, Silanus and Marcia came out to join Kaeso in the garden, and shortly afterwards lunch was brought up to them. During the meal a messenger from the Palace brought the brief guest-list for the following night, which Nero was graciously submitting for Silanus' inspection.

There was Petronius, whose artistic and literary competence and cynical *savoir-vivre* had long made him an intimate favourite of the emperor. There was the vile Vatinius, because of his amusing side, which was not without its profundity. After all, Nero liked to make him repeat: 'Caesar, I hate you because you're a member of the Senate.' There was the impecunious Vespasian, one of Vatinius' favourite butts. Vespasian was to be accompanied by his two sons, Titus and Domitian, whom he was trying to launch. Titus was a great booby of twenty-five, but Domitian, who was twelve years his junior, seemed a little smarter. There was Coccius Nerva, a friend and distant cousin of the emperor and a fashionable poet at court, one of those precious young men who are old before their time. There was fat, insolent Vitellius, whose company at table and in his orgies Nero had come particularly to like: in an ocean of platitudes Vitellius' cynicism had something healthy and comforting about it. And contrary to all expectations, there was Otho.

'What's Otho doing here?' asked Marcia. 'I thought he was still in Lusitania or Hispania Tarraconensis.'

'Lusitania,' Decimus corrected her. 'It's old Galba who's currently governor of Hispania Tarraconensis. Otho was called back for a curious court case. Before he left for the banks of the Tagus, he was in debt up to his ears – or more accurately over his head. Among other shady incidents, he persuaded some imperial slave, who was hoping in return for some post or other in charge of I don't know what, to give him a million sesterces. Well, the post of course turned out to be non-existent. When a rich slave, who in most cases will have made his money by fraud, is taken for a ride by an even bigger crook than himself, he has difficulty getting his money back. Since he has no legal standing, how can he bring a case other than through his master? And it isn't usual for him to want to confide in *him*. Unluckily for Otho, the slave in question was freed and appointed to a position of responsibility in the Department of Aqueducts. Burning for revenge, he stirred up other victims of his debtor, who formed a syndicate of plaintiffs and besieged the praetor with their complaints. As a result the Senate itself sent for our dishonest friend, with Nero's approval of course, to ask him to account for his actions. On top of the rest of his troubles there was a little matter of a charge of maladministration in Lusitania. As there's nothing to be scraped out of a province as poor as that, the slightest exploitation becomes immediately noticeable.

In the Senate T. Clodius Eprius Marcellus was put in charge of the prosecution. Everyone knew what that meant. Marcellus himself just got off on a charge of grand larceny in Lycia, and, like Vibius Crispus or Vatinius, he and his tear-jerking eloquence are wheeled out whenever those in power want to settle a score with someone.

Marcellus was already polishing up his speech when Nero suddenly stopped the whole business. Perhaps Poppaea put him up to it. It would have been difficult not to get some mud on her in the process of sifting through her ex-husband's escapades.

Otho thought he was ruined and was very frightened, but for the moment he seems to have got off with nothing worse than a scare. Probably that's all the emperor intended when he let him be recalled. Our dear emperor likes to keep those who offend him on tenterhooks, until the time comes to pull the rug out from under their feet. If Otho has been invited to dine at my table before returning into exile, you can bet your boots that it's because the scent of his fear sharpens Nero's appetite.'

Silanus sent back the guest-list with the marginal comment: 'I hate Vatinius, because he ought not to be a member of the Senate.'

Marcia and Kaeso were appalled, but he observed: 'Vatinius already detests me. I represent in his eyes everything he can never hope to be. But Vatinius can only act if Nero lets him. Nero is like a dog, the scent of fear makes him want to bite. It's an attitude which makes political sense, in that fear is usually a sign of a bad conscience. I have nothing to reproach myself for, and Nero couldn't give a damn if people have a dig at Vatinius. He despises him as much as the rest of us.'

During the afternoon Kaeso went back to his room, and Marcia came to keep him company. She tried to have a trivial, relaxed, confident conversation with him, and frequently referred to things in the past. But there was no longer any safe ground. Kaeso looked at her as if she were a complete stranger. Eventually he asked her: 'How many of your ex-lovers will be at dinner tonight?'

Marcia thought for a moment, and said:

'Only three or four.'

'Three or four? Aren't you even sure any more?'

'I had a short affair with Vitellius, who was quite generous. Otho borrowed 20,000 sesterces off me, which I have naturally never seen again. As for Petronius and Nerva, I can't be sure. We were all in the dark at the time. I don't know who I was with, or whether it was several men or the same person several times. But what does it matter now, Kaeso? If we were all in the dark then, shouldn't we be prepared to stay in the dark now?'

'So you sometimes did it for free?'

'Well, I had to keep people interested, silly boy!'

The return of the tablets filled with writing in Paul's hand gave Kaeso a good excuse to bring this painful exchange to a halt. The speed of Paul's reaction was remarkable, as though Kaeso had put his finger in a wound.

'Paul of Tarsus to his dear friend Kaeso.

You are right. You are always right. How could it be otherwise? You are young, quick-witted, your memory functions better than a clock, you have studied rhetoric and philosophy at your leisure, you have Roman good sense and Greek finesse, and you speak your mind, because you belong to a society where even ignoramuses and imbeciles speak their mind.

What am I beside you? I have studied little except Jewish law, and Christ who came to fulfil it. And even where the law is concerned, a Gamaliel or a Philo knows far more about it than I do. My knowledge of philosophy is superficial. My rhetoric is all extemporized. The fact of constantly being on the move and constantly getting into hot water is beginning to make me feel my age. And my faults don't help. I know that I am intolerant of contradiction, and that my reasoning is sometimes dubious. I have said a lot and written a fair amount: in so doing I can now see that I have given impressions of my thought which are divergent or even contradictory. Some people accuse me of having betrayed the Law; others of having betrayed Christ; and others of having betrayed myself. The closer I get to dying, the more I become aware of my ignorance, inadequacies and weaknesses.

But what does your power of reason or mine matter! Is it reason which causes us to be born, live and die? As you must be aware, since you came to me for guidance, reason only opens very narrow domains of everyday experience to us. It helps us train a horse or smoke a cheese. It has never solved any essential problems, because they do not depend on its narrow and prosaic lights. Life and death are beyond all reasoning. And the more fundamental an experience is, the rarer it is. One cannot be born twice, so one cannot, as the saying goes, "learn from experience". Even you, who will die twice, have not learnt anything from your first taste of death.

There is, however, an experience, just one, which doesn't need to be repeated to become perfect. That is the experience of faith. If I were to sum up the grand design of my mission, and the whole spirit of our Church, in a single word, I would use the Latin word *conversio*, which means "turning around". That describes the physical impression which I had near Damascus. After that shock, I certainly did not know any more about the world, but I had been "turned round" in such a way that I was looking at it from a new angle. The uncertainties which had been worrying me up to then became completely secondary next to that one indelible truth: Christ had taken upon himself all the sins, all the mistakes, all the ignorance of those who have faith in Him. From that moment a believer's weakness becomes his strength, because Christ helps him to bear the burden. Standing firm at the centre of all things, He stretches out his two arms from the Cross over all human history.

Yes, you are right a hundred times over. I have never known how to speak to slaves or how to answer all the questions they put to me. I have only been able to say to them: "Christ died for your sins as He died for those of your masters, and He will have pity on you all on the Day of Judgement."

So you will not be going to the house of Eunomos. I shall see you shortly. I am having my toga ironed and I shall take a bath.

Fare well, my little rationalist!'

Kaeso was delighted to get out of Communion at the house of the notorious Eunomos. He was getting himself baptized to make an impression on Silanus, on his father, and perhaps on Marcia. He could see no advantage in being seen in public with a band of Christians. A rash lot like that might end up in trouble. The less he had to do with them, the better it would be.

When Silanus came to visit him in the late afternoon, Kaeso took the opportunity to show him Paul's last letter, and asked him his opinion of this sort of literature.

'It's an interesting point of view,' Decimus declared. 'This fellow Paul really seems convinced that he brought you back from the dead, since he maintains that you'll die twice.'

'The doctors had given me up for dead, and apparently I certainly looked like it. Paul can be excused for believing it was a miracle, and it's not out of the question. The Christians aren't the only people who claim to bring people back from the dead. Aesculapius was supposed to have effected resuscitations of the sort, and in the temples of Epidaurus, Cnidos, Kos, Pergamum and Cyrene miraculous cures are legion. Even in Athens, where scepticism flourishes, there were some while I was staying there.'

'What a pity your memories of what happened are so vague.'

'That doesn't prove anything either way.'

'The uncertainty is annoying. A doctor who can resurrect his patients can earn higher fees.'

'I've already told you that Paul wasn't interested in money,' said Kaeso, laughing. 'And you read the rest of his letter for yourself . . .'

'Yes. He's obviously a fanatic. He says himself that he sees the world differently from the rest of us. As for being disinterested, we shall see. As my grandfather warned me, it's the honest women who've cost me the most.'

'You can't have come across many.'

'It's just as well. I shouldn't have a *nummus* left for Marcia!'

It suddenly occurred to Kaeso that if Decimus could be persuaded that he had really died and come back to life, that would be an excellent motive for conversion and baptism, indeed the only motive which it would be difficult to argue about. However, so as not to baffle Silanus unduly, he ought to improvise a Paradise with a touch of the Stoic about it . . .

'I do have a few hazy memories of the other world, like occasional rents in a veil. But what is odd is the way the images elude me or dissolve into sensations, feelings, retrospective viewpoints. I can see whiteness . . . Yes, we were all in white togas . . .'

'Togas?'

'On reflection, there may have been some Greek or barbarian clothes. That's a detail. I could be wrong about the shapes and even the colours, for there was a dazzling light everywhere. But this divine light transmitted a whole host of scientific and moral information. My mind was filled with the Stoic world order. I could understand everything, and nothing surprised me any longer. Could I have been dreaming?'

'It would have been a fine dream.'

'In any case, the trip must have taught me a foreign language, since Paul revealed to me that I spoke to him in Aramaic, the most commonly spoken language in the near East.'

'But you've forgotten it again?'

'Completely. Just as children forget their mother tongue if they stop speaking it at an early age.'

Silanus left in a very thoughtful mood. Like his father and Marcia, Kaeso was a past-master at the 'lie pious'.

❈ CHAPTER ❈
8

Silanus' *familia* had been busy throughout the day of the IV of the Nones of May, scrubbing, polishing and decorating the house. By evening it looked absolutely delightful. There were garlands and wreaths of spring flowers everywhere, and as the emperor was so fond of amber that he had it strewn all over his amphitheatres, it had been scattered here and there, supposedly at random. To ward off any bad joke on the part of Cicero, Silanus' art collection, which Nero was likely to want to look at, since he was among other things passionately interested in painting, had been displayed around the area where the dinner would be held, and the critical citrus-wood table had been carefully locked away in the gallery. On his previous visit, at the party Silanus had given when he moved into the villa, the emperor had lingered for half an hour in front of the *Prometheus* of Parrhasios of Ephesus.

This famous painting, for which Silanus had paid 7,000,000 sesterces, was particularly brutal in its realism. The artist, taking artistic scrupulousness to a rare degree, had painted Prometheus' torture from life, using a condemned criminal as his model. But whereas the liver of the legendary hero had kept growing again as fast as the vulture gnawed it away, the entrails of the condemned criminal had not been endowed with that marvellous ability. Parrhasios had therefore been obliged to use an inevitably long string of prisoners. The eagle, who was very well trained, had stuck to his task and had indeed got better at it each time. However, Parrhasios, who had died nearly five hundred years earlier, was principally famous for his effeminate erotic male figures.

Yet again the head chef at the Palace had been asked about the emperor's tastes. Had they changed recently? Doubtless Nero still liked the rarest delicacies, but his taste for diet foods was expanding with his artistic ambitions. Hence his more and more marked penchant for any vegetable with a definable virtue. He ate dishfuls of blood-cleansing dead-nettles and tall health-giving elecampanes (the endless consumption of which had helped that old reprobate the empress Livia to reach the age of eighty-six). He browsed on houseleeks to make the tone of his voice bright. Unfortunately, as he ate these diet foods on top of his already extraordinary standard food, he was getting fatter and fatter.

Early in the day Silanus' chef had sent his assistants on the rounds of the city markets to buy up all the finest and most therapeutic vegetables. The choice was staggering. The Romans, being peasants at heart, still clung to a mass of wild plants, while at the same time experienced horticulturists were developing and perfecting new species and varieties every day. It was of course in spring that the competition between wild and domesticated vegetables was at its keenest in the markets. It was then that both types were particularly sought after, because at the end of the winter everybody was dying for something fresh.

There were displays of delicious little beans, turnips, swedes, carrots, horseradish and radishes, celeriac, beetroot, caraway, salsify, Egyptian beans, fennel, onions, shallots, garlic, sow-thistles, and bulbs of gladiolus, asphodel, wild orchid, star of Bethlehem and scilla, all of which were deadly poison if eaten in large quantities.

The Romans were also very fond of all the young spring growth on plants and bushes, if cut before the leaves opened: wild and garden asparagus shoots, of which the market-gardeners of Ravenna grew such splendid specimens that you needed only three to the pound, delicate little shoots of broccoli and baby gourds, samphire, broom-rape, convolvulus, wild strawberry, hop vine and cardoon; tender shoots of ruscus, white and black bryony, fig and vine.

There were also eryngium leaves, lettuces, dandelions, chicory, cucumbers, endives, garden cress and watercress, purslane, water parsnips, fenugreek, mallow, celery, spinach-beet, orach, amaranth, patience-dock, sorrel, mustard, nettles, heliotrope, bugloss, plantains, giant fennel, marsh-mallow, elm buds and a dozen different types of cabbage.

After a shopping expedition of that kind, Silanus' kitchens looked like a kitchen garden. The emperor would have plenty to choose from.

As the guest list was more selective than had been expected, it had been decided not to put out the *triclinia*. A single *sigma*, comfortably stuffed, had been set out in the upper garden.

Towards evening Tigellinus' police had politely presented themselves to check that the dinner would take place in complete safety, and had gone away satisfied. The garden was well enclosed, out of sight and out of bowshot – with a sufficiently flexible bow a trained assassin could transfix his victim from a considerable distance.

After an idyllic and confident start to the reign, relations between the emperor and the majority of the Senate had begun to deteriorate six years previously, and after another three years had become frankly bad. Tigellinus was constantly on the watch for an assassination attempt. So security measures had been strengthened, and the emperor, who had become more and more fearful, was now unwilling to run the slightest risk. Like Tiberius he tried to discourage plots, or rather to prevent such plots being carried out, by constantly moving around within and outside the city. As far as possible Tigellinus would even prepare various potential programmes and Nero would select one at the last moment. Contacts between sovereign and ordinary people, previously so frequent, had been reduced to the indispensable. And in the palace porticoes carefully-angled mirrors, designed to reassure the emperor that there was no one behind him as he walked, had made an incongruous appearance. (They were to prove incapable of saving the life of Domitian.)

When they withdrew, the police left a cordon of the Praetorian Guard spread out around the villa. This could mean one of two things to passers-by: either the emperor was visiting, or the owner was in the process of committing suicide. A dozen German guardsmen were posted in the atrium, together with a few trusted gladiators, including Ti. Claudius Spiculus, Nero's favourite bodyguard. A group of inspectors and food tasters stayed behind in the kitchens. Since the death of Claudius his adoptive son had become very mistrustful of mushrooms, and they were not allowed on the menu when he dined with friends. These treacherous items of food could still be found out of season, either dried or preserved in oil.

Just as night was falling, the Prince and his retinue – without Vatinius – arrived from the Palatine, shortly after Paul. Decimus, Marcia and Kaeso received them in the brightly lit atrium. Nero showed his *savoir-vivre* by pretending not to recognize Marcia and Kaeso.

Decimus introduced Paul as follows:

'Cn. Pompeius Paulus is an eminent doctor who specializes in miracle cures. He has just saved the life of my future adoptive son. I was determined that you should meet him, because I hold your good health even more dear than that of my close relatives.'

'A true Roman citizen at last!'

Everyone laughed at the Prince's little quip. Paul was in fact the only person present draped in a toga, and it did not suit him at all. Among friends the emperor liked loose-fitting Greek clothes, without even a belt, and his companions followed his example. Silanus and Kaeso, being in their own house, wore simple tunics.

Nero went on:

'And a true Roman matron, exactly like her statue! You see, Silanus, I took the trouble to find out one or two things before I came, so as not to be short of a compliment. May I congratulate you on making such a good match. You could have married an aristocrat who was only too capable of looking after herself, such as your sister Silana, but a woman like that would only have caused you trouble and obliged me to scold you. You wisely preferred discretion, modesty and decency.'

'I only remarried out of regard for you, Caesar!'

'And I'll bet that it's also out of regard for me that you're preparing to adopt a young man of such obscure birth but so very handsome.'

'You guessed right.'

'We left Vatinius in a low dive with awful toothache. The inevitable consequence of so much poison passing through his mouth. You're quite right not to want him in your house, and especially right to tell me so so frankly. To princes frankness is a sign of a clear conscience . . . or of the most profound dissimulation. It's a quality both you and Vatinius cultivate.'

The reference to Silana opened up a still unhealed wound.

In the second year of the reign, nine years earlier, Decimus' sister had tried to avenge her two dead brothers by conspiring with Domitia, Nero's surviving aunt, to bring various potentially fatal accusations against Agrippina, and had nearly succeeded in causing her untimely death. Seneca and Burrhus, by their impartial inquiry, had just saved her life. Silana was extremely rich, had neither children nor morals, and was already past her prime at the time. During the reign of Claudius she had bought herself C. Silius, who was reputedly the handsomest man in Rome, but had then lost him to Messalina. It was as a result of this latter intrigue that Silius and his imperial mistress had eventually met their deaths. As Nero was ostensibly reconciled with his mother, he sent Silana into exile. After the murder of Agrippina she had come back to live near Rome but had died before being authorized to return to the city itself.

Nero dumped the case containing his precious cithara into the arms of Vespasian, as though to reproach him for his lack of sensitivity to music. They went to take a look at the furniture, chatting as they strolled. Then they went into the cloakroom to put on their *syntheses*, went up into the garden and stretched out on the vast *sigma*. The emperor was naturally at the top end, followed by Marcia, Kaeso, Silanus, Petronius, Nerva, Vitellius, Otho, Vespasian, Titus and Domitian, with Paul modestly placed at the bottom. As the *sigma* was a segment of a circle, the apostle thus found himself lying opposite Nero, with the serving tables in between them.

With his blue, rather unfocused gaze – as yet unclouded by the effects of drink – Nero looked at Paul with curiosity. Kaeso felt he ought to make a supplementary introduction:

'Paulus, who is a Roman citizen of the old school, is Jewish by religion.'

'Poppaea and Acte are sympathetic to the Jews. It must be the only feeling they have in common apart from love for myself. I myself am favourably disposed towards them. Those in Palestine are rather unruly but the rest more or less give satisfaction. Seneca once told me that the rabbis maintained that a single god was responsible for creating and organizing the universe. An interesting idea. We could add this god to our pantheon as the crowning touch. I don't quite understand why the Jews banish all gods but their own and won't even make the usual sacrifices for form's sake. It really is rather irritating of them to attach more importance to ceremonies than we do ourselves.'

It was in Kaeso's interest that the Christians should have as few difficulties with those in power as possible. He seized the chance to smooth away a potential problem:

'Forgive me, Caesar, for touching on a political problem on a purely private occasion . . .'

'Feel free. I am at the service of the public night and day.'

'Cn. Pompeius Paulus is considered heretical by most rabbis, for obscure theological reasons which it would be out of place to discuss here. In the meantime, Paul's sect has converted numerous Jews, and even, so I'm told, a number of Greeks and Romans, who would accordingly refuse to throw the customary grain of incense into the flames on the altar of Rome and Augustus, should they by chance be called upon to do so. These new converts, whether Jewish, Greek or Roman, should surely, in all justice, enjoy the same dispensation from sacrifices as the orthodox Jews, given that converts to standard Judaism already enjoy it by definition.'

The Emperor addressed Paul.

'Are you a Jew or aren't you?'

'Caesar! I'm a Jew, the son and grandson of a Jew. I come of stock going back to the founding of the Jews. I'm even more Jewish than Abraham, since my doctrine assimilates the whole Jewish tradition, brings it to its natural fulfilment and extends it.'

'That's your opinion. But Kaeso tells us that most rabbis look on you as a renegade.'

'Because they are blind men in the land of the blind.'

'Put yourself in my place for a moment. Isn't it up to the majority of the Jews to define who is and is not a Jew? If your brothers reject you, what can I do about it? If you're to benefit from the dispensation on sacrifices, you should make it up with the other rabbis. What is your sect called?'

'I am a Christian.'

The name seemed to ring a bell with Nero.

'Tigellinus told me that the Chief Rabbi in Rome has complained about the Christians. He claims that they ignore the laws of the Empire, despise its customs and manners, and even stir up troubles. Some of them have apparently got themselves worked up to the point where they imagine that the great Stoic conflagration, which Seneca has wisely predicted as coming after the end of my reign, will in fact happen in the near future. It is not healthy to go around predicting catastrophes. If they're slow to come, there's a danger that somebody will give them a helping hand, don't you think?'

'As God is my witness, you have been misinformed. The Christians may have their own customs and manners, but in my writings I myself encourage them to respect the laws. Rather than wanting to stir up trouble, they pray every day for the welfare of the Empire and of your august self.

As for the end of the world which you mention, it's true that our Holy Scriptures allude to it, though without any precise date. Those who suppose that it's close at hand are going beyond what is written in the texts and cannot claim the support of anyone in authority in my sect. Like all rational people, I personally think that the end of the world is not necessarily going to happen tomorrow, and that your reign, which began under such favourable auspices, will finish even better than it began. The Christians will work to that end wholeheartedly.'

'Be that as it may, only true Jews have the right to be dispensed. If the majority of them convert to Christianity, then there won't be a problem.'

Nero turned away to talk to Marcia. The incident was over. Paul gave Kaeso a grateful look, although his well-meant intervention had not got them anywhere. It was obvious that, the way things were going, the Christians would never get the precious dispensation.

The Emperor was praising the pictures which decorated the verdant scene of the festivities. Marcia herself had supervised the placing of the lighting, which was intended to show the paintings to their best advan-

431

tage, and Silanus had decided how far away they were to be from the observers at the sigma.

'The way you have set out the pictures shows the eye of the true art lover,' said Nero. 'A given light will have a positive or negative effect on a given painting, and each painting will have been intended to be seen at its best at a particular distance. People are too inclined to forget the fact.'

The first course was no less appreciated. On an immense platter the chef had arranged a vast mosaic of sea food and small fresh vegetables, representing Phoebus Apollo in his chariot, a delicate allusion to the mythological splendour of the Emperor.

As usual, conversation revolved around aesthetic and artistic questions, and around Nero's successes and ambitions in these areas, which were the only things which really interested him. The courtiers had plenty of choice when it came to flattery.

Nero, the new Apollo, had driven chariots round the track at the Circus Vaticanus, which had been closed to the public for the occasion. Nero, the new Hercules, had almost strangled a lion in his imperial embrace – but the event had been cancelled when they could not find an animal docile enough. Nero had written religious poetry, improvised plays, lyric, erotic and satirical verse, and dramatic poems and tragedies such as *The Bacchants* and *The Mutilation of Attis*. Nero had written music and songs, some of which had become popular, an unmistakable sign of their composer's talent. But he was passionately interested in the old legends of Troy, and had concentrated his efforts principally on a long epic poem in honour of the Trojan War, the *Troica*, where the young shepherd Paris played the main role. It was his ambition to give Rome a new *Aeneid*, which would have served as a sort of preface to the Virgilian epic. In the figure of this Paris, a charming sensualist, sporting and carefree, as cruel as Achilles, as devious as Ulysses, part plebeian, part dandy, the emperor portrayed his own predecessor and model. The work was nearing completion, but the poet was having terrible difficulties with the burning of Troy. For Nero's nature, rich as it was in both Apollonian and Dionysiac qualities, a complex mixture of the classical and the baroque, was not well-equipped to conjure up such a scene. The requisite dash, grandiloquence, and exuberance went very unhappily with the pursuit of the rare and precious word, the elegant expression and the sophisticated turn of phrase. The more the writer sweated over it, the more the fire had the air of an exercise. Nero was well aware of the fact, and his disappointment had become a source of almost obsessive concern.

Fortunately there was always his talent as an actor and singer to distract him from these Cyclopean labours. Before a carefully selected audience the emperor took a keen delight in acting in plays by Euripides, his favourite tragedian, or by Seneca, with a mask which reproduced his own features or those of his beloved Poppaea, for he liked playing women as well as men. He was also prepared to hazard himself in mimes and even in comedies. But though declaiming gave him a thrill, it was singing, to his own accompaniment on the cithara, that he liked best of all. After lessons with the famous Terpnos he had even reached the point of seeing himself as a professional citharist. His great ambition was to sing passages from his *Troica* to a vast public dumbstruck with admiration. Sculpture, painting and architecture were all secondary in his eyes.

Petronius, Nerva and Silanus all took an authoritative part in the discussion. Otho and Marcia prudently confined themselves to paraphrasing points they were certain they had understood. Vitellius made the odd joke, Vespasian, without Vatinius to get at him, did not dare open his mouth. Titus yawned quietly, and Domitian devoted himself to one of his favourite pastimes, which his biographers were to be so unreasonable and unkind as to hold against him. His right hand would suddenly stretch out and catch a fly, the fingers of his left hand would carefully remove its wings, and the insect, bewildered by its changed condition, would crawl about until a sharp tap put an end to its uncertainties. Biographers who are in favour of gladiatorial games might have the decency to put up with the martyrdom of flies without complaining.

It was clear that Nero was the only one who took art seriously. Nerva pretended to, and even for Petronius and Silanus it was only one source of pleasure among many.

The emperor's isolation was sad and gave grounds for concern over the future of the regime. In the Hellenized East, where art was one of the reasons for living, no dynasty had yet dared to give it pride of place in the State. And now, here in Rome, where art was hardly more than an external sign of being very rich, a sovereign was concentrating his ambitions on it. There was a danger that the marital incompatibility between a ruler who was a born artist and a Senate of antique-dealers might end in a *crime passionel*. According to the most deep-seated Roman traditions Nero was a monster of bad taste, since enlightened taste consisted in treating art as of secondary importance.

Kaeso was acutely aware of the split and the potential drama. As he remained silent, Nero asked him:

'What about you? You've hardly said anything up to now. What's your

433

opinion on the question: should the artist work for an élite or for the masses?'

'In the first place I don't think that it's work if it's pleasure. As a divine reward for his genius, the true artist is the only man guaranteed against the burden of mere work. Artists are like gods. The gods don't work, do they?'

'Well said. An excellent reason why I should feel even more divine than I had supposed. What then?'

'I think, Caesar, that the question is a misconceived one. Philosophy, whose job it is to tell us about the nature of Beauty, Justice and Truth, tells us that where we find the first two we shall also find the third. But pure art is a domain in which, by definition, notions like justice and truth have no place. An action which is just and true will always be beautiful, whereas a beautiful statue is neither true nor just: it's beautiful in itself, independent of all criteria which are not of an artistic nature.

The point of this banal introduction is to recall that art is logically part of a vicious circle, and nothing can break the curse, since in aesthetic matters the criteria of judgement are themselves borrowed from aesthetics. So that art is both judge and defendant in the same case. As a result it's impossible to lay down unquestionable rules for what is beautiful and what is ugly.

In consequence the approval of either an élite or the masses will never tell us anything about the quality of a work. In a situation of this sort the connoisseur may be as mistaken as the man-in-the-street. In the total absence of fixed criteria, given that all judgements have only individual value, all appreciation will be capable of endless qualification.

Doubtless on the basis of our anatomy and physiology, and the awareness we have of them, one might determine rules of harmony outside which a work of art would run counter to universal common sense. But such rules would lay down what one should avoid. They would have nothing to say about how to create a masterpiece.

So the artist finds himself condemned to a solitude which is both his curse and the source of his grandeur. As a social being and an altruist he ardently seeks human contacts and wants to be understood and liked by the greatest possible number of people. But he soon realizes the vanity of such a quest. When he's not understood, he's in despair: when he's favourably received, he's aware that this confirmation isn't enough to allay his misgivings, which are all the more painful the more talented and scrupulous he is.

You, divine citharist, are in the most unhappy position ever faced by any artist in the history of mankind. Many mediocre artists take comfort in the enthusiasm of their audiences. But the enthusiasm of *your* audiences is worth even less to you than the equivalent would be to your rivals. When your verses and your singing are praised, how can you ever tell whether it's the emperor or his work which is being applauded?

You could take refuge in a deep forest and play only to the wild animals. But the gods must have something else in store for you. If they have given an emperor the genius which they normally bestow on ordinary mortals, there can only be one explanation for their whim. They want you to surpass yourself. They're hoping that, for the first time ever, the sincerity and unanimity of the audience's delighted response may constitute a criterion of truth in this shifting ground where no such criteria have previously existed.'

Nero was impressed by this very sensible speech, finishing on such a perceptive piece of flattery. After a moment's silence he said:

'Despite your youth you talk about art as well as Petronius does, and you understand the true nature of the problem. Yes, I'm very unlucky and can only escape my lot by surpassing myself. Thank you for telling me so so clearly.'

At this point Vitellius cut in: 'The Roman concept of art is that it should be a permanent vehicle of education at the service of the State. And it's only too true that there's no unquestionable rule for distinguishing beauty and ugliness. However, art must do its job. To get out of this impasse there's a simple solution, which is particularly appropriate given that the majority of Romans are totally indifferent to artistic problems. Let the Emperor lay down once and for all what's beautiful and what's ugly, and all those who disagree can be thrown to the lions.'

'Then I'll start by laying down what you can and can't eat, you great philistine,' cried Nero.

After the first course came fish which the chef had amused himself by disguising as vegetables. Then came a third course of meat disguised as fish.

The Emperor noticed Paul and asked him:

'What are the aesthetic views of the Jews?'

'Just the same as everyone else's, Caesar. Neither the Jews nor the Christians will ever cause you any trouble on that score.'

'What do you mean by that?'

'That the difficulty of Justice and Truth already gives us so much difficulty that we've no time for the moment to bother ourselves about aesthetics. As far as we're concerned you can go ahead and follow Vitellius' advice. You give us your definition of beauty, and we'll put it at the top of our Creed. We can always change the paragraph from reign to reign.'

Nero frowned, as though he found this accommodating attitude suspect.

'So when it comes to it, you're not interested in beauty as such?'

'On the contrary, we feel such respect for it that we're waiting for it to be precisely defined before we take an interest in it. Isn't that wise? And isn't it a form of wisdom guaranteed to assure the tranquillity of governments?'

'What with Vitellius, the Jews and the Christians,' sighed Nero, 'I'm well set up for artistic support.'

Marcia remarked: 'Everyone knows that the Jews are so far from any interest in formal beauty that they condemn all representations of the human body, and violently attack masterpieces of painting and sculpture. I'm sure that left to their own devices the Christians too would be quick to destroy paintings and statues.'

As Paul said not a word, under Kaeso's amused gaze, Nero asked him:

'You heard the charge. What's your answer?'

Paul was extremely put out. He invoked the Holy Spirit, but for once it offered him no decent escape-hole.

Eventually he said:

'For religious reasons the Jews won't allow statues in their own buildings, but they don't attack other people's statues. The Christians take the same line as the Jews, but in a more adaptable form, to take into account the sensibilities of new converts. What shocks Christians is not sculpture or painting in general, but the fact of worshiping a god in a material and not a spiritual form. That is why we continue to hope, as Kaeso told you just now, that your justice and kindness will grant us the same dispensation as the Jews have.'

When the desserts came, and the chef's imagination surpassed itself, the wine-jugs had been filled with crushed ice. The excellent wines liberally imbibed since the hors-d'oeuvres had put everyone in an amiable and jolly mood.

Impishly Kaeso threw the ball back to Paul:

'I think you're dodging the issue. Caesar and Marcia asked you what would happen to the statues in Rome if the city became Christian. Would you destroy any and if so which?'

Paul threw Kaeso a pained look of reproach and replied with eminent subtlety:

'In a Christian Rome the Emperor himself would be Christian, and it's not my habit to discuss the Prince's decisions.'

They all laughed at this neat evasion, Nero more than anyone.

'I promise you,' he said, 'that the day I become a Christian I'll destroy all the statues of myself. But it'll take a long time, because there are so many.'

Silanus, who was in the habit of sniffing out potential dangers a mile off, was not at all pleased with the turn the conversation had taken. Whatever the curative gifts, real or supposed, of this Paul, he was a compromising fellow and Kaeso had been unwise to take up with him. It was time for a diversion.

The master signalled to a freedman who was acting as master-of-ceremonies, and gave him discreet instructions to increase the percentage of wine in the blend in the jugs, to leave the lights around the paintings but reduce the light around the *sigma* a little, and to bring on the fortune-teller whom he had been keeping in reserve in case she was needed. The Emperor liked his hosts not to bring on entertainments between courses: wasn't he there to provide those himself, if the fancy took him? But despite his chronic artistic jealousy, not even Nero could see a fortune-teller as a rival.

In the dimmed light, which had something unsettling and mysterious about it, the woman appeared. She was thin, dressed in black, with a swarthy skin, jet-black hair and eyes. It was impossible to guess her age: it was as if the gift of second sight had placed her outside time. This Melania, a native of Mauretania Tingitana, had an outstanding reputation and was in enormous demand. Instead of working with a huge paraphernalia of accessories, she simply read the lines in people's hands.

The Emperor, who already knew her, graciously presented her with his palm, and said: 'Do as you usually do. Don't tell me the truth unless you can see something nice.'

Melania scrutinized the august hand for a long time and said: 'You still have years ahead of you which will seem long and you'll be regretted by the *populus* when you die.'

'Can you tell me the name of anyone who truly loves me?'

'There are at least two: Egloge and Alexandria.'

This statement raised a few murmurs. They were the names of the prince's old nurses.

Nero impatiently withdrew his hand. 'Try someone else. You aren't telling me anything I don't already know.'

The woman looked at Marcia's hand, let it go without saying anything, passed on to Kaeso, then Silanus, still without a word, tried Petronius, still said nothing, then arrived at Nerva . . .

'Good news at last. You'll be emperor, but only when you're very old. You'll only see the purple for long enough to have yourself buried in it.'

As Nerva was all of eleven years older than Nero, the news inspired sinister reflections. Nerva hurriedly removed his hand and shrugged his shoulders, taking those present as witness to the implausibility of the prediction. There was nothing to suggest that Nerva, who was an amusing dilettante, was destined for such an honour. He was of course related to the Julio-Claudians, but quite distantly so, and his fidelity to the Emperor, who had heaped rewards on him, was not in doubt.

Nero himself hastened to reassure Nerva, who was finding it difficult to get over the incident.

Melania looked at Vitellius' hand, and lingered over it doubtfully, as if hesitating as to whether or not she should speak.

She finally announced: 'You too will be emperor.'

Vitellius sniggered. He was twice Nero's age, he was one of the senators most closely associated with the present regime, and his family's title was a fairly recent creation.

Otho was hanging back, so Vitellius took his hand and presented it to the fortune-teller, with a cry of: 'What about Otho here? Is he going to be an emperor too and make up the threesome?'

The woman studied the palm of the dissipated Otho and declared: 'I shall make you laugh again. Even Otho will be emperor.'

The atmosphere had relaxed a little at the revelation concerning Vitellius. Now it relaxed completely. Otho was hardly older than Nero, and no one took him seriously. His greatest claim to glory was that he had praised his wife's charms to the prince until Nero succumbed. His greatest error lay in supposing that he still had a husband's rights after the flattering event.

Melania, who was most put out, took no notice of Vespasian and made as if to withdraw. The latter, full of curiosity, held out his palm, and soon the visionary declared yet again: 'Here's a fourth emperor.'

There was an explosion of funny quips. Vespasian was a dull, cautious soldier of fifty-five who did not seem at all a likely candidate for the job. But when Titus and Domitian were also in turn credited with the purple, the general merriment turned into hysteria. With Nero, surely that made seven emperors round the table?

Nero, who was in tears of laughter, dried his eyes on a napkin and asked Melania: 'Can you tell us which out of all this lot is to succeed me?'

438

The answer was some time coming.

'Can't you tell? Or are you keeping the answer to yourself?'

'Master, your successor is not here.'

'Will he be a child of my own blood?'

'I see your successor in Spain.'

'Then it must be Galba, who's all of sixty and a complete nonentity!'

'I don't know. Show me his hand and I'll tell you.'

'In the meantime don't forget to look at the hand of Paulus. All we need is a Jewish emperor.'

Paul did not dare refuse his hand. The woman looked at it particularly carefully.

'There's more here than eight emperors!'

And suddenly Melania fell back on to the fine gravel path, screaming and foaming at the mouth, a prey to a fit of hysteria or epilepsy. Amid her random mutterings were recurrent snatches, phrases and whole passages from the most striking of Cicero's speeches, from the famous '*Quousque tandem Catilina . . .?*' to '*O audaciam immanem*' from the Second Philippic. The phenomenon was extremely bizarre in a fortune-teller from the edge of the desert, who spoke only popular Latin.

The distressing impression left by this scene was made still worse by Paul's efforts to exorcise the unexpected demon by crying: 'Leave this woman, foul fiend, in the name of the Son of the Virgin!'

After a few last spasms, the possessed woman fainted away, relaxed, and Silanus hurriedly ordered his slaves to spirit away the heap of black rags, which had already done its worst.

So calm was restored, but the guests were still in a state of shock, as they called for fresh draughts of wine and chatted in low tones. Petronius, whose self-possession, as a result of his robust scepticism, was remarkable, was the first to raise his voice. He asked Paul:

'You sometimes take on the job of calming down lunatics. How do you explain the fact that certain people have a gift for predicting future events, some of which do in fact come true? After all, Otho may very well one of these days become emperor of the Ethiopians or the Iazyges. And how, too, do you account for the fact that a madwoman can quote texts which she doesn't know, in a literary language which is also unknown to her?'

Paul being at a loss for an answer, Kaeso replied for him:

'Since I first met you at Baiae, Petronius, you've lost none of your presence of mind. These facts are inexplicable in a universe where the gods are subject to Chronos. Such gods couldn't know the future, since

439

like us they would be prisoners of time. But the Jewish god whose authority Paul acknowledges creates time and space the way he would grow beetroot. He's capable of anything and everything. Consequently he knows the future as well as the past and the present. The gift of the fortune-teller is therefore a provisional and partial participation in divine omniscience – or in the knowledge of the Devil, since the Jewish Satan must know as much as their god about these matters.'

'What an ingenious hypothesis! You more or less prove the existence of the transcendent god which some philosophers have already hypo-thesized, on the basis of the indirect evidence of the dual vision possessed by the creatures he has created, be they holy or demonic?'

'Can you think of a better explanation?'

'I shouldn't even care to try. I haven't practised philosophy among graceful ephebes. I'm just a short-sighted Roman.'

A few voices began timidly to ask Nero to sing. Marcia was particularly pressing:

'Please don't hang back any longer. After that rather unnerving interlude we need to be charmed, and my stepson and I have never had the good fortune to hear you. We're anxious to find out whether your reputation hasn't been exaggerated. The crowd of base flatterers who besiege you couldn't tell a cithara from an oboe.'

It was an unanswerable argument. Nero was dying to sing. He sat on the edge of the *sigma*, carefully took his cithara out of its case and its protective cover, and tuned it.

Modern composers had brought to the large concert cithara a great number of technical improvements and harmonic refinements, but for intimate evening parties the emperor preferred the instrument used by intransigent purists, the antique seven-string lyre as used by Terpander. Its very limited possibilities showed off the finger skills of the virtuoso. Disdaining to use a tortoise-shell plectrum, Nero played his seven-string instrument with just his fingers, with his nails cut very short. In com-petitions cithara playing was divided into two separate classes – with or without a plectrum – because the effect of the two techniques was so different.

Marcia murmured to the artist:

'You have, I hope, noticed the salad of houseleeks at the end of the third course? We were thinking of your voice.'

'There's nothing I could find more touching than such thoughtfulness. Would you like me to give you a piece from my *Dominicum*?' (The emperor's most highly praised poems had been made into a collection under that name.)

'Why not an excerpt from this *Troica* which you've been hiding up your sleeve all this time, keeping us on tenterhooks?'

'There are a lot of verses in it still to be polished. My burning of Troy isn't going at all well.'

'You can sometimes ruin a work by trying to make it too good. It seems to me that a fire in particular should only be half-polished.'

'You may be right,' said Nero with a laugh. 'So be it.'

Raising his voice so that everyone could hear he said:

'At Marcia's request I'm going to sing you a passage from my *Troica* for the first time. I have to confess that Terpnos gave me a few suggestions about the music.'

When the cries of ecstatic thanks had died down, the imperial voice rang out to the accompaniment of the imperial lyre. The singer's voice, which was a little indistinct, had a pleasant sweetness but lacked fullness of tone. It seemed more suited to performing to a gathering of friends than at a public concert. One could see why the Emperor hesitated to hazard himself on a vast stage. But at least the voice was well-pitched and had evidently been the object of careful preparation. The cithara technique was in any case excellent. The touch was perfect in its precision and showed exquisite refinements of effect, and the sound closely matched the singing.

But it was the poetry which was the strong point of the performance. After a baroque period Nero had more or less come back to the demands of a Vergilian classicism. The result was astonishingly harmonious verse. One was instinctively aware that every word had been chosen, carefully weighed, its placing considered, to obtain the maximum effect.

Kaeso, who was more sensitive to the poetry itself than to the music or the singing, reflected that it was a great misfortune and a great risk for so talented a poet to have become emperor. If Nero came to a bad end, and his very name was cursed as Caligula's was, what would survive of all his works? Perhaps the emperor was secretly afraid of the same thing. In his implacable efforts to stay on his throne and wipe out all possible rivals, in his frenzied desire to assure the succession for a child by Poppaea, the will to save his verses from oblivion must play a large part.

From time to time Nero slid a murderous look at young Domitian, who had quietly captured a large fly. His father dug the boy in the ribs, and the fly limped away, spinning on its one wing.

The poet struck a last chord and looked modestly at his feet. His face showed the genuine anguish of the creator waiting for the reactions of his public. It was not easy to give any genuine reassurance to a man con-

441

demned to express his talent in conditions so false and artificial. It was in the interests of flattery to live at close quarters with genius.

After the obligatory silence, which was thought to convey ecstasy, everyone weighed in with their own compliments and comments.

Nero had just sung of the deceptive peace which had brought reassurance to the Trojans after the false departure of the Greeks. It was a peace which was the harbinger of the general destruction of Troy by fire, and the beauty of one verse was particularly striking:

COLLA CYTHERIACAE SPLENDENT AGITATA COLUMBAE

(The neck(s) of Aphrodite's dove gleam(s) in motion)

The adjective, subtly placed at the caesura, referred forward to the final genitive in a flight of musical sonorities, set off by an elision, and all the suppleness of Latin grammar had been used to profit in the ordering of the words.

Petronius and Nerva, discreet occasional collaborators on the *Troica*, found it difficult to praise the author without praising themselves, but the others did not have the same motive for restraint. The most competent comments were those of Silanus. They seemed to have an effect on the emperor.

Vespasian, who did not know what to say, stupidly asked: 'Were there doves with more than one neck in Trojan mythology?' His naïvety raised a roar of laughter. His family were not of senatorial rank and his education had been rather neglected.

Nero patiently explained: 'Nowadays it's poetic licence, in Latin poetry, to employ a plural instead of a singular to give greater weight to the expression. "Colla agitata" is thus put for "moving neck". And don't make fun of this faithful soldier, the rest of you. It's not ignorance which is shameful, it's the refusal to learn.'

Kaeso broke in. 'The use of the plural here seems to me all the more effective and significant in that it reminds one of the Greek philosophical maxim "You can't step into the same river twice". Here the brilliance of the feathers is, like the flowing water, the result of a host of movements. What difference is there between saying "the water of a river" and "the waters of a river"? In the same way the bird's neck gleams all the brighter for the constant motion. It's the close succession of images which produces the impression of brightness, and basically there is a separate neck in each of those images. It's wonderfully closely observed.'

Nero was enchanted by the remark, and in recompense he started singing and playing again, while his audience got down to drinking. The poet took great care of his condition, and rarely let himself get drunk. His audience too took good care not to overstep the limit. Truth lives at the bottom of an amphora, and not all truth is best seen naked.

At the end of a charming little piece taken from his *Dominicum*, the emperor took a brief rest and drank a cup of chilled wine. Then, as Domitian was searching around for a compliment, Nero offered him one: 'If I were you, I should say: "Caesar, your singing is so beautiful that it makes the very wings fall off the flies. Even Orpheus didn't go that far."'

Domitian blushed bright red. Vespasian and Titus looked for a hole to crawl into.

It was very characteristic of the emperor to postpone his vengeance if something was done to offend him.

And the singing started up again, in an unfailing flow, to this circle of friends, most of whom were thinking of something else altogether ...

❧ CHAPTER ❧
9

As the emperor was afraid that the cool night air might damage his voice, the assembled company had retired into the drawing-room, where they continued their drinking and conversation, but in scattered groups. Nero, who was very slightly tipsy, had spread himself out on the sofa cushions, between Marcia and Kaeso. Petronius formed another group with Nerva and Silanus. Vitellius was talking to Otho, and Paul to Vespasian and his sons.

Vitellius said in Otho's ear: 'It's nearly time for the big speech about Agrippina. As Marcia and Kaeso haven't heard it before, Ahenobarbus will surpass himself.'

Pursued by the furies of remorse, Nero was indeed in the habit, at the end of banquets, of referring to his mother, if he felt himself at all among friends on whom he could rely. And of course what came out was not the official version but the truth, in so far as one can expect the truth at all from a creative artist who is permanently preoccupied with performance and effect.

With his hands over his eyes, Nero murmured: 'It's at night that she visits me and reiterates her cruel reproaches. If I'm asleep, it's a nightmare, and if I'm awake, the memory is even more cruel. It's too, too utterly unbearable!'

Kaeso, who was slightly drunk himself, asked:

'Who are you talking about?'

'Who else could I be talking about but my mother? I had a mother, and I had her killed.'

'You must have had a good reason.'

'You're talking like a child. Could anyone ever have a good reason for killing his mother? Can you think of one?'

'Agrippina herself, so they say, was responsible for the deaths of a lot of people, sometimes for no particular reason.'

'Yes, indeed she was ... L. Silanus, for a start, whom she falsely accused of incest with his sister Calvina. Agrippina wanted to get Octavia's fiancé out of the way so as to make sure that I could have the hand of that unfortunate princess. Then she drove Lollia to her death, on the pretext of having supposedly consulted Chaldean magicians, but her only crime was having nearly married Claudius. Then she attacked Calpurnia and left her with nothing but her life, just because she was jealous of her beauty. Then she arranged the death of Statilius Taurus so that she could get her hands on his gardens. Then she had my poor aunt Domitia Lepida, of whom I was very fond, accused of sacrilegious magic, and the consequence was her death. She was afraid that that particular relative might have more influence over me than she herself did. Then she poisoned Claudius to get me the throne. Then there was the stupid murder of M. Silanus in Asia. Thanks to my mother I came to the throne weighed down with crimes for which I was not responsible. I make no mention of her scandalous affair with the freedman Pallas, which lingers in everyone's memory ... But was all that a good enough reason for killing her?'

'You had better ones later, I believe.'

'Agrippina certainly wanted for herself the power which she'd worked so hard to put in my hands. She was the most authoritarian woman who ever lived. While she was alive I was just a puppet in her hands. She claimed the right to make every decision and run everything. Was that a good enough motive?'

'Power cannot be divided. But I think there was something else too ...'

Nero fixed Kaeso with a haggard look, turned to Marcia, then back to Kaeso, and said, lowering his voice:

'Yes, there was something else. When Agrippina realized that I was trying to get out of her grasp, she threw her last weapon into the balance against me. I soon realized with horror that she was planning incest as a worthy final touch to the edifice of her crimes. And how could I have stood out against her advances? Ye gods, how beautiful she was! To put it in a nutshell, I had her killed so as not to give in to the temptation.'

The relevation was a surprising one, and guaranteed to have an effect on Kaeso, who said:

'There you have all my sympathy. How else could you escape from the attentions of a mother prepared to misuse you like that? It's a fault of an entirely positive nature to kill someone to protect one's virtue. You win the esteem of every critic that way. In your place I don't know whether I would have had the courage, but I certainly wouldn't have lacked the will.'

'Ah, I can see that you understand me, and that gives me great pleasure.

What courage it took! As always happens when you don't see to something yourself, everything went wrong. After the wreck of the galley which should have taken her to her doom, Agrippina survived by swimming; and in front of her very eyes her stupid maid Acerronia, who was crying out that she was the emperor's mother in order to get herself saved, was beaten to death with boathooks and oars. It was a horrible way for Agrippina to learn that she was doomed.'

'It was absolutely justified. We should defend ourselves against women who are dead set on enslaving us. There's only one solution for clinging mistresses, possessive wives and lustful mothers: into the water with them all! And if the water isn't enough, a good clout with an oar will finish the job off. If a boy was unlucky enough to sleep with his mother, what freedom would he have to become a man?'

Tearfully Nero threw his arms round Kaeso. They understood one another all the better under the inspiration of alcohol.

The absurdity of this touching scene cut Marcia to the quick, but she could only fret in silence, while the rest of the audience – with the exception of Silanus, who was completely thrown, and Paul, who paid no attention – felt a nascent disquiet and jealousy at the skill with which this boy, who yesterday was still an unknown, had managed to get himself into the emperor's affectionate embrace. It did not occur to them that Kaeso owed his success to his sincerity.

The prince calmed down again and picked up his lyre, but instead of singing, he announced:

'I've made up my mind, and you shall be the first to know. This year will see us in Egypt and Greece. There I shall sing to an audience of connoisseurs, and when I come back, my reputation will ensure that I'm a success in Rome.'

The approval was not as keen or as general as Nero had expected. Petronius, Kaeso and Silanus all preserved a notably embarrassed silence. Nero was aware of the fact and looked questioningly at them.

Petronius, who was all for frankness when he thought it would serve any purpose, ventured to sum up his thoughts in a striking phrase:

'There's nothing to stop you going. But will you come back?'

'What's at the back of your mind?'

'The fear of risks you ought not to run. But they seem so obvious that a young man like Kaeso can describe them to you as well as I could.'

Petronius was quite happy to put Kaeso in the hot seat instead of himself, with the possibility of disavowing his opinions if he said something stupid. And if he spoke the truth, the emperor's disappointment would rebound on him, not on Petronius.

Silanus signalled to Kaeso to keep quiet, but he took no notice. 'What I fear, Caesar, is that you'll be chasing a dream. It will take much more than the approval of the Greeks to teach the uneducated Roman *plebs* to appreciate your singing as it ought to be appreciated. What they'll applaud is you, and they could do that tomorrow. This same *plebs*, who are now so favourable to you, are easily seduced by false rumours. If you're unwise enough to leave for the East, they'll get worried, they'll fear for their food supplies. And your numerous enemies in the Senate will exploit the situation as a way of destroying you. The Senate and people of Rome have a traditional deep-seated mistrust for the East. Your ancestor Antony went there too, but he didn't come back.'

Nobody dared to contradict Kaeso. Nero walked up and down for a moment, then asked Silanus for his advice.

'You know the mentality of those senators who are hostile to me – what do you think?'

'I might also be thought to know the minds of the others as well, seeing that you're in my home among close friends and show sufficient confidence in me to ask the question!'

'Of course. Well?'

'Kaeso has said bluntly what we are all thinking. We're afraid for you, and afraid for ourselves as well, since we've hitched our star to your wagon. I won't deny that a majority of the Senate would prefer another emperor, more heedful of its views and interests. When it comes to it, you know that as well as I do. You ought to take that bias into account and not tempt fate. If you do leave for Greece, you would be wise to take the Senate with you – your friends because they *are* your friends and your enemies so that they can't intrigue behind your back.'

'That's good advice. In that case I can leave you in Rome on your own, because you like and dislike me in equal quantities.'

'It's true that I'm not interested in either flattering or harming you, and you can trust me on both scores.'

The emperor sat down again in some irritation.

Petronius suggested:

'Since Rome isn't ready to hear you, and Corinth is rather too far, why don't you have a trial run in Naples? It's a Greek city and the people there have taste. When Tiberius was on the throne, there was still an *ephebia* on Capri.'

'That's not a bad idea.'

Kaeso made his own suggestion:

'For some time there's been a rumour going around that you're about to leave for the East, and the *plebs* needs reassuring. If you announce officially that you're deferring the trip until better times, they'll be overjoyed, and the schemers in the Senate will be thrown off-balance. It would be to your credit to renounce the plan, but it may as well serve a purpose too.'

'That's not a bad idea either.'

Marcia got up to go to the lavatory, and Nero said to Kaeso in low tones of complicity:

'You have a very seductive stepmother. From the way you reacted when I was talking about my mother just now, I have the feeling we may be brothers in misfortune.'

Kaeso was very disturbed by this remarkable piece of intuition, and made a feeble attempt to defend himself.

'Women like that,' went on Nero dreamily, 'need a master's hand to keep them in order.'

'Unfortunately they're incorrigible.'

'Have you given in?'

'Not yet. I'm doing my utmost to get out of it, but it's not easy.'

'What you need is a galley on which to send her off for a cruise . . .'

'I'm only prince of a very small patch . . .'

At the other end of the room Paul was trying to get a little metaphysical disquiet into the head of Domitian, who, being only thirteen, was a possible convert. Domitian was far from suspecting that thirty years later he would have his cousin Flavius Clemens condemned to death and his wife Flavia Domitilla deported to the island of Pandataria on a charge of Christian 'atheism', and that this Domitilla would give her name to a catacomb, whose ground she had given to her Christian community.

When Marcia got back, the emperor gave Kaeso a friendly tap and got up to go. The relevations that the unfortunate stepson had, with no malice aforethought, given away in confidence had suddenly made Marcia into another Agrippina, in Nero's eyes. It was all there: the dishonourable sleeping around in a shady past, the passion to possess and dominate by whatever means, the combination of a voluptuous body and a proud look. How many men had been entrapped by Agrippina's body before she put out the lures to snare her own son? But in making love with Nero, as with the others, she would only have been thinking of her own ambition. There are women whose natures drive one to despair: the more you learn about them the more you discover that they are impenetrable. You can only really possess them in death.

Kaeso insisted on accompanying Paul back to his lodgings at the Porta Capena, with a little escort of slaves bearing torches. It was the middle of the night, and near the eastern end of the Circus Maximus they kept walking on programmes for the races, containing the list of the horses and chariots which had excited the day's passions. Theatres and amphitheatres also had their programmes. A man would sometimes lend one to a woman sitting next to him as a way of getting to know her. And amid the flotsam of human and racing passions were torn female undergarments, debris from the crazy nocturnal processions and orgies of the Floralia, which had just finished.

Kaeso was rapidly sobering up in the cool night air. He was beginning to regret having made his plaintive confidences to Nero, although he was quite glad to find that someone so famous had undergone the same sort of martyrdom as he had. Only the rebellion of modest sons could set a limit to the lustful ambitions of mothers and stepmothers.

Paul was still dazed at having heard art and aesthetics talked about the whole evening. His ears were still buzzing with Nero's singing and the sound of the lyre. For Kaeso, on the contrary, what was astonishing was the fact that in all the Jewish and Christian scriptures there was no mention of any sort of beauty but moral beauty. They were certainly the last books to get Nero to read.

In front of the house of the Christian Jew at the Porta Capena there was a fountain.

Kaeso said to Paul:

'Isn't it high time you baptized me? I certainly know more about your religion than Christians who can't read or write. At the lavatories in the Forum you yourself told me that one could be a perfect Christian with very little instruction. I've listened to you with patience and interest, I've taken an interest in the future of your sect, I've given you what advice I can, I've shown you Nero as you wanted, and twice at that: as *imperator* in the glory of the *pulvinar*, and in a pleasant relaxed state at my future adoptive father's house. As for my faith, as long as I profess your Creed you're incompetent to judge, and it's in the hands of god alone. So don't keep me hanging around any longer!'

'For a boy of doubtful faith you're in a great hurry.'

'I have my reasons, which are nothing to do with you. I swear they are honourable.'

Paul hesitated.

Despairing of getting what he wanted, Kaeso added: 'I'll make you an honest bargain. If you baptize me, I'll tell you why I wanted to be baptized. If I've sinned, Christ will pardon me through your mouth, for there's a sense in which it's precisely in order to be faithful to your god, as defined by you, that I absolutely must go through this confounded baptism.'

Paul was becoming more and more hesitant. Kaeso saw that he had taken the wrong line and tried to think of a way round it:

'Do Christians baptize their children?'

'Naturally they baptize them if they are about to die, and even before that, since their souls are purer than ours.'

'So baptism has an effect on its own, independent of the predisposition of the person baptized?'

'I can see what you're getting at! Kindly don't compare the innocence of children with the possible wrong motives of a being endowed with reason. Baptism is the sign of the approbation of faith, present or future. It requires innocence in all cases.'

'But I'm as innocent as a lamb! I have no evil intent. On the contrary.'

'Do you have faith?'

Paul was determined to get him to lie. For the sake of peace and quiet Kaeso gave in.

'Yes, I do,' he said. 'What more do you want?'

'Do you believe that Jesus died on the Cross for your sins?'

'I can even believe that he died for my sake alone, and that if God had only created one man he would still have been prepared to come down to earth and die for him. In the eyes of a logical god what difference can there be between a man and hundreds of millions of men? Is God a grocer trading in pardons? Did he decide to have himself crucified when the number of sinners reached twelve, or twenty-four? The Holy Spirit bids me tell you that Jesus would have died to re-open Heaven to Adam and Eve if on leaving their terrestrial Paradise they had been eaten by a crocodile.'

Kaeso had a talent for raising theological issues of the most ridiculous kind.

Paul sighed: 'Jesus did indeed die for the sins of each of us individually. Do you believe in the resurrection?'

On this point it seemed unnecessary to lie.

'What does that matter?'

'I don't think I can have heard you aright.'

'You yourself told me that the resurrection played a very secondary role in your system, such that it could be suppressed without any inconvenience.'

'You're joking! I have said and written: "If Jesus did not rise from the dead, then our faith is in vain."'

'Then you have a bad tendency not to grasp the meaning of the story you're telling.'

'What do you mean?'

'Just think for a moment. Christ's death for our sins re-opens to us the Paradise closed by the sin of Adam and Eve. It serves a purpose. But what purpose does the resurrection serve? It proves to us that Jesus is god and prefigures our own resurrection. But our resurrection was already an article of faith among the Pharisees prior to the birth of Christ. And as for the famous proof, all I have to do is affirm that I don't need that proof in order to believe, and it immediately becomes of no interest whatsoever. Have you understood now, O ye of little faith? I believe Christ died for my sins, whether or not he rose again from the dead.'

Kaeso's logic was terrifying.

Paul, however, retorted: 'Jesus rose again precisely to convince those who didn't have the same faith as you, a faith which you must admit is of a rare kind. The resurrection is a fact, predicted by Jesus himself. You must believe in it, whether or not you need it as a prop to your faith. Is that clear?'

The silhouette of the Circus Maximus was beginning to stand out in the first light of dawn. Kaeso gave in.

'OK, I believe in the resurrection,' he said. 'But I do wonder whether it was a good idea on God's part. It may perhaps persuade a few people to believe, but it will probably dissuade more. But then perhaps that's what your god is aiming at? I get the impression that keeping the company of the Jews for so long has made him mean with his illumination. The resurrection may well become for humanity in general what circumcision is for the Jews: a barrier carefully designed to keep Paradise for an élite. Can't you see the strange contradiction in the theology of your sect? Here's a god who sheds his own blood and who strains his ingenuity to make sure that the proofs of his sacrifice are highly dubious . . .'

'What would become of our free will if even men of little faith were condemned to believe by what was indisputably obvious?'

'There would always be some who prefer the Devil to God, since the fallen angels, who believed in God even more firmly than you do, turned their backs on him.'

'Men are worth more than angels, because it was for mankind that Jesus sacrificed Himself. And true love is never imposed by force.'

Paul made Kaeso kneel by the fountain and baptized him: 'Kaeso, in the name of the Father, the Son and the Holy Ghost.'

Kaeso got up joyfully and asked for a certificate of baptism.

'A certificate? That isn't usual. What would you do with it?'

'It's easy to see that you don't have the Romans' sense of administrative efficiency. Certificates of that sort allow the "priests" to count their sheep. As far as I'm concerned, if one day I want to get myself martyred like Stephen, I absolutely must be able to present the judge with a certificate so that there won't be any judicial error. Can you think of any misuse to which one could put a piece of papyrus of that kind?'

Paul shrugged his shoulders, asked Kaeso to wait a moment, took a large key out of his belt, and prepared to open the house door. It had not been bolted and barred, because he was out.

As he could not manage it, being unused to Roman safety locks, Kaeso gave him a hand. These locks, which were easy once you understood the principle, had the one quality essential in a lock – they were unpickable. The keyhole was considerably offset in relation to the mechanism, which had to be operated by a right-angled key.

Paul soon returned and gave Kaeso a slip of papyrus on which he attested to having baptized 'Kaeso Aponius Saturninus' into the Christian faith on the night of the IV to the III of the Nones of May; and on the instructions of the young man he added 'in the consulship of C. Lecanius Bassus and M. Licinius Crassus Frugi'. Kaeso refrained from telling him that he should have abbreviated his first name, because it was followed by his family name and surname. This failure to observe hallowed custom was of no importance.

It was at this point that Paul reminded him: 'Didn't you promise to confide to me the honourable reasons why you were so anxious to be baptized?'

'Yes, thanks to God and you, I had myself baptized so as not to run the risk of having to sleep with my stepmother.'

'What an extraordinary answer! Did you suppose that baptism would give you a special gift of grace to withstand that particular temptation?'

Kaeso made up his mind to tell Paul all his troubles in detail. Paul had a lot of experience of moral issues and might be able to give him some good advice. But as Kaeso proceeded with his explanation, Paul began to frown.

After some thought he said severely: 'It's difficult for me to condemn you, because the intentions behind your action were praiseworthy. It's not normal to give up a fortune of that size out of self-respect. But I hope you aren't expecting me to congratulate you. You have deceived me shamefully, using all the resources of your education and intelligence. You used baptism into our faith for honest ends, but they are secular ends. You thought only of yourself, and God played no part in your decision.'

'If the Christian god exists,' Kaeso protested, 'I must have been thinking of him subconsciously, because Jesus said to Mark: "Whosoever does God's will is my brother and my sister and my mother." It must be god's will for me to get away from my stepmother's pressing attentions.'

'It's not the will of the Christian God that you should demand baptism without possessing faith.'

'In those circumstances perhaps my baptism is void . . .'

'Your wrongful act is not. If you don't repent, God will punish you.'

'To repent, I should have to have faith. God couldn't reproach me for not believing, since that isn't something for which my will is responsible.'

'God has given you more tokens than many others.'

In his irritation Kaeso let off steam:

'He has indeed sent me your person as a token – and you were responsible for that impious piece of stupidity in your letter to the Romans: "He shows his mercy to those whom he wishes, and He hardens those whom He wishes against him . . . Who in fact can resist His will?" So, by yet another contradiction, but one which seems to lie at the heart of your dubious personal creed, you sometimes assure me that Jesus died for me, and at others that God could capriciously harden me against accepting his grace, thereby damning me in advance. Why shouldn't that be my case? And if it is, you should reproach this god you've invented and not me. I'm only the instrument of his gratuitous malice. Moreover, if god is worse than Nero, and chooses his elect by a throw of the dice, what use is your preaching? You're of no more use than the flies with which Domitian amuses himself.'

'Upon my word, baptism inspires you. You tax me with being contradictory, and your excuse for not believing is that you take exception to a definition of God on the grounds that, in your opinion, it's personal to me.'

'I'm simply saying that if an intelligent man were inclined to believe in the Christian god, the aberrant caricature of him which you give would be enough to put him off. I'd rather be in hell with honest people than in

453

heaven with a god who hardens my heart at will and judges me with no regard to my actions.

Of course, you'll claim yet again that what you said doesn't properly represent what you meant. Just as when you maintain that faith without action is sufficient in itself, whereas James, who knew Christ better than you, affirms the exact opposite.

"Man's vindication lies in his actions and not in faith alone," he writes in the one letter of his I've been able to see. And he goes on: ". . . Wasn't Rahab the prostitute vindicated by her action in taking the messengers in and letting them leave by another way?" James is making it plain to you that foreign prostitutes will be saved by their good works sooner than the sort of people you're so fond of. If ever I come to believe, it won't be your sort of faith. It'll be the sort of faith that James and Mark and even Luke have – and I can't say I find your influence over the latter a particularly good thing.'

'I don't care if you keep your prejudices against me, so long as you acquire a faith like James's. Each man finds his own way to God, and I can't claim to have explored them all.'

'I don't have any prejudices against you. I quite like you, with your "thorn in the flesh": it's something which I nearly felt myself.'

Paul gave a start: 'What are you talking about?'

The escort of slaves, who had withdrawn a respectful distance, were beginning to get restless. Kaeso had to call them to order. It was now daybreak and the city was beginning to stir.

'I was only quoting you . . .'

Kaeso had not expected Paul to pick up the reference, and he was embarrassed by his insistence. He had taken Paul's phrase as a discreet confession. He now realized that the author had not intended it as such.

'I only know what you say about it . . .'

'But I don't say anything else.'

'Let's forget it. Anyway, I could be wrong . . .'

'It's important to me. I want you to tell me here and now what you thought you understood.'

Paul seemed anxious.

'You really want me to tell you?'

'Yes.'

'You won't be angry with me if you find the truth upsetting?'

'The truth has never hurt me. All truth comes from God in some way.'

Weighing his words carefully Kaeso gave in to Paul's demands.

'Your Lord, Jesus, had women all around him and knew how to talk to them. You only ever refer to them to call them to order, and to insist that they be modest and self-effacing, as if standard male brutality needed the support of your voice. It's absolutely clear that you only love these women in theory. I've never seen you look at a pretty girl with frank, innocent pleasure. And among all Jesus' disciples you make yourself conspicuous by not marrying. Though you were educated as a Pharisee – and the Pharisees are vigorously in favour of marriage – you weren't married, as far as I know, before you became a Christian, and yet you must have been about thirty at the time. Jesus hasn't given you any inclination for marriage either. You're not a eunuch, you're not impotent, to the best of my knowledge, and yet you don't seem to indulge in any sort of sexual activity. Then again, you're very harsh on the subject of sodomites and inverts, and even lesbians earn your hostility.

So, since your flesh is, shall we say, alienated, despite your sensitive, passionate, irritable and highly-strung nature, and yet is not at first sight actually incapable in any way, what can be the meaning of the phrase "thorn in the flesh" which apparently slipped from your pen by accident? It's a very precise phrase. It's not a thorn in your soul, and yet as far as your flesh is concerned it's only a thorn. One can see at once that it's a very secondary form of discomfort for you, that you master it and look down on it, although that doesn't prevent it from being painful from time to time. Probably you see it as a mark of your god's care for you, something permanently reminding you of the necessity of humility and offering proof of the wonders he can achieve with the most frail and fallen of instruments, people whose wounds are of long standing and incurable.

What I'm getting at is this. Your hostile indifference to women and aggressive rejection of homosexuals surely entitle one to see you as a repressed pederast? I swear by all the gods that I admire you for it, and yet I feel very sorry for you. Ordinary men already have enough trouble staying chaste if marriage doesn't come to slake their lust – to employ a turn of phrase you'll find familiar. But what can one say about the man who knows he must deny all aspirations of the flesh until death delivers him from them? The chastity of the homosexual is all the more meritorious because his temptation is double. Your heroism makes me feel there really must be a god behind you. Is my compliment misplaced?'

Paul washed his hands and face at the fountain and came back to Kaeso.

'You haven't spared me any criticism, and it's taken you long enough to come up with the slightest compliment. In the eyes of a boy who has been a member of the Athenian *ephebia* I might appear to give grounds for such suspicions. My life-style is certainly out of the ordinary. If your diagnosis is correct, it would be the best proof that the Holy Spirit breathes where it will, and that we are responsible for our acts if not for our tendencies. Let my example, be it real or only hypothetical, serve as a lesson to you when Satan pursues you. I must say goodbye to you now. I shall be leaving soon.'

'My compliment isn't the cause of your going?'

'I shouldn't go for so trivial a reason. I'm going for the sole reason that I had great hopes of you and they have been bitterly disappointed.'

'Do at least stay long enough for Silanus and Marcia to reward you. They're wondering what you'd like . . .'

'I can't make any profitable use of that household. Or of Nero. The only important form of beauty in life will always escape him. What would give me pleasure is for you to stop playing at being a pretend Christian. In the meanwhile read my letters more carefully. I've never undervalued good works. I merely meant to say that the value of actions lies in their being consequences of faith and as such sanctified by the redemptive sacrifice of Jesus.

One day – and I see that day as soon – you'll get yourself killed because of that certificate that you so thoughtlessly wheedled out of me just now. On that day, before the sword comes down on your neck, an act of faith can still save you and retrospectively make all the good deeds in your life into one long act of prayer. At that moment, if not before, remember what I've just said.'

With this sinister prediction Paul sadly embraced Kaeso and went into the house.

By now the day had well and truly begun and there was no need for an escort when going round the town. Kaeso dismissed his attendants and walked slowly back to Silanus' house. It was the second time Paul had made a prediction of the sort to him and it was very probable that it was of no more value than the wanderings of Melania, who was decidedly on the decline. But it left an impression nonetheless. A prudent golden rule of the old Roman religion in which Kaeso had been brought up as a child was that one should never get on the wrong side of a god, whoever it might be, because any little tinpot god could still cause you far more trouble than a man. And the Christian god was a force to be reckoned with. The mad elephants which had trampled on the crowd in the Circus Maximus in Pompey's day were nothing compared to the Christian god, if he existed. But did he? There was a high probability that at the heart of the universe there were gods to organize a whole heap of things. Or rather one god to organize a whole heap of things. Or a god on the Stoic pattern, whose confused and diffuse quality would seem to make him all the more easy to accept. But a personal god, creator of the universe, was a different story. Even though his existence was merely hypothetical, it was hardly reassuring, if there was half a chance that Paul had actually had anything to do with him. And Paul's belief was absolute. In any case, baptism seemed to bring nothing but bad luck, given that the Christians, beginning with Jesus himself, had had endless trouble. Jesus died for the sins of the Christians, and as if that were not enough he required them to die for him afterwards. Paul had seemed to find it quite natural that Kaeso should get himself beheaded for a ridiculous certificate.

Kaeso was in a hurry to show the document to Silanus. It would be a nasty moment, but then he would be free. His health was now restored and he had no reason to linger at the house of Cicero.

As he went up the steps which led by the shortest route to Silanus' house, Kaeso was surprised to find that a small detachment of Praetorian guardsmen were still on duty. He had a nasty feeling that something unpleasant had happened.

He at once asked the centurion of the guard the reason for their presence. The man replied. 'Shortly after the guests had left, the emperor sent a litter to fetch your stepmother, and I have instructions not to let anyone leave. But you can go back in.'

Kaeso hurriedly did so and rejoined Silanus, who was walking up and down the peristyle, watched with concern by his most trusted freedmen.

'What's this I hear? The emperor has abducted Marcia? It's unbelievable news.'

'For hours I've been asking myself what could have got into him. It's totally uncharacteristic of him to behave like that. You talked to him for a good part of the evening – have you any ideas?'

Kaeso revealed to Silanus the interest which his and Marcia's beauty had aroused in the prince during the races, when of course he was unaware of their rank.

The incident did not seem to throw much light on the situation. Silanus remained puzzled.

'Marcia said nothing about that little misunderstanding. I assume she didn't want to alarm me. Anyway, it isn't at all clear what it has to do with what's happened tonight.'

'I agree. Perhaps it's just a vulgar joke from a man who's had too much to drink? Supreme power is an incitement to scare people on the cheap. Remember Caligula. He used to call senators to the palace before dawn, and they thought their last hour had come. Then when the poor things had been sitting around on a dais for ages, he would suddenly appear, accompanied by flutes and wearing those sandals with little concertinas underneath, and would perform a languorous dance for their benefit.'

'But Nero isn't mad.'

'There's always a touch of madness in anyone who can do whatever he pleases. What brain could stand up to the dizzying effect of total power?'

'Whether or not the emperor thought of me in this affair, his whim has put me in a very unpleasant position, possibly even a dangerous one. My slaves and those of the prince will talk, the whole city will gossip about it, people will watch for my reactions, as though there were anything I could say or do . . .'

Marcia's situation did not seem to worry Silanus unduly. It was true that the victim's virtue could no longer be said to be exposed to much risk.

Kaeso felt he ought to assure Silanus of one thing: 'Whatever happens I can guarantee that Marcia didn't do anything consciously to attract or excite Nero.'

'That goes without saying. She'd have to stay faithful to you, wouldn't she?'

It was the first time that Silanus had so baldly revealed his suspicions. Emotional stress was obviously responsible for the slip. Probably he hadn't believed a word of Marcia's false confession, though his letter to Kaeso, implicitly acknowledging the situation, had appeared to accept it.

Kaeso was saved from having to reply by a noise from outside the doorway: Marcia was back. She soon appeared in the pale sunlight of the second hour, walking briskly and with an animated look in her eyes, as if nothing abnormal had occurred.

'I'm absolutely starving,' she said. 'I've been on a boat trip.'

Marcia went off in private with Silanus while Kaeso gave himself up to the wildest of guesses.

After a very long interval Silanus rejoined Kaeso and said:

'Marcia would like to see you and reassure you. As far as I'm concerned I must admit that I'm quite out of my depth. People are certainly right when they say that truth is stranger than any fiction.'

Marcia was stretched out in a housecoat in the shadowy bedroom.

'What's all this about a boat trip?'

'Well, the litter took me at a trot down to a small boat anchored over by the docks. I was made to sit on the deck and we were rowed up river. Doryphoros, one of the freedmen closest to the emperor, was in charge of the whole thing, and was very polite to me. We went under the Pons Sublicius, the Palatine bridge, the Pons Fabricius and the Janiculum bridge. At the Vatican bridge the sun began to rise. We went past the arsenals on the right bank of the river and eventually weighed anchor opposite Agrippina's gardens. There a huge cage was very carefully winched on board and lowered into the hold. There was some growling from the cage, and Doryphoros told me that it contained a Mauretanian lion.

The freedman then asked me to go down into the damp dark hold, which was lit only by a nightlight. He undressed me, tied my hands behind my back and fixed them to a ring in the hull at about waist-height. Then he took a whip, opened the cage, and verbally encouraged the animal to jump out, which it did with no further ado.

It was a fine lion with a superb mane, but with a soft white stomach and a little rat-like penis. When Nero disguises himself as a lion, that's the detail that gives away the imposture.

The animal attacked me, roaring loudly, with a curious mixture of brutality and tenderness. Sometimes it licked me with its rough tongue, breaking off to cry "Mummy, mummy, why have you abandoned me?" in a touching, tearful voice. At others it bit me with its sharp teeth, heaped obscene insults on me and reproached me for my loose morals. It was perfectly obvious to me what role I was supposed to play, so I whimpered away on the theme of "You wanted my body, you great lout, and yet you had me killed."

From time to time Doryphoros gave the animal a good crack of the whip across the rear to encourage it to repent. In the end the lion turned its hind-quarters towards its trainer, who took advantage of the fact to inflict the ultimate outrage on it, despite the difficulties raised by the long hairy tail, which kept on getting in the way. Even a well-practised Greek doesn't find it easy to bugger a lion.

The emperor withdrew, hanging his head, and Doryphoros acknowledged, as he untied me, that I played my part perfectly. Silanus thinks so too. What else could I have done?'

Marcia's complete calm gave pause for thought.

'Have you often had to deal with nut-cases like that?'

'All men are nut-cases, Kaeso. The only difference between Nero and the rest is that our prince has the means to put his fantasies into practice, and that he does it with an undeniable sense of theatre.'

Marcia was looking at a cameo encrusted with emeralds, showing Nero in his divine glory, which Doryphoros had given her as a thank-you gift from his master.

Kaeso did not feel in a position to reproach Marcia for her behaviour. The incautious way in which he had spoken to Nero had clearly had more than a little to do with the incident. The emperor had seized on the opportunity to relieve his feelings of sorrow as an orphan, but it was also obvious that the scene had been staged as a gesture of fellow feeling towards his young friend.

But that was the last thing he could tell Marcia.

Kaeso congratulated her on being in such good form and told her that he was going back to his father's house until the adoption. Marcia did not want to run the risk of antagonizing Kaeso by insisting that he prolong his stay.

Before leaving Kaeso thanked Silanus for his hospitality and informed him of Paul's approaching departure.

'A piece of good news at last,' said Decimus. 'That fellow is nothing but trouble. It wouldn't surprise me if he'd put a spell on Marcia or Nero.'

Obviously it was not the right moment to talk about conversion. But one day either way was of no importance to Kaeso. There were still a dozen days to go before the Ides.

At home his father was in a deep sleep and Selene was bathing to wash away the traces of the night's outrages. Her master was a very poor sort of lion in comparison with the king of the species.

Kaeso felt the need for a complete change of mental horizons. He wanted to look at something beautiful. He undressed and indiscreetly joined Selene, whom he found splashing about in the little warm pool.

'I'm a Christian,' Kaeso called out gaily to her. 'I've even got a certificate of baptism.'

'Then keep your eyes off me. You're not allowed even the tiniest sin now.'

But where did sin, which was everywhere and nowhere, begin and end?

❧ PART FOUR ❧

⁂ CHAPTER ⁂
I

When the emperor woke up again, about the fifth hour, after his nostalgic river trip, he thought of Egypt and Greece, and of his impatience to visit them at last and try out his voice there. But the reservations recently expressed by Petronius, Silanus and Kaeso, which were in fact the same as those of Tigellinus, spoiled his dream. When he thought about it, the situation hardly seemed ripe for a trip of that sort. He would leave too much trouble behind him and dangerously disappoint an anxious populus. The *plebs* could not do much to protect the prince, but it could contribute to his downfall, even if only by passive complicity. So he would have to be patient, use cunning yet again and consolidate his authority first. Any citizen, however insignificant, could sing where he liked, but not a Nero!

Feeling humiliated, angry and above all afraid, the emperor sat up abruptly on his couch, making Sporus jump. Young Sporus, one of his favourite male concubines along with Pythagoras, the priest of Cybele, had, contrary to rumour, come to Nero already castrated. He was as faithful as a setter.

'What's worrying you this morning?' asked Sporus. 'Have you had a bad dream?'

The emperor replied testily: 'Reality's enough to worry me, I don't need dreams.' He got up brusquely, and went and consoled himself with his building plans.

In a room next to his bedroom lay an astonishing vast scale model of the new city of Rome as Nero would have liked it to be. His first teachers, Anicetus and Beryllus, then the learned Stoic Chaeremon, had held up for his admiration the fascinating town planning of the Greek cities of Asia and Europe. Their orderly, open vistas, the achievement of a model process of colonization, formed such a happy contrast with the random little alleys of old Athens, where the only intellectually satisfying features were the use of space afforded by the Acropolis, and in particular the *agora*, between the Stoa of Attalus and the Hephaestion. But at Pergamum, Miletus, Alexandria, and even in the Piraeus, it was not only the centre of the city which flattered the eye; the popular quarters too had been the subject of geometrical planning. Everything was absolutely straight, everything crossed at right-angles. The attentive eye of the administrator or the policeman could run easily from one side of the city to the other. There were no more secrets.

In Rome Nero's attempts at town planning had run up against insurmountable obstacles. Even the construction of his new palace, the Domus Transitoria, between the Palatine and the Esquiline, was not making much progress. It had been brought virtually to a halt by irritating problems of space and compulsory purchase. The low-lying, sordid regions of the city which the prince knew from the inside, as a result of having nightly found his entertainment there in his youth, were guaranteed to stand up to the assaults of both reason and art. Though many a disaster had inflicted substantial damage on the city, it had always been rebuilt at random. The only positive feature of this disorder was that the height of the apartment buildings and the narrowness of the little streets were a guarantee of shade in summer.

What a difference there was between the disorder of the real Rome and the Rome of Nero's model. The Domus Transitoria, at the heart of the city, had spread out to take on the dimensions of a veritable little city itself, with everything else leading into it. The most astonishing feature was not the extremely luxurious quality of the buildings, dominated by the 120-foot high statue of Nero. It was the way in which the symmetrical gardens still favoured by landscape gardeners had been replaced by rolling vistas of forest, pasture and vineyard, around a huge lake, where tame and wild animals alike would come to drink. Whereas stone had been tamed, Nature untrammelled had resumed her rights. Even the slum districts of the city now had wide avenues, vast squares, dozens of fountains, waterfalls and stretches of open water fed by new aqueducts. This orgy of running water had not satisfied the imagination of the architects Severus and Celer and their engineers. Across the former slum area there was also to be a network of canals bearing water from the sea at Ostia. This would provide an effective safeguard against fires. New rules had moreover been devised for the placing and construction of *insulae*. Their height could be reduced, and every building was now isolated at the centre of an open green space, and flanked with porticoes, as an extra precaution against fire.

Faced with such an attractive model, one began to wish for a major disaster which would level the old Rome to the ground. But Gauls bent on arson were no longer in plentiful supply. Even the most violent fires only destroyed small areas, one whole district at most. And earthquakes in that region were far too feeble to give much hope.

Nero sighed deeply. Perched up on the Palatine he felt cramped. The temptation came to him yet again to clean the place out, to set the whole filthy city ablaze, so that modern builders could immortalize his name by their genius. There was no doubt that the temptation was artistically justified. But was it politically opportune?

There would be one immense advantage. With Rome destroyed the prince would appear in all his paternal splendour as the only hope. The *plebs* on the bread-line, who owned virtually nothing anyway, would lose all they had. Many senators and rich men, who did not give a damn for the regime when in the safety of their own four walls, would be punished for their treason by the disaster and reduced to begging for his aid. Not only would it give great moral satisfaction to watch the destruction of a large number of insolent villas, stuffed to the eaves with booty from centuries of plunder and prevarication, but there was the additional advantage that for years all other problems would sink into insignificance beside the need to rebuild. The saviour prince could, without too much risk, briefly abandon his building-site of a city, and visit the East for a concert tour.

There was, however, a hypothetical danger. If ten or twelve out of fourteen districts all burned down at once, people would suspect that there was a human agency at work behind the disaster rather than a divine one. It was an unfortunate coincidence that the emperor was known to be writing about the fire of Troy: his own poetry would point the finger of suspicion at him. But imperial propaganda would have a rational argument at its disposal. If Nero had wanted to burn Rome down with impunity, he would have stuck to two or three districts and would hardly have been so stupid as to be working on verse about a fire at the same time. The very scale of the disaster and the unfortunate coincidence of the *Troica* would be evidence of the innocence of the august architect and poet.

The emperor thought for a moment of all the masterpieces piled up in Rome, in private houses as much as in public buildings and squares. They would be sure to be destroyed in the flames and the inevitable pillaging which would follow. But he did not linger over the point. Kaeso had confirmed him in his deepest and most instinctive feeling: beauty and ugliness were matters of opinion, whether popular or supposedly informed. The only indisputable artistic reality was the pleasure which the artist himself found in creating. He could be wrong about other people's art, but his own pleasure bore witness to the value of his own. As a result other people's work had, when it came to it, little importance. A true artist did well to detach himself from his own creation once he had

465

experienced the pleasure of creating it out of nothing. It was doubtless difficult to detach oneself in this way, but it was good for one. At all periods of intense artistic activity, people had despised, forgotten, condemned and destroyed without a second thought the forms produced by preceding ages and now judged imperfect, had they not? And look how many painters had abandoned their usual style of work and dedicated themselves to searching for something new. The antiquarian mentality was an indication of aesthetic impotence.

If Rome were swept clean of masterpieces and copies alike, a new sensibility could flower outside the beaten paths of tradition. There was something stilted and stifling about contemporary official art. A disaster which would give work and inspiration to countless artists would be sure to blow away the cobwebs.

Nero sighed even more deeply. It was gambling for high stakes, but the higher the risk, the greater the profit. Yet a very understandable fear held him back from crossing this incendiary Rubicon. Future generations would undoubtedly guess the truth and would approve the sacrifice. But the present generation had no taste, no leaning towards the limpid beauties of Greek-style town planning. Was it his task to make these philistines happy despite themselves?

In a very thoughtful mood he left the tempting model, and set out on his morning stroll, which took him, with a small escort of the German Guard, as far as the nearby *pulvinar* in the Circus Maximus. It was not yet catching the rays of the rising sun.

The beggars and the homeless had abandoned the steps of the monument before daybreak. In the afternoon it became a place to stroll, like the Appian Way or the Campus Martius. But in the morning the track was the refuge of a few idlers briefly fleeing the feverish activity of the Forums, and the guild of soothsayers, who were particularly successful with women, conducted their main activities there.

The clients, supposedly as a rite of purification, were first obliged to go once round the track at the double. They could be seen puffing round in a duck-like waddle, all tangled up in their clothes. With their hearts and pulses racing and their critical faculties reduced they would then allow their features and the lines of their hands to be examined by the seers, and with trembling fingers would draw a little cube of poplar or pine wood from a basket, with a mysterious mark on it which was supposed to help in the accurate prediction of their future. It was forbidden by law to make predictions about people's deaths, but the law was difficult to enforce.

As he looked at the familiar sight from the shade of his *pulvinar*, the emperor wondered which cube might have his destiny and the destiny of Rome inscribed upon it.

At the same time of day the rejects of the profession, magicians from Armenia or Comagene, tended to be plying their trade among the jostling crowds of the Velabrum, alongside the fishmongers, oil-sellers and other pedlars. There they read the future in the palpitating breast of a dove or the way an egg reacted to hot ashes. And once their credulous customer had been dispatched, they would discreetly eat the proffered egg, whose white surface, beneath the shell, would just have gone brown in the heat of the little portable brasier.

Like most aristocrats Nero had more confidence in the 'diviners', who specialized in the interpretation of dreams, and particularly in the Chaldean astrologers, still known as *mathematici* or *genethliaci*. These last determined the *thema* or *genesis* of their trusting clients from the position of the stars at the moment of their birth, and attached great importance to the signs of the zodiac. These were still based on the science of astronomy as they had been at the time of Hipparchos, 200 years earlier. They were unaware that, as the equinox goes back thirty or so degrees every 2,150 years, in about the twenty-eighth century from the founding of the city of Rome Aries would correspond to the constellation of Pisces. But, at that rate, around the year 26,500 by the Roman calendar the equinox would have gone full circle; once again there would be a wonderful coincidence between the signs of the zodiac and the constellations, and consequently, a positively Neronian accuracy of prediction.

As for witches and wizards, they preferred to work in secret and had some of the heaviest trade. While the official augurs and *haruspices* made people smile, the Romans, paradoxically, had the greatest confidence in charlatans who plied their trade in private.

The emperor's glance accidentally fell on Silanus' box, and the fresh and pleasant memory of Marcia and Kaeso came sharply back to him. Nero had enough common sense to put politics, on which his life depended, before the little pleasures which his position afforded him.

He went back to his apartments, called for a secretary, and having totally forgotten what Kaeso's precise civil status was, dictated a note to Silanus:

'Thank you for entrusting Marcia to me for a few hours. We experienced a great moment together. In her gracious company I was initiated into the status of "lion" in the religion of Mithras. But that involves awesome mysteries, and I am not allowed to tell you more.

467

Your Kaeso is a charming boy. I like his intelligence, simplicity and frankness. He is as handsome as the Apollo of Antium, and he can talk as well. Following Petronius' advice I shall shortly be leaving for Naples – on the seventeenth of the Kalends of June, the day after the Ides of May to be exact. All the court and my beloved *augustiani* will accompany me. There is a place for Kaeso in that élite corps, offering him fine prospects. I very much hope that he will come with us. I shall look after him as carefully as I did Marcia.

Farewell.'

Nero absent-mindedly instructed this message to be sent 'to the father of K. Aponius Saturninus', and the secretary, after making inquiries, accordingly wrote at the top: 'L. Domitius Nero to M. Aponius Saturninus' and dispatched the tablets accordingly.

The note arrived at the *insula* during lunch, and had the effect of a thunderbolt. Kaeso was in the process of introducing his father to the beauties of Christianity, and had drawn a veil over his stepmother's little misadventure. Marcus therefore learnt in one fell swoop that his ex-wife had been abducted and returned, that the same honour awaited Kaeso, and that the letter could not be intended for him.

Kaeso was appalled. After all the efforts he had made to escape from Marcia's carnal attentions, it looked as though he might fall into the hands of an emperor whose erotic intentions were much less to his taste. Most young Romans would have crawled up the Palatine on their hands and knees for a chance to become one of the emperor's favourites: his bounty was legendary. But Kaeso was made of other stuff.

Marcus, on the contrary, was enchanted by this extraordinary distinction, and was inclined to think that Kaeso might have been clever enough to earn it during the course of the night. The role of old-style Roman father, however, discouraged him from showing a glee which would have been in bad taste. Having read and re-read the letter aloud, and sliding over the unplumbed mysteries of Mithras, one of the least well-known of foreign gods, Marcus expressed the guess that the letter was probably intended for Silanus, and added, in a fairly neutral voice:

'The emperor has spoken. There is nothing for it but to obey. You must think of yourself as a soldier carrying out an order, Kaeso. If the emperor found you ungrateful, the insult could well undermine Silanus' position, and consequently Marcia's, not to mention your own.'

'Soldiers only have to be prepared to shed their blood,' said Kaeso. 'I

468

have the impression that the emperor is hoping for something rather different.'

Marcus casually remarked: 'He already has Pythagoras, Doryphoros and various others at his service. You'll only ever be in the rearguard of the troop.'

The mention of Pythagoras and Doryphoros accorded with the sexual principles which Marcus had dispensed to Kaeso previously, for everyone was pretty sure that they performed honourably active service for Nero. But it was equally common knowledge that the emperor liked catamites, as his liaison with the notorious Sporus, among others, proved. This double appetite was quite remarkable and furnished a permanent source of gossip.

Selene was upset on Kaeso's behalf, but could not prevent herself from feeling a certain delicious secret pleasure at the idea that free men too were sometimes obliged to endure sexual practices against their inclination.

To Marcus' considerable annoyance she observed: 'I think it's difficult to predict how the emperor will enjoy our Kaeso, from the front, the back or sideways, but it's certain to be a tangibly rewarding experience.'

Kaeso shouted in exasperation: 'And what if I don't want to be enjoyed at all? Do I look as if I'd make a good slave?'

He grabbed the tablets, got up from the *triclinium* and left the room.

It was a fine protest, but it did not offer any solution to his new problem. If the whim took him, Nero could have Kaeso buggered by thirty legions.

It was abnormally warm weather for spring. Kaeso felt the need to breathe more freely. He began to climb one of the staircases which led to the flat roof of the *insula*. From the fifth floor above the mezzanine the stairs went on up to the roof, but the wretched hovels in which the tenants on the sixth floor lived were accessible only by ladders which the owner took away, like those which led to the mezzanine floor above the shops, when the tenants got into arrears with their rent.

Kaeso made his way through the bushes, hencoops and drying washing and reached the parapet on the south side of the building. Immediately beneath him, like the frozen waves of a sea of brick and stone, were the red-tiled roofs and green roof-gardens of the *insulae* of most of the Subura. Beyond could be seen the numerous monuments of the Roman Forums, dominated to the right by the Capitoline, and in the background, at a height of over 1,000 metres, by the Palatine. That was where Augustus, Tiberius, Caligula and Claudius had lived, in palaces old and new, palaces burned down, rebuilt and modified. What a collection of tyrants, some hypocritical and covert, others brutal and cynical! At least Claudius had been original in his eccentricity.

Like his father after the dramatic auction, Kaeso felt crushed, scandalized and at a loss. The difference was that this was not a question of money. Given the incident with Marcia, Nero was quite clearly after his body. And against someone in Nero's position certificates of baptism would carry no weight. It was all the fault of Paul and his childish curiosity that he had fallen into the emperor's clutches.

The prospect of becoming one of the *augustiani* – '*augusteioi*' in Greek – was already enough to send shivers down Kaeso's spine. In the space of five years the number of these good-for-nothings had increased tenfold, and was now about 5,000 in all. A tenth of these young men were recruited from among the sons of senators or knights, the rest were plebeians. The band was commanded by a member of the senate, and the leaders got as much as 400,000 sesterces. The *augustiani* could be recognized by their luxurious clothes and their long curled hair. Their only function was to accompany the emperor, support him with their flattery, and cheer him when he appeared on stage, and more particularly when he sang. This gigantic claque had even been divided into teams, each trained to applaud on a certain rhythm, and the variety of these rhythms had been compared to the different rhythms used by rowers of galleys. Nero, who had a thing about Greekness, had taken the wonderful idea of this troop of flatterers from the companies of 'royal boys' – the *basilikoi paides* – with which the dynasties of the Seleucids and the Lagidae had surrounded themselves, and which provided reserves of pages and catamites. It was a kind of *ephebia* dedicated to an individual instead of to the State. The *augustiani* were absolutely committed to the emperor: their only ambition was to please him. For Kaeso they represented domesticity at its most horrendous.

Under the impulsion of an increasing sense of distress Kaeso found himself being drawn, against his will, towards Marcia, the only refuge and source of advice which he could think of in a situation of that kind. Despite the deceptions and disappointments which had piled up, his old filial instincts suddenly came back to him. He ran down the stairs, with the fatal tablets still under his arm, and hurried off towards Cicero's house.

When he arrived at the Carinae, between the fruit market and the house of Pompey, Kaeso stopped for a moment to get his breath back. He had just remembered that he had entirely forgotten little Myra and had left her at Silanus' house. He was irritated by this piece of absentmindedness, which was a clear sign of his mental state – as irritated as Marcia had been the afternoon when she left her silk parasol in a copse in the Campus Martius. (It was particularly difficult to lose a Roman parasol, as they had no mechanism for closing them up.) Kaeso was beginning to go through the hard apprenticeship of the slave-master, who is the owner of objects which persist in presenting a human appearance. To be entirely responsible for an animal which is too intelligent and too sensitive is not always a sinecure. Even from the simple standpoint of the law, the slave-owner could be brought to court for damage inflicted by his slaves on a third party. At the baths Myra had blown kisses to Nero. If she had kicked him in the teeth, it would have been Kaeso who had to explain her conduct.

The visitor was asked to wait in the peristyle for a moment. He had got Marcia up from her siesta, and she must have had to redo her make-up. She finally received him half lying down in her boudoir: she was draped in a négligé of a delicate material which had probably come from India or the East.

'Why are we so fortunate as to be favoured with a visit from you so soon after your return to the *insula*? You look utterly wretched.'

With a word of explanation about the mistake in the address Kaeso threw the tablets into his stepmother's lap and looked at her with a woebegone look of entreaty.

Marcia read the text and thought for a moment. She was well aware of male prejudices, and could read her Kaeso like a book. On the basis of her encyclopaedic experience she could have given him a lecture on the erroneous, conventional and artificial nature of questions of dignity in love, where every gesture, eternally repeated and alike, had, at bottom, only whatever value one chose to put upon it. But she knew that she would only sink lower in his estimation without managing to convince him. She would have to deal with the Kaeso she herself had helped to form by her traditional instruction. Having diverted him from the pederasts of Athens she would now have to convert him to a less intransigent position, because matters of the highest importance, which involved their general safety as well as the possibility of wealth, were suddenly hanging by a thread from a common or garden matter of sexual preference. It was enough to make one weep: Marcia had always hoped that her stepson would be spared the troubles which had marked her own life. But it had taken only a trip to the Circus and a dinner-party for the emperor to have an unforeseen – though not unforeseeable – whim. She

471

should have guessed what might happen and have prudently got Kaeso out of the way of all possibility of exciting imperial lust.

'Well now, my young friend,' she said severely, 'if I believed in the gods, I should say that they hadn't wasted any time in punishing you for the contempt you heap on me. I hope you're as agile at getting out of this tricky position as you are at avoiding me.'

Kaeso hung his head and looked so sad that Marcia's heart was touched.

'Come, come, all is not lost. You'll certainly have to go to Naples. Nero wouldn't forgive you if you tried to get out of it. He would have every right to suppose that Silanus and I had been put out by that absurd little episode on the boat and had turned you against him. That would be absolutely guaranteed to endanger all our lives. Once on the trip you'll probably have an opportunity to avoid the unpleasant duty which appears to be lined up for you. Our emperor is fickle in his tastes, and there's no shortage of handsome boys among the *augustiani*.'

'But how can I get out of the task in question if the issue specifically arises? What used you to say to men whose advances you wanted to turn down, so as not to upset them too much?'

Marcia could not suppress a smile.

'There weren't many advances I had to reject. In your case I can't really think of any appropriate excuses. But there are two ways of going about it, a good and a bad. If you try to curl up and hide at the back, the Emperor is all the less likely to forget about you because your very discretion will make you noticeable. And if he's hurt by your behaviour, you're sure to get exactly what you're trying to avoid. The thing to do is to make yourself noticeable in a way which is to your advantage. Get into a relationship with the emperor based on friendship, esteem and confidence. Make yourself useful, indispensable even. You're more intelligent and more cultivated than most of the blockheads who make up the *augustiani*. Nero likes his friends to be really gifted people, and he can be surprisingly tactful towards them. If he's seduced by your intellectual charm, he'll be careful not to rush things, for fear of losing you. Remember that, fortunately, he isn't short of lovers to play either role in bed with him. Your best hope of protecting yourself is to be able to offer him other forms of satisfaction than the ones he can get with any boy.'

The good sense of the advice was impressive, but it was designed to diminish the risk, not to abolish it.

With an effort Kaeso asked:

'If, despite all my attempts to raise the level of our relationship, the emperor's passion for my body reaches the critical point, what particular form of . . . activity do you think he'll want me to engage in?'

'I know what's worrying you. Unfortunately the answer isn't obvious. If you were built like a German guardsman, or if you hadn't yet grown out of childhood, we should have a clear indication. But you have perfect looks: you have that touch of virility which makes women melt and the suggestion of feminine grace which attracts sodomites. It isn't even certain that Nero knows precisely what he wants. He can be calculating but he's also impulsive. He's capable of mulling over a problem for years and then committing himself on a hunch at the last moment.'

Marcia and Kaeso spent some time going through all the best known of the Emperor's favourites, active and passive, looking for resemblances to Kaeso which would be a basis for expectations and probabilities. Kaeso seemed more cut out for active service, the only sort which allowed a man to keep his good reputation.

With frank motherly solicitude Marcia could not refrain from adding: 'The divine nature of our beloved Nero is so resolutely ambivalent that it's not out of the question that he might ask contradictory services of you before fixing his preference one way or the other.'

At that Kaeso sank down beside Marcia, and she took his hand tenderly.

'You really mustn't exaggerate the importance of this possible fooling around, you silly child. Isn't it a matter of "Needs must when the devil drives?" Would you by any chance be considering a Stoic suicide as a way of escaping from a little purely temporary unpleasantness? Think of the Jews, who hold suicide to be a crime – whereas I think of it as a piece of stupidity in most cases. What's the point of giving up living if you're no longer present to enjoy the pleasure or even the discomfort of a new state? Think of that eccentric fellow Paul, who gives sight back to the blind and awakes the sleeping. If Nero had abducted his old carcass and raped him, do you suppose he'd have ended his life for such a trivial cause?'

'He certainly wouldn't. Paul recommends slaves who find themselves in a similar position to endure their misfortune patiently, not to enjoy it more than they can help and to pray hard.'

'What a very wise doctrine. One can pray on all fours just as easily as on your knees.'

'According to Paul "everything comes out to a Christian's advantage in the long run".'

'He said it, not me!'

Marcia pressed Kaeso's curly head to her bosom and stroked his hair.

'There's nothing to be afraid of. You'll always be the same Kaeso to me. Emperors come and go. A relationship like ours stays the same.'

The perfume rising from Marcia's body began to have an unsettling effect on Kaeso. He thought it wiser to sit up, and asked:

'What's worse – to refuse a man your active or your passive favours?'

'If Nero offers himself to you in the woman's role, he'll be terribly put out if you don't leap at the chance. Whereas a catamite can use a certain amount of coquetry and prolong his defence without upsetting his suitor unduly. It's all a matter of tact and restraint.'

'Now I don't know whether I should try to pass myself off as a German or a young lad.'

'What advice did your father give you?'

'He had difficulty hiding how pleased he was. After all, he's been used to living off other people's charms for years, hasn't he?'

'You're unfair to him. Life hasn't treated Marcus kindly, and he loves you dearly. You're his pride and joy, and he only wants your happiness. He would never deliberately give you a piece of bad advice.

And while we're on the subject of advice, the most important thing is not to defer your adoption, which is at present scheduled for the next Ides. Then you can leave for Naples with that to protect you. Nero had no second thoughts about raping young Aulus Plautius, because the boy's relative obscurity left him with no defence. Raping the son of a Silanus would be another kettle of fish. The act would have political overtones, and the emperor would only dare do it if he'd decided to wipe out what's left of the family of the Torquati – in other words, my husband and his nephew. Up until now there's nothing to suggest that he has any such intention. On the contrary he's showing you his favour in the most pleasant of forms.'

'The fact of being Silanus' wife didn't protect you from a little minor misuse.'

'Your position as an adopted son would bear no comparison with mine. Nero's police must have told him that one more nutter would make no difference to me, whereas your reputation is intact. And you're fortunate enough to be a man. High society accords a great deal more importance to a man's arse than a woman's, and Nero knows the people he has to deal with, despite his eccentricities.'

'What if I refuse both the adoption and the trip?'

'That would be the surest way to ruin all three of us. Nero is mistrustful, touchy and vindictive over many things. This invitation to go to Naples is an order, Kaeso. To give a helping hand to Fate, you should mark yourself off from the other *augusteioi*, who happily adopt Greek manners and dress, by wearing sober, dignified Roman-style clothes, which will emphasize all your most manly attributes. And so as not to leave any doubts about your tendencies, the obvious thing is to take little Myra along with you. Those are the final pieces of advice from someone who loves you dearly, and you'll appreciate what it cost me to give the last one.'

Kaeso kissed Marcia on the forehead and withdrew to take the tablets to Silanus.

The boy had no desire whatsoever to drown himself in order to escape from the emperor's hypothetical attentions. But it seemed to him quite clear that if one were to come out of dishonourable situations with one's head high, Stoicism preached a moral code which was superior to that of the Jews and Christians. The acceptance of suicide gave man sovereign liberty, free from all conjecture. That was a long way from the tearful submission recommended by Paul and his disciples. In the life of Jesus himself, who wanted to be exemplary in all things, there was a disappointing lacuna on this subject, which was a continual source of embarrassment to his disciples. The Gospel according to Mark would have had a more moving and socially relevant aspect if the young Jesus had had to serve briefly, despite his opposition, among the slave catamites of a Roman procurator, and his mother would have caused purer tears to be shed if she had been obliged to begin life like Myra. Paul would then have been in a less difficult position in talking about virtue and patience to slaves of both sexes.

After Kaeso's return to his father's house, Silanus had retired into the 'poorman's cell' which had been set up in one of the dark, narrow prisons in the slaves' quarters. There, unshaven, he had stretched himself out on a pallet, and covered himself in a patched cloak, before the disgusting remains of a beggarly meal. The 'poorman's cell' was a delicious Stoic custom. From time to time sybaritic Stoics retired into the most obvious discomfort and deprivation so as to meditate on the vanity of all things human and on the self-mastery which permitted one to dominate them. After a cure of that kind they came back to pleasure with a redoubled appetite.

As he came in, Kaeso accidentally knocked over the pitcher of warm water which accompanied the meal and offered to fill it up again. But the temporary pauper made a weary gesture of indifference. 'What's the point? Shan't I soon lose my life? If Nero has sexually abused my wife on

475

a pretext of honouring Mithras, he must have decided to sacrifice me. Following his usual habit he'll play at cat and mouse for a while, but I'm done for. I can feel it in my bones.'

Kaeso protested. Silanus' lugubrious appearance was pitiful. There was only one way of restoring any hope to the patrician. Kaeso resigned himself to revealing to Decimus that there was very probably a cause and effect relationship between his own unguarded words during the preceding evening and the rather peculiar boat-trip which had so suddenly followed it. He at once asked the unfortunate husband not to breathe a word of what he had said to Marcia.

Decimus was dumbfounded. He murmured:

'You mean that that scoundrel disguised himself as a Mauretanian lion in order to nibble Marcia's pussy because a few chance remarks from you made him see her as another incestuous Agrippina?'

'In a word, yes. And I'm confirmed in my suspicions by the cruise itself. You know as well as anyone how Agrippina temporarily escaped from death. So it seems that the affair has less to do with you than you thought.'

Silanus' face lit up.

For form's sake, although he knew that Silanus must suspect his wife's real feelings, Kaeso respected Marcia's lie more overtly on his own account:

'I only had to refer to the sexual relationship which Marcia and I briefly enjoyed before we knew you. The Prince's sick imagination became excited. How could I have known what would happen?'

'I don't hold it against you.'

Kaeso hurriedly changed the subject.

'Here are some tablets bearing the imperial seal. This note will make it plain to you more easily than I can that, far from seeking to hurt you, Nero is well disposed towards those who are dear to you. Rather too well disposed, in fact.'

Decimus glanced at the contents, whose import was indeed only too clear. It provided him with further food for thought.

'There's one thing which must be clearly settled between the two of us. If you decide to respond to the Prince's pressing invitation, it must be for Marcia's sake or your own. I should look on it as shameful to ensure my own tranquillity at the cost of such an unpleasant sacrifice.'

This declaration had all the necessary nobility without being imprudent. Silanus hoped that the thought of Marcia's, or his own, best interests would be sufficient to make Kaeso see reason.

Kaeso told Silanus what advice his father and Marcia had given him, and he added:

'Seneca recently praised to me the charms of an accommodating opportunism, which the Stoics call *eukairia* in Greek. But he was very insistent that there are limits to it. Do you see Nero's invitation as an extreme case, and how would you handle it if you were in my place?'

'Since despite myself I am, by the force of events, both judge and interested party in this wretched business, it's hard for me to add my advice to your father's and your stepmother's. But I wouldn't wish, either, to appear to have no interest in what happens to you. I'll speak to you as though you were a foreign friend in trouble.

The wisest Stoics have never had recourse to suicide except as a last resort, when they were bereft of even the slightest hope of being able to lead a life in conformity with their dignity and merit. A suicide for inadequate reasons is far from being exemplary. Nero's whims don't last long, and you have brilliant prospects in life. These considerations seem to me sufficient to encourage you to adopt a *eukairia* which would preserve the future. After all, the prince may not require the worst of you, and he may forget you as rapidly as he noticed you in the first place.

If you want to seize on this as a pretext for withdrawing from an existence which you find disappointing and burdensome, my surgeon is at your disposal. But Marcia would follow you to the grave, and would tear my eyes out before doing so.

At all events, act as you think fit and my esteem will follow you in death or in life.'

These paternal observations carried the weight of good plain common sense. Kaeso thanked Silanus warmly and withdrew to the accompaniment of affectionate wishes.

It was hardly the right moment for categorically refusing the offer of adoption. In any case, the emperor's nascent passion had relegated the problem to a secondary level. On the other hand, if Nero's fancy for him was likely to be only a passing whim, the adoption would condemn Kaeso to return to the poisoned atmosphere of the Silanus household. That was a danger not to be overlooked.

In the atrium Myra, looking completely unrecognizable, was waiting for her young master. Marcia had given her one of her blond German wigs. The child's face had been carefully made up to make her look several years older than she was. She was wearing the long Greek linen tunic called a *khiton*, held in at the waist with a gold belt. Over that was draped a gracious Ionian cloak, the *pharos*, and a shawl. On her head she had a *tholia*, the pointed hat often seen on Tanagra statuettes. And the fine sandals had heels sufficiently high to give the impression that she was a little taller than was the case.

Myra herself was absolutely delighted. 'Marcia told me that I looked like a little boy and that in the future I should look like a woman. What do you think of it all?'

Kaeso smiled and complimented Myra. Marcia really was not omitting any detail which would make his task easier. Such solicitude was very touching.

❧ CHAPTER ❧

2

Marcia had arranged for Kaeso and Myra to be taken back in a litter, which was also somewhat weighed down by the collection of pretty clothes which she had given the child. Myra was chattering away, full of excitement at the prospect of leaving for Naples, for Marcia had mentioned the forthcoming trip to her.

'She told me that the emperor had a great affection for you, that we should be part of his suite, and that I must be a credit to you. It's the first time I've ever been asked to be a credit to anyone, and I've no experience. Please, you must be sure to explain to me exactly how you want me to behave.'

Kaeso was not quite sure what to say. He was himself a prey to unpleasant thoughts about the nature of basic honour, that irreducible minimum of dignity which everyone hopes to preserve through life's hazards and torments. It was as though Marcus, Marcia and Silanus were in collusion. Each in their own particular way was pressurizing Kaeso to resign himself to his fate in what seemed to him a contemptible fashion. Even Selene, who instinctively gave very perceptive advice, was evidently taking the whole thing very lightly. How very isolated the last few hours had suddenly made him feel!

The litter had come down as far as the Triumphal Way, between the Palatine and the Caelian, a small road running from the 'head' of the Circus Maximus to the Via Sacra, and then on to the Capitol. In the old days triumphal processions used to form up in the Campus Martius, cross the Circus Flaminius from west to east, skirt the Capitol and the Tarpeian rock, come into the city by the Porta Triumphalis, cross the lower part of the Velabrum by a first Via Triumphalis, then the Circus Maximus, and come out at the eastern end on to a second Via Triumphalis. (It was along this second road that Kaeso's bearers were now trotting.) The whole circuit was more than three Roman miles long. Caesar had spent the night before the triumph celebrated on the occasion of his Gallic campaigns in the temple of Venus adjoining the theatre of Pompey.

Posterity had not held Caesar's catamites against him, but his reputation had suffered from the story that he had played the passive role with Nicomedes. Even during his Gallic triumph the legionaries had sung in chorus: 'Caesar conquered the Gauls, Nicomedes screwed Caesar, but that was his only triumph' while Vercingetorix, who was to be strangled shortly afterwards, asked for a translation.

When the litter arrived at the Via Sacra, Kaeso, who was haunted by the thought of Caesar, impulsively instructed that it should turn around and go towards the Porta Capena. Paul had probably not left yet, and Kaeso, in a state of complete mental confusion, felt a strong desire to tell him of his troubles and doubts. Paul was an irritating fellow but he inspired a contradictory mixture of mistrust and confidence simply through the strange quality of absolute conviction which animated him. What people in trouble most want is categorical assertions. There was no point in going to see Seneca. He would surely be of the same opinion as Silanus. Stoics of his sort would not cut their wrists unless they had been buggered against their will for a long time. They had a keen sense of degrees and nuances of experience. An extra advantage of a last consultation with Paul would be that the apostle could foretell the future and might know which way round Nero wanted to enjoy Kaeso.

Paul was on the point of leaving and was packing his few possessions. He was in something of a hurry because Kaeso had delayed him, and Peter's arrival had been announced as imminent. Peter was supposed to have already arrived in Ostia, where he was staying in an apartment block near the new harbour built by Claudius. Paul and Peter no longer had much to say to one another and preferred not to meet. Though united in Christ they had nothing else in common.

Peter was rustic, obstinate, and had little education. He had been brought up in the old rural Jewish tradition, was consequently very attached to its customs and would have liked them better preserved. But after irritating debates Paul's ideas had won the day, and the Law had been cut about to make it easier to attract Gentiles. It was a decisive choice, but it generated uncertainty and bitterness. The Apostles had in practice given up trying to persuade Israel and use it as a leaven for the patient conquest of the world. The bridges with a whole past of faithfulness to the letter of the Law had been noisily broken. And yet its riches were many and not easily replaceable. The revolutionary concern with immediate effectiveness had led to the repudiation of circumcision, the sabbath, forbidden foods . . . These innovations had hardly helped the Christians to convert Jews. And the reproaches which Paul's supporters directed against the Jews had a certain excessive and painful quality about them, which Peter instinctively felt and was distressed by.

He was also distressed by his intellectual inferiority to his brilliant bourgeois second-in-command. Paul could speak and write fluently. He could dictate the way he spoke, whereas Peter, whose public appearances were few and far between, was reduced to giving his secretaries, Silvanus, a former friend of Paul's, or someone else, a few ideas to develop.

Peter did, however, have the advantage of the mysterious authority which Christ had conferred upon him. He was one of those who had shared Jesus' public life and had seen Him after He rose from the tomb. Whereas the vision with which Paul had been honoured was a purely private matter.

With his robust good sense Peter was aware that Paul was sometimes carried away by his own eloquence, and that, because he was by nature inclined to take his ideas through to their logical ultimate, he risked leading his inexpert audience or readers into error. This was particularly the case when it came to problems as delicate and complex as the justification of faith and predestination, not to mention the burning and shocking question of the Lord's return amid the general conflagration of all the elements. From time to time Peter allowed himself a tactful attempt to put Paul on his guard.

Kaeso was made to wait in the hall of the Christian Jew's house, while little Myra stayed outside in the litter. Paul was disagreeably surprised by Kaeso's visit. He wondered what the boy could still want with him. He had just been reading a letter from Peter which had put him in a very bad mood. The secretary had expressed himself in very carefully chosen terms:

'Treat the lord's forbearance as salutary, as our dear brother Paul has also written to you, in accordance with the wisdom given him. He says so, moreover, in all the letters where he speaks of these questions. There are obscure points in them which uneducated people, lacking firmness of purpose, misinterpret – as they do the Scriptures – with disastrous results.'

Paul was cut to the quick. He murmured: 'So with the feeble wisdom given to me I'm supposed to be spreading dangerously obscure ideas. If people aren't to risk perdition in reading me, they need not only education but firmness of purpose. He might as well come straight out and say I'm a public menace. And how politely it's all put.'

Paul did up his bag and asked for Kaeso to be shown in. After all the visitor could hardly say anything more disagreeable to him than what he had just read.

He received him very coldly: 'I'm leaving immediately on foot for Pozzuoli, where I shall take a boat for the East. I'm surprised to see you again. I thought we'd already said our goodbyes. Anyway, I can't give you much time, so be quick.'

Kaeso did his best to sum up the situation in a few words. 'You wanted to see Nero and we showed you him. But on the same occasion I caught Nero's eye, and he wants to make me one of his passing favourites. To put it briefly, I've gone from the frying pan to the fire, and the second is a great deal hotter than the first. You're partly responsible for the situation, if only because you called me back to life when I'd escaped all troubles of the sort for ever. And you claim to be a man of truth, an expert in ethics, which is easy, but also an expert in practical day-to-day morality, simply on the strength of your Jewish descent. So you're well placed to tell me how to behave honourably. If the emperor's libidinous intentions towards me become more precise, what am I to do?

There are many people's interests at stake. To deal with myself first, I should personally only be risking my career, which I've already sacrified to get out of having sexual relations of an incestuous sort, as I told you this very morning. However, my stepmother is the wife of Silanus, who has presented me to the emperor as his future adoptive son. Silanus is one of the last surviving descendants of Augustus: his life hangs by a thread. If I seriously offend the emperor – and you know how touchy homosexuals are – Nero, who doesn't like Silanus, would have a good excuse to drive him to suicide by the hypocritical procedures of which you must have heard. Another point is that my father's income derives exclusively from titbits of work passed on to him by Silanus, and the latter's ruin would undoubtedly lead to the former's, not to mention my stepmother, to whom I owe so much.

So, naturally, I'm wondering what to do. Surely, from an ethical standpoint I'm in the same position as a slave whose conduct is excused by the fact that it's forced on him, even though rebellion would only rebound on himself? What freedom of action, in fact, do I still have apart from suicide, of which you disapprove, or flight, which would be equally disastrous to me and those close to me? Where could I hope to find a refuge unknown to the police? What would I have to live on? Anyway, as you advise mistreated slaves against running away, what right would you have to advise me to do so? And lastly, should I refuse to give in to the emperor's whim on the grounds that I've been baptized, which would run the risk of bringing down premature and unnecessary trouble on the Christians?

I've been as brief as I could manage. I hope you'll be equally brief and clear.'

Paul walked nervously up and down the room for a long time, deep in thought. Then he replied:

'I find it very touching that you persist in placing so much confidence in me, despite having well and truly deceived me. You're quite right in saying that homosexuals are touchy, and I can see that the dangers are by no means slight for you and above all for those who are dear to you. But may I first know whether I'm giving a consultation to a young philosopher or to a Christian neophyte? Which class of person is my reply supposed to be addressed to?'

'My reason for coming to see you is precisely because philosophy doesn't seem to offer me a decent solution to my problem.'

'Then Christian will speak to Christian. At the risk of making serious mistakes, there may certainly be a morality of preferring the lesser evil in public matters, when human misdemeanours oblige us to choose between two undesirable solutions. That is why Christ said that, as far as possible, we should render unto Caesar those things that are Caesar's and unto God those things that are God's.

But in the domain of private morality, where the word of the Lord rings out unambiguously and without fear of contradiction, our duty is always clear. So you should know what your duty is, in theory and in practice. One must use one's body only for the glory of God.

Your problem today is that, in a lawless State, the ruler's whims are likely to weigh on a free man just as heavily as on a slave, and to place the same constraints on his person, with the added aggravation of the fact that the freeman has relatives and friends who may suffer if he revolts. The necessary evil constituted by slavery suddenly seems to spread like a plague to the detriment of a few imprudent and unlucky people.

But there's a great difference between the position of a slave and your own, and the laws are the expression of that difference. When a master abuses a slave, he sins against God, but he doesn't commit a crime according to the provisions of an over-tolerant civil law. Whereas if Nero claims the right to misuse you, one way or another, he's acting against the provisions of his own laws and committing an abuse of power in an area where divine and imperial law undoubtedly coincide. You therefore have the right, and even the duty, to resist his attack, because you can legally defend yourself. The choice of a reasonable means of doing so lies with you.'

Kaeso thought about this fine-sounding statement and observed: 'Since Roman law gives the right to resist an attack of this sort by force, I think I would even be morally justified in killing my aggressor in the last resort. Should I then virtuously wave my bloody baptismal certificate under the noses of the Praetorian guards, as a piece of pious propaganda for your cause?'

Paul looked grim again but could not hide a wry smile. He had hoped to find in Kaeso a choice vehicle to carry Christianity into the upper circles of the aristocracy. The murder of the emperor by a baptized Christian sensitive about his honour was certain to have the opposite effect.

'As a last resort you do indeed have the right to resist by force. But you must think of the consequences. An assassination of that kind would condemn large numbers of innocent people to death as well.'

'So if I slept with Nero to guarantee the safety of you and your brethren, there wouldn't be any sin?'

Kaeso's logic was exasperating. Paul was obliged to declare: 'Yes, there would be sin. I only meant to say that there are probably other ways than violence to get you out of the sexual abuse of which you're afraid.'

Kaeso asked: 'The emperor is shortly leaving for Naples, to make his public debut as a singer there. He's asked me to go with him. Do you advise me to obey?'

'You can accompany him without fear. You'll come back from Naples untouched.'

'Another vision?'

'A very abstract one.'

'In the tiresome situation in which I find myself, no precaution should be neglected. I feel that if you gave me the Holy Spirit, I should see things more clearly and be more readily able to discover a means of protecting myself in conformity with your prudent wishes. Don't you agree?'

Paul protested:

'The Holy Spirit isn't an apotreptic of that sort. In any case, as you yourself confessed, your faith is largely a pretence.'

'Only partly. You've made an impression on me and I agree with you on many points.'

'While there's even one little point of difference, it's out of the question!'

On a table lay the slim book-rolls which Paul had lent Kaeso and which he had sent someone to fetch earlier in the morning. There was also Peter's letter, which had put Paul in such a bad temper, and a thin cheap *tomus* which had not been made available to Kaeso. Paul's haste to get his belongings back after the disappointment which Kaeso had inflicted on him was remarkable. Only good Christians should own good books.

Because he had never seen the *tomus* before and because of its unusual format, it caught his attention and he glanced at it.

'Who is this Jude, and why didn't you give him to me to read?'

Paul answered with bad grace:

'He's the brother of the dead James and very "Jewish" if I can put it like that. He has taken over certain baseless superstitions which are current on the margins of traditional Jewish circles. I wanted to spare you his references to works of doubtful authenticity.'

'Meaning?'

'The story of the assumption of Moses, for example.'

'What does "assumption" mean?'

'The taking up into heaven of a believer who has died in a state of sanctity. For the present Christians only acknowledge one assumption, which we call "ascension" because the subject of it raised Himself up to Heaven on his own – the ascension of the resurrected Christ.'

'So even the oldest of Jesus' companions aren't free of doctrinal error?'

'We all agree on a common basis of belief as summed up in our Creed. On other points discussion is free until the Church takes a definitive stand.'

Paul approached Kaeso, put his hands on his shoulders and said to him:

'There's one point on which you and I are in total agreement: sodomy is an abominable sin. And I affirm that to you as a man whom you have accused of being a closet pederast and ashamed of the fact.'

'Shed a bit more light for me, will you? Of course it's a crime, and contrary to human rights, to impose sexual relations on someone who finds them unpleasant. It's equally a crime to prevent someone having legitimate sexual relations. In my opinion, when you tell fathers to keep their daughters virgin, you're committing the same crime which could be held against Nero where I'm concerned. But we've already talked about that, and you didn't dare to contradict me. Now I'd like to know why free homosexual relations should be any more worthy of condemnation

485

than their heterosexual equivalent. You know what the Greeks think about it, and plenty of Romans have come to share their view.'

Almost unnoticed, little Myra, who was getting restless in the litter, had crept into the house and ferreted about among the people packing their bags to accompany Paul along the Appian Way as far as Pozzuoli, and even beyond in certain cases. Despite the artifices heaped upon her, she still had the air of a child, and they had found out that she was accompanying the noble Kaeso. After climbing the stairs in search of her master, Myra had pushed open the door of Paul's room, which a slave had pointed out to her.

On seeing her Kaeso put a finger to his lips and signed to her to go and crouch in a corner.

Paul was distractedly trying to find a clear, satisfactory reply. Eventually he said:

'The key to our beliefs on this question is that God is a father, who naturally wants to have as many children as possible. Consequently all ideas and practices which serve to hinder the free reproduction of the human race are to be condemned.

You know that Greece and Italy have been becoming depopulated to an alarming degree – it was Greece that started the trend. It's no longer certain that that trend can be reversed. Since children give a lot more trouble than pleasure, there are in fact only two good reasons for having any: devotion to the State, which needs citizens and soldiers, and religious beliefs. It's only rational to have children if one is looking beyond pleasure to the defence of causes which go beyond the individual. It was from the moment when traditional religious beliefs and patriotism began to decline in the city-states that the number of births started to drop in an alarming manner, to the point where governments themselves are permanently concerned about them and trying to come up with remedies. But the only remedy is the true God. Only the Christians are capable of reversing the tendency.

Sodomy is rejected by the Gospels as it was by the Old Testament, because it deflects man from the divine plan.'

'What if there came a day when the population outstripped the available resources?'

'That could only happen through the fault of mankind: idleness, improvidence, waste, prevarication and disorder. In any case an accident is no reason to question a rule. On the contrary, it should encourage one to intensify it.'

'Christ had no children. Neither have you. And I thought you told me that voluntary chastity was considered a state superior to marriage by Christians and even by some rather unorthodox Jews. How are you going to get yourself out of that contradiction?'

'I'm chaste so that I can dedicate myself more fully to God. Sodomites renounce chastity to dedicate themselves to man and his pleasures. One must judge a thing by the ends to which it is directed. The means are secondary.'

Myra, in her corner, suddenly exploded with laughter, making the two improvised theologians turn towards her. She was covered in confusion.

'And what's so funny?' Kaeso flung at her in irritation.

'Oh Master, do forgive me. But I overheard you both saying such strange things. All about a Father god who wants lots of children. Well, I'm a child. And like all little prostitutes I'm afraid of the moment when I start to have periods, because in my trade having a child is a disaster. The brothel owner beats you to punish you for your carelessness, he makes you have an abortion or exposes the child as soon as it's born. Hasn't this Father god you were talking about rather forgotten the likes of me?'

After a painful silence Paul suddenly burst into tears and gestured wearily to his visitors to go.

As they were going down the stairs, Myra said to Kaeso:

'Why did what I said make your friend cry? Did I teach him something he didn't know?'

'Paul's too sensitive for a theologian. He lives in a dream. His great scheme is to repopulate a world which is drying up for want of vigour and brotherly love. But history has laws which make his hopes impossible. The more civilized society becomes the fewer children are born. The most prolific countries are the most barbarous ones. We must choose between the pederastic dialogues of Plato and the childish burble of the Germans.'

'I can't follow you.'

'That's because I was talking to myself. What I meant, my poor child, was that the sterility of the brothel is a clear sign of civilization. Uncouth barbarians living in forests or on the steppes don't need brothels. But if the unthinkable happened and Rome did away with its brothels, the whole city would end up like a whorehouse instead. And if one day there are Christian cities, there'll be Christian brothels as well, where Paul's successors will go and weep hypocritically on Sundays. Your troubles have hardly begun.'

It was getting late. Kaeso told the bearers to head in the direction of the new Baths of Nero, where he relaxed for a long time in Myra's company. The girl's nascent breasts and the fine down on her girlish genitals which had already seen so much service made a touching contrast with the immensity of the echoing rooms and their decoration of voluptuous mosaics. Kaeso began to be worried for Myra's sake, like a man whose own future is uncertain, but who, in a moment of weakness, takes in a stray cat.

In the rest room, while Kaeso and Myra were dozing side by side, buried under a hired long-haired *gausapa*, Kaeso suddenly said to the child:

'The emperor's interest in me is too much for my own well-being. There's nothing more treacherous than a palace. Lots of favourites come to a sticky end. I'm wondering what I ought to do with you. You would be upset if I sold you to a *leno* again, wouldn't you? Even if he were a good one – if such a thing exists.'

'There's no such thing as a good *leno*. I should like to work for an old madam who specializes in expert young courtesans. And if I were good at it, when I grew up I could have girls to work for *me*.'

There was nothing one could say when faced with Myra's brand of level-headedness.

Despite the favourable circumstances the girl was so intimidated by Kaeso that she did not dare risk even the smallest caress. She finally screwed herself up to ask:

'Perhaps you're not interested in women?'

'When I was in Athens I had hetaeras who cost a lot more than you, and I think I found an appropriate degree of pleasure in them, although it was always the same thing.'

'That's even more true with ordinary prostitutes.'

'In reality all that sterile writhing around and to-ing and fro-ing seems absurd as soon as you think about it for a moment.'

'Have you ever had a boyfriend?'

'I've never fancied one in the least.'

'What *do* you fancy then?'

'I want to be left alone. But unfortunately I'm very handsome. Men and women swarm round me like flies. I was constantly pursued in Athens, and it's even worse in Rome.'

'What you need is a grand passion.'

'I've already got one, but it doesn't seem to do me any good.'

'If you become the emperor's favourite, you're not going to have much of a time of it.'

'Well, it isn't settled yet.'

'If Nero takes you as his catamite, you've got one stroke of luck. He has a very small winkie.'

Kaeso burst out laughing and changed the subject. Sooner laugh than cry.

During dinner Kaeso went on with his attempts to educate Marcus in the principles of Christianity, without trying to rush things. He began on a light, philosophical tone. As Silanus no longer had any illusions about the nature of Marcia's feelings for Kaeso, the presentation of the certificate of baptism was now more of a polite formality. This transparent lie would have something touching about it, since Kaeso had gone to such lengths to be in a position to produce it. But with Marcus it was different. It was under his roof that Kaeso would have to live after he rejected the projected adoption. It was therefore necessary to present Marcus with a picture of Christianity which was attractive enough to justify a sincere conversion, would soften the blow and would leave him disarmed as far as rational argument went. If Kaeso were suddenly to 'see the light' in a religious sense, Marcus would have to accept it: it was a well-known phenomenon. Whereas it would have been much more difficult and much more unpleasant to get him to understand that Kaeso had thrown a billion sesterces down the drain for fear of finding himself sexually under Marcia's thumb. A man who was prepared to dispatch his son with military efficiency into Nero's bed would find the excuse far too trivial. Jesus was the most effective and elegant solution.

Moreover, Marcus' ingrained disquiet and mistrust had been lulled by the proximity of the adoption and the emperor's show of favour. He listened to Kaeso with particular care because he prided himself on his knowledge of philosophy and was happy to see the young man taking an interest in him after weeks of indifference or barely concealed repulsion. Marcus was far from perceiving the abyss which opened up behind the boy's remarks. He saw in them a purely temporary obsession. And – like Kaeso with Paul earlier – he played the game, asked questions and thought up objections. The debate was further enlivened by Selene, who, to oblige Kaeso, took a malicious pleasure in pretending to hold favourable opinions of a religion which she detested. So there were two pseudo-Christians preaching the true faith to someone who did not give a damn about it. When, after a philosophical approach to the phenomenon, Kaeso put on a troubled, thoughtful look, it was enough to enrage the most merciful of heavens, whatever god were occupying it.

After dinner Marcus, who had drunk less than usual, went off looking lecherous with Selene. Shortly afterwards she reappeared in the would-be atrium, where Kaeso was dreaming in the moonlight.

She sat down next to the boy, who asked her:

'You've lived in Alexandria and Canopus among sculptors, painters, poets, singers and actors. Given the liveliness of your mind I don't suppose for one minute that all they appreciated about you was the sculpted perfection of your body. Though you saved me from Marcia's tiny hands, I now look like falling into the great paws of Nero. Can you throw some light on the artistic mentality for me?'

'I'd prefer to say something reassuring to you, but you'll find the truth more useful. As you know, there are a number of different moral codes, with pretensions to specific or general validity. The Jews and Christians have their own. So do those who believe in false gods, whether one is talking about the pretentious Stoics or just the man-in-the-street. Even the atheist Epicureans have a moral code. And setting aside universal and national doctrines, if you look at the ideas and conduct of this or that small section of society, you discover that each one has its own special ethical code, and that everybody more or less obeys rules which are intended to defend his or her own interests. Soldiers, gladiators, *lanistae*, *lenones*, prostitutes, tradesmen, and thieves all have their customs, their prejudices and a certain concept of honour.

But there is one exception. Not only do artists have no morality, but they actually like to be immoral, because it's their natural inclination to make fun of the morality of others. There's nothing surprising in this attitude, since one obviously couldn't deduce even the smallest definitive rule of conduct from the exclusive, fanatical cult of forms and sounds. And the fact that the artist is permanently afflicted with terrible doubts about the significance of what he creates makes him all the more excessive and unpredictable in his behaviour. The uncertainty undermines and unbalances him. Sometimes he'll leap for joy at the stupidest of compliments. At others he'll sink into frightful depression when criticized by someone with no knowledge or authority. An artist is like a ship continually searching for an anchorage or a harbour where it can rest for a while. He never stays the same, he's for ever piling up contradictory experiences in his vertiginous onward flight.

So one can't rely on an artist in any respect. They drift from mood to mood according to circumstance. They can be pleasant or cold, kind or cruel, sensitive but superficial, disinterested but thoughtless, wasteful, provocative, vain, inclined to rapacity and contemptuousness, hedonistic. And dishonest, in the sense that their expressions of enthusiasm are only of as much consequence as the moment which inspires them. Artists are by nature antisocial creatures, dominated by passions, capable of anything and everything. In a state which was properly run their birth and reproduction would be prevented. If your father were an artist he would be even more corrupt than he is.

Pious Jews would blush to be the parents of anyone with the least artistic pretensions, and unpleasant experiences have led me to share their religious convictions. But the abomination of abominations is undoubtedly an artist-emperor, who can use his absolute power to further his dangerous obsessions. So watch out. You're going into the lion's den, and his whimsical predilection for playing at being a bedside rug only makes the situation more alarming. Sooner or later the rug will get up and bite you.'

Clearly Selene's Jewish upbringing was in part responsible for this sinister vision, but it coincided too closely with the traditional old Roman prejudices for Kaeso not to find it disturbing. He confirmed Selene's fears by recounting Marcia's impromptu boat trip.

'What you've told me only half surprises me. In many of the prince's improvisations you can, in my opinion, see a desperate effort to react against Agrippina's authority over him, which is said to have been crushing. The true artist can only free himself by trampling his parents under foot – it's another one of his basic traits, and one of the least attractive. I've never heard an artist say anything nice about his father or mother. They're always suspected of having been obstacles to his wonderful vocation.'

'Then what's your advice to someone in a mess like mine?'

'It's not up to a slave to preach human dignity to a free man. And since you're my sole source of protection, it's clearly in my interest for you to stay on the right side of both Marcia and Nero, though the latter is more important than the former. The only chance you have of getting round an artist is to flatter his talents. But there is a great crowd of flatterers around him and you'll need to be a genius to stand out.'

'Among the artists you've known, which were the ones most to be avoided?'

'Sculptors, painters, singers and actors have no concept of morality. But poets and writers sometimes say what they mean and behave more or less honestly. Not of course because they are poets and writers, but perhaps because their art derives in part from the precision of their judgement. A statue or a picture "means" what the public thinks it means and its quality is continually being reassessed. But if a poet puts into verse: "In the public lavatories I met a lad as beautiful as Cupid", although you can discuss the technique of the verse till the cows come home, everybody will grasp its meaning in the same way. The arts which address themselves to the organs of sight or hearing "mean" little or nothing. Those which address themselves to the intellect establish a more precise form of communication between men. This characteristic makes a poet more like the rest of the human race than other breeds of artist.'

'You mean that a poet is still a normal human being precisely in so far as he is not a poet, and leaves no margin for interpretation.'

'Precisely. The most mediocre poets are also the most normal and certainly the most widely understood.'

'Well, Nero is a real poet, and by temperament sensitive to every possible art form.'

'He is possessed by an absolute form of madness, and it would be wise to keep out of its way. One last characteristic of the artist: because of his extreme sensitivity, and the pathological lack of confidence which inevitably goes with it, he will be timid and mistrustful.'

Kaeso leant his head on Selene's knees and whimpered: 'What's to become of me?' The fact that he now felt completely bereft of support strengthened the effect of the slave's remarks. Her wisdom was the fruit of bitter experience.

'Whatever you can achieve and perhaps whatever you want . . . Everyone reacts in his own way to the degree of freedom which changing circumstances accord him. I, for example, am still free to say to you that it's not proper for you to put your head in my lap. If the master suspected your feelings for me, he'd take it out on my body.'

Kaeso hurriedly sat up.

Selene went on: 'It's good for a man to have a moral code of some kind, but he shouldn't overdo it. Just as there's a form of artistic madness which is at the opposite pole to all concept of decency, so there is a form of moral madness which is even more distressing to see, because it plays havoc with very worthy people and they're inclined to spread it.

It's a warm, bright night, thieves and muggers will still be knocking back their after-dinner wine and so is the master. If you'd care to follow me to the Aventine, I'll show you an instructive sight which you won't forget: a model of virtue.'

Kaeso's curiosity was aroused. He fell in behind Selene, who went first to the kitchen and took a large *placenta*, made from flour, semolina, dried powdered cheese and honey. She hid the cake under her cloak. Kaeso, on the off-chance, hid under his the short sword which had already done him a good turn in his encounter with the *vespillones*. And they set off.

The brightness of the evening showed up the charcoal graffiti and various placards which lovers left on the door of their beloved's house. Tomcats attract the attention of potential mates by urinating all over the place. Aspiring Roman lovers, those whose desires had not been fulfilled during the discreet hour of siesta, were in the habit of standing on their beloved's doorstep, while her husband or protector was away, and leaving glaring traces of their feelings, in which expressions of the most humble fidelity jostled with outbursts of extreme rage and spleen. And just as people found the inscriptions on tombs a source of entertainment, so they did those on doors, some of which were absolutely studded with laments and panegyrics which the mistress or the husband could not be bothered to have erased. And of course neighbours and passers-by did not scruple to add their own comments. Sometimes the door was decorated with a garland of faded flowers or a burnt-out torch, as a reminder of hours of waiting in vain. Most of the inscriptions were in verse, which often reproduced a fragment of poetry which the passionate suitor had declaimed or a fragment of a serenade which he had sung.

At the entry to the Forums Kaeso stopped for a moment to read two new quatrains on a door whose two panels looked like a biographical sketch:

> Oh rather let the breeze's whim
> Blow your boat o'er the deep,
> Than put your faith in Flavia,
> Who ne'er her word will keep.
>
> Aquilo is more trustworthy
> Than Flavia's word will prove,
> Boreas more predictable
> Than Flavia's fickle love.

Kaeso said to Selene:

'This is the first time I've ever known you go out. Are you taking that cake to some particularly virtuous lover?'

'From time to time I take a few cakes or sweets to my old uncle Moses, who has no teeth left. Seven years ago the Romans picked him up and sold him into slavery after a riot in Jerusalem. Like the rabbi Samuel, who got hold of his address for me, he's a Pharisee of the old school.'

'He must have been pleased to see you again?'

'Surprised rather than pleased. The last news he had had of me was that I was still a prisoner in my Alexandrian brothel.'

'What happened to your parents?'

'By the time I was reduced to slavery my mother was already dead. My father died of grief. My brothers and sisters were split up and I'm not sure what happened to them.'

At the Porta Capena Kaeso and Selene had difficulty getting past the carts which were hurrying into Rome to ensure its re-provisioning. They went round the Aventine to the east and then climbed up the slopes of the hill towards the bread market and the Portico of Minerva. At that time of day, in this industrial quarter close to the docks and the warehouses, activity was concentrated in the flour-mills and bakeries, where the work, in shifts, only stopped after midday. Nobody had made their own bread at home for years. The air was full of the dull grinding of the mills and hazy with smoke from the roasting-chambers and ovens.

Close by the market stood the premises of the firm of Pansa. It was both a mill and a bakery, and one of the biggest. Pansa himself, who was a power in his guild, produced starch for pastry-cooks, by soaking grain in water which was frequently changed. By carefully pulverizing it in great wooden mortars he then obtained, dependent on the fineness of the sieve used for sifting, three qualities of flour, the pure wheaten flour used for cakes, ordinary flour, and coarse flour mixed with bran. Pansa also had a roasting chamber, because, despite the overwhelming competition from easily hulled grain, hard or soft, some people still stuck to the traditional types of grain which, since they could not be winnowed, had to be roasted before they could be ground. The type of grain known as *far*, whence the word *farina* (flour), was the first grain known to man and was still thought the noblest by some. Virgil had refused to acknowledge any other. But Pansa, following the Greeks, also roasted barley and millet, for the preparation of polenta, and even some ordinary grain. Roasting it made it keep better and gave the flour a sweeter flavour, by turning part of the starch into dextrin.

Selene asked Kaeso to follow her closely and plunged into the vast hangar where more than 100 half-naked slaves were working busily in the infernal heat of the grills and ovens. A supervisor nodded to Selene as they passed through on their way to the mill-stones, which were close to the kneading-troughs. She stopped in front of one of these stones, which were being turned by a wretched group of blind men. Slaves with no

494

source of protection who had lost or almost lost their sight were often sent to the mills.

These devices had been designed with remarkable practical intelligence. The grain was milled between an upper female cone, which turned, and a fixed lower male cone, which was fitted with an adjustable spindle allowing one to grind to different degrees of fineness. The female cone was symmetrically surmounted by an identical reversed cone which acted as a funnel. To get a new mill, all you had to do was turn the whole thing upside down. The former funnel then became the grinder and the former grinder became the funnel. This model was used throughout the Roman world, and was worked by either humans or animals, who pressed against wooden bars arranged laterally.

Kaeso wrinkled his nose to keep out the acrid smell of sweat coming from the streaming, panting bodies. In a low voice Selene said to him:

'The thinnest one is my uncle Moses. You can't even tell what his features are under that wild beard which covers his face. It's equally difficult to tell what's going on in his mind. Moses is what they call "strong-minded"; he's stubborn through and through. He's only ever known the Law, the whole Law and nothing but the Law, and he's guided by his conscience the way an animal is guided by its instincts. In Jerusalem he was compromised by his association with a band of zealots, crazy revolutionaries who dreamed of chasing the Romans out by force. His misfortunes haven't changed him. If anything they've hardened his character still more. For years he's been going round and round, attached to his mill-stone, on a diet of thin gruel and beatings. For this sort of work it's better to be blind: anyone with good eyesight would soon become dizzy. When they use donkeys they have to cover their eyes.'

'It's all very sad, but why is this man a model of virtue? And, if you'll forgive me for saying so, your virtue is clearly less than his, since with the 100,000 sesterces which I gave you you could have bought up and freed 300 wretches like him.'

'Buying him out was my first thought. But the evening when I mentioned my intention to him, with a little present of sweets and cakes to back me up, he answered – and remember that I am his niece – "I should feel less free if I escaped from slavery thanks to the impure money of a prostitute."'

❖ CHAPTER ❖
3

Kaeso rubbed his eyes, which were irritated by the smoke from grills, lamps and torches, and sat down on a brick seat which ran along the bottom of a wall. He tried to focus on the lesson Selene was trying to teach him. In front of him, chained to one of the two wooden arms of a mill, was a being of the strongest moral principles, dissuaded from suicide by his religion, going round and round like a squirrel in a cage. In splashing about in his evening gruel the old man had got it everywhere, even in his hair, which made him look all the more absurd.

Kaeso finally asked Selene:

'Why didn't rabbi Samuel buy Moses out, using your money?'

'Because that would have meant tricking my uncle, who would have been bound to suspect something. There's no one crazy enough to buy an old blind slave who's not fit for any work but the mill. Moses isn't worth 200 sesterces.'

'What about yourself? Why didn't you ask my father to agree to your release? 100,000 sesterces is a lot of money to him.'

'I'm already worth 70,000, and Marcus is very attached to me. What would be most to my advantage is to persuade him to free me in his will. A pretty woman with no money is never free.'

'To come back to your uncle, would he be on his guard if I offered to buy him out?'

'He's close to death now, and that makes his virtue all the more cautious. Anyway, it pays a blind man to be mistrustful.'

A baking session was just finishing. They had opened the iron doors, and were taking all sorts of loaves out of the line of ovens which ran all along one side of the hangar. To do this they used the long-handled spades which they had previously used to put the bread in. At the same time the fashioning of a new load of loaves for baking was being completed.

One oven was devoted exclusively to white bread made with pure wheaten flour, the *panis candidus*, which was much the most expensive. Other ovens were reserved for white bread of the second quality, which in the old days had satisfied the rustic tastes of Augustus in his old age. But most of the ovens were producing plebeian black bread, much of it made from the grain distributed by the services of the *Annona* to those qualified to receive it. There was also 'wholemeal' bread, made from unsifted flour, and even common bran bread for dog food and for those slaves who were least well looked after.

Fat Pansa appeared and, with a frown, checked the quality of the baking and the precise shaping of the new loaves. These were very various, though the majority were round cobs split on top into fours. He paid particular attention to the *panis ostrearius*, which was intended to go with oysters, and then to the plebeian loaves with erotic pretensions, a collection of phalluses and vulvas, arses and nippled breasts, which were sold at a high price to rich layabouts who were bored with *panis candidus* and appreciated the tonic and laxative virtues of this common food.

All around Pansa, who was famous for his awful temper, the supervisors and slaves concerned held their breath. One day, thoroughly fed up with a scrounging apprentice, Pansa had without thinking pushed the boy into the open mouth of an oven which was in the process of being loaded. The whole ovenload of bread had been spoiled. The Prefect had nearly made a lot of trouble for the brutal owner, but at least the necessary discipline had been re-established.

At the sight of Selene Pansa's face lit up – he was a great womanizer – and he came over and spoke very amiably to her. To sleep with Selene, who pretended not to understand what he was after, he would have roasted a dozen bungling apprentices.

Selene introduced Kaeso to Pansa, who promptly became still more amiable: Silanus' steward was one of his big customers. Conversation naturally turned to the question of buying out Moses, one to which Pansa had given plenty of thought, since he would happily have handed the old man over to anyone in exchange for a few small favours from Selene. There were in any case plenty of blind men in Rome. Certain proprietors were even ready to give their blind slaves away gratis to anyone willing to take them. But while Moses remained suspicious and obstinate, there was nothing to be done. At Pansa's establishment at least the old man got a decent plate of gruel to eat. What would happen to him if he quarrelled with Selene and were left all alone without work in this monstrous Babylon? Would he even be able to find a Jew to take care of him? He wouldn't get fat by begging, since the fact that most blind beggars were frauds made the public rather sparing in their charity.

Pansa graciously had Moses untied and replaced before his turn, and led him firmly by the wrist to the bench where Kaeso and Selene were sitting. The slave had a tendency to walk in circles, from having to go round and round the same way all the time. Mill slaves quickly forgot how to walk in a straight line, and Moses had been breaking his back in the job for three years now. Finally, after a last caressing glance at Selene and a final exchange of *politesses* with Kaeso, Pansa went on with his inspection, trailing in his wake the tall athletic Nubian negro who served as his general handyman and bodyguard. Pansa was very proud of his negro – it was his only trace of snobbery. Slaves of that colour, given their rarity, reached very high prices, and were usually to be found only in great houses or in the arena at the amphitheatres, where they were the ultimate in popular luxury.

Selene put the cake down in her uncle's lap. He touched it with visible repugnance, as if this *placenta* carried with it a suggestion of debauchery and infamy. Clearly it was the only concession that he would ever make, the only benefit of the doubt that he would ever give, to the surrounding impurity.

Without great hope of convincing him Kaeso said to Moses: 'My name is Kaeso, and I'm the younger son of Selene's master. I recently had a long and sympathetic talk with rabbi Samuel, because I was thinking of converting to Judaism. The moral beauty of the creed has had a very forcible effect on me. My circumcision has been postponed until I have received more instruction, but in the meantime I have the greatest respect and esteem for the Jews in general and the Pharisees in particular. That's why I understand and admire your refusal to regain your liberty through the intervention of your niece. Through no fault of her own she's undoubtedly obliged to live an unworthy life. But would you do me the honour of believing me if I assure you that I should like to buy you out with my own money, simply as a token of friendship?'

The old man went on eating his *placenta* without reacting. However, sensing Selene's impatience, he said to Kaeso:

'I lost my eyesight three years ago, but my ears have become correspondingly more sensitive to lies, and your Greek rings false. You're not interested in me. You're only acting for Selene's sake: you must be hoping for her favours, if you haven't already enjoyed them. Everyone knows that in Rome sons don't scruple to rape their father's concubines when they feel like it. Let me die in peace. There are no favours I can hope for except from the Almighty.'

There was nothing much they could say to that. Moses had resolved according to his own lights the problem which continually tormented

498

Seneca and many other Stoics. At what moment did it become appropriate to refuse the compromise and corruption of this world once and for all and take mental refuge in a more attractive universe? Was it a question of degree or of nature? Should one say no at once, straight away, in a matter of no importance, or should one wait patiently, though choking with disgust, until some major event signalled the advent of a breaking point. It was unclear whether Moses' decision was a sign of senile imbecility or sublimity.

Kaeso suddenly remembered a rather bizarre passage in the Gospel of Mark: 'John said to him: "Master, we saw a man driving out devils in your name, and as he was not one of us, we tried to stop him." Jesus said: "Do not stop him; no one who does a work of divine power in my name will be able the next moment to speak evil of me. For he who is not against us is on our side."' So not only did Christ and his followers have the power to perform miracles, as Paul's miracle cures seemed to prove, but Jesus himself thought it quite natural that anybody could perform miracles if they used his name.

Suddenly, urged by a strange inner force, Kaeso said to Moses: 'You're a man of truth and you have the right to be told the truth. I should confess to you that the rabbi Samuel made such difficulties about becoming a Jew that I got into contact with representatives of the Christian sect, who undoubtedly have gifts which are out of the ordinary. A certain Paul, for example, cured a blind man in my presence in the Cattle Market, in front of the Temple of Patrician Modesty, by simply rubbing his eyes with the very scarf which I'm wearing this evening. According to the Christians it's written that to cure a sick man it's enough to invoke the name of Jesus. Would you accept it if Christ gave you back your sight through my agency?'

At this name the old man lifted his head and stared with his sightless eyes in the direction of the creaking mill. He seemed to be in the grip of old emotions. Eventually he said in a slow voice:

'When I was fourteen or fifteen or so – I had been under our Law for a few years – I followed your Jesus for a while. Many people claimed he might be the Messiah. He was certainly a very clever conjuror. He had an astonishing trick where he produced huge quantities of fish and bread, but he couldn't get a shoulder of lamb out of an empty sack. I also saw him cure several of the sick. Since I've been turning this mill and eating filthy gruel, I've sometimes wondered about Jesus' talent for multiplying loaves. He was so gifted he even managed to produce warm bread, as though it had just come straight from the oven.

The pack of ecstatic women who clung round him were besides themselves over it.

But I gave up following Jesus when he started to attack the Law and to grant remission of sins. That is the privilege of God alone. What are all the miracles in the world compared with a single verse of the Law? Jesus claimed in his defence that someone possessed by devils can't chase out devils. But there are plenty of learned men who maintain that Satan's cunning easily extends to that. I want nothing to do with this Christ. We were right to condemn him for blasphemy.'

'They say that he came back from the dead unaided.'

'That's the crux of the matter. I was with Jesus when he brought the daughter of the chief priest of the synagogue, Jairus, back to life. But only a God can come back from the dead unaided, and Yahwe could not and would not take on human form. Don't talk to me about your Christ. I've had all the illumination I need – the light which has been enlightening Israel since the days of Abraham.'

The logic of the old man's declaration was impeccable. At a period when miracles were commonplace, and where the distinction between the ordinary and the extraordinary was imprecise, the only truly convincing miracle was to come back to life unaided. Everything else was of dubious significance, within the grasp of any school with an ounce of *savoir-faire*. What counted against the Christians was that the only definite miracle they could offer, the cornerstone of their whole edifice, was flatly beyond belief, for a reason which was even more metaphysical than physical. A god who is careful of his reputation does not go to the lavatory.

Kaeso said to himself that if science were more advanced, and if the distinction between the miraculous and the normal were clearer and better defined, many of Jesus' miracles would perhaps look more convincing. For the time being the incompetence of scientists was a factor creating a degree of uncertainty.

Moses went on: 'I have all the less scruple in turning down your well-meant offer because you mentioned Paul. He's a thoroughly bad lot, full of hatred for the pious Jews who condemn his fantasies, and against the Law, every letter of which remains a living reproach to him, no matter what he says and does. In the few writings of his which I read in Jerusalem before I was taken prisoner by the Romans, he constantly accuses the Jews of having crucified his Christ, which is doubly untrue. In the first place Jesus crucified himself, because he knew quite well that to claim divine incarnation was punishable by death under the Law. Second and more important, while the Law which was applied to him certainly affects all Jews, those who condemned him and handed him over to the Romans were only a tiny minority. It took a generation before most Jews had even heard tell of the misfortunes of Jesus, and the majority is only an accomplice after the fact, even if that fact is something for which it is justly prepared to take the credit. But how could an ignorant Gentile grasp those nuances? So you can see a feeling of mistrust and hostility towards the Jews developing among those Christians with a Gentile background, although that feeling can only be justified against the handful of educated Jews who were actually responsible. The truth, of which Paul claims to be the apostle, would be improved if in his letters he replaced the term "the Jews" by a more precise expression: "Some Pharisees and Sadducees in Jerusalem". I'm beginning to wonder whether Paul doesn't get himself beaten up by Jews from time to time on purpose, so as to help keep the confusion alive.'

Kaeso was not very interested in this point of view. He wished the old man luck and withdrew with Selene.

On the way she asked him:

'Did you draw the right lesson from all that?'

'Unfortunately I could see two contradictory lessons to be drawn. Is Moses a touching model of steadfastness or the ultimate example of the most pernicious and stupid fanaticism? I don't expect you to answer.'

Instead of going back to the insula via the Porta Capena, Kaeso and Selene crossed the Aventine, went round the western side of the Circus Maximus and came down into the Forums by the Clivus Sublicius. The night was drawing on and clouds hid the last quarter of the moon. At that time of night such a route, where the open spaces were more numerous, was likely to be safer. They passed between the temple of Bona Dea and the altar of Jupiter Elicius, kept Pollio's library to their left, went along the front of the temples of the Moon and Juno Regina, came down the steep part of the *clivus*, crossed between the temple of Pompeian Hercules and the temple of Flora, then between the plebeian temple of Ceres and the entrance to the Circus Maximus, and arrived in the Cattle Market. There, once upon a time, a bullock which was about to be sacrificed had escaped from the priests, climbed the stairs of a modest apartment block, and thrown itself off the third floor, a wonder which had marked the beginning of the Punic Wars. Every stone in Rome had a story to tell. Everywhere the gods gave signs. Only the Judaeo-Christian god observed total discretion. Being followers of a sole god the Jews only wanted a single Temple – their synagogues were merely places to meet and pray, and no sacrifices were performed there. And the Christians had still not thought of putting their incarnate god, and the slivers of bread into which he had been made, into monuments specially built for the purpose.

There was something ghostly about a Rome stripped of its crowds and animated only by the occasional nocturnal traveller or by the rounds of the Watch. It was the moment when vengeful spectres came out of their tombs to terrorize those negligent persons who had not done what was necessary to keep the dead at a distance. Cicero would be prowling the corridors of Silanus' house, much put out by the tranquil philosophy of the new owner and the insulting contempt shown by Marcia.

In front of the temple of Patrician Modesty Kaeso said to Selene:

'One of the good things about the Jewish and Christian religions is that the living are no longer troubled by the dissatisfied dead. No more errant souls. They're kept prisoner in hell or heaven, and their heirs can sleep in peace. I can't imagine that any one has ever seen a Jewish ghost.'

Selene agreed that the concept of a Jewish ghost was unorthodox. But she added: 'According to rumour the Christians are busy concocting a whole system of trafficking with the dead. Since their god took on human form they are for ever praying to Jesus to intervene in their affairs, and they think that some of their martyrs can also have an influence. There's nothing Jewish about ideas of that sort.'

A posse of filthy blind men emerged from the shadows of the nearby portico of the Basilica Sempronia and launched into insistent demands for alms. Kaeso and Selene began to walk faster, with the blind men (who seemed to have less and less difficulty in seeing) at their heels. Eventually the beggars began to run, intent on beating up the two passers-by. Kaeso and Selene made off through the alleys of the upper part of the Velabrum and finally took refuge, quite out of breath, in the Aequimelium, which was currently being restocked with pigeons, chickens and rabbits. This market specialized in the little victims which the poor offered up as sacrifices.

'There would be more point,' said Selene, 'in blinding those who pretend to be blind than in curing those who really are. The Christians ought to use their talents to put all the thieves and murderers who infest the city out of action!'

Kaeso explained to Selene that, as far as he understood, Christian miracles were not a social gesture. Christ could have multiplied the shoulders of lamb – or even the legs of lamb which the Gentiles ate without worrying about the impure sciatic nerve – in such a way as to feed the entire earth, he could have cured every illness and made men lose the bad habit of dying, but he had preferred merely to offer a few miniscule examples of what he could do. Never had a miracle-working conjuror showed himself so sparing with his gifts. As far as Kaeso knew, in a period of twelve or so days Paul had limited himself to one cure and one resurrection, although they hadn't seemed to tire him much, and Luke, although a doctor, had simply kept his arms crossed. When it came to amateurism, Paul was a classic disciple of his Lord.

'But in that case,' said Selene, 'why do the Christians allow any miracles at all?'

'I assume they must be intended as demonstrations. They give, in an off-hand way, a glimpse of what could be done if they cared to do it. But they hold back so as to make the patient understand that famine and disease are nothing besides sin. That's the only sickness which really counts. And it's certainly true that if everyone became completely virtuous and charitable overnight, food would be better distributed and digestive systems more peaceful. But from their paradoxical standpoint the Christians aren't entirely wrong. Even the philosophers say that it's the soul which needs caring for first and foremost.'

Kaeso and Selene had taken refuge in a labyrinth of cages piled one on top of another, all containing pigeons. Some way off the work went on by torch or lantern light, for though the night was bright, the inside of the market was dark. Sometimes a wavering light would catch Selene's profile, as she stood pressing close to her master's son in her fear. She had never been more beautiful.

The pigeons, which had been woken up by their cart ride, were also snuggled up to one another. Perhaps the Holy Spirit, of which Paul made so much use, had disguised itself as a pigeon to show that cooing tenderness (even of an edible variety) was of more value than discursive intelligence? When it came to it, the Christians were intuitive and only used reason as an accessory.

Kaeso suddenly felt a rush of physical desire and his hasty hands spoke for themselves. Instead of struggling foolishly, Selene stayed motionless, with her legs together, and tried an appeal to reason. 'Do you by any chance want to prove Moses right in his prejudices? He imagines the most distinguished Roman families as just so many brothels where fathers and sons share out the slaves of both sexes under the indifferent gaze of their immoral wives?'

It was enough to make him lose his temper. The Athenian ephebes, and Marcia and Nero, among others, had pursued Kaeso with their attentions, even certain Greek hetaeras had seemed to take a frank pleasure in his company, and when for once in a while he actually wanted a girl – a girl who had been sleeping with anyone and everyone for years – she lectured him on morality. But just as he was about to give in to his impulse, he realized the baseness of his conduct and said instead: 'Forgive me. I gave you my word I'd protect you against Marcia, and I must also protect you against myself. I shall never take advantage of you as so many others have, and I'll never force you into acts which might displease you. It's your friendship and esteem which I especially value. I ought already to be very grateful to you for your devotion and advice.'

Selene kissed Kaeso's hand and said in a friendly voice:

'If I were a young Jewish girl of fifteen, and you were a Jew, and your parents asked my father for my hand in marriage, I should be delighted. You have everything needed to set a virgin dreaming.'

They extricated themselves from the pigeons, and for greater security followed a team of sewage disposal men along the 'Vicus Jugarius'. The Forums were deserted, the Subura was slumbering and they reached the *insula* without any further disturbing encounters.

Kaeso passed a bad night, his sleep constantly broken by nightmares and periods of wakefulness. He had the impression of being at a turning point in his life, and all the roads open to him were dark. There was no midway path between the requirements of dignity, whose effect would be catastrophic, and the surrender of principle which, though excusable, did not of itself definitively exclude all danger. Men like Moses turned mills, men like Paul got themselves stoned, the most rigorous Stoics found a way out in noble suicide, but the very caresses of Marcia and the emperor were a trap. He would have to make a choice, like it or not, because the scheduled dates of both the adoption and the departure for Naples were close.

When dawn broke Kaeso felt the need for a change of air, and withdrew for a time to the family *ludus* by the Appian Way, to be among healthy, brave men whose good sense might be contagious. Myra insisted on going with him.

After a pause during the winter months gladiatorial activity had theoretically started up again, but there was still a shortage of clients. Aponius' men, for want of Roman *munera*, were reduced to putting on shows in Italian towns. The kind of ambitions which generated frequent *munera* had died with the Republic and its aristocratic leaders. Since then every emperor had imposed his own mark and rhythm on the profession of gladiator. Caesar had been fairly liberal with *munera*, but during the best bouts he could be seen openly doing his correspondence in his box.

Augustus had shown a gentlemanly interest in gladiatorial performances, and had taken pride in a show of bountifulness. Tiberius had retreated into an aristocratic disdain which had been the source of his unpopularity. Caligula had added his measure of lunacy in this area as in all things. Claudius had been an addict, and was held back from doing more only by his avarice. And with Nero, whose aesthetic repugnance was well known, *munera* had become quite rare, but exceptionally luxurious and unpredictable. Everybody at the *ludus* always hoped there would be a big spring show staged. So, as in many another barracks in Rome and the West, Nero's desire to leave for Greece was a sore point. There was already little enough fighting in the arenas of the city. There would be virtually none if the emperor went away.

The unbearable Amaranthus had been killed outright in a brawl in Ravenna and replaced by an old *mirmillo* to whom the emperor Claudius had previously granted his freedom on the grounds that he was the father of a large family. It was an even rarer occurrence among gladiators than among other social groups, and the exemplary nature of the privilege had raised a laugh. Not knowing what else to do the man had signed up again, and still went around with three infants clinging to his tunic while his cadaverous mistress was doing the washing. The Greek, Dardanus, had finally shacked up with a shifty-looking young lad who was always asking him for money, and Capreolus had just been wounded in the hip by a Gaul in the arena at Pompeii. But the lanista Eurypylus and the charioteer Tyrannus and his two stallions were still the same as ever.

First thing in the morning Kaeso would go out riding along the road, then he fenced furiously. After siesta he would go and bathe in the nearest baths, which were close to the Appian Way behind the joint temples of Honour and Virtue. At meals, for which he supplied little extras in the way of wine and food, he forced himself to take an interest in the conversation of Eurypylus and his pupils, which always revolved around professional matters. And after dinner he would be sure to visit Capreolus, who was improving slowly and took his meals in his room. The Jew was troubled by the fact that he had been wounded in the hip like Jacob in his struggle with the Almighty. He was almost inclined to see it as a mark of election. Since that metaphysical struggle the Israelites had given up eating the sciatic nerve of animals, and this bizarre custom continually posed unpleasant practical problems. If there were no expert butcher to hand to take the nerve out of the appropriate part of the animal, they had to abandon the whole of its rear quarters. The strictest Jews absolutely refused to touch it. Another rule that Paul had got rid of!

During the day Kaeso succeeded in not giving much thought to his troubles. But at night, in the darkness of his little room, he was a prey to fits of acute anxiety and to nightmares which made him scream and scream, until Myra got up from her pallet and put her cool hands on his brow. There was unfortunately nothing else she could do to comfort him.

In his new surroundings one of the most persistently painful aspects of Kaeso's state of confusion was that he had got to the point of wondering whether the seriousness of his case was real, or whether his imagination was responsible for the worst of his suffering, like a sick man who cannot decide whether he has a cold or leprosy. The vast majority of young Romans would have gone quite happily from Marcia's arms to those of the prince. Was the paralysis afflicting Kaeso divine or human in origin? Was it a sign of holy dignity or an absurd moral luxury?

The constant company of the gladiators, with their basic appetites, showed Kaeso quite clearly how far notions of good and evil were dependent on opinion and sensitivity. Opinions can change with the wind and sensitivity varies with the individual. Scepticism was unfortunately the last doctrine which could be relied upon to produce a decision when it was absolutely necessary to do so.

After three days of havering Kaeso made up his mind to go home. On the morning of the Lemuria, a *dies nefastus* when the souls of the dead had to be appeased, he walked back along the Appian Way, followed by Myra, who was rather worried by her young master's condition. The Ides were four days away and Nero's departure for Naples had been officially announced.

Shortly before the Porta Capena, on the right-hand side of the road, were the temples of Honour and Virtue, behind the tomb of the *gens* Marcella and the adjoining tomb of Camilla, the sister of the three Horaces. In killing his sister on a delicate point of patriotism Horace had perhaps taken honour and virtue too far. On the other hand, didn't ordinary virtue usually take its inspiration from excessive virtue? It was in any case striking that the temples of Honour and Virtue had been built outside the city walls, as if to signify to the perceptive observer that honour and virtue were not qualities conferred on the body politic once and for all, but ones which had to be the object of a quest, to be undertaken only by the best . . .

Once through the Porta Capena Kaeso turned off towards the house of the Christian-Jewish tent-maker, which was slightly off his normal route. He left Myra at the door, with instructions to behave herself, and went into the house, which seemed deserted. Even the concierge was not to be seen.

In fact everyone was gathered together to take part in a sacred meal, and as he was now baptized, Kaeso was entitled to partake of it. So he mingled with the faithful.

The element of segregation, which seemed an essential part of the Christian religion, offered food for thought. The sacrifices which were a part of Greek and Roman official religion took place in front of temples, in the public square. Whereas the followers of Jesus, following Oriental custom, would not allow non-initiates to be present at their ceremonies.

An ascetic-looking preacher, with a shrill voice and a fanatical gleam in his eye, was delivering a speech in Greek on the eschatological and apocalyptic themes which were so frequently discussed by the Christians. Jesus had predicted that his disciples would be grievously persecuted, and had put them on their guard against false Christs and false prophets who would be attractive and ingenious enough to deceive even the elect. He had announced in horrifying terms the ruin of Judaea and the Roman occupation of Jerusalem and the Temple. He had predicted that the Jews would be driven out of Palestine and scattered until, in turn, the day of the Gentiles was over. And this appalling catastrophe had inspired him with terrible allusions to the end of the world and to the Last Judgement, when he would come back in glory to gather the elect together in a blaze of light which would no longer owe anything to that of the fading stars. Jesus had moreover prophesied that the fall of Jerusalem would occur before those of his own generation were dead. Many of his shocked audience had become mixed up about these stories of the end of the world and the Jews and supposed that the Last Judgement would take place soon. True, the best prophets take a strange delight in remaining vague and avoiding the sort of specific detail which would encourage people to take them seriously. Jesus had prophesied in the stock style of the Jewish eschatological and apocalyptic tradition, without dates. So far none of the three predictions had come true, and it was not within ordinary human powers to foresee that as far as two of the three were concerned the machine was already relentlessly working towards a prompt verification of the Lord's words.

The echo of these prophecies of disaster had been so resounding that the first generation of Christians had had difficulty in freeing themselves from an apocalyptic mentality. The persecutions and the fall of the Temple, though imminent, seemed of little importance beside the Last Judgement, though its relative deferment offered something of a breathing space. But these Christians benefited from their lack of perspective in the sense that fear of a general judgement to the accompaniment of great trumpet blasts drew from them virtues which the fear of a close, fatal but purely individual Judgement would not have been sufficient to produce. In their innocence they did not yet know that each man's death is the end of the world for him, and that the end of the world is therefore something entirely common and private.

Kaeso was astonished at the importance of this apocalyptic dimension to the Christians. He was suddenly discovering a religion of disaster, of which Paul's rationalist activities had barely made him aware. For a cultivated Roman with a veneer of Greek culture the phenomenon was particularly interesting, because it called into question the fundamental concept of time. To Rome and Greece time represented a process of cyclic evolution. One went from golden age to iron age, and when the wheel had completed a full cycle, it all started again. Humanity did not progress: it went round in circles. But by claiming to be God, the incarnate Jesus had smashed the eternal wheel of time and substituted a linear movement. After the golden age of earthly Paradise and the Fall men were moving slowly but surely towards Christ, whose death and Resurrection summed up the whole of history. After which, the game was over, the world was entirely superfluous and events ceased to be of any interest. One could die in peace, whether sooner or later made no difference, because one was saved. The linear movement did not represent progress: the direction of the line had been broken by the imprint of God.

The preacher had a lot to say about fire: the flames with which Jesus had threatened hardened sinners, the flames awaiting Christians during their persecution, if their Lord was to be believed, the flames of the Last Judgement, whose heat was already perceptible in this abnormally dry and warm spring weather . . . Kaeso asked his neighbour the name of the speaker and was told that it was Eunomos, the rich imperial slave who ministered to the emperor's pleasures. Kaeso was astonished, and with good reason.

But his very astonishment suggested its own explanation. Perhaps the apocalyptic exaggerations of this Eunomos reflected the exasperation which he felt after day at being condemned to work with prostitutes and catamites. Others might have felt the same at being condemned to the mines. Instead of cutting his wrists, he comforted himself with visions of planets and stars in free fall amid a host of avenging angels.

A bearded, elderly-looking man who, Kaeso was told, was Peter, the leader of the sect, added a few words to Eunomos' speech:

'My children, the world is in the grip of fear. Children fear their parents, wives their husbands, slaves their masters. Soldiers fear their centurions, everyone fears the emperor that God has given us, and, still more everyone fears death, which is our common lot. This universal fear is not always positive in its effects, and we, as Christians, must be careful not to add to it. What have we to fear if we carry out the will of Christ at every hour of the day? Are we not promised life eternal? I shared Jesus' life for several years before I betrayed him three times because of fear, and I can tell you that I never felt afraid of the Lord. On the contrary, I only felt safe in His company, and we are all safe now, whatever happens, because He and the Holy Spirit are close to us and will remain with us until He returns in glory. His return can be a source of fear only to evil-doers.'

After an orgy of hell-fire these simple thoughts were attractive and made one overlook the mistakes in his Greek.

Peter blessed the bread and wine and distributed it. Kaeso had a share. After the final hymn, which was in a form of modern popular poetry where, instead of a rigorous metre, the last syllables of the Greek verses rhymed, Kaeso was presented to Peter in the presence of Eunomos, who evidently played a role in the community befitting his financial standing and closeness to the emperor. Paul had not boasted of the bitter disillusionment he had experienced with his very difficult proselyte, and Kaeso's reputation was unblemished.

Eunomos hastened to explain to Peter the wealth and status which Kaeso could expect as Silanus' future adoptive son. The whole Church in Rome stood to benefit from it.

Kaeso said to Peter, in a Greek which he strove to make very simple and with every syllable clearly enunciated: 'I was only very recently baptized by Paul after a very rapid course of instruction and I have just taken part in one of your holy feasts for the first time. You know how fascinated many Romans are with cooking and original recipes. I should love to know exactly what I was eating. Paul was very sparing with details in the matter, yet it seems to me to be of major importance.'

Peter frowned, hesitated for a moment, and finally answered:

'You're more open about your curiosity with me than I was with Jesus, but that isn't meant as a criticism. So I'll tell you what I know. The evening before Passover the Lord blessed the bread which He was giving out to us with the words: "Take, eat, this is my body." Then, raising a cup of wine, He gave thanks and made us all drink some, saying: "All drink some of this, it is my blood, the blood of the new testament, which is going to be shed so that the sins of many men may be redeemed." And He asked us to do the same in future, in memory of Him. That's what I saw and heard on that occasion.'

'Was the Lord talking metaphorically?'

'We fervently hoped so. It was already hard enough to get the Jews to accept the idea of an incarnate God. Actually eating God on top of that would be making things unnecessarily difficult. We were all nudging each other and trying to get each other to ask the Lord the relevant questions. But nobody dared, for fear of getting an answer that was too hard to swallow. Even John, who was a very close friend of Jesus, kept quiet. Afterwards everything happened terribly quickly, and there was no time to raise the issue again. How were we to know that the Lord would be torn from us a few hours later? He had alluded to the fact – but does anyone ever believe in the death of those they love?'

'And you didn't ask Christ after his resurrection either?'

'I'd like to have seen you do it! Before the Lord's death we hardly dared ask Him questions. Everyone just pretended to understand. And after the Resurrection we were hypnotized, like birds. Jesus left His footprints beside the Sea of Tiberias. He ate grilled fish before our very eyes. And yet He'd just come out of the tomb. But after Pentecost, with the help of the Holy Spirit, we faced up to our memories. Then a long speech made by Jesus at Capernaum came back to us – John remembered it more clearly than the rest of us: "My flesh is truly food and my blood is truly drink. He who eats my flesh and drinks my blood remains in me and I with him. Just as I am sent by the Father, who is alive, and I live by the Father, so in the same way he who eats me will also live by me."'

'Metaphorical again perhaps?'

'We have proof of the opposite. In fact, many disciples had taken the statement literally and thought that Jesus had gone mad. He said to them: "Does my language scandalize you? What will you say when you see me ascending into Heaven, whence I came?" At that point a number of disciples left the Lord and He let them go, when all He needed to say to keep them was: "I was talking metaphorically." So for Jesus the Eucharist was as miraculous as the Ascension. Do you see why we're inclined to believe that Jesus meant exactly what He said?'

Kaeso was left speechless by this accumulation of mysteries. After a prudent silence he said: 'During Jesus' lifetime you could have been more wide-awake. It seems to me that if I'd had access to a god, I should have kept on at him with intelligent questions.'

Peter answered with a smile: 'Most of us were humble, timid people.

Perhaps Jesus avoided being surrounded by educated types like you precisely so as not to be tormented in that way. His legal father was a village notable in Nazareth, and after studying in the synagogues He could have stayed exclusively in the company of learned men if He chose. But He preferred to trust in me, a man who had never studied anything but fish.'

'Well, you only betrayed him three times.'

'I hope my more learned successors will betray Him as rarely!'

'May peace be with you for as long as you only want to know the things that are important to you!'

Eunomos courteously saw Kaeso out, and the latter seized the opportunity to ask him:

'Unfortunately Nero has a weakness for me and has invited me to Naples. I find this extremely embarrassing, as you can probably imagine, since your own life is far from easy. From your knowledge of the emperor would you say that he was likely to be very angry with me if I turned down his advances?'

'He wouldn't be angry if he were absolutely convinced that you're not interested in men or that you're acting on moral principle. Unfortunately our emperor, being more Greek than Roman in mentality, is convinced that homosexual tendencies are natural, and is also deeply persuaded that nobody's life is run by virtue. If you disappoint him, he'll suspect that your attitude conceals a hostility which is political in nature, and then the worst is to be feared.'

'Then let's hope the Apocalypse occurs before my trip to Naples!'

'You're a free man.'

'I have a father, brother and stepmother who are dear to me, and the noble Silanus has conceived a liking for me.'

'Then I can only feel sorry for you.'

On the doorstep Kaeso pointed to Myra, who was playing fivestones near the fountain, and recounted to Eunomos the circumstances which had led him, in a moment of weakness, to encumber himself with the child. 'I paid 7,000 sesterces for her, but I'll willingly make you a present of her if you can find her a suitable position at the Palace.'

Eunomos ran a critical eye over Myra and said: 'There's no such thing as a "suitable" job at the palace for anyone. In any case, as far as I can tell without undressing her, she's too skinny. Nero and his friends like them chubby.'

Kaeso embraced the specialist with distaste – as it was the custom among the Christians – and went off with Myra, who, after all, was the least of his problems.

❧ Chapter ❧
4

As he was walking round the edge of the fruit and early vegetable market which had been set up near the Busta Gallica at the start of the Via Sacra, Kaeso came across Niger, a very ugly middle-aged slave whom his father had acquired to help his Syrian chef. This individual, who claimed to be called Yajniavalkya, had been nicknamed Niger for simplicity's sake, because his skin was very dark, although he had non-negroid features and his black hair was absolutely straight. Niger had been carried off near the Indus by the Parthians, they had got rid of him at the Arab market in Petra, and he had passed from dissatisfied master to dissatisfied master until he finished up at Rome in Marcus' household, where he drove everyone to despair. Probably because his progress westward had gathered speed in proportion to the growth rate of the disillusion which he inflicted on his owners, Niger, who claimed to speak fluently a mother tongue of which no one understood a single word, could get by adequately in Persian, but his Greek was halting and his Latin rudimentary. By eating a most peculiar diet he had been reduced to a skeletal state, and looked as though a puff of wind might blow him away. The problem was that Niger obstinately refused to eat meat, fish or even eggs, and constantly found something unacceptable in the gruel he was given. You could almost have suspected him of trying to commit suicide – the height of ingratitude in a slave. He was, however, virtually unpunishable. Though, with his gentle, absent-minded air, he carried out some minimal task at a snail's pace, the slightest beating would have been the death of him, thus causing him to lose the little value which he still possessed.

Niger had just bought a huge cabbage, which he seemed to be having difficulty carrying. Kaeso relieved him of the vegetable, which he swiftly passed over to Myra, and tried to find something pleasant to say, but could not on the spot think of anything. He intuitively sensed that the man possessed an unusual secret.

In street Greek Kaeso said to the slave:

'When will you make up your mind to eat like everyone else? You can't

512

have special meals cooked for you, and you have a talent for detecting the smell of meat everywhere. You'll end up by falling sick and dying. What do you think you're up to?'

'I'm not worried by death – it's birth I'm worried about.'

'Your death's your own business, but you're not responsible for your birth.'

'That's just a barbarian prejudice. Forgive the epithet. A barbarian is, for each one of us, someone who doesn't speak our own language, wouldn't you say?'

Yajniavalkya was suddenly speaking excellent Greek.

'Why did you pretend to speak Greek so badly?'

'It's always in one's interest not to understand properly a language in which people are trying to give one orders. I know Sanskrit, Persian and Greek. It's my Latin which is weak, but that's no loss. The vocabulary is too concrete for an unfettered mind.'

'Thanks for the compliment.'

'One only has to look at you to tell that you belong to the only aristocracy which counts, the aristocracy of those who are concerned with truth, who search for it constantly, and whose minds never rest until they find it. It's a very small élite in every country and can be recognized by its air of being in a foreign land. Truth is a country which demands allegiance to itself alone. It unites its adherents everywhere, but divides us from the majority of our fellow countrymen.'

Kaeso's curiosity was awakened. He told Myra to take the cabbage back to the *insula*, and sat down with Niger on the shady terrace of a café overlooking the crossroads which led to the district of Carinae. From this terrace you could see the huge temple of Tellus, on the left, where Antony had assembled more than 900 senators after Caesar's assassination. On the right stood two altars, set up in the year 86 from the founding of Rome, for sacrifice to expiate the crime committed by Horace in murdering his sister. And across the road which led in the direction of the Portico of Livia a beam of wood shaped like a yoke had been laid, which Horace had been made to go under as a form of punishment. It was still there, and was called 'the sister's beam'.

'How could you have as much education as you claim,' asked Kaeso, 'and make so little use of it? Isn't that grounds for doubting your wisdom?'

'The Parthians snatched my carcass from a monastery twenty years ago and in that time I've learnt to hide my intelligence. In any case the people hereabouts are scarcely in a state to absorb anything new or true that I could offer them. As far as essentials go they live more or less completely in the dark.'

'And what, in your view, is essential?'

Niger, who never drank wine, wetted his lips in a weak tisane and said:

'The story goes that when a traveller from India disembarked at the Piraeus, Socrates struck up a conversation with him to find out about the philosophical beliefs current in his native parts. When he said to the Hindu: "For my part I'm trying to know man," the latter replied "To know man you must first know God." This traveller must have taught Socrates a thing or two, for the doctrines of Plato shamelessly plagiarize Indian philosophy. The borrowings aren't acknowledged, but they are obvious to anyone who can read.

Since you studied philosophy at Athens, you'll certainly know something about Plato's dialogues, particularly the *Phaedo*, in which he describes Socrates' exemplary death – he drank hemlock out of respect for the laws of the city. The thoughts which Plato attributes to Socrates on that solemn occasion are of special value and have the air of a testament. Now, the dying man declares that our eternal and fallen soul exists prior to our birth, which is only, when all is said and done, a re-incarnation. He suggests that drunks will be reborn as asses, tyrants as wolves. Only philosophers will manage to rid themselves of their bodies, interrupt the cycle of constant rebirth and finally achieve a satisfactory stable position, participating in the essence of the divine.

Plato, like most plagiarists, is, however, rather incoherent. He's aware of the importance of the idea of re-incarnation, since he gives it a prime place in his dialogues, yet that place is nonetheless a rather small one for such a fundamental truth. One feels that he's been playing with a foreign notion without entirely assimilating it, without seeing or extracting its indisputable merits. And the Pythagoreans are no more enlightened in this respect.

In India we have long ago learnt to distinguish the essential from the secondary. Among the supporters of the old Brahman religion there are monists, who think reality is a single phenomenon, deists, pantheists, even atheists. Among the Buddhists, who have been spreading through India for 500 years and are beginning to make an impact in China, there are agnostics, personalists, sceptics and nihilists. But these are merely differences of schools of thought and of no significance to our wise men. The true sage is only interested in his own salvation, in the four noble truths recalled by Buddha, about which Brahmanists and Buddhists are in complete agreement: existence is painful, it is produced and renewed from life to life by desire, there is a deliverance from existence which is itself obtained by deliverance from desire. Our philosophers are therefore experts in meditating on a void, where the elements of the conscious mind vanish, in order to achieve a state of illumination which will deliver them from the fatal cycle of rebirths, provisional hells and paradises – even re-incarnations in the guise of some god or other, for the Hindu gods also suffer, are degraded and die.

As for what happens to the soul when it is relieved of its burdens by the breaking of the chain of miserable reincarnations which act as a barrier to perception of the truth, opinions differ. Many Brahmanists maintain that the self in some sense continues to exist within the universal soul. But I find the Buddhist approach more reasonable, given that all suffering derives from the self. They imagine a nirvana, where the individual consciousness is more or less dissolved. On this point Buddha said: "Belief in, or denial of, survival within nirvana is equally to be rejected. Do not worry your heads over those sorts of problem." Surely the essential is to break the alienating chain of rebirths?'

The digressions of this sickly ascetic in pursuit of illumination were interesting, not least because of the reference to the *Phaedo*. Plenty of Greek philosophers had expressed opinions favourable to ideas of metempsychosis, but Plato's fame had given a particular importance to the supposed last words of Socrates (which had been reported to Plato, who was in fact ill and therefore not present on the day in question). However, the strange doctrine was only current among a limited intellectual élite. As Yajniavalkya had observed, the Greeks had dismissed the idea as a foreign import of no significance. For such a surprising theory to attract the credulous masses, one would have had to develop a code of conduct to go with it, e.g. a prohibition forbidding the consumption of donkey or wolf flesh for fear of biting impiously into a drunk or a tyrant, or better still a whole technique for abolishing all trace of desire, leading to a total detachment which any superficial observer might mistake for complete stupor. But the Greek people had healthy appetites and no wish to curb their desires. So Pythagorean and Platonic metempsychosis had remained at the stage of somewhat far-fetched theory.

Paul, who knew a little about Plato, had reacted against such ideas and the *Phaedo* had stuck in his throat. For Jews and Christians a dialogue of the sort was unfortunate. Plato's other writings could be readily assimilated to Jewish-Christian thinking, but metempsychosis was too much to swallow. Paul had one day confessed to Kaeso: 'We could manage without the *Phaedo*. From what I've been told about it in Jewish circles, it's a ridiculous stain on a body of otherwise great work.' If Christianity ever had any success there would doubtless be Christian apologists who would dishonestly annex Plato by making careful excisions in the text.

All the same, in the meantime it was curious to discover that the transmigration of souls was the basis of religious thought in a land as vast and populous as India, with which trade contacts had become more settled in the past few generations. Roman gold was even beginning to pile up in Hindu coffers, which was a very tangible form of transmigration.

Kaeso said to Niger:

'You haven't got the slightest proof of your theory of perpetual re-births. And your pessimism is just a fancy. To refrain from desiring anything at all is certainly the best way of avoiding disappointment, and it is ingenious to reduce religion to such painless techniques. But the Romans prefer to quench all their appetites, at the cost of some moments of disappointment. And if that means that they come back as wolves in another existence, well, wolves with strong jaws and plenty of courage can still have a good time occasionally.

Philosophers of your sort, who might be of more value if they carried more weight, need treating like geese: you cram a delicious mash down their throats through a funnel, and they are reborn in the form of *pâté de foie gras*.'

A century earlier the consul Metellus Scipio and the knight M. Seius, who owned huge flocks of geese, had taken the recipe for *foie gras* from the Greeks. And since then, enormous tender livers were obtained by stuffing the birds with a mash made basically from figs. The livers were eventually marinated in a mixture of milk and honey, and left to swell. Goose liver *pâté* had rapidly become the symbol of culinary luxury. Whereas the standard word for liver in Latin was *jecur*, it was already becoming usual to call a fattened liver *ficatum*, because of the figs used in feeding. And the day would come when the word *ficatum* would be used for any liver, as if the poorest citizens had themselves been fattened up for the tables of the rich.

Worn out by the speed at which they were walking, Niger lent on his companion's arm. Kaeso asked him:

'If I understood you aright, you refrain from eating meat so that you can be reborn in a higher state, perhaps even obtain definitive liberation from the disastrous chain of incarnations. So your present appearance must be the fruit of your actions in earlier lives?'

'Exactly.'

516

'So that one's virtues determine the status into which one can expect to be reborn, unless one achieves nirvana?'

'That's what I told you. Everyone in India knows it.'

'What happens to your freedom then?'

'Only the basic qualities and conditions of the rebirth are pre-determined. Thereafter one is still free, under this or that outward guise, to behave stupidly or to detach onself, within the pattern of one's new existence.'

'So rich Hindus can reasonably despise the poor, since the latter are morally responsible for their own condition. And if the wretches turn rebellious, one is in a position to prove to them that they are laying up even worse forms of existence for themselves.'

'That's why the poor Hindu, whose ignoble state is his own fault, is a model of patience. In India the people never revolt. They are much too afraid of being reborn in the form of unclean animals, as a punishment for their stupid and imprudent sins.'

'You have invented perfect social stability.'

'I prefer to think of it as perfect tranquillity for the soul.'

Niger stopped to get his breath back and added:

'In India not only does the general system of belief encourage the masses to be virtuous, but so does the organization of society into castes – priests, soldiers, merchants and peasants – each of which lives a separate lifestyle. (There are also untouchables who have no caste. They don't count and we have nothing to do with them.) Since definitive freedom from the world of appearances takes a long time for most people, it's good for the individual to have a superior caste before his eyes, and to know that a certain degree of wisdom on his part may allow him to be reborn a member of that caste. The priests, who are the highest caste, because of their past merits, hope to become gods if they do not achieve their liberation.'

'An admirable system.'

'There's another stimulus to lead a good life: the desire to be reborn with a very pale skin if one has experienced the disgrace of being born with a black or very dark skin. At Rome skin colour has no part in the esteem in which people are held. You merely despise ignorance. But our priests believe that a dark skin is a punishment for deplorable acts in an earlier life, and particularly for deplorable thoughts, because we think that thoughts are more important than acts, because the former condition the latter. I myself was a member of the merchant caste, and the colour of my skin had a bad effect on trade. The reason why I adopted Buddhist ideas was in part because Buddha does not take the caste or colour of an individual into account.'

'If I were a black untouchable in India I should be obliged to perform miracles of virtue!'

'Indeed, for many people the path to freedom is interminable. For thousands of years you go forwards and backwards through deceptive appearances. You will appreciate that the hope of reaching my goal prevents me from making any sort of compromise.'

'Do you still retain that desire?'

'It's the only one we're allowed. Suicide would inflict a disastrous rebirth on us.'

Kaeso and Niger had arrived at the Forum Cuppedinis (where special foods were sold), and were standing in front of displays of monstrous goose livers, whose arrangement was mouth-watering. The owners of de luxe shops spent much time and effort on making their shop-fronts look striking, and these were known by the jolly name of *oculiferium* (eye-catcher). The display of a certain Heracles was particularly effective: a pyramid of *foie gras* in terrines was dominated by a superb stuffed goose with a vast funnel down its throat.

Niger was looking at the sight with evident disgust. Kaeso said to him:

'My natural sense of justice is offended by the fact that poor Hindus are encouraged to lose the little they have by so-called priests who have everything they want and for whom detachment is merely the luxury of a spiritual exercise.'

'Surely detachment is in everyone's interest? But our poor have another role to play as well. Among all the exercises intended to uproot egoism and exterminate desire so as to attain illumination, charitable thoughts and even actions have a place of honour. Buddha offered himself to a hungry tigress who, in desperation, was preparing to eat her own cubs. Our philosophers are charity itself.'

'I'm willing to bet that the finest charity for would-be Buddhas is to go and beg food from the poorest members of society.'

'It is indeed a signal honour for them to feed a future Buddha.'

Kaeso's black humour was something to which Niger was evidently oblivious. Faced with such a state of things Kaeso suddenly gave way to a fit of truly Roman anger. He went up to Heracles, who had been supplying Marcus ever since the family fortunes took a turn for the better, and whispered to him: 'You see that slave who's come to us from India? He's a tiresome philosopher that my father paid 1,200 sesterces for. He's made up his mind to die of hunger, because of some doctrinal nicety. I can see three good strong slaves stacking *amphorae* in your store-room at the back. I want them to get hold of Niger, stuff that nice large funnel down his gullet, and feed a good-sized goose-liver down it. There'll be a good tip for your men, though stuffing that skeleton won't be difficult.'

Heracles and his assistants were much taken with the idea. Nothing pleases muscular louts more than mistreating and upsetting a sickly intellectual. Kaeso found an excuse to send Yajniavalkya off to his destiny, the three brutes leapt on him, thrust the funnel into his mouth and started administering the wonderful product to him, while his young master strolled up and down, feeling very pleased with himself, in front of the *oculiferium*.

Niger came tottering out, his eyes popping out of his head, and with *foie gras* dripping from his mouth. Kaeso took hold of the slave by the elbow and pushed him towards the *insula*.

'You can thank me,' said Kaeso, 'for finding a way of saving your shaky state of health without your being in the least responsible. Every time you refuse to eat your stew I shall send you off to Heracles. But you won't always get *foie gras*. Given your absolute lack of responsibility this procedure will do nothing to hinder your progress towards illumination.'

Niger belched up a dribble of *foie gras* and stammered:

'It's your own progress to liberation that your action will hinder, you madman.'

Now that his anger had abated, Kaeso felt slightly ashamed of losing his temper, and asked his victim:

'What in fact do you want to eat?'

'Well-spiced rice boiled in plain water.'

'Rice is a ruinously expensive foodstuff in Rome. We get it in very small quantities from India and Babylonia and from some parts of Syria. It's barely used except in medicine and in some *haute cuisine* for thickening and binding sauces. And Indian spices are pretty expensive too. I'll ask Selene to prepare you some rice in that fashion, but only once. After that you'll have to be more accommodating.'

When Kaeso got back to the *insula* with Niger, who was dribbling *foie gras* everywhere, Marcus threw up his hands.

'In the name of all the twelve great gods, that's *foie gras*. The most useless of all my slaves is belching *foie gras*. Have you gone mad, Kaeso?'

Kaeso seized the opportunity to attribute this treatment to the doctrines of the Christians, who were thought to coddle their slaves with unceasing love and attention. During lunch he expatiated on the theme of Christian love with infectious enthusiasm. He had no difficulty proving that if

519

everyone 'loved his neighbour as himself', to use that fine expression from *Leviticus* which Jesus so happily borrowed from his Father, the world would be a better place. There would be no further need to do your utmost to flee from the world of outward appearances like a naïve Plato or a cowardly Hindu.

Kaeso's sudden passion for the Christians was beginning to worry Marcus, who had difficulty following him. The whole Roman tradition went against the idea of taking love to the point of feeding your slaves on *foie gras*.

Kaeso was particularly pleased with the incident. A touch of mystical madness would not go amiss when it came to cutting the ground from under Marcus' feet with the coming terrible revelation.

The Ides of May, the date for which the adoption was scheduled, were fast approaching and it would be very shocking to back out at the last minute. Silanus would never forgive him, and the *praetor urbanus* would swallow his ceremonial *fasces*. The following day there would be the Games, commemorating Augustus' dedication of the Temple of Mars Ultor. The day after that there would be a second round of the Lemuria – better to chase the dead away twice than once. And the day after that was the eve of the Ides. So there were only three days left. He had reached absolutely the last possible moment for writing to Silanus – and in an affair of this kind writing seemed preferable to breaking the news in person.

Instead of taking a siesta Kaeso withdrew to the library, took papyrus and pen, as befitted the outstanding importance of what he had to say, and hesitated one last time before making the decisive turn of the tiller which was to change the course of the galley of his days. But that was the price he had to pay for liberty, and Kaeso desperately wanted to stay free.

He was dipping his pen in the inkwell when he became vividly aware of quite how angry his father, whom no conversion to anything at all would pacify, was going to be.

Marcus was indeed likely to lose a very great deal because of the particular nature of the Roman law on adoptions. This started from the principle that no civil law could prevail over the laws of blood and religion. For example, an adopted son became the brother of any children which his new father might beget, contrary to expectations, after the ceremony, but he did not acquire any legal relationship with his adoptive father's wife. Similarly an adopted son had the right to have the adoption annulled and to reassume responsibility for the cult of the family into which he had been born if his natural father died without issue. At the same time, in the majority of cases, an adopted son remained his natural father's heir and vice versa. If a very rich Kaeso were to die in Paul's absence (and there seemed to be no known examples of resurrections outside a three-day period), Marcus would share in the inheritance. Kaeso happened to know this particular point of law: Marcus knew it still better.

His poor father must already be enjoying the formalities of the adoption in anticipation, for they had everything to delight a lawyer's heart. The natural father first went through the fiction of selling his son as a slave, for one *as*, to the adoptive father, so that his paternal power over him was dissolved. Then the adoptive father sold the boy to a third party, which put him in a position to be reclaimed: lastly the adoptive father reclaimed the child, who, in the absence of any protest from his new proprietor, now legally became the son of his adoptive father, enjoying the right of *agnatio* (paternal consanguinity). While the formalities of adoption were bizarrely complex, those of *adrogatio*, which concerned those whose father had died, were more simple. In the absence of a father, the approval of an assembly of the Roman people, reduced for the purpose to a few symbolic *lictors*, was all that was required. It was not the custom to adopt daughters, since they were not considered capable of perpetuating the family cult and offering up sacrifices in their own name.

In the library Kaeso found Marcus' presence weighing too heavily upon him. He took his writing-case and withdrew into his own room, but his sense of constraint only grew worse. The room brought back to him his first memories of Marcia, which went back to the days when he shared it with his brother. She had so often come there to look after him or to calm his fears at night. And after Marcus junior had been moved into a room of his own, relations between Marcia and Kaeso had become more intimate and collusive. The child had confided everything to his mother without a second thought and she would instinctively find just the right words to send him off to sleep. How distant all that was – and at the same time how very relevant to the present.

In the end Kaeso shut himself up in his brother's room and wrote the following letter to Silanus:

'K. Aponius Saturninus to D. Junius Silanus Torquatus, greetings.

This letter will come as no surprise to you. What may perhaps surprise you is my decision to tell you the truth after hesitating to do so for so long. But the kindness which you have shown me in the past and which you were willing to show me in the future puts me under an obligation to explain myself absolutely clearly. To come straight to the point, I think it better to decline the honour of the adoption which you had envisaged.

In that way I shall not be a prisoner of an ambiguous and dangerous situation, in which sooner or later I would have been obliged to behave in an unworthy fashion. Even if you, in your friendship, had tolerated it, I should have been less tolerant towards myself.

You once wrote something very true to me: you said that when it came to love one should not pay too much attention to ways of doing things or to situations but should follow one's natural inclinations, because "nobody else can experience pleasure for us". By refusing to be adopted I think I am taking your advice. I still think that pleasure and love are serious matters, and that we should not commit ourselves to them unless there is a prospect of our remaining true to ourselves throughout the experience. At my age one is not inclined to make love because it is to one's advantage, or out of gratitude, sympathy, pity, fear or habit. Your good opinion of me will help you to understand that I would have blushed to run the risk of doing so while under your roof.

Marcia will be very disappointed that I am not in a position, when all is said and done, to lead the shared life in your dual affectionate company which she was hoping would result from my youth and your pleasant philosophy. I don't need to warn you that you will need to keep a very close watch on her health and not leave her alone with slaves who are too obliging. Make her see that my filial love for her is eternal and that, if you allow it, as soon as I get back from Naples I shall pay her respectful visits as often as I can. She would deal me a fatal blow if she despised an existence which is dearer to me than my own. I am willing to shed my blood for her – but not more.

Since I have made up my mind to tell you everything, I ought also to tell you that the contacts which I have had, in the state of cruel doubt in which I found myself, with Seneca, the Jews and the Christians have all probably played some part in the firm decision at which I have arrived. I had already noticed in Athens how inclined philosophers are to make elementary problems complicated by the use of uncontrolled language. In fact, the solutions which reason and experience offer us are very few.

One can accept a materialism whose elements are at the mercy of chance. It's a hypothesis which suffers from considerable weaknesses. One wonders how chance contrives to sustain constant order among the innumerable phenomena which derive from its blind activity. One also wonders what clear and definite moral code one could derive from the random interplay of Epicurus' atoms. Social morality becomes very doubtful. Even individual morality is subject to the whim of States or individuals. Another equally insoluble question is: how could atoms which have no power of thought or will of their own have emerged from the void, and what force sustains their errant life and organizes their distribution? When it comes down to it, chance explains nothing at all, because its very existence raises fundamental questions.

Alternatively one can accept some sort of pantheism, where divine elements are diffused throughout, and mingled with, matter. This sort of theory gives a better account of the undoubted order manifest in the world than the preceding one, but it has its own weaknesses. It is difficult to deduce a precise ethical system from the organization of the elements, even if one presupposes it to be divine in origin, and one can see the Stoics oscillating between extreme rigorousness and deplorable compromise. Seneca appears to have spent his whole life moving towards a state of irrepressible disgust, which one could reproach him for not having experienced sooner. You yourself present the picture of a man probably more racked than he seems. Moreover, if the gods are mixed up with the world, the problem of their existence, half material and half spiritual, remains unanswered. To claim, as Plato and certain peoples of the far East do, that fallen souls transmigrate according to their merits through a variety of forms until an excess of virtue draws them out of the dungheap is simply a way of avoiding the main question instead of resolving it. Why should this decline occur, and why should material appearances be adjudged "bad" *a priori*? This fundamental pessimism introduces an unfathomable contradiction. If the gods are in the world, why should the world be something to shun and despise?

A third possibility would be, like the Persians, to imagine a constant titanic struggle between a god who creates good and a god responsible for evil. This childish notion simply transfers to a transcendental plain the contradiction from which pantheism suffers in the immanent. Dualism will never attract logicians to its cause.

Or else one can adhere to a faith in a unique personal god, outside everything and creator of the visible and invisible universe. Both the advantages and disadvantages of the idea lie in its sublimity.

The existence of the world, and of space and time which provisionally condition its movement and forms, finally receives an explanation which is intellectually satisfying, and against which only logical arguments of a dubious nature could be raised. But such a god is, by his very nature, utterly unknowable, and it is at first sight impossible to know what he could want. Once god is outside the world, what sort of relations could one have with him?

If you want to achieve a working morality on a rational basis, there is an immeasurable void to fill. It is a leaking barrel, like the one the Danaids tried in vain to fill. Into it the Jews and the Christians have poured different water, but of the same type. For the Jews, God said what he wanted on Sinai. For the Christians, Jesus, the son of this same God, took human form to give supplementary information. Twice a bridge is supposed to have been established between God and his isolated creatures.

Such notions of divine communication might tend to make one smile if, over and above the baldness of the supposed facts, they did not offer something utterly new. God is supposed to have created men out of his paternal love, and it's out of love for all responsible creatures that his son is said to have sacrificed himself, to redeem sins which were simply the product of the unfettered malice of the impious. So that the key to this new religion is love. That makes it of interest not only to philosophers but also to the humblest and least intelligent among us. All the cavils of reason take second place to the trusting smile of child to father. A filial love suddenly gives meaning to the universe.

There is no reason to be impressed by the fact that Jesus and the Christians have accomplished miracles. A miracle, given how little we can know of it, proves nothing in itself: it is the miracle which needs to be proved by the motives behind it and the worth of those who accomplished it. Miracles are merely the accessories of a truth, and the love of one's neighbour might be the greatest of all miracles to engage our attention.

If one needed proofs in order to love, I should be more inclined to see them in the fact that the only god of love showed himself to Moses about 1,000 years or so ago, in other words to the representative of a wild, nomadic people who could not, in the normal evolution of its beliefs, have conceived of transcendent solitude as the intimate love of a god without equal. In *Exodus*, one of the oldest Jewish texts, one can read of this extraordinary event, which is more disturbing than all the miracles imaginable: Moses asked god what name he should call him by, because for a primitive man, anxious to get a grip on a protective divinity, the knowledge of his name is essential if incantations are to work; and god replies: "My name is 'I am'", meaning by that that he is the only constant and necessary form of existence. If you can believe that a shepherd managed to invent that, your philosophy must be very inadequate. And as for those who would doubt whether Jesus proved that he was the son of the Father and of the same nature as he, I can produce a piece of evidence from Luke which is part of the Christian oral tradition, and which is again one of those things that no one could make up: when the Jews were expressing surprise that Jesus could have known Abraham, he retorted: "Before Abraham was, 'I am'."

Would I really become a Christian? I have reached the point of thinking that Judaeo-Christianity is the most satisfying doctrine for those who aspire to a well-ordered moral life, and for those endowed with the exacting merit, or the admirable weakness, of claiming that they have discovered an answer to the myriad questions which trouble them about the nature of man and his eventual end. And I find Christianity superior to Judaism, which has confined itself to a single race and risks remaining prisoner of it for ever. But is the truth necessarily closely bound up with what, one fine day, we happen to find attractive?

I have to confess that I accepted Christian baptism at the hands of Paul with the ulterior motive of making it impossible for myself to take responsibility for your family cult. I now feel thoroughly ashamed of having thought of playing a trick of that sort on you, and humbly beg you to forgive me. I can only plead in my defence the difficulties in which I found myself plunged and from which I could see no honourable way (for myself or anyone else) of extricating myself. The instructive example of your own frankness and scrupulousness should have dissuaded me from such cheap, calculating behaviour. All I needed to do, surely, was to speak to you as though you were the father to me that you wanted to be.

You will understand that I have at present many reasons for renouncing such an adoption, reasons which are deeper and more praiseworthy than this frivolous baptism. I find myself impelled to this course of action by everything I have learnt from the best Stoics, Jews and Christians. Even the good old sense of Roman *dignitas* which my father inculcated into me as a child – though he himself has proved so poor at putting it into practice – pushes me in the same direction. Added to that is the insurmountable repugnance which I feel at finding myself in any sort of false position. So I hope that you will accept all these as sufficient motives, and that I may continue to enjoy your esteem if not your entire approval. That esteem would be a great help in consoling me for the undeserved disappointment that I find myself inflicting on you completely unintentionally. My actions would look like base ingratitude if you did not for your part make a cordial effort to understand me. I hope that your natural nobility of soul will help you.

I hope Marcia will fare as well as you.

P. S. I am trying to get my father to take my baptism seriously. I cannot think of any better way of pouring soothing oil on the fury which will shortly possess him. You know how important money is to him.'

Kaeso re-read the letter with a sigh. It was far from satisfactory. He had the impression that he had not been able to express adequately what he was trying to communicate. But he had had to stir up so many thoughts and feelings in so short a time that he couldn't have done any better in the state he was in. So he crossed his Rubicon, rolled up the papyrus and put his seal on it.

He felt a belated wave of remorse. He hadn't said as much about Marcia as he should have done, nor had he spoken about her in the right way, although she had never been out of his mind as he penned the lines.

So he took up some tablets and wrote to his mother:

'Kaeso to his very dear Marcia, affectionate greetings.

The last time I had the pleasure of seeing you, you quite rightly drew my attention to the fact that my adoption by Silanus might encourage the emperor, if not to respect my person, at least to treat it with a certain amount of consideration. But the austere education I received has in no way prepared me for the indispensable element of prostitution involved. Why did you let me get such an exaggerated idea of your virtue? If Nero, despite my newly-acquired eminent social position, happened to pinch my bottom in a corridor and an unfortunate reflex movement led me to punch him in the teeth, it would be highly preferable at that moment for my adoption to have been publicly announced as indefinitely postponed. I want to face the Cyclops with no arms but virtue and native cunning. I do not want to run the least risk of compromising a man I respect and a woman I adore. So let us talk about my adoption at some future date when circumstances are more favourable.

In the meantime you are still the first and only woman in my life. I love you for everything you have taught me, everything you have hidden from me, for the extraordinary love which you have never ceased to bestow on me, a love so fine, so strong and so total that no man could be worthy of it or able to respond to it as it deserves. Forgive my inadequacies. But remember that they derive in part from the image of you which I held for so long. It is the image which I prefer, one of calm and confidence. The new Marcia has too confusing an effect on me for me to be able to look her in the eyes. The best way for me to remain faithful to you is to condemn myself to disappointing you, but your rich experience should have taught you how futile the area of experience in question is.

Aren't we both above that sort of thing? It is only a proof of love to those who have no better proofs to offer. I would sleep with anyone to save your life. But you are not just anyone: you are the one and only Marcia, the Marcia who brought me up and formed my character, the Marcia who has given me all of herself and who could not add anything significant to the gifts she has already made. There is something literally uplifting about my passion for you. I belong to you in my entirety, but on a vertical plane. Try to love me the way that I love you.

Take care of your health as before. Your existence is indispensable to my happiness.'

Moved by his own eloquence, Kaeso finished his note in floods of tears. Nero too, according to all those who saw him, had shown great signs of emotion during the meal which preceded Agrippina's boat trip. A man does not condemn his mother to death or solitude without a certain feeling of regret.

Yet what could Kaeso have done which was worthy of his legitimate and entirely innocent ambitions? He had, without knowing it, shared the little prostitute in the *popina* with his father and, with the thoughtlessness of youth, with his brother. He had allowed Selene to do him a small favour before going back to the demands of her master's bed. He had almost shared Marcia with Silanus. And having insulted Marcia's modesty, the emperor was in a strong position to outrage his. Was it not entirely to be expected that a sensitive being should be thoroughly disgusted by all this promiscuity and incest?

Before going to the baths with Myra, Kaeso sent the tablets off to Marcia. It was only on his return from the baths that he dispatched his letter to Silanus. In that way he hoped that Silanus, warned by Marcia of the fresh postponement of the adoption before he himself received more frank and definitive explanations, would be in a position to prepare his wife gradually for the inevitable.

❧ CHAPTER ❧
5

Early the following morning a messenger from Silanus brought this note for Kaeso:

'Decimus to Kaeso.

Both your letters arrived while I was out. Marcia could not stop herself breaking the seal on the second one, and her indiscretion was punished by the bitterness which a comparison of the two versions occasioned. I myself am touched by the comparison, since Marcia freely offered me her letter to read. So your thoughtfulness in sending off the letters in succession had, unfortunately, the opposite effect to the one intended.

Marcia, overcome with grief, has spent the night in floods of tears. I don't know what to do to console her, and I cannot think of any argument which I could produce to make you change you mind, since you seem to be totally unaware of the heartbreaking cruelty of your attitude. Does one argue with a Horace or a Brutus? Oh, there's no doubting the esteem – the only too high esteem – in which I hold you. Your youthful, barbarous intransigence is enough to make virtue seem hateful, if there were any trace of it left in the world. I only hope that those gods who are indulgent to human weaknesses, the ones who inspire me with the most confidence, will not cause you promptly to regret your attitude.

I too had come to love you, I was prepared to do anything for the sake of your happiness, and I shall hardly ever see you again. In refusing to assume responsibility for the perpetuation of my family sacrifices, you are in fact sacrificing Marcia and me.

May you fare better than we shall.'

To hear those heart-rending accents reverberating within him made Kaeso feel ill. He ran to look for Selene. He found her just getting out of her bath in a first shaft of sunlight. The master's bed gave Selene a wild desire to bathe, and she would succumb to it even before the water in the family baths had heated up. Kaeso brought her up-to-date on developments and let her read Decimus' note, which had been written in Greek, as had Kaeso's two letters. Greek was a language better suited to the expression of emotion and philosophical ideas than Latin. Caesar himself had died by his own son's hand with a Greek phrase on his lips. Silanus, too, instinctively expressed his sorrows in Greek, and all the more naturally because his feelings for Kaeso had perhaps become somewhat more than paternal.

'Well,' said Selene, 'I salute you as a member of a rare species. Marcia and Silanus are at your feet, the emperor lets his gaze run lovingly over you while waiting for a chance to let his hands do the same, and here you are bucking like a mule, because of your lofty pretensions to remain the sole proprietor of your body. When it comes to it, you appear to treat all philosophies merely as pretexts to the same end. Yet at first sight the dignity you lay claim to seems a very precarious one. If you suddenly become inflamed with desire – and the liberties you took with me that night among the caged pigeons show that it does happen – there's no metaphysics will long hold you back from throwing all virtue to the winds. You're a very clumsy hero, and completely ignorant of the age you live in. Greek mythology, which has been copied by the Romans, teaches us that the only conceivable hero, to the mass of ordinary people who are ruled by a passion for physical pleasure, is the man who gives himself up heart and soul, like a tool of destiny, to flattering conquests. You're behaving like an athlete who refuses to run in a race because he doesn't like the look of the other contestants. There's no place nowadays for the heroism of abstention. The Jews end up turning mill-stones and the Christians have got off to a bad start.'

'It's enough if I'm a hero in my own eyes.'

'It's the privilege of free men to prefer solitude amid the ruins which their virtue has piled up to triumphal procession between suspect temples. Personally I should simply like to have the choice. I admire you of course, but as a friend I feel alarmed for your sake.'

There was good reason to be alarmed. Kaeso had set himself up as Selene's protector, but, the way things were going, who was going to protect *him*?

Selene added a reprimand to her warning:

'Niger was vomiting up *foie gras* all yesterday evening and told me of the disgraceful treatment which you'd subjected him to. It was a very extravagant act of violence and makes me wonder how mentally stable you are. Haven't you read "An eye for an eye and a tooth for a tooth" in our Bible? Every act of violence brings another in its train, and the real guilty party is the one who starts it all off. Do you suppose a plate of rice will be enough to wipe away the insult?'

'We had a philosophical difference of opinion. Niger thought that to be born into misery was a punishment for sins committed in previous existences, and that poor people with black skins are more abject than anyone else. He refused to eat meat for fear of chewing a negro who had been reborn as a chicken. It was good to teach him a lesson which would expand his mind and his stomach at the same time. Otherwise he would have ended up by dying of hunger.'

'Where on earth did he get such an extraordinary prejudice against blacks? They're highly sought after here.'

'It's apparently a prejudice current in India. One can only hope that such a piece of stupidity doesn't gain any wider currency. Otherwise the price of black slaves will drop like a stone and they'll be less well treated.'

'Niger's madness is no excuse for your own. Imagine Nero, impelled by a sense of natural justice, thrusting an imperial funnel into one of your orifices . . .'

'In the name of Zeus, there's no sense of justice that could impel Nero to anything!'

Although the notion of natural justice seemed to derive from childish superstition, the perspective was nonetheless disturbing. Amid the debris of traditional Roman religion a host of superstitions had flowered and every Roman had been infected by them.

Since Kaeso had broken with Marcia in such a painful fashion, he had experienced a stealthy growth of interest in Selene. He had lost a mother, friend and confidante who was at the same time only too sexually attractive. For a boy of his age it was a large gap to fill, and Selene had the particular merit of being on hand. On reflection his father's incontestable rights were rights of ownership rather than of love, and the noble minds respect the former less than the latter. Anyway, it is only the first step that counts, and Selene herself had cheerfully taken that already.

'Do stop looking at me like that!' said Selene. 'You look like Actaeon watching Diana bathing. Take care, the old dog isn't far off.'

Marcus' heavy tread could indeed be heard. Kaeso blushed and turned aside from the temptation.

It was scandalous that Selene could refer to her master as 'the old dog' without an informed listener daring to take offence. It was very strong language. The philosophers of the Cynic school probably took their name from the Cynosarges, the gymnasium where they originally used to meet, but there was an even more certain connection with those shameless dogs whose prolonged bouts of breathless coupling offer a first lesson in the facts of life to little children. From frequent close contact with Greek philosophers worried about provocation and scandal the young dogs themselves had contracted marked homosexual tendencies. All that could be said in Marcus' defence was that his 'cynicism' was preferably directed at women and was relatively discreet.

At this point a messenger from the emperor burst in, quite out of breath. Kaeso was summoned to the palace, immediately. Bearers of the emperor's messages within Rome always left at top speed and arrived panting for breath. It was only in mid-journey that they were to be seen comfortably installed in front of a jug of iced wine in some friendly *popina*.

Selene helped Kaeso drape himself in his finest toga, while Marcus showered him with unnecessary advice, whose honourable platitudes disguised thoughts to which he could not admit. At last he embraced the boy and said: 'Years ago I too climbed the Palatine, but I came back stripped of all I possessed. The wheel of Fortune has turned again and you have everything to hope for if your wisdom and prudence are equal to your other gifts. If the occasion arises, please assure the prince of my eternal loyalty.'

A large part of the Palatine had been colonized either by imperial residences or by buildings ancillary to such residences. Private houses, such as those of Silanus, Clodius or Scaurus, had become few and far between. The imperial quarters had ended up as a sort of city apart. Augustus had started it by building a fairly modest villa near the *pulvinar* of the Circus Maximus. This had burnt down in the year 756 from the founding of the city, and had been rebuilt by public subscription on a rather more luxurious scale. Between the winding *clivus* of Victory and Livia's little house Tiberius had had a vast palace constructed, and Caligula had expanded it still further. The Flavians in their turn would build between the villa of Augustus and the palace of Tiberius, which was in theory Nero's habitual residence. But, as much from choice as from a concern for his personal safety, the emperor had begun to spend most of his time in the heart of this or that garden, whether it was imperial property or belonged to one of his freedmen. He had at his disposition, on the Pincian, the gardens of Sallust, Lucullus and his ancestors the Domitii. But he preferred the area near the Esquiline gate, where the gardens of Maecenas, Pallas and his freedman Epaphroditus could offer him hospitality. He was particularly fond of staying in the gardens of Lamai and Maia, a stone's throw away from the cavalry barracks of the German Guard.

Kaeso was taken to the palace of Tiberius, though the Emperor was not there, and shown into the room where the model of the new Rome was laid out. The eunuch Sporus was waiting for the visitor. Sporus shared his master's passion for these architectural fantasies. They appealed to his still childlike nature, and he never missed a chance to wander among the projected marvels.

Kaeso saw a brunette with curly hair leaning over the vast model. She was dressed in a long pink tunic. It could have been a slightly younger Poppaea, and for a moment Kaeso wondered whether this was indeed the empress. But the young person's bust was too flat and the visitor was soon relieved of his doubts . . .

'I'm Sporus. You may have heard of me.'

The high voice was melodious and the expression very fond and gentle.

'I know of you by repute,' answered Kaeso, 'and like everyone I know of the esteem and affection in which the prince holds you.'

'I am indeed fortunate enough to be counted among his closest friends and am perhaps the only one of his freedmen in whom he has total confidence. He knows I shall never betray him. I wish I could say as much for the others. I think Helius and Polyclitus are to be relied upon, as are Petinus, Patrobius and Pythagoras. But I wouldn't put much money on Epaphroditus or Phaon, or even that brute Doryphoros, who has the same name as the ambitious supporter of Octavia whom my Master had put to death two years ago.'

It was the moment to keep a diplomatic silence. It would have been extremely unwise to get mixed up in the jealousies and tortuous quarrels of Nero's freedmen.

Taking Kaeso's silence for assent Sporus went on: 'It's because of the exemplary intimacy with the Master which I enjoy that I am receiving you this morning. Nero has confided to me that you are to be part of his immediate entourage on the coming trip to Naples, and he wants me to put you in the picture.'

Sporus explained to Kaeso that for form's sake he should call on Mam. Correlius Afer, a person of the rank of praetor who was the head of the *augustiani*. This Mamercus had his quarters in a palace building which served as headquarters for the *augustiani* of noble blood, while those of plebeian extraction used an annexe to the drivers' club in the Campus Martius. On the strength of this interview Kaeso would be officially enrolled and given a flattering rank. But that was a trivial matter in comparison with the signal honour of being included in the exclusive little group immediately around the emperor.

With a seriousness which showed that he was coming to the point, Sporus added: 'Nero spoke of you in very friendly and flattering terms. You've made a very favourable impression on him, and I'm delighted. There are only a very small number of us who truly love our prince, without any ulterior motive. I pray to the gods that you may quickly become a member of this élite of the heart. Because of his ever-alert sensitivity, Nero has a certain gift for judging the quality of his fellow men.'

Kaeso protested the warmth of his feelings. At the same time he was trying to think. The surprising nature of what Sporus was saying encouraged cordial frankness in return, though such an attitude was not advisable at court. But despite everything perhaps there was more to be lost by trying to be clever than there was to be won.

'The emperor's display of open friendship had dissuaded me from taking up Silanus' offer of adoption – though Silanus' loyalty is of course irreproachable. I wish for no other father but the emperor himself. I'd be grateful if you would communicate the news to him.'

'Nero will be pleased with your handsome decision. He certainly has no precise cause for complaint against Silanus, but he doesn't get on with him very well. As Epicurus would have put it, their atoms are incompatible. That does away with a possible shadow over your relationship. Trust in the prince and you won't lose by the exchange.'

Kaeso decided to dive straight in . . .

'I won't disguise from you the fact that I do feel just the tiniest bit worried . . .'

'About what?'

'It's a rather delicate matter.'

'Then let me guess. Perhaps you have no experience with boys and are apprehensive about getting into my Master's bed, even rather frightened at the idea of what he might make you do?'

Kaeso's embarrassment gave away the accuracy of the diagnosis. Sporus gave a charming smile and reassured him: 'You have a quite wrong image of the emperor. You must be judging him on gossip. You'll have been told about the rape of young Plautius. Believe me, he did everything he could to get raped. You can trust me when I tell you that Nero has never forced anyone to make love to him, either way up. Why should he? Aren't there legions offering themselves for his sexual fulfilment, and isn't the desire to give pleasure one of an artist's first concerns? From his real friends Nero only takes what they are prepared to give. I think you have enough charm and wit for your company alone to be a memorable asset.'

As Kaeso did not seem to be entirely convinced, Sporus announced: 'I know the emperor better than anyone, and it's only fair to him that I should describe him as he is, with a tenderness which will give my words more truth than a neutral account would.

Nero is generosity itself. He came to the throne utterly disgusted with the crimes, treason and violence which had served as the appalling setting for his childhood years. The beginning of his reign was reminiscent of the golden age. People still talk about that *quinquennium*, the famous five years of peaceful authority, which are certainly a contrast with the degradation of the present. But the prince is not responsible for that. His bounties have been repaid with ingratitude, his trust with lies and plots. To prevent his throat from getting cut he has had to act with severity on occasion, but he still finds blood as unpleasant as a stain on a picture.

It's not true that Nero had Britannicus killed, though Agrippina was in fact threatening to use the boy against him. Why should he have been so stupid as to poison him in public when so many more discreet ways of disposing of him would have been open to him?

He had to get rid of Octavia, whom he had divorced on grounds of sterility, because a rioting crowd of her supporters, who'd been secretly stirred up by his worst enemies, had caused havoc throughout the Capitol and the Forums and was on its way up to attack the palace.

As for the death of Agrippina, he told me himself that he'd talked to you about it. Remorse for what he did will pursue him to the end of his days.

That makes him a pretty restrained tyrant in comparison with Tiberius and Caligula. How could one expect such a man to tyrannize his friends? Despite everything Nero wants to believe that there is such a thing as true friendship. He needs to believe in it to help him endure the burdens which oppress him. And a true friend is such a rare and precious thing that the Prince would put him on a pedestal rather than upset him. What ought to worry you is the prospect of not being worthy of the sensitivity and affection he will show you.'

There must be something in what Sporus said. It was usually quite difficult to detect where reality lay when faced with the eulogies of hired panegyrists of the regime on the one hand and the charges levelled by its fiercest opponents on the other. The uprising in favour of Octavia had been short-lived but violent. The statues of Poppaea which had been distributed around the city, to show to all and sundry the affection in which the emperor held that graceful citizen of Pompeii, had been thrown down and mutilated, and the statues of Octavia put back in the Forums and even in the temples, as if a thoughtless or perverse people had wanted to impose sterility on a monarchy which had already done so much for it. Octavia's sad martyrdom had indeed been mixed up with a political plot which might seem disturbing. The Roman populus was very attached to Nero and the revolutionaries must have been bought or have been taken from the clientele of hostile senators and of imperial freedmen who were enemies of Poppaea. As for Britannicus, his mysterious sudden death was no closer to being cleared up.

'I'm delighted to hear all this,' said Kaeso. 'May I ask you something else? Does the fact that it was you the emperor asked to receive me indicate that I'd be expected to play a role – if my inclinations lead me in that direction – similar to yours?'

Sporus burst out into silvery laughter, and anwered: 'I hope so for your sake. The prince is fonder of his passive lovers than his active ones. They have a difficult part to play. How can one master the Master of the world while displaying a suitable degree of modesty? The difficult problem for an active lover is to guess at exactly what point the humiliation of the beloved starts to become painful to him. The Doryphoros who lost his life two years ago, in addition to his unwise political imbroglios, was possibly maladroit in his sexual activities with Nero. When one's Greek name means "spear-bearer", one mustn't abuse the quality. If you're paid the immense compliment of being treated as a man, your youthful inexperience may make things very tricky for you. I'm warning you as a friend. Whereas passive lovers have more room for manoeuvre.'

This specialist advice was very unpleasant.

Kaeso sighed:

'I suppose Nero's sudden changes of mood are all part of his artistic temperament?'

'On the contrary. Artists are naturally amiable, because their basic inclination is to make people like them and to pay the greatest possible attention to other people's opinion of them. Provided one can avoid upsetting them, artists are the easiest people in the world to live with. You'll find out that, taken overall, Nero is nowhere near as touchy as people say. Even when it comes to art, he accepts criticism when he can see that it's justified and that there's no malice behind it. At the moment what is at the forefront of the emperor's mind is his confrontation with the Neapolitan public, leaving aside for the moment the prospect of what might follow. The city has been Greek for 750 years and there are plenty of well-informed people there. As the date of the performance gets closer and closer, Nero becomes more and more fraught and nervous. We could do with your help in calming him down. The whole thing is so important to him.'

'But the theatre will be stuffed with his supporters, won't it?'

'Exactly so. That's the insoluble dilemma. Nero detests sycophants, but he can't manage without them. Although, with good reason, he sees himself as an experienced performer, he's not at all sure of himself, and it takes him enormous efforts to overcome his nerves even in front of the best-disposed of audiences. Many performing artists suffer from the same problem, and one can only feel very sorry for them.'

Kaeso went on asking Sporus about his master, using the prince's amorous overtures towards himself as the excuse for his indiscreet questions. It was natural for a future favourite to find out all he could from an expert, so as to be in a better position to give every satisfaction.

In the end Sporus perceptively asked: 'Is the point of all these questions to find out how to give my Lord the greatest pleasure or how to avoid him?'

Kaeso was evasive:

'I wouldn't want to make you jealous or upset you, and both reactions would seem entirely natural. Your beauty and the affability of your manner towards me have inspired immediate affection in me.'

'I long ago gave up being jealous: all that matters is what will give the prince pleasure. I have a special place in his affections which no one could take away from me. And your success would worry me not at all, since money is of no interest to me: I already have more than I need.'

Kaeso changed the subject of conversation to the architectural model. Sporus gave him an extensive, enthusiastic commentary on it. The contrast between the dream and reality was enough to take one's breath away.

Feeling vaguely troubled, Kaeso observed:

'I see that my modest apartment building in the Subura has been replaced by a little lake with swans on it.'

'The emperor can afford to rehouse you as befits your merits.'

'Jupiter will have to strike the whole of the old city down with thunderbolts for the realization of a plan of this kind to become possible.'

'Then let's pray to Jupiter!'

It was time to go and present himself to Correlius Afer. Sporus put Kaeso in the capable hands of a court usher. Although the morning was drawing on, the palace seemed asleep and the atmosphere was heavy. Nero must be taking his ease in some garden or other. Kaeso had very little trust in the prospect of princely delicacy which Sporus had dangled before his eyes, and the cynical advice of the invert, a species always anxious to recruit others to their band, had made his flesh creep. Yet this advice had been similar in kind to what Marcia had suggested when she had seen feminine coquetry as a way of putting off the key moment. Kaeso was very unhappy.

Correlius, one of those court officials with a finger in every pie, had just woken up after a broken night. He dealt with Kaeso with mechanical and sleepy politeness. To him the candidate was only yet another ambitious young man in a hurry who was eager to get to the top by lying on his stomach: he'd seen plenty before. Correlius even showed just the slightest hint of the same contempt that Marcus had noticed in the attitude of the elder Vitellius, when he had gone to ask him for his support for a sycophantic, incestuous marriage. Social climbers who have actually arrived enjoy the luxury of despising those at the bottom of the ladder who have no choice when it comes to their means of climbing. Kaeso was touched on the raw by it.

Right up to the eve of the Ides Kaeso gobbled his meals up so as to have time to lecture his father on Christian principles. He was still convinced that this was the best tactic to soften the fatal blow. The young man had been well trained and had little difficulty in playing the credible role of a naïve boy caught in the web of eastern charlatans of above average cunning. Kaeso's incontestable moral ambitions helped to create the illusion. Furthermore, it is typical, surely, of a certain sort of defenceless adolescent to become the victim of metaphysical infatuations.

Marcus was well aware that young people who have fallen prey to such crises should not be attacked head on. That would simply have led the boy to a display of eloquent contradiction and to dangerous attempts to surpass himself. In the process his prejudices would have been confirmed in a lasting form. The best course was to be patient, assume an air of importance and wait for this unexpected storm of stupidities to pass. From time to time Marcus would interpose a common-sense objection, learnedly compare Kaeso's resurrection to those attributed to Aesculapius or Asclepias, and seize every opportunity to insert judicious advice on how to behave with Silanus or at court, which was naturally his fundamental preoccupation.

By the evening before the Ides Marcus had reached the point of knowing more about the Christian religion than any other upper-class Roman with a traditional upbringing. If the material had been worth the trouble in his eyes he could have drawn up a short account of the history of the movement, explaining and illustrating its doctrines. Such a book would have found a place in the currently fashionable public readings where authors publicized their works in person. But Christian doctrine, though a plentiful source of wit and humour when looked at from a certain angle, was basically offputting to the average educated Roman.

Towards the end of dinner, despite Kaeso's discretion on the point, Marcus inevitably stumbled over a discovery which he thought would bring Kaeso back to his senses.

'If I've understood the essence of this new religion properly, these Christians of yours, like the Jews, aren't allowed to take part in sacrifices offered by the State or by heads of families, and, with all the more reason, can't offer such sacrifices themselves.'

'Yes indeed. I hadn't thought of that.'

Marcus gave a loud laugh. 'I could become a Christian, since I don't have much to lose by it. But as Silanus is counting on you to perpetuate the cult of his *gens*, it would be a pity to disappoint him for so little.'

Selene pretended to approve of this view, and Kaeso looked impressed by the force of the argument. Contempt for his father, whose capacity for compromise and despicable actions seemed limitless, had brought Kaeso to the verge of hating him. In the attempt to be plausible and dignified he had given the most objective summary of Christian doctrine that he could manage, and had limited his deception to giving an appearance of conviction which was far from representing his real state of mind. What he had to say ought to have interested any honest man. But Marcus, crushed by the weight of traditions which he betrayed the more he paraded them, had felt nothing, understood nothing, and remembered nothing of the essence of what was clearly at stake. His denseness, the way in which his mind was closed to any substantial or sublime idea was enough to drive Kaeso to despair. It was almost as if he were one of the huge flock of the damned whom Paul's caricature of a god took pleasure in leading astray right from their dubious birth.

Marcus, who had drunk rather too much, motioned to Selene to follow him and withdrew, leaning on the arm of his slave. In the doorway Selene turned her head and threw the pseudo-Christian a last look full of sadness and concern. There is a critical point beyond which the imprudent swimmer who has struck out to sea is no longer capable of getting back to the coast. Selene had the impression that Kaeso was about to cross the fatal line, and that he would take a lot of other people down with him.

As night fell Kaeso wrote the following lines to his father:

'Kaeso to his respected father.

Silanus has agreed to postpone the adoption. With reason he fears that a lack of flexibility on my part, in the role which the gods have now assigned me, could damage him if I were closely tied to him by all the majesty of Roman law. The fact that the masterly education which you gave me was aimed at the magnificent goal of turning me into a true Roman makes me all the more inclined to behave like one. So prepare to be proud of me yet again and share my disgrace as bravely as Mucius Scaevola if things turn out as badly as is to be feared.

Do you remember? I was about ten. Marcia and my brother and I had stayed in our seats at the amphitheatre during the lunchtime interval, because you wanted your sons to see the interlude put on for schoolchildren, which was going to present some of the most exemplary pages of our history. The condemned thief illustrating the sacrifice of Scaevola was not at all Roman. He had been gagged to stop him from shrieking in an inappropriate way and his hand had been attached to the brazier so that he would put his heart into playing his unpleasant part. That didn't stop the wretch from writhing about; he was a mediocre actor unable to live up to the requirements of the scene being staged. Yet there was enough instructive truth left in what we saw for your eloquence on the subject to have a moving effect on us, and I have never forgotten the lesson. Like Mucius we must pay the penalty for our mistakes and where possible not make any. Better to have your finger in the fire than up an imperial arse-hole.

By an extraordinary coincidence, which gives one food for thought, the Christian moral code, of which I have spoken enthusiastically to you, is identical on many points with our old Roman code, as if all the gods had agreed at the beginning of time to grind a single type of grain, from which man has made slightly different types of bread in different places. Such unanimity is disquieting and encourages one to good behaviour. Another point in common between our ancestral customs and Christian virtues is that both have been inspired by epic and not myth. The Greeks feed on myths. They invented them and endlessly polished them, and once we had brought those poetic dreamers to their knees we provisioned ourselves from their store. But our traditional education, which first and foremost concerns the will, repudiates any form of destructive, fatalistic mythology. Instead it essentially appeals to the cult of very real historical heroes, whose lives are instructive to us and show us the way. Similarly, for the Christians, Christ is not a myth but a flesh-and-blood hero like Horatius Cocles or Mucius Scaevola, combining epic and didactic dimensions. Any strong, binding religious creed must base itself on real people whose good example can be followed, rather than Greek will-o'-the-wisps.

So all that you have taught me and all that the Christians have preached to me leads me to honour you in a way which you would never have dared to hope.

Fare well.

Your grateful Kaeso.

p. s.: I am leaving straight away with Myra. Why say in person what one can write?'

Kaeso sealed the tablets with a smile. Marcus was going to reap what he had sown with such constancy, and the shock would terrify him and drive him to despair. Moralists are always astonished at being taken at their word, and it is sometimes amusing to exaggerate one's courage, so as to give their ideas some consistency and bite. After all, for Kaeso to make a plausible Scaevola, you'd *have* to tie him to the brazier.

Kaeso and Myra, who were travelling light, went to spend the night in the *ludus* by the Appian Way. They found the gladiators liberally celebrating a piece of unexpected good luck. After Naples the emperor was going on to Beneventum, where the dreadful Vatinius was putting on a magnificent *munus* in his honour. All Marcus' troupe of gladiators had been hired. Eurypylus, who had still not got over the news, was beaming all over his face. They were hoping that Nero would feel it was his duty, as a friend, to be present at a show which had been staged especially for him. The emperor had an aesthetic prejudice against displays of bloody brutality and always took a lot of coaxing before he would put in even a momentary appearance in an amphitheatre.

When Kaeso announced that he would be a member of Nero's retinue, he was asked half-seriously, half-jokingly, if he would take the opportunity to appear in the arena with his father's gladiatorial *familia*.

For more than half a century the emperors had been producing contradictory legislation about the presence of senators and knights in the arena. The result was that things were allowed in practice which were strictly forbidden in theory. Men of good birth were constantly to be seen incurring the 'disgrace' of the *munera* of their own free will, either because of a passion for the art, or in the hope of making a fortune, or simply to curry favour with an emperor who looked more or less favourably on this particular form of loss of status. And in any case the mass of spectators exerted constant pressure on the authorities, since a gladiator's aristocratic origins increased the value of the sacrifice in a very touching way. The crowd preferred a free man to a slave, a knight to a free man and a senator to a knight. So nobles wanting to fight got a good price for themselves when they signed a contract of *auctoratio* with a *lanista* or took an engagement for a single appearance by direct arrangement with the impresario staging the show. It was easy to get round even the most explicit imperial prohibitions, since an aristocrat who was in the normal way banned from participating in Games could always fall back on the device of getting himself excluded from his order by deliberately incurring some judicial stigma which automatically 'freed' him.

With Nero the period of doubt was over. To win favour with the *plebs*, and also because he was by nature anticonformist and liked to stir things up, the Emperor openly encouraged knights, senators and even their wives to appear in the arena or on the stage. The deepest-dyed traditionalists among the members of the senatorial order were duly scandalized. The appearance of married women of noble blood as gladiators seemed especially designed to throw the old guard of the Roman Senate into paroxysms of rage. Husbands had already lost all authority over their wives. The spectacle of half-naked blood-thirsty viragos disembowelling each other was merely calculated to foster revolutionary thoughts in the last remaining obedient wives.

The gladiators' unexpected suggestion struck Kaeso like a blinding flash of light. It offered both a temptation and a reassurance. Greed, a passion for fighting, or the desire to attract the emperor's benevolent attention were not the only motives which drew some nobles to gladiatorial combat. There was also that fashionable malady, *taedium vitae*, the disgust with life which would suddenly overwhelm a disappointed lover, a bankrupt or an incurable misanthrope. By a paradox which added a certain extra spice to the spectacle, the very intensity of such emotions made the combatants particularly dangerous opponents, who fought with exceptional desperation. The man who has nothing to lose doesn't hold anything back; he doesn't calculate his risks; and he often saves his life precisely by trying to lose it. Old stagers of the arena had been completely disconcerted and outdone by young lunatics who were capable of anything.

For the first time since the banquet at which he had become aware of Marcia's passion for him, Kaeso felt that destiny was offering its prisoner a way out other than the Stoic suicide whose passivity he instinctively rejected. The arena was a form of moral and social suicide, but it left a door open on basic hopes, and the relative modesty of such hopes meant that there was no danger of disappointment. You made the sacrifice of yourself to the emperor and the public. Thereafter nothing mattered any more. You found freedom by sloughing off your outer self and detaching yourself from everything around you. It was a form of Hindu asceticism for men of courage who knew perfectly well that no one rises from their ashes as a cow or a sheep. Yes, if things went badly for Kaeso, there was always the arena.

The following day, the Ides of May, should have been the day of the triumphal adoption. Marcus, on waking up, found his son's tablets near the family *lares*, had a heart attack, and lay unconscious on the tiled hall floor for a moment. Selene found him there, and, thinking he was dead, fervently thanked Heaven for the first favour her master had ever done her. But Marcus came to, groaning, and leant against his slave's bosom. The sense of shame which he had been suppressing for so long that he had been able to suppose it anaesthetized and harmless had suddenly come back to choke him. But no one can change from one moment to the next. His plaints to Selene were only the 'n'th variation on a well known rhetorical exercise: the lament of an unfortunate model father over the outrageous ingratitude of an unworthy child. Selene tried to console him, pointing out that perhaps the adoption had merely been deferred, as Kaeso himself claimed. In a wheedling voice she added maliciously that Kaeso would probably prove much more reasonable at court than his letter suggested, and went on to describe in graphic detail, and with a trace of amusing crudity, the most intimate of the favours which Kaeso would have to suffer from, or bestow on, the emperor. They were, she argued, really matters of no importance, and she herself had had to suffer the same without losing any sleep over it. When Marcus realized that she was poking fun at him in the most outrageous way, he slapped her face with a cry of rage and hurried off to his room to brood unseen over his sorrows. Marcia, for her part, had given up her laments and was scarcely even crying any longer. She had become the very picture of silent despair, and nothing that Silanus said or did seemed to awake any response in her. She looked as the statue of Patrician Modesty might have done on receipt of the news of the death of a favourite son at Trasimene or Cannae.

Silanus should have known that broken hearts cannot be mended by thoughtful attentions. What is necessary is, on the contrary, to bring the person concerned out of himself as energetically as possible, because despair on that scale is always a luxury which requires leisure, concentration and tranquillity. Cold, hunger, toothache, headlong flight before a pack of unreasoning wolves are all good antidotes to lovesickness, because it is entirely the product of an imagination left to its own fantasies. Marcia herself could have remembered that her female slaves forgot their heart-aches, unless she herself were the cause of them, when beaten. But the first and most alarming symptom of lovesickness is that the patient stares at his or her navel in solitary state and absolutely refuses to be cured.

Kaeso spent this fateful day with a feeling of having done his duty. His mind had been taken off his troubles by watching the gladiators preparing for their big moment at Beneventum. They were busy sharpening the points and cutting edges of their blades, and polishing their armour and weapons. Tyrannus and his driver were polishing up their chariot, grooming the two stallions, making a detailed examination of their hooves, and judiciously selecting the horse-shoes for the journey.

During the night Kaeso woke up with a feeling of freedom which roused his sexual appetites. He invited little Myra to join him in his bed, but the feeling that he was abusing a defenceless child suddenly under-mined his vigour. It was, however, an entirely false impression, which must have derived from an ideal world which had little or no relation to reality, for Myra underwent the ordeal with unaffected pleasure.

As Kaeso seemed to be having difficulty getting going, Myra put her hand on his forehead and said: 'Stop thinking. Don't think about any-thing. It's not what's going on in your head that counts.'

Every prostitute who wanted to get on in life had her own recipe for making her customers overcome impotence, and Myra's derived from penetrating psychological insight. When a child gives advice as judicious as that, her age tends to be forgotten.

❧ CHAPTER ❧
6

At dawn the next day, the XVII of the Kalends of June, Kaeso and Myra were caught up in the whirlwind of the emperor's departure. For a trip of some importance – and in his own eyes the importance of this trip was decisive – Nero took the whole court with him. It was an entire city, or an army, setting itself in motion all of a sudden, in the most unbridled luxury. Like tributaries arriving at the main river, glittering processions kept sweeping up from all directions to join the main cortège as it spewed forth from the gate chosen for the exodus for hours on end. Between two ranks of legionaries of the urban cohorts, who were there to keep the crowds of sightseers back, there processed units of the cavalry of the German Guard, detachments of Praetorian guards (to music), selected gladiatorial bodyguards, the emperor in his chariot, the emperor's wife, the emperor's lovers and catamites, the emperor's mistresses and con-cubines, the emperor's friends, the senatorial courtiers who were hoping to become the emperor's friends, the *augustiani* (both noble and plebeian), representatives of the principal ministries and offices, who did not want to lose contact with serious matters during the journey, a swarm of imperial freedmen and slaves specializing in every sort of job, a squadron of dispatch riders on their Mauretanian thoroughbreds, and the friends, lovers, catamites, wives, mistresses, freedmen and slaves of all those who were in a position not to travel too much on their own. Outside the city gates were thousands of private vehicles and heavily-laden baggage-wagons waiting to fall in behind. With them were the silver-shod she-asses which supplied milk for the empress's baths.

Myra had been popped in at the back of the line, but Kaeso was put in the relatively small group of Nero's friends who walked just behind the litter of Poppaea. He was delighted not to have been relegated to the company of the long-haired *augustiani*, who looked thoroughly stupid when one saw them in a compact troupe.

By the end of the morning the imperial chariot was approaching the Porta Capena. Nero had personally taken the reins and was driving a *quadriga* with a team of white horses selected for their calm temperaments.

He was wisely taking things at a gentle pace. Despite numerous trial goes in private on the track of the Circus Vaticanus, the emperor had never proved capable of controlling difficult horses, and he was very touchy about this failing.

Kaeso was chatting to Petronius when, level with the temple of Mercury which rose on the left, the procession stopped for a brief moment, a bottleneck having occurred in the immediate vicinity of the Gate. Suddenly Kaeso saw a half-veiled woman in a dark-coloured dress staring at him. She was perched on the edge of the ornamental round pond of lustral water which had been laid out in the centre of the open space in front of the building. He barely recognized the tragic face: it was Marcia. The procession was already starting up again. Overcome, Kaeso gave a friendly wave of his hand before turning away to follow. He had been struck with a presentiment that he would never see Marcia alive again. He was seized by an impulse to get out of this current which was dragging him blindly on towards lands which were foreign to him. He wanted to run to Marcia, ask her forgiveness, submit to her will entirely and find the ultimate peace which compromise would bring. But he still went on his way with his eyes misty with tears.

Petronius took him by the arm and asked:

'Are you weeping at leaving Rome?'

'I'm weeping at leaving my mother. I'm not sure I shall ever see her again.'

'Has Marcia fallen ill since Jupiter – or so they say – abducted her for a few hours?'

'No, her affliction has a quite different source.'

And he added spontaneously: 'She loves me in a way I can't reciprocate.'

After a silence Petronius went on:

'That's a situation straight out of a play. But it doesn't make it any less crucial or full of potential dangers. When stepmothers start pursuing their stepsons there's always an orgy of death at the end of a tragedy. Stepmothers are reputed to take love seriously.'

'Don't I know it! That's why I've given up the chance to become Silanus' adoptive son.'

'That's a considerable price to pay for your freedom.'

'Yes, especially as Silanus was prepared to accept the situation. But it doesn't leave me free for all that. Nero has suddenly taken an excessive interest in me.'

'That takes us from tragedy to comedy.'

'The mood of the play depends on how I play my part.'

Petronius let go of Kaeso's arm and pointed at the imposing harem walking in front of them.

'You'd be quite wrong to draw attention to yourself amid such a large chorus. I know my Nero well. He's the most charming young man when you know how to handle him. He's overtaxed and his sexual powers are considerably reduced. After a few insignificant formalities he'll leave you in peace. It'll be up to you whether or not you do well out of the relationship . . .'

Petronius knew how to phrase things in an elegant, reasonable way.

Kaeso asked:

'Since you know the emperor well, can you tell me which side of me is likely to please him?'

Petronius laughed heartily and answered: 'That's difficult to say. If you're worried about ending up like Sporus, your best chance would be only to risk yourself in his company when he's just left his wife or one of his catamites. Eros can't be ready to shoot his quiverful all the time.'

The advice seemed excellent because it was so simple. But to put it into practice required precise information every day, which would be difficult to get in an absolutely reliable form. Kaeso found the absurdity of his situation more and more painful.

In an absolutely charming way Petronius put Kaeso in the picture about the particular psychology of sodomites and inverts. It was a difficult task, for the laureate of the unnatural could play both roles at once, simultaneously or successively, and still take an interest in girls as well. But Petronius was a poet and novelist, trained to talk well about things with which he had barely come in contact. His air of competence in his subject was enhanced by the fact that, though he himself did not have a specific reputation for homosexuality, he had placed the two heroes of his latest low-life novel in positions which left no doubt at all about their sexual tastes.

'To sum up,' he concluded, 'the confirmed sodomite often presents all the characteristics of superabundant virility, physically and mentally, whereas the chronic invert is very likely to adopt the manners and reactions of a woman. But I've seen people who are ambivalent switching in a curious way from one tone and look to another entirely the opposite, depending on whether their mood of the moment made them feel like playing an active or passive role. It's as if they had a double personality. Actors have a special gift for it, since their temperament trains them day in, day out, to seem on stage to be what they're not or what they'd only like to be.'

Petronius had been talking in a rather loud voice, and there were naturally a large number of homosexuals in the emperor's small personal retinue. A voice from behind them rang out: 'Oh sure, when the gays do their rounds in the moonlight, like a laurel wreath on the imperial brow, the double nature of their personalities stands out a mile.' There was an explosion of guffaws and Petronius promptly changed the subject.

Once they were through the Porta Capena people of higher rank got into their carriages or litters and the procession became strung out along the Appian Way towards the nearby point where the Via Latina, which led to Campania by a more northerly route, branched off. To make the task of organizing the journey simpler, it had been arranged that Nero and his immediate followers would go by the Via Latina while the bulk of the party went on down the Appian Way, which first reached the sea at Tarracina, after the Pontine marshes. The Latin Way went through regions full of gentler, more charming valleys. A third convoy had concurrently left Rome by the Porta Raudusculana and had taken the Via Ardeatina, which hit the coast at Ardea, south-east of Ostia. And the heaviest baggage had already left by boat a few days earlier. When the emperor went a-travelling it was no small matter!

The journey to Naples took three days, for those travelling at a normal pace. But nothing was normal where Nero was concerned. Senatorial speed was already slow: imperial speed gave the local population all the time in the world to admire what they saw. When the court was on the move it had preserved the old Roman custom of banqueting until an advanced hour of the night, which meant that there was no possibility of an early morning start. And the frugal al fresco lunches themselves turned into wearisome feasts. The emperor also had to find time to put the finishing touches to his singing, under the professional direction of Terpnos, and his elaborate exercises required supplementary halts.

On the first day they only got as far as Tusculum. The following day they slept at Agnani, the day after that at the Volscian capital of Fregellae. On the fourth evening the party divided up between the two neighbouring localities of Casinum and Interamna in Latium (there was another Interamna in Umbria). Finally they spent a night at Capua so as to organize Nero's entry into Naples, which was to be accomplished with the same pomp and circumstance as his departure from Rome. The rich city of Capua was abuzz with life the whole year round, but at the preceding stops the imperial party had unleashed their ostentatious luxury on sleepy little Latin towns which had long been bled dry by the tentacles of the vampire which dwelled upon the seven hills. The upheaval caused in such places by the court was all the more shocking to the inhabitants because the emperor, with his ever alert generosity, had set up free brothels at every halt, for the benefit not only of those accompanying him but also of those who had the honour to receive him.

Every evening Kaeso ate with Nero and his closest friends. Vitellius and Petronius were always included in the party. As Cn. Pompeius Paulus had predicted, the emperor seemed very little interested in Kaeso. He was visibly haunted by the spectre of prospective failure on the Naples stage, to the point at which he no longer dared discuss the subject. The best way of keeping Nero's confidence up was to ask him to sing for the small circle of his most faithful admirers. But he was anxious to save his voice for the great day when it would have to win over and dominate a sea of unknown faces, and he spent his sleeping hours with lead discs on his chest.

The emperor had another reason for feeling frightened and confused. A triumph at Naples would be a powerful encouragement to extend his trip as far as Corinth, and his bags had been packed with that in mind. But the prospect of leaving behind him a Rome which was unsettled and unreliable gave him pause for thought. Nero had come to hate the old Rome, which dragged at his august ankles like a ball and chain. As he was making his majestic progress toward the Porta Capena, the lowest of the *plebs* had been heard to cry pitifully: 'Master don't abandon us. Come back soon.' The warning was one to heed.

Kaeso cultivated the company of Petronius with particular interest and pleasure. This privileged friend of the emperor had been nicknamed 'the arbiter of elegance' on outward criteria, but his most elegant attribute was his wit. He had all the charms – and the occasional faults – of such a quality.

The loss of belief in any fixed values swiftly leads to a keen interest in outward form, where an artistic sensibility – or what claims to be such – can be given free rein. When metaphysics has failed, you have to fall back on your senses, which a disillusioned sceptic may find less deceptive. But the sybarite, who has put his energies into turning his existence into a little paradise of grace and beauty, is very rarely a man of strong character. Petronius resolved this contradiction in a nonchalant way which would have deceived a superficial observer. This man who indulged in every form of pleasure with an aristocratic moderation, this man who lived mainly at night, like Athena's owl, was in fact extremely unaffected by fear or corruption, never gave way to malice or envy, and was said to be a reliable, kindly and discreet friend. It was as though this hedonist was slowly burning himself out for want of anything better to do. He stood permanently outside his own enjoyment, ready to lose his smile and leave the theatre once the comedy had ceased to amuse him. There was nothing philosophical about his detachment. It could be seen as in harmony with the old Roman tradition which regarded the arts and letters as elegant superfluities in which a gentleman would have been ashamed to involve himself too deeply. Petronius was an artist at arm's length, and the excellence of his aesthetic judgment possibly derived from just that distance which he had been able to put between himself and the favourite object of his preoccupations. He tried to imbue the most baroque of Nero's extravagances with a little good taste, never insisted, and was all the more readily heeded. People wondered what he might have achieved if he had devoted himself to producing something worthy of himself. But he had resigned himself to passing as the shadow of what he might have been, without leaving an imprint proportionate to his genius.

One fine evening Petronius and Kaeso were out taking a walk after dinner in the Latin countryside immediately around Tusculum. Behind them, beyond Cicero's villa, they could hear, on the clear night air, the noise of the brothel which Nero set up wherever he went. From the heights where the little town had been built they could see the Via Latina winding its snake-like way through the valley, and beyond it, away to the South, the mass of the Alban mountains, which evoked memories of so many moments in history. It was there, on the banks of the Lacus Albanus, that the first Rome, Alba Longa, had been built. By day they would have been able to see as far as the coast.

Kaeso was asking in some concern about Petronius' health, for his weariness was visible. The latter replied:

'I'm as well as a condemned man can be. And since I've nothing against anybody, the fact that most of the emperor's friends are in the same position isn't enough to console me.'

When Kaeso protested, Petronius explained:

'It's our upbringing which condemns us. And what can one do against one's upbringing?'

'You're getting more and more oracular.'

'I'll tell you a story which may make my point clearer. I have the irreparable misfortune to inspire confidence in other people, and one of my friends recently had the bad idea of asking my advice. Because of his hostility to the present regime, of which he makes no secret, he was invited to a select gathering where the master of the house eventually sounded him out as to his possible participation in a plot to overthrow the emperor. Out of prudence rather than conviction he put off agreeing to do so, and ever since then has been pursued by the fear of one day being compromised in this criminal affair, despite the fact that his only crime is to have kept his mouth shut. My friend felt trapped and did not know what to do. An instinctive horror of informing, which he imbibed with his mother's milk, held him back day after day from putting himself in the clear by betraying the plotters – a betrayal, moreover, which the whole of high society would have thought infamous.

Do you see the problem? Nero has three sorts of friends. Those who want to assassinate him. Those who wish him no harm but wouldn't inform on others to save his life. And those who would sell their nearest and dearest for a kiss from the emperor. That shows you the degree of solitude in which he lives, and the amount of confidence he can afford to place in those closest to him.

If I find myself among the false friends of the second category, it's because of a certain concern for style. I'd happily denounce a slave. If absolutely necessary, I'd be prepared to denounce a freedman. But it would be more than I could stomach to deliver men of my own class into the hands of Tigellinus. And I can sense that you're no informer either.

You can see what sort of a massacre this rotten situation could end in. Every year the number of those who know, who've got wind of something, who suspect something and yet have said nothing, is increasing. One day the storm will break, and by degrees, as person after person is tortured, a whole crowd of smart people whose only crime is that they couldn't bring themselves to speak up sooner will go inexorably to their deaths. It will probably be the beginning of the end for the regime, but it won't collapse of its own accord. Someone like Seneca, who knows even more compromising secrets than I do, is branded with the same fatal mark as I am. High society will lament the cruelty of a Nero who can shed the blood of a man as honourable as his old tutor. There will be few historians prepared to point out that it isn't a usual part of a tutor's moral code to allow the assassination of a pupil who has heaped every sort of favour on him. That's the way of the world, and it gives me little chance of enjoying a natural death. But then, despite the convictions of Stoics and Platonists, is there conceivably such a thing as a natural death?'

If Petronius was to be believed, the court was an even more dangerous place than the arena.

'Why then,' asked Kaeso innocently, 'does the number of nobles and senators who have sworn to get rid of Nero get bigger every year? It's not such a crime to turn one's nose up at the old Roman traditions and follow in the footsteps of Alexander or Antony. The essentials of our civilization all come to us from the East and an eastern concept of political power will inevitably impose itself sooner or later. The prince can't remain "first among equals" for ever, when his supposed equals are a bunch of senators who have long lost all political effectiveness. Augustus shored up that fiction after a fashion, but it was already tottering in the days of the great Caesar.'

Petronius scythed the top off a tuft of grass with his cane and thought for a minute before revealing the secret:

'The greater part of the Senate doesn't give a damn about lifestyles or even politics as long as its material interests aren't affected. When people like that accuse Nero of becoming Hellenized or playing the oriental despot, that's quite obviously merely a hypocritical manoeuvre to get the superstitious lower middle classes and *plebs* on their side by pandering to the fact that the lowest cobbler fancies himself a Romulus. The man in the street is much more sincerely attached to the glorious phantoms which prowl the Alban Mountains than any aristocrat is.

Seven years ago Nero became consul for the third time so as to make his wish to influence the current situation quite plain. A grandiose project for tax reform was submitted for the approval of the Senate. It had been under debate for a year or so in the Imperial Council, and I'd heard very precise and credible rumours of what it contained. You know what the present system is. It's the result of our multiple conquests. The cities which were burned to the ground have been rebuilt but fiscal discrimination remains. Indirect taxes, which by definition fall most heavily on the poorest, traditionally form a fundamental resource of the Treasury. They are raised by companies of *publicani*, who are capable of advancing the money to the State, and who get a fat percentage of the money they collect. The farther away a province is, and the more difficult it is to keep a check on what's going on, the more money these tax-farmers help themselves to, and the more scandalous the profits they make. So, Italy escapes their exactions relatively lightly. The importance of direct taxes is constantly growing, but Roman citizens in Italy are exempt from them.

Nero's plan was unprecedentedly daring. He wanted to reduce or abolish indirect taxes and replace them with a general direct tax, to be paid by all subjects of the empire, including citizens.

You can imagine the fury of the senators, who are obliged by law to keep a considerable amount of capital tied up in property in Italy. For the first time it was being proposed that they should pay contributions proportionate to their income. They'd have lost even more, since the abolition or reduction of indirect taxes on the circulation of provincial goods would have lowered the cost of imports and thereby compelled the Italian landlords to sell the produce from their estates at a lower price.

The complaints of the Senate at this naïve, idealistic proposal were so vociferous that the young emperor had to accept a derisory compromise which largely respected the interests at stake.'

'What stopped Nero from going ahead regardless?'

'He could have massacred the Senate. But he'd only have had to replace it with another which would have defended the same privileges. Nero can have a senator killed and confiscate his estates to add them to the immense imperial properties, but he can't kill everyone and confiscate everything. He wouldn't have the administrative capacities to run such an enormous area of land. And the injured parties in the Senate had the support of all the knights involved in tax-farming and even of many ordinary citizens in the Italian peninsula. It was only the Roman *plebs* who had anything immediate to gain from the business, because the cost of food would have gone down.

The Senate has never forgotten that nasty shock and neither has Nero. His sincere desire for the public good had come up against a wall of money, and given the immensity of his ambitions he needs money more than most. The emperor has dreams of a new Rome built on a geometric pattern, where the German and Praetorian cavalry could get round with ease if there were riots. And he spends vast sums on the Greek-style artistic and gymnastic competitions which he has tried to introduce, not to mention the usual ruinously expensive spectaculars in the circuses and amphitheatres, which have never been more lavish. That's the cause of the great split between emperor and Senate. Nero wants to bring those egoists to heel, to reduce them to the level of ordinary citizens, to make them subject to common law, in the hope of bringing his famous tax reforms forward again one day. All those whose fortunes he wants to reduce, so as to assure the State of more equitable, regular, plentiful and healthy finances, are working hard to get rid of him as soon as possible. Sword or poison, any means will do. I wouldn't give you an *as* for his life. And that's a pity. This new tax policy is the only remedy for our financial ills. Otherwise one day there'll be a financial collapse which will eventually make it impossible to pay the armies the Empire needs to protect it against external enemies and to maintain good order internally.'

'So rather than betray a criminal friend, you'd condemn the Empire to destruction?'

'I'm afraid so. It's all a matter of upbringing . . .'

Amid the dazzling pomp which accompanied the entrance into Naples Kaeso found this conversation quite unreal. Sightseers had come piling in from all the neighbouring colonies and *municipia*, mingling with the exuberant and adulatory native Greek population to get a close look at an emperor who was preparing to make a public appearance on stage. Even Caligula hadn't dared to show such provocative contempt for all the best Roman traditions. While the imperial chariot was slowly progressing towards the *agora* of the Greek city, Vesuvius was emitting black smoke, as if to show that the gods of Hades looked unfavourably on Nero's audacity.

The emperor shut himself up for two days with Terpnos to get himself keyed up for the terrifying event. The performance was scheduled for the X of the Kalends of June, the festival of the Tubilustrium, the purification of the war trumpets, under the patronage of Vulcan. Kaeso and Myra spent these two days in the villa which Petronius owned near Herculaneum, a house quite small in size but luxuriously elegant, with a superb view over the gulf of Naples from Capri to Ischia and Procida.

Petronius had brought only one mistress, an aesthetically perfect freedwoman called Isis, and a dozen slaves who formed a modest little *familia* with the twenty-odd male slaves charged with the protection and upkeep of the villa. As Kaeso did not enjoy Myra's company so much that he wanted to be stuck with her for ever, he offered her to Petronius at the beginning of his stay in thanks for his hospitality. But his host was reluctant to accept the gift. Petronius Arbiter had fewer than 300 slaves, but they were all equally valuable and he could see no advantage in encumbering himself up with this skinny shrimp, who could offer only very basic pleasures. Petronius was afraid that his refusal might have hurt Kaeso's feelings, and offered him the free run of Isis during their stay in Herculaneum. But Kaeso in turn refused. Petronius had already thrown a girl into his arms at Baiae. He found something a trifle suspect about this habit of passing on one's mistresses to one's friends.

Petronius eventually explained his habit on the second evening, while the two of them were dining alone together in front of a sea as smooth as milk. Myra and Isis, who found all conversation of a certain level boring, were elsewhere.

'I have on principle always been careful,' Petronius admitted, 'to exclude all risk of falling in love from my life. Given the chaos and destruction caused by that redoubtable malady one can't be too careful. The surest way is to pick mistresses who are full-buttocked and empty-headed, attributes which are very widespread among women. Then you can have peace and total satisfaction. The only problem left to solve is the tiresome one of jealousy. And there's nothing which deals with that so well as the liberal practice of that form of asceticism which consists in giving pleasure to one's friends. The first time I saw you at Silanus' house, full of youth and innocence, I already thought you worth a little flattering attention. The mistress I was honouring at the time seemed just right to make three people happy.'

Petronius' views on marriage bore a similar stamp of wisdom. 'The fatal boredom of marriage would perhaps be tolerable if there wasn't an additional potential hazard which dissuades me from trying the experience – the possibility of fathering a child. Children spend their time destroying the hopes you have placed in them. As my father, who thought me an utter good-for-nothing, so forcefully expressed it: "Having children is simply a way of increasing one's potential for unhappiness." Not even one in a hundred is a success. To produce one who turns out the way you want you'd have to get a prodigious number of concubines pregnant, and the game isn't worth the candle. The only people who can have children without trembling at the idea are country bumpkins dominated by the obscure forces of instinct, and fanatical philosophers short of an audience who fall victim to the illusion that, by increasing the size of their family, they can enlarge the number of people who pay attention to them and perpetuate their ideas. And women also sometimes want children, because, in their shortsightedness, they fail to realize that their sons will be like the men who have deceived and hurt them. Agrippina is an excellent example of the dangers of pregnancy.'

As pessimism such as Petronius' was very widespread, it was hardly surprising if the empire was becoming depopulated.

During these two days, in addition to receiving last-minute advice from the great Terpnos, Nero was rehearsing a Euripides play with his favourite actors. He had decided to stage the play as an *hors d'oeuvre* to the performance proper. Meanwhile, feverish preparations were going ahead to provide him with a tailor-made audience, because his reception was a matter of national importance. Tigellinus, who had stayed in Rome to expedite matters in hand, had worked on a plan with a team of specialists, and now, on the spot, precautions were being taken to prevent the slightest risk of a hitch. Everybody was terrified at the mere thought of the emperor experiencing a humiliating failure, and nobody could think how to tell him that he would have absolutely nothing to worry about. So while Nero was in a state of anguish at the prospect of facing a sea of connoisseurs who would be difficult to please, his audience would in practice be more artificial and indulgent than ever before.

The largest of the theatres in Naples, which had been made in the lazy Greek style by excavating a hill, facing the sea, had been rejected as too small. Instead, an immense wooden theatre had been put up Roman-style in record time on a flat piece of ground in a suburb of the populous city. Everyone who was anyone at court, the senators and the *augustiani* were to occupy the front rows, along with the members of the town council. Higher up would be distributed a vast, predominantly Greek crowd. It had been filtered with minute care, each man having to present his own personal entrance *tessera*. Higher still would be a number of Greek women and children, similarly selected, and their numbers were to be increased by the addition of the cream of the prostitutes whose services had made the journey more pleasant. The highest tiers, at a distance from the stage where faces were no longer identifiable, would be filled with Praetorian guardsmen in civilian clothes; and the blond giants of the German Guard would form a ring around the top of the building so as to deal with the slightest sign of unrest.

Furthermore, during those two critical days the major part of the invited audience was constantly being summoned to take part in rehearsals, for which they were rewarded with banquets and little presents. It was necessary to organize the applause in such a way that the emperor had a vivid impression of spontaneity and informed appreciation. A second company rehearsed the Euripides play with this enormous claque, and a singer and cithara-player then went through the pieces which Nero mistakenly supposed he would be the first to perform. The crowd of spectators had been divided into sections, each provided with a claque leader whose job it was to give the orders and co-ordinate the performance of his group to the best of his ability. Kaeso had been assigned to the *augustiani*, who were responsible for the 'discreet applause', the sort which required perfect timing and the greatest sensitivity and skill. Petronius couldn't stop laughing at such a masquerade.

From dawn onwards on the feast of the Tubilustrium the theatre gradually filled up, and the performance of Euripides' *Hercules furens* started early. Nero had thought that the Greek citizens of Naples would be capable of responding to his favourite author, whom the Roman *plebs* had been unable to appreciate for years now. By taking the role of Hercules in a play he knew well, and in which he had often performed in private, he was counting on getting the 'feel' of his audience and becoming attuned to the demands of a big public performance, so as to be on his best form for the singing which was to follow and which was what really counted as far as he was concerned. There was another advantage to a high tragedy: the fact that it was obligatory to wear a mask. The amplifier would give his rather weak voice more carrying power, and he would be able to get it in trim, ready to accompany the cithara after the interval. Nero wasn't much worried about playing the part of Hercules. He had played plenty of other characters, both male and female: Orestes, Creon, Nauplius son of Palamedes, Thyestes and Alcmaeon, Attis and Capaneus, Antigone, Niobe and Melanippe. He had even had no difficulty with Candace in childbirth.

Overcoming his nerves at this moment of capital importance, the emperor succeeded in making a good impression. He was helped by the warm atmosphere created by his, as he saw it, well-informed and dis-interested audience, and by the fact that he was surrounded by old stagers who took every opportunity to give him the limelight. A tragic mask was, moreover, an excellent protection against the threat of stage-fright, and the masks of the other actors allowed them to prompt their master discreetly with any verses which, through nerves, he forgot. Nero gradually thawed out and gave it everything he had. There were a great many more mediocre actors, and the audience had been expecting worse. It looked as though he was going to have a partly-merited success.

Towards the end of the play Hercules arrives at Thebes just as his wife and three children, already prepared for sacrifice, are about to die. His unexpected arrival saves them, and he is loaded with chains to be sacrificed in his turn. It was the most moving moment of the play, and the audience was keeping religiously silent, when a young soldier came rushing out of the wings, waving his naked sword, and made a dash for the prince.

Private Liber, from a poor family in Lucania, had for a time guarded sheep in the area of the Via Popilia which linked Capua to Rhegium in Sicily. Fed up with sheep, especially the ewes, which lacked the charms of the 'little fillies' of Grumentum or Bruxentum, he had opted for a military career and had recently been stationed in Campania. His only artistic experience hitherto was of the arenas and the pornographic theatre of the cities of that region, where fortunes accumulated from agriculture and trade had allowed the local magnates to distinguish themselves by their patronage. The violence and crudity of shows in Pozzuoli and Pompeii were legendary.

Up until the punishment of Hercules, Private Liber had been guarding one of the entrances to the machine room, which stretched under the boards, in front of the wooden 'stage wall', and had been amusing himself watching how the scenery was moved. From there he could just hear the faint sound of the applause and ovations which punctuated the performance. The total silence which had set in with the scene of Hercules' punishment had aroused his curiosity, and he had succumbed to the temptation to climb up a few steps and risk taking a squint, not having the least idea of what to expect from a classical tragedy. He only knew that Nero was to play an important part in a play which, from his basement, he supposed was bloody and lewd.

The unexpected sight of the emperor groaning under his burden of chains had completely robbed him of his self-control and all capacity for thought or analysis. A shepherd cannot attend the picturesque and dramatic executions of criminals condemned to death without what little critical faculty he possesses being dulled. Thinking that some vile attack was being made, Liber had drawn his sword and rushed to the rescue, harking only to the call of duty and hoping for promotion.

The eruption of this threatening brute plunged the whole stage into the most ghastly confusion. The intruder was wrestling like a lunatic to free Nero from his chains. Nero, for his part, thought his last hour had come. Guards had rushed in and were trying to overpower the assassin. And the actors were emitting shrieks and groans which at last sounded genuinely tragic.

After a brief moment which seemed an eternity the nature of the mistake began to be clear, and it occurred to someone to raise the curtain.

The fainting emperor had been taken into the sumptuous dressing room which had been organized for him behind the 'stage wall', and there, with his mask and boots off, he was lying with teeth chattering and eyes staring wildly. Artists are usually too sensitive for physical courage to be their strong point.

Out among the audience, the assassination attempt was still being taken at face value. The leaders of the claques, out of their depth, no longer knew what instructions to give and the most contradictory rumours about the emperor's fate were rife.

Once the first shock was over, those closest to Nero had rushed to get news, only to find themselves kept at a distance from the dressing room by a tight cordon of Germans, Praetorians and gladiators. There was Poppaea, alternately threatening them and beseeching them in her attempt to force a way through the barrier, Sporus in such a state of despair that he had lost an earring, the freedman Pythagoras (the emperor's favourite lover, whom he was thinking of marrying just to enrage the Senate), and of course Vitellius, Nerva, Petronius, Kaeso and lots of others.

A Praetorian centurion finally detached himself from the guards and announced that the emperor wished to speak to Petronius, Nerva and Kaeso, a remarkable selection under the circumstances. As a true artist mindful only of his responsibilities, Nero, neglecting wife, lover and catamite, wanted to speak first to friends whose artistic experience inspired confidence in him. Petronius and Nerva were his usual advisers in such matters and he had thought well of Kaeso's remarks at the dinner given by Silanus.

As he guided the three visitors to the prince's room, the centurion Sulpicius Asper confided to them: 'The attacker turns out to be an idiot whose sole intention was to rescue the emperor. When the Livys of the future come to tell the story, nobody will believe it.' Asper omitted to add that he would have been delighted if the emperor *had* been assassinated. For many of the Praetorian tribunes and centurions, even for Faenius Rufus, who shared the key office of Praetorian Prefect with Tigellinus, the appearance of a Caesar on the public stage brought disgrace on the whole army. Praetorian officers were primarily recruited from the ranks of an Italian bourgeoisie which was totally unprepared for such scandals.

Nero at once said to his three friends: 'Will there ever be an actor more unlucky than I am? How can years of hard work and aspiration be undone in such an utterly ludicrous way! There's no punishment good enough for the wretch who did it. How could I possibly go back on stage now? I just don't know *what* to do . . .'

Nerva had to admit that the extraordinary mixture of tragedy and farce had killed the performance stone dead, and that it seemed impossible to lower the curtain and stage the end of the play.

Petronius made a practical suggestion. 'Asper assured us that this idiotic attack was intended to rescue you from a dreadful fate. Now there's a fine example of courage and loyalty which could be a source of inspiration to many Praetorians. The more stupid legionaries are, the more you can trust them. There's no point in discouraging anyone. I'd advise you to get the laughs on your own side by rewarding this brave fellow. Do you want me to see to announcing it to the public?'

Kaeso thought the plan a very clever one, and Nerva was on the whole inclined to favour it. Nero eventually came round to the idea and sent them away. 'Petronius can go and do what he suggests. That will get the situation back to normal. You two can go too. I need to be alone before I sing. What it is to be an actor!'

So Petronius went out on stage and announced in a loud voice, in prefect Greek: 'You can all be reassured. Caesar has asked me to tell you that he is well and that he will sing for you as arranged, as soon as he has had a little rest. As for the play, it finished on a *coup de théâtre* which even Euripides himself, for all his genius, would have had difficulty imagining. A soldier with more loyalty than education, on seeing his emperor laden down with chains, rushed to free him. If every legion copies such devotion, our tragedies will be much more pleasant. This brave fellow has earned the promotion which Nero has granted him at my request and that of all his friends. You can see that Hercules is not always enraged: he has his moments of clemency when at Naples.'

The claque-leaders now knew exactly what to do. While the blue skies were filled with laughter and flattering cries of approval, Private Liber, who had been tied up like a Gallic sausage, was hurriedly released.

A good hour went by. Nero called Petronius in again, and he came back and said to Kaeso:

'There seems to be an impasse. Nero has got as far as the ladder which leads up to the stage, and he's just standing there, clutching his cithara, incapable of going a step further. He's terrified of appearing on stage without a mask. I didn't know what to say to boost his morale.'

Kaeso in turn went to see the prince, who signalled that he should be admitted into his presence. He was in a pitiful state, rolling his eyes desperately in the half-light of the wings, rooted to the spot with stage-fright. A sense of shame prevented him from going back. Kaeso asked the guards to withdraw a little way. He went up to the wretched man and said to him in a confidential tone: 'You're a great singer. I could tell that when I heard you at Silanus' house. The greater a singer, the more susceptible he is to crises of confidence, and no artist could go out and sing after such a shock as you've had. But you're not only an incomparable artist, you're also the Lord of the World. The emperor must take the singer by the hand and get the situation under control. I'm going to tell you an old trick which will help you out of your difficulty. Stop thinking about all those filthy people stinking of garlic and onions out there. Sing as you usually do. Just sing for the little circle of sincere friends who know your worth and are constantly expecting you to surpass yourself. If you like, just sing for me. I'll sit in the front row, among senators who'd be delighted if you made a fool of yourself, and our eyes will gaze into one another's until the last chord from your cithara dies away. But in the circumstances don't think of me as a girl. A Greek god can't give the best of himself for a woman. Sing for me as the young man that I am, sing to please me and snap your fingers at the whole of the rest of the universe. Venus will grant you success.'

There was already a gleam in Nero's eye. The emperor stood up straight and murmured: 'By all the gods on Olympus, I'll do it. I'll isolate myself with you to score my success, and you shall share in it.'

Kaeso, who would have settled for less, respectfully took the emperor by the arm and drew him towards the steps.

With his gaze amorously fixed on Kaeso, Nero sang until mid-afternoon. He went through all the hits in his repertoire and finished with selections from his *Troica*. The applause was long and loud; the spectators had fortunately not been distracted from attending to their own lunch-time sustenance. The emperor, who was in seventh heaven, had the impression that he had never sung better. In fact about three-quarters of the spectators could not hear him properly, but given what was at stake that was a trivial detail.

Nero finally fell silent, in a state of exhaustion, tore his gaze from Kaeso's and went off to rest on his laurels. The organizers and the audience were as relieved as he was.

Petronius asked Kaeso: 'Whatever did you say to make him do it?'

'I told him to sing just for me, like a girl in love.'

Petronius smiled. 'Your fear of being taken for a Sporus inspires you with divine ideas . . .'

❊ CHAPTER ❊
7

The theatre had been empty only a short while and an army of workmen was just about to go in to dismantle it, when the upper half of the building collapsed with a frightful crash. Nobody was hurt. It was evident that the hand of a god had been at work, because there was clearly no natural reason why a building of that kind should stand up to the enormous weight of the spectators and then be unable to support its own weight a moment later. Petronius and Kaeso, who had got out of their litter to look at the cloud of dust floating over the debris, were divided in their views. Petronius saw it as a sinister omen, Kaeso as a manifestation of an attentive providence which did not want a sinner to die, even if he were an artist.

Such accidents were only too frequent, particularly in amphitheatres. They were so expensive to build out of stone, because of their size, and because they had to be built on flat ground wherever it was impossible to take advantage of the bowels of helpful hillsides. In Tiberius' day the inhabitants of Rome were for a long time deprived of gladiatorial games by the cruel emperor, and *munera* were organized in the little cities round about. Accordingly, greed led to the building of tottering amphitheatres intended to house a mass of deprived Romans. The most famous of the resulting catastrophes, the one at Fidenae, had resulted in a whole body of preventative legislation which was more or less observed. For practical reasons wood had continued to be chosen as the common building material: those parts which could be dismantled could thus be used a number of times. The whole world did not have the sort of money which allowed the Pompeians to build in stone. Nero himself had used wood for his amphitheatre in the Campus Martius, and restricted his prodigality to the vast sums expended on its lavish decoration. In the old days Rome had also seen a most original solution to the problem: a circular wooden amphitheatre which opened in the middle so that the two parts, pivoting back to back, could be used as theatres. But a technical refinement of this sort was only possible in buildings of a modest size. The machinery and the wheels would not have coped with too great a weight.

In the late afternoon banquets were thrown in all the main squares of Naples to reward the hospitable populace for its appreciative reception of the emperor's golden voice. Nero himself dined later with a few friends in the gardens of a rich villa on the local riviera. He had once been very fond of public banquets, which had provided him with so many opportunities to offer himself in all simplicity to the natural, sympathetic affection of the *plebs*. But he had had to give up exposing himself to the dangers they presented.

The emperor was radiating intense joy at having come out of all his troubles so well: he had, in a sense, proved himself a real professional. After years as a promising amateur he saw the prospect of further stage appearances opening up before him: Greece, Asia Minor, Egypt, the East. To celebrate his success more guests had been invited than usual. Most of the time Nero preferred to dine as the Greeks do, in all-male company, so as to enjoy interesting conversation. Hetaeras and catamites, if present, were merely looked on as decorative extras. But on the memorable feast of the Tubilustrium, Poppaea and a few trendy married women had also been given places on the cushions of the *triclinia*.

When Petronius and Kaeso arrived, the emperor was in the middle of recounting for the 'n'th time (each time with more embellishment) how Kaeso had helped him to recover his talents instantaneously. What delicate constitutions artists do have! He rushed up to the young man, and showered him with kisses, caresses, promises and compliments.

'Come into my arms, you divine, glorious boy. Thanks to you I've now won a new reputation which is dearer to me than the Empire or life itself. Come close and let me get a proper look at you: you know my eyesight isn't too good at a distance. I was singing to a face lost in the mists of Olympus. I even wonder whether at one point I wasn't singing to Vatinius!'

Poppaea thanked Kaeso in her turn, with the utmost graciousness. She was ferociously jealous and expended much energy on getting rid of female rivals who might damage her, but very sensibly she looked kindly upon new male favourites, who at least had the very definite virtue of keeping the emperor away from scheming women. She had not shed all trace of prejudice against catamites, with their feminine charms, but imperious imperial lovers were always welcome. From time to time they were able to strike chords within the emperor so deep no woman could reach them.

Kaeso, whom everyone but the emperor looked on as a courtier of genius, had no difficulty in playing the modest innocent, since, taking an entirely relative moral stance, he had only thought of protecting his rear, so to speak. This modesty merely added to his charm.

Kaeso was placed 'below' Poppaea, who was herself stretched out 'below' the emperor. Nero was anxious to know what impression his art had made. Nerva and Petronius indicated one or two points on which minimal further progress was possible. Vitellius declared that since the Master's voice had already demolished a theatre, he ought to be sparing with his effects. Only Vitellius' notorious ignorance allowed him to get away with such heavy-handed jokes. Kaeso suggested that it would be in the interests of the divine citharist to sing for a more attractive young man than himself, but Nero protested: 'It's all decided. I shall sing for you at Corinth, in the great theatre at Pergamum, and in the shadow of the Pyramids. I need your confident gaze to sustain me: it sums up the look of all the men I should like to enchant.'

Nero added that he was composing a song to thank the gods for having spared so many precious lives by preventing the theatre from collapsing sooner. The people of Fidenae had been less fortunate in the days of Tiberius.

A courier had been instantly dispatched to Rome with news of the miracle. Tigellinus could also thank the gods. If the upper parts of the theatre had collapsed on hundreds of Praetorian guardsmen in civvies, it would have been hard for him to explain away desertions on such a scale to the emperor. Nero liked to spoil the Praetorians, who had brought him to power. At the same time he was afraid of them, and, with the two prefects, kept a close eye on the troops, to spot any black sheep. Unfortunately for him it was the shepherds whom he should have mistrusted. The dimwits in the German Guard, who were by definition insensible to the old traditions of Rome, gave less cause for alarm.

The celebrations went on into the middle of the night and – as Nero had already sung more than enough for one day – were for once enlivened by a series of entertainments which alternated, according to a carefully planned progression, between the serious, the amusing, the erotic and the obscene. All of it was of a very high quality. Taking advantage of Nero's temporary absence at the latrines, Poppaea started to flirt with Kaeso. He was very surprised. The emperor was not jealous by nature and was used to taking part in group sex, which he liked to be gracefully choreographed, but the virtue of the empress was kept spotless, for the good reason that Nero was determined to have a successor of his own blood. Kaeso eventually realized that Poppaea was only using her charms to find out what her husband could have been up to with Marcia on a boat on the Tiber in the depths of the night, as rumour had insistently proclaimed.

Kaeso was evasive and waited until Nero could hear his reply too. 'I was there when my stepmother returned. She's a woman no longer in her first youth, and her lifestyle has become very austere since her marriage to that old Stoic Silanus. Marcia was still trembling all over. Caesar had done her the honour of initiating her into the cult of a foreign god called Mithras, whom our legionaries have brought back from Armenia. Apparently king Tiridates is an adherent of this strange sect. According to Marcia a huge lion plays a part in the ceremony, to test the courage of neophytes, who are principally recruited from the army and among women of warlike character. The postulant has to put his or her head into the animal's mouth, pat its rump, pick up its cock and fearlessly grasp its balls. If the hero doesn't get eaten, he's admitted to the brotherhood. Marcia smelled of lion for several days, to Silanus' great alarm. He was as shaken as she was proud.'

Nero confirmed his story. 'That's approximately what I told Poppaea. No one makes up a tale like that. One of these days I'll go into the arena dressed as Hercules and strangle a lion or kill one with a club. That'll add a new lustre to my reputation.'

At the end of the festivities the emperor announced that he had finally decided to go on at least as far as Corinth. His tone brooked no argument. Nero was attracted by Corinth because of its mixture of a new-style Greekness with a Roman element. He felt only contempt for Athens, which he saw as an ageing city worn out by the demons of democracy, and he had no more time for Sparta, which had doubtless died fighting but was now only worth a brief tourist excursion. What attracted him were the great deeds of Alexander and in particular the regimes which Alexander's heirs had set up and got to work, where a king-god imposed his charisma on mixed populations who were in principle united in their love of, and respect for, their ruler. He was expecting the East to provide him not only with informed applause but also with political lessons. However premature his dream, it nonetheless reflected the deeper nature of reality.

The aristocratic government of the big Greek maritime cities, after interludes of tyranny, had succumbed to the egalitarian appetites of middle-class businessmen and traders. But democracy had also had its day. For reasons of communication the only conceivable form of democracy was a direct form, in which government was in the hands of as many citizens as will fit into a public square. Such a solution was inapplicable to political groupings on the scale of kingdoms and empires. This direct democracy had itself been a factor in the destruction of the cities in which it had been rife, since citizens who really do have the freedom to regulate their own taxes have only two ways of sparing themselves: crushing the rich to the detriment of the economy or getting the money from successful wars. But even then you can't get money out of the conquered indefinitely. The future lay with new Greek-style tyrannies. What was wanted was an enlightened absolutism capable of receiving the assent of the majority no longer just at the city level but at that of immense territories.

To make the young Nero reject tyranny Seneca had given him Xenophon's *Hiero* to read: a long lament by the ill-starred tyrant of Syracuse against the risks and problems of the job. But what the adolescent had remembered was the encouragement given by the second speaker, the poet Simonides, who considered that a virtuous tyrant should be capable of attracting loyalty. Simonides' arguments reflected the position of the author, a man all for law and order, who was shocked by the failure of the Greek city states. The innocent Nero had long cherished the ideals contained in Simonides' moving peroration, and had tried to put them into practice in the first five years of his reign:

'I tell you Hiero, it's against the heads of other states you must compete. If you make the city you govern happiest, you can be assured that you'll be the winner in the finest and most magnificent contest in the world. In the first place you'll immediately secure what you really want, the affection of your subjects. Secondly your victory will not be proclaimed by the voice of a lone herald: all the world will speak of your virtue. You'll be the cynosure of all eyes, a hero not only to private citizens but even to many foreign powers; you'll be admired not only in your own home but by the general public. And you'll be free to go wherever you choose in complete safety, at home or abroad. For you'll have an endless successsion of people anxious to show you the clever, beautiful or good things which they've created or discovered, and of people anxious to serve you. Every visitor will be devoted to you, everyone not in your presence will long to be there. They'll not just be fond of you, they'll adore you. As for good-looking young men, you won't have to chase them; they'll be chasing you. You won't have to worry about anything; everyone else will do the worrying for you. Your subjects will obey you of their own volition; you'll find them looking after you without your requesting it. And should any danger arrive, they'll be not just allies, but zealous protectors. You'll be laden with presents, and have no shortage of friends to bestow them on. Everyone will rejoice at your prosperity, everyone will fight to defend your interests as though they were their own. Everything your friends possess will be at your disposal.

So take heart, Hiero. By enriching your friends, you'll enrich yourself . . . Look on your country as your private estate, your citizens as your comrades, your friends as your children, your children as yourself. And try to outdo them all in good deeds. For if you outdo your friends in goodness, you'll have no need to fear that your enemies may harm you. If you do everything I've just said, rest assured that you'll be blessed with the finest and most precious gift in the universe. You'll be happy without being envied.'

At the end of a banquet at which a great deal of drink had been consumed, the emperor would sometimes hear with painful nostalgia the echo of that sublime hymn to intelligent and generous despotism. He had believed it. He had believed it only too well. He had lavished fortunes to make himself loved, he had lavished still more to disarm hatred. Terrible experiences had made him sceptical about the gratitude he could expect from his fellow men. Seneca had warned him: 'Money is ephemeral and gratitude more ephemeral still', but it was too late. He needed more and more money to buy loyalties which became more and more dubious. Hiero's disenchantment was the inevitable price to pay for power.

One of Simonides' statements had, however, left more of a mark on Nero than any other: 'As far as handsome young men are concerned, far from having to win their affections you'll have to fight off their offers.' In the desert in which even the best of emperors was condemned to live there was a strong temptation to reinforce loyalty with love, and as Xenophon had implied, it was not women's love that could build a rampart of effective devotion around a ruler. Amid all his virtues Nero had seen himself as obliged, if only by political expediency, to give free and unashamed rein to his latent homosexuality. But the 'sacred battalion' which a solitary man can build up by the constant gift of himself nonetheless remains too small to undertake a campaign.

Over Poppaea's head the emperor indicated to Kaeso that he would like to finish the night in his company. It seemed to him the natural conclusion to such inspired singing. But with that excess of delicacy to be found only among the very young Kaeso protested: 'First you must give the empress an heir: she has never looked more beautiful.'

Nero could only thank him for so elegant a reminder of his first duty.

As the emperor was in a hurry to set foot on Greek soil, early the following morning the court was already en route, in a certain state of chaos, for Beneventum, which was reached in the late afternoon. The modest local amphitheatre, which was very old, had been passed over, and Vatinius had had a suitable wooden amphitheatre built. Its super-structure dominated the town and the green countryside of Samnium, which had once run with blood during the ferocious 'war of the allies' between Rome and her Italian neighbours. It was to be hoped that the wood taken from the Apennine forests would prove to be of better quality than that used at Naples. The problem now was to bring forward by a day the hunt and *munera* arranged for three days' time, but the change of programme occasioned no difficulty in a town of relatively modest size.

Kaeso left his baggage at the country house of the friend of Petronius who had offered them hospitality, and hastened to contact his father's gladiators, who had arrived the night before. They had travelled very slowly, because they had been engaged as reinforcements for the con-veyance of 200 gladiators from the prisons of Praeneste, a little town close to Tusculum, which served as a reserve supplying 'livestock' for the Roman games. Gladiators under contract, who fought in pairs, were a minority in the arena. At the end of an afternoon there would be fights *gregatim,* in other words, in a confused mêlée reminiscent of the conditions of war. The combatants would be prisoners captured on the battlefield or individuals who had been condemned to this fearful extremity by the courts. The magistrates, like the legionaries, lent a hand in the task of filling the arenas of Rome, Italy and the provinces. Both prisoners and condemned criminals had a double interest in showing themselves good fighters. When the official responsible for the Games stopped the fight, the few survivors would be kept for another show, and it was not unusual for the crowd to ask for mercy for this or that man who had particularly distinguished himself. Bandits and runaways, and prisoners who inspired so much mistrust they could not even be reduced to slavery, had the choice between fighting in the arena, on the one hand, and the hangman's axe, death by wild beasts, crucifixion or the dreadful hell of the mines, on the other. It was always these conscripted gladiators who revolted, as the runaway and bandit Spartacus had once done, and the burghers of the tranquil cities of Italy were not reassured by the sight of a large mass of such desperados in their midst.

After Interamna on the borders of Campania the rumour had suddenly spread among the 200 wretches that half of them were to be blindfolded for their fight at Praeneste. Such a spectacle was found particularly entertaining by the spectators, who would be sure to tease the *andabatae* by giving them wrong advice. This band of involuntary gladiators profited from the general drowsiness during a short rest, when they were not shackled together, to hurl themselves in concert on their undermanned escort, using their handcuffs to cosh them and the chains which linked them to strangle them. The business could have got badly out of hand if a number of those who had rebelled had not taken advantage of the aggressive instincts of the more determined ones and made off in the direction of the vineyards on Mt Massicus. Four soldiers had been badly injured but all the gladiators were safe. A dozen or so mutineers had got clean away and thirty more had been massacred on the spot, in the rage engendered by their treachery. The gladiators under contract cordially despised a miserable crew barely good enough for launching a show.

While Kaeso was hearing the story of the adventures the gladiators had been through on this eventful expedition, Petronius, who had just emerged from his host's baths, received a letter from Marcia to Kaeso. She had addressed it to Petronius, because it had occurred to her that amid the mass of courtiers the courier would have less difficulty finding such a famous man than a young man who was almost unknown. Marcia had entrusted her dispatch to one of the private postal enterprises whose journeys were notoriously slow, as their messengers had a tendency to zigzag across the main routes so as to serve as many clients as possible. Had time ceased to be of importance to her? The letter in question had followed Kaeso to Naples and thence eventually reached Beneventum.

At the same moment the emperor was digesting, to his intense vexation, the contents of a dispatch from Tigellinus, which had travelled with, among others, a letter from Silanus to Kaeso. The imperial *tabellarii*, who kept going at full speed night and day by the fastest roads, were not, in principle, available for public use. But there was a certain amount of latitude: if a *tabellarius* was not too loaded, he would, for a good tip, accept a little private correspondence as well. This was an irregular form of post. You had to keep an eye open at the Central Postal Service in the Campus Martius or at some relay station along the way. Sailors and friends who travelled were similarly asked to act as couriers.

With his usual clarity Tigellinus was raising tiresome difficulties.

'C. Ofonius Tigellinus to Nero Caesar Imperator, greetings.

Marcia, the wife of Silanus, died by poisoning the day after your departure. Her maids claim that it was suicide and there is no reason to doubt their word. Their mistress had seemed depressed for some time.

However, she left no document to explain her action, she confided in no one, and Silanus, with his usual hauteur, has not deigned to enlighten us, if indeed he is in a position to. Marcia was not, apparently, suffering from any serious illness, and there is no evidence that she has had an affair with anyone since her re-marriage. Her death is a mystery of a kind which inevitably arouses curiosity and over-excites the imagination.

No sooner had her death been registered at the temple of Libitina than an increasingly elaborate rumour began to go the rounds among all those who are sworn to do you harm. Marcia, the image of Patrician Modesty, is supposed to have killed herself because of a sense of shame and despair caused by the fact that you abducted her one night and subjected her to frightful outrage and brutality.

You asked me for information about this woman before dining with Silanus, and you will admit that, in the circumstances, the idea of her shame is even more implausible than that of your lubricious cruelties. But you are aware that for years there has been no slander, however incredible, which your enemies will baulk at in their attempt to undermine your power.

My spies have reported to me that for three days every discontented member of the Senate, every pressure group, every nest of conspirators plotting to destabilize the State, has been filing through the atrium to pay its respects, with appropriate hypocritical lamentation, to the embalmed corpse displayed there. Musonius, Thrasea and Cassius Longinus have naturally been prominent. What a difference between the discreetly conducted marriage and these noisily public condolences! And these icy-lipped Stoics actually managed to keep straight faces as the weighty name of Lucretia flitted from mouth to mouth. I'm only a knight, and not a very well-educated one at that, but I seem to remember that it was after the rape and suicide of Lucretia that the victorious revolt against a tyrannical monarchy broke out in Rome, and handed power over to the very people who would like to get it back today. It is no accident that they are so loudly invoking the name of Lucretia: it is a symbolic expression of a hope and an intention.

When Seneca himself put in a saccharine appearance, I felt that the time had come to prevent you from being jeered at and insulted any further, during your temporary absence. I invited Silanus to hurry up the obsequies, and even to get them over at night-fall, so that the crowds would be smaller or at any rate less visible.

As Silanus had shut himself up in an enigmatic silence, it was difficult to know what part he might have played in this abject comedy. But at the very least he must have been an accomplice. No one saw him protest against the stupid lies which his visitors were hawking about, though he could easily have done so. And he did not find the title of Lucretia an excessive honour for a wife so virtuous that in earlier days she occasionally went so far as to pick up her customers at the baths or under the porticoes.

Since I wanted to have an entirely clear conscience, I courteously paid him a visit the morning after the funeral. He was crouching in the "poor man's cell" which Stoics build so as to add a bit of spice to their pleasures. He seemed completely lifeless, and greeted my indignant remonstrations by saying in a dreamy voice:

"Yes, I married a Lucretia without realizing it. She has shown me the path of dignity. No more compromise."

These strange remarks could be taken as semi-confessions. I suddenly thought of a possible explanation for Marcia's suicide. Suppose that she was compromised, possibly against her express wishes, but compromised nonetheless, in a conspiracy in which her husband played a leading part. If she despaired of its success, and was overcome with remorse or anguish, might she not have preferred that way out to the prospect of a condemnation which would destroy her good name? When I suggested this to Silanus, he merely shrugged his shoulders.

I felt that I had a right to arrest his freedmen and interrogate them at leisure. A man who lets his emperor, a near relative, be insulted and remains odiously indifferent to the fact is clearly capable of anything. If he is not yet part of a conspiracy, he soon will be. He is a living insult to the emperor.

These interrogations were vigorously conducted, and though they did not precisely bring any conspiracy to light, they did provide evidence for a certain number of supplementary charges.

Silanus was spending enormous sums of money, and they were increasing. Perhaps he did not expect to live long? In any case the effect of his prodigalities was to enlarge what was already a considerable clientele and make this descendant of Augustus very popular.

On the pretext of the need to administer his enormous fortune efficiently Silanus had organized his freedmen into a veritable little government, with titles analogous to those of ministers and ministries.

On the strength of some leak from an unknown quarter he did not hesitate to speculate on the devaluation, the announcement of which, as you know, was postponed.

All his freedmen – and the evidence is corroborated by the slaves –

agree that Cicero's ghost made frequent appearances in the villa on the Palatine which previously belonged to the old bore. Marcia and Silanus are both even supposed to have spoken to the ghost. I feel I am justified in wondering whether they may not have asked it about your state of health. Cicero was hostile to Caesar, and his ghost is unlikely to be friendly to you. You will notice how often the opposition are revealed to be involved in magical practices. This impiety is one of their typical characteristics.

A further very marginal point. As the houses of Clodius and Scaurus have long been part of the imperial domain, Silanus' villa is one of the last private residences on the Palatine. It would be in your interest to acquire it to make it easier to realize our rebuilding projects in this area.

To sum up, since Silanus seems to be virtually inviting condemnation, it would, in my opinion, be an excellent occasion to get rid of someone who is dangerous because of his name and his immense fortune, and because of the murky hopes which could be placed in him. Sooner or later people like that give way to the attractions of an ambitious revolutionary plan. Better to nip it in the bud than have to deal with the consequences.

This alarum is a pressing reason for me to advise you not to go over to Greece at the present moment. Whatever my own devotion and un-shakeable loyalty to you, I could not entirely answer for the situation here. You must deal with Rome before you think of leaving it for long.

The first time you talked to me about your desire to build a new city to immortalize your reign and make your subjects happy, I was, I have to admit it, shocked by your grandiose dreams. I wondered whether you were one of those people whom the gods like to lead astray so that they can destroy them more easily. But long pondering on the matter has finally convinced me of the superiority of your inspired vision. And I am in a position to tell you that the whole thing is possible, that it would be exceptionally desirable just at the moment and that I have the matter in hand.

Aesthetic questions are not my forte, but you have always been satisfied with my political and administrative advice. A Rome which was clearly rebuilt on the Greek pattern would be much easier to govern. It could even be allowed to spread over a larger surface area. The current piling-up of buildings causes a multiplicity of insoluble problems. And from a political point of view it is becoming more and more urgent to crush the Senate, that hydra whose poisonous heads are constantly growing afresh. It is also becoming more and more urgent to establish an effective control over the fickle lower classes. Hostile or dubiously reliable citizens cannot carry out two different activities at the same time: conspiring and re-building. A carefully planned catastrophe will make you master of the situation.

All it will take, with the weather and the wind in our favour, is a small number of agents especially selected for their capacity for hard work, who will keep their mouths shut for fear of being torn to pieces. Success will be complete, because verbal instructions will have been given to reduce the number of people available on fire watch. It won't be possible to prevent some unpleasant accusations being levelled against you. But we can get the best of this summer's idiots, as we can the idiots of the future, by retorting with the common-sense argument that the idea is too far-fetched. An inspired ruler can get away with anything once he exceeds the limits of plausibility. For the man-in-the-street will certainly see no more in the accident than the chance play of destructive forces. The profound, beneficial underlying reasons for it will escape him. How could we expropriate without the money to rebuild? However, an élite, both today and in the future, will guess the truth and approve the sacrifice.

So, my divine master, come and preside over the painful birth of a new Rome, without roots, where every stone will speak only of your glory. It would be a good idea, before the storm breaks, to lay on Games such as have never been seen before, so that the old city disappears at the end of a joyful and unforgettable apotheosis, summing up all the pleasures of the past and heralding all the pleasures to come. I will see to that too. And if sacrificing me as an accomplice will one day help to secure your position, I promise you my co-operation in advance.

Hasten home. Fare well!'

When he got back to his host's house to take a bath and change for the evening Kaeso stopped to chat for a moment with Petronius. The latter seemed to be thinking of something else. Eventually he said: 'A letter has arrived for you from Marcia, followed by a letter from Silanus which must be more recent since it came by the imperial courier. I imagine that the only news you could be getting from Rome will be bad news. In such cases I usually postpone reading the letter, or even ask a freedman to give me a summary of its contents. But perhaps, like most young people, you're in a hurry to know the worst?'

Kaeso was. During the whole trip he had contrived to put both Marcia and Silanus out of his mind, but now they only came back to him with all the greater force. His hand was trembling as he broke the seal on Marcia's dispatch . . .

'Marcia to Kaeso.

I was proud of you as I saw you go. The handsome Kaeso walking behind his emperor towards a brilliant future was the same little boy whom I found in a feverish state on the honeymoon night of my 'marriage' and to whom I gave a first night of love without his even having to ask me. It was the same boy whom I proudly took with me to the baths, and on whom I lavished my kisses, my secrets and my advice. And it was the same young man who has caused me so much worry. My success was complete, and I had no regrets for the pains, public and private, which I had to suffer to obtain it.

I am dying of sorrow, but I have no one to blame for it but myself – or some unknown god who plays with women's hearts and inspires in them passions which can have no fulfilment. My last and most ardent wish is that my death should not be a burden to you. Treat it as one of those blows of fate which it is not in our merely human powers to ward off. What I have accepted and endured so discreetly in your service did not of course give me any special rights over you, beyond the right to continue to serve you in the same way, with your affectionate, condescending approval. As you expressed it so well in a letter which was not addressed to me: 'At my age one is not inclined to make love because it is to one's advantage, or out of gratitude, sympathy, pity, fear or habit.' A young man of distinction should only make love because he is in love. I think of myself as lucky because, ever since you were very young, I have only made love out of love for you. And I am certain that, had the need arisen, you would have done the same for me ... with any other woman but myself. I thank you for your generous attitude, which makes us quits, really.

I don't know whether I brought you up the right way, that is, in a way which serves your best interests. I think I did the best I could, trusting to my own good intentions and feelings. My heart may sometimes have misled me, but I feel that in the long run it was a fairly reliable guide. As I say my last farewells to you, one thing above all others comforts me. I have constantly observed that the greater a man's qualities, the less effect upbringing has on him. You have a noble genius in you which sets you above others. There was nothing I could suggest to it which it did not know already. Doubtless I did not deserve to supervise your natural progress, because all I had to offer you was love, and that love you were one day to judge excessive. But I shall never forget that part of it which you deigned to accept, and I cannot help believing that you would have preferred not to have to endure it from anyone else.

When you come back along the Appian Way, wave to me. Wherever I may be, my one sweet love, I shall still love you.'

Kaeso uttered a low moan, dropped the letter-roll in Petronius' lap, and started to weep. He could not speak. Petronius ran his eyes over the Latin text of the letter and said:

'A truly exceptional woman. Her fate illustrates only too well, alas, the dangers of passion. It was for your sake she married Silanus, wasn't it?'

'Yes,' admitted Kaeso with a sob, 'just for me, so that she could have all of me. I only understood when it was too late.'

'It wasn't her first act of devotion?'

'How could I have guessed?'

'Don't reproach yourself for anything. Marcia herself among the shades would be upset if you did. It's in the nature of passionate love never to meet an equivalent reciprocal passion and never to find rest outside death. Marcia had the life she wanted. A man in the grip of passion may waste his life on an obsession, but the obsession is one which he accepts willingly, cultivates and makes into his reason for living. Perhaps, deep down, such people have more will-power than sensualists.'

Kaeso did not feel strong enough to read Silanus' letter, and he asked Petronius to summarize it for him until such time as he was in a state to look at it himself. Petronius read and reread the Greek text, which was in the patrician's own hand-writing and barely legible, so as to be able to separate the phrases and understand it properly.

'I shall read you the whole thing. It deserves it.

D. Junius Torquatus to his dear Kaeso, greetings.

Despite all my precautions Marcia poisoned herself the morning after you left, because she could not face another day without you. She died instantaneously with your name upon her lips. There is no point in re-proaching you for your part in this: you will reproach yourself more bitterly than I could. And I must reproach myself for not having kept as close an eye on her as I should have done. I could not even bring her back to life. In Paul's absence I was referred to a fellow named Peter, who sent word that resurrecting suicides was not his business. The bizarre narrow-mindedness of that sect is fearfully disappointing. It is true, of course, that Marcia would probably have done it again.

I hardly dare speak of my own misfortune in this context, and yet they stem from it with the astonishing logic of the absurd. All that section of the Roman nobility which swears only by Cato of Utica, or at the absolute outside by Augustus, has seized on the opportunity to make Marcia's death into a bloody reproach to the emperor. The pretext is that she is supposed to have ended her life like Lucretia, following the nocturnal rape to which Nero is supposed to have subjected her. If I hadn't been the victim of it, I should have thought it an excellent joke. But the joke was made worse by the fact that among the most strident of the mourners there were doubtless some who, out of sheer envy, were stirring things up for the pleasure of getting me into trouble.

To satisfy the legitimate desires of Tigellinus, who persisted in asking me for explanations which would clear the emperor's name, I would have had to explain that a married woman of the *gens* Junia with an appropriate 'past' had been raped for a laugh by a friendly, joking Nero, and that she had only poisoned herself out of despair at being rejected by her stepson, whom I had been prepared to adopt.

Without Marcia and you, whom I should have liked to unite in a single enveloping feeling of love and good will, I felt that the time had come to allow a fiction so flattering to my ancestors free rein and to withdraw from life with all the undeserved dignity which the gods were offering me, to bring me back to a proper sense of self-respect.

Why let things drag on? I have had everything I could want in life except you, and this is a magnificent opportunity to exit with my head high. I may never get another like it.

I have made my nephew my principal heir. I am leaving a few statues and pictures to the emperor, along with the citrus-wood table which once belonged to Cicero – he has been very touchy lately. I am also bequeathing a suitably large sum of money to Tigellinus and a few others. To you I am leaving the Gallic necklace which Manlius Torquatus once won in single combat. Caligula took it away from my family, and Claudius gave it back to us. Since you are a prodigy of virtue, you will of course make good use of it. I would have wronged you if I had left you anything more than a souvenir. Your disinterestedness would be an eternal example to Roman youth, if circumstances permitted it to be more widely known.

I have rewarded the most meritorious of my slaves and freedmen and am now waiting for the surgeon. I shall have my wrists cut in solitude, like a sage, instead of having a little celebration with my close friends, as that poseur Petronius would doubtless do if he were reduced to such an extremity.

I have only one thing left to say to you. When you travel along the Appian Way, remember that I loved you.'

Reading this letter sent Kaeso into floods of tears again. Petronius seemed a little less moved by it than by the previous letter.

'Forgive me for being indiscreet, but what can Silanus mean by the strange expression "raped for a laugh"?'

Kaeso, choking back his sobs, clarified the point. Petronius found it significant.

'Men will put up with their wife being raped, but not for a joke. I imagine that Silanus committed suicide in part to avoid looking ridiculous. His sense of pride must have stifled him. What an admirable, Roman death! We may not know how to live, but at least we know how to die.'

'I wish it was me who was dead instead. I've made my mother die of grief, and Silanus, who was so well disposed towards me, would still be alive if I hadn't brought bad luck on him.'

'He brought the bad luck on himself. You clearly have no responsibility whatsoever for this fatal misunderstanding.'

Petronius did his best to reason with Kaeso at some length, and with some success, since the latter was receptive to intelligent arguments. Passion had killed Marcia, his sense of pride had killed Silanus: Kaeso had only been, at worst, the virtuous tool of fate. If fate had such virtuous tools at its disposal, it looked as if it could not be as blind as people claimed. It was even capable of smiling on one occasionally, since the funeral of Silanus obliged Kaeso to return to Rome with all speed, and Nero could not take offence at the fact.

Kaeso would, however, have to take his leave formally. After a dinner party at which the emperor had seemed worried and absent-minded, Kaeso asked to speak to him in private, told him of Marcia's death and Silanus' probable suicide, of which Nero was still unaware but which hardly surprised him, and ended by asking for his permission to return to Rome at once, so as to be able to pay his last respects to his stepmother's husband. The bodies of aristocrats were normally on view for a week, a delay which in summer posed a considerable problem for the embalmers.

Without referring to the letter from Tigellinus, Nero asked whether the correspondence he had received threw any light on the precise reasons for this double suicide. Kaeso felt obliged under the circumstances to imitate Silanus' discretion and not say more than what the emperor might already know or be able to guess. So he declared: 'As far as I can tell Marcia must have killed herself because she suffered from the incurable ennui which is the worst of the currently fashionable maladies, because doctors don't usually have any talent for amusing their patients. Decimus and I were powerless when these crises became really serious. Apparently in her final moments my stepmother kept saying 'Only Nero knew how to entertain me.' Silanus was very much affected by his wife's brutal end, but the final blow seems to have been the stupid slanders against you which irresponsible senators were apparently putting about in this context. The rumour was that Marcia had followed the example of Lucretia because you had attacked her virtue. I am however in a good position to know that your virtue and hers were about the same.'

The emperor thought for a moment and eventually said in the most friendly of tones: 'I'm very sorry to hear about Silanus' death. It provides me with yet another reason to mistrust the Senate. And I'm still more sorry that Marcia should have left us. As you revealed to me one evening, her passion for you went beyond the bounds of the acceptable, but she had every quality a mother should have, and I'm happy to think that she had pleasant memories of me.'

The imperial voice took on a coaxing tone:

'But couldn't you, nonetheless, put your departure off for a moment? I should like to offer you some consolation for these redoubled blows that have struck you . . .'

'Please forgive me and understand my position: I've just lost a dear friend and a second mother. Not even Venus herself could console me tonight. I have no appetite left for anything and I have a migraine.'

Poppaea often suffered from migraine too.

'Well,' said Nero, 'I won't be so cruel as to detain you. I'd hoped to travel through Greece and Egypt in your delicious company, but I think I'll return to Rome myself after Vatinius' *munus*. Serious matters require my presence there.'

'I'll come and throw myself at your feet as soon as you get back.'

'On your way then, and my good wishes go with you. I shall immediately give instructions for your journey to be as smooth as possible. The moon is shining bright for you.'

Nero gave Kaeso an affectionate kiss. He had a cast-iron excuse for not lingering. It was the ever-attentive and jealous Marcia's last present to him.

❊ CHAPTER ❊
8

Kaeso entrusted Myra to Petronius, who was to bring her back to him on his return to Rome. Then, with the aid of the ever fresh and lively horses of the imperial postal service, he set off at a dash for Rome. He had been relieved to be forced to abandon the child in this way. Despite all her good will, she had in some indefinable way disappointed him. Perhaps the shameful influences to which her negative education had inescapably subjected her had been too much for a girl of fragile will-power. Kaeso reproached himself for not having expended as much care and attention on her as he ought to have done. He had treated her like a dog, and then had leapt on her when he was feeling desperate. He could have found the time to pay her more attention, take a paternal interest in her desires and suggest better ones. He had behaved negligently and egoistically, and the cares which had overwhelmed him were a poor excuse.

At the relay-station in Capua, which adjoined an inn full of 'little fillies', Kaeso suddenly wondered whether Jesus's teachings, despite his leading minister's prudent attempts to adapt to circumstances, were not guaranteed to deliver a fatal blow to slavery as an institution. The gap between the rights of the property-owning classes and the requirements of a stringent moral code was so great that it was more or less intolerable. There was also a striking parallel between the anguish of a tyrant who wanted to behave generously and the problems of a slave-owner who wanted to mould his stock of slaves in his own virtuous image. In both cases the deprivations of any element of freedom became a crushing burden on the narrow shoulders of the well-meaning master. In both cases it was a depressing and disappointing experience, because it was an attempt to assume an impossible pseudo-paternity. But what would slaves or even whole peoples have done with their freedom, given that they were incapable of enjoying it wisely or elegantly?

Kaeso slept for a few hours at Capua, and rejoined the Appian Way as dawn began to break.

He was riding under a dazzling sun through the neatly set out and well cared for vines of the Falernian region when his head began to throb with a terrible migraine. Perhaps the gods were punishing him for having lied to the emperor like a frigid concubine. For a second time, as on the occasion when he had apparently died, a fever reduced him to delirium. The rows of vines seemed like pursuing armies, the vengeful ghosts of Marcia and Silanus barred his way, the ears of his mount were suddenly those of Nero, Paul was walking beside him laughing sarcastically, and high in the cloudless sky the three Christian gods, wearing the eyeless helmets used by *andabatae*, were bickering in a scandalous fashion.

The Son was complaining: 'I was born too soon into a deaf and blind world. I wasted my time and I suffered in vain. My God, my God, why have you forsaken me yet again?' The Father was turning round and round, not knowing which saint to trust himself to, but the Holy Spirit cried out as it sharpened its sword: 'The impossible faith can only be founded on the blood of martyrs. Blood! blood! What we need is blood.' And all of a sudden these three tragic actors in search of an audience pointed at Kaeso and shrieked in chorus: 'You are our beloved son, and we've got worse things in store for you yet!'

Kaeso mechanically wiped his mouth and slid down at the feet of his horse in a faint.

A peasant on the way back from his vineyard hoisted him over the back of the horse and took him home.

Although the illness was not as serious, it followed the pattern of the previous occasion, developing in alternate bouts of violent fever and complete prostration. For seven days Kaeso was treated with all the resources of rural medicine – herbs gathered in scrupulously observed conditions and made into bitter brews, massages with wolf fat, and various sorts of broth in whose preparation imagination ran riot. On the morning of the eighth day, the Kalends of June, the patient began to come to, after taking a restorative thin soup which smelled of warm blood-sausage. This was made from toads' intestines and menstrual blood collected from virgins. The second of these ingredients was much harder to obtain than the first in a wine-making region where the girls were easy. They had had to go as far as Cales, where there was a brothel-keeper who always kept a few virgins on hand as a special treat for rich customers. The beneficial effect of the mixture was the best proof that in cookery, as in love, it is all in the mind.

The Kalends of June were the festival of Carna, the goddess of the human entrails. M. Junius Brutus, a distant ancestor of Silanus, had asked this goddess for the strength to conceal in his inmost heart his plan to drive out the tyrant Tarquin so that the upper classes could trample on the people at their leisure. This first of the Brutuses known to history had become one of the earliest Roman consuls, and, in his gratitude to the goddess, had raised a temple to Carna on the Caelian, which Augustus had had restored, along with many others. (Perhaps Silanus had prayed to Carna when he was coping with the indiscreet Tigellinus.) At a later date the cult of Carna, the goddess of beneficial secrets, had become associated with that of Mars, the god of effective violence, and Juno Moneta, the goddess of fruitful premonitions. That way you could be covered for everything.

Kaeso was interested to see the head of this rustic household make an offering of beans and bacon to this divine trinity, such food passing as classic restoratives in the country.

Before setting off on his journey again Kaeso spent another three days with his kindly hosts in a Virgilian bucolic atmosphere which gave him a lot to think about. Virgil had created sham rustics, just the way townsfolk, who are very careful not to run the risk of being disappointed by actually meeting the real thing, like to imagine them. But, with a poet's intuition, Virgil had sensed a great truth which showed through the artifice in places. Man's dialogue with Nature is a constant factor for wisdom, circumspection, dignity and virtue, provided that the country dweller is in a position to do the cultivating himself and can draw a reasonably comfortable living from the soil. In Virgil's day the modest farms which had provided the bulk of citizen-soldiers for the legions had in large part been swept away by the irresistible forces of 'progress' represented by the vast aristocratic estates, devoted to speculative stock-raising and crop farming. People had got into the habit of expecting Sicily or Africa or Egypt to provide corn which Italy refused to produce. Since then things had got worse. The rural slaves had become '*coloni*', prior to becoming serfs. What Kaeso had before him was what you might call an archaeological rarity: peasants who were more Virgilian than Virgil, and who were not even homosexual. Perhaps the requirements of growing and producing fine Falernian wines explained this survival? Top quality vine-growing is an elaborate art which is not compatible with the approximateness of the way things were done on the *latifundia*.

The master of the house had given up his own room, behind the classic Campanian atrium, to Kaeso. He had been taken in and looked after without being asked for anything in return. The questions which he had put about the bullocks or the poultry, about vine growing or the diet of the dozen or so slaves who were all crowded into an outbuilding, were all answered in a friendly fashion. Old Tullius treated his slaves with as much care as his bullocks or his hens. His wife and five grown-up children were obedient to his commands, and he presented a picture of a peaceful, well-balanced man who expects more of himself than of other people.

At dawn on the day before the Nones of June Kaeso took leave of his benefactors, who indignantly rejected the very idea of payment. But, in a charming custom which had generally fallen out of use, Tullius engraved his name on a piece of wood, with Kaeso's underneath, broke the piece of wood in two, and gave a piece back to the traveller. In the old days the Romans had always shared with their guests the *tessera hospitalis*, which served as a recognition-token. Whilst *tesserae* were hardly ever seen any more, the expression 'to make a friendship token (that is, a *tessera hospitalis*) with someone' still existed, in the sense of forming a strong bond with someone. When Sulla had 12,000 proscripts executed at Praeneste, he let one off because he had ties of hospitality with him. And quite recently Piso had rejected with horror a plan to assassinate Nero under his roof, despite all the difficulties inherent in doing so elsewhere. These links of hospitality had even extended to whole towns and nations, which had a privileged relationship with Rome or with this or that Roman official. Hence the laws relating to ambassadors, which made their persons sacred.

Kaeso was very moved as he put the fragment of *tessera* in his bag. He felt that before him he had, in the person of Tullius, the traditional solidly-rooted father that Marcus would like to have been, but of which he had only been able to provide a caricature. As Kaeso's horse had been promptly returned to the postal service, Tullius had offered him a mule to help him reach the next relay station without wearying himself. In bidding him goodbye Tullius had said: 'Since you're in the habit of talking to Nero like I'm talking to you now, be sure not to mention me. My grandfather once gave old Augustus, who was on his way back from Baiae with a very small group of attendants, some refreshing water from our well. In thanking him the emperor said: "Do you know, I'm jealous of your happiness." One jealous man as important as that is honour enough for any family!'

For a naturally taciturn man so much eloquence was remarkable. What an astonishing family! Though the lack of decent bathing facilities was beginning to get Kaeso down, he would happily have gone on boarding with Master Tullius, so as to be able to enjoy an imperial happiness amid his vineyards.

As he was still weak, Kaeso chose to hire a gig with a cover to protect him from the sun, rather than use imperial post-horses all the way home – the Post kept its ultra light-weight vehicles for the *tabellarii*. Since Silanus would have rejoined Marcia a week before, he completed the journey without hurrying. It was in fact only on the VI of the Ides of June, towards midday, that he came within sight of Rome. Although his strength had more or less returned, his health still gave grounds for disquiet. The coast of Latium was being ravaged by marsh-fever, but Tullius had assured him that his illness was not the same, a negative diagnosis which got Kaeso nowhere.

Shortly before the mausoleum of the Silani a new inscription attracted Kaeso's attention:

'Though a victor on every battlefield I succumbed to the sheer number of my doctors.'

A surgeon had put an end to Silanus' life, but at least he was acting under instructions.

Kaeso got the attendant to open the tomb for him and was shown the two most recent marble sarcophagi. Silanus's, which had been made some time ago, stood out from the others because of the bas-reliefs on it, representing fish and aquatic plants. Marcia's had not yet received the attentions of the sculptors, but in the already engraved funerary inscription Silanus had expressed both all his disdain for the regime under which the gods had thoughtlessly called him to live and die, and all his contempt for vulgar proprieties:

CHASTE AS LUCRETIA SHE BROUGHT HAPPINESS TO ALL THOSE WHO KNEW HER.

Kaeso was overwhelmed. He had to lean on the attendant's shoulder to come back to reality.

The Subura apartment block, plunged in the torpor of siesta time, offered a sad and disquieting spectacle. No one had done any housework and most of the furniture of any value had disappeared. Kaeso came in without knocking and woke up Selene, who was sleeping draped over a bench in the would-be atrium.

'What happened to you then? The court came back with Myra in tow, and your disappearance was yet another source of distress to your father. Even Nero asked after you several times.'

Kaeso gave a brief account of his trip, explained why he was delayed and asked what had been happening . . .

'The chain of disasters unleashed by your virtuousness is growing longer by the minute. You've opened a Pandora's box, and now that all the bad things have flown out, there turns out to be no Hope at the bottom after all.'

'What do you mean?'

'At his wife's nocturnal funeral Silanus coldly told your father that he'd manage without him in future, since Marcia was dead and you'd caused the adoption plan to be dropped. Marcus, who'd been trying to kid himself that the adoption was still on the cards despite all the evidence to the contrary, collapsed, and his clients had to bring him home. He'd been counting on Silanus' protection and on Nero's friendship for you, and on the strength of his expectations he'd been living beyond his means and incurring ill-considered expenses. The rumour of Silanus' contemptuous rejection of him, which had been rather public and particularly hurtful, spread like wildfire among his creditors, all of whom came swooping down so as not to be the last to get their pickings from the modest spoils. The apartment building and what's left of the furniture will be auctioned off on the festival of Summanus. Marcus is drinking like a fish to take the edge off his torments, and has become strangely confused. He keeps saying: "Another auction? But I've only just finished with the last one." He's clinging, as a last forlorn hope, to the idea that the emperor will be so charmed with you he'll heap you with presents. So you can guess how upset he's been by your mysterious absence. And if it means anything to you, I can add that I'm none too sure about what's going to happen to me. If I'm to be sold again, who knows what hands I might fall into? They could be even worse than the ones I'm already in.'

Kaeso's recent attack of fever had brought him close to death for the second time, an experience which makes most people cling all the more tenaciously to the things of this world, but causes the most austere moralists to feel even more detached from them. For some time he stood lost in thought in front of the Priapus fountain, which was an invitation or a dissuasion, according to how you looked at it. Then he said to Selene:

'I've already promised to look after you as an attentive master or a respectful lover would. Marcia can't hurt you any more, and I shall protect you from whatever harm anyone else may wish to do you. There's a disturbing resemblance between us. Our only value in the eyes of the world around us lies in our exceptional beauty. I'm in a position to get mine to perform miracles if I want to. The day your safety requires it, I shall regard it as my duty to put all my powers of seduction at your service. But you can't expect me to debase myself that far for an ignoble father or even for myself, given that I'm not sufficiently fond of that self.'

Kaeso asked Selene to write Nero a letter in Greek for him:

'Kaeso to Nero Caesar Imperator, greetings.

I was struck down by a malignant fever and fell off my horse while riding through the vineyards of Falernum. Kindly peasants found me unconscious and took me in. I have only just got back to Rome, and it has been my first care to dictate this note to you to reassure you as to my well-being. I am still very weak, but happily my convalescence is progressing normally. As soon as I am well enough to appear before you, I shall be sure to come to see you and reaffirm my loyalty and affection. I am proud of having been able to be of service to you, in such a simple way, in circumstances which are of great importance in your eyes. But I only did my duty. You owe me nothing in return, and your friendship and respect are all that I could possibly want. Material gifts could not make me more attached to you than I already am. Perhaps you do not hear people say that every day. That is probably because you do not have with most people the special relationship you have with me, in which the two of us are drawn together by the exercise of a particular tact and trust.

I have now been struck down by a different kind of fever. I am sure you will be happy to learn that I have fallen madly in love with the beautiful slave who is penning these lines for me. Forgive this weakness, which is momentarily distracting me from thinking of your benevolent majesty alone.

I hope that your health is better than your faithful servant's. Your very weaknesses are still a source of blessing to the state. I cannot aim so high.'

Selene sighed. 'I doubt whether Nero will appreciate such disinterestedness, and Marcus will appreciate it still less. You'll finish him off. I suppose you think that it's up to him to tickle the emperor's fancy himself if he wants to improve his finances?'

Kaeso made no reply, but went in to see his father who was just emerging from a muddled sleep.

Despite all the disappointments he had experienced, Marcus let out a cry of joy on seeing Kaeso – Mercury, messenger of the gods – who perhaps held the fate of his family in his hands.

'I hope you haven't been stupid enough to quarrel with the emperor, have you? In that dreadful letter you left me before you went off, you were just trying to frighten me, weren't you? To teach me a lesson, in a childish fashion? I forgive you.'

'Nero and I are on reasonably friendly terms. I even had dinner with him.'

'Good. Then nothing's lost. Selene must have told you how things are . . .'

'On what grounds am I supposed to ask the emperor for money? As an *augustianus* I have 120,000 sesterces per annum. That money is of course at your service.'

'A fat lot of good 120,000 sesterces would be! The bailiffs are at the door. Ask Nero as a . . . friend. I need 900,000 sesterces. What's a sum like that to the emperor?'

'He's surrounded by people asking him favours.'

'But I'm told he's particularly fond of you. He kept on sending for news of you in your absence.'

Marcus realized that he should have begun by expressing his grief at Marcia's death or asking after Kaeso's health. He hurriedly made good his omission. Then the unfortunate senator came back to the point, stressing in pitiful tones, and with much touching detail, the situation to which a certain lack of common sense, but more particularly terrible bad luck, had reduced him. He said rather less of the services to which his son would have to expose himself to get his father out of his plight.

It was beyond Kaeso's powers of self-control to tolerate such an unpleasant display for long. He asked: 'What's stopping you from going and asking the emperor for the money yourself? Nero holds you in great favour.'

Marcus sat up on his bed. 'What makes you think so?'

'He said to me one evening: "Marcus should come to the palace more often. With little wings he'd make a lovely cherub."'

Marcus turned bright red and gasped for breath like a fish out of water.

Kaeso changed his tone. 'I've already told you in writing, and I'll say it again. I deeply regret having to disappoint you, but I'm only acting in the way you honourably brought me up to act, in conformity with the traditional Roman values which you drummed into me day after day, and in whose virtues I have always believed. A Roman debauches himself for pleasure and not for a handful of sesterces. I should be confirmed in my attitude, if I needed to be, by the fact that for some time now I have shared the moral views of the Christians, who eventually baptized me and admitted me to membership of their community. As a Christian I'd remind you that we're all accountable before God for the use we've made of our bodies, which He made in His own image, bodily as well as spiritual, since Jesus came down among men and took on the most common and humble of human forms. A Christian jealously preserves his virginity as a precious possession which will prove him more flexible and more disposed to good works than those of the faithful enmeshed in the web of marriage. If he gives in to the temptations of the flesh, it will be by marrying a virgin and staying chastely faithful to her. All the rest comes from Satan and leads to Hell. So don't say anything more to me about Nero and all his glories. They will pass, like the waters of the Tiber under the bridges of our filthy city. It would be better if you'd follow my example and prepare yourself for an eternity of happiness in the arms of my mother Pomponia.'

Marcus was dumbfounded. He could barely think straight. But one thing, beyond his worst fears, was perfectly clear to him in all its horror. The Christians had driven his precious Kaeso stark staring mad. And what could you say to influence a madman, and get him to see a few reasonable, practical considerations? He was overcome, and could only murmur:

'I suppose it was also to please these Christians that you broke with Silanus, threw Marcia into utter despair and hastened my downfall?'

'You know perfectly well that a Christian can't carry on an idolatrous cult.'

'Ah! So that was the reason.'

But there must have been something else as well. Marcus had been very surprised by Marcia's suicide: she was such a tough-minded, intelligent woman. Marcia would not have killed herself simply because a planned adoption had been called off. Marcus forced himself to think, and suddenly made a discovery which went through him like a flash of lightning.

'You're a liar. You didn't give up a fortune for a foreign god. Marcia killed herself because she loved you and you wouldn't return her feelings. That's the key to it all, isn't it? You can't deny it.'

Kaeso felt an access of rage against this man who corrupted everything he touched, and who had hit upon a secret which he, Marcia, and Silanus had discreetly preserved.

'It was your intention to prostitute me to Nero to save the tottering fortunes of this house, which is itself a fragment of the fortune amassed by your slave and freedmen ancestors, who got rich by their own spare-time whoring. You lived, and for years made me live, on the proceeds of the prostitution of your wife and niece. You grew fat on the sweat of her charms, and drowned your shame in drink. Would you also have liked me to prostitute myself with Marcia on Silanus' lap? It was a proof of Marcia's ineffable sense of pride that she only slept with people for love of me. Where's your pride, you slob? What lessons has your wisdom still got to offer me?'

Marcus changed from red to very pale. He finally answered in a toneless voice: 'My pride is the same as Marcia's. At every dishonour we shared,

586

we'd say to each other: Kaeso will be free, rich, and happy. All that dishonour for nothing. But don't spare my self-respect if you're sensitive to Marcia's. My shame is at your service too. I admit that you didn't ask for anything. But is one supposed to wait for the children to ask before one gives them something?'

This pitiful declaration would have touched Kaeso if he had been fonder of his father. Instead of feeling compassion for him, he said something unfortunate: 'A mother's shame can be borne in silence. A pimp's shame is not in the same bracket.'

Suddenly touched on the raw, Marcus leapt up, hurled himself at his son, and slapped him across the face, shouting: 'Get out! Get out! May all the furies pursue you! Parricide! Matricide! Your birth cost the life of your mother Pomponia, but that wasn't enough for you. I hope those devilish Christians choke you!'

Kaeso retreated into the alley outside, pursued by a Marcus who was beside himself. In a little while his father threw all the insolent boy's clothes out into the dust. The whole neighbourhood had come running to witness the classic scene: the noble Roman father driving out his ungrateful son with the appropriate stock insults. While Kaeso was collecting up his things, a circle of indignant traditionalist Romans, whose grandfathers had all served as bum-boys to their affectionate masters, added their jeers to those of Marcus.

When her master had gone back indoors, Selene helped Kaeso to retrieve a toga and put it on. She said to him sadly:

'The final achievement of your virtue is to get yourself insulted by the crowd. Our prophets knew plenty about that. Do you still want me to take your note for the emperor to the palace?'

Kaeso nodded, but suddenly remembered that Selene had had a Greek upbringing and that the Greeks shook and nodded their heads to mean the opposite of what was commonly meant. Fearing that she might have misunderstood him, he expressed himself more clearly: 'Yes, yes, yes! I don't care who insults me, I shall sleep with whom I like, or I shan't sleep with anyone.'

Like Marcus, Selene had the impression that Kaeso was on a slippery slope and past the point at which he would listen to reason from people with experience. Myra, who had been woken by the row, had watched Kaeso's expulsion in consternation. He seemed to have forgotten all about her as he struggled ridiculously under the weight of togas, tunics, loin-cloths, and shoes. The spectacle had both moved and shocked her deeply. She had the greatest of respect for fathers, for she herself had had the very best sort, the sort of which all perceptive and sensitive children dream, an unknown father, that eternal mythological figure to whom any quality you like can be attributed the more cruelly his absence is felt. Kaeso must certainly be at fault. But he was her master, he had been good to her, and it was not his fault if he made love with his head.

Myra ran after Kaeso, picking up various trinkets which he had dropped on the way, including his ephebe's *petasus*, which he had kept as a souvenir, and the lead collar used on runaway slaves, which the blacksmith had come and sawn off the child's graceful neck.

'Look! Here's your hat and my collar. But by Leda's twin sons, what have you done to make your father drive you out of the house like that?'

'Apparently I tried to be virtuous.'

'Well, you certainly did it differently from anyone else.'

Kaeso could not help smiling. He went and found a porter to carry his stuff out to his father's *ludus*. As a refuge it seemed particularly appropriate: it would soon be changing hands.

Marcus stopped drinking to take stock of the situation, but it was, alas, irremediable. Marcia, who had given him so much good advice and had kept him going, had been wounded by the arrows of Eros, the last of which had killed her. He had never been able to have any positive influence on the course of this fatal passion, which he had never suspected until it was too late. Silanus had swiftly followed Marcia into the tomb, and in his lifetime had already deprived him of all protection. Once again he found himself an out-of-work-lawyer, his creditors were becoming impatient, the dispersal of the rest of his patrimony by auction was approaching, and without the minimum property qualification he would be barred from the Senate, just as he would be expelled from his own house. He knew no trade, he felt old and tired, there were already too many beggars in Rome, and he could not expect any help in his misfortune from the high and mighty Arval Brethren.

But all of this was trivial compared to the dreadful insults thrown at him by Kaeso. Marcus had struggled for twenty years to set up his beloved younger son – not to mention his older brother – and he had been nurturing a viper in his bosom, only to find the creature now erect and hissing with pride and contempt. Kaeso had never loved him. Otherwise he would have been as understanding towards his father as he had been to Marcia. Who can flatter himself that he achieves the goals he sets himself in life?

Kaeso's ingratitude, his lack of good sense and flexibility, had brought ruin where shining palaces should have sprung up. Marcus had received the most heart-breaking of all knife-wounds at the hand of his dearest child: decades of tolerating shameful sacrifice had been in vain, their only reward further shame. Two auctions in life was one too many. It was time to make his exit.

But Kaeso had not acted alone. Christian fanatics had helped to turn him against Marcia, and Silanus and Nero. A young Roman carefully brought up in the old ways by his parents does not give way to the most intransigent madness unless his mind has been sapped by strange and perverse doctrines.

Throughout the afternoon Marcus prowled around like a bear, sometimes in one empty room, sometimes another, racked with paternal grief and a prey to self disgust, yet possessed by a growing hatred of all things Christian. Selene and the slaves watched him uneasily.

Towards evening, with no thought of dining, he shut himself in his study, and by lamplight wrote a long letter to Flavius Sabinus, Vespasian's brother, who had replaced Pedanius Secundus as Prefect of the City. Pedanius, a friend of Seneca, had fallen victim to an unpleasant morals case. Sabinus, who was a well-balanced and serious man, inspired more confidence in Marcus than Tigellinus did. He would know what to do.

'M. Aponius Saturninus to Flavius Sabinus, greetings.

My friend, I want to make a formal complaint and to ask you for your help.

I had a son, Kaeso, a flawlessly handsome, intelligent and friendly boy, who was the comfort and hope of my old age. The most distinguished of the nobility were fighting one another to adopt him, the emperor himself had an affection for him, and when he was in Athens the *ephebia* lavished its friendships and intellectual benefits on him. Now the Christian sect has taken him away from me. He has been seduced from all his duties and reduced to a state of blindness and madness which would inspire me with more pity than revulsion, if he had not replied to my offers of good advice with the most wounding insults. I had to drive him out, and my life is no longer worth living. You will appreciate the infinitely pernicious nature of this new sect if you remember that the boy is no illiterate, credulous common lad who has been lured away by Christian enticements, but a young man who possesses every gift of intellect and sensibility, lovingly and farsightedly raised in a very strict senatorial environment, where the traditional glories of Rome have constantly been held up as objects for his meditation. The cunning of these people is unbelievable. If

589

they are allowed to go on unchecked, they are clearly capable of upsetting and perverting a constantly increasing mass of people.

These Christians are still relatively unknown, and I would not be at all surprised if your knowledge of them was rather vague. However, in the inept hope of converting me into one of these mad visionaries, my unfortunate Kaeso spent days on end talking to me about the doctrines and mores of the people who had abused his good faith, innocence, and sincere and estimable desire for moral perfection. A Jewish slave-girl has completed my education on the subject. I am consequently in a better position than anyone to tell you about the Christians, what sort of people they are, what they want, and how they can unequivocally be recognized, so as to render them harmless as soon as their cup of iniquity overflows.

At first sight it would be easy to confuse the Christians with the Jews, because the founder of the sect, one Jesus, a carpenter, was a Jew by birth. But in fact it was the Jews in Jerusalem who themselves condemned this adventurer to death for blasphemy, because he had the gall to declare himself not only Messiah, but also son of the eternal father and equal to god in all things. In the reign of Tiberius our procurator, Pontius Pilate, approved the verdict and had the sentence carried out. Since then the Jews have always protested when the Christians are over-hastily identified with them, and they have been right to do so. The Christians have in fact abandoned a large part of the prescriptions of the Jewish Law and introduced new doctrine pregnant with serious consequences. They claim that their Jesus was resurrected from the dead three days after his death and walked around for another forty days while waiting to ascend to Paradise with a quick flick of the heels.

You will certainly be wondering why a fable of this kind should be of any significance. But experience of public affairs must have repeatedly shown you that what is important to the magistrates is not how reasonable or otherwise certain beliefs may be: that is not within their sphere of competence. However aberrant or dubious a belief, what matters is whether it is or is not shared, whether it does or does not spread, and what effect its characteristic aspects have on public order. I can assure you that the Christians have managed to get people to believe in this resurrection. Many slaves and ordinary people have been convinced by it, and it is set fair to impose its supposed truth on people of the highest rank, as the unforeseen mischance which has struck me so eloquently proves. Belief in the resurrection of Jesus, otherwise known as Christ, is in fact the first sign by which a Christian can be recognized, and it is extraordinary enough to make the identification simple.

Moreover such a belief necessarily makes the lunatic who believes it absolutely intractable, and inspires him with total contempt for, and the most dangerous hostility to, all ideas, convictions and customs which do not happen to coincide exactly with those of the religion of the supposed resurrectee. How could it be otherwise? A man who can bring himself back from the dead is divine in essence, and his word must therefore be superior to that of any other man. Absolute intolerance of the most monstrous variety is the force which activates all Christians.

An inquiry would bring you spectacular confirmation of what I have said, particularly as regards the following points:

Christians believe that virginity is superior to marriage, that a man should have only one wife and stay faithful to her, that if a married couple separate re-marriage is immoral for such time as the divorced partner is still alive. In fact, re-marriage is in any case frowned upon, and Christian priests are not allowed to re-marry. Given the depopulation threatening the Empire, the antisocial side of this inhuman doctrine is starkly obvious even to the least well-informed. Are people no longer to be allowed to divorce a sterile wife? And if a woman is disappointed by an impotent old fogey, is she to be denied the pleasure of seeking offspring in the arms of an Adonis? Whether one likes it or not, Romans of both sexes have won perfect freedom in marriage, even the freedom not to marry and to derive the greatest of pleasures from concubinage instead. It is not within the powers of a religion to send a revolution in mores of that sort into reverse. History teaches us that as far as this sort of thing goes, once a right is acquired, it is acquired once and for always. But that does not make the unrealistic pretensions of the Christians any the less revolutionary and potentially trouble-making.

The Christians think that homosexuality is a crime which should be severely punished. Plato, thou shouldst be living at this hour! The time has come to disguise yourself, so that Christians get a more flattering image of your talents. Poor Sporus! The time has come to seek impotent refuge on the flaccid bosom of a sympathetic hetaera. The Christians take a charitably condescending attitude towards the more standard weaknesses, and are on the whole inclined to tolerate female brothels, on condition that the girls are kept hidden in the most abject of conditions, and deprived of all freedom, all dignity, and all honourable entertainment and distraction. Divine whores, beware of the Christians, who think copulation should be done in the dark.

Christians believe that any abortion, even when authorized by the father, and any exposing of a child are crimes that just laws should pursue and punish. The Roman law which authorizes a father to punish his son with death has fallen out of use, but the right to have only such children as he sees fit is surely the first and most sacred right of man?

Christians believe that any device or activity designed to prevent an inopportune pregnancy is a sin. The only reason that Christians are reluctant to declare such faults as crimes is because they doubt whether an effective policing of the issue could ever be carried out. Our Christians sometimes show good sense, but only to confuse us.

Christians frown on horse-racing, because of the betting which it encourages. They abominate gladiatorial combat, because they think that human blood should not be shed for entertainment. A fine piece of impiety, if one remembers that the original purpose of these confrontations was to provide a sacrifice acceptable to the shades of a dear one. But they particularly abominate the theatre, on the grounds that it is supposed to excite unhealthy passions. Even the noblest tragedies disgust a Christian. The least pornographic entertainment gets him in a terrible state. Plebeians, whose daily bread it is, beware of the Christians. They will only allow porn behind closed doors!

The founder of the sect, an illegitimate son (according to the Jews) of a Roman auxiliary soldier, expiated his follies on the gibbet. That is probably the explanation for the Christians' cowardly revulsion for blood and violence, which is almost as strong as their peculiar hysterical rejection of pornography. Against all common sense and public order some of them go so far as to claim that to use weapons even in self-defence would be a sin, and the blood of animals shed in your *venationes* makes them faint. If one listened to them, our legionaries would throw their arms into the Rhine, nothing bigger than a chicken would ever be put to death, and the science of surgery would cease to progress, in the absence of vivisection of human bodies. For everyone knows that the results of observations done on animals cannot always be transferred. From Jesus on his cross the Christian still derives a natural penchant for everything humble, poor, vulgar and dirty. Unable to bear the sight of nudity at the baths, these fanatics have given up washing. They even feel a distaste for the slaves to whom they are everlastingly preaching a freedom incompatible with their condition. The ignominious cross can also be reasonably seen as connected with the absurd and suicidal taste for suffering which the Christians exhibit and to which they attribute the highest value. Reasonable people avoid suffering. Christians court it. So there should be no hesitation in exposing them to it. They enjoy it.

The Christians, who initially recruited among the Jews, have borrowed from them the strongest repulsion for all the plastic arts, which they dare to describe as 'idolatrous'. Left to their own devices, they would indulge in an orgy of blind destruction which would annihilate all the masterpieces of Greece and Rome. In fact, people have long known that no precise connection can be established between art and morality. To Christians, even the purest form of art is superfluous and harmful. It titivates the senses in such a way as to distract man from what is essential in life, which is invisible. O Phidias, whom the visible did not discourage, beware of the Christians. When they hear the word 'statue', they reach for their hammers.

And the holocaust would not be limited to the plastic arts. The Christians would burn any book in which the least word or phrase, the least allusion, contradicted their obsessions – in other words more or less the whole of extant literature. Only books of the sect itself would be spared, and not for long, for the Christians are always quarrelling about pointless chimaeras. As soon as one looks at all closely, it is difficult to find two who believe the same thing.

As you can see from this brief sketch, never in the history of mankind has a religion arisen so contemptuous of the society in which it is proposing to establish itself. The Christians detest our basic civil and military laws, our pleasantest and most politically necessary customs, even the appearance of our gods as defined by the chisel or brush of our most inspired artists. They carry their rejection – this you will find scarcely credible, and the lawyer in me is deeply shocked by it – to the point of daring to set up their own sectarian courts, so as to remedy the shortcomings of our universal courts, which were unable to modify the laws to take account of their lunatic fancies. Out of this total contradiction between their own laws and those of the Empire the Christians have even developed a clever argument in their own favour which has impressed some naïve people: to wit, that, naturally, men anxious to make converts would not have invented such shocking and unpopular doctrines, therefore, obviously, a god must have inspired them with them.

While they wait for this new god to impose his authoritarian domination, Christians are prone to take up two entirely different positions. Part of the time they talk of love, mercy, gentleness. The rest, they heap frightful contempt and abuse on divorcees, homosexuals, abortionists, partisans of a pragmatic approach to marital relations, even all the wretched people who try to find relief from their boredom in the Games which are so liberally provided. A Christian only loves his neighbour if his neighbour is as like him as a brother. Beware of the Christians, all you brothers of dissimilar character!

Let's get back to the Law, since respect for the Law is what keeps Rome alive. It would be difficult to bring a hard-and-fast case against the Christians over their strange special courts. They might well be able to pass them off as harmless, conciliation services, set up to take the pressure off the ordinary courts. On the other hand the Christians clearly fall foul of our criminal code when they claim benefit of the dispensation from sacrifices, which is granted only to the Jews. A Jew is a citizen of a very precise nation, whereas Christianity is ostensibly designed to discourage anybody from the worship of the nation and the Empire. The Christians are trying to break open the Jewish ghetto and turn the whole Empire into an immense ghetto where not even the Jews would have a place any longer. The Christians hate the Jews for the pointless reason that the latter will not give any weight to their divine resurrections. The Jews give as good as they get. If one day you were to start on a general round-up of Christians, get the Jews to help you. It is just what they are waiting for. Our police still find it difficult to tell a Jew from a Christian, but it is in the interest of the Jews to see there are no mistakes.

You will also get help from the lowest levels of society, to whom the Christians, with their affectation of bizarre and arrogant virtue, are a living reproach. The fact that the Christians have adopted some of the characteristics of a secret society also helps to give them a bad reputation. Their priests have no distinctive mode of dress, as if they were ashamed of their position, and the whole filthy pack hide away in corners to take part in ceremonies which are said to have very strong cannibalistic overtones. Initiation is in the form of 'baptism', by immersion in an icy bath, which is why many Christians have runny noses in winter. On close inspection, all the symptoms of an 'illicit superstition' are there.

One last fact, and a particularly disturbing one. Many Christians are convinced that their Christ will soon return to reward the good and punish the bad. This return will take the form of an incendiary and apocalyptic conflagration which leaves Rome as mere hot ashes under the moonlight – if the moon has not gone up at the same time. The charitable Christians talk of nothing but fire and flames. They exude hatred of Rome and all it represents. That constitutes a public danger.

Please take my warnings seriously. I got them, three times over alas, from an impeccable source. You will perhaps object that a religion so contrary to human nature could not have any long or durable success. Sooner or later, doubtless, human nature will reject Jesus and his intolerable requirements. But the well-known hypocrisy of the priests and their astonishing capacity to adapt the impossible to the everyday could make a temporary existence last much longer than predicted.

My friend, I want to lodge a complaint about the enticement of my son. He is a shadow of himself since they "baptized" him, and is now on his way, in a zombie-like dream, to some form of absurd martyrdom. I want to lodge a complaint that so many legitimate hopes have been disappointed. I bring the complaint in my name and in the name of the Senate. I might even dare to say "in the name of the emperor", since the Christians daily drag his name through the mud just because some of his friends have the misfortune to displease them. I lodge my complaint in the name of Rome, which has triumphed over all nations and has nothing left to fear but itself.

Fare well. My vengeful pen falls from my hands.'

❊ CHAPTER ❊
9

Marcus carefully re-read this communication to Flavius Sabinus. He had had the greatest difficulty in finishing it, although he was starving hungry and possessed by the inspiration of pure rage. At several points his ideas became all muddled, at others failures of memory brought him to a standstill. And he had been disturbed by abnormal, exasperating phenomena: the inkwell slily changed place, the ink made itself too thin or too thick, one of the hooks holding the papyrus came loose and the papyrus itself crumpled between his feverish hands and suddenly curled up like a snake. The very chair he was sitting in creaked, the lamps blinked and went out, although there was not a breath of air in the little study . . .

In fact legions of good and bad angels were fighting an epic battle around Marcus' head, in the heart of this tiny room where they scarcely had room to unfurl their wings. The battle was all the more uncertain and confused because there were not only good and bad angels. There were also angels in the know and less well-informed angels, who had belatedly come running because of the size of the stakes. The improvised actions of the latter caused chaos in both camps. The divine angels who knew the inside story of the affair kept encouraging Marcus, comforting him, inspiring him with the most effective and striking expressions, as he began to flag under the redoubled blows of fate. The intelligent evil angels, for their part, were doing their utmost to stupefy the writer and make him abandon his plan. For they were well aware that Peter's church badly needed a long series of intermittent, localized, clumsy persecutions, if it were to establish itself and survive. By throwing its martyrs in the face of the world as so many irrefutable pieces of evidence of the decisive Resurrection, the church would spread and prosper. But the tender-hearted and naïve little angels of the lesser choirs, faced with the prospect of such a carnage of martyrs, kept trying to hold back Marcus' furious hand, while the incompetent young demons in the other camp, excited by the smell of so much spilt blood, were quivering with communicativeness. There had not been so fierce and so contradictory a battle since the Judas affair. The sublime angels of Yahwe could still remember the emotion which that utter traitor had aroused in them when his scruples had momentarily come close to changing the course of events and causing the Redemption to misfire.

Marcus happened to have fewer scruples. The letter was eventually well and truly complete and ready to do its work.

Everyone in the house was alseep. Marcus went to the kitchens and took a stiff drink of unmixed wine. Then he came back to his study to bid his elder son farewell.

'M. Aponius Saturninus to his very dear son Marcus, greetings.

Kaeso has become a Christian, he refused to be adopted by Silanus, Marcia has poisoned herself, Silanus cut his wrists. I have driven Kaeso out and cursed him, I am ruined, and there is nothing left for me but to die as Cato of Utica did.

If only I had preferred you to Kaeso! You have never given me anything but satisfaction. I should have liked to leave you a better inheritance, but I am confident that your courage will help you to get on as you deserve. In throwing myself upon my sword, my last thought will be of you, for it is very important for your career that I die before my ruin causes my expulsion from the Senate. If you feel that I might have been more attentive in my affection for you, perhaps my blood will be some compensation.

Think of me as a very unlucky man whose noble desires were constantly crossed. I must have been born under a baleful star. There is nothing one can do against such stubborn ill-luck, except to act as a devoted Roman for one last time. I really did love you, you know.

Fare well, and beware of Kaeso.'

Marcus fell heavily asleep over his desk, and it was there that dawn awoke him. He finished putting his affairs in order by adding to his will, which under the circumstances was a very theoretical document, a codicil providing for the freeing of Selene, in the vain hope that the weight of debts would not exclude this piece of posthumous largesse. But he could not bear the idea of giving Selene her freedom while there was breath left in his body.

He roused a good-for-nothing slave, and instructed him to go and leave the note for the tribune Marcus at the Central Postal Service, and then to take the deposition for Flavius Sabinus to the offices of the Prefect of the City, on the lower slopes of the Esquiline, facing the Palatine on the left and the Capitol on the right. Then he went back into his room, where Selene was sound asleep, and took down his sword, which had never previously been of any use to him. Faced with this Stoic suicide, he felt his courage drain away somewhat. But there was nothing he could do to get out of it, now that Marcus junior had been informed of it.

Really and truly, Marcus had no desire whatsoever to kill himself. It was a pity that a good surgeon cost so much. If he used his own sword there was a grave danger that he would botch the job, but any of his slaves would have been even more clumsy than he was. They might even do it badly on purpose, with a malicious sense of pleasure. Marcus thought for a moment of sending for one of his gladiators from the *ludus*, but his nerve failed him at the thought of his executioner coming closer and closer, step by step, along a route he knew so well.

Time was running on. Marcus stupidly wondered if it was a favourable day – as if there could be good and bad days for committing suicide. The previous day had been the feast of Mens, the goddess of courageous intelligence, to whom the Senate had consecrated a temple on the *Inter duos lucos* area of the Capitol after the disaster at Trasimene, so as to stiffen the morale of the terrified citizens. Mens must have been helping Marcus with his final correspondence. There was a festival of Vesta that day: it was also a festival for bakers. The day after next would be the festival of the nurse of Bacchus. And two days after the Ides was the Festival of Ashes, when the ashes from the hearth in the temple of Vesta were annually thrown into the Tiber. None of the possible days was very inviting.

Marcus was suddenly afraid that Selene might wake up and catch him in the ridiculous position of hesitating on the brink of suicide. This childish fear pushed him into action. He lent the hilt of the sword against the wall and rapidly and randomly blundered on to it.

The noise of Marcus' fall and his accompanying cry roused Selene with a start. She opened her eyes and saw her master lying on his back at the foot of the bed, with a sword sticking into some part of his shapeless stomach. He was losing blood profusely and calling for help in a weak voice.

'What do you want then?'

'I think I've done it wrong. Fetch a doctor.'

Selene uncoiled herself in a leisurely fashion on the couch and said to the suffering man:

'It looks to me as if you've done the job properly. Just be a bit patient. Rome wasn't built in a day.'

'Get a doctor, I tell you. You can see I'm dying.'

'You don't seem to be able to make up your mind what you want.'

Selene, out of a sense of prudence, was finally going to stir herself when Marcus, who had been trying to crawl to the door, lost consciousness. She took advantage of this to lie down again. A lake of blood was gradually spreading through the room.

After a moment Marcus re-opened his eyes, which were already clouded with death, let out a strangled cry, vomited black blood and stared at Selene in horror, as he prepared to take with him to the grave the image of inextinguishable hatred which she had so abruptly revealed. With his mouth full of blood he spluttered:

'What have I ever done to you?'

'You dared to lay hands on me, you fat uncircumcised pig! You dirty old goat! You sick dog! You slimy snake! You old windbag! You filthy drunk! You dared to touch a Jew. May Hell swallow you up! May your shrieks lull me to sleep every night!'

While Selene was taking her time over giving him the full benefit of her opinion of him, Marcus was still hanging on to life. This was becoming worrying. The morning was drawing on. At any moment a slave might come in to take his master's orders and hear a last whimper of revenge.

Selene got up, skirted the pool of blood and gently placed her bare foot on the dying man's throat. With a sinister gentleness she pressed until she reduced to almost nothing the ribbon of air which her master was desperately trying to take in. But his face must not go blue or it would excite suspicion. So Selene relaxed her pressure, then tried the trick again, while quietly muttering fresh insults at him. The fourth time Marcus had a little spasm and stopped breathing. Unlucky to the very end, he had trained his sights on the Christians and had forgotten the Jews, whose women are still less inclined by nature to forgiveness.

Selene then opened the door of the room and cried: 'Help! The master is dying! The master is dead! He killed himself while I was asleep.'

As soon as he got back to Rome, the emperor had published an edict definitively fixing the date of his departure for the East as the morning of the Festival of Vesta, on the V of the Ides of June. The prince assured his faithful subjects that his absence would not be a long one, that the peace and prosperity of the State would not be affected by it, that every precaution had been taken to make sure that the provisioning of the city on a regular basis was guaranteed. Such a declaration had caused astonishment. People wondered why Nero, having got as far as Beneventum on the road to Greece, should have come all the way back to Rome to make an official announcement that he was leaving again.

On the morning of the festival of Vesta, while Marcus was putting an end to his life, Nero was going up to the Capitol to sacrifice to the gods on the occasion of his leaving the city. He was accompanied by all the leading figures of the State, by everyone who was anyone in the city and by a large crowd of priests.

There were the patrician major pontiffs in conical hats with pompoms and the plebeian minor pontiffs, eminent guardians of the rites, under the authority of a permanent high priest, who was none other than the emperor. There were the ministers of the altars, whose job it was to offer up the sacrifices. They were called *flamines* because they replaced their heavy pointed helmets with veils when they were in their light summer clothing: the *flamines* were also both patrician and plebeian, and were helped by a King of Sacrifices who also dealt with the calendar. There were the *flamines* of Hercules, who served at the Great Altar which stood facing the starting-posts in the Circus Maximus: by an astonishing departure from custom, which had its roots in legendary times, they were drawn from the ranks of public slaves. There were the *quindecimviri*, who looked after the Sibylline books (which were kept in two gold coffers under the statue of Palatine Apollo) and were responsible for consulting them. There were also the *epulones*, who organized the sacred banquets in the temple of Jupiter and elsewhere. There were augurs and *haruspices*, who had the essential task of determining the will of the gods. The augurs were distinguished ornithologists, who took the auspices by observing the flight of ospreys, buzzards, eagles and vultures, and the flight and cries of ravens, crows, green woodpeckers and various kinds of owl. For this reason soldiers on campaign used common or garden chickens, for fear of not always having a suitable and right-minded bird available in the sky at the appropriate moment. The haruspices, who examined the entrails of sacrificial victims, were much less well thought of than the augurs. There were also the members of various specialist colleges, priests of Augustus, Luperci, Salii, Arvals and Fetials. A whole section of society which for centuries had been ensuring that Rome lived in harmony with its gods: a whole world which the Christians had sworn to dispatch to oblivion. The ceremony had also attracted representatives of the numerous unofficial cults, Egyptian and Syrian, which were only admitted on condition that they make an act of allegiance to the traditional gods of the city of Rome. That was the price which the Romans exacted for toleration. After all, they were on their own ground.

The Corinthian temple of Jupiter Capitolinus had three naves. The middle one, which was the largest, was mostly open to the skies, an artifice which went marvellously well with the majesty of the king of the gods, whose statue, at the far end of the nave, seemed to stand between earth and sky. The two other naves were dedicated to Minerva and Juno, such that Jupiter was placed between his wife and daughter, providing a tutelary image of the Roman family.

The emperor went and stood in silence for a moment in front of the father of all the gods. The huge ivory statue, draped in a purple toga, held a spear and a golden thunderbolt, and beneath its crown, shaped to suggest the rays of the sun, its face was painted vermilion. Scipio Africanus had also come to speak with Jupiter before taking a serious decision.

The god gave his advice to his suppliant. Then Nero walked up and down for a time among the treasures which the centuries had piled up in the temple precincts: moving military trophies, which testified to the conquest of the world, precious booty, the offerings of foreign rulers, consuls, emperors, even private citizens. Jewellery, crystal, gold and silver plate, works of art, all jostled for space, the rarest items being concentrated behind the grills which kept the three statues of the gods out of the reach of common mortals. In front of Minerva's grill was a statue of that goddess offered by Cicero when he went off into exile, and behind the grill Cleopatra's jewels were a particular object of admiration.

From the terrace which ran around the temple, and which was equally cluttered with trophies and statues, the greater part of Rome could be seen. Nero lingered on the western side, which immediately overlooked the temple of Bellona and the Circus Flaminius. In the distance, in the sunshine, the silvery waters of the Tiber, beyond the Tiber island, seemed abnormally low. It was getting hotter and hotter, and the marked shortage of spring rain was threatening many crops. Then Nero looked to the south.

The emperor seemed to be saying au revoir to the city, but it was more a case of adieu. His poet and gambler's eye replaced the jumble of filthy slum blocks which disgraced the Velabrum, the area around the Forums and the Carinae, with pleasant apartment buildings of a reasonable height, flanked with graceful porticos and standing amid green gardens. These islets of happy tranquillity were served by majestic avenues and gay waterways. Between the Palatine and the Esquiline, as a reward for the imperial architect, an immense palace rose from the earth amid woods, waterfalls and rolling meadows. It would take twenty years . . .

And in this new city, a new race would be born to acclaim the greatness of its prince. Along every main road in Rome, with their sumptuous monuments of polished marble and gilded bronze tiles, grateful parents were urging towards the palace joyful processions of prepubic hermaphrodites, whose rosy behinds twinkled at Caesar.

Such a vision would have driven away the last remaining doubts of a far less daring and benevolent ruler. The emperor, full of his vast plans, came slowly back down the steps of the Capitol, accompanied by the Vestals. He intended to accompany them back to their nearby residence. It was the done thing to make one's farewells to the sacred fire of Vesta, the permanent hearth of the Roman people, before setting off on a long journey.

The *atrium* of the Vestals, a building of relatively modest dimensions but roofed with bronze from the sack of Syracuse, had been built in the heart of the Forums, near the house of Numa, which had for a long time been the residence of the Pontifex Maximus. Beneath a cupola vented to allow smoke to escape the sacred flame was burning on the goddess's altar. The Vestals were also responsible for the mysterious Palladium, whose preservation was as important to the safety of the empire as was the permanence of the fire.

The emperor stood for a while looking at the hearth. He pondered on the fact that a Rome worthy of him would rise out of the ashes of the very same fire which was supposed to insure its protection. The paradox was calculated to please a mind free of contemporary superstitions.

Nero's gaze fell on the Vestal Rubria, who was smiling at him as if to wish him *bon voyage*. There was a detail about this fresh-faced spinster which inevitably excited the emperor's depraved imagination. It was rumoured that the chastity of the Vestals was not as total as it should have been, and that the assiduous practice of solitary vice had made them develop amazing clitorises. Nero was very tempted to find out: he was sometimes possessed by a vision of being buggered by a band of randy Vestals, with the chaste Rubria playing a particularly unbridled role. Slander, which is always so perceptive, was not entirely wrong in attributing impious practices to Caesar. But the case of the Vestals was like other similar matters. If only out of political prudence, the emperor only put into practice a derisory fraction of his fancies. If virtue can be defined as a favourable relationship between one's vicious desires and their possible realization, Nero was exceptionally virtuous, and had the even more exceptional virtue of not being aware of the fact. But in a confused way he suffered from being deprived of such pleasures, and the creation of a new city would be a happy compensation for so much restraint.

The emperor smiled back at Rubria, and suddenly began to tremble all over, calling on his greatest talents as an actor to give the impression of a hero visited by a divine, premonitory trance. The naïve Vestals held their breath. Exhausted and barely able to stand Nero eventually lent against Rubria's shoulder, and said, as he gazed at the columns of smoke going up to the sky: 'No, I certainly shan't leave. I've seen the despairing faces of the citizens, I've heard their secret laments over the trip I was about to take. I know how unhappy they already were about my short absences, accustomed as they are to regarding the emperor's presence as a protection against the blows of fate. The Roman people has its rights over Nero. Since it seeks to hold me back, I must obey.'

These moving words were promptly reported to the uneasy and sulky crowd which had amassed along the imperial route, and there was an explosion of joy and gratitude. The *plebs* loved Nero, despite his tactless contempt for ancestral traditions, the cult of which was, for many of the poor, their only practical opportunity for respectability. The common people recognized themselves in him, and shared, with an intensity sharpened by their relative deprivation, his rather vulgar taste for every sort of pleasure, luxury and extravagance, and for the theatre, an art principally directed at the masses, whom the aesthetes despised. Moreover, the provinces had never been better governed, nor had the activities of senators and knights in a position to abuse their powers ever been more closely monitored. But the closest bond between prince and people still lay in their common hatred and defiance of the arrogant and lying aristocracy.

Thunderous acclaim followed Nero as far as the Palatine. He was weeping for joy at being so well understood. The procession, which had assembled without enthusiasm for the long trip, broke up again without a word.

Kaeso had not even been sent for.

The matter of Marcus' assassination was dealt with briskly.

A keen attachment to property – particularly other people's – had led to the development of a monumental body of civil law in Rome. It was the domain of the praetors, and abounded in special jurisdictions and possibilities for appeal. Criminal cases, which came under a variety of courts, hardly roused any interest except where politics was involved, and their simplicity offered a strong contrast with the interminable minor complexities of civil cases. The simplicity was increased by the fact that a people who bear the stamp of common sense do not bother with prisons to inflict what are always ineffective penalties on wrong-doers. Prisoners in Roman gaols were merely awaiting some form of execution.

Citizens condemned to death were always dispatched outside the sacred soil of the city. They were drowned downstream from the Pons Sublicius (or Aemilius), beyond the Porta Trigemina: they were thrown off the Tarpeian rock; they were beheaded by sword or axe in a nearby suburb: they were strangled in the dark hole of the Tullianum prison, which was so deep that it was regarded as foreign territory. The only other criminal penalties provided by the law for citizens were deportation, exile and banishment, none of which cost the State much, as the victim paid the costs.

As for slaves, their masters themselves took responsibility for keeping them in order. They could be loaded down with chains, whipped or put in the stocks. Metal collars would be put on the necks of runaways, or they could be branded on the forehead with the dishonourable F for fugitive. They could be prodded with goads like oxen, a method which revealed a certain Virgilian nostalgia for rusticity. When an inquiry demanded it, a master would unwillingly hand his slaves over to the police, fearing that they might spoil them, for the evidence of slaves was only legally admissible if given a patina of truth by beating, or the use of branding irons or other instruments of torture. Except in cases of conspiracy or sacrilege the law forbade the use of a slave's evidence against his own master, but the State then had the resource of buying suspects and then interrogating them with no holds barred. A slave condemned to death was normally crucified, a punishment considered very painful, thrown to wild beasts, decapitated during the interval at a *munus* or executed during a play.

The contempt in which the criminal police were held had led to the responsibility for their activities being put in the hands of the *triumviri capitales*, young men who were undertaking their first duties among the *vigintiviri* and were therefore on the lowest rung of the magistracy. Fortunately, when State interests were involved, the Praetorian Prefect and his specialists would intervene. Still more fortunately, the inexperience of the *triumviri capitales* was compensated by the routine of their investigators, who, for want of abstract ideas, had learnt to be very observant.

Marcus' death was thus explained there and then. A policeman asked Selene to show him the soles of her bare feet, and then asked her: 'How come the dust of this room, which hasn't been swept for some time, is both on your feet and on the dead man's throat, while his clenched hands are free of it? Did the senator rub his throat on the ground?'

There was nothing even an intelligent Jewess could say to get out of that one. Of course it was standard practice for a master to be aided in his suicide by one of his servants, but in such cases it was usually a question of freedmen or male slaves. In any case, no Roman who had killed himself by running himself through with a sword would have asked to be finished off with a foot on his throat.

Since this dusty crime was more than enough to ensure her condemnation, Selene hastened to admit the bloody deed itself, so as to avoid being tortured, except by her own conscience. She got off with a good beating, which allowed those carrying it out to admire her body at their leisure and for free.

When Kaeso and Myra sought refuge at the *ludus*, he was grieved to learn of the death of Capreolus, who had been killed outright at Beneventum by an old *secutor* from Cisalpine Gaul. Dardanus, worn out by the demands of his boyfriend, had suffered a sabre blow across the face. The father of the large family had come home on a stretcher. And Tyrannus had lost Bucephalus, probably by accident. It was not usual to attack the horses, which were there to make the event last longer, to the satisfaction of all concerned. Out of a sense of propriety no one mentioned Capreolus over supper, and the laments about bad luck were all directed at Bucephalus, to whom mythological qualities were attributed. But, very obviously, when talking of Bucephalus they were all actually thinking of Capreolus, who had left fond memories with everyone. Vatinius had not spared any expense in engaging the best people available, and yet Nero had only presided for a very short time and had not even bothered to turn up for the morning hunt.

Kaeso suddenly felt a desire to escape from the funereal atmosphere. He was both relieved to have got away from his father's house and at the same time deeply upset at having had to flee from it in such circumstances. The atmosphere at the *ludus* was not guaranteed to improve his state of mind. Another, more pressing reason to make a move was that the emperor, dissatisfied with his letter, might persist in searching him out, and it would take his emissaries no time at all to find him among his father's gladiators – or what was left of them. There was still a considerable temptation to provide himself with the excuse of convalescing in a place unknown to anyone.

While Marcus was breathing his last, and Nero was staging his little turn for the benefit of the Vestal virgins, Kaeso and his slave-girl were leaving the *ludus*. During the afternoon they found a modest room in a fairly respectably kept inn on the outskirts of Aricia, a charming little town not far from the Appian Way, on the banks of Lake Albanus, at the foot of the mountains of the same name.

Kaeso had given an assumed name. He had nothing else to do but meditate on his past and think about his dark and uncertain future. It was very disconcerting and painful to cause such unhappiness and misfortune to people he loved and respected. He was only trying to obey the voice of his conscience as best he could. But that voice was made to seem all the more weak and doubtful by the fact that most people were apparently satisfied with what they heard from quite different voices. Myra did what she could to amuse Kaeso, but she could not do much.

The inn-keeper had lost a 'little filly', who had died of fever, and asked Kaeso to sell him Myra. It was a tempting solution in the impasse in which he found himself. But though he sang the praises of the inn to the girl, it was all in vain. All he could get from her were tears and entreaties, and he had not the heart to force her into it. Perhaps the baptism was at work in him? He thought bitterly that when the day came when all slaves came to love their masters, it would be an intolerable burden on the latter.

Kaeso had been moping at Aricia for a week with no source of distraction other than lake-side walks, when the news arrived that this year Nero had decided to lay on some sensationally splendid Ludi Apollinares for the benefit of the *populus*. Dedicated to Apollo, to whom the emperor was particularly devoted, these games had been introduced during the second Punic War, in the hope of winning a victory over the threatening Hannibal. They lasted eight days, from the eve of the Nones to the day before the eve of the Ides. On the seventh day the anniversary of the birth of Julius Caesar, who had given his name to the month, was also celebrated. Such festivals involved the use of the theatre, the amphitheatre and the Circus, under the presidency of the *Praetor urbanus*.

Kaeso's attention was once again drawn to Rome. He was tempted to make a quick trip back to the *ludus*, to find out whether the emperor was still interested in him and get news of the *insula*. He was worried about Selene. The auction had been fixed for the festival of Summanus, the god of nocturnal thunder and lightning, which came just after the lesser Quinquatria dedicated to the Aventine Minerva, the festival of actors. This was now in full swing. Only five days separated Kaeso from the disastrous event which would doubtless see the sale of Selene to some rich womanizer. And for want of money he would not be able to do anything about it. He had used up what Silanus had given him, and the

606

Palace had only allowed him a very small advance. As for the 100,000 sesterces which Selene had placed with rabbi Samuel, they did not come into the issue, since in principle they were legally the property of the creditors, who would have confiscated them if they had known of their existence. Still, by presenting the money as his own, Kaeso might have been able to intervene.

It was less than two hours' walk from Aricia to the *ludus*, on a road which was well frequented by day. Kaeso was worried that he might run into a messenger from the emperor, so after lunch he told Myra to go and find out the news. She was to be sure to be back before nightfall.

In the afternoon Kaeso, without even Myra's prattle to take him out of himself, went as far as a little lake known as 'the wooded lake', through pretty countryside scattered with superb villas. The two famous pleasure-boats of the emperor Caius were still there. They were the inimitable ultimate in the art of boat-building. The men in charge of them would take you over them for a small sum, with interesting commentaries: U-shaped cast-iron stern posts; artistically caulked hulls, rust-proofed, padded with waterproof wool, and then lined with sheets of lead fastened with bronze nails; precious wood put together by the techniques of cabinet-making; metals soldered with a perfect finish; anchors with moving stocks; unique stern-post tillers; towing apparatus, ventilators, chain-pumps; drainage pumps with double pistons; use of an alloy of bronze and nickel (then a very rare metal); wildly luxurious baths and sitting-rooms and a roof of gilded bronze. Two boats as crazy as their original owner.

It was almost night when Kaeso got back to the inn and found Myra waiting for him in their room. One look at her told him that the news was none too good.

'Well?'

'Eurypylus was afraid that I might get muddled, so he gave me this letter for you. As he writes slowly, it made me rather late back. I think you'd better sit down to read it. Things couldn't be much worse.'

Kaeso obediently sat down and said as he broke the seal: 'There couldn't be anything worse than the news of my mother's death.'

In a Greek whose spelling was very tentative but syntactically passable, the director of the *ludus* expressed himself as follows:

'Eurypylus to Kaeso, greetings.

On the morning of the V of the Ides of this month your father was found dead in his room in the presence of the slave Selene, who admitted under torture that she had run him through with a sword, then choked him by putting her foot on his throat, because he was slow to die. There's no smoke without fire, of course, but I could not say how much of the charge is true. Apparently Selene tolerated your father patiently enough – I can vouch for the fact that he was temperamentally morose and difficult – and he had freed her in his will. Marcus was threatened with ruin and had plenty of reason for committing suicide. An unfortunate action in the course of a bedside quarrel is however a possible explanation. You will probably be in a better position to guess what happened than I am.

Because of the hot weather Marcus' body was displayed for only five days, and the funeral was yesterday. It was surprisingly elaborate – the Arval Brethren must have paid the bill, out of professional solidarity. The ashes have been put in the tomb of M. Aponius Rufus, until the dead man's fine mausoleum is finished – if it ever is. Soon the *ludus* itself will be sold up, probably at a low price. These are very hard times for a private *ludus*. The inheritance will be worth even less if all the master's slaves are crucified, which is possible under the terms of the law.

I hope that, despite everything, you are in good health. I am, as ever, at your service, and you can count on me and my connections for anything that is in our power. Since your father's tragic death everyone has been looking for you, not least Selene, who managed to smuggle a desperate note out of the Tullianum. But the emperor, whom Myra says you are worried about, seems to have forgotten about you.'

Kaeso gave a cry of pain. He wanted to go straight back to Rome, but Myra made him see sense: 'What would you do at this time of night? Your apartment in the Subura is empty. If Selene hasn't already been crucified, it won't happen tonight. And if she's still in the public prison, they won't let you see her tonight either. From twilight to dawn the officials and executioners are busy with their own affairs and aren't available to anyone. Why don't you go into the city tomorrow morning at the first hour instead? Then you may be able to do something.'

Kaeso spent a terrible night. A dramatic chain of events, in which he had played his part, had led to his father's death on top of those of Silanus and Marcia, and Selene and the slaves had been put to death, or were about to be. But even if it was not already too late, how could he do anything to stop it?

The law which provided for the crucifixion of all slaves present under their master's roof at the moment of his murder by one of their number was being applied more rigidly than ever. An example had been the extermination of the 400 unfortunate souls of the *familia* of Pedanius Secundus. At the beginning of Nero's reign, when the emperor was still nursing the hope of ruling in harmony with the Senate, the most implacable of the *patres conscripti* had even taken things to the point of publishing a decree which also condemned to death those slaves freed according to the terms of the will, whom justice had previously spared. It was a strange paradox that, while most slave owners were becoming more easy-going under the influence of new ideas, the traditionalists in the Senate lived in a state of fear and suspicion. Though the period of slave revolts was long over, and the immense majority of slaves were entirely quiescent, conservative senators maintained that, from time to time, a memorable example should be made to keep the slave population in a state of fear. Nero's supposed predisposition to favour the humblest doubtless played a part in this anachronistic display of cruelty. But the example came from above. Had not Augustus crucified a slave who had roasted a fighting quail he was fond of? The murder of a senator and Arval brother, even if he were among the most despised members of his class, was guaranteed to upset all the Stoics in the Senate. No mercy could be expected from that quarter. Since Kaeso had no money, he could not resort to the expedient of corruption, which was in any case very unreliable. The last resort was an appeal to the emperor. But he had lost interest in Kaeso as a result of his ungracious letter.

It was appropriate that Aponius had rejoined his brother beneath a shocking inscription paying homage to improvidence. Where did foresight get you?

As he lay there, unable to get to sleep, Kaeso's feelings for Selene became heightened by the dangerous situation in which that amiable Jewess found herself. He finally realized that he loved her much more deeply than he had imagined. Or at least he imagined he did, which, where love is concerned, comes to the same thing. Amid the hecatomb which his virtue had caused, Selene alone remained, with her serene beauty, ever-alert intelligence, attentive sympathy, sensible counsel, caustic humour and original moral code. She was another Marcia, one he could rightfully love, and misfortune made her even more moving. In any case, Kaeso had sworn to protect her, hadn't he? And she had trusted him. The charges against her seemed ridiculous. He clung to the hope that there had been a judicial error which could be proved in time.

Before dawn he entrusted Myra to the inn-keeper, who promised to look after her as though she were his own daughter, hired a horse and set off at a gallop for Rome. All manner of empty carts were coming in the opposite direction at this time of day. At the Porta Capena, at day-break, he handed over the sweating animal to an agent of the hirer and ran off to the Tullianum, a small prison at the eastern foot of the Capitol. As he was approaching the sombre façade in rough-cut Alban stone, he had a nasty shock. Some boys, who had arrived too late to follow the procession of condemned criminals from its starting point, were turning round and hurrying to catch up the convoy – its route was well-known. In earlier days Kaeso had also played truant with his brother when there was an execution of slaves or foreigners. Such expeditions were in fact the only disciplinary lapses which Marcus tolerated. Since his values had been formed on the old Roman model, to his mind such executions were as educational for the young as the butchery which took place in the amphitheatre. The sight of suffering hardens a man to the point of only half botching his suicide.

A child confirmed to Kaeso that it was indeed the slaves of Aponius who were to be punished. They were to go across the Subura and climb up as far as the Esquiline Gate, near which lay the piece of ground called the Sestertium, where executions were carried out. Kaeso wondered how, in his early youth, he could have enjoyed such sights, and even have bet nuts on how long this or that crucified victim would hold out. The executioners and soldiers seemed less cruel than the little boys, and were even willing to offer some of their rough wine to those whom it was their unpleasant duty to dispatch.

Kaeso stumbled on towards the Porta Esquilina. Nothing could have stopped him from being present at the execution, but he knew what he would see too well to want to hurry.

Weakened by torture Selene would be crossing Rome for the last time, carrying on her shoulders the horizontal wooden cross, bound to her forearms. On the Sestertium field were a forest of posts, which were changed when they started to rot. Selene would be stripped, stretched out on the ground, and the executioner would nail her on to the cross-bar. There were two ways of doing it. Professional executioners, who were experienced and skilful, put the nail into the wrist through a narrow space surrounded by bone, which the point of the nail enlarged without breaking anything. In so doing they split or severed the median nerve, which made the thumb drop on to the palm of the hand. Amateur executioners, who were incapable of such precision, preferred to put the nail in just above the wrist, between the radius and the ulna. In both cases the arm was sufficiently firmly fixed to make any other sort of bond more troublesome than useful. The arms were in fact supposed to stay free around their nail so that the condemned man could indulge in gymnastics which might go on for hours, if not days. Then the horizontal piece of wood would be fixed to the upright post, and they would nail down the delicate arched feet which were supposed to have stifled the senator Aponius. There were two ways of doing that too. Either the nail went through the two insteps, one on top of the other, or else the feet were set side by side, resting on a block of wood as in the former position, so that they could be nailed sideways on, with heels together, making the victim appear to twist round.

Then a long wait would begin, since death on the cross was a form of asphyxiation. In the lower position the pectoral and intercostal muscles were paralysed by the weight of the body hanging from the nails in the two wrists, and it was impossible to breathe. Selene would push on her nailed feet to get a few gulps of air in the higher position, until the pain became intolerable and she dropped back. And so on. Only in the higher position could the victims say a few words. When they no longer had the strength to pull themselves up, they lost consciouness, and asphyxia did its work. To finish off those who persisted in breathing for longer than had been expected, all that was necessary was to break their legs with a sledge-hammer. Those who were apparently dead were finished off with a sword or spear, which was less effort.

In his despair Kaeso wanted to pray. But who could he pray to? The Romans were rather sceptical of the effectiveness of prayer and were preoccupied, from a religious point of view, with knowing whether such and such a moment was or was not favourable for this or that action, an attitude which showed a distinctly practical spirit. The fashion for eastern religions had indeed made people familiar with the reassuring notion of a god who was ready and waiting to answer specific prayers. The Christians were the classic example of such a way of thinking. They never stopped praying, either in praise of God or to ask him for some favour or other. But Kaeso's philosophical training made it difficult for him to accept such fancies. He was quite prepared to burn incense to a possible Creator, if that might please him. But how could God have intervened in the course of events without being in contradiction with himself? For if man was free, divine intervention, even if one supposed it possible, negated the human liberty which was absolutely indispensable if God were to be thought free of responsibility for all the evil in the world. A God who cheated over the freedom which he had granted got himself into a trap from which he could not extricate himself with honour. There was no point in reproaching him for not cheating more often, so that everyone

611

could be happy. This simple consideration had constantly prevented Kaeso from attaching the power of definitive conviction to Christian miracles. What was the importance of miracles, if, by them, God merely showed up how scandalously miserly he was with his gifts, given his extraordinary capabilities?

And yet, despite all his philosophy, as he climbed up the Esquiline in pursuit of the dreadful convoy, Kaeso let himself go and started to pray. 'O Christ,' he murmured, 'since You are apparently able to do anything, even to throw divine grains of sand into the blind wheels of our liberty, save my Selene, and I shall believe that Your powers of reason are superior to mine.'

The procession was now in sight. Kaeso quickened his pace, elbowed his way through the crowd, and ran his eyes over the condemned. The pitiful *familia* of Aponius was indeed there, plus a few unknown slaves. A soldier was even carrying Niger's piece of wood on his shoulder, since the slave found it hard enough just to hold himself upright. But Selene was nowhere to be seen. With his heart beating fast Kaeso presented himself to the junior officer in charge and asked him what had happened to her. The man replied that the *triumviri capitales* had received instructions from the Praetors' office that the prettiest girls were to be kept for the Ludi Apollinares. That was all he knew.

❧ CHAPTER ❧
10

So Selene was safe for another twenty days or so. The news flooded Kaeso with joy and hope. Now he had room to manoeuvre. Better still, he had, it seemed, discovered through force of circumstance the magic formula which allowed him to establish personal contact with Jesus and to have an effect on him. It would be very cruel of Jesus to save Selene for only a few days. Any way, he was a Jew, wasn't he? And for that reason he was inclined to offer particular protection to people of his own race. The Christians were instinctively hostile to the Jews, but that was just an emotional reaction which contradicted their Lords' words. For Jesus had only ever attacked a few Pharisees whose excesses were suspect. His attachment to Israel was blindingly evident in a number of his speeches. He had wept over the ruins of Jerusalem, which the Christians were quite prepared to accept with stony hearts as a punishment for attachment to the letter of the Law. Yet Christ had accepted the yoke of this Law for thirty years before rejecting some of its details. A Jewish Jesus could not let a Jewess be crucified.

It occurred to Kaeso that Jesus had insisted on experiencing suffering on the cross. But that was his affair, and had nothing to do with Selene. There could clearly be no cause-and-effect relationship between one cross and another, since Selene was not even a Christian. Abraham, Jacob and David had not been Christians either, and they had not been crucified. At first sight it looked as though being a Jew was a good insurance against it.

Crucifixion was then so current that Jesus' entirely run-of-the-mill sufferings were not such as to move the heart of a Roman, who was more likely to be sensitive to the particularly shocking fact that a god should have chosen to be punished like a slave or a criminal without rights of citizenship. It was the metaphysical and social aspects of Christ's sufferings which struck a Roman first, and seemed so scandalous.

Out of a sense of kindness and propriety Kaeso went with the procession as far as the Sestertium field. After all, the slaves had belonged to his father, and he had known some of them. It was not their fault if an outdated senatorial law had held them to be accomplices in a hypothetical crime in which they had had no part. On the way Kaeso chatted amiably to the junior officer, who was flattered to have such attention paid him by a senator's son and *augustianus*. It was Kaeso's charitable ulterior motive to persuade the soldier, who did not seem an unpleasant type, to alleviate the punishment, in the very small measure possible.

As a boy he had noticed that cutting the median nerve caused considerable extra pain. Perhaps the executioner would agree to put the nail in a little higher? And a hammer blow on the legs before the accepted time was always a possibility.

The fact that Selene was provisionally safe gave Kaeso such a feeling of satisfaction that it could easily be seen on his face. The officer was under the impression, till disabused by his interlocutor, that the pleasure of revenge was the cause.

For a large tip, and with the tacit approval of his superior, the executioner was persuaded to put the nails between the radius and the ulnus, but his honour as a specialist was offended by the procedure. On the other hand he had no objection to not nailing the victims through the heels, which would have been the more painful way.

Kaeso walked among the low crosses for a few moments, with a word of encouragement for this or that slave, in circumstances which unfortunately made the pointlessness of his remarks only too obvious. It would have been hard to say whether the women suffered more than the men from their treatment, which was also an offence against their decency. At any rate it was the Syrian cook, a fat and greedy man, who groaned the loudest. As the victims' feet were quite close to the ground, they could easily be given a little wine to moisten their open mouths, and Kaeso insisted that the soldiers should give them this derisory form of relief more frequently.

Having finally obtained agreement that they would be finished off as soon as was decently possible Kaeso could see no further reason for prolonging his presence. The most urgent task now was to see to Selene. And the sight-seers, a mixture of tearful friends and sick voyeurs, were beginning to get on his nerves.

But before going he thought it appropriate to make a Christian exhortation to Niger, and said to the Hindu: 'Now you must be able to see how false your beliefs are. If past virtues caused you to be reborn in the form of a man of property, what sins in your present life made you deserve what you are now going through? Your only thought was to avoid suffering by expelling desire, and through no fault of your own you have suddenly been subjected to the worst possible form of suffering, which no pain-killer can cope with. Can't you see that the great problem man has to face is not how to avoid suffering but how to find a meaning and a purpose for it? Neither Plato nor the Indians have managed to do so. But the god of the Christians has interesting revelations on the subject. Trust in him and you won't forget it.'

Niger was exhausted, his efforts to hitch himself up and his consequent collapses were getting more and more rapid. It was clear he would not last long. Profiting from a moment in the higher position he replied in a jerky voice: 'An excellent lesson . . . but it comes at the wrong moment . . . if I'm reborn a Christian . . . I'll let you know!'

Conversion is a difficult art and Kaeso had not yet got the hang of it. Though it *was* Sunday.

The first thing to do was to make contact with Selene and find out the precise circumstances of his father's death. Equipped with these details Kaeso would be able to prove the condemned woman's innocence, although justice took little interest in what happened to a slave. The law would be particularly unwilling to admit it had made a mistake, since the bulk of the *familia* of the dead senator had already been put to death.

At the headquarters of the *triumviri capitales*, which was installed in an outbuilding of the City Prefecture, no difficulties were made about informing Kaeso that the young lady he was interested in had been imprisoned in the great *vivarium* or game-reserve at Ostia, under the responsibility of a well-known trainer called Cethegus. That was all Kaeso needed to know. He immediately set off for Ostia. Whilst he was quite familiar with the gladiatorial scene, he knew next to nothing about the world of the *venationes*, the remarkable morning hunts in the amphitheatre, and nothing at all about animal training. Masses of animals intended for the Games were constantly arriving in Rome from the most distant provinces of the Empire, and the *vivaria* where they were kept in the meantime were a familiar sight in the suburbs. But the largest was at Ostia, because many animals, especially the heaviest ones, naturally travelled by sea. This was inevitable in the case of animals from Africa or the further reaches of the East.

Claudius had had a new harbour built to the north of the city: Trajan was to enlarge it. Close to the quays of this new port, amid the mountains of broken *amphorae*, lay the great *vivarium*. The risk of the wild animals escaping had caused it to be banished to this zone of night-soil heaps, a long way from the *insulae*, which, though most towns in the interior were free of them, had sprung up at Ostia as in some other large trading towns along the coast.

Towards the middle of the morning Kaeso was admitted into this strange place, perhaps on the strength of his appearance and status, and with the help of a discreet bribe, but principally because he claimed to have an important communication to make to Master Cethegus. Bribery had become a characteristic feature of the society.

Kaeso was taken across parks containing lions, bears, panthers, elephants, different types of deer, ostriches, onagers, all the game you can imagine, from the most common species to the most rare. There were even ponds containing seals, hippopotami, and crocodiles. Amphitheatre hunts played an important part in ridding the empire of animals which were dangerous or whose numbers were becoming too large. But there were also familiar animals such as horses and donkeys, as it was from the *vivaria* that theatre directors took the materials for their lavish stagings. For example, 600 mules laden with presents might be needed for a tragedy. And trained acts, by both wild and domestic animals, had their place in the entr'actes at the theatre, as they did in the interludes at the amphitheatre and the Circuses.

Kaeso was eventually taken into a vast square hangar. In the middle was an enormous cage, which must have been intended for training dangerous beasts. Round the edge was a line of stalls in which various animals could be seen.

Cethegus, accompanied by subordinates, was in the middle of inspecting the inmates. He was as hairy as a wild boar, and his little eyes shone fixedly with a hypnotic gleam. You immediately felt uneasy in his company. Kaeso, who wanted to see how the land lay, with a view to handling him better, presented himself as a noble *augustianus*, a personal friend of the emperor, interested in animals and wanting to stage an original show for some friends. The imperial *ludus* and *vivarium* were not averse to a little private custom: it helped them keep costs down. There were *munerarii* like Vatinius, who could afford to stage a whole day's show at Beneventum, and there were others of more modest means.

Cethegus needed no persuading to talk about an art in which he was passionately involved, and Kaeso's charm was an additional stimulus. He was delighted that a young nobleman should take an interest: most of the time children of the senatorial class had more of a taste for the *venatio*, which allowed them to go into the arena without tarnishing their reputations, as long as they only did so on an amateur basis. Hunting was after all a smart occupation. But high society rarely got worked up about the secrets of animal training.

Cethegus' greatest triumph were some elephants who could do tight-rope walking. He had succeeded in getting them to go along two parallel cables. He also went on at length about other successes, involving lions, tigers and such like or members of the horse family. Under the guidance of Kaeso, who was patiently manoeuvring him towards the topic which interested him, he eventually declared:

'But all that's nothing compared with the difficulties of training an animal and a condemned criminal together for the theatre, the way the public wants it these days. They're always after something new, demanding more and more off-beat sex and violence. The exciting moments which new plays by successful authors are written around are incredibly difficult to pull off, without risking the kind of failure which would look absolutely ridiculous. The night before some shows where my professional reputation is on the line I can't eat or sleep.'

'And what exactly is the . . . source of the difficulty?'

'It's twofold. Part of it is the animal, the other part the man. In order to respect mythology, which imposes very precise requirements on the genre, I have to get an animal used to a diet or to sexual habits which aren't necessarily natural to it. The Caledonian bear, for example, prefers honey to human flesh, and is a very timid creature. It becomes confused and paralysed with fear at the sight of such a sea of spectators. In the same way a billy-goat or an ass has no natural interest in human females, and all sorts of precautions and tricks are indispensable to get them going. The animal has to become familiar with the girl, live with her for a time, and she will only attract him if you rub secretions of nanny-goat or she-ass on heat between her legs. So you can see the work it entails. You really have to be in the profession and to have been trained by an attentive father. As for the humans, there's no problem when it's just a question of their being eaten. But it's harder to get the girls, who've got to do a bit themselves, to collaborate. Once they've been substituted for the actress, ready for the animal's final assault, they tend to panic. To encourage them, you have to promise to strangle them on stage or after the curtain comes down, and not to crucify them, which is what would happen to them if they weren't lucky enough to be appearing on stage. But that's not always enough to get the best out of them. I have to alternate between the stick and the carrot, as I do with the animals.'

Cethegus put his hand on Kaeso's shoulder and offered the following superficially banal reflection, to which his professional experience gave a certain depth: 'If anyone tells you that animals and men are the same species, don't you believe it. Training methods may coincide at many points, but they differ even more. Men know they've got to die. Animals don't. Despite all my experience and good will I've had to send unsuitable girls to the Sestertium. There's something unpredictable about bipeds.'

Cethegus just happened to have a beautiful slave in hand who was going to appear in the *Laureolus* on the III of the Ides of July, the last day of the Ludi Apollinares, in the great theatre of Pompey. This play, which was always a huge success, was to stay in the repertoire for 200 years. It had every ingredient guaranteed to please an audience. It illustrated the life of a terrible bandit, arsonist and sex-fiend, who in the end was fittingly punished for his excesses by crucifixion. There was a fine flexibility about such a plot, and scenes with which the public was beginning to get bored were easily revamped. The final crucifixion was in fact the only obligatory piece of bravura. Before his contact with Greek philosophy had extended his mental horizons, Kaeso, together with his brother, had enjoyed the highly-coloured and titillating realism of this spectacle. How far away those happy days now seemed.

Kaeso and Cethegus had arrived in front of the crucial stall. In a corner sat Selene, her head down. She was chained by the ankle and the chain was too short for her to strangle herself. Cethegus had clearly born in mind the propensity of two-legged animals, who knew they were going to die, to commit suicide. In the opposite corner a huge gentle-eyed Calabrian donkey was mechanically pulling at his halter in an attempt to go and join his companion, who was giving off a delicious smell of she-ass on heat. And like many a husband who tries to imagine that he is with someone else (and vice versa), the donkey, who was in a permanent state of semi-erection, kept looking lovingly at Selene, whose ears seemed to be gradually getting longer. But her back was not yet marked with the miraculous cross which had distinguished the breed since the flight of the Holy Family into Egypt.

At this incongruous sight Kaeso let out a loud laugh, so as to make Selene grasp at once that he was only there to play a role which might turn out to her advantage.

He asked Cethegus:

'Is the donkey allowed to practise before the actual performance?'

'It would be a useful precaution, and I used to do it with little adolescent donkeys. But the public now demands adult animals with huge organs. The girl can only take it once.'

The sorry situation was beginning to inspire in Kaeso an increasingly

Christian frame of mind. He mentally thanked Jesus for having had the foresight to create such huge donkeys.

He went on: 'What a beautiful girl! What a perfect figure! She must be a very expensive slave. It's a waste to give her to a donkey for the pleasure of spectators with no taste, who would be satisfied with any girl.'

Cethegus explained that the slave was supposed to have murdered her master and that the law could not take that sort of thing into consideration. Selene could already thank her beauty for the fact that she had not been crucified on the spot. She would make the most of the time she had left.

Anxious to bring Selene some comfort, whatever happened, Kaeso suggested:

'As most of the scenes in the *Laureolus* are interchangeable – I've never seen it the same twice running – and dogs, who as a breed have long been used to living in close proximity to man, are perfectly willing to serve a woman, wouldn't it be simpler to call on some large mastiff? It would be less likely to tear her apart and wouldn't even need rehearsing?'

'It's easy to see you're no specialist. After coitus, dogs have an astonishing erection which prevents immediate separation. And you know that in the theatre there mustn't be any moment when nothing is happening. The action has got to keep going at a good pace. A sexually satisfied dog would introduce a pause which could only be filled with boring dialogue. And a dog can even turn out to be dangerous, as a result. I had a track-hand from Boeotia, a bit of a wilting violet, who had a weakness for playing dirty games with his dog, which was a hefty brute. One evening the animal had done its stuff and was lying on his master's back when a cat went by with its tail in the air. The impetuous lover went bounding after his feline prey and took his master's innards with him like a trophy. The boy died of course. A fitting end for a Greek, and a lesson in virtue to us Romans.'

The cruel gleam of amusement in Cethegus' eye gave no hint of virtue. Another Roman whose traditionalism was worth no more than Marcus's!

Cethegus' assistants, seeing that the conversation was going on a long time, had left the hangar, with its penetrating smells and its occasional echoing cries of restless or exasperated animals.

'The state of that donkey gives me an idea,' Kaeso suddenly said. 'He's getting ready for a brief moment of happiness which plenty of mortals would give a lot for. If he doesn't object, could you leave me alone with this beauty for just long enough to . . . press my suit with her?'

So saying Kaeso flashed a few gold coins in the palm of his hand.

It was a very irregular request, but Cethegus let himself be persuaded and left the hangar in his turn.

Kaeso at once climbed over the barrier and threw himself at Selene's feet.

'I love you. I love you more than ever. I love you eternally. I realized it when I saw you in my mind's eye walking towards the Sestertium with your cross on your back. How awful this is for both of us.'

Selene roused herself from her lethargy and looked at Kaeso the way Niger had done as he struggled with the acute problem of breathing. There are situations in which even the most moving orator can do nothing. Kaeso belatedly had the good sense to realize this.

'But what use is love to you now?'

'Exactly. Cethegus is promising me only too much of it.'

'Tell me how this miscarriage of justice came about, so that I can move heaven and earth to get it put right.'

'That would be difficult. After running himself through on his sword, Marcus, who had freed me, begged me to finish him off, so I pressed on his throat with my foot, and the dust off my instep was found on his neck. To avoid pointless torture I confessed to having stabbed him – at his request of course, but there's nothing to prove that I'm telling the truth. Marcus left nothing in writing announcing or even giving a hint of his fatal intentions. A slave told me that he had posted letters to Marcus junior and the Prefect of the City. The investigating agents were honest enough to check out the letter to the Prefect, but it contained nothing to clear me. Marcus junior may be able to, but that will be too late. Even the imperial post would have difficulty doing the round trip to Vetera and back in such a short time. I need saving here and now, and you're the only person who can do it. I need a pardon from the emperor.'

The jealous donkey was getting restless. Selene added crudely: 'An animal each.'

Kaeso promised to do the impossible and the conversation at last took a very loving turn, since Selene was in no position to reject Kaeso. Her suitor kept asking, 'Do you love me?' and she kept replying, 'Of course, how could I fail to love a boy who's so devoted to me?' But she gently reminded him that he should be asking Nero that question first. She also reminded him that she had 100,000 sesterces deposited with Rabbi Samuel which could be of use.

Kaeso tore himself away from his beloved after managing to give her a kiss on the cheek, roughly in the area of her mouth. As he was getting out, the furious donkey took a piece out of his tunic. It was a crazy situation.

Kaeso went to thank Cethegus, and found him with his assistants. He was in the middle of treating the foot of an African elephant, a species somewhat less than docile. Numidian rhinoceroses and Hircanian tigers were also awaiting his attention.

Kaeso had to wait. In the distance, among the mountains of broken *amphorae*, the sails of cargo boats could be seen going by in the sun, as they left Ostia or prepared to come into the harbour. Once inside, they manoeuvred with precision in the calm waters, thanks to the sensitive lateral rudders which worked like sculls.

When Cethegus was free Kaeso took him aside and said to him without beating around the bush: 'That girl is truly extraordinarily beautiful, and I want her. What's to stop you producing another for the *Laureolus*? One corpse is as good as another. If you're prepared to do me a favour, there's 100,000 sesterces in it for you.'

Cethegus weighed up the pros and cons. He was visibly caught between greed and caution. But in the end he declared: 'That's a pretty expensive enthusiasm you've acquired for a slave you've only just seen. I suppose you've known her a long time. I'm sorry, I can't help you. In my position I make plenty of money, and I wouldn't want to risk losing my job, even for a large sum like that. Anyway, as a slave of the Imperial Household, I should lose a lot more than my job. What you're asking is a crime punishable by a shameful death. And even if I were weak enough to say yes, there's no way of doing it and getting away with it. There's a close watch on all the animals here. And do you suppose that pretty women condemned to death grow on trees? You're wasting your time with me. But I love lovers and gold coins. I'll close my eyes to a few more visits.'

As he was seeing Kaeso out, Cethegus added: 'I like you. I'll give you a piece of advice. If there's a way out, it'll be in the theatre itself. The authors and producers can fiddle around with the play as they see fit. Go and see Turpilius from me: he's got a little house on the lower slopes of the Janiculum. He's in charge of the staging of the *Laureolus*. He's a Roman citizen and very poorly paid, like every one who works in pornography – there's too much competition. If he gets caught trying to make 100,000 on the side, he won't end up on a cross.'

Kaeso thanked Cethegus in suitable fashion and spent the afternoon looking for Turpilius. He had constantly been seen in places where he turned out not to be, from the Aventine baths, of highly dubious reputation, to a whole series of sleazy establishments along the banks of the

Tiber. He finally arrived home on his own, in a somewhat unsteady condition, when it was quite dark. Kaeso was waiting for him on his doorstep, from which he had watched twilight fall over a city stretching out towards the dying light.

Once he was absolutely certain that the noble Kaeso was not the bailiffs, Turpilius freely opened his door to him and showed him into a modest interior where the most artistic disorder reigned. By the light of his lamp the host made an unconvinced attempt to tidy up, quickly tired of the impossible task, took a jug of luke-warm wine out of a cupboard instead and cordially invited Kaeso to explain the reason for his visit. Turpilius was a pleasant young man, with a face that was already somewhat worn, and seemed to take life very lightly.

'It was Cethegus, the famous animal trainer at the game reserve in Ostia, who gave me your name, in connection with an affair which could bring you a good sum of money. But I can see you're an artist. Perhaps you're not interested in money.'

'By Minerva, that's a filthy slander! Artists only despise money in so far as they're incapable of earning any. What inexpiable crime have I got to commit for you? Honest work, as the porn trade proves, never brings in a penny. You can speak freely. For twenty sesterces I'm your friend till dawn.'

'On the contrary, it's a good action I have in mind . . .'

Kaeso, who had nothing to lose, set out his problem in detail, stirring a passionate interest in his listener. Turpilius even forgot to drink. The orator finished by saying: '. . . To work out what trick would fit the bill we must begin, I think, by taking a close look at the scene in which Selene is supposed to take part. Perhaps it would be easier to modify it than to change it.'

Turpilius was absolutely in agreement.

'It would be particularly disagreeable to change it, because there's already a host of scribes at work on the programmes, where it's presented in mouth-watering detail. Anyway, there's my artistic self-respect to consider. That little scene, which has no dialogue at all in it, is entirely my own work. It's a gem of pure theatre, combining bestiality, horror and a good laugh. But one also has to think of the better class of spectator. The surprise I have in store for them will give them an extra reason for priding themselves on their superiority.'

'What do you mean by that?'

'Imagine this poignant situation . . . Laureolus' wife brings in an armful of hay for the donkey, but, with ignoble ingratitude, it leaps on

622

her and rapes her on the self-same hay. The condemned criminal will be substituted for the actress behind a pillar in the stable. The actress has just been making love with the bandit in the room next door while the donkey – for a little extra spice – is playing the voyeur. The victim of the rape calls for help. Laureolus comes rushing in, but too late to prevent the irreparable from happening: his honour is lost. So, as a good Mediterranean, a man from our southern territories, without a second thought, instead of beating the donkey he strangles his wife. Isn't that an amusing twist? Something to appeal to the *plebs* and Petronius at the same time?'

Time was when Kaeso might have been amused. But those days were over.

'I don't see,' he said, 'what could be changed in that to save my Selene . . .'

'Let me think . . . I've got it. It's child's play. Now listen carefully. The actress who is to play the part of Laureolus' wife, a slave called Cypris, who spent ten years on the streets in the Subura, is credulous by nature. If we promise her a good sum, she'll do the necessary to get Selene out of her tight spot. There just won't be a substitution.'

'What about the strangling?'

'Cypris will think it's going to be a pretence. She'll also think that the police have been bribed or that they won't look too closely and will accept a coffin full of rocks. But you'll appreciate that Cypris will actually have to be properly strangled, because outside the theatre the authorities will be waiting to check that there are the right number of corpses. Cypris will do just nicely. Anyway it'll be cheaper in the long run to get away without paying the girl anything than to try bribing the police, who cost the earth once there's a whole series of people involved. My solution is simpler and more economical. Anyway, from what I know about women, it isn't the strangling Cypris will be worrying about, it's the donkey. But we could play around with that detail in the scenario – choose a less alarmingly endowed example or another animal which the victim preferred.'

Kaeso was horrified and disgusted. 'But you're suggesting murder,' he murmured.

Turpilius protested. 'The crime is helping a condemned criminal to escape. When you kill a slave, you pay up the price and that's that. Cypris belongs to the State, which has plenty of better things to do than worry about what's happened to her. Anyway, if you're overcome by a fit of morality, you might look at the problem this way: either we sacrifice a completely worthless slave, or we sacrifice the woman you love. Both of them are perfectly innocent. Do you think you've the heart to let Selene die just to save someone you don't even know? All my experience is telling you plainly that there's no other way round it. You can convince yourself of it. I think Laureolus will do the strangling for a small fee. Playing bandits has turned him into one.'

Ever since he got back from Greece Kaeso had found himself knee-deep in the most tricky matters of conscience. He seemed to have taken out subscription to them. Either he had got on the wrong side of the gods, or he was following an insufficiently precise moral code. The Jews and Christians were brilliant at avoiding problems of conscience. They always knew straight away what they should do.

Turpilius cleverly pushed the point that Cypris was a poor, unfortunate girl with no talent, whose future would never be more than a long downhill slide. She had hoped to come up in the world by going from prostitution to porn, but she clearly didn't have a vocation for it. Her public copulations were plainly lacking in uninhibited enjoyment. And Laureolus, with all the good will in the world, could not do all the work for both of them. Cypris would leave this world for another and better, without even realizing it. And after a last love scene which would have given her a final inflated view of her professional talents, she would die on the boards, a touching and admirable death such as every rich and successful actor wanted.

There was something disturbing about the argument. Mothers who threw their children on the rubbish-heaps also consoled themselves with the idea that they were sparing them the hazards and disappointments of life. When murder puts on the face of virtue, it is a sign that a moral force is developing, which is capable of persuading people to believe in it.

For this charitable act of euthanasia Turpilius only wanted 50,000 sesterces. He thought he could get the actor playing Laureolus for 10 or 12,000 and would need to spend as much again to ensure the indispensable complicity of one or two subordinates at the critical moment.

Despite the entirely new strength of his feelings for Selene, and the fact that she was condemned to the most depressing of intimate meetings with a randy donkey who had probably been through it all before, Kaeso hesitated. When a young man who wants to do the right thing morally, but lacks a practical doctrine, gets mixed up, even at arm's length, with matters of conscience, there's a risk that he will get inextricably trapped in their complexities. Another matter of conscience was already taking shape. The sacrifice of the poor Cypris was necessary only if the prince refused to pardon Selene for Kaeso, a trivial detail for a man of such amorous disposition. Should Kaeso expose himself to the tyrant's whims to save Cypris? His Roman education inclined him to see such self-sacrifice as excessive. For Selene, of course he would. But why should he for a bit of aimless flotsam like Cypris?

Kaeso asked for a few days to think it over. Turpilius, whose feminine side was perceptible, then made him some indecent proposals which he declined with exquisite politeness, on the excuse that Selene had cast a spell on him. When you have barely escaped having Nero, you don't voluntarily go screwing a Turpilius at cess-pool emptying time.

Kaeso had a longish chaste sleep in the house of Turpilius, who bore him no ill will, and went off early to find Rabbi Samuel, who lived quite close, the Janiculum being next to the Trans Tiberim. Rabbi Samuel knew all about Selene's misfortune, but a scrupulous Pharisee was not going to hand back 100,000 sesterces just like that.

'You claim,' said the rabbi, 'that Selene, in the most extreme distress, wants her money back to pay for a possible defence. I wouldn't presume to query the fact that you've been authorized to reclaim the money by my co-religionary. But I can't quite see what a woman who has been con-demned to death could do with 100,000 sesterces, and I feel justified in presupposing that they might be employed illegally.'

'Selene is innocent. What has Roman law got to do with you?'

'It has a great deal to do with me. It is written in *Exodus*: "Do not oppress the foreigner. You have learnt from experience what it is to be a foreigner, since you have yourself dwelt as such in the land of Egypt." In the land which Providence has given the Jews and which no one shall ever take from them, the Jews are required to treat their guests in con-formity with the law. The laws and customs of the foreigner will be tolerated, and even respected, in as far as they do not seriously conflict with Jewish Law, which is superior to all others, because it was dictated by the Almighty. The Jews of Palestine today are morally justified – setting aside questions of expediency – in resisting the Romans by force, because the Romans are occupying their territory against their will. But that's an exceptional case, which has no bearing on the general rules of hospitality. Vice versa, I would insist, Jews accepted into a foreign country are obliged by their religion to obey local laws in every case where they don't pose an insurmountable problem of conscience. Roman criminal law, whether it be excellent, good or dubious, is what it is. It's not up to the Jews to question it in Rome. I am responsible for Selene as for all the Jews in the city. If you put those 100,000 sesterces to an illegal purpose and get caught, it's the whole Jewish community in Rome which would suffer the consequences of my incautious pity. In any case, it's not even certain that Selene is innocent.'

Kaeso protested. 'She is. She certainly is. I'm the dead man's son and I'm telling you so. The murder is completely unproven, and still would be even if there were any legitimate motives for it.'

'Aren't you blinded by jealous passion?'

'The love of all men, Jews as much as the rest, obliges me to say that a victim of rape has the right to defend herself by force. My father has raped that slave often enough for his murder to be justified a hundred times over.'

The rabbi looked at Kaeso with a sympathetic curiosity.

'You're talking in terms of divine justice, of which the Romans know nothing, and which most Jews have difficulty accepting. But I'm obliged to take account of a less ambitious view of justice here.'

After some hesitation Kaeso admitted the truth. Rabbi Samuel said to him: 'Your embarrassment proves my point. Even to save a Jew one cannot murder one of Yahwe's creatures, however fallen she may be. What do you know of the divine plan for Cypris? She shouldn't be made to act as scapegoat for a person who has been condemned in a court of law, whether or not there was a judicial error from the moral or formal point of view. The law is the law. That's what Plato reminded us, when he portrayed Socrates accepting an unjust sentence, on the grounds that the law of the city is the foundation of all conceivable order.'

All Kaeso's arguments and entreaties met a brick wall. He had Yahwe and Plato against him.

Rabbi Samuel finally added: 'Even if I wanted to, I couldn't give that big a sum back to you in time, since at Selene's request it was invested at a high rate of interest in maritime trading business. I didn't tell you so sooner, because I wanted an opportunity to enlighten you on where your duty lay.'

Kaeso was shattered. He wandered off through the crowded streets of the Trans Tiberim. Despite himself his steps led him towards the palace. The sun was already high in the sky when he sought an audience with Sporus. He was hoping to sound him out, and perhaps get him to act in his interest, before trying to obtain a more august interview.

Sporus agreed to see him. He was getting dressed, in the hands of his 'maids' who had bizarre transvestite voices. A large well-polished mirror reflected his graceful image.

'May the gods be with you, Kaeso. You're a rare visitor. Nero has withdrawn into the gardens of Epaphroditus and is working even harder than ever on his fire of Troy. It'll be an astonishing piece.'

After the standard civilities, Kaeso said to Sporus: 'I've just recovered from an illness. I was laid low with a fever and am barely in a state to reappear at court. It's bad news for me that the emperor has cut himself off like that, in the grips of his creative genius, because I have a favour I should have liked to ask him. It's one which might touch his aesthetic sensibilities. In consequence of my father's death a slave girl who was wrongly suspected of having played a part in it has been condemned to finish her days in the *Laureolus* at the Ludi Apollinares. It's a slave famous for her beauty, whom Silanus once bought for a huge sum of money, and it would be an irreparable loss to sacrifice her in such a vulgar fashion, or even to sacrifice her at all. I have to admit that this little matter is really upsetting me. If I'm not fortunate enough to see him in the next few days, could you ask Nero, who can't refuse you anything, to pardon this girl? Her name is Selene.'

A swishy boy swathed in a diaphanous fabric was plucking his master's eyebrows, while Sporus emitted gentle little squeaks.

Eventually Sporus said: 'The emperor still holds you in high regard. But he nonetheless confided to me that he'd received a note from you which had upset him.'

He impatiently dismissed his boys, turned to Kaeso and went on: 'Nero never condemns anyone to being his lover. The imperial couch is not a galley where you have to take an oar against your will or against the current. What upset my master was your alternate pursuit and rejection. Yes, don't protest. You behaved like an irresponsible coquette, who enflames his victim's senses in the name of affectionate friendship and then refuses to go the last step. You must understand that that sort of behaviour just isn't on with Nero, who has no time to waste. He was particularly annoyed because he had very tender and sincere feelings for you – as I can fully understand. Why didn't you just say to him straight off 'I don't like men'? You would have stayed on the best of terms. In such circumstances the last favour that Nero will grant you is a pardon for a pretty woman. You can't expect the impossible from human nature.'

In vain did the supplicant plead that it was all a mistake, and offer every possible service. Sporus stayed as cold as marble. Kaeso found himself in the painful situation of a young man who is very willing to prostitute himself in a good cause, but who can't find an opportunity. Marcia had had more luck than he.

Sporus finally got up from his chair, asked Kaeso to sit down beside him on a sofa, and confessed to him with fluttering eyelashes: 'If I add my entreaties to yours, I could perhaps, despite everything, obtain from the compassionate emperor the pardon which, I presume, you're more anxious to have than you admit. But would I be able to count on your gratitude? Do you know that you're divinely handsome?'

Another occasion for scruples, and one which was maddeningly delicate.

'My unshakeable loyalty to the emperor,' argued Kaeso, 'would restrain me from inflicting such an insult on him, however much I might wish to. You're even more beautiful than I am.'

Sporus smilingly blew that objection out of the window. 'Nero's well aware that he can't concern himself with me all the time. He's good enough to allow me a few harmless distractions on the side. We've been friends for so many years. He knows that my passion for him is a spiritual one, but that he isn't exactly my type. So we're rather like one of those old married couples, who have a little fling from time to time which has more tenderness than passion about it. Be nice to me and you won't regret it.'

Sporus' hand began to wander. Kaeso got up abruptly.

'I'm not interested in men. I'd make an exception for the emperor . . . guided like you by a passion of a higher order. Don't ask me for more than that.'

'Then there's no need for me to detain you longer.'

Having upset Nero, Kaeso had now contrived to alienate Sporus. And his finances were at rock bottom. Before leaving the Palatine he went to the headquarters of the *augustiani* to get as big an advance on his pay as possible, but he was met with an ill-will that bordered on rudeness. The *augustiani* had to wait their turn for advances, like poets at the bookseller's, and to get anywhere you needed the sort of special protection which Kaeso now lacked. To be precise, the bright rays of the imperial sun no longer shone on him.

Kaeso went for a walk through the Forums at midday, thinking with bitterness and anguish of all his mortifying setbacks and trying to work out how he could possibly help Selene.

The longer he walked through the noisy, motley crowd, deaf to everything but his own thoughts, the more aware he became of a truth whose scandalous starkness astonished him. The cascade of misfortunes which had swept him away since he had left his mother's skirts to look for a career worthy of himself derived exclusively from the permanent lust of which he was the object. Bright-eyed Marcia, dull-eyed Silanus, the Athenian ephebes, the emperor of Rome, Turpilius, Sporus and lots of others – they had all taken their cue to harass him. And the only love which he had found, a love which had been hounded until it ended up between the hooves of an ass, Selene, to give it its name, was so weary of love that she was more or less indifferent to his declarations of affection. Perhaps Paul of Tarsus was right to think of all profane love, best and worst alike, as a waste of time, a more or less futile expenditure of energy. Paul was lucky enough not to be good-looking, and not to have to make much effort to defend his extraordinary virtue.

What Kaeso could not win by his charms he would have to conquer by force of arms. As with all those who were right down on their luck, the gladiator's art offered him its deadly embrace, the chance of making money fast and the kind of glamour which bowled girls over. Even Selene would look more kindly on Kaeso if she owed her life to his valour.

Kaeso went back to the little *ludus* on the Appian Way. After lunch Eurypylus gave him a letter of recommendation for one of the best-known of the imperial *lanistae* in the great *ludus* on the Caelian.

❧ PART FIVE ❧

PART FIVE

❧ CHAPTER ❧

I

The great *ludus* was a world of constant bustle. It contained Atimetus, the imperial freedman responsible for managing it, the *lanistae* under his authority, who dealt with the engagement or re-engagement of gladiators and supervised their training, the instructors, referees, doctors, armourers and all the secondary services necessary to the arena. And of course, the gladiators themselves. Some were slaves, others free men under contract, and they ranged from the musclemen, whom every tart adored, to the effeminate *tunicati*, who were usually confined to the role of *retiarius*, the lowest of the gladiatorial grades. By day an intensive training programme was carried out: by night there was a constant stream of giggling girls, discreetly veiled women, and fancy-boys with painted eyes.

On the afternoon of the same day, immediately after siesta, the *lanista* Liber – another of the emperor's freedmen – agreed to see Kaeso with considerable interest. To celebrate Nero's decision to stay in Rome, and to mark the sacrifice of his career as a singer which he had just agreed to make for the sake of the *plebs*, the Ludi Apollinares to end all Ludi Apollinares had been announced. To lay on these games, Tigellinus had had lavish credit facilities opened. Nothing was to be neglected in the determination to increase the Emperor's popularity and put it on a solid basis.

It was intended that the prodigious memory of these Games should linger long over the ruins of the city, offering a guarantee and a promise of fresh liberality. The gladiators, previously somewhat neglected by an emperor whose tastes were too refined to include them, had therefore received tangible favours, and there were plenty of gladiators who would finally find full employment for their talents in Rome and not have to give private lessons in Italy or the provinces. Nero had even promised to preside over the *munera* himself. Naturally there was no shortage of money to attract aristocrats into the arena. And the lower classes loved to see members of that arrogant class, which the emperor had been constantly edging towards destruction, sacrificing themselves to the popular interest. Kaeso, the son of a senator and

Arval brother, was therefore a catch, guaranteed to be a draw and flatter the imperial obsession.

The applicant could have taken his business direct to a representative of the *Praetor urbanus*, who was still in theory the presenter of these highly traditional Games. Recourse to such a *munerarius* would have relieved him of any possible consequences until the special contract had been drawn up. But Eurypylus had recommended him to deal with one of the emperor's *lanistae*, who could give him the benefit of his advice and of the training available in the *ludus*, which was particularly necessary since the aspiring gladiator was not exactly in the best physical shape.

Kaeso insisted that he should be engaged for a single fight, and of course asked for a signing-on fee which Liber thought excessive, even given the flourishing state of his finances.

'You seem to be unaware,' he said to Kaeso, 'that the standard fee for a *tiro* or novice is not usually more that 2,000 sesterces. Even for re-engaging a *rudiarius*, an experienced veteran, the ceiling is normally 12,000. I know you're a good-looking young nobleman, and I'm only too happy to take those qualities into consideration, but let's not overdo it. The contract you have in mind wouldn't even be given to a well-known aristocrat who'd been driven into the arena by one of those scandals that the sentimental general public adore. I can't see what, in your past history, I could base exciting publicity on . . .'

Kaeso suddenly had an inspiration.

'I'm signing on because I've been crossed in love.'

'I don't want to be offensive, but you couldn't come up with a more banal reason than that.'

There were some empty tablets on the table. Kaeso took a stylus and slowly wrote, before Liber's astonished eyes:

'K. Aponius Saturninus to Nero Caesar imperator, greetings.

My beloved, what a way to treat me! For nights on end I was lucky enough to feast in your lap, breathing your heady perfume, drinking in your words and thrilling to your singing. At Naples – remember Naples, you ungrateful man – it was by gazing into my eyes that you regained control over your voice and your lyre, and became more master of them than you already are of the universe. Unfortunately a serious illness struck me down, and when I came tottering to find you, you had already forgotten me. I lived only to please you, I am nothing once you pass me by without a glance and I cannot even touch the hem of your robe. So I dedicate myself to you, just as in olden days our generals, despairing of the outcome of a battle, threw themselves on their enemies' pikes, to win from the gods the victory which was eluding their swords. I shall soon die in the arena before your very eyes, the victim of your disdain, but my shade will still follow your glorious and funereal apotheosis, seeking in the Apollonian wheel-tracks of your chariot the kisses which you deny me. And as my bloody body is dragged to the morgue, you can say in a dreamy voice: There goes a boy who really loved me.

Farewell. My last breath will rise towards your box in a final loving reproach.'

Liber, who felt very doubtful, scratched his head. Eventually he said:

'That's certainly original, and it's got everything necessary to get the public excited. But are you sure you're on safe ground? Nero may find your letter amusing, but he might also have you put to death for your insolence even before you make it into the arena.'

'He won't. He was in love with me and that's why he's giving me the cold shoulder.'

'I don't understand.'

'I refused his advances. It's only for the money that I want to fight.'

Liber laughed and said to Kaeso:

'You're a smart operator. Making honourable amends like this for such an affront to the emperor ought to touch his heart. But if you leave the arena alive, he's likely to take you at your word.'

'That doesn't matter, as long as I've got the money.'

'I'll forward the letter. If the emperor takes it the right way, I can put about some tempting rumours on your account and increase the sum due under your contract. Nero might even add a little himself. From my own funds I'll go as far as 20,000 sesterces, putting things at their best.'

'That's not enough.'

'All right, 25,000, but that's the absolute maximum. If you win, the presider will give you a prize in kind as well.'

'Not worth much.'

'You can take it or leave it.'

Kaeso went back to Aricia to wait for his new letter to Nero to have its effect. Night and day he could think only of Selene, especially when the local donkeys started braying. The humble, gentle donkey, whose image had soothed Kaeso in his sheltered childhood, now took on in his painful imagination the demeanour of a monster thirsting for debauchery. And if, when out walking with Myra, he saw a peasant beating his donkey, he would encourage him shamelessly. The relations between men and animals are anthropocentric or mythological.

From grilling Kaeso Myra had got a glimmer of the true situation, and she sympathized whole-heartedly with the victims of a love story which set her dreaming. She even offered to put in a bit of service among the 'little fillies' at the inn to improve Kaeso's finances, but her master blocked his ears and cried: 'Just don't mention the subject to me again.'

A few days passed. On the morning of the feast of Summanus, while Marcus' last remaining possessions were being sold up, a note arrived from Liber:

'Liber to Kaeso, greetings.

The emperor was so affectionate as to add 50,000 sesterces to your fee. I myself will go up to 30,000, the way now being open for some exciting publicity, which, rumour has it, Nero will be flattered by. The gods are clearly on your side, and that encourages me to offer you the best possible contract. Farewell. I look forward to seeing you shortly.'

Kaeso hurried off. Nero had indeed forgiven him, but only on condition that he risk his skin as a punishment for his off-hand behaviour. The way to Jesus was the way of the cross. If you followed Nero, you got your face smashed in. It seemed that the road to love was paved with atrocities.

Liber agreed that Kaeso should go into the arena only once, but in return, to add to the drama, he would have liked him to face a *suppositicius*; in other words Kaeso would have fought an opponent and his replacement in succession.

'It isn't often done, but this would be a perfect opportunity. At all events, what have you got to lose? If I'm to believe Eurypylus, you're too skilful to get killed outright, and if you have to give up the struggle, Nero will be there to show you mercy. The public will never allow such a pretty love story to end in death.'

Kaeso had no confidence in the public, and less still in Nero, who was probably waiting avidly for the moment when he could give the 'thumbs down'. Eurypylus resigned himself to a straightforward contest, but was honest enough to warn Kaeso:

'Since I'm staking my reputation and a full-scale publicity campaign on this saga, if you're only going to face one opponent, I can't pair you with an unknown *tiro* or a third-rate veteran. And there's no question of pitting you against some young noble novice whose situation would be like your own, because your two histories would clash in an unfortunate way. I'll be obliged to put you against a gladiator who is, if not famous, at

636

least reasonably well known. But I'm afraid that you won't be able to cope with an expert.'

'Provided I've already got the money, it doesn't matter a damn.'

The first four days of the Games were to alternate between races and theatrical performances. The interest of the second four days was to be concentrated on the *Stagnum* (pool) of Agrippa in the Campus Martius, which the emperor had found just right for his extraordinary projects. Men were working on cleaning out the bottom of the pool, which had already been drained. On the first day there would be a gigantic hunt there from morning till night, with floods of human and animal blood soaking into the sand which was to be put down. On the following day the pool would be filled up with water again, and there would be a *naumachia* illustrating the battle of Salamis. On the third day, in the arena which would have been dried out yet again and covered in fresh sand, the gladiators would be on the rampage from dawn till night-fall, with all the more fervour for the fact that it was the anniversary of the great Caesar's birth. Throughout the evening and night of the fourth and final day an immense banquet would be served. The spectators invited would eat on the banks of the pool; the emperor and his special guests would feast on floating platforms, the pool having once and for all been refilled with water. At the same time, other smaller banquets would be delighting the élite of the loyal *plebs* in numerous of the public squares throughout the city. To work up an appetite, and perhaps to remind people that hunts, mock sea-battles and gladiators were not the ideals of an artist-emperor with no taste for blood, in the morning there would have been a performance, in the theatre of Marcellus, to half-empty rows of seats, of a boring tragedy by Euripides, and after snack-time, to the packed hemicircle of the theatre of Pompey, a performance of the vulgar *Laureolus,* the glaring contrast between the two plays summing up Nero's complex character. The lavish expenditure necessary for putting the Stagnum Agrippae to such bizarre use was also a mark of the emperor's tormented mind.

Kaeso was, then, to make his appearance on the anniversary of Caesar's birth, at the end of the show. The most exciting item was always kept till last. After the feats of the best gladiators there were only the mad elephants battling against a choice group of intrepid hunters. But there was a problem of what weapon and what form of protection to choose – the *armatura* as it was called in Latin.

Many types of *armaturae* derived from specialities which went beyond the bounds of sword-fighting proper and required special aptitudes and a long training: fighting from chariots or on horseback, *retiarii* and their pursuers, *velites*, etc. But the big names in gladiatorial combat had above all made their careers in the two *armaturae* which had constantly found favour with the public and the emperors: those of the *mirmillo* and the *thraex*. The *mirmillo's* equipment was heavy: helmet, rectangular shield (the *scutum*), a leg-guard on the left leg, an arm-guard on the right arm, and a sword. The *thraex* also wore a helmet, but his shield was circular (the *parma*), and he had two greaves to compensate for the reduction in size of the shield, an arm-guard on his right arm and a short sabre. Stronger men preferred the *mirmillo's* equipment, more agile and highly-strung men had a tendency to fit themselves out as *thraeces*. For generations, just as the Blues opposed the Greens, so the quarrels of the long versus the round shields, the *scutarii* versus the *parmularii*, had been going on: every emperor interested in gladiators had been a supporter of one or the other of these forms of *armaturae*. Caligula had sworn by the round shields. Nero was inclined to favour the long ones, though not, it would seem, fanatically. After some consideration Kaeso chose a round shield, on the grounds that the equipment was better suited to his build and his temperament.

It was not done to stage a fight between the two men in the same *armatura*. A classic pairing was a *mirmillo* against a *thraex*. Liber suggested to Kaeso that he should fight a man by the name of Pugnax, a free man of about forty and a native of Switzerland. After thirty-two victories this *scutarius* had been freed from all his obligations, but he had soon signed up again and won another seven victories. Kaeso had no reason to say no.

Since everything appeared to be in order Liber went on to draw up the contract of *auctoratio*, which Kaeso then took to show to the appropriate tribune of the *plebs*, whose offices lay between the Circus Maximus and the Tiber, in an offshoot of the temple of Ceres. As a contract of this sort gave a *munerarius* or a *lanista* temporary right of ownership, potentially extending to issues of life and death, over the person of a free man, it was normal for the authorities to check that the man concerned was, from a legal point of view, of an age, and in a fit mental condition, to abdicate his autonomy in such a serious way.

Kaeso was relieved to get out of this sinister place, where all sorts of poor people came to claim bread from the *aediles*. He set off for the family *ludus*, wanting to ask Eurypylus' advice about the terms of his contract.

The latter congratulated Kaeso on the exceptionally large size of the fee, but he drew in his breath at the name of Pugnax.

'You could have run up against someone more dangerous, but not someone more difficult to beat. The fellow comes from the mountains, and he's like a rock himself. He stays cautiously lodged behind his great shield and waits for his opponent to make a mistake. He never loses his cool, he's got as much experience as he has stamina, and he tries to win by wearing his opponent down. In a fight of that sort the spectators cat-call the *thraex*, who can never be aggressive enough as far as they're concerned, until he loses his temper, uncovers himself and Pugnax seizes his opportunity. His stab blows aren't fast, but they're very accurate.'

'What can I do against this Swiss rock?'

'Be more patient than he is – and patience isn't the most obvious virtue of youth.'

'Do you think he'll try to kill me?'

'Unless he has it in for you for some private reason, no. As you know, by tacit agreement gladiators try not to inflict fatal wounds on each other. Of course, an accident can easily happen. But just keep calm. The risks of serious injury are slight, and in cases of defeat the spectators are inclined to pardon a man who's fought well. In every ten fights between gladiators who are equally matched, there are no more than one or two deaths.'

'But this is precisely a case of gladiators who won't be equally matched!'

'Whatever you do, avoid insulting Pugnax in the hope of making him lose his temper. All you'd do would be to make him turn nasty. At Beneventum Atticus, a Corinthian Greek, lost his cool and called him a cuckold. Pugnax is still a cuckold, but Atticus isn't around to tell him so.'

If the risk of death was one in ten at each encounter, Pugnax was four times as good as the average, since he was coming up for his fortieth fight. But, to avoid frightening Kaeso, Eurypylus had told him something less than the truth. A change was already under way which was to triumph in the two following centuries. Disappointed by the circumspection which the gladiators practised for perfectly comprehensible reasons, the audience was increasingly inclined to be unwilling to show mercy to losers. Cutting a vanquished fighter's throat, which had once been a punishment for obvious cowardice, was tending to become a normal conclusion, and clemency had to be earned by exceptional bravery. There was nothing surprising about a slide in that direction. When it came to it, the masses did not come to the arena for the beauty of the spectacle or the skill of the fighting. They wanted the pleasure of holding the life of a broken man, full of unspoken entreaties, in the palms of their hands.

Before putting his seal on the contract, Kaeso went to find Turpilius and check that he was still willing. Artists are volatile people who get sudden enthusiasms and lose them just as suddenly.

Turpilius was in the Theatre of Pompey, working on his production and surrounded by actors and the stage hands who worked the machinery. He took Kaeso aside during a scene change and told him in lowered tones that he was only waiting for a good advance to set the plan in motion. He nodded towards a large girl with stupid eyes some way off. This was Cypris . . .

'She's a Greek from Canopus, near Alexandria. You can see she's none too bright.'

Kaeso could well have done without this confrontation.

He asked about a point of detail which was worrying him:

'At Athens, at the beginning of a performance in the theatre of Dionysius, I saw a condemned girl raped by a donkey, but the soldiers guarding her dragged her right up to the animal.'

'Yes, that does happen, but if you allow that sort of thing it destroys all the poetry. Here in Rome, as far as possible, the soldiers of the escort are not allowed on stage unless their presence is justified by the scenario. The police trust the actors to keep an appropriate eye on the victim. Anyway, how could she escape? And we do treat the wretched girls with more humanity than their usual gaolers. They get them drunk on wine, make them childish promises, tell them tales. Here we know how to handle things. Similarly the police never have anything to complain about when there's a Cethegus around to keep a close eye on every detail.'

'Isn't there a risk that the soldiers will notice that the corpse isn't the right one?'

'I shall bribe the verifier with 5 or 6,000 sesterces, just as a precaution, though since he won't suspect anything, he probably wouldn't look that closely.'

'But Selene has fairer hair than Cypris.'

'Their emotion makes them sweat and that makes it look darker.'

Turpilius had an answer to everything.

In a final fit of scruples Kaeso hurried off to Ostia, arriving there before midday, to inform Selene of what was afoot and get her agreement. He thought that perhaps a Jewess might instinctively reject the scheme on moral grounds, as Samuel had done.

Selene, who was threatening a hunger strike, had been put into isolation in a separate cell, and her chains had been removed.

Once she heard the plan, she was suddenly full of hope:

'That's a wonderful scheme. But be careful that you don't get taken for a ride by this crook Turpilius. He could take your money and then decide it was wiser not to give you anything for it.'

'I've already thought of that. Turpilius will probably be afraid to act. But he'll be still more afraid that a desperate gladiator might run him through with his sword.'

'Always supposing you survive the *munus*, which is the day before the *Laureolus*.'

'I shall survive it, because I love you.'

To complete his reassurance of Selene, Kaeso revealed to her that his relationship with the emperor seemed to have taken a new turn. The hard-pressed slave was suitably impressed.

'How good you are to me! You're putting your wits, money, courage and body at my disposal.'

'I'm even getting involved in a shameful murder.'

'What do you mean?'

'This poor girl Cypris, who's going to be raped by an animal and then strangled . . .'

Selene started to laugh:

'The Greeks destroyed my family's grocery business. It's their fault I'm here. I don't give a damn about one Greek more or less.'

'Rabbi Samuel has strong reservations about it.'

'That holy man, according to what you've told me, had strong reservations about giving me my money back. He should have had the decency not to give himself the luxury of any extra scruples.'

The Jews hated the Greeks as much as the Romans. Their more amiable prejudices were reserved for races with which they had never actually come into contact. Either they were a sullen lot or their Yahwe liked to keep them at daggers drawn with everyone.

Selene expected Kaeso, following in his father's footsteps, to make imperious advances to her, and was already looking for friendly pretexts to defer the unpleasant task. But Kaeso had no such thought in his head, his natural sense of elegance restraining him. The more of yourself you give, the less inclined you are to ask for anything in return. You don't just leap on a woman who is condemned to death and hasn't had an opportunity to fix her face. Kaeso was putting off till later the shared delights he had in store for them both.

He swore he would be back as often as possible, stopped in Ostia to take a swim, for the smell of the game-reserve clung to his skin, and went straight back to spend the night at Aricia. Since he had fallen in love, he no longer laid a finger on Myra, who was naïve and sentimental enough not to be astonished by this reaction. She was even rather proud at sharing the life of the hero of a novelette.

The following morning, with Myra and their luggage, Kaeso moved into the great *ludus*, where he tidied up the last details of his contract. Then, with some other novices, he swore the gladiators' terrible oath, by which they accepted in advance 'chains, whips, red hot iron and death'. Seneca had compared the gladiators' oath to that of a wise man face to face with an adversity for which there is no remedy. In fact only uncontrollable gladiators were ever chained up, and the whip and red hot iron were only there to recall the most timid elements to a sense of their duty, when the killing sent them into a panic. At high-class fights they were only there for form's sake, as part of the decor.

Kaeso finally got his fee. That night he took 25,000 sesterces to Turpilius. He found him at home, with his 'n'th jug of wine.

As Turpilius was counting the *aurei*, which shone in a fascinating way, Kaeso made sure to say to him: 'That money comes from a contract of *auctoratio*. On the day before the *Laureolus* I'll be fighting the famous gladiator Pugnax, who's won thirty-nine victories, at Agrippa's pool. I'll make no more than a mouthful of him. If you betray me, I shall rip open your stomach, and if any mishap occurs to me during the *munus*, my gladiator friends will come and make mincemeat of you. Your life depends on my Selene's. Agreed?'

Turpilius had turned very pale and dropped the glittering *aurei*.

Kaeso went on: 'You gave me your word, and I'm not putting up with any perjury. If you want to stay in one piece, and you want the other 25,000 sesterces, you must just stick to what we agreed. Denouncing me to the police won't get you anywhere. You won't have any significant proof to hold against me. In any case, like a lot of gladiators, I'm on very intimate terms with Nero, and I know just how to get what I want from him.'

The thought of the imperial gladiators scared Turpilius stiff. He hastily launched into a flood of assurances, protesting his good faith and declaring that he was going to put everything else on one side immediately and rework the scene so as to introduce an animal acceptable to a broadminded Greek from Canopus.

Kaeso went back to the *ludus* feeling more or less reassured. From now on he was obliged to adopt an exceptionally regular life-style. He would get up at dawn. After a substantial breakfast he would devote the morning to physical exercise and weapon training, either in a covered room or in the great training arena with its surrounding porticos, under the direction of a gym instructor or a fencing master, who also provided verbal instruction during the rest periods. At lunch time they all sat at communal tables and ate a meal which was designed merely to take the edge off their appetites until dinner. In the afternoon they were free. After siesta they could bathe without leaving the *ludus,* which had good baths and even a little library: this mostly contained works on medicine and athletics, for there were plenty of gladiators who had known better days and had varying degrees of education. The dinner, which finished before nightfall, provided a diet of healthy and plentiful food, which had been the object of dietary research. They had tried to adapt it to the requirements of men who had to expend enormous amounts of muscular energy. There were several dining-rooms, which satisfied the Roman taste for hierarchy. The élite gladiators on big contracts had a room of their own, but their wine ration was no bigger than anyone else's. Another room was reserved for the concubines and children of the combatants, who paid the cost of their board themselves. The freedom which the gladiators were allowed was limited by the need to keep themselves in perfect condition: it was in their own interest as much as in that of the *ludus.* Any man who let himself go was soon called to order, and punishments ranged from being gated to detention in the slave prison.

In this very special place there accordingly reigned a sense of team-spirit, a camaraderie, which was rarely allowed to slip and was indispensable to the maintenance of good morale. After a few days in the *ludus,* it was easier to understand why disorientated *rudiarii* should sign up again, disappointed by their return to civilian life. The gladiatorial barracks dispensed a sort of family discipline, where all cares except the need to survive were banished. And that was the least of worries for individuals incapable of running their own lives themselves.

As a result of the auction of Marcus' property, his modest *ludus* on the Appian Way had been sold up, and most of the gladiators still left had had their contracts taken over by the *lanistae* of the Caelian barracks. The arrival of this little group could not console Kaeso for the loss of Capreolus, but the familiar figures helped to mitigate the sense of solitude a little. Tyrannus, however, had left for Verona, and Eurypylus for Pergamum, where the *ludus* was famous.

Gladiators who lived with an official concubine were allotted a small room of their own. It was an unexpected gift from Myra to Kaeso. The girl was overwhelmed by the atmosphere of the *ludus* and naturally very worried by the danger her master was running. But she would not hear of being freed. She was well aware that freedom would only have been the beginning of new misfortunes.

Kaeso then had the brilliant idea of bequeathing Myra in his will to the Christian Jew at the Porta Capena, with a request that he should free her when she reached the age of twenty. At the same age she would receive a legacy of 5,000 sesterces, on which in the meantime her new master would have been receiving the interest. Kaeso wrote as follows:

'Young Myra was exposed to a long period of dishonour at the hands of hardened sinners, who abused her innocence and her tender age. But she is a pleasant, sensitive girl, grateful for all that is done for her. Please take her in, in memory of me, and treat her as a sister in Christ, as I have always faithfully done myself. Myra needs a firm and devout hand, which I am sure she will find under your roof. God will reward you for what you expend on her, and she will be a respectful and devoted freed woman to you.'

The virtuousness of the Christians constantly obliged him to tell lies. Kaeso explained to Myra, with the help of details and examples, how to behave with the Christians, what she should do and not do, and should and should not say.

'And I'm not to sleep with anybody?'

'Only a virgin husband, if a good one can be found, and they're rare.'

'These Christians are nuts.'

'Listen, bird-brain: the Christians may be round the twist, but entrusting you to them is the only way to keep you out of the hands of a pimp. You ran away from a brothel: I want you to promise not to run away from the Christians, even if you find them a bit odd. For, if there were nobody but true Christians around, there wouldn't be any more brothels. Understood?'

'But there'll always be false Christians, and so the brothels will do a roaring trade.'

'Don't argue, just do as I say.'

Myra snivelled for ages, imagining Kaeso as good as dead. These peculiar Christians did not sound at all promising.

When Kaeso was not too tired, he would hurry off to Ostia at the end of an afternoon, and bribe his way to a brief moment's courtship of Selene. He would talk for both of them with deep passion, a passion which would have been infectious in other circumstances, and if it had been addressed to anybody else. The fear which racked Turpilius had obliged Cethegus, who was used to the whims of authors and directors, to replace the huge Calabrian donkey by a sweet little donkey foal, who looked as if he might have been keeping his virginity for a Christian marriage. The revamped scene of intimacy looked as though the experience would be less painful for the victim. Meanwhile, Selene found Kaeso's love especially tiresome in that she genuinely liked him and was grateful to him, and her critical situation obliged her to put up with his passion without protest.

Fearing that Cypris' misfortune might excite unnecessary pity in Kaeso, Selene took every possible occasion to slander the Greeks, using convincing arguments. 'The Greeks are an impious race of pederasts, lesbians and contemptible slaves, who only manage to reproduce themselves by accident. They're insanely arrogant. The Romans open up their city to the people they've conquered. They try to assimilate them little by little. But in all the states which sprang up in the footsteps of Alexander, the Greeks are still behaving as though they're in temporary occupation of conquered territory. Everywhere, without taking the slightest notice of the natives, they've founded purely Greek cities, which are autonomous and isolated, like pieces of straw on an unknown sea. The day that Rome can no longer provide the military back-up, those contemptuous, parasitic cities will promptly be swept away, and the oppressed peoples will begin to breathe again. In that part of the world the Romans and the Greeks have divided the job up between them: the Romans run the place, but it's the Greeks who occupy it. And they can't tolerate the least competition, though they've no home country but their provisional colonies – and those have been depopulated by their debauchery. In Alexandria there's an aggressive Greek population which is permanently causing trouble for the Jews. And, of course, after every riot, the Prefect scolds the Greeks and puts the Jews to death. When I was still a child, thousands of Jews were executed, with refinements of cruelty which you can't imagine, in the city's great theatre. I expect Cypris was there cheering.'

Kaeso reminded Selene that the Jews also lived in isolation and were trouble-makers, but she answered:

'It's virtue makes the Jews cut themselves off. The Greeks do it to fornicate.'

Virtue always easily wins the day when it comes to talk. It only finds things difficult in practice. That was just what the donkey seemed to be saying, though, unlike the emperor sporting in the baths, it seemed to have a very large organ for so small a donkey.

On the evening before the Kalends of July, in infernally hot weather, Turpilius came to visit Kaeso, who received him in the *ludus* cold bath. Turpilius seemed very depressed, and trembled as he whispered:

'Forgive me for disturbing you in your bath, Achilles, but I think I've taken on more than I can chew. The ghost of that great idiot Cypris is haunting me night and day – though I'm the first to be surprised by the fact . . .'

'Are you trying to make fun of me?'

'I wouldn't dare. It's just that I was wrong about myself. Artists like me, we live in our imaginations. When harsh laws ask us to dream up aesthetically satisfactory punishments for condemned criminals, we feel that these punishments, and their victims, aren't real, they're just part of the story, part of the stage set. Thanks to you, I've suddenly realized that the donkey and Cypris and Laureolus are all real live creatures. It's making me ill. So I've brought your money back. Please take it.'

'You're just worried that something will go wrong, and you're putting on a turn for my benefit.'

'What I'm principally afraid of is you, and the band of tigers around you.'

Kaeso got out of his bath, led Turpilius to the armoury, had it opened, and showed him at great length the glittering collection of helmets and shields with filigree work, arm- and leg-guards, javelins, tridents, swords and sabres.

'This is what you should be dreaming about,' he said to Turpilius. 'There's plenty of food for thought here.'

He took up a straight-bladed sabre, felt the cutting edge with his index finger, and added:

'As true as my love is just like Achilles' love for Patroclus – in other words, ferocious and without the least pity – you'll get a taste of this sword-blade, at my hand or a friend's, if my Selene doesn't survive safe and sound.'

Turpilius was dripping with sweat, from a mixture of heat and fear. As he escorted him to the *ludus* door, Kaeso went on:

'The other day you rightly made me see that it was a question of sacrificing Selene or Cypris. How can you dare to prefer that prostitute to the noble and innocent young girl who's my most precious possession?'

Turpilius whimpered: 'But I see Cypris all the time, I've even slept with her, after my boy-friend left me . . . for a gladiator, at that.'

Kaeso grabbed Turpilius by the shoulder:

'If you want a close look at Selene, go to Ostia and say I sent you.'

'No, there's no point. I'll do what you want, as far as I can.'

'You'd better do *everything* you can . . .'

'Yes, everything. Just don't hurt me . . .'

646

In the days which followed Turpilius wrote to Kaeso several times, in wax made soft by heat and tears, to keep him informed in veiled terms of the progress of the operation. The actress had been 'sounded out', and had 'courageously accepted the proposal' for a sum of 7,500 sesterces payable in advance, and the same again if the operation was successful. Laureolus had asked for a small supplement, but the humble verifier had proved reasonable. All that mattered to him was that he should see a corpse go out, which could have fooled him. Obviously the absence of a corpse would have obliged them to bribe all the soldiers in the escort, and that would have been very expensive, even supposing that they were all prepared to play ball.

Kaeso breathed again. Yet he continued to feel a certain amount of discomfort. He was well aware that Paul would have shared the Rabbi Samuel's prejudice. But surely that was an exaggerated ethical position?

In the days leading up to the Nones, when the eight days of the Ludi Apollinares began, Kaeso took a closer interest in Pugnax, a quiet fellow who said little and did everything calmly – which was perhaps the reason why his Belgian concubine so readily equipped him with horns. He was always looking for her in every corner, with a sad and disillusioned air.

It was generally accepted that it was not a good thing for future opponents to get friendly. Such contacts, even if they did not lead people to pull their punches, were liable to encourage illicit arrangements, swindles and deceptions. It was tempting for a novice gladiator to buy the indulgence of a stronger man, or for two experienced gladiators to come to an agreement about staging a spectacular fight without doing each other much damage. But there was nothing to guarantee that an opponent would keep his word, and legitimate mistrust counselled abstention from such arrangements.

Kaeso spent a long time watching Pugnax training. His style of swordplay was very prudent and left no openings. At most he would occasionally lunge with a deep sigh like a lumberjack chopping down a tree. Pugnax watched Kaeso's efforts for only a brief instant, as if to confirm himself in the impression of his opponent's mediocrity which he had already formed. He had met several eager and lively young men, capable of good swordsmanship, but he was still alive, massive, heavy and confident in the effect of his own solidity.

Kaeso's natural growth of interest in the Swiss led him to open up a conversation with him as the *mirmillo* was coming out of the baths. He said amiably to him: 'I hope you won't mind my saying that I'm very proud that I shall soon be fighting someone as good as you. I'm well aware that it isn't my experience which has earned me this honour but my late father's rank, and the imperial love story, which is only too widely known.' It was indeed the case that Liber's publicity, supervised by the director Atimetus, had born fruit, and Kaeso had quickly become the object of much curiosity in doubtful taste.

Pugnax looked at Kaeso in silence and eventually said:

'It's an honour for me to meet a noble in love. I was once in love too. I didn't die of it.'

And with this mild encouragement he went on his way.

When Kaeso went for a walk in the town, he could not help remarking the many notices of the forthcoming entertainments painted on walls or shop-fronts, following the official general proclamation. There were specific posters for the Circus and theatre; and with even better reason the complicated *munus* at Agrippa's pool had its own posters.

In view of the importance which he attached to these Games, the emperor had finally decided to become their *editor* himself, pulling rank, on the grounds that he was the lavish *munerarius*, over the praetor and his college who would normally have borne the title. (The other classic religious Games were the responsibility of the curule and plebeian aediles.)

The official notice of the *munus*, after much imperial huffing and puffing, gave the place and dates. First on the list were the gladiatorial games, with the number of pairs to be presented. While the generosity of the praetors and aediles was prudently restrained, the emperor could stage as many fighters and pairs as he liked, which in the event turned out to be forty-odd. It was a large number, even for a whole day, as there were to be group fights as a little extra. So as not to distract the spectators' attention, only a small number of pairs of high-quality fighters were presented at the same time: indeed it was standard for there to be only one pair at a time. Then the notice gave details of the sea-battle, where more than 1,500 condemned criminals were scheduled to kill each other, in a very confined space. And finally there were the extras: the *venatio* which, in conformity with popular demand, was to be full of lions, bears and panthers; the awnings, which were all the more necessary with the sun as fierce as it was; the sprinkling of saffron-coloured water, the distribution of prizes, and the concluding feast. There was always a crowd standing around reading such notices, which people tried to leave uncovered as long as possible, as a sign of respect for the generous *editores*. Here and there could be seen notices which had piously been preserved for several generations. When the memory of a bad emperor – or one said to be such by the Senate at any rate – was condemned, his name was merely scratched off the notice.

But the real excitement was over another sort of publicity: the papyrus handouts, abundantly distributed, which gave the composition of the pairs, this information being indispensable for betting. In many inns it was displayed on a wall, and the innkeeper would put up the results at the end of the *munus*. So you could place your bets and find out the result without leaving your favourite *popina*. Such programmes also, of course, carried all such information about the matched pairs of gladiators as was calculated to interest the public.

As he came down from the Caelian towards the Forums, Kaeso would now avoid the family house where his parents had once lived. But he sometimes stopped at the *popina* where he had had lunch with Paul and Luke, and where his father had got drunk and had his toga stolen, in days of which Kaeso knew nothing. One afternoon he ran his eyes over the composition of the pairs, which had recently been written up and was the subject of all conversation inside and outside any inn close to the great *ludus*. All Pugnax' victories were listed, and then at the end: 'K. Aponius Saturninus, *tiro*, despairing catamite of the emperor'. Kaeso was given at seven to one. It was enough to put him off betting on himself.

The curse of sex was still with him. Even when he took up a sword, it was his arse which featured on the poster. In his declaration of love for Nero he had used terms sufficiently neutral to sow doubt and leave things open. But the uneducated *plebs* preferred a male emperor to a female one, and so Kaeso's reputation was settled. The organizers had carefully avoided giving him a stage-name, to show his noble origins more clearly, and heighten the emotional effect of his disappointment in love.

On the third day of the games, two days before the gladiatorial combat and hunt, the usual parade took place. Atticizing Greeks called it the *propompe* – or *exoplasiai* in popular Greek – to distinguish it from the proper procession which opened the *munus*. When the baths had closed, the forty pairs of gladiators paraded through the busiest streets, from the barracks on the Caelian to the theatre of Balbus, with its back to the Tiber and its rear stage wall next to the great Corinthian portico of Cn. Octavius, the conqueror of Perses. There the matched pairs of men stood side by side, stripped to the waist, and struck poses or flexed their muscles for the benefit of fans and gamblers. The horses of the *bigae* and *quadrigae* stood at the starting ropes before an event in just the same way.

There were a large number of top-class gladiators there, since the cream of the *ludus* was being used for the occasion. But the keenest interest centred on Kaeso's beauty and misfortunes. The plebs on the corn-dole and the lice-ridden lowest class shouted jokes and obscenities at him, while the tight-knit tribe of Roman homosexuals thrilled with especial sympathy for him, going so far, in their emotion, as to shout at Pugnax: 'Child-eater! Christian!' It was the first indication Kaeso had of what a very bad reputation the Christians had among the ordinary people. Pugnax, who had heard worse before, remained as impassive as a Swiss oak-tree.

That evening Myra, who had followed the *propompe* with passionate interest, naïvely said to Kaeso: 'Now you're famous.'

But it wasn't the sort of fame of which Marcia, or even Marcus, had dreamed.

CHAPTER 2

On the evening before the opening of the bloody *munus* the traditional *cena libera* was served to the gladiators and the various categories of condemned prisoners. This carefully prepared meal was called 'free' because relatives, friends and even the general public were admitted to watch it. It was a favour exclusively granted to those men and women called to risk or lose their lives in Games at the amphitheatre. Ordinary condemned criminals and victims of the pornographic theatre were not entitled to it. Naturally it was the *cena* of the most famous gladiators which attracted the most attention, and lovers of pathos found what they wanted in the spectacle. Some gladiators were unwise enough to drown their fears and sorrows in drink. Some had no appetite. Others made their wills, and commended their concubines and children to the care of friends. Sometimes an old father or a trembling mother, though dishonoured by their son's *infamia*, could not help coming and embracing him for perhaps the last time. The gladiators' feast was first and foremost a spectator event, providing an additional opportunity to gauge the morale of this or that champion at leisure.

As night began to fall, and the lamps and torches were lit, a crowd formed around the eighty gladiators, of whom Kaeso was one, in a room in the *ludus* decorated with greenery and flowers and opening on to a courtyard planted with trees.

Kaeso ate and drank in moderation, opposite Pugnax, who was behaving just as usual, with the difference that his Belgian concubine was standing behind him and watching Kaeso uneasily. Women who depend on a man tend to get worried over trifles. Though it is true that the probable is never definite.

Suddenly Kaeso saw, quite close, a fellow by the name of C. Furius Mancinus, the son of a quite distinguished knight, whom he had liked and thought well of during his school days. Furius looked ill at ease, but nonetheless he had come. Kaeso took the opportunity to leave the table, where the food was not up to the standard of Silanus' house, and went to meet his friend.

'It's kind of you to have come.'

'We've rather lost touch with each other, but misfortune brings people back together. I heard, as every one did, of your father's tragic death and ruin. But I must admit that I didn't expect to find you in a *ludus*.'

'My contract is for one appearance only, and I have been paid right royally for it.'

'I can guess . . .'

'Whatever you guessed would be different from reality. The day may come for you too, when you'll have to risk your skin for cash. I have at least the great honour and consolation that the money isn't for myself.'

'I'll bet you need it to ransom a chaste fiancée who's been kidnapped by pirates.'

'Actually, I have several fiancées in that plight.'

They joked together for a moment, then parted, with a touch of emotion.

Indiscreet people pressed Kaeso with vulgar or stupid questions, There was surprise at the presence of Myra at his heels. It was even suggested that she must be a boy.

Kaeso withdrew to his room with the child and had difficulty getting to sleep. The appearance of Furius had brutally brought back to him a whole past life, with its illusions and legitimate hopes. The loving mother and respected father had vanished. He had had to ruin his reputation in an uncertain cause, his very life was at risk, and he still lacked the certainties or illumination of a faith or philosophy to sustain him and drive away his feeling of malaise. Events had suddenly moved faster than his feelings or ideas could cope with. He had had no time to analyse himself or pull himself together. He was preparing to die in a mental fog, with no other assurances than those dispensed by his confused instincts.

The races and theatrical performances of the first four days of the Games had already roused much enthusiasm, and the emperor had had the satisfaction of being acclaimed in the Circus with more unanimity than usual. The four days of celebrations in the gardens of Agrippa, which were to follow, were being applauded in prospect.

Kaeso heard very favourable reports of the *venatio*, where hundreds of wild beasts had fought and been put to death, after tearing apart an exceptionally copious ration of condemned criminals, whipped on by the animal trainers towards the claws and jaws of the famished predators. For, while the gladiators, the animal-trainers and the intended victims banqueted before a *munus*, the animals went without food. The sight of the condemned criminals wending their way to the amphitheatre from one direction and the wild beasts from another, the former in chains, the latter in cages, was always much enjoyed.

Kaeso also gathered that the sea battle, in which the Greeks had cut up and drowned the Persians yet again, had given every satisfaction, although it had been marred by the scandalous suicide of some spoilsports – Germans of course. Those people were really good for nothing but to be used as bodyguards or model mercenaries.

During these two memorable days Nero had taken himself in hand and had actually presided over the Games most of the time, even making an effort to look as though he were enjoying it. Such an evident desire to please the people was touching.

It was the rule for gladiators to enjoy a complete rest in the days immediately preceding a *munus*. Kaeso had plenty of time to write to his brother and bid him farewell. He gave him all the latest news and asked him whether his father's letter to Vetera threw any light on the circumstances of his death. His own letter, despite all his efforts, lacked warmth. Kaeso held it against Marcus junior that he had let him down, although he understood very well that his brother could not have done otherwise, since he had only acted in accordance with his nature. How could two brothers brought up in the same way be so different? Had Pomponia perhaps been unfaithful? Should Kaeso, to crown the rest of his disgrace, have been called 'son of Spurius'? In his present state of bitterness no further unpleasant trick of fate could have surprised him.

On the afternoon of the day before the anniversary of Caesar's birth, when the actual gladiatorial *munus* was to take place in the pool of Agrippa, Kaeso hounded Turpilius with exceptionally horrific threats. Yet, if he died the next day, there would be nobody to carry them out. Whom could he trust? Then he paid a last visit to Selene. Kaeso recounted his plan to flee with her – and the 100,000 sesterces in Rabbi Samuel's safe-keeping – to a distant country where both of them could begin a new life. Perhaps Carthage, where life was supposed to be sweet for lovers? Selene gave silent approval. In her mind she could already hear the footsteps of the soldiers who would be coming to fetch her, and Kaeso's romancing seemed even more superfluous than usual. She did, however, let him kiss her on the mouth, which was good of her. By a nice paradox prostitutes tried to keep this favour for their favourite pimps, and not even all Kaeso's devoted acts entitled him to be thought of in those terms. It is true that Selene was only going on hearsay: she had never loved any man.

The imminent approach of his contest pushed Kaeso into securing metaphysical assistance for himself, and he had difficulty in warding off a superstitious frame of mind. The official patron gods of gladiators did not inspire him with much confidence. Philosophy offered him only very vague resources in such a crucial moment. Since the day when he had shed his childhood *bulla*, on the morning of his assumption of the *toga virilis*, Kaeso had had no amulet. Paul had refused him the gift of the Holy Spirit, but it was not out of the question that that mysterious person might bring him luck. Paul himself had had difficulty knowing what the Spirit wanted, and only made it speak with some hesitation and reservation. It rather seemed as though its most remarkable quality was that of acting in complete contradiction to common sense, pursuing un-fathomable ends by the simplest and yet also the most out-of-the-way routes. Since the Holy Spirit had a tendency to do the opposite of what was expected of it, it was quite capable of defeating Pugnax.

When he got back from Ostia, Kaeso elbowed his way across the Pons Sublicius, which was crowded with beggars and wretched prostitutes, and reached the Trans Tiberim, where Peter, according to the Christians at the Porta Capena, had chosen to take up residence. The apostle was in the middle of dining with friends on the third floor of a mediocre apart-ment block in the Jewish quarter. He probably preferred the atmosphere of the ghetto because it reminded him of the neglected traditions of his youth.

A cushion was pushed forward for Kaeso in front of the common dish. The relative isolation of the Christians had the advantage of ensuring that they had not yet heard about the recent exploits of Marcus' son, and Kaeso still enjoyed a certain amount of prejudice in his favour. Peter saw no objection in principle to imbuing Kaeso with the Holy Spirit, and as he ate, he checked his knowledge of the creed, which was first class. He accordingly held up this young Roman noble, who already spoke of Heaven with more elegance than he himself did, as an example to those present. But things went a little astray when he asked Kaeso to recite the 'Pater'. . .

'Didn't Paul teach you the "Pater"?'

'I'm afraid not. I should have remembered.'

'Indeed you should. Jesus himself taught us to pray in this fashion. Say after me: "Our Father, which art in Heaven . . . Hallowed be thy name. Thy Kingdom come, Thy Will be done on earth as it is in Heaven. Give us this day our *arton epiousion* . . ."'

Kaeso frowned and said: 'For the poor to ask God for *arton*, made from white, wheaten flour, is a good idea, but what is the meaning of *epiousion?* The Greeks use this term to make reference to a vague future, tomorrow, or even to the same evening.'

Peter, who was not very good at Greek, hesitated.

Kaeso went on: 'After all, Jesus spoke in Aramaic. Can't you remember exactly what he said?'

Peter scratched his head, rather put out. He finished by admitting to the guests, who were drinking in every word, that his memory had failed him. 'I shall have to check in the Aramaic gospel of Matthew,' he said. 'The main thing is that the essential idea should be clear.'

He continued: 'And forgive us our trespasses as we forgive those who trespass against us. Preserve us from temptation and deliver us from evil.'

Kaeso thought he ought to offer an excuse for his ignorance. 'I couldn't spend as much time with Paul as I should have liked. In any case, that learned gentleman is inclined to interest himself in theology at a very high level. It's difficult to keep his feet on the ground. He floats. I should also say that I read the gospel according to Mark on the banks of the pool of Agrippa, and I didn't find this "Pater" in it. Didn't Mark know about it?'

Everyone protested, but had to admit that Kaeso's justifications were good ones.

At the end of the meal Peter made the new Christian kneel and laid the Holy Spirit upon him.

Kaeso got up and asked: 'I suppose that in future I shall know for sure what's good and what's bad?'

The answer was not easy. Peter limited himself to saying: 'If you keep all the commandments of Jesus, and if you pray hard, the Holy Spirit will indicate the right path to you. He only enlightens those who deserve enlightenment.'

Covered in blessings Kaeso went back to sleep at the *ludus*. He had never felt Marcia's loss more keenly.

Early the next morning Kaeso embraced the weeping Myra, who had energetically refused to come to the fight, and ran to join his comrades as they set off on foot for the amphitheatre, amid an already dense crowd.

The gardens of Agrippa were unrecognizable, now that they had been invaded for days and nights on end by swarms of workmen and spectators. The copses themselves had served as improvised sleeping-space and picnic grounds. To the north and south of the sand-strewn floor of the pool two vast stretches of wooden tiered seating had been put up, presumably so that the spectators need not have the sun in their eyes at any time; in the space to the west had been built some rustic cottages, and in the space to the east some smaller houses, close to the portico and temple of Bonus Eventus (Success) which ran on from the Baths of Agrippa. Over this strange amphitheatre the sailors of the Misenum fleet had stretched an immense awning of sky blue, scattered with gold stars. In the middle of it was a gigantic glittering Nero, represented in glory in the chariot of Apollo. The emperor and VIPs were to sit on the south side of the arena, to judge from the still empty *pulvinar*. But the tiers of seats and even the lawns between the houses, were visibly filling up.

Under the seats on the southern side had been installed dressing rooms, an infirmary, a weapon store, rest room and massage room, all for the benefit of the star gladiators. It was on this side that the Gate of the Living opened, while the Gate of the Dead and the mortuary were to the north.

At the beginning of the morning, with the praetor presiding in the emperor's absence, the spectators had had to sit through confused mêlées of such co-operative condemned criminals as had not been used for the sea-battle. Nero and his suite arrived towards the middle of the morning, while a largish crowd was watching the end of an entertaining presentation of *andabatae*. Now the really interesting events could begin.

Shortly afterwards the superb traditional procession came into the arena, to a unanimous ovation. At the head were the *lictors*, then came the band, with the full brass section playing a vigorous march, to the booming accompaniment of a great hydraulic organ. Then came the publicity chariots and the sandwich-board men, followed by the men carrying the palms for the victors, and the representative of the curule magistrate who was acting as *editor* – in this case the emperor. Nero had honoured his friend Vitellius by entrusting him with this role, and he fulfilled it all the better for adoring gladiatorial games. Next came officials proudly parading the gladiators' decorated helmets. As shows in the amphitheatre were a summer entertainment, the combatants put their helmets on only at the last moment, since the sun and heat would have turned them into kettles. Moreover, that particular day the temperature was overpowering. Then came the grooms, leading the horses of the mounted fighters who were to open the show with their graceful duels: the riders themselves walked behind their mounts. And at the rear of the procession came the forty pairs of gladiators, on foot, with weapons and shields.

Kaeso, who was in the middle of the troupe beside Pugnax, was struck by the soft aquarium-like light reigning in that place of carnage. The two flights of luxuriously decorated seats, black with people, seemed to him like the jaws of a monster about to devour him. Pugnax said to him:

'Those people don't count. In a moment you'll be alone, with no one but yourself to rely on. Then you'll forget that anyone's looking at you.'

The procession circled the arena. As it passed beneath the *pulvinar* Kaeso recognized, among others, the figures of Sporus and Petronius in the emperor's immediate entourage. The latter, briefly and discreetly, raised his thumb, as though to say that, if it were left to him, he would get him out of this wasp's nest. This mark of sympathy was comforting.

When they had returned to the rooms under the south side, a long and trying wait began, since Kaeso was not to fight until late afternoon. Under this vast wooden structure the accumulated heat was even more uncomfortable than outside. Kaeso went up to look around from the top of the staircase. There was in any case some advantage to him in knowing the mood of the public.

The horseback duels were over, and four pairs entered the lists, including a *retiarius* and his *secutor*. Following a procedure with which Kaeso was familiar from having attended dozens of *munera*, the men went first to greet the emperor, who was to preside over their feats of arms. Since the disastrous business of the *'morituri te salutant'* at the Claudian sea-battle on Lake Fucinus, everyone was careful to avoid a formula which could be thought of as bringing bad luck. Next, the equipment and weapons were checked: this was a task entrusted as a sign of honour to friends representing the imperial *munerarius*. The chief umpire, who had a long staff, then reminded the gladiators of the correct rules of combat, while the rods, whips and red hot irons, which would probably not be used, were being prepared. Once the formalities were over, the pairs separated, each with its particular umpire. The gladiators, still bare-headed, then attacked one another in a formalized way to warm up and give an idea of their style: this was the *prolusio*, to which Ovid had rightly compared his first polemical sallies. But these elegant demonstrations could not go on for long or the audience would get bored. At the first sign of impatience among his guests, 'president' Nero, who took his job very seriously, signalled to a messenger dressed as Mercury. The messenger then communicated to the relevant parties the order to begin battle. Some children brought the gladiators their helmets; each of the four umpires raised his staff, which had been dividing the chests of the opponents; the rhythm of the orchestral accompaniment became more throbbing; and the iron hammer made the bronze gong well and truly ring out.

Pair followed pair like this until the midday break, when their number went from four to three. By the interval forty-two gladiators had made an appearance. Two had been killed outright, one of them, who had run on

657

his opponent's sword in an excess of impetuosity, by accident. Five more had had their throats cut by their opponents after mercy had been refused. Yet three of those had fought with an honourable enough vigour. They had only abandoned the fight, by raising their finger, kneeling or throwing away their shield, after a series of serious wounds. But none of the five victims had been a public favourite, such as Petraites, Prudes, Hermeros or Calamous, who always rounded off the end of the programme. So it looked as if the public, too long pampered, was becoming more and more demanding; as if the less important gladiators had less and less chance of rousing sympathy; as if the threshold above which a good reputation could excuse a failure was becoming higher and higher. Such a development, which made the fights more and more violent, certainly heightened the beauty of the occasion, but it reduced the hopes of survival for the novice or average gladiator. At Beneventum, where Marcus' gladiatorial *familia* had been thrashed, of the twelve *tirones* engaged by Vatinius, two had been killed, one seriously wounded and three had had their throats cut for 'inadequacy'.

If he were defeated, Kaeso's life would depend on the dubious effects of the publicity which he himself had stirred up to increase his fee, for the emperor, precisely because he was not much interested in gladiatorial combat, had been following the majority all morning. Even if he very much wanted to save Kaeso, that would not weigh heavily in the balance against the unpleasant prospect of displeasing the public. Nero might even play at Brutus, and sacrifice, with crocodile tears, a pretended favourite to the law of the greatest number. It was slippery ground.

Kaeso felt quite depressed. He went back, ate a few olives and drank a goblet of water with a dash of red wine in it. Then he went back up for a breath of fresh air. The interval was being used to fit in the ceremony of *vapulatio*: a group of recently engaged *tirones* were struck with canes as a symbol of their entry into the profession. They would take part in a forthcoming *munus*. Kaeso had of course been exempted from the ceremony on the grounds of his immediate participation.

A little further off some *paegniarii*, gladiators with buttoned foils, were fencing for the amusement of those spectators who had remained in their seats.

An unexpected breeze reached Kaeso, and he stretched his head out of the stairwell. He happened to be in the section of seats reserved for the Vestal Virgins, most of whom had withdrawn. But a little way off on his left sat Rubria, looking weary. She was being vigorously fanned by a small slave. Where clemency for the gladiators was concerned the opinion of the Vestals was particularly important. Kaeso coughed, and with a charming smile offered the lady some of the olives left in the palm of his hand. Rubria initially gave the intruder a very haughty look, but Kaeso was irresistible, and she finally took an olive with the very tips of her fingers.

'Who are you then?'

'You'd recognize me if I'd kept my breastplate on after the procession.'

Rubria started and stared at Kaeso with a mixture of curiosity and disapproval.

'Why are you looking at me like that? I'm said to be in love with Nero. But you know that that's not true. I'm no more Nero's lover than you are, despite all your charms. And if you're looking disapproving because I'm a gladiator, my answer is that I'm not doing it from choice, any more than you chose to be a Vestal. Some emperor must have selected you when you were very young. A hostile destiny marked me out in the same way.'

Rubria was somewhat mollified and asked:

'What do you want?'

'I just want you to raise your thumb nice and high if I should get into any trouble.'

'What is there in it for me?'

'At nightfall I'll abduct you, and we'll run off and be happy on some secret desert island. There you can embroider slippers for me, do the housework, cook my meals, look for shells for me, catch rabbits and hedgehogs which you'll roast over an open fire, while I shall be amusing myself with my favourite monkey on a bed of sweet-smelling leaves. And if you think of anyone but me, or if you let the fire go out, you'll go and cut switches for me so that I can give you a good whipping.'

'It's just as well I've never married.'

'Then since I've been able to convince you of it so easily, raise your thumb for me. And get your dear sisters to do the same.'

Rubria looked towards the Gate of the Dead. Nearby, the soldiers were quietly decapitating those condemned criminals who had been cowardly enough to refuse to fight.

'I'll ask for mercy,' she said, 'if I think you've fought bravely enough.'

'I shall do the impossible to please you.'

'Don't try too hard. I've bet 300 sesterces on Pugnax.'

That was an element in his favour. The spectators had a tendency to sacrifice those whose defeat had made them lose money.

As the *paegniarii* were leaving the arena, the heralds began to announce the punishments, of a mythological or legendary sort, to be inflicted on some redoubtable bandits. The best known of these, one Galerius, had committed robbery, arson and torture in the Pontine marshes, an area particularly difficult to police. A chariot burst in, driven by Achilles and dragging behind it the ferocious Galerius, in the role of Hector's corpse. The tow-rope was round the victim's heels and he was uttering terrible screams – he was obviously under-rehearsed for the part. Preparations were also being made to crush a Sisyphus under a rock.

Kaeso could not take his eyes off his Vestal. He suggested; 'If you're worried about the idea of abduction, I'll wait twenty years for you to complete your term of office, and then tender bonds of marriage will unite us. I'll make love to you in all the positions in the book, and you'll give me nuts and sweets.'

'If I want to, I can give up my office in seven years' time.'

'By Venus and all her attendants, I'd never have believed you could be a day older than twenty-two – well, twenty-five at the outside . . .'

'Nonsense, you wicked flatterer.'

But Galerius would not keep quiet. He had just gone by at a gallop behind his *quadriga*, in front of the deserted *pulvinar*, letting out wild shrieks and a stream of insults which showed his total lack of penitence.

Profiting from the fact that this madman was momentarily being borne away in the opposite direction, Kaeso looked deep into Rubria's eyes and sang in an undertone, to a fashionable tune:

> 'Keep for the goddess proud the finest of your gifts,
> Keep your ripe lips, and keep your jutting rosy tits,
> Keep your round dimpled arse which every heart enflames,
> And keep the fleecy slit where many fain would come.
> Of all those raffish charms which lord it o'er the Games
> The only bit of you I yearn for is your thumb.'

'Did you just improvise that?'

'How could I have possibly done so? Like every young Roman, I've been thinking of you for years. You're the finest ornament of your college.'

The intolerable Galerius went round again, and the cries of delight from the remaining members of the crowd half covered Kaeso's last phrases. The rock had finally crushed Sisyphus, whose legs, sticking out from under it, were jerking in the last spasms of the death agony. You had to have a really tight grip on the instinct for self-preservation to be able to go through a near-the-bone flirtation with a middle-aged Vestal Virgin in such peculiarly inappropriate circumstances.

Rubria eventually became cross: 'Stop making such sacrilegious suggestions, and go back into your hole. You're not the first to have tried to
trade on my good nature.'

Before obeying, Kaeso said to Rubria: 'Remember that you're possibly
the last pretty woman to whom I shall ever speak, and then you'll forgive
my boldness. Keep these olives as a souvenir. If I die because of you, the
stones will remind you of your hardness of heart.'

The show restarted, but Kaeso could no longer face watching it. From
three pairs at a time they went down to two, then to one, under the chief
umpire. The programme had arrived at those gladiators whose list of
honours ran to forty or so victories. As the afternoon wore on, the
proportion of those who were carried off on a flower-strewn stretcher,
led by a Charon, to the sinister Porta Libitinensis grew smaller. It was in
nobody's interest to sacrifice a top-class gladiator lightly. But Kaeso had
only slipped in among them by accident. As time passed, the waves of
excited cries rose higher and higher, and the music became more and
more throbbing.

Towards the end of the tenth hour Kaeso and Pugnax put on their
armour in silence, helped by the attendants, while the preceding pair were
fighting. Kaeso thought for a moment of Selene. Everything seemed to
have been organized as well as it could be: his will, in which a codicil
provided for the final payment to Turpilius and his accomplices, had been
deposited with the Vestals, and the money he still had left was safe in the
coffers of the great *ludus*, under the guard of Atimetus. The trumpets
finally rang out to announce another victory. Henceforth Kaeso was wise
enough to think only of himself.

He was to keep a confused memory of the preliminaries of the fight
and its banal *prolusio*, during which he tried not to give away his tactics.
The din all around him, the shouts, and music, reached him as though in
a dream.

Suddenly he was aware of himself, with a helmet on his head, face to
face with another, threatening, helmeted figure.

It was expected that Kaeso, when faced with an adversary whose
careful, defensive stance was well known, would adopt an attacking
attitude appropriate to his *armatura* and still more to his youth. At the risk
of temporarily disappointing the public, Kaeso had decided to adopt the
opposite tactics, so as to oblige Pugnax to undertake a degree of swordplay
which was not habitual to him nor suited to his temperament.

Kaeso bided his time, therefore, despite the whistles and boos, until the

Swiss, if only for the sake of his reputation, found himself compelled to attack, though unwillingly, and to tire himself out earlier than expected. As Kaeso was well endowed for evasive action and capable of making dangerous counter-attacks, the clashes beneath the great imperial *pulvinar* were interminable. Kaeso had regained his self-control, and Pugnax, who was beginning to feel his age, was huffing and puffing with irritation inside his helmet.

After a particularly brutal attack Kaeso's sabre broke. The umpire at once came between them, an identical weapon was brought immediately, and the fight began again, with the impartial encouragement of the crowd. The sweet young girl whose talents Kaeso had already appreciated at Silanus' house was fighting at his side on her organ, and getting the most beautiful effects from it.

Pugnax was getting close to exhaustion. He wanted to get the whole thing over and was beginning to make mistakes. Realizing the fact, he took refuge for a moment in a restful passivity until the indignant cries of the crowd shook him out of it.

Staking everything, he hurled himself on Kaeso and wounded him in the right leg, above the greave, while he himself was wounded in the left shoulder. He was now having trouble holding up his heavy shield, but Kaeso, who was in great pain, found it equally difficult to move at all.

Pugnax' helmet started to speak, and Kaeso suddenly heard: 'Shall we give up together?'

Sometimes the audience would ask for two gladiators, who had reached the end of their strength without either being able to win, to be allowed to retire without victor or vanquished. Equally two exhausted gladiators would sometimes ask for their own *missio* by laying down their arms at the same time. The public, according to its mood, would then decide whether to send them off or have both their throats cut. Pugnax, who was always careful, was counting on his reputation and his wound to get him an honourable dismissal, which would have the side effect of also benefiting Kaeso, who had been incapacitated by a wound in the same way as Pugnax.

The difficulty lay in the problem of exact synchronization. The course proposed could conceal a trap, such that the naïve would raise a hand only to find that their opponent, having made the suggestion, did nothing.

Kaeso replied: 'Let's each go back a few steps and put our armour – you your *scutum* and me my *parma* – down simultaneously.'

Pugnax took a step back, Kaeso two, and they slowly let their shields drop.

The gesture unleashed a storm of opposite reactions. Some fanatics wanted them both put to death. Others were for a *missio*. But gradually a majority emerged for continuing the fight, and the Emperor eventually transmitted to the umpire a decision to that effect.

The seconds summarily cleansed their wounds and the struggle recommenced. The blow which Pugnax had received turned out to be fairly superficial. But Kaeso, whose leg was getting stiffer and stiffer, was losing a lot of blood, and inside his overheated helmet the sweat was running down into his eyes. Pugnax, who was dragging his shield like a dead weight, nonetheless felt that he had time on his side, and took no more risks.

The time which was passing seemed an eternity to Kaeso. The bizarre idea flicked through his mind that time in eternity, instead of being longer than human time, was perhaps, on the contrary, much denser. But he refused to give in.

When Pugnax had the impression that Kaeso, who was turning on his wounded leg, was all in, he attacked him in decisive fashion, but, in an unexpected gesture of courtesy, instead of striking him with the cutting edge of his sword, he hit him hard with the flat of the blade across his sword arm. Kaeso dropped the weapon from his numb hand, immediately threw away his shield, and hastily raised his left arm to the *pulvinar*, under the protection of the umpire, who had hurried over to him.

Audience excitement, which had been steadily mounting all day, now reached its peak. At all points of the compass the spectators leapt to their feet and indicated their preference. Thumbs went up and thumbs went down, togas flapped on the lower white tiers where the well-off citizens sat. The pandemonium reigning beneath the awning penetrated Kaeso, who up to then had been totally absorbed in his fight, like a whiplash. Nero was enigmatically waiting to see a trend develop, which was a bad sign, since the president had the right – though admittedly he rarely used it – to impose his own decision, especially when his name was Caesar. But perhaps the emperor was hoping for a majority in favour, so that all he would have to do was to accept it. Petronius and Poppaea had their thumbs up, and so did Sporus, who was not one to bear a grudge. Rubria had turned hers up immediately, and some of the other Vestals had followed her example.

However, to Kaeso's surprise, the crowd was gradually shifting the other way. And soon revealing shouts gave the explanation. Despite all

Nero's efforts, a shameless homosexuality, insolently flaunted as a badge of honour, had not won the hearts of the Romans. Many senators were hostile to it, preferring to conduct their debauches in private. And the *plebs* were more hostile still. Their touchy sense of patriotism was irritated by any sort of Greek behaviour. To these considerations was added, among the majority, a kind of sporting desire, often to be observed, to do the opposite of what the emperor wanted. It was no longer a question of whether Kaeso had fought well or not. On this anniversary of the Punic Wars, the crowd, by crushing an impudent imperial catamite, had it in mind to give their Master a warning and a lesson on the cheap.

A wave of despair swept over Kaeso, and at random he called on the name of the Holy Spirit.

Then, step by step, despite everything, the homosexual party began to gain ground. The bisexuals, the specialists, all those who had 'come out', were throwing themselves frenetically into the struggle on Kaeso's behalf, winning over, a block at a time, all the others who had tried it, who had pretended to, who had played touch-my-willy with their little friends when they were very young. And it began to be clear, to everyone's surprise, that it was an unexpectedly large number of people. Kaeso suddenly had a brilliant idea of stripping himself virtually naked, thus showing off his magnificent body, and he held out his arms towards all the men of good will who actually judged other people on the courage they showed. A delirium of pederastic desire swept across whole tiers like a bush-fire. A Hellenizing Emperor could scarcely remain insensible to it for long. The future of a Rome freed from prejudice rose before his dazzled eyes like a luminous phallus.

Petronius whispered in his ear: 'You can hardly kill an Apollo during the Festival of Apollo.' Rubria was trembling with well-intentioned excitement and all her sisters were now caught up in the wave of emotion. The Holy Spirit, which simply could not do without Kaeso for the success of its mysterious long-term plans, was deploying good angels all over the stadium to do some persuasive publicity for the cause by dropping a few insinuating words in the right ears.

Nero sighed and gave in. His august thumb turned up, amid a blend of imprecations and acclamations.

Saved by a coalition of gays and Vestal Virgins, Kaeso walked slowly towards the Sanavivaria, the Gate of the Living, while Pugnax, who was rather forgotten in all the tumult, climbed up to the saffron-scented *pulvinar* to receive the palm, victory garland and *aurei* yet again.

*

664

Deep in the bowels of the building Kaeso's wounds were washed and dressed more carefully. And, though his contract was finished, Liber offered him a few more days' hospitality. Then he went back to the *ludus* in a litter, and found Myra biting her nails outside the great gate. The sight of her master more or less in one piece threw her into transports of joy. Kaeso immediately sent a reassuring message to Selene, via Cethegus. Then he fell into deep reflection. Rabbi Samuel's reservations on the subject of that fool Cypris suddenly hit him hard. He realized that he had only been spared by a miracle brought about by a Providence working in his interests and without consideration of his merits. He had just been given his life back a second time, and yet he was preparing to destroy another life in a way which was even less excusable than it had been previously, since the emperor's clemency to him now gave hope that such mercy would also be granted to Selene. If Selene were spared, she would doubtless be replaced at a moment's notice by another girl in the same case. But then it would be the path of justice which was responsible and not Kaeso. The crux of the affair, a fresh occasion for scruple on top of so many others, was whether he should put up with the probable 'favour' of the emperor, no longer to save Selene but to get off the hook a contemptible and stupid girl he did not even know. For mortals of coarser clay there could have been no possible reason to hesitate. But Kaeso was full of finer feelings, and the temptation to act humanely was strong in him.

During the dinner hour Kaeso sought refuge alone in his little room and meditated on this urgent problem with all the mental capacity he had left after the fearful pressure of emotion to which he had just been subjected.

All his education had inclined him to hold slaves and even the *plebs* as negligible, essentially in the name of a cultural prejudice. There's no contempt to equal that of the educated for the ignorant. No contempt is more ineradicable or more hypocritical when it pretends to disappear, for education secretes its own poisons which colour the pride of their victim with the most reasonable of outward appearances. The Romans had once imposed themselves by the sword. Eventually, when the sword had become blunted, culture had come to its aid, to help firmly establish the domination of the educated at the heart of the empire. An astonishing symbol of this was the stylus, which as well as writing in soft wax could also on occasion be used as a dagger.

But chance had brought Kaeso into contact with the Christians. Their offbeat theology, in its shattering simplicity, seemed independent of all education – though doubtless intellectuals who were expert in Greek would eventually turn it into a complex reflection of their favourite civilization. Paul had already been working on it. But it was to Peter, and men like him, that Jesus had entrusted his Church. And Jesus had chosen to address the universe in a regional dialect unknown to the majority of the inhabitants of the Roman world. Divinely despising Greek and Latin, he had been sufficiently sure of himself to hope or foresee that no translation into the language of the intellectuals or the conquerors would ever succeed in erasing the essentials of his imprint. This religion of the poor in spirit was quietly overthrowing the present and future domination of the pen and the sword with a few simple strokes. Mark, in his rough Greek, told Kaeso that God the Father made no distinction between his children once they agreed to make none between themselves. Equality was in the process of descending upon the world.

Kaeso was well aware that the poor were not very attractive. They were for ever trying to get other people to feel sorry for them so that they could take them for a ride, and they were even more selfish than the rich of the old school once modest success had dragged them out of the mud. But it was not a question of being charitable to Cypris. It was merely one of being just to her, because God, who did not have to account for his actions to anyone, had taken the trouble to create her and make her grow.

The more Kaeso thought about it, the more he had to admit, without enthusiasm, that this Cypris had the right to survive and to go to Hell by the road of her own choosing.

According to the 'Pater' of Peter, moreover, God only forgave those who forgave others. But to forgive, you had to be alive. If Kaeso had Cypris killed, how could she ever forgive him? The irreparable character of the event frightened him. It was always possible that a vengeful God might ask victims for their advice before forgiving their murderers.

As the summer twilight fell, Kaeso sighed and took up his stylus:

'Kaeso to Caesar,

May I see you tonight? I must put your generosity to the test yet again. Forgive me for not having asked enough of your goodness before. I shall not behave like that again. My leg is hurting me but I shall come to you on my knees if necessary. Fare well.'

Kaeso gave the note to Myra, with the strictest instructions that it must get through tonight, and a quite large sum of money to help get past the barriers of subordinates. But, alas, Kaeso's notoriety was now such that

Myra would probably have no difficulty in getting permission to hand it to the emperor in person.

The consoling feature for Kaeso in this situation was that it was more than likely that sooner or later the emperor would send for him for proof of his 'spectacular' devotion. It would have been a pity to sacrifice Cypris, only to find that he had merely deferred for a short while an unpleasantness which was inescapable.

Myra soon came back from the nearby Palatine, where one of the minor freedmen of the immense imperial *familia* had promised to forward the letter as soon as possible. Nero was dining that evening in Piso's superb villa on the Pincian. The Prince thought of this patrician as a friend and often stayed at his villa in Baiae, where he liked to get away from it all. If the emperor was still alive, it was because Piso, heroically adhering to the principles of traditional hospitality, had got it into his head that the one place Nero was not to be assassinated was in a house belonging to *him*. Sometimes events of the greatest importance are called off by destiny for the most disconcertingly trivial reasons. If Piso had been less hospitable, Peter and Paul would have died in their beds wondering why they had been overlooked for martyrdom.

Towards midnight Kaeso received a few charming lines from Piso.

'C. Calpurnius Piso to K. Aponius Saturninus, cordial greetings.

You are the man of the day. Everybody wants to meet you – we are all queuing up behind the emperor, who is still much moved by your bravery. To make your acquaintance all the faster I am sending a litter for you, with a triumphal escort, and am having a few titbits put aside for you which will be a pleasant change after the nut cutlets in the *ludus*. You have set the hearts of every Roman fluttering even more wildly than those of our Vestal Virgins, you devastating boy! See you soon!'

A postscript added; 'I was very fond of your stepmother, an exquisite woman who used to speak of you with all the affection of experience. By a miracle of love you have inherited her beauty. I raised my thumb for you just now in memory of her.'

Kaeso really felt one of the family. He tarted himself up and went out, limping.

❧ CHAPTER ❧

3

Nero, with Vitellius as his sole companion, was dining in all innocence in the serried ranks of a group of assassins. In attendance, stretched out on their couches with a smirk and a pretty word on their lips, was a notable proportion of those who, the following year, would get caught red-handed at the last moment.

First there was Piso, a handsome and ostentatious man of sceptical tendencies, much smitten with tragic theatre, whose contribution to a conspiracy was a distinguished family name and a reputation for idleness which encouraged the dishonest.

Then there was Faenius Rufus. The emperor had thought it clever to divide the office of Praetorian Prefect between Tigellinus and Rufus, but one of the two apples was rotten, and it was not the lesser of the two.

And Lucan. In his bitterness at not being able to declaim the final books of his *Pharsalia* in public, because they contained a condemnation of the regime, he accused Nero of professional jealousy, forgetting that the emperor had lavished praise on his verse for as long as it had flattered him. When arrested Lucan would offer the pathetic spectacle of a man ready to denounce his own mother and all his friends to spare himself the unpleasantness of torture.

And Seneca, accomplice in murder by his discreet silence.

And senators such as the debauched Scaevinus and the high-living Quintianus, who were enraged at a few satirical verses of the emperor's. And ambitious knights, such as Senecio, Proculus and Natalis. And even a freedwoman who was a close confidante of Piso, the intriguer Epicharis, who was to strangle herself in a covered litter, with the band of her bra, between two interrogation sessions.

Along with plenty of others, all of them were, or would be, in the plot.

Kaeso was received in a very friendly fashion. Satria Galla, Piso's much-loved, depraved wife, whom he had taken off one of his obliging friends, even gave up her place beside the emperor to the seductive guest. The banquet had reached the last course.

Nero had drunk more than usual, perhaps because he was not in the mood for singing that evening. He apostrophized Kaeso with a pretended abruptness: 'So, you bad boy, there's nothing to which you won't stoop to move me to mercy? An amphitheatre is barely big enough for you to trumpet your despair. If all my friends were like you, we'd spend our whole time at *munera.*'

Kaeso went through the act of looking contrite.

Vitellius declared: 'You were too good to this rascal. We must clear the arena of people with aspirations like his. Personally, I gave the thumbs down – out of pure cruelty, of course, but also to prevent this insolent fellow's example being followed by every *augustianus* hoping for your favour.'

Nero was delighted, and had to admit it. 'Yes, I was too good to him. My virtuous people were demanding that impudence be punished, but I preferred to listen to my heart. Hasn't Seneca been preaching the merits of clemency to me for years?'

Seneca was gnawing a carrot in melancholy fashion and used this as an excuse for not answering. Public affairs were taking on a lunatic aspect, which discouraged all comment. The older the philosopher got, the more mysterious he found human nature. What was this fellow Kaeso, who had once come to see him on a tricky point of ethics, doing here?

The conversation became general. It was principally about the gigantic closing celebrations scheduled for the following evening on Agrippa's pool. Tigellinus had promised to organize the most enormous orgy in recorded history, and the event stirred the imagination. For days and days the emissaries of the talented and devoted Prefect had been trying to persuade, or bribe, a large number of still relatively young women of the Roman aristocracy, by means of promises, presents and even shadowy threats, to get them to agree to show their devotion to the Emperor by filling the brothels designated for them on the banks of the pool. Caligula had already taken a vicious pleasure in dishonouring the most virtuous wives of the *nobilitas*, and had not recoiled before the most cynical and scandalous acts of violence. Nero was more interested in the size of the operation. He wanted to do things on the grandest scale possible, and hence was bringing pressure to bear, by every technique of suggestion and persuasion, on all those who had virtually no reputation left to lose. Caligula had been mad. Nero was a moralist concerned with efficiency and high yield. In his hostility to the least trace of hypocrisy he wanted hundreds of women to give themselves up publicly to the sort of de-bauches in which up till then they had only been prepared to indulge behind closed doors. He wanted to expand the discreet promiscuity of the upper classes until it embraced the whole of the State. And fortunately for a sovereign whose views were so broad and so deep, there were many husbands, fathers and brothers at court prepared to put their shoulders to the wheel to ensure that the brothels were suitably filled and did not shame their august organizer. Of course, the professional prostitutes would not be forgotten at the fête. With unprecedented generosity, the emperor had even decreed that brothels should be free all the following evening throughout the city. Agrippa, in his long-ago days, had paid for baths and barbers: Nero was going one better.

Seneca reflected that this regiment of married women at the heart of an orgy of wild group sex was a new and rather disturbing factor, for the Hellenism on which the Emperor prided himself provided no model for anything of the kind. When it came to the infamous, Nero was beginning to manage on his own, without further reference to any past, be it Roman or foreign. Greece would be represented around Agrippa's pool and on its calm waters by a troop of carefully selected passive homosexuals.

The guests, who had drunk as much as Nero, were jokingly trying to persuade Seneca to send his wife Paulina to the brothel. The philosopher was gently protesting; 'She's too old, she couldn't manage it any more, she has such trouble with her sciatica . . .'

Kaeso felt that the conversation was taking place in some dream world. Only the jabs of pain in his leg brought him back to earth.

In the garden where the *triclinia* had been set out, a ravishing Leda appeared with her Olympian swan, which had perhaps benefited from patient instruction by Cethegus. After an admirably organized erotic exhibition, the sacred union took place . . . (Was the swan just pretending?) . . . and while the creature – whether satisfied or merely tricked – winged its way back to Olympus, Leda flexed all the prolific muscles of her most intimate anatomy and laid two enormous eggs. She immediately broke their shells and with a show of pious amazement took out the gilded statuettes of the two pairs of divine twins, Castor and Pollux, and Helen and Clytemnestra.

Kaeso was trying to whisper into Nero's ear, in a rather confused fashion, that his Selene was having problems with a donkey . . . a quite small one, but tenacious . . .

The emperor cut him short. 'I can't refuse you anthing. You spilled your blood for me. Send for some tablets, write what you like and you'll have the guarantee of my seal.'

Kaeso gave the order to release Selene immediately. He had to rub the words out several times, because his hand was trembling so much with joy.

Nero added: 'This Selene of yours will need to recover. Say that she is to be taken to the little house of Albinus Macedo, on the lower slopes of the Caelian. It's a part of an inheritance recently left to me. I'm delighted to put it at your disposal, to shelter this modest idyll of yours . . . What, in fact was the slave accused of?'

After a moment's silence Kaeso answered: 'She's supposed to have murdered my father. But she's innocent.'

'Those we love are always innocent. Anyway, if every murderer was condemned to death, where should I be? – I, who was obliged, alas, to kill both my wife and my mother?'

At this recurrent painful memory, the emperor's eyes became wet with tears. But he soon recovered, put his seal on the tablets, and ordered them to be taken to Tigellinus straight away, even if it meant waking him up. When Nero wanted to be obeyed on the instant, Tigellinus was the one man he could rely upon to do it.

Kaeso passionately kissed the beringed hand with its liberating seal, while the Master stroked his hair, as Marcia had once done.

Nero rose to his feet, heavily, made some amiable remarks to Piso and his wife, and even to Seneca and Lucan, then, after a last cup of refreshing wine, called for his litter and motioned to Kaeso to accompany him. His gait was rather tottering and his voice muzzy.

The huge litter, whose soft cushions were dimly lit by a nightlight, set off for the gardens of Epaphroditus, with an escort of gladiators and Praetorians, at the even rhythm of its twelve muscular bearers. A thin ray of moonlight came between two badly-drawn curtains.

Suddenly the emperor blew out the nightlight and threw himself on Kaeso, with all the awkwardness of a large, timid man who has had too much to drink. There followed a very strange and confused struggle on the cushions of the attractive litter. Nero had been utterly spoiled by the gods: he liked women, active men and passive ones, and had every means available to him to satisfy his whim of the moment whenever he chose. By day he hardly knew which way to turn. By night, after a drink or two, at the mercy of the movements of a swinging litter and in the arms of a partner who had more will than skill, the fundamental ambiguity of his sybaritic and sensual nature reached a peak, and his fleeting ideas and uncertain gestures contradicted each other. Sometimes in a treble voice he would beg: 'Take me, glory of the arena!'; at others he would threaten in masculine tones; 'Just wait and I'll screw you rigid, you randy rascal!'

Kaeso, half-stifled by the pawing of this affectionate overgrown boy, who dreamed only of being loved for his own sake, no longer knew what role he was supposed to play. When things seemed to have taken a precise turn one way or the other, the litter, which the bearers were having difficulty in controlling, would give a bump and take them back to square one.

At the crossroads of the Via Salaria and the Via Nomentana an over-worked cushion burst, and a cloud of feathers spread over the scene of the action, making any precise manoeuvre difficult. Out of breath, covered in feathers, absolutely done in, the sweating emperor collapsed on Kaeso's chest muttering a string of inconsequential words.

At the Porta Viminalis, drunken singing abruptly roused Nero. He coughed noisily, gave instructions to the bearers to stop and got out of the litter, with Kaeso holding him up. In the torch light they looked like two huge disorientated white swans.

The bearers tried to keep straight faces while they got the feathers off. The litter was given a rough clean-out, and the emperor, after vomiting against a wall, reinstalled himself in it. Despite the state of his leg Kaeso preferred to continue on foot, and asked the escort to slow down. His leg had perhaps saved his virtue, for on several occasions Nero had scrupled to push on, assuming that the groans of the wounded hero were the cries of a virgin in pain.

Kaeso was walking beside Spiculus, who had risen from the arena to become commanding officer of the gladiators in the imperial bodyguard: he was to be cut down by Galba for his fidelity to the last of the Julio-Claudians. Spiculus tactfully turned the conversation to Kaeso's fight, which he had watched from the *pulvinar*, and complimented him, as an expert, on his intelligent tactics, which deserved to have been more successful. Kaeso had the impression that some of the Praetorians had been looking at him a bit sideways, and commented on the fact to Spiculus, who answered contemptuously: 'They come from the country and are shocked by anything and everything. The only people who watch over the emperor without asking unnecessary questions are the Germans and the gladiators.'

They went into the gardens of Epaphroditus. At the door of the villa Nero seemed to have bucked up a little, and before going up to bed, he said to Kaeso, as he kissed him; 'Thank you for what you have just done for me. I shall never forget it.' It was not at all clear what he was referring to. The wine must have confused his memory.

Kaeso was exhausted. He spent the night in a comfortable room, where he slept a deep and dreamless sleep. Birdsong awoke him. He imagined Selene waking at the same moment in the little house on the Caelian, full of gratitude and ready to love him. The events of the night before came back to him, and the emperor's last words gave him an idea for a ruse which Ulysses would have envied. After tidying himself up, he asked to be admitted into Nero's presence. The emperor was still in bed but was already dictating his correspondence. He made a sign to his secretaries to withdraw, and Kaeso threw himself on the foot of the bed.

'Divine Lord, since our return I have been haunted by remorse which prevented me from sleeping. Will you ever forgive me for having done you violence with such discourteous alacrity? Is it a sufficient excuse that I had been waiting for the moment for so long? Please say that I haven't upset you, and that you're still my friend despite my gladiatorial manners.'

A shadow of perplexity crossed the august brow. But the emperor had no reason to mistrust Kaeso, and, when it came to it, he was not put out to be rescued from such disagreeable doubt so easily. He gave his hand for the repentant boy to kiss and said, with a severity to which his dreamy blue gaze gave the lie: 'You deserve that I should dismiss you. And that's what I shall do ... until this evening, when you're to meet me by Agrippa's pool.'

Kaeso did not wait to be told twice. He hurried off to the Caelian, much comforted by the success of his manoeuvre. In this sort of affair, it was important to get off on the right footing. With Nero's very ticklish honour satisfied so cheaply, Kaeso would perhaps pass into the ranks of honorary lover sooner than he had foreseen. There were so many people vying for the Prince's favours ...

The little house crouching inside its little garden near the foot of the Caelian was charming. Tigellinus, who was ever zealous, had put seven slaves of the imperial *familia* at Selene's service, and she was already relaxing in the modest but well-fitted baths, next to the kitchen. While waiting for her to emerge, Kaeso glanced around the ground floor and the single floor above, which were very well furnished, and asked the names of the servants of both sexes, who seemed of good quality.

Selene soon joined Kaeso in a bedroom under the eaves, and fell at his knees with the most ardent expressions of gratitude. Kaeso hastened to raise her to her feet. She was thinner, there were dark circles around her eyes, and she had never seemed more touching. Sitting on the bed, hand in hand, they told each other at great length all they had been through and all their hopes and fears in the course of those terrible days. Selene was very amused by the trick which Kaeso had played on Nero. Kaeso finally raised the question dearest to his heart:

'Since my father freed you in his will, the least I can do is to carry out his last wishes, but to do so, you need to be legally in my possession. Now, since the liabilities of the estate far outstrip its assets, at the moment you're in the power of the creditors. I shall have to buy them off before I can have any legal authority over you.'

'My money is at your disposal.'

'Rabbi Samuel wouldn't let go of it quickly. I must have enough of my own left to settle this business.'

'Is there no limit to your kindness?'

When all was said and done Kaeso thought it more courteous to sleep with Selene after she had been made a freedwoman. He spent the whole morning hurrying around to get the matter settled. First he managed to get the trembling Turpilius to cough up. Then he paid off the syndicate of creditors, who were only too pleased to take 6,000 sesterces in cash for a slave who might be physically exquisite, but who had been convicted of the murder of her master and had thereby become virtually unsaleable. Finally he went and had Selene entered among the freedmen on the Census registers, in the Atrium of Liberty near the Porta Sanqualis. It was the simplest way of giving a slave complete and irrevocable freedom, though it could also be done by appearing before a consul or praetor, or by will. Wills could also be used to get one's own back on troublesome slaves, since the dead owner could forbid their liberation for a period of fifteen or twenty years. The other methods of granting freedom, by the written or oral testimony of a certain number of friends, or by the old ceremony of officially admitting the slave to the master's table, only created a freedom which could be revoked. Anyway, plenty of masters ate on familiar terms with their slaves without the latter being freed as a consequence.

The news of her definitive freedom threw Selene into a state of extraordinary delight, which Kaeso found very moving. She was very pleased with the idea that her value as a slave had collapsed as a direct result of her conviction for murder. While she was taking the precaution of gradually choking Marcus with her foot, a vengeful Providence had been lowering the value of her charms. How good of Yahwe it was to improvise like that, using such fine symbols.

After lunch Kaeso and Selene went upstairs and lay down side by side. It was siesta time, the right moment for so devoted a lover to enjoy at last those rights of ownership which, having had them in his possession for a mere three quarters of an hour, he had, with great tact and sensitivity, so promptly abandoned. Selene put up with his advances with amiable patience, but lay there with her legs together, as if she were on the cross, and did not return his kisses. An immense, and very surprising, sorrow rapidly filled her magnificent grey eyes with bitter tears.

'What's the matter? I can see you aren't weeping for joy.'

Selene answered in one breath: 'Don't touch me. I'm a Christian. I've been baptized.'

Kaeso was shattered. Selene explained:

'Christianity is a religion which most Jews have only a partial, not to say caricatured, knowledge of. As a result of your own efforts to get to know its doctrines, which you wanted to pretend to adopt so as to mislead your father about your real reasons for disappointing him, I became better acquainted with it. And I realized that all I had ever been told about the Christians was untrue.

In the Ostia *vivarium* a handsome old man with a white beard, who had been a slave since the cradle, used to bring me my soup and empty my bucket. It was also his job to rub between my legs with secretions of she-ass on heat, to keep up the large Calabrian donkey's appetite. He was full of brotherly tact, and regularly turned his head away as he did it. And he always took care to say a word of encouragement and comfort to me as he took his equipment away. What a contrast he made with Cethegus. That brute, I can now confess to you, was perversely turned on by your chaste and only too short visits. As soon as you'd gone, he would abuse my charms, or what was left of them.

I would have guessed from the pleasant old man's exquisite manners that he might be a Christian, even if he hadn't told me so himself, to make me stop crying. There's something more unbending and chilly about Jewish charity. The fear of committing an impurity sometimes paralyses the most generous impulses in a Jew. The old man's humble visits continued to trouble me. I was afraid of the emotion they aroused, and yet at the same time I was longing for them. Perhaps grace had already entered me via that ambiguous female organ, whose attractive mouth, with its V for victory or viper's head, is the source and recipient of all the best and worst in a woman's life.

One night, after – thanks to you – my donkey had shrunk, I had an incredible experience. While I was imploring heaven to come to my aid, I suddenly saw a luminous cross on the back of the virgin donkey-foal. At first it lit the whole stable, then it gradually grew fainter and fainter until it was like a glow-worm, and eventually it disappeared. It was like a dream, but the memory of the dream refused to fade.

Up to that moment I'd thought that the idea that a god could have died for me was utterly absurd. Now it struck me in all its indescribable obviousness. The light of the Resurrection reaches right into the heart of the most abject prisons, to remind the most despairing of sinners that all flesh purified by the cross is promised to eternal glory.

Since all your efforts to help might come to nothing, there was a good chance that I'd suffer an ignoble death. The fact that I was still racked by this threat must have favoured my conversion. Nonetheless, I'm still surprised by it. Shortly before the soldiers were due to come for me, to shut me up in a building adjoining the theatre, I asked the obliging old man to baptize me. At that very moment you were fighting for me in front of Nero. I felt certain that the baptism would bring us both luck, whether in this earthly vale of tears or in the new Heaven.

Now that I've been freed from sin by Christ and from involuntary association with infamy by your enlightened help, I shan't hesitate to say to you: henceforward, look on me as a loving sister, who would be delighted if you shared her faith. The act you had to put on must surely have left some trace of the truth in you, mustn't it? If it's ordained that your blindness should continue and you're troubled by vulgar temptations, send for Myra at once. I'm not jealous. My deepest love is no longer vowed to this world.'

Kaeso's mind was in a state of upheaval. It was certainly not out of the question that Selene had profited by his example, and was using Christian self-denial as an excellent argument for tactfully preserving a freedom dear to her. But, like all really good liars, the freedwoman had achieved a moving air of sincerity. She had contrived to give her account those little touches which are not realistic, and yet give the deceptive impression that they could not have been invented. Kaeso was not attracted by the prospect of se_ching the Ostia game preserve to check on the existence of a handsome white-bearded old Christian, with a talent for anointing a woman's crutch. Love made him trusting. He began to talk of marriage.

At first Selene treated the proposal with sympathy. Her reservations consequently made all the more impression.

'If you're really fond of me, don't tempt me like that. You're young, handsome, noble, the emperor's favour smiles on you, and you're sure to find an advantageous marriage with a young girl as the finishing touch to your good fortune. Nobles do sometimes discreetly set up house with a

676

woman who has recently been freed. They never marry one. Just think of the sort of life I've led, all the men I've been forced to sleep with, the last of whom was none other than your own father. Do you like the thought of incest? The fact that it took a more or less official form would make it all the more serious. Who would you dare introduce your wife to, if you married a woman older than you, whose reputation was indelibly stained by her experience of the brothel and of an unmentionable liaison? If I were weak enough to agree to marriage, you would soon be reproaching me for it. And you'd be right. I must act sensibly for both of us.'

Far from convinced, though disturbed by her arguments, Kaeso made unsuccessful loving protestations, then resigned himself to going and finding Myra. He could not in any case simply abandon her in the nearby *ludus*.

Before leaving the barracks Kaeso insisted on thanking Pugnax for having avoided taking off his forearm. The Swiss made this striking remark: 'If your profession is violence, you don't like pointless violence. It's amateurs who go in for cruelty.' Kaeso felt that such a fine sentiment ought not to go unrewarded. He gave Pugnax 10,000 sesterces. The Swiss took it without a fuss and said: 'A disinterested gesture is beyond price, and so is a free man's arm. I'll take this money as an advance on a commission.' Unfortunately there was no one left whom Kaeso wanted murdered.

In his absence, large quantities of clothing and various presents had been delivered for him from the palace, and Myra proudly showed them to him. Nero never wore the same clothes twice, and he liked to encourage wastefulness in his entourage, saying that it was good for trade. He had consciously adopted the opposite attitude to that of all the old Roman moralists, who had learnt from the earth that good harvests are followed by bad, and therefore preached the virtues of thrift and restraint. Selene, for her part, pursed her mouth and looked at the wages of sin with the air of moral superiority appropriate to a Christian virgin who needs no more than the providential veil of her long hair to hide her charms.

A message had arrived that a litter would come for him at the eleventh hour. Kaeso got a Jewish surgeon to renew the dressing on his wound, dressed in Greek style, punctually installed himself in the litter and set off to the feast. Although Selene saw luminous crosses on the backs of theatrical donkeys, she had as yet no confidence in Christian surgeons. Admittedly, the Christians were more interested in last moments, or in resurrections. They liked to have the last word.

On the way Kaeso saw that the whole of Rome was getting ready to celebrate. A monstrous banquet, such as not even Caesar himself had ever given, was to be held in various of the city squares.

The only tiny shadow in this climate of joy under a brilliant blue sky was the rather disturbing growing shortage of water. The heat and drought had reduced the Tiber to a filthy ribbon unwillingly flowing between two heaps of rubbish which the drop in the water level had uncovered. The quantity of water brought by the aqueducts, which had been expanded and extended for centuries, was also dropping in an alarming fashion. The Marcia, the Anio, the Tepula, the Julia, which came from the mountains of Latium or Sabine country, now delivered only a very inadequate quantity of water: the Virgo and the Appia, drawn from the nearby Roman countryside, were almost dry; the Alsietina, which furnished the Janiculum quarter with water from Etruria, had kept a reasonable flow, but the three Claudian springs, once so pure, and Nero's aqueduct, which had been added to complete the supply to the Caelian, now only yielded occasional, muddy water. There had not been such a shortage for six or seven years, and old men were calculating on their fingers and comparing all the 'dry' years they had known.

The shortage, however, was partly artificial, for Tigellinus had carefully persuaded the Imperial Council that they should profit from this exceptional reduction in flow to carry out all sorts of repairs at reduced cost. The far-sighted Nero had supported the proposals.

Tigellinus was having the time of his life. Indeed he hardly had time for life at all. He was too busy doing three things at once: arranging unforgettable celebrations, preparing to burn down the city, and planning all the emergency measures which would allow the emperor to appear a diligent saviour after the catastrophe. The fire was merely to be a somewhat unpleasant intermediary between the benefactions of yesterday and those of the morrow, between the still rather constricted pleasures of the past and those of the future, which would sate every possible sense. Never had a minister been charged with such a responsibility. Tigellinus knew it, and was proud of the fact.

This pride had its source in his inmost being. Tigellinus was a knight by birth. But two quite different sorts of knight had emerged from the hard-working people: business men who farmed out indirect taxes and looked no further than their immediate profits; and the Civil Service knights who had got into all sorts of aspects of administration, with a success which derived in part from the fact that they were the only competent people between a senatorial class which wanted to do absolutely nothing and an uneducated *plebs* which was incapable of doing absolutely anything. But the administrative knights nonetheless kept up dealings with the *plebs* from which they had come, and had maintained a number of friends and connections among them. The habit of public affairs, and the experience of a civil service which paid great attention to the requirements of hierarchy, had given them a sense of the State as an entity and a taste for planning the future. Whereas the upper echelons of the aristocracy had idly assimilated themselves to Rome in order to pillage it, the Tigellinuses worked hard and pillaged relatively little. The administrative knights had reached the top of their class, and the majority of them were likely to remain there for a long time. So that there was every reason for them to nurture a violent prejudice against the hereditary aristocracy, and this prejudice, under the pressure of disinterested or envious feelings, was capable of developing into hatred. Tigellinus detested the Senate as strongly as Nero mistrusted it. This community of outlook and sensibility formed a strong bond between the two men. Torturing an aristocrat was a real treat for the Praetorian Prefect. He always greatly regretted the far-sighted suicides which condemned his henchmen to a certain degree of inactivity.

Thus, for Tigellinus burning down lots of palaces belonging to the *nobilitas* in between provocative celebrations, and a lengthy rebuilding programme in which the State would have the final say, was an act of piety, which flattered all his instincts, good and bad. He had tried to foresee every eventuality, according the fire a privileged place in his calculations, for his destiny and the emperor's were intimately linked. Day after day he had found ways of lessening the water flow, of sowing disorder among the units of the Watch, of recruiting a small number of accomplices who would be forced to keep their mouths shut for ever by the, to them, unexpected scale of the catastrophe. He had selected the most favourable points for the 'action', and had even worked out how to protect a small number of monuments. It was particularly important to save the temple of Jupiter Capitolinus, because it would be impossible to get the considerable treasures which it housed out of the way before the critical time without people talking.

Tigellinus was well aware that after a coup of that sort, his fate would be inextricably tied to the emperor's. But he had confidence in the regime's ability to keep the Senate under control, and the great fire could only be a help in this respect. The hypothesis that Nero would try to get rid of him he found implausible. Nero only killed out of fear, and was not ungrateful to those who served him intelligently and effectively. On this last point the future was to prove him right.

Once again Kaeso found Agrippa's Pool unrecognizable. With a swiftness which seemed almost magical the gardens and copses had been cleaned up. The rows of tiered wooden seats to the north and south had been replaced by an army of tables and couches, where the bulk of the guests were to sit. And on the banks of the pool, a vast gold and ivory covered raft, reserved for the emperor and his friends, was waiting to float out. It was to be drawn by gracious galleys, whose oarsmen had been recruited from an unexpected quarter. To cock a snook at the traditionalists in the Senate, Tigellinus had recruited exclusively gay crews. Sodomy was a seaman's speciality, since women stayed in port, but that secret had never been revealed with such blinding cynicism. All these queens, garlanded with flowers, were chattering as they awaited their Master's arrival.

Important guests were already queuing in front of the raft, among them a group of Vestals, including, Kaeso noticed, Rubria. Another surprise. Since most women tolerated cruelty much more readily than lewdness, the Vestals normally only went to the amphitheatres and Circuses. On rare occasions they might attend the theatres, if the violence was devoid of sex. But the respect due to them made it impossible to invite them to shows which would make them blush.

Kaeso greeted Rubria, thanked her for having raised her thumb in his favour, and they chatted for a moment in a desultory fashion, while guests of all ranks thronged along the banks or in the approaches to the raft. Rubria seemed ill at ease, either because Kaeso's charm or his reputation were having an effect on her, or because the preparations for the fête were of a kind to disturb her sense of decency. For years the rumour had periodically gone round the city that this or that Vestal had a lover, but the authorities had given up taking such things seriously, and everyone was satisfied when suitable discretion on the part of the suspects allowed them to be given the benefit of the doubt.

Rubria kept glancing nervously round at the effeminate crews, whose nature ought, logically, to have quietened her fears. Kaeso whispered to her: 'Rumour has it that this reception is going to end in an unbridled orgy. Nero said to me as recently as yesterday evening: "I've had enough of the Vestals' hypocrisy. Tigellinus has persuaded me that they should be regularly examined by midwives. It's the only practical way to be sure of their virtue." The first examination is to take place this evening after the dessert. Vestals worthy of the name will be taken home with all honours before the whole thing turns into an orgy. The others – if there are any, that is – will be kept and buried alive under the weight of handsome, lively boys.'

Rubria gave a start. With a Nero, and a Tigellinus to advise him, anything might happen. When Kaeso smiled mockingly at her, she blushed at having started so naïvely, and said furiously: 'You're the one who should be buried like that,' and turned her back on him.

Nero was arriving with a small escort of Germans, to general acclaim. The great open litter stopped before the gangplank leading to the raft, the emperor got out and gave the signal for the 'embarkation to Cythera' to the accompaniment of a musical aperitif. As soon as the passengers were in place beneath the awning of azure silk, the young rowers chosen for the occasion flexed their feeble muscles and the raft slowly left the bank, stirring in its majestic path a plish-plash of tiny waves and a light breeze, as gentle as the caress of an amateur galley-slave.

By a bizarre and scandalous departure from the norm which had caused an enormous sensation, the dark, handsome Pythagoras, a priest of Cybele and the emperor's official lover, had taken the best place on the *triclinium*. Nero, swathed in filmy material, was reclining 'below' him. To Kaeso this extraordinary sight was, if anything, reassuring.

There was nothing else memorable about the meal. The Greek pleasure of elevated conversation, which had for Kaeso been the sole point of interest at all the banquets in Athens, was impossible in such a noisy crowd, who had come to eat in anticipation of better things. Kaeso was not at the emperor's *triclinium* but at another, between Vespasian, whose conversation was pretty dull, and a very young man of senatorial rank, P. Cornelius Tacitus. This Tacitus was apparently making his debut in high society, and seemed as much worried as excited by the prospect of the disorders which were to follow. He would have liked to visit the aristo-cratic brothels on the west bank, but was afraid that he might run into one of his maternal aunts. He was by nature a man of taste and discretion, and was repelled by the prospect of the common prostitutes who had been distributed among the little houses opposite. Kaeso pointed out to him, with a certain logic, that in a profusion of naked women social distinctions ceased to have much importance. In fact the equality preached by the Christians could just as well be obtained by the global practice of total shamelessness.

As darkness was falling over the gardens of Agrippa, the nautical feast came to an end, amid singing and laughter, on the brightly lit raft. The two villages of debauchery had also lit their lamps, but the decorative furry and feathered animals with which Tigellinus had stocked the pool and gardens had innocently done their copulation in the sunshine, and were now looking for a place to sleep. As the raft got nearer and nearer to the senatorial brothel, the prostitutes from its plebeian counterpart began to crowd in increasing numbers along the other bank in the simplest of clothing, and their plaintive invitations came wafting across the water, attracting the attention of those guests who had been feasting around the pool and were waiting impatiently for the imperial raft to come ashore. This was to be the signal for the rush for the spoils to begin. Eventually the prestigious craft moored in front of the chalets where the women of good society were waiting inside – a last concession to decency – and Nero set foot ashore, preceded by the inverts from the tow-boats and followed by his favoured guests. A great cry went up from the rutting crowd, and utter chaos of the most pornographic sort was unleashed everywhere.

Like a flock of frightened sheep the Vestals, with Rubria at their head, came hurrying over to Kaeso and asked him to extricate them from this collective madness. Rubria clung on to his arm, and begged him insistently for his help. Kaeso took a torch from the hands of a servant and tried to guide the women towards the exit, against the current of the incoming crowd. It was a very difficult manoeuvre to attempt in the midst of such disorder. Despite all his efforts he lost Vestal after Vestal, and soon there was only Rubria left. She had lost her distinctive headdress and her red hair was gleaming like fire in the fitful light of the torch. To get out of the press he thought it best to cut through the woods, but there the torch ran out of combustible material and went out. In the pale moonlight Rubria clung despairingly to him. He put his arms around her to reassure her and they fell down on to the thick scented carpet of green pine-needles.

Rubria had already lost her virginity. Kaeso scolded her.

'It was Caligula,' she admitted in tears. 'He raped me like a savage the very day he picked me. I was ten years old.'

That damned Caius! Was there nothing he wouldn't do?

At the entry to the gardens Rubria found her litter and thanked Kaeso for having protected a virtue which needed to remain permanently above suspicion. Kaeso was about to go home when Tigellinus came up. He had come to run a critical eye over the results of his work, and perhaps also to have a little fun, for he was a great womanizer who also had a taste for boys. One day when he was torturing a servant of Octavia, to force her to confess her mistress's supposed depravities, the girl had spat out in his face: 'Octavia's genitals are purer than your mouth!' The spicy little story had gone the rounds of the whole city. Even torturers were sometimes indiscreet.

Kaeso could not leave the fête so early under the eye of the Prefect. He even had to go up to his litter, greet him and thank him for everything he had just done to help him. Tigellinus amiably invited him to sit beside him, and the litter headed for the heart of the tightly-packed crowd.

After congratulating Kaeso on his exemplary fighting Tigellinus asked him what he thought of the evening, and Kaeso answered:

'Since you share my devotion to Nero's true interests, I must speak the truth to you as I see it, rightly or wrongly. Whatever you do, you'll never persuade the majority of the Senate to collaborate with the regime. But why feed the hypocrisy of this irreducible group and discourage those who might otherwise join you, or at least remain neutral, with gratuitous excesses like these? Without agreeing with those moralists who would call them a crime, it's prudent politics to see them, quite simply, as a mistake. Don't you know that you can't change morals by decree? It's as pointless to attempt to precipitate immorality as to restrain it, the way Augustus in his sober old age tried to do. Surely every man lives at his own rhythm, a prisoner of his upbringing, which weighs heavily on him but is still the most effective reference point in a moment of crisis? As you've just seen, I had to escort a panicking Vestal out. How long is Rome going to put up with this sort of serious attack on her traditions? Your boldness frightens me, for the emperor as much as for yourself.'

Tigellinus kept silent for a long moment, and Kaeso thought he had offended him. But he roused himself and said: 'I entirely agree with you. Rome can't tolerate for more than a few days what's going on tonight. It would sooner disappear. But until then I must follow Christian principles.'

After Selene's prodigious revelation Tigellinus' took the miracle to its ultimate. Kaeso's astonishment made the Prefect think that the boy had never heard of the Christians. Tigellinus confessed to him; 'They are a more or less Jewish sect of no great importance, but I've been given what purport to be the words of their founder, a fellow called Jesus whom Pontius Pilate, before he got killed, sent to the gibbet in the reign of Tiberius. It's absolutely crazy the amount I have to read in order to keep public order. Well, I must admit that what this Jesus had to say made a deep impression on me. Philosophers are in the habit of anathematizing vice and lauding virtue to the skies on their way between two brothels. Jesus stands out from the ruck in a unique manner. Instead of wasting his time attacking vice, an activity which had never yielded any fruit, he pardons sinners except for one class: hypocrites. Tonight's feast must

683

give him a lot of pleasure, and I shall remind him of it if I ever have the honour of meeting him.'

Kaeso argued that, as far as he knew, Jesus was equally against scandal, but Tigellinus said to him laughingly: 'For form's sake, only for form's sake. As hypocrisy is a sin which can't be forgiven, it's difficult to be virtuous without hypocrisy, while the most glaring sins, which can still be pardoned, protect you for certain from this dangerous vice.'

As the litter approached the pool, it was having difficulty making its way through an excited throng of people who would never have been found guilty of hypocrisy. Roman matrons with their breasts dangling and their hair streaming in the wind, their faces streaked with the overflow of their debauchery, were fleeing from the houses with an insatiable pack at their heels. The tufts of dark hair standing out on their naked bodies looked like so many wild rabbits scampering around the gardens. Young galley slaves on a spree were obscenely groping the Prefect's tall Nubian porters, who were consequently allowing the litter to pitch and toss like a drunken pleasure boat.

They had to get out. Tigellinus guided Kaeso to the doorway of a house and invited him in: 'Come along, together the two of us will besiege and screw the frigid Senate.'

When Kaeso found an excuse not to come in, Tigellinus seized him by the ear; 'Bloody hypocrite. You're tired because you've just had Rubria in the bushes. Watch out for the good Jesus!'

Kaeso was caught off guard and defended himself without conviction. Tigellinus' policeman's nose was astonishing. The emperor owed it to him that he was still alive.

The Prefect shrugged his shoulders and went in alone.

Kaeso, who felt drained, was free to go home and sleep.

✥ CHAPTER ✥
4

Kaeso lingered a moment, rather like one of those travellers who have difficulty tearing their eyes away from a view because they doubt whether they will ever have a chance to see it again. After the first burst of enthusiasm the celebrations had taken on a more relaxed pace. There was no more screaming; people were trying to get their breath back.

Beside the pool Kaeso bumped into Eunomos, whom Tigellinus had made responsible for recruiting the inverts for the galleys. The apocalyptic preacher had had to select them, arrange them on the benches by height, skin colour and even speciality, so as to avoid pointless disputes as far as possible, and offer the most peaceful and decorative of sights. Though well inured to Nero's fantasies, his disgust and exasperation were extreme, and he was feeling particularly desperate because all his efforts to get transferred to different work had been in vain. Before his abrupt conversion he had made the emperor and Tigellinus dependent on his excellent service, and he could not now neglect his task on the pretext that a new god had told him to do so.

At the sight of Kaeso Eunomos' face became inscrutable. While Peter and his immediate entourage were still in the dark about the depravities of this highly suspect Christian, someone in Eunomos' position could hardly avoid being in the know. But the first attribute of a slave, even a rich one, was to be polite. So it was Kaeso who tried to justify himself in a few phrases, before he had even received the slightest reproach.

'Like you, my poor Eunomos, I've had to prostitute my talents and even my body. Not, it's true, to save my life, but to guarantee the safety of someone dear to me . . . and even the life of someone else who was less so. We've both drunk from the same cup of bitterness.'

'Enough said. It's not for me to pass judgement on you. Enjoy the evening while you can. The fire from Heaven is close and it will sweep away all this filth. Then shall there be weeping and wailing and gnashing of teeth. Remember what happened to Sodom.'

'I can't. I was too young at the time. But let me give you a piece of friendly advice. Since you're willing to leave it to God to judge me, why don't you also leave it to him to judge the world – and to fix the date for the judgement? You know that there are always fires in Rome. If the Christians pray for fire and rejoice at every catastrophe which a vengeful God sends in punishment, they'll end up by getting themselves accused of being responsible. People will say that, if there's no smoke without fire, there's no fire without a Christian.'

'Jesus predicted that there would be great persecutions against us. I'm ready for them.'

'Jesus didn't say you should do everything possible to bring them down on your own heads. I'll bet that to get yourself out of the indescribable situation which your burning virtue finds itself exposed to you would, without actually looking for martyrdom, be relieved and grateful if it came your way.'

'How can you doubt it?'

'Your own words condemn you, and unfortunately they risk condemning many others, less innocent than you perhaps, but who are weak enough to cling to life.'

'For all the respect which I owe to a gladiator who is an intimate friend of Nero, you'll forgive me if I express surprise at your remarks.'

'Instead of being surprised by good sense, take your example from Jesus, who frequently slipped out of the hands of those who wished him ill and only let himself be captured at the hour fixed by his Father. Or take your example from Paul, who's always looked after his own skin by a relentless insistence on procedural niceties. Even a life which has received scandalous publicity at the hands of an imperial artist in a public garden is still worth living on the whole. Your suicidal mentality does not conform with the instructions of the Gospel. I find it particularly worrying because I myself, who have no vocation for suicide, risk being compromised sooner or later by your inflammatory linguistic excesses. Commit suicide if you must, but try not to take everyone else with you.'

'How attached to the things of this world you are!'

'If God took the trouble to make it, it can't be as bad as all that. You're as pessimistic as a Hindu I knew. And he had more reason than you to be bitter: he ended up on the cross, a martyr to bad luck for which he had no responsibility.'

'Oh come, just look around you . . .'

A lady came titupping up, surrounded by four enormous Germans, who were making a rampart around her with their bodies. Who could possibly need their virtue protected in such a manner on a night like this? The answer was Sporus. The eunuch seemed upset. He kept wiping his eyes with a handkerchief which he drew from the wide sleeve of his dress. Seeing Kaeso he stopped: Eunomos bowed deeply and discreetly withdrew.

'You're awfully well guarded this evening.'

'I have to be. These days no attractive person can go out in the streets without being importuned.'

The statement, which was clearly not intended to be funny, showed a remarkable lack of awareness, given the context.

'And what's the cause of your touching sadness?'

'How can you ask? Don't you know that my prince is getting married?'

'But I thought that Poppaea . . .?'

'Oh, she'll only be a witness. This is to be a real marriage, a marriage between two men. Pythagoras is marrying Nero the day after tomorrow at Antium. The ceremony will have everything. They're going to consult the auspices, the emperor will have the flaming veil of a young bride on his head, they'll be escorted with torches to the nuptial bed, and he'll shriek just like a young bride used to in the old days. Nero is determined to be married in the town where he was born.'

However extravagant the concept, such a piece of news had the virtue of being in a certain sense in harmony with the night's celebrations.

Kaeso tried to console Sporus:

'Since Pythagoras is one of the emperor's favourite lovers, a match of that sort doesn't give him much more than he already has, and doesn't take anything away from you. I'd have expected you to have got over that sort of jealousy.'

'It's nothing to do with jealousy. It's a question of honour!'

Sporus was very concerned about honour. After the tragic death of his master, rather than expose himself to unhealthy curiosity on the stage, he was to prefer to commit a discreet suicide.

'And how does it affect your precious honour?'

'Nero had given me to believe that I should be the first to be married. Now he has promised me that I shall be able to take the marriage veil during the Greek trip, but that doesn't alter the fact that I shall be second.'

At the pinnacle of progress, having invented the homosexual marriage, and wanting, with a very Greek concern for balance, to sacrifice to both the active and the passive joys of hymen, Nero had had to solve the problem of knowing which marriage should precede which. The problem was all the more thorny for there being no precedent, no manual of etiquette to offer a possible solution. Inspired innovators often find themselves faced with problems of this calibre.

'Well,' observed Kaeso, 'one of them had to happen before the other. If Nero had married you both at the same time, what could he decently have worn? It's difficult to imagine a wedding garb which was masculine in front and feminine behind. Be a bit reasonable.'

'Elementary gallantry should have ensured that I had first place. When people go to dinner with a gay couple, they give the flowers to the wife.'

'What arguments did the emperor put forward for inflicting this cruel disappointment on you?'

'He said to me: "I have good reasons for consummating the union which, of the two, shows the greatest contempt for all the stupid Roman traditions. In a little while people will inevitably think differently."'

'So as far as he was concerned there was a political element in the choice. That ought to be a comfort to you.'

Sporus dabbed at his eyes again. His make-up had run on to his cheeks. Kaeso pointed the fact out to him and helped him tidy it up.

'How kind you are to take an interest in me. I feel so lonely.'

With four body guards watching over him, in the midst of a crowd in the grip of elementary lusts, poor Sporus felt lonely. The heart had its own turmoils, to which the flesh was oblivious.

Somewhat pacified Sporus said to Kaeso: 'I have a disappointing piece of news for you, which I'm sorry about. Just now when I was bitterly reproaching Nero for making an exhibition of himself with Pythagoras, he said to me: "You're not the only one in trouble. Kaeso was a terrible disappointment to me. Since I can't remember at all what he did to me during that obscure pillow fight, I can be excused for thinking that he isn't very good at it. He's still my friend, and my doors are still open to him, but he won't be coming to Antium."'

Kaeso had great trouble in looking touchingly upset. Sporus took him by the arm in a friendly way and confided: 'Never mind, there are 500,000 sesterces for you to pick up from the Paymaster General. My charming prince is still generous even to those who fail to please him. But money shouldn't be everything in this world. Those who are most faithful to Nero – and I hope you'll be one of them – are often those who have the least. In any case, this failure should be a lesson to you. Even the most banal of love acts can't be improvised in a cloud of feathers, still less the kind of finesse needed between a love and his beloved, since that takes one out of the realm of common sexual relations where animal instinct serves as a guide. If you'd had a little experience in my arms, you'd have had rather more success.'

Kaeso bewailed the fact that it was too late. 'I feel that the career in which I'd have shone has come to an abrupt stop.'

'It's never too late to learn and improve.'

'Those four magnificent hunks you have with you will give you more pleasure than an apprentice.'

'But I'm afraid of them . . .'

Kaeso had great difficulty in shaking Sporus off. He left the pool and headed for the exit, stepping more and more gaily out as he realised how happy he was to have escaped from the emperor's attentions without the least quarrel. Since the extravagances of the regime risked bringing it crashing down sooner or later, it was in any case preferable not to be seen among the emperor's most constant companions.

Kaeso rested for a moment under an arbour, where a senator and a catamite were sleeping, wrapped in the folds of the same *toga praetexta*. A strange thought, in which Nero and Jesus mingled, struck him.

Creative passion inevitably leads the artist to despise all tradition, since the artist who believes in himself is condemned to leave the beaten track and constantly invent new forms. Where art is concerned, once all dubious criteria are set aside, only one type of judgement commands instant acceptance: this is a copy, this is new. The true artist, whether he likes it or not, is a revolutionary to the core. Nero was a typical improviser living in a state of permanent revolution, always looking beyond what had satisfied the lazy supporters of routine and repetition.

Jesus also claimed to have brought something new, but his was a once-and-for-all innovation, since he was god, and therefore had no time for researching and retouching. In a few phrases he had smashed the traditions of the Jews, the most traditional race on earth, and had proposed a revolutionary truth to all mankind, with no tradition behind it.

Nero – in the name of forms and what could be perceived by the senses – and Jesus – in the name of the invisible – had linked hands to abolish the past. Each had taken his system to its logical end. Between the demands of these two irreconcilable enemies was there a middle term, a zone of calm and reason for men of good will? Or would Jesus and Nero fight it out until vice or virtue definitively triumphed, drawing more and more troops, who were less and less orderly, into their battle of ideals as the generations passed?

In any case, between Nero and Jesus there was a similarity which threatened to make the conflict eternal: the beautiful and the ugly were not susceptible to proof; neither was the Resurrection. Men only fight vigorously for causes which go beyond all experience.

Kaeso thought for a long time. Nero disgusted him and Jesus disturbed him. It was possible, even probable, given the excessive nature of the two pretenders, that their war would come to nothing or only be a flash in the pan. The important thing was to stay prudently on the sidelines.

The air had acquired a certain chill, which announced the approach of dawn. The senator awoke for a brief instant and covered the shoulders of his boy, who was shivering, with a free end of his toga.

Along an adjacent walk Cethegus and one of his assistants, leading a billy-goat, were walking towards the city. The animal seemed tired and was pulling on its rope. More human than rams, billy-goats, like dogs, could be abused by expert women. Tigellinus, with his thirst for perfection, had seen to it that degraded women in pursuit of new sensations should have everything at their disposal. Selene had once recounted to Kaeso that, in nomadic tribes in the East and Egypt, the women slept with their goats when the men were at the pastures, while the latter would from time to time find relief in the vertiginous vaginas of mares on heat. And she had claimed that the Jewish custom of chasing into the desert a goat bearing the burden of the sins of the people of Israel had its distant origins in the bestial indulgence of too often neglected Jewish women. Of course, it was always the women who were in the wrong. And it cost less to sacrifice a goat than a mare.

Kaeso nearly ran up to Cethegus to ask him about the handsome white-bearded old man, but he was ashamed of his mistrustful curiosity, and stayed put. When it came to it, he was afraid to be told what he already knew only too well: Selene did not love him and probably never would. There was a curse on him. The object of ardent desire throughout Greece and Rome, he had had to refuse Marcia's great passion, and yet his own passion for Selene seemed fruitless. Was Heaven punishing him for having rejected Marcia and having refused to help his father by the derisory sacrifice which had finally served to prolong the useless existence of a creature like Cypris?

On his way back to the Caelian Kaeso reflected on love, and came to some new conclusions. The brightest and best sort of love was clearly that in which sex played no part. Jesus had said so, and Plato before him had sensed the same thing. It was therefore tempting to reduce physical love to its lowest and most banal forms of satisfaction. Surely all the unhappiness of lovers came from their attempts to make the matter-of-fact sublime, like people who made a fetish out of food, and, instead of simply eating, fell on their knees in front of a haunch of meat no different from any other. Where love was concerned, the old Roman traditions gave a lesson in simplicity and good sense to those capable of following it. Even so it was inconceivable that a girl such as Selene should dare to refuse a Kaeso indefinitely.

The unfortunate thing was that the young master no longer had any right to oblige the recalcitrant girl to have sex with him. True, freed-women were even less pampered by the law than their male counterparts. Like the latter they were obliged to respect their patron and perform all sorts of services for him. Their former master also served as the guardian legally responsible for their marriages and their will. The right to leave their property more or less as they wished had only been granted to mothers of four or more children, to encourage large families. But in principle freedwomen were free to sleep with whoever they liked. '*Dura lex, sed lex.*' The days were over when patrons had power of life and death over their freedmen.

Kaeso reached home at dawn. He wandered into the wrong room and found Selene and Myra asleep in each other's arms, a sight which might of course be entirely innocent but which put the final touches to his bad mood. The fact that Kaeso neglected Myra and Selene neglected him was not a reason for them to become as close as that!

Five days passed, during which the atmosphere in the house was op-pressive. Kaeso did not dare precipitate matters with Selene, and con-tented himself with throwing looks at her which alternated between the lustful and the fawning. Myra made herself even smaller than usual.

Selene, with impressive calm, played the role of the model freedwoman. She took the house in hand, and everything was in perfect order, even the food was excellent. She had not only a natural authority over the slaves but also the knowledge which comes from a long experience of all the tricks to which slaves are prone. She was everywhere and kept an eye on everything. Having once come across a valet with his hand feeling the obliging behind of a kitchen maid, she personally whipped the offending hand and bottom, to make it plain to everyone that working hours were sacred. Kaeso had nothing to do but get on with life, while Nero, in a see-through dress, was inaugurating the new era of conjugal homo-sexuality, which should have led to common or garden trigamy. For the emperor was no less interested in women. After the death of the pregnant Poppaea in the course of the following year, he was to marry Statilia Messina, who would philosophically serve as a witness, in Greece, at Nero's marriage with the amiable Sporus. If the fashion had spread, the lawyers would have had a field-day. In the meantime Kaeso had no wife, lover or boyfriend, and he was withering up from frustrated love.

On the morning of the XV of the Kalends of August, the anniversary of the disaster of Allia, which had let Brennus penetrate as far as the walls of the Capitol, it occurred to Kaeso to ask for the famous torque which Silanus had left him in his will. It turned out to be a barbarically beautiful necklace of interwoven gold bands. The object inspired bitter thoughts in him. What would Manlius Torquatus have done if a slave he had just freed had insolently refused to oblige him in any way? He was, after all, asking very little of a girl to whom, even if she lacked the feelings for him which she ought to have had, one man more or less could make very little difference.

Marcia too had asked very little of Kaeso, and had not got it. But Kaeso did not make the comparison. For the first time in his life he was walking blindly in the footsteps of his libidinous father.

On the excuse that it would be lacking in respect, Selene had obstinately refused to lie on the garden *triclinium* beside Kaeso. She would eat sitting up in a chair, which made it easier for her to keep an eye on the service. The refusal was not calculated to put Kaeso in a good mood. It made it plain that many others would follow.

Dinner on the XV was particularly gloomy. A torrid and tiring south wind had been blowing since midday, which had made them hesitate as to whether or not to eat in the garden. They had had to accumulate stores of water, because the hundreds of water-towers which regulated the flow in the city had become as capricious as they were inadequate. Myra, encouraged on the quiet by Selene, had paid careful attention to her appearance and tried to attract her master's attention by all sorts of clumsy coquetry. She knew perfectly well that only time cures the lovesick, but her humble sympathy made her keep trying.

At the end of the meal she sang for Kaeso's benefit a Greek song from Canopus which Selene had taught her in bed. Its melancholy obscenity reduced the pangs of love to their most modest proportions:

> 'So learn, all you lovers so gloomy,
> Who search for perfection in vain,
> That since in the dark every cat becomes grey,
> All pussies are really the same.'

Twilight was falling. It was rutting time. To brace himself up for the attack he was planning Kaeso had been drinking, despite his conscience, which kept whispering: 'Careful! up to now you may have made mistakes, but not for the wrong reasons. You're preparing to commit a truly

692

abominable sin in a little while, one to make even Nero blush. You're going to infringe a freedom which you created with your own sin. Heaven will never allow it.'

The tune got on Kaeso's nerves. He dismissed Myra with a wave of his hand, and said to Selene, using a lie to find out the truth:

'I met Cethegus in Agrippa's gardens during the orgy. You're not a Christian and you haven't been baptized.'

'Well, that's better than being baptized and not being a Christian.'

'You admit you lied?'

'It wasn't exactly a lie, for two reasons: in the first place, I lied out of politeness: in the second, you weren't stupid enough to believe me, since the otherwise unnecessary idea came into your head – or so you say – to check my story.'

'In other words you wanted to get round me tactfully.'

'Exactly. There's no necessary connection between gratitude and love.'

'Some women are capable of making the connection. Especially when the suitor had every virtue.'

'You have every virtue but one. You're a man, though I'm prepared to concede that that isn't your fault.'

'How very broad-minded of you.'

Selene got out of her chair, came and sat on the edge of Kaeso's couch and said:

'If your mind wasn't clouded by what people call love, you would have more than enough intelligence to understand me. I was made a plaything by men when I was very young. What so many men have destroyed in me no one man, even a Kaeso, can restore. Liberty, in my eyes, is first and foremost the hope that no man will ever touch me again against my will. And it's my will that no man should ever touch me again.'

'What you say doesn't surprise me, but . . .'

'What "but" can there be?'

'I'm not asking you to find ecstasy in my embrace like a wild maenad. I myself am not obsessed by the physical manifestations of love. It's because I think too much, according to Myra. It's a fact that I'm constantly being disappointed. What I feel never matches up to what I'd hoped. You can see that I wouldn't be a very demanding lover or husband for you. I'm only asking you to let me love you as a tender and respectful friend. And since you claim to feel some friendship towards me, you could perhaps make a tiny effort to accept my loving advances, since you made plenty of effort to learn to put up with brutal aggression.'

Selene lightly ruffled Kaeso's hair with the back of her hand.

'Do you realize you're sounding like an Athenian in a debating contest? But you're arguing like a novice. Your arguments can be turned against you. Why should I make a tiny effort, if it's only going to lead to your disappointment? And in fact it couldn't do anything else. What you're lusting after isn't Selene: like Narcissus at the bottom of the stream you're looking in me for the reflection of your own disturbing image, and you'd drown before you could grasp it. I can't do anything for you. Despite deceptive appearances we're not made for love or for each other. But I'll be happy to give you everything a woman can offer, except myself. So be sensible. Be satisfied with the possible, and stop chasing a myth.'

As Selene got up, Kaeso said to her: 'If there's any truth in what you say, and your knowledge of men makes me suppose there is, it's in my interest to destroy the myth, to be disabused as soon as possible. Please look on me as a sick man who needs curing. You've already skilfully administered a pleasant remedy which should have set the cure on the right tracks. Sleep with me two or three times, I shall get better and better and we shan't need to speak about it again. That's a very modest demand for a former master to make.'

'A former master has no right to make any demands of that kind.'

'Most *patroni* wouldn't think twice about sleeping with freedwomen they fancy.'

'Because they harass them until they give in. After so many protestations and proofs of love, do you by any chance feel like persecuting me?'

'You listened to those protestations, you accepted those proofs. And were more than happy to do so.'

'I was a slave. I had to save my life. Now I'm free and my state of health is fine.'

At that point Selene went up to bed without Kaeso, whose exasperation was growing.

Myra reappeared, edging along the wall, and timidly suggested: 'Selene is in a bad mood. May I sleep with you?'

'Don't be a hypocrite! You're not worried about disturbing Selene, and you don't give a damn about sleeping with me. The only reason you're making sheep's eyes at me is just to get me to leave Selene alone, when she's making a fool of me.'

'Selene is pefectly capable of looking after herself.'

This anodyne remark was all that was needed to send Kaeso bounding up the stairs. He threw open the door of Selene's bedroom like a whirlwind. She was brushing her hair at her dressing table. In the tones of a Manlius

694

Torquatus he promptly declared: 'Enough of this farce. I love you. I want you. Take your clothes off.'

Selene turned and retorted coldly: 'And I have to undress myself as well? Just the way your father ordered me to the first time he saw me? What if I refuse?'

'You know perfectly well I'm going to have you sooner or later. Why not now? My father's ghost will learn to live with the idea.'

Selene weighed up the advantages and disadvantages. A great weariness came over her, and she began to worry about the 100,000 sesterces still in the hands of Rabbi Samuel. She had still been a slave when she deposited them, and Kaeso could dispute their ownership.

In the end she gave in and said: 'You spoke of two or three times, long enough for you to become disillusioned. Under the circumstances wouldn't it be appropriate for you to pay me a suitable price for these therapeutic favours?'

'I'm not prepared for that degree of disillusionment.'

'Then you'll get what you paid for.'

Selene started to undress herself slowly, carefully folding and hanging her things up as she went. Kaeso felt like crying and looked the other way.

Suddenly, through the wide open window, Kaeso saw immense flames at the semicircular 'head' of the Circus Maximus, where an additional quantity of oak and pine beams had recently been stored for repairing the huge edifice for the Ludi Apollinares. Behind the Palatine, in the hollow where the temple of Murcia stood, the superstructure of the Circus must already be in flames, for thick clouds of black smoke had appeared over the hill and were drifting towards the Velabrum, born in streamers on the wind. From the 'head' of the Circus a wall of fire was visibly advancing on the Caelian, cutting round the Palatine the other way, to the east. The scale of the catastrophe was stupefying. It had taken all the fascination which Selene exercised over Kaeso for him to take so long to become aware of the disaster, especially as it was accompanied by an ever-increasing din.

The naked Selene went up to the window. The moon had been full the previous night. It was brighter outside in the city than it was in the room, which was only lit by the weak light of a single lamp. But soon, at the rate the flames were going, Rome would have no need of moonlight for its illumination.

For a moment Selene stared at the spectacle with a wild joy which she could not conceal. Eventually she said, carelessly stroking her genitals:

'Well, it looks as if you'll have to wait for another day to have me. The Christians must have set fire to Rome to prevent you committing a sin. It's time I got dressed again.' Selene's accusation was only superficially a joke. For centuries Providence had been moving mountains, to give birth to mice whose cries interrupted a consultation of the auguries, and thus brought the politics of a great State to a complete standstill.

Selene's jubilation astonished Kaeso.

'Why are you so delighted? Because you've escaped from me, or because Rome is burning?'

'Both.'

'I may have upset you by my passion, but what has Rome done to you? If Rome wasn't there, the Jews would be much worse off. They're surrounded by a wall of hatred. The Romans may put restraints on the species but at least they preserve it.'

'Who was ever grateful for the restraints put upon them?'

'Any intelligent animal which would get eaten if it were free.'

Outside the door the terrified slaves were setting up a plaintive commotion. The fire was being driven on by a wind from the south which showed no signs of slackening. It looked as though it would reach the Caelian in a few hours. Though the houses there were less dense than lower down, there were numerous sea-pines which would provide it with more fuel. Kaeso pushed the door open and ordered the slaves to get all the precious objects together.

Myra, who had taken the opportunity to force her way through, was expecting comfort from Kaeso, as though the situation were on a human scale. As Kaeso could only sigh, she helped Selene get dressed, throwing an occasional reproachful look at her abusive master as she did so.

'I haven't touched Selene,' Kaeso said. 'She only stripped off to enjoy the penetrating heat of the fire.'

Selene sniggered: 'The Romans have built cities everywhere which are of no use to any but the rich and beggars. What good have they ever done anyone else? What would the majority of the population have to lose if all the cities burned? All they do is waste what the countryside produces.'

Kaeso said: 'On that principle what use is Jerusalem?'

Cicero's house had already gone up in flames, and the fire, which had swamped the Circus Maximus from the west, was moving swiftly towards the Tiber. Its advance seemed irresistible.

In the middle of the night the lower part of the Velabrum went up, a notable part of the Palatine was in flames, and at the foot of the Caelian the fire was sweeping through the old and new Curiae. Kaeso thought it prudent to abandon the house before an influx of refugees made it difficult to get away. He took his *familia* up to the great *ludus* to seek provisional asylum there. Moreover that was where most of his cash was to be found. It was not the moment to be going up to the Palatine to ask for 500,000 sesterces.

Left without instructions the gladiators had decided, despite the furious protests of the inhabitants, to knock down the buildings abutting the barracks so as to make a barrier to the fire, which kept moving north, although a rather less violent east wind had replaced the initial south wind. Kaeso, in thanks for the hospitality granted him, took part in the demolition work before taking a few hours sleep. His leg was still hurting him.

In an oven-like atmosphere, obscured by the continually renewed smoke, it was difficult to make out the dawn.

Rome burned non-stop for seven days, the time it took Yahwe to create the world from the energy of light. Once Tigellinus and his trusted aides had got the fire really going, it had simply been a question of letting the monster run its course, whipped up by the prevailing south and east winds.

The fire had first rushed through the lower quarters of the city, where the crowded *insulae* on both sides of narrow, winding streets had encouraged its constant progress. While it took its time to finish off the palaces and *villae* on the Palatine, it had devastated the Carinae, reduced the Forums to ashes, reached the river and gaily launched itself into the Velabrum and the Subura. When the wind was in the east, fresh outbreaks of flames in the rear of the destruction fitfully destroyed the Aventine and the docks, industrial regions where numerous warehouses contained an inexhaustible supply of combustible materials.

Then the fire launched a full-scale attack on all the hills surrounding the basins in which its inferno already raged. It began with the Caelian, which was the nearest to the original flames and suffered terribly as a result. Then it made fierce sorties against the Esquiline, the Viminal and the Quirinal, but with limited success. The rich or well-off inhabitants of these heights were more thinly distributed, and had plenty of staff, who had time to get organized. Nonetheless some of them suffered considerable destruction. As for the Capitol, where Tigellinus had wisely concentrated the cream of the fire-brigade, it had been more or less spared.

During the last two days the flames had completed their task across enormous acres of temples, public monuments and well-stocked markets in the southern zone.

697

On the morning of the VIII of the Kalends of August, the twenty-fifth day of July, the wind fell, the fire seemed to be under control, and it was supposed that things could not get worse. But in the late afternoon the splendid villa which Tigellinus had appropriated outside the city walls, in the Aemilian quarter between the foot of the Quirinal and the Septa Julia, flared up like a torch, the fire spread to the whole area, and only died down on the morning of the VI. The graceful Portico of Pola, and the huge *Diribitorium*, built for the distribution of soldiers' pay, had burnt down, and the disaster had spread, to the north of the Palatine, as far as the Circus Flaminius, which was razed to its foundations. Eight days and ten nights of fear.

Of the fourteen administrative areas of Rome, inside, outside or straddling the old walls of Servius, three had been completely wiped out, and seven largely destroyed. Two, the Esquiline and the Quirinal, had suffered only marginal damage, and only two had got off scot-free: the Trans Tiberim, on the right bank and therefore defended by the Tiber, and the Porta Capena, which lay outside the walls and up-wind of the Circus Maximus, as far as the winds which had for the most part favoured the propagation of the fire were concerned. A good half of the 4,000 *jugera* (2,500 acres) of more or less built-up land had fallen victim to the gigantic bonfire, but at least two-thirds of the inhabitants were affected, for the ravages had been most complete in the lowest-lying areas of the city where the population was the densest. The homeless amounted to the incredible total of almost a million.

Since the emperor – an abnormally far-sighted man for an artist – wanted to expropriate land at no cost to himself, so as to make the architects happy and create a dream city, the result of the fire was, in his eyes, a remarkable one, far outstripping his wildest hopes. Tigellinus, though as pessimistic about human nature as the Christians, had rightly foreseen that a large number of Romans would collaborate in the task wholeheartedly. But even he had never thought there would be quite so many. What policeman can ever flatter himself that he really knows the underworld of a big city?

At every ordinary fire a crowd of vile wretches would emerge from the shadows in search of a good opportunity for theft and plunder. Profiting from the disorder they would offer their assistance, nay insist on it, so as to have a better opportunity to pinch anything that came their way. The bravest of these salvagers would try, on the quiet, to help the fire on, so that the flames would spread in the most fruitful manner. The Watch were constantly overwhelmed by the numbers and insolence of these abominable scoundrels. And when there were only a few walls left standing, another sort of scoundrel would send a pleasant-seeming business-man round to see the grieving victims and buy the site for cash, at a very low price, for a speculative building project. Crassus, the glorious con-queror of Spartacus, had once made a fortune out of endemic fires. One could not help wondering whether he had not lit some of them himself.

For the lowest and most wretched among this rabble of incendiary parasites Nero's great work had been the signal for a general and enthusi-astic mobilization. Processions of rats had come crawling out of every hole in the city to get a bite at the cheese before it melted. This scum would stop at nothing. They would lie in wait outside a burning house and ambush a respectable citizen, laden with gold and abandoned by his slaves, who would desperately cling on to his sack while the desperados hurriedly raped his wife or daughter. They would throw torches in through windows or into stair-wells to flush out the game more swiftly. They would force their way into the more modest and accessible houses, and hasten their evacuation with kicks in the rear, claiming that the Praetors' Office or the Prefect of the Watch had authorized them to do so.

A host of amateurs, ready to try anything once, had soon flocked to join all these professional arsonists and specialists in public disaster: out-of-work boxers and gladiators, deserters, runaway slaves, beggars, all the categories of cut-throats and muggers which Rome concealed in her skirts. And every day reinforcements had arrived from the surrounding country. After the festival of sex in the gardens of Agrippa there was a festival of fire for all those who had nothing and no one to lose.

To continue and complete Tigellinus' work, the Rome of the shadows, filled with long-suppressed feelings of hate and revenge, had spontan-eously come out into the light and smoke of the prodigious sacrifice.

In his villa at Antium, a wonder of wonders, where an extraordinary profusion of the most famous Greek masterpieces were on display, the young bride Nero had set to work on his *Troica* with such passionate enthusiasm that he forgot his conjugal duties as a gay wife. The emperor was perplexed by a really important problem, relating to literary creation in general and more specifically to poetic creation. How far is genius dependent on original experiences and passions? Did the imagination derive from a given context or from the mysterious inner depths of the individual? Nero was struck by the fact that Virgil had spent a very uneventful life, not to mention Horace, the son of a freedman responsible for auctions. If genius and imagination depended on favourable external factors, surely someone in Nero's position should have been streets ahead of the competition? What life could be richer and more exciting than his own? That was where the great fire of Rome took a place of major interest in the imperial preoccupations. It would be of incomparable value as a test case. A host of poets great and small had already described vast cities in flames, without ever having been privileged to see any in that condition. Nero would be able to see whether, after contemplating Rome at the best possible moment, in a sea of fire, this unique and unforgettable experience would or would not have a decisive influence on the quality of his verses. And after all, even if the results of the experiment were less than satisfactory, Rome would not have burned for nothing . . .

These considerations discouraged the emperor from proceeding with the polishing of his poem, and he abandoned the epic for occasional odes. When he was officially informed that the fire was under way, he was looking out over a calm sea and busily working at a little ode, in major archilochians with alternating catalectic iambic *senarii*, in which he reproached the god Tiber with having let Rome perish for lack of water. At the important news Nero turned pale, let out a cry and raised his hand to his heart. Tigellinus and he were naturally the only people in the secret, apart from the subordinates who had carried out the plan.

For several days the emperor redirected into poetry his feverish impatience to return to Rome and enjoy the new tragedy with a fresh eye. Lying in wait in his Praetorian camp, under a sky heavy with smoke, Tigellinus kept him hourly informed on the progress of the production, so that his Master, a sublime actor on the biggest of stages, should make his entry at the moment when the set would be at its finest. Nero must not arrive too soon, because he was to present himself as a saviour, and would have been reproached for his inaction.

Only on the fifth day, shortly before noon, did the emperor, who had come round the city to the east – it being no longer possible to approach it from the south – arrive at the gardens of Maecenas, through the Esquiline Gate at the top of the hill of the same name. The friend of Augustus and Virgil had had a belvedere built there, from which in his day you could look over the whole of the peaceful city.

Nero, cithara in hand, dreamily climbed the steps of the observatory, and stood silent, for a long time, before the fantastic sight. The lower-class Rome of the old marshlands was barely more than embers glowing in the wind. The Aventine and Caelian were crowned in flames which were beginning to lick at the other hills. A whole nation of poor tenants, pursued by the fire and the looters, was surging towards the Campus Martius in total chaos. At the foot of the tower where he stood, his

German bodyguards, who were keeping away even his most intimate friends, were in the process of discovering that civilizations may be mortal.

Nero wept emotionally over the heaped ruins of his motherland, and the emotion was not entirely assumed. He struck a few chords, but inspiration eluded him. Clearly the special quality of the poet was to add to external experiences an essence which he could only draw from inside himself, and the more extraordinary the external experience, the more difficult the task. What genius could have mastered such a situation and translated it into art? Faced with his masterpiece Nero felt impotent, disillusioned and utterly alone. He wept in earnest.

❋ CHAPTER ❋
5

As soon as Nero had come down from the observatory, he spent whole days of superbly energetic activity in nobly attempting to remedy what might appear to be irremediable. At the risk of having the salvagers taken for arsonists he ordered fire-breaks to be burned across the bottom of the Esquiline. He had all the available gardens and monuments still standing, even the Pantheon of Agrippa, opened to the multitude of dazed refugees. To house the homeless he saw to it that huts were put up in the open spaces of the Campus Martius. Furniture was brought from Ostia and neighbouring municipalities. The provisioning of the city with basic essential foodstuffs was assured, the price of corn lowered to three sesterces. All available forces swooped on the looting rabble, to provide fodder for future Games.

With some difficulty Tigellinus had obtained permission to burn the Aemilian district, where he lived, as an extra. The argument which carried the day was: 'To give you a good alibi, divine creator, we have sacrificed your palace on the Palatine. With all due respect, shouldn't I be allowed the right to be your brother in misfortune?' And so, with a breeze which was still blowing the right way, the most built-up area of the Campus Martius had gradually gone up in flames, up to the foot of the walls of Servius.

The popularity of the emperor, who paid more attention to the material interests of the *plebs* than his predecessors had done, was happily at its height. Nero, struggling against the devouring flames on the new front, the Circus Flaminius, had been acclaimed more enthusiastically than ever, and trusting, suppliant hands had stretched out to him from all sides. The greatest claim to glory of governments which have unleashed disasters is to palliate them with feeling and panache.

The great *ludus*, like a stone ship anchored in a tempest of fire, had survived the critical period undamaged. With entirely military foresight, after brutally demolishing the surrounding houses, some of the gladiators had seized a large quantity of food in the great market which Nero had set up on the Caelian, near the villa and gardens of the Annii, where

Marcus Aurelius was one day to be born. Others had stocked up with water. In an apocalyptic atmosphere they had spent their time feasting, fornicating and sleeping, only getting up to keep a look out for fire and to massacre anyone who tried to force their way in to camp in the training arena. It was difficult to tell refugees from bandits.

At the end of five days of this pattern of life, the rumour went round that Rome had been wiped out. As fire surrounded the *ludus* on all sides, they had forgotten that such a thing as laws existed, and primitive appetites had been unleashed. Selene's beauty had made an impression on everyone. On the evening of the festival of Neptune – but who was still thinking about the calendar? – four of the most famous gladiators abducted Selene before Kaeso's very eyes, contrary to all traditions, and fought over her with all the more passion for the fact that, inevitably, one of them was always unable to join in. The authority of Atimetus and the *lanistae* was no more than a memory now, and no one gave any thought to seeing that justice was done to Kaeso, who could do nothing but eat his heart out. But his legitimate rage was coupled with a feeling of sombre satisfaction, for he was inclined to see in the incident a providential punishment for the ingratitude which Selene had heaped on him. Myra, who did not have the same reasons for conniving in the penalty paid, wept and offered to replace Selene, but they laughed in her face.

On the morning when the disaster seemed finally allayed and under control, the hurricane of madness abruptly blew itself out, order was re-established, and Atimetus confined himself to whipping the guilty parties, whose deaths would have been too high a price to pay and would have caused public regret. When Selene emerged from the gang-bang, she seemed unchanged. She said to Kaeso: 'You'll notice the surprising improvement in my status. If I'd still been a slave, you'd have received payment for damages. But since you've freed me, you can hope for nothing more than a whipping from the same canes if you dare lay a finger on me.' Kaeso's hostile reaction was sanctioned by one of those cutting phrases at which Selene was an expert. Contrary to all masculine logic, the more she was abused, the less rights to her Kaeso had. It was enough to drive him mad.

With other gladiators Kaeso was requisitioned the same day to re-establish order, and, shortly after, to organize the evacuation of the victims of Tigellinus' last exploit.

For all those who had lived there, had memories of it and were attached to its traditions, Rome presented a touching sight, which irresistibly brought to mind the Apocalypse constantly predicted by the Christians.

The low-lying areas which had suffered the most were also those which had contained the largest number of monuments of some antiquity. Most of the temples and basilicas were now no more than calcinated ruins, the sanctuary of Vesta and Kaeso's will had gone up in smoke, and in the Campus Martius the flames from the Circus Flaminius had spread to the temple of Jupiter Stator, of which only a stretch of blackened wall remained beside the almost untouched Baths of Agrippa. The Subura was a pile of hot ashes. It would have been difficult to tell where precisely Marcus' *insula*, the house where Marcia had watched over the young Kaeso for so many years, had even stood. Most of the Romans who had escaped premature cremation or dissolute murder seemed to be wandering around at random, like ghosts risen from the grave, or were searching through the rubble with haggard faces, looking for a past which was dead and buried.

In the days following the cataclysm a crowd of labourers were seen to start tracing a new communications network across the ruins. Its size gave cause for astonishment. At the same time the old public squares were being cleared and enlarged, and new ones were being built, of even more ambitious proportions. The plan so carefully meditated was at last hurriedly being put into action, with fanatical enthusiasm, under the impassioned gaze of a visionary Nero.

Once freed from his obligations Kaeso spent his free time paying court to Selene in a way which was now more entreaty than threat. To make her weaken he had recourse to all his intellectual and emotional resources, but in return was treated as a spoiled, capricious child.

In compensation for the wrong done to him Kaeso was authorized to stay at the *ludus* with his *familia* until the end of the month, since, naturally, the house on the lower slopes of the Caelian had been razed to the ground.

On the morning of the III of the Kalends of August the traditional sacrifice was made to *Fortuna huiusce diei* on her altar in the Campus Martius: this was a first manifestation of a religious life which was pressing to restart with particular fervour, because of the immensity of the misfortune which had occurred. The day when he destroyed the Cimbri Marius had vowed to build a temple to this manifestation of Fortune, and it had just burnt down between Cicero's house and the Palatine Palaestra. To bring themselves luck the Romans had built large numbers of temples to Fortune: Fors Fortuna, Fortuna Luculli, Fortuna *equestris, obsequens, publica, privata, respiciens, virginalis, virilis*. There was even a plain Temple of Fortune, and Fortuna Primigenia had two temples to herself. A solemn invocation to this *Fortuna huiusce diei*, who had given such cause for complaint, seemed auspicious.

It launched a craze for sacrifices, (which meant the Arval Brethren ate themselves silly), for Rome could only have burnt down as a result of some impiety or other. It was necessary to appease the enraged gods, discover who was to blame and purify the city of them. The Sibylline books, which had a quick answer to everything, advised offerings to Vulcan, Ceres and Proserpina. Married women made offerings to Juno in the form of *sellisternia*, banquets specific to goddesses, who ate sitting upright, whereas at *lectisternia* the gods had the honour of lying down. Such an anachronistic discrimination was enough to put Juno in a bad temper. The more she was fed, the more manifest her mysterious wrath became. Nobody knew what to do. What impiety could there be in Rome, under a man like Nero?

When the emperor had returned to the house of Epaphroditus, after sacrificing to *Fortuna huiusce diei*, he got the young Epictetus to read to him. This was the boy whom Silanus had regretfully sold to the freedman to please Marcia. The slave was gifted with a keen mind and could declaim the pederastic odes of Pindar in a delicious manner, but he was already parading the Stoic views which were to establish his reputation in adulthood. Nero, who had never cared for the Stoics, had come to detest them. It seemed clearer every day that they had discovered a particularly hateful form of opposition, which was difficult to define in legal terms and punish: passive resistance. Some resisted by appearing to approve of what they secretly disapproved of. Others contemptuously withdrew into their own magic circles and threatened to cut their wrists to attract sympathy as soon as the slightest pressure was put on them. But they were all adept at a surly non-violence, and, like all pacifists, they were hypocritical accomplices of the excesses which their passivity encouraged, for they were quite ready to protect, by cowardly silence, the assassins whose supposed aim it was to put an end to such excesses. Seneca, who sometimes flattered the emperor in the hope of restraining and controlling him, and at other times 'cut' him, with pursed mouth, personified the dual tendencies of Stoicism. The secret energy of this vegetarian seemed to derive from another world.

As, with the naïve pride of those who discover philosophy, the young boy was mouthing the famous dictum of the Stoics, 'Endure and abstain', Nero lost patience with him and said: 'I warn you, young Epictetus, be on your guard against that insinuating doctrine. It's out of place in a free man, and more still in a slave. Aren't you obliged in any case to put up with what you can't prevent? And how can you abstain from what's imposed on you? Being a Stoic was of no great help to the late Silanus, your previous master. He had nothing to put up with but pleasures, and he couldn't find anyone to impose anything on him at all. But I doubt whether that's so in your case, where Epaphroditus is concerned. Stoicism is good only for the rich who are weary of excess in everything.'

The boy retorted: 'It would seem, divine Lord, that I've gone into early training for being rich and world-weary.'

The emperor burst out laughing, gave Epictetus an *aureus* and said: 'It's just been devalued, but it's still too much for a false philosophy. At any rate, don't call me "divine Lord". The Romans prefer to wait for my death to deify me. During my lifetime I'm only a god in Egypt and the East.'

'What a promotion when you go and sing there! But how sad when you come back. Personally I prefer not to change nature when I travel.'

Nero laughed again, although the slave had twisted the knife in the wound. Fortunately the trip to godhood was now possible.

The day before the Kalends of August, Selene and Myra, who had gone out to get some fruit from Nero's market, did not come back for lunch and could not be found. They had left all their belongings in the little room which, because of the overcrowding of the *ludus*, they shared. (Myra had very little but Selene rather more.) It seemed impossible that they could have run away. Kaeso, who was terribly shocked and worried, did not know what to think. Selene set great store by the clothes and the few, relatively inexpensive pieces of jewellery which Aponius had given her, and by the few thousand sesterces which she had saved up. It was not at all clear why she should have willingly abandoned them. As public order was far from completely re-established after the fire, Kaeso thought it likely that they had fallen victim to marauders. In the absence of bodies, and as in any case they only had small change on them, murder seemed unlikely. If they had been attacked by rapists, they would have philosophically allowed them to get on with it, and would have arrived back a little late. The probability was that they had been abducted and set to work in brothels, though women usually ran that particular risk at night.

After the biggest disasters, astonished to find themselves still alive, people are gripped with a feverish desire for pleasure. They can not have enough of sex and food. The rich set a conspicuous example and the poor do their damnedest to follow it. There were still a few brothels of various types standing in the Aventine area. Those on the Caelian had been destroyed, but those on the Esquiline, Viminal and Quirinal, of which there had, it is true, never been many, were mostly still intact. In these three districts rather classy brothels were becoming popular in the areas around the city gates. The legions of prostitutes from the Subura and the Velabrum had been placed all around the Campus Martius, to provide entertainment for the refugees, to whom Nero had had vast quantities of free tokens distributed. The impotent and the exhausted sold them to the sex-obsessed for a mouthful of bread, and the girls were worn out. The streetwalkers, whose professional pride was riled by this disloyal competition, had never walked the streets so determinedly.

If Selene had been a victim of some unscrupulous pimp, her beauty would have led to her being confined in a discreet establishment of the most superior sort. Whereas Myra had doubtless wound up in some third-rate knocking-shop. It was absolutely certain that they would not have been set to work in the open air.

Kaeso sent the servants, who were of no further use to him, back to Tigellinus with a graceful expression of thanks, and, with a sinking heart, set about going through all the brothels in the city. Despite the scale of the destruction they could still be counted in hundreds. The office of the *aedile* responsible for prostitutes was no more than a memory on the map of the Velabrum. For the time being, no help could be got from that quarter.

Each afternoon, as soon as such establishments opened, Kaeso would rush off to those which seemed the most plausible. For, with a praiseworthy desire to be fair, he was thinking not just of Selene, but also of Myra. His quest would go on late into the night, since the smartest brothels kept happily going into the small hours. His visits were terribly unrewarding. For the whole of the first half of August he expended his energies and hopes there, usually sleeping on the spot, worn out but racked with anxiety, for the price of a night's sex, and letting the girl whose services he had theoretically purchased lie beside him so that she could get some rest.

The brothels of Rome, with their variety of attractions, became confused in his mind: exotic beauties with unusual and picturesque specialities, from pale Breton girls to Nubian negresses; little girls barely past puberty who had been exposed to the most painful assaults; women who were expert at bestiality; women with whips, women who were whipped, women who performed with other women. The common-or-garden brothel, in its Biblical simplicity, seemed more healthy than these secret establishments lurking behind fine trees.

One night in mid-August Kaeso dozed off for a moment in a luxury establishment on the Aventine beside a slave who, for running away, had been subjected by a pitiless master to an unusual form of punishment. Some wealthy womanizers experienced a perverted pleasure in buggering a woman whose vagina had been infibulated. The unfortunate girl was a Christian, and spoke of Jesus as a loving and helpful master, who watched over her closely and aided her in her troubles. Jesus' ability to insinuate himself everywhere was food for thought. Kaeso asked the girl whether she really believed in Christ's resurrection. She answered: 'I don't just believe: I know.' She was luckier than Kaeso.

The following morning Kaeso happened to walk past the ruined bakery of Pansa. It occurred to him that uncle Moses might be able to give him some news of Selene. But Pansa said to him: 'The fire swept through the shed so suddenly that we didn't have time to unchain the mill slaves. I also lost my three donkeys.'

Moses had refused Selene's money and had been burned alive. But what did that matter, if he had won his bet and was now in the exclusive Jewish Paradise?

Kaeso realized that the thought was absurd. Moses had not made any bet. He had reckoned he was on to an absolute certainty. A bet implies that you only half believe. Those who bet on the next world consequently never have the strength to attain it, and are left betting outside the gates of Heaven, which they thought they could get through cheaply. Kaeso was only at the betting stage, and his vague bet 'for' condemned him just as surely as if he had bet 'against'. At the entrance to the Jewish and Christian paradises there must be a large notice saying: 'NO GAMBLERS'.

Despairing of Rome and its sinks of iniquity, both noble and plebeian, Kaeso went as far as Ostia, and even reproached himself for not having gone there sooner. It was possible that Selene and Myra had been kept there for some time before being sent off to some distant land. There, too, he drew a blank.

One morning, after he got back from Ostia, Kaeso went over the Pons Sublicius to question Rabbi Samuel, a last dice-throw in the game of chance. It was the XIV of the Kalends of September, the nineteenth day of the month of August, the joyful festal day which marked the opening of the grape harvest and the sad anniversary of the death of Augustus.

Rabbi Samuel had no information. But there was a trace of embarrassment in his attitude. Samuel had the whole list of possible lies at the ends of his fingertips: sacrilegious lies, hateful lies, self-interested lies, lies occasioned by a sense of propriety, or human respect, lies which could be tolerated or excused, lies which are a matter of choice, advisable or indispensable lies, white lies . . . And he had a very precise idea of all the circumstances in which moral casuistry could be employed. It was difficult to catch him on the wrong foot. Yet nobody who is anxious to do things according to the book can ever cover every possible contingency. Rabbi Samuel was lying, and lying clumsily, because he was not sure that he was justified in lying.

This embarrassment opened Kaeso's eyes in a cruelly illuminating way, just as, at the banquet to celebrate his assumption of the *toga virilis* at Silanus' house, he had had a lightning vision of the truth. The difference was that Selene would not be there to give him advice. She had come to the rabbi's house to get her money back, and was now leaving Rome with Myra for a future from which Kaeso was for ever excluded. It was typical of her intelligence and calculation.

But he had to get to the bottom of it. Kaeso imparted his suspicions to Samuel and added: 'If by any mischance you've assisted in this flight, you've put yourself in a very difficult position. You yourself assured me that you have the greatest respect for Roman law, where your faith isn't in question. Aren't you aware that freedmen owe assistance and fidelity to their former masters? *Patroni* can exile their freedmen twenty miles from Rome as a punishment, but in no case can a freedman himself evade his obligations. Still less so in the case of a woman, whose property should normally revert, after her death, to her ex-master, to whose guardianship she is irrevocably subject.

This shameful flight is in itself a serious crime. To make it worse, it was my intention to set up a profitable business with the 100,000 sesterces which I'd handed over to Selene while she was still a slave. It was understood between us that after she was given her liberty, she'd be in charge of the business, and the profits would be shared. Still worse, Selene has taken with her a very young female slave, belonging to me, whom she has seduced and perverted by the most unspeakable and grotesque love-making.

You have doubtless become her accomplice – I hope, for your sake, absolutely unintentionally – in crimes which are punishable before a Roman court. I shall spare you only if you admit all, in such a way as to increase my chances of recovering the runaways. Where are honesty and good faith to be found these days, if even rabbis, the light of the world, indulge in such underhand dealings?

So talk. I have the emperor's ear and am in a better position than most to get my rights.'

Samuel was in a cold sweat.

'As Almighty God is my witness,' he whimpered, 'I've been as much deceived as you. I saw Selene once, during the afternoon of the eve of the Kalends of August. She did indeed ask for her money back, with any interest which might have accrued, and she seemed in a great hurry to have it. What reason did I have for not making honest efforts to give it back as soon as possible? The girl had been cleared of the charge against her by an imperial pardon, and she'd just received her liberation from slavehood. As far as the runaway slave goes, as you can well imagine, she didn't breathe a word about her to me.'

'Wouldn't it have been wise to put me in the picture?'

'Yes, it certainly would. I was guilty of a serious lack of care.'

'Why did you lie to me just now?'

'Before bringing trouble on one of my co-religionaries I was waiting to be better informed. I now am, and I concede that you're legally in the right. Fortunately the damage can be remedied. I saw Selene again yesterday, and she was getting impatient. I don't know where she's set up house with her young friend, but she's supposed to be coming here the day after tomorrow, in the evening, because I'm expecting the money to arrive at any moment. The devaluation has put the knights in a good mood, and I had fewer difficulties than expected. I beg you, however, to wait until Selene has left my house before you have her arrested. This is a house of prayer, and any unnecessary violence would be out of place.'

While waiting for the great moment, Kaeso went and stayed with Turpilius, who did not dare refuse him hospitality. Kaeso's ideas and feelings were in a tragic state of chaos. The only woman in his life, after all the sacrifices, both heroic and shameful, which he had made for her, had preferred the considerable dangers of flight to a peaceful relationship of great advantage to her, or even a very honourable marriage. And on top of that she had deprived him of a child to whom he had showed nothing but kindness. Sometimes he was overcome with a desire for vengeance, at others he felt like throwing himself in the Tiber – or would have done, if the river hadn't been almost dry. Had he only expended time, effort, and money, only sacrificed his honour, his love, his very life's blood, so that two ungrateful lesbians could run off and make a fool of him? Many a time Kaeso was on the point of hurrying off to the police of the Trans Tiberim, an area full of refugees, to arrange for the trap to close. But at the last moment an obscure force restrained him.

At dawn on the decisive day, the festival of the god Consus who presided over the gathering in of the harvest, Kaeso, who was exhausted and deprived of all impetus to action, could not make up his mind what to do. He eventually had the impression that his heart was physically cracking apart, his soul detaching itself from his body and breaking free of all that restrained it, his mind soaring to unforeseen heights. Calmly and without ulterior motive, as though there were nothing else he could do, he went to the Palatine, where the Imperial Treasury had by now re-opened its portals, and drew his 500,000 sesterces. Then, in a temporary building which had been put up between the Porta Sanqualis and the Via Flaminia, he had Myra's name entered in the list of freedwomen. Finally, he went back to Turpilius' house and wrote to Selene:

'Kaeso to his dearest Selene, greetings.

I cannot face seeing you again. In addition to the 100,000 sesterces, which I hand over to you unconditionally, Rabbi Samuel will give you the 500,000 sesterces which I gained by sporting amid the flying feathers with a drunken Nero. I have just freed Myra irrevocably. You will now be in a position to look after her as well as I can – it will not be difficult for you – and perhaps better. I looked for you in all the brothels of Rome with increasing anguish, and only learnt one lesson: like a god – and I am as handsome as one – I take pleasure in making a gift of the best thing within my power, freedom, and I shall not go back on that gift. I set you free of everything, except yourself, your rights and duties. Consult your intelligence with even more perspicacity than you have shown in advising me in the past, and treat others as I have treated you. Do not hold it against Rabbi Samuel that he betrayed your secret to me. You know that Jews resident in Rome cannot show contempt for Roman law without putting their whole community at risk.

Without you I am overwhelmed with a feeling of disgust at life. I have given away so much freedom that there is none left for myself. I shall sign on again at the great *ludus*, where I shall sense your perfume on the air. But four gladiators are enough for you. Have no fear that I shall make a fifth. I shall wait for you to come into the arena and take me by the hand, and death will doubtless prevent that wait from being too long.

I shall have a modest tomb built for myself on the Appian Way. When you pass it, remember that I loved you more than anyone. It is the source of my misfortune and my happiness.

I hope you and Myra are well. But when the great Games are announced, don't bet on me: you would probably lose your money.'

*

Kaeso took the 500,000 sesterces to Rabbi Samuel, who was infinitely relieved at this unexpected outcome, and went to renew his contract at the *ludus* for three fights and 18,000 sesterces. His amorous entanglement with the emperor could not keep his price up indefinitely.

That night a note came for him from Selene:

'Selene to Kaeso.

You're a better man than any rabbi, and that's saying something. I could almost believe that Paul's baptism is having a good influence. One day when you're having Nero from behind, take advantage of the fact that he's got his back turned and baptize him: the double aspersion might turn him into a model emperor. Myra kisses your hands and is only sorry you didn't screw her more often. I find your decision to sign up again upsetting. I think, however, that I'm only a pretext for this whim. It's in your nature to despair, because you ask the impossible of life. I hope you'll live long enough to realize the fact and become reasonable. Fare well. I have learnt to love you as you deserve.'

Kaeso's tears flowed into the furrows made in the wax by the Greek letters. The heavens, satisfied for the time being, poured stormy cloud-bursts of water on to the parched countryside, and the god Tiber swaggered in his river bed.

While Kaeso was so prematurely achieving a *taedium vitae* worthy of Seneca – but with the attenuating circumstance that it was a question of leading others to their deaths rather than himself – Rabbi Samuel, with characteristic application, was putting the finishing touches to the tiresome task which the Chief Rabbi had set him.

Aponius' memorandum complaining about the Christians had finally reached the Prefect of the City, who had run his eye over it without enthusiasm, regarding it as the distressing product of a disordered imagination. Flavius Sabinus, a level-headed man and good administrator with no time for unnecessary problems, could see nothing in the elucubrations of senator Aponius which could undermine the rule of law, since the crime of unlawful intent was unknown in Rome.

Doubtless the Christians, as their accuser claimed, refused to sacrifice to the gods of the State, in particular to Augustus, who had attained divine status by apotheosis, and the goddess Roma. Every emperor attached great importance to this patriotic imperial cult, which remained the strongest link between the reigning Caesar and all his subjects throughout the empire, and offered a panacea for all disturbing local peculiarities. Every provincial capital, every *municipium*, had its altar to Rome and Augustus, and the most devout worshippers came from among the lower classes and even freedmen who had, generously, been given the right to take part in the cult. This imperial religion, a pure formality which involved no painful requirements but was the occasion for pleasant banquets, played a part in Romanization, peace and social progress. But, when it came to it, the adepts of the cult were by definition volunteers, with the exception of all the people who were absolutely obliged to take part because of their positions. Accordingly, only the official representatives of the Jews were called upon to make a formal expression of their adherence and respect, in accordance with a unique procedure which excluded all appearance of idolatry. It would have been ridiculous to waste one's time chasing up ordinary individuals to ask them whether or not they were willing to sacrifice in this or that manner.

In any case there was no shortage of completely batty sects in Rome. Before interfering with them the authorities had always waited for either clear contraventions of the law or serious disturbances.

One last point encouraged him to file the memorandum in the archives without more ado: the unfortunate complainant had just been killed, and the Christians had clearly had nothing to do with the case, since it was a Jewess who had confessed to the crime. In the context of the inquiry into the senator's violent death the police had come and consulted the memorandum, in which Aponius had written that his life was no longer worth living. But if everyone who had come out with that phrase had committed suicide, there would not even be enough undertakers for the funerals. So the matter seemed closed.

Sabinus had fought like a lion to save the buildings of his Prefecture, on the lower part of the Esquiline, from the fire. He was proud of having more or less succeeded, never having seen, on the vast model in the palace, the brand new premises which Nero had tastefully prepared for him as a replacement for his present ageing quarters. Aponius' memorandum had barely been signed.

It would have stayed forgotten on its shelf until the rats finished eating it, if, from the beginning of August, more and more insistent rumours had not begun to spread, accusing Nero of setting fire to Rome out of pure mischief or as a choice way of stimulating his poetic inspiration. Everyone knew he was writing the *Troica*, which was to be a glorious pendant to the *Aeneid*.

The futile and totally implausible enormity of such accusations, whose source was unknown, should have condemned them to instant ridicule. But the senatorial opposition leapt on this crumb with alacrity, and helped to spread the slander via its numerous clients. Consequently the rumour had constantly grown and become embellished, every day adding to it a new motive for suspicion and hostility. Certain witnesses whose word could be believed had even seen the ghost of Cicero slipping out of the house of the late lamented Silanus, for it was well known that ghosts cannot endure fires. And Cicero, who was kicking his severed head along the ground (his hands having also been cut off) had made the most precise accusations, punctuated with resounding cries of '*O tempora! O mores!*' A government is in a difficult position when it comes to proving beyond all doubt that such evidence is suspect.

Nero and Tigellinus had certainly expected a few rumours of the kind. Initially they had put up with them patiently, in the conviction that idiocies of the sort would be short-lived. But by mid-August the rumours were being openly proclaimed, and the emperor was beginning to look sideways at his prefect, as if he suspected him of having made a shamefully incompetent blunder. Tigellinus was getting more and more nervous, and sensed the urgent need to invent a reason for a procession or an entertainment of some sort. But despite his keen nose for such things, he could think of nothing which would have the right effect.

It was at this point that one of the policemen who had been to check on Aponius' memorandum had mentioned to the Praetor's agents that a senator who had since been murdered had accused the Christians of being capable of setting fire to the city to satisfy their leanings towards an apocalypse. On the offchance Tigellinus had gone to take a look at the letter. It had offered him, literally, a blinding flash of inspiration.

Governments endowed with foresight always have a few groups of social misfits to hand to serve as scapegoats when trouble arises. The ideal scapegoat, naturally to be suspected of each and every crime, must above all have the essential characteristic of appearing to imperil the very basis of the society which is imprudent enough to give him refuge, so that a feeling of acting in the public interest will stifle the least sense of pity during the course of the repression. But it is very difficult to dispose of entirely credible scapegoats in sufficient quantities at the crucial moment when they are needed. Even the most skilful chefs sometimes fail to get a sauce to come out right.

The Christians, however, were tailor-made for the requirements of Tigellinus and the emperor. They were typically anti-social and intolerant, and stood, in all respects, for the opposite of traditional Roman values, as

714

much as for the opposite of the values of Nero's Rome. To these significant attributes they added the advantage of being unfamiliar to the majority of the population and even to most educated people, the further advantage of mass activity among the lowest class and slaves, in a manner which looked like that of a secret society, and even the advantage – and this was the finest and least expected point of all – of public declarations of an incendiary turn in the guise of apocalyptic theology. Since the Christians had made such efforts to shock everybody and commit every possible imprudence, it would not need much slandering to turn them into a bogy capable of scaring the Senate just as badly as the plebs. And it was not out of the question that they might genuinely present a danger to Rome! If they had not burnt the city this time, they would burn it one day. And when they did so, it would be the new Rome, the splendid Neropolis, city of luxury and pleasure, to which the emperor wished his name to be for ever attached.

Tigellinus was ecstatic. He at once had the precious memorandum copied and recopied and sent to the emperor himself and all the permanent and occasional members of the Imperial Council. At the same time he put all other work aside and ordered an in-depth inquiry to be carried out swiftly on these terrible Christians, who had not up to then been the focus of his attention. Confused police reports lazily persisted in muddling them up, more or less, with the Jews, of whom, on the contrary, Aponius had promising things to say.

The obvious thing to do was to contact the Jewish community in Rome, since it might come in useful some time. So the Chief Rabbi had been asked to give his advice on the formal complaint made by the late senator, and had entrusted the task of drawing up a reply to Rabbi Samuel, after agreeing the general drift with him and a few other Jewish leaders. Samuel had a great reputation for fairness.

The evening of the day after Kaeso's second and final visit, Samuel took his work to the Chief Rabbi, whose headquarters were in the Porta Capena district. They worked over the text in detail and corrected it together, sealed it with the seal of the Chief Rabbinate and sent it off.

Tigellinus took cognizance of it the following morning, the X of the Kalends of September. It was the festival of Vulcan, the god of fire, and while a red calf and a boar were being sacrificed to him, the Prefect (a total unbeliever) read these pious lines with keen pleasure:

'The Chief Rabbi of Rome to C. Ofonius Tigellinus, Prefect of the Imperial Bodyguard, greetings.

With an increasing sense of concern, the Jews have been trying for a generation, through their learned men, to draw the attention of the Roman authorities to the dangerous character of the Christian phenomenon – dangerous, that is for the Jews and for the Christians themselves. To all these authoritative warnings there is now added that of the late Senator Aponius, which could have been avoided if we had been heeded sooner.

A complaint lodged by a member of the Senate naturally rouses your curiosity about these Christians. In the context of your inquiry you encourage me to make any useful comment possible on the Aponius memorandum. As we have long suffered from the blasphemies, insults and provocations of the sect, we are indeed well-placed to know it, especially as, unfortunately, it sprang from our bosom, by a deplorable mischance, and has dared to misappropriate our Sacred Writings and use them for purposes of impious propaganda.

I can therefore confirm to you that Aponius' assertions are, taken as a whole, entirely accurate. This is not surprising, given that he was abundantly informed by his 'baptized' son and by a Jewish slave who was happy to oblige.

The similarities and dissimilarities between Jews and Christians can very clearly be seen from this honest communication. Like the Christians, the Jews hold sodomy, abortion, onanism, pornographic entertainments and violent Games, mixed bathing and the worship of idols, to be sinful. But they do not make the least claim to deprive the Greeks and Romans of them. On the other hand, the indissolubility of marriage preached by Jesus is in direct contradiction to Mosaic Law, not to mention common sense and human nature. I shall pass over both the invention by the Christians of two extra divine figures, supposed to form, with Yahwe, an unexpected Trinity which recalls the Capitoline Triad and others such, and Jesus' supposed resurrection, which is impossible, since our Yahwe, by definition, cannot take on human form. I prefer instead to convince you of an alarming truth. This gross caricature of Judaism which is being hawked around by uneducated Christians is effectively directed at absolutely anybody, as Aponius very well perceived. As such it aims at dissuading the subjects of the empire from the imperial cult. How could our dispensation from idolatrous sacrifice, for which we give daily thanks to Rome, be extended to the general mass of Roman citizens, provincials and freedmen, without irreparable damage? Yes, Aponius is right to say that the Christians are breaking down the walls of our ghetto. And to allow this process to continue would be to allow the potential undermining of the very foundations of Rome. Since I am confident of being understood by an enlightened emperor, I will not hesitate to stress the fact that the religion of Israel is so much at odds with all other known religions that it obliges those Jews who respect its Law to live in pious isolation. Since we constitute a specific race, this has no tiresome consequences for Rome at all. You know how few Romans have themselves circumcised. But there is not simply a total opposition between the Christian religion and the traditions of Rome. The Christians' sole aspiration is to convert as many people as possible, and they have no desire whatsoever to withdraw into a ghetto. In theory – forgive what is an absurd exaggeration when one thinks of the eternal character of the empire – either Rome or the Christians will have to be destroyed, since, whereas the Jews propagate themselves by marriage, the Christians do it by the Word.

In all justice I must make it plain that the charges of cannibalism made against the Christians are not correct, although they have encouraged them by lunatic pronouncements, since they go around saying that they eat the flesh and drink the blood of their Jesus during sacrificial ceremonies from which non-initiates are excluded. As it is known that Jesus died long ago – and was probably buried – the man-in-the-street who was not in the know had every reason to imagine that young children were being sacrificed in his place. It took the Jews themselves some time to get to the bottom of the matter. In fact the Christians eat bread and drink wine which they imagine to be the actual flesh and blood of Jesus, who died on the cross. As a result, as far as we Jews are concerned, the Christians are much more repellent than any cannibal, seeing that, on their own admission, they do not eat human flesh but dare to devour the supposed body of the Creator. An illusion of this kind will give a Roman such as yourself a good idea of the contagious folly which characterizes Christianity.

As far as the question of whether this collection of scoundrels is or is not incendiary by nature is concerned, fear of bearing false witness deters me from making a definitive affirmation. What is certain is that the Christians, who have borrowed so much from us and then distorted it, have also gone in for apocalyptic pronouncements. As the Greek word indicates, these are divine revelations in the form of visions pregnant with symbolism. For more than 200 years this offshoot of conventional prophecy has been fashionable in Jewish circles, where it excites the talents of *aficionados* with impetuous and confused imaginations. Our learned men do not encourage activities of this kind, since it is not easy to tell a false vision from a true one, and the interpretation of the symbols merely unleashes sterile discussion. There are no apocalypses in our canonical writings, and I hope we shall be spared them for many years to come. Another reason for reservations about the genre is that since apocalypses deal with human destiny and our ultimate end, they are full of terrifying disasters which are guaranteed to upset ordinary people to no good purpose.

Left unchecked by their incompetent leaders, the Christians have not imitated the cautiousness of our rabbis. They have gone in for apocalyptic preaching with enthusiasm, and Jesus himself is attributed with terrifying visions in which the destruction of Jerusalem is linked to the end of time, which many believe to be close at hand. If you read Christian writings, you are struck by the fascination with, and importance of, fire. The Christians consign to the eternal fires of Gehenna all those who have the misfortune to displease them.

It is undeniable that there is among the Christians a prevailing climate of eschatological excitement which is extremely unhealthy, and could certainly encourage some of them to use unheard-of criminal methods to hasten the final conflagration which they fear and at the same time hope for. The risk is particularly serious because the many small Christian churches already established in the east and in Italy function in a chaotic state of improvisation, and have recruited most of their supporters from people who have nothing, and whose very condition inclines them to despise and hate the established order. It is in the nature of a Christian to reject all authority except that of his own conscience, which is formed by the ravings of his imagination.

We have not yet heard it said that the Christians could have set fire to the city, but it is clear that the worst elements among them might have been tempted to do so, being very particularly shocked, in their indiscreet intolerance, by the splendid banquet which you recently staged for Caesar on Agrippa's pool. An inquiry would certainly not be out of place. However, if even a small number of Christians took it upon themselves to carry out this hateful criminal act, the majority could have had no part in it. I strongly advise you to use the chance to introduce an effective and farsighted policy against the Christians as a whole, designed to ensure the complete destruction of this unnecessary sect.

Bear in mind that the Christian shares with the Jew, of whom he is a wayward cousin, what is at one and the same time a quality and a defect: violence and adversity strengthen his faith, and sweetness and tranquillity dilute it. Given the way in which the Christians have cunningly spread throughout the empire, I do not think that hunting them down as criminals will ever get rid of them. Such activities would be too localized, too

718

episodic, and would only make them more tenacious. It is the majesty of civil law, constant and universal, which must little by little obliterate the Christians by subjecting them to discouraging discriminatory legislation.

So, take a census of the Christians. Load them down with special taxes. Bar the schools to them, forbid them entry to the army, the legal profession and all public office. Deny them what they claim to detest – brothels, public baths, the Games – and they will want to go there more than ever. Let their bodies, on pretexts of hygiene, be banished to distant cemeteries. And above all, make it illegal to free Christian slaves, for it is through the murmuring of slaves in their master's ear that Jesus contrives to turn the heads of the rich and powerful. Be patient. It will not take more than two generations for Christianity to give up the ghost. No religion can stand out against the feeling that it has become a source of social embarrassment. None, that is, save my own!

To put it briefly, since the Christians detest the institutions and mores of the empire, and yet aspire to live scattered across it, justice urgently demands that they should be made to vegetate in isolation until they are forgotten and die out. In the shifting sands of history a Christian ghetto should be temporarily added to that immortal monument to piety and fidelity, the Jewish ghetto.

We, who are respectfully submissive to the authority of the laws of the empire, will, if you require it, furnish you with more precise information to enlighten your justice, so that all tiresome misunderstandings may be avoided. Given the progress made by the sect, it is no longer only the unfortunate Jews who would run the risk of being confused by the police with the Christians or with individuals suspected of being such.

I have a painful confession to make to you. It is because too lengthy and serious a period of study was required in order to become a Jew that young Kaeso strayed into the clutches of the Christians. We have been told that Paul of Tarsus, who claims to be a Roman citizen, is supposed to have been responsible for this aberrant conversion. Peter, the nominal head of the sect, is illiterate, but Paul, who is exceptionally well-educated for a Christian, is disconcertingly active. It would be a good thing if a stop were put to his activities.

We humbly pray that the Almighty will heap you with all the blessings which your rare virtues merit.'

⇘ CHAPTER ⇙
6

By the VI of the Kalends of September Tigellinus had at his disposal a persuasive dossier of weighty evidence. The measured views of the Chief Rabbinate – which were all the more impressive for being so restrained – had in their turn been communicated to Nero and to every possible member of the Council, and the inquiry into the Christians had come up with surprising results. Until then the police had only come across them through the Jews, who were the object of special surveillance in Rome as everywhere, and indeed in Rome more than anywhere else. Tigellinus' *agents provocateurs* had finally flushed out the real Christians from their highly unexpected lairs, without much difficulty, for their prey, being accustomed to living in relative peace, hardly bothered to hide. Cases of disquieting infiltration into the 'nobility' were noted, but one fact in particular made a striking impression: the perverse jubilation of the Christians at the disaster which had just hit Rome. While the Jews rejoiced secretly, in their heart of hearts, the Christians, once persuaded to open up, blessed the heavens for having burned down Sodom, for having wiped out Babylon. Their happiness was all the more expansive for the fact that a God who did not want the death of all sinners had carefully preserved the areas of the Trans Tiberim and the Porta Capena, where the majority of the Jews and Christians lived. In the wind of madness which had blown through Rome, Christians had even been seen burning down a number of modest brothels and baths of dubious repute, and they could with reason be suspected of having set fire to a little oriental temple which had made prostitution piously remunerative. At the first signal from the Praetorium, the police flattered themselves that they would be able to get a rapid confession from the suspects and swell their numbers appropriately.

As Tigellinus had hoped, the emperor not only jumped at the prospect of such a providential distraction, but added to this purely political consideration a personal motive for showing himself pitiless. The Christians had taken their sacrilege to the point of establishing a foothold among the most lovingly treated of his favourites. That Kaeso could be a Christian was a constant source of terrified astonishment to Nero. How could the progress of a criminal sect be stopped when it could hide behind the most delightful and charming of exteriors? If Kaeso was a Christian, why not Tigellinus or Vitellius? The deceptive wiles of the Christians seemed unlimited. Once convinced of the truth of the flabbergasting news, Caesar, beside himself, had hurried off to have purificatory and relaxing enemas administered to him, just in case. And thereafter he kept repeating to his close friends, who were almost as shocked as he was: 'I killed my mother, a Christian laid me among the feathers, abusing my trust and my tenderest feelings. Where will my misfortunes end!'

At the end of the morning a decisive meeting of the Council was held in the *Tabularium*, in the hollow between the Arx and the Capitol, the palaces of the Palatine being in ruins. This great edifice was a particularly good choice. It housed the Tables of Roman law, which the Christians had flouted, and from the Council chamber there was a view over the pitiful spectacle of the Forums which the sect had burned down: the Cattle Market to the right, the Forums of Caesar and Augustus to the left, with the old Roman forums in between, separated by the blackened remains of the great Basilica Julia, whose roof had fallen in.

The emperor was anxious to get the best advice, and also preoccupied with clearing his own name and accusing someone else with the maximum glare of publicity. So he had not contented himself with summoning the usual members of the Council: the Praetorian Prefects, the Praefectus Annonae and the Prefect of the Watch, all members of the 'equestrian' class, the Prefect of the City, from the senatorial class, the freedmen in charge of financial and legal departments, petitions and communications with the provinces. The two *consules suffecti*, who had taken over from the ordinary consuls, were also there, so that they could bear witness to the Senate of the justice of the decisions to be taken. Seneca himself had been prized out of his shell. This had only been achieved with great difficulty, for he was mistrustful of the regime and had not been invited for a long time. But Nero was counting on his good offices to enlighten those senators suspected of spreading the slanderous rumours. Similarly, he had sent for Paetus Thrasea, the leader of one of the most important Stoic circles. After a period of limited co-operation Thrasea had taken refuge in a disdainful opposition, based on moral principle, and had taken many discontented senators with him. But he was thought to be an honest man, hostile to lies. Lastly, the emperor had called upon the services of Vitellius, who was to inform the senators favourable to the regime, the Arval Brethren and the members of a number of other influential colleges.

Nero asked Tigellinus to address the meeting, and the Prefect gave a long, but clear and precise, account of the subject. It was obvious that the disaster which Rome had just suffered had originated with the Christians, and that all the characteristics of the sect made it extremely disquieting. So they should defend themselves by taking action. But it was the first time that Rome found itself in conflict with lunatics of the type. What legal and physical means was it appropriate to use to get rid of this scourge?

Very sensibly Tigellinus made a distinction between the arsonists proper, of whom he had a full list at his disposal, and the mass of ordinary Christians, who were innocent of the crime. No one would ever believe that all the Christians had helped to burn Rome down. But measures needed to be taken against the mass as well, for while they had not set fire to anything, they had at the very least been hoping for the disaster, had awaited it with impatience and had rejoiced at it unrestrainedly. If only the actual criminals were punished, a movement as dangerous as this would produce others sooner or later. It therefore seemed legitimate to impose penalties on those who were accomplices in spirit, as a safeguard. On this last point it was necessary to establish what would be the most effective steps to take, something which was by no means self-evident at first sight.

With ostensible deference Nero then asked his former tutor, Seneca, to speak: he was curious to see how he would cope.

Without actually suspecting Nero as such, Seneca was completely unconvinced that the Christians were guilty. The only thing entirely clear, in his eyes, was that Tigellinus, whom he despised and cordially detested, was letting off a thick smoke screen so as to hide the accusations being levelled against his master. So he was evasive, to embarrass the Prefect, and said in a gentle voice:

'It is a fact noted by everyone that the spread of the gigantic fire was aided by the criminal initiatives of individuals greedy for loot. Possibly these included some Christians. Personally I should be more inclined to react against the stupid rumours spread against Caesar. That the Christians may be guilty to a greater or lesser degree is one thing. The reputation of the emperor whom I brought up and instructed is another, and close to my heart. I am astonished that, with all the means at your disposal, Tigellinus, you have not yet been able to discover the source of these rumours and demonstrate their stupidity by punishing the slanderers? It must surely be the first example of a suspicion of this kind being levelled against a reigning emperor?'

'Unfortunately you have an exaggerated idea of the means available to me. It is very difficult to silence rumours which seem to originate in very different quarters, as if they were entirely spontaneous in character.'

'And what, in your opinion, could be the explanation for such a surprising spontaneity?'

'A whole series of unfortunate coincidences. What can be done against coincidences for which the gods alone are responsible?'

'Which coincidences did you have in mind?'

'There have been plenty of other dry summers, but for the first time half the city, and the most heavily populated half at that, burned down, just at the moment when the emperor, who is passionately interested in revolutionary urban planning, was working on his *Troica*. I myself have had my share of coincidences. I have been accused of setting fire to my own villa in the Aemilian quarter to get the fire started again, and of having thrown the organization of the water service into disarray by untimely repair works.'

'Those are indeed two amazing coincidences. I suppose it wasn't you who burned Rome down, by any chance?'

'I don't find that funny. When people start looking for coincidences, they come popping up like rabbits. There are coincidences which work the other way. The Christians of the Trans Tiberim and the Porta Capena took good care not to get burnt.'

'The Tiber protected the Trans Tiberim, and the wind was blowing from the south and east. If it had blown from the north-west for half a day all the southern suburbs would have gone up too.'

'That is very possible. At any rate, the best way to silence the insulting rumours about the emperor is to discover who is really responsible. I flatter myself that that is precisely what I have done.'

Nero intervened. 'Tell us, Seneca, what you think should be done to the majority of these Christians?'

After a moment's reflection, Seneca replied:

'It's not in the traditions of the Roman legal system to formulate laws against religious and philosophical creeds. This abstention seems to me to be based on a very wise principle. Despite all our efforts and our intellectual curiosity, we know very little about the gods or the order of the universe. Everyone has the right, under our rule, to think, write and speak what he likes, as long as he or she is not so grossly lacking in politeness as to make a formal attack, involving excessive terms which contravene the law, on the gods of Rome itself (who, let it be said between ourselves, are not such as to inconvenience anyone).

When troublemakers appear, it's consequently our healthy custom to deal exclusively with individuals, in the context of specific crimes involving public order, since our laws cannot demean themselves by taking up a position on ephemeral doctrines, of which the most attractive can never be more than probable, and the worst have nothing certain about them.

For as long as Rome is Rome, and the least concept of law exists, the Christian religion cannot be outlawed. But Christians can legitimately be punished if they contravene, clearly and explicitly, our criminal and civil code.

Let the Christian fire-raisers, if they exist, be punished. As far as accomplices are concerned, since their degree of guilt remains to be defined, let them also be punished according to the laws at present in force. But it would be contrary to equity for people to be brought to trial simply because they bear the title of Christians, since that would come down to condemning the religion rather than the individual responsible.

I am, however, disturbed, as you all are, by the decidedly antisocial character of the Christians, and it seems a good moment to oblige them to recognize the common law of the empire. They cannot argue, as the Jews can, that they are a unique nation, so as to obtain a unique right.

We have, on previous occasions, expelled philosophers and members of sects who are considered subversive, but they were foreigners. The Christians, however detached on a religious and moral plane, are part of us. If they really are dangerous, and we expel them, they will spread the contagion far and wide, since we have now conquered the whole world. The only solution is to assimilate this foreign body. And we have an elegant legal formula at our disposal for doing so.

Let every person convicted or suspected of being a Christian be required to sacrifice to Rome and Augustus. Those who accept will no longer be Christian, and those who refuse will be put to death for treason and *lèse-majesté*. What could be more reasonable and more legitimately Roman? It's no longer Christianity which is being prosecuted. It's merely a question of punishing those inhabitants of the empire who refuse, for whatever motive, to pay the homage of fidelity to the emperor which the law theoretically imposes on everyone.'

This appeal to fundamental Roman law, and the practical and juridically ingenious proposal which concluded it, had a great success. Flavius Sabinus, the two consuls, the Praefectus Annonae and the Praefectus Vigilum, some departmental heads, Thrasea and even Faenius Rufus,

Tigellinus' colleague at the Praetorium, all supported it with varying degrees of enthusiasm.

Nero's brow darkened. He urged Tigellinus to reply, and the latter hastily began:

'That is a typical laywer's suggestion. It entirely sacrifices effectiveness to hazy issues of principle. What's the problem? We have on our hands a collection of people who are actual or potential arsonists. And what does Seneca suggest? That the Christians should be given a pleasant little test! Tell me, Seneca, out of a hundred Christians obliged to choose between death and abjuring their faith, how many victims do you suppose I shall have?'

'Maybe a dozen. But from what I know of the Jews they'd give you your fill of corpses. If you want blood to please the *plebs*, why don't you persecute the Jews? You'll gain on all counts.'

Tigellinus took his audience as witness to Seneca's lack of awareness of the issues:

'Here we have a philosopher who is for letting the Christians punish themselves. According to Seneca the Christians should have the choice. May I draw your attention to the fact that the Christian community in Rome is still very small. If we apply Seneca's method, all we shall get our hands on is a tiny handful of Christians who elect for a sort of Stoic suicide after mature reflection. The danger represented by the sect will barely be reduced, since most of those who abjure their faith out of cowardice will remain Christians at heart, with an increased hatred of Rome and the Emperor. Worse still, they'll become Christians again as soon as possible. I have, in fact, been told that the Christians spend their time sinning, pardoning themselves, absolving themselves and starting again. They seem to have achieved the perpetual motion of which mathematicians dream! Seneca is claiming to be able to deal with a human situation by a hypocritical legal artifice. But when it comes to it, he doesn't know men as well as he flatters himself in his works that he does. Otherwise he'd know that you can't make people change their minds by inflicting a momentary humiliating fear on them.

However, on three points I think Seneca is right. Firstly, it isn't up to us to condemn the Christian religion. Anyway, religions are constantly changing. If Christianity catches on, how many forms of it will there be in 400 or 500 years? The emperor would have to turn himself into an Eastern theologian to work the whole thing out. Secondly, expelling the Christians from Rome would in fact come down to spreading the infection to the provinces, which are already sufficiently ailing. Thirdly, it is indeed the arsonist, and not the holder of certain religious tenets, whom the law should punish. We're working in the interests of the people, and the people couldn't give a damn about doctrine. It isn't doctrines which get crucified, it's men, and it's men the people want to see.

So it seems to me expedient, when all is said and done, to condemn all the Christians in Rome we can lay hands on, on a charge of incendiarism or complicity therein. If, to please Seneca, we get tangled up in subtle distinctions about various degrees of complicity, we'll never extricate ourselves, large quantities of guilty persons will escape punishment, and the Christians will burn Rome down every summer, for the perverted pleasure of lining the lawyer's pockets.'

Seneca, who was a lawyer with well-lined pockets, inquired:

'Where in our legal code can you detect a concept of collective criminal responsibility punishable by death?'

'When your friend Pedanius Secundus was murdered, the 400 slaves of his *familia* were crucified. Isn't Rome worth at least as much as that old fool Pedanius?'

'But they were only slaves.'

'Most of these Christians are slaves, freedmen and foreigners. Very few Roman citizens have been baptized.'

'From a legal point of view I find the idea of laying the blame on citizens in an affair of this kind very serious. Who, in any case, would you get to swallow the idea that citizens could have set fire to their own city?'

'And what principle of justice would you invoke to allow Christian citizens to be spared? Anyway, isn't it better to wipe them out while their numbers are limited?'

'The way you're going, you'd better apply your new law to the Christians in Egypt, Greece and the East as well.'

'It's precisely the fact that I'm only invoking the law against those responsible for the burning of Rome which allows me to leave the rest in peace. In that respect I'm more moderate than you. You're prepared to harass all the Christians in the empire with your bizarre and far from watertight system. Indeed, I'm not just more moderate, but also more respectful of tradition from a legal point of view, since I don't think it's ever the State's job to root out any religion, whatever it may be. If, moreover, I had the pretension to undertake such a task, I'd prefer to apply the excellent methods proposed by our Chief Rabbi, who is by definition an expert on fanaticism.'

'Why don't you just admit that what you really want is masses of condemned men for the Games?'

Vitellius broke in: 'Well, and so what? After going through so much, aren't the ordinary people entitled to a little offbeat entertainment? I'm a plain man at heart, and I'm not ashamed to say: "The Christians will make a good show." It's not every day that a whole population of fire-raisers gets grilled. It's Seneca who should be ashamed of himself. He makes digs at the butchery in the amphitheatres, with disgust dripping from his pen, but he disguises himself in a Gallic hooded cloak and goes and enjoys them in secret, from a seat among the tarts and the urchins. He'll weep over the Christians, because he's a philosopher. But you can bet your boots that he'll be there to see them sizzle. He's a hypocrite.'

The outraged Seneca was gibbering with indignation. The emperor, who had some difficulty preventing himself from smiling, called Vitellius to order.

From the beginning of the meeting of the Council Seneca had been well aware that it was with Nero's tacit approval that Tigellinus had been manoeuvring to get permission for this repellent mass extermination. Seneca could not understand this sudden fit of cruelty in a man who, up till then, had abstained from gratuitous bloodshed. He made an attempt to reason with Nero.

'Aren't you afraid, Caesar, that your reign, which has been so brilliant thus far, will be tarnished by a massacre whose usefulness would seem debatable?'

'You don't realize how far Christian vice will go. The hypocritical Christians excel at disguising themselves so as to take advantage of good faith and innocence. They even lurk beneath the toga. They're lavish with their show of friendship and love, they'll shed their blood, if necessary, just to wheedle themselves further into your good graces, and once in your bosom the snake will finally bite! The Christians are monsters of dishonesty and pretence. They must be unmasked and crushed before they get to work in earnest. Fire-raising isn't the least of their talents . . .'

Seneca, who recalled having recently seen Kaeso at Piso's house, and who had received copies of Aponius' memorandum and the advice of the Chief Rabbi, suspected that the idyll between the young man and Nero must have gone sour, and that the favourite's 'baptism' had had something to do with it. The emperor must of course have received a rude shock at the idea that he had accorded his favours to an ambitious fellow to whom setting the emperor's entrails aflame was only a routine piece of training for projects on a grander scale. Seneca searched his memory and recalled how Kaeso had come to consult him amid the future ashes of the Palatine library. Then he had only been envisaging keeping company with the

Christians as an ingenious expedient for declining Silanus' offer of adoption. Seneca felt an impulse to say to his naughty imperial pupil, after the Council: 'Don't get cross about nothing, little Lucius. Kaeso's baptism was only a pretence.' But could he actually guarantee that? A man such as Paul of Tarsus was quite capable of catching Kaeso in his own trap. Anyway, it was Seneca's prudent principle never to get mixed up in other people's lovers' quarrels, especially when they were homosexual. Gays were as touchy as a man who's been flayed alive, a factor which discouraged any form of rational intervention. So Seneca preferred to let Kaeso justify himself, if the need arose.

His thoughts came back to the planned blood-bath, which shocked his sense of proportion and his sensibilities as a jurist. Nero's reign was marked by a propensity for the worst forms of innovation. After the most monstrous exhibition of group sex ever known to man, they were now going, for the first time in human history, to exterminate in cold blood a host of individuals who, according to highly dubious criteria, were being labelled as unassimilable criminals. It was no longer a question of putting to the sword, in the heat of action, the inhabitants of a town that had been taken by storm, or of cutting the throats of proscribed men in the atmosphere of mingled hatred and excitement roused by a civil war. Nero and Tigellinus had, after mature reflection, just invented genocide on grounds of national interest.

Seneca wondered whether a third innovation would not follow the first two: expropriation by fire, with a view to brilliant town-planning on the scale of an immense metropolis. The rules and regulations which were to govern the construction of the new Rome had already appeared, and people had been struck by their breadth, precision and wisdom. The houses were to be in straight lines and isolated from one another, kept to a prudently low height, and surrounded, as a protection against fire, by porticos for which the emperor was prepared to pay the costs, after clearing the ground at the state's expense. Subsidies were being offered to speed up the work. Rules were laid down for the use of wood, and the use of fireproof stone from Gabii or Alba was made compulsory for the most exposed parts of buildings. Everybody was obliged to keep a whole range of fire-fighting equipment permanently available. The water service was to be reorganized and made subject to stricter control, until such time as rivers, even the sea, reached the city via aqueducts which would complete the chequer-work pattern to be created by the broad new avenues spreading out from the imperial Domus Aurea, a building already rapidly rising from the ground between the Palatine, Esquiline and Caelian hills.

The ships which had come up the Tiber laden with corn were carrying back rubble to fill in the marshes at Ostia. Such measures could never have been improvised in the course of a few weeks.

But Seneca rejected the suspicion which had only flitted across his mind. How could a sage, despite the most blindingly obvious indications, understand the madness of genius? Seneca was only a small-scale artist, on wax or paper.

He found his impotence distressing. He had tried to buy off the emperor by offering him the prospect of a sacrificial test of more than doubtful efficacy as a sop to his pretended or genuine anger. Seneca himself would have been very surprised to know that emperors in the two succeeding centuries would use his scheme as their constant and preferred form of repression. But a man as superficial as Tigellinus did not give a damn about the eradication of Christianity, which he doubtless saw as a transient phenomenon. Deaf to the far-sighted counsels of the Jews, all he wanted was glittering celebrations through which the emperor's popularity could be re-established. The only comforting consideration was that, as the genocide was opportunist, it would probably not occur again.

While the precise programme for the festival of extermination was being discussed, Seneca, feeling very weary, asked permission to withdraw. As he went, his eyes caught those of his friend Thrasea. This brief confrontation completed the philosopher's feeling of depression. Thrasea was visibly unaffected by his part in the disappearance of the Christians from the city. It was not only Nero's Rome which the Christians could not swallow, but Augustus' Rome as well, whereas Thrasea's paternalistic Stoicism could, if absolutely necessary, have come to terms with the latter. Why had the Christians taken their negative attitudes to such extremes?

The Cattle Market was now reduced to a building site. While Seneca's litter was crossing it, he caught sight of Kaeso, who was in the middle of freeing Marcia's statue from the rubble in the ruined Temple of Patrician Modesty, with the help of a few workmen. Luckily the marble was undamaged. Kaeso had been to ask L. Silanus, Decimus' main heir, to make him a present of it, and the young Stoic nobleman had done so with a somewhat contemptuous readiness. Lucius adhered to the rites of the old Roman religion only for form's sake, and looked on Marcia as a tart who had exploited his uncle's weaknesses.

On seeing Kaeso, Seneca stopped his litter some way from the statue, which had been raised up and dusted off with the intention of loading it on to a cart. Kaeso meant to put it in one of the porticos of the *ludus*. It was the only image of Marcia that he had.

Seneca sent his bearers some way away, to be sure that he and Kaeso would not be overheard, and said: 'It's come to Nero's ears that you had yourself baptized. He's particularly upset by the news, because the Christians are suspected of having set fire to Rome. They're threatened by the greatest danger at any moment. I can't tell you any more: I've just come from the Imperial Council, where I couldn't make the voice of reason prevail. I've already told you more than I should have done. I hope I can trust you to keep my warning secret. Though you'll be doing me a service if you betray me: I've lived much too long.'

Kaeso reassured Seneca and said:

'As I've already given you to understand, I only hung around the Christians to get out of being adopted by Silanus. I don't attach much importance to this baptism.'

'Then you'd better explain as much to the emperor, as soon as possible, and pray to the gods that he believes you. Otherwise you'll come to the same tragic end as all the rest.'

Kaeso thought for a moment, stroked the smooth cheek of the statue, and finally made up his mind to answer.

'I think it'll be more than I can manage to provide such an explanation.'

'But it's a matter of life and death.'

'Tigellinus begged Silanus to deny the rumours according to which Marcia, whom you see here in all her modesty, was supposed to have committed suicide like Lucretia as a consequence of the dishonour inflicted on her by the emperor. It would have been very easy for Silanus to admit to the Prefect that his wife had in fact renounced life because I had refused to make her my mistress under the roof of an obliging adoptive father. He preferred to preserve his honour by keeping silent. His action imposes a similar obligation on me. I can't give Nero a convincing reason for my incongruous baptism without revealing the secret which was the cause of Silanus' death. I owe the homage of silence to Marcia and Silanus: they both died out of love for me.

One final consideration is enough to persuade me, if I needed it. Although I'm not a Christian, I see no reason to exonerate myself of being one. You know as well as I do how tiresome the faults and naïvely rash actions of the Christians can be, but I've spent enough time with them to know that they didn't set fire to the city. Either the disaster was an accident, or, as I'm inclined to believe, the real villain is that megalomaniac, Nero. In the Palatine palace I saw an immense scale model in which tomorrow's Rome was set out in the minutest detail. The premeditation was there for all to see. If I die in the company of Christians, I shall die among innocents. Nowadays that's a rare privilege.'

'That is a noble attitude, worthy of a true Stoic.'

'I've driven too many people to their deaths to refuse to add my own to the list. My only remaining ambition is to be murdered by riff-raff.'

'I should admire your virtue more if I didn't have a feeling that the exercise of your touchy sense of honour has been encouraged by personal disappointments which have been an untimely barrier to your enjoyment of life.'

'I can't dissent from that view. I eluded Marcia. I eluded Nero. The woman I loved eluded me. It's time for me to escape from myself. In less than twenty years I've discovered what it's taken you more than sixty years to learn. Life is a bad dream, and we shouldn't be afraid to wake up from it.'

'I can't think as fast as you, and I'm still weak enough to indulge in a little dreaming. But, despite my past faults, I too, I must confess, long to awaken. I hope the awakening will allow me to rejoin you and continue this exemplary conversation, along with Zeno, Socrates and their like. May all the gods protect you, and if there's only one, may he welcome you with all the more favour. I should have liked to have had lots of pupils like you, instead of Nero.'

'They wouldn't have done you much good.'

'I might have died a natural death. That now seems less and less probable . . .'

While the cart set off towards the *ludus*, Kaeso ran across the ruined Circus Maximus to the Porta Capena, told the tent-maker of the approaching threat to the Christians, and suggested that he warn as many as possible of his fellow-believers at once. But unpleasant rumours had reached the man's ears about Kaeso, and as he could not admit the identity of his source without giving Seneca away, his fears merely seemed alarmist. The tent-maker's objections to spreading panic on the strength of hearsay were very much to the point:

'Suppose that your warning were worth believing, where could the Christians, whom everyone knows, possibly hide? You're also forgetting that lots of Christians are slaves and freedmen, who haven't the right to go off when they feel like it, and that foreigners and citizens would be admitting their guilt if they took fright at every official threat.' Peter was due back from Pozzuoli that evening. He would be told about Kaeso's visit.

On the doorstep the Christian Jew made a remark which was very characteristic of people who are about to be exterminated because of some label or other:

'All my neighbours like me and think well of me.'

Kaeso sadly retorted:

'All your neighbours hate you precisely because you set them a good example. Do you think that people like to be taught a lesson?'

When a young man has reached that degree of wisdom, it's understandable if he finds life on this earth a burden.

The night was calm. Light showers heralded the onset of autumn. At first light on the V of the Kalends of September, the Praetorian Guard and the Urban Cohorts surrounded the Trans Tiberim and Porta Capena districts, and methodical house-to-house searches began. In what was left of the other parts of the city, and in the encampments in the Campus Martius, the police were likewise busy. It was a public holiday, the anniversary of Augustus' dedication of the Altar of Victory in the Curia. Nero, who had the occasional fit of religion, thought the gods would be favourable. And indeed, the whole operation went perfectly, with the enthusiastic cooperation of the Jews and the local population, who at last knew who to blame. The bulk of the Christians were completely bewildered, thought there must be some mistake, and let themselves be led off like sheep.

As the victims were brought in, Tigellinus anxiously counted his flock. According to all the information he had been able to collect, the Christian community in Rome, which had only started to spread in the reign of Claudius, still contained too few baptized people to provide fodder for the shows he was hoping to stage. As the emperor had given him a free hand, he had given orders to spread the net very wide, and not to bother with theological considerations, which were in any case incomprehensible to the police and soldiers whose job it was to carry out the arrests. So, while 'priests' and 'bishops' and those who were undoubtedly their flocks were arrested, lumped in with them higgedly-piggledy were spouses of different religions, sympathizers, be they fervent or lukewarm, adolescents in receipt of instruction, friends of the family who happened to be in the house . . . The important thing was to get a lot of people. Tigellinus told himself, very correctly, that the most glaring errors would be easy to put right at a later date, since the parties in question would be sure to protest and bring forward evidence to support their case. Anyway, public rumour is rarely wrong.

Tigellinus had given instructions that mothers were not to be separated from very young children. This was ostensibly a humanitarian measure, but he had it at the back of his mind that the deaths of these babies would have a striking effect on the plebs, showing them clearly just how repellent and dangerous Christians were. This was yet another novelty, even in a reign already so prolific in innovations. But it conformed to the logic of the concept of collective guilt. You couldn't leave the seed of arsonists to grow and flourish. Anyway the habit of exposing children at birth was an equal incentive. Was an eighteen-month-old incendiary really less guilty than a day old superfluous mouth to feed?

By evening Tigellinus was reasonably satisfied. Those who – rightly or wrongly – energetically denied being Christians were relatively few, and the show could go on without too much worrying about numbers. Anyway, extra searches were to take place right up to the end of the month.

So as not to upset the Senate, whose approval of the genocide was desired – but also because it would have been particularly hard to get anyone to believe that nobles or knights had set fire to Rome – Nero had resigned himself to leaving undisturbed the very few individuals of both orders, senatorial and equestrian, who could be convicted or suspected of being Christians. The knights, both businessmen and civil servants, had in any case proved very unreceptive to Christian preaching. Only one baptized knight had been found, and he worked in the offices of the corn-supply department. Tigellinus found this sterling resistance to the poison by public functionaries another cause for satisfaction.

Nero had, however, ordered that an exception should be made in Kaeso's case. His condemnation ought not in principle to upset any senator. His father's reputation was highly dubious, and the boy's own gladiatorial *infamia* fitted perfectly with his dealings with the Christians.

Towards the first hour on the V of the Kalends of September, almost before dawn had broken, troops came to arrest Kaeso at the *ludus*. In his case a Praetorian tribune and a sizeable detachment of guards had been sent, in case, out of *esprit de corps*, the gladiators made any trouble. The tribune, Subrius Flavius, was to be compromised in Piso's conspiracy and himself executed the following year, after having the insolence to call the emperor a ham actor and incendiary – which only goes to show that some sorts of calumny take a long time to die out. He was an archetypal soldier of the old style, and was to spend his last moments grumbling because his grave had not been dug strictly according to regulations.

Before entrusting himself to Subrius' care, Kaeso piously embraced Marcia's statue: it was difficult to tear him away from it.

Subrius was astonished and said to him:

'I'd heard that what the Christians want most in life is to break up our idols.'

'Don't believe everything you hear about the Christians. Anyway, it wasn't an idol I was embracing.'

In a fit of black humour Kaeso went on: 'It's a statue of Mary, the virgin mother of Jesus Christ. If you embrace her, she gives you whatever you want. I've just asked her to grant your promotion.'

Subrius scratched his head under his helmet and asked:

'What's the difference between this statue and ours?'

'Roman statues represent gods that are dying; Christian statues represent people who are alive, in Heaven, and can help bring us happiness. You've just seen the first of them.'

'Are you by any chance taking the mickey out of me?'

'Oh no, absolutely not . . .'

After a moment of deep emotion, Kaeso had quietened down, and during the journey he chatted in friendly fashion with Subrius. He was being taken to the Tullianum. Subrius explained that the intention was to pack the majority of the Christians into a variety of places, wherever there was room. But Roman citizens and the leaders of the sect were entitled to the distinction of being housed in the public prison. As there was no such penalty as imprisonment for citizens, only people who had been condemned to death were kept in the Tullianum. They were strangled in the underground chamber, brought out feet first, and their bodies were put on view on the nearby Gemoniae steps. Alternatively they left on two feet and went to be executed elsewhere.

It was only a short way from the Caelian to the Capitol. Soon the massive sinister façade of the Tullianum could be seen crouching at the foot of the hill between the Clivus Asyli and the Vicus Fori Martis. The entrance was framed by two huge lateral staircases which ran up to two-thirds of the height of the building.

As he handed Kaeso over to the gaolers, Subrius said to him by way of consolation: 'People rarely stay here long.'

Kaeso cast a last glance over the Forums, which he might well never see again. But they were no longer the same Forums which had been the ornament and delight of his childhood. Of those, Nero the artist had eliminated all trace, thereby depriving the Romans of their memories, so as to make new ones which fitted in with his own views.

The Tullianum was the simplest prison which ever existed. Its inmates had to make do with a single room lit by a small barred skylight. It was a quadrilateral room, broader at one end than the other, entirely built of rough stone, vaulted and relatively small. It was about fourteen feet high, twenty-five long, and eighteen wide (on average). Ancus Marcius, the fourth king of Rome, had built this masterpiece of solidity, from which escape was impossible. And Servius Tullius had dug a more or less circular dungeon about twenty-two feet in diameter under these living quarters. This part of the prison was barely taller than a man, so there was no temptation to try to commit suicide by throwing oneself through the narrow communicating hole. This totally unlit dungeon was used only for executions. It was there that Vercingetorix, like many before him, had been strangled after Caesar's triumphal procession. Caesar never forgave him and his barbarian followers for wasting so much of his time at an important moment in his career.

The ground floor room was rapidly filled, more or less, with Roman citizens. Kaeso initially found their company tiresome, for the most part. They kept complaining, protesting and calling for their lawyers. In their legalistic, logic-chopping little minds they were shocked that a law of collective responsibility which was just about acceptable when applied to slaves could be applied to them. It was, it is true, the first example of such flagrant abuse of the law. And they found the terms of the accusation another cause for scandal. No citizen had ever previously been persecuted for his religious beliefs, and the idea that Roman citizens could have set fire to their own city was glaringly improbable. As Christian citizens, they had thought of themselves more as citizens than as Christians. Nero was brutally reminding them of the terms of the Gospel.

However, some of them, Jews or Greeks by birth, seemed less surprised. They could remember the bloody disputes between Jews and Christians which had caused upheaval in the East from time to time, under the uncomprehending and negligent arbitration of the Romans. Even in Rome short-lived riots had occasionally set the Christian Jews and the Jews of the Trans Tiberim against one another. (The Porta Capena district was more middle-class and had always remained calm.) These Christian Jews and Greeks understood better than the native Romans that Christianity had all the right qualities to arouse general hostility sooner or later, and that there would come a day when the Emperor had to take sides.

It upset Kaeso to see the true Romans under such serious illusions. They clung to the idea that it was all just a judicial error, while what they should have been doing was preparing themselves to face death. Kaeso tried to explain that there was no mistake, and that Nero, whom he had had the honour of meeting at only too close quarters, knew exactly what he was doing. But he found it difficult to get them to understand.

During the last days of the month the process of filling the prison was completed by the arrival of those leaders of the sect who were not citizens. Most of these were Jewish, Syrian or Greek priests and bishops. Being more accustomed than the native-born Romans to keeping a wary eye open for trouble, they had got wind of what was afoot and tried to escape. Finally, at the beginning of September, on the IV of the Nones, the anniversary of the battle of Actium, a last place was found for Peter. He had been arrested on the right bank of the Tiber, in the gardens of Caesar, where he had gone and camped discreetly among the refugees to whom Nero had given shelter there. But one of Tigellinus' Jewish agents had tracked him down. Peter did in fact have the characteristic appearance of a pious Jew, but Jesus had got him out of the habit of washing his arms to the elbow before eating, as was the strict custom among the Pharisees and even among the average God-fearing Jews.

Peter was shattered. He would have expected a disaster to strike Jerusalem
– Jesus had predicted the destruction of Jerusalem in the near future.
Yet it was Rome which had burned, and the Christians were accused of
setting fire to it. But after all, if Jesus had not said a word about the
incident, it was perhaps because what happened to Rome was of relatively
little importance compared with what happened to Jerusalem? Jesus was
not a Jew for nothing. There was another reason for Peter's surprise and
distress. The size of the cruel and dishonouring persecution was out of all
comparison with the troubles they had encountered hitherto, if only
because it was a persecution ordered by Caesar himself, in the capital of
the world. The Evil One had been laying it on rather thick, which made it
all the more obvious that Heaven had let him. Was the end of time at
hand?

The apostle tried to comfort his faithful, but he was having difficulty
comforting himself. Kaeso's conversation was the only thing that cheered
him up a little. That was scarcely surprising. What could a Christian in
distress expect from another good Christian in the way of consolation?
Nothing of which he could not predict every detail in advance. Whereas
Kaeso remained, at heart, insensitive to the metaphysical dimension of
the events. The injustice of the extermination of the Christians did, of
course, touch him, but only in the same way as any other dreadful historical event of which he had previously heard. Since his misfortune was of a
personal nature, it was only to be expected that he should keep his spirits
up and look at the situation objectively. His calm attitude had an in-
vigorating quality in that general atmosphere of religious despair.

Since the gaolers did their usual work without any particular animosity,
and showed the consideration due to Roman citizens, the condemned
were able to keep a few contacts with the outside world. Kaeso and the
other well-off inmates had some decent food brought in, and everyone
shared in it. But terrible news gradually filtered in through the stoutly-
made closed doors.

Since the days of Tiberius the emperors had been laying out gardens, and extending them, in the area of the Vatican Hill, which rose to the north-west of Rome, beyond the Campus Martius and the Tiber. Nero had put the latest grandiose touches to them and had also finished the Circus, which Caligula had started by digging out part of the hillside. The beauty and calm of these gardens, far from the hustle and bustle of the city, were much appreciated. But because the Circus was so far away and had two rivals, it had attracted very small audiences. Nero, who had discreetly made his first clumsy attempts at driving a chariot there, was very fond of the setting.

The fire had destroyed the Circus Maximus and the Circus Flaminius, Nero's vast wooden amphitheatre and even the ancient amphitheatre of Taurus, to the south of the Campus Martius. The obvious thing to do, therefore, was to take over the Circus of Nero, in the gardens of the same name, and hold the Games there, until such time as something better was available. Exceptionally, all types of entertainment except plays were to be shown there. (The three Roman theatres had been left untouched by the scourge.) And in fact lots of refugees were still camping out in the waste-land areas of the Campus Martius, and for them the Circus of Nero was quite close.

From the Ides of September onwards there were a succession of races, hunts, gladiatorial fights at all levels, and various athletic competitions, not forgetting the long-awaited executions of condemned criminals, in which the lion's part was reserved for the Christians.

They were torn apart by wild beasts, crushed by elephants, forced to appear in all sorts of legendary poetic deaths. Little children, sewn up in animal skins, were hunted by savage dogs while their mothers were being disembowelled by panthers. But the emperor's concern as both aedile and artist found its most memorable expression in the first attempt at lighting the city by night. From Rome to the Vatican gardens the Triumphal Way and the bridge were lit up by rows of Christians covered in pitch and impaled or crucified in the late afternoon, and then set on fire at nightfall. The gardens were similarly lit. And in the Circus the shows went on at night by the light of incendiaries burning around the rim of the vast building. Although roasting flesh was not the most pleasant of smells, the whole scheme was madly original and the good old *plebs* could hardly fail to appreciate the fact.

At the same period there was such an abundance of condemned criminals that the three theatres outside the city walls were playing continuously. They were staging pornographic productions which raised this exacting art to heights never before achieved. Nero had entirely understood that Euripides was no longer appropriate. To win back and firmly establish a popularity which the catastrophe had brought into question again, he had nobly decided to pay less attention than ever to his own delicate personal tastes. On stages quivering with excitement there could at last be seen on a grand scale the fulfilment of that requirement in the best Roman tradition, that virgins should not be put to death. Donkeys, billy-goats, dogs, a whole unexpected menagerie of animals, and the least sensitive and most self-confident actors, all indulged themselves with gusto until such time as a picturesque death had its effect. The ecstatic public cheered its emperor, and the long-standing theatre buffs shook their heads in melancholy gratitude and wondered whether, after that, there was anything really spicy left to see?

Sometimes, on those mild September nights, as Nero was driving his chariot through his brightly-lit gardens – and wrinkling his nose in disgust the while – faced with the cries of joy of a delighted populace he would ask himself: 'What would it have been like if I'd been a cruel man?'

In the Tullianum even the most indignant of the Roman citizens had finally fallen silent, if only out of a sense of shame. They only risked being strangled or beheaded, which were minor unpleasantnesses compared with the fate awaiting the others. They had in any case lost all hope of surviving, and were beginning to grasp, in the claustrophobic and promiscuous atmosphere which grew constantly more oppressive, that they were living through an unparalleled period in the city's history and that they must nonetheless die like true Romans.

Apart from an apocalyptic bishop who had started to 'speak in tongues' in a way which exasperated everyone, those leaders of the sect who were not Christians were preparing themselves for martyrdom in a peaceful but not particularly enthusiastic fashion. Physical fear of what they were to undergo haunted them day and night. As this was the first persecution worthy of the name there was no precedent from which they could draw inspiration for their thoughts or on which they could model their behaviour. Where martyrdom was concerned the poor things were absolute pioneers.

To keep their spirits up they sang and prayed. Peter blessed and distributed the bread and wine, when there was any available. Kaeso abstained: his first communion had not left an indelible mark in his memory – a fact which, it has to be admitted, was entirely his own fault, since God only ever gives us what we bring Him.

As dawn approached, Peter would awake with a start, moaning pitifully. For, though many cockerels had been roasted for Nero's banquets, those belonging to the guardians of the Capitol were still in full voice, and the gaolers themselves had a little poultry-yard, and sold the eggs to the captives at extortionate prices.

One morning Peter confessed to Kaeso, who was sleeping wrapped up in his cloak beside him:

'There are cocks everywhere, in town as much as in the country. There's nowhere I can go to sleep without fear of being woken in this cruel way. I know what time the cocks crow in every place I've been through. In Jerusalem they start much earlier than in Rome – while it's still pitch black. But, in any case, once the first cock has given the signal, the others all take up their trumpets, and the music goes on and on, to shame me all the more for my repudiation of Jesus. Every time I used to wake up shouting and weeping, my late wife, who was my inseparable companion, would kick me in the shins.'

'It would have been more charitable of Jesus to call on the services of a nightingale.'

'Even a cock is too sweet-voiced a bird as a punishment for what I did.'

'I read in the writings of your secretary Mark that Jesus is supposed to have said to you: "I tell you this . . . before the cock crows twice you yourself will deny me three times." Was it after the horrible bird's first or second crowing that you realized your offence?'

'After the second, as I told Mark myself. But now one is enough!'

'Why do you let Luke put a false version around?'

'What does it matter? Will there ever be a Christian stupid enough to get in a stew over details like that?'

'Yes, I can see your point of view. But if, despite Nero, your religion conquers the world, stupid Christians will become legion.'

Of course, Peter invoked the protection of the Holy Spirit, asking it to spread its wings over the Church. Hope was an intimate part of his make-up.

But his body was the weak point.

Kaeso had had long talks with Peter. He had told him the story of his excessively short and action-packed existence, and Peter, in turn, had confided interesting information about himself to Kaeso. Faced with a fellow Christian, a man of scruple is condemned to play the part of the Christian. Faced with an amiable, unprejudiced stranger, the tragic actor can take off his conventional mask, and the man beneath will appear in his relative nudity. With Kaeso, Peter sought relief from the long periods of constraint, which had been particularly severe because he had not been at all prepared to play the overburdening role for which the Divine Director had cast him without prior consultation. So Kaeso was getting to know him very well. He was a simple man, and he found him more sympathetic than Paul, who was always so complicated and tormented.

In the light of this sympathy the affair of the denial took on its proper proportions in Kaeso's mind. Peter had lived with Jesus for a long time, and had loved him deeply and without reservations from the start. And yet he had been capable of denying him in circumstances whose gratuitousness might seem baffling. He had merely been asked, in a courtyard, whether he happened to be a friend of the accused. There was nothing to suppose that such people would be troubled in any way, and indeed they had not been, as long as they kept quiet. Peter had not been playing a trick: he had not conned the enemy as a way of being of service to his Lord. For absolutely no reason he had been paralysed by an insensate terror, and had denied Jesus three times, despite every fibre of his personality, simply because he was devoid of physical courage. It was only his body that had spoken.

Kaeso said to Peter:

'You're scared stiff, aren't you?'

'Who wouldn't be, in my position?'

'I think you're more frightened than other people. But you've got plenty of excuse. You were told long ago that you would share the same fate as Jesus, whose cockerel wakes you up with a start every morning. That's enough to undermine you. And then, unfortunately, you're timid by nature. To be more precise, you find it harder to bear fear of suffering than suffering itself.'

'Yes, yes, that's it exactly. I envy your gladiator's sang-froid.'

'You've got to react against it.'

'But how?'

'You've got to prepare yourself for your crucifixion the way gladiators prepare themselves for a fight. I have, as you know, briefly been a gladiator, and as a lad I saw plenty of victims of crucifixion squirming on their crosses. So I'm well placed to advise you.'

'I'm listening.'

'In the first place you should say to yourself: "I've signed a contract. I shan't escape from my assignation with death."'

'Yes.'

'Then you should say to yourself: "Whatever I have to go through will seem pretty long to me, but in fact it will only take up a very brief space of time."'

'Yes.'

'You'll also have the advantage of the fact that, in moments of high emotion such as love and death, time stops. The minutes no longer seem to keep coming one after another. Since you'll be unaware of what precedes or follows, you'll only suffer for a moment.'

'The Greek words you're using are not very familiar to me, but I can grasp the gist. When Jesus was transfigured, time stopped then, too. I couldn't say how long it all took.'

'That's an excellent analogy. You'll be transfigured by your suffering, and the sand will cease to run in the timer. A century will seem like a wink.'

'I would still prefer a wink.'

Kaeso laughed roundly, and went on:

'To be really sure, you need to know the right technique.'

'Isn't that the executioner's business?'

'No, it's also a matter for the victim.'

Kaeso gave Peter a detailed explanation of the mechanics of death by crucifixion, with its alternation of high and low positions, the victim being able to breathe in the former but asphyxiating in the lower.

'I already knew all that. Like everyone else, I imagine. So?'

'In the Sestertium field,' Kaeso went on, 'I've previously noticed a difference in behaviour between city slaves, who had never prepared themselves to die like that, and footpads, who, like you, had long foreseen that they would die on the cross. The slaves stretched up on the balls of their feet to get a bit of air, with that instinctive reaction which makes the most wretched of men cling to life, and those who were as strong as you are prolonged their own agony in consequence. Whereas the bandits stared in hate at the soldiers, sightseers, and curious children, and didn't hesitate to deprive them of their due by drawing themselves in and fighting as hard as they could against the upward movement which instinct required of them. So much so that some conscientious executioners would be irritated by such insolent cheating, and would jab their spears at these individuals who huddled up in the lower position, so as to stir them into taking a good breath of air. The victim of crucifixion who succeeds in controlling his movements – though it does take a lot of will-power – dies very quickly.'

'That's not what Jesus did, though he was big and strong.'

'The crucified Jesus still had things to say, and could only say them by pulling himself up.'

'If the good robber had applied this technique used by hardened bandits, he might well have died before he could repent.'

742

'You've been doing penitence for long enough already!'

'For sins like mine . . .'

'Well, I'll teach you another trick, which couldn't be confused with suicide and is equally effective. Unless you're determined at all cost to suffer as much as possible?'

'I am too humble to be so presumptuous.'

'That's a variety of humility which does credit to your good sense. The device in question won't work if a condemned man is brought to the field of execution with his cross-piece on his back, and the upright poles are there waiting for him. But we've heard that crucifixions are being carried out to provide public lighting across the Campus Martius and the gardens of Nero and right up to the *spina* in the Circus Vaticanus, which is a sandy space on either side of the obelisk. What's more, there are a lot of people to crucify every evening, and soldiers in a hurry aren't in a position to choose their sites, because Nero, who's an artist, is after an orderly, decorative lighting effect.'

'What are you getting at?'

'When the soldiers are dealing with light soil, where the upright posts would have to be sunk a long way into the ground to avoid the risk of their tipping over, it's customary to place the cross-bar at a quite low height above the ground and at an angle, so that one arm is pointing in the direction in which the cross seems likely to tilt. This gives maximum stability and the victim is crucified head downwards. In that position asphyxia is very rapid. So make every effort to be crucified like that. There may be some virtuous Christians among the executioners. If necessary, try to change places with someone who doesn't know any better . . .'

It was Peter's turn to laugh.

'That would be an unpleasant thing to do to anyone. But there are indeed some Christians among the soldiers, and they may not have been denounced yet.'

'I hope so for your sake. Better burn dead than alive. And the Christians can always say that you had yourself crucified upside-down out of humility . . . I can see from your smile that you like the idea. That's the smile you must have had in the days – before you met Jesus, of course – when you used to sell "off" fish to toffee-nosed Pharisees.'

This time they laughed together. A cock belatedly let out a strident crow, and Peter's expression changed. Kaeso made a renewed effort to get his spirits up:

'If you want to walk with an unfaltering step to meet your fate, as befits a leader, you really must give up weeping over the fact that you denied your Master. Tell yourself that Jesus was a wonderful judge of men and that he chose those around him accordingly. Why did he choose the criminal Judas if not deliberately so that he'd betray him? And why did he choose you, and put you at the head of his Church, if not so that you could deny him like a coward, in the most unforgivable way?

Just remember this: your successors will be named by men; but you were designated by Christ in person, when you were only thirty-odd years old. One can only conclude that you represent his ideal for the post. You're of very humble birth. You only had a very rudimentary education. You're not a brilliant speaker or writer. Your works, despite the talents of a few secretaries, won't be of great significance. You're a bit of a coward. And you're best known for having betrayed Jesus, like Judas – with the difference, in your case, that, out of love for him, you preferred to stay alive afterwards.

Well, personally, I've got this to say to you: as a man who's been chosen from thousands by Christ, after mature reflection, as an incomparable example for all Christians in the future, and particularly for your immediate successors, it's high time you learnt to hold your head up. You'll be raising your feet to Heaven soon enough. Through your timid voice Jesus whispers to us that education and money encourage pride, that the less a leader says, the fewer stupid things he risks saying, that the kind of courage which really counts is the courage to admit one's faults and mistakes frankly and openly, repent of them and try to put them right, and that the most important virtue is that of not despairing at having committed such faults. Peter, you'll go a long way . . . when you're dead.'

Peter felt a little better. The idea that Jesus could have picked him out precisely because of his modesty and his fallibility reduced the significance of his insufficiencies and betrayals.

Kaeso went on:

'Luke told me that an angel once got you out of Herod's prison, that you walked on the water and brought a dead man back to life. Those were the days . . .'

'God does miracles for us, or through us, while He needs us for His service. His grace no longer works when we only need it for ourselves. I know that, today, my hour has come. But you have been of great comfort to me, and I should like to do something for you.'

'If it's in the service of God, then a miracle must be possible?'

744

'Of course. And I should love to give you faith, the ultimate in miracles. What's the obstacle?'

That was a question to which the answer was both very simple and very complicated. Nonetheless Kaeso tried to give an answer.

'I nearly slept with my stepmother, who brought me up and whom I adored. I drove her to suicide. I also drove to the same end a man who loved me and had shown me very great kindness. In the process I sexually abused a young girl, condemned my father to death by my indifference, and would have raped his concubine, whom I'd just freed, if Nero hadn't set fire to Rome. After my appearance in the arena I was, briefly, the emperor's favourite. I planned the assassination of an actress. I had myself baptized as part of a pretence I was staging and asked for the gift of the Holy Spirit as a talisman. I continually deceived and disappointed everybody. And yet I'm intelligent, and my intentions have always been of the very best. So naturally I wonder what ill-intentioned imbeciles get up to. Perhaps they do good?'

'I can see what's worrying you. You have the impression that man is the plaything of accident and chance, that the relationship between intentions, actions and results is uncertain . . .'

'I even feel that the better the intentions, the more deplorable the consequences.'

'I can understand you, precisely because I feel just the same. For years on end we've been preaching pure love non-stop, and only getting hatred in return. What we're going through now is the crowning reward of our actions.'

'To judge from this massacre, your intentions must have been even better than mine. Take things easy, do!'

'If things are as they are, it's because the Gospel of Jesus Christ has put the Devil into a state of frightful rage, and nothing exasperates him more than good intentions. As soon as he spots a good intention anywhere, the Devil hurries off to twist it, vitiate it, make it look ridiculous, and see that it turns out disastrously. He hopes that the Just will become weary. But the Just are tireless. Even you, here in this horrible Tullianum prison, after all your disillusions, have still been prepared to spend your time giving me courage, with great kindness and much ingenuity. The scandalous distance between our good intentions and what actually happens should not trouble us. It's a sign that God has called us to thwart the plans of the devil. It's a very abstract idea, but it can be seen everyday . . .'

'You never fished that Greek adjective "abstract" out of Lake Tiberias?'

'I think I learnt it from Paul . . .'

'Oh dear! You're on a slippery slope. It's time for you to withdraw before you ruin your fine reputation for simplicity. Jesus never talked like that.'

'He spoke more beautifully than anyone else. And you can trust His word, because I saw Christ risen from the dead as well as I see you now. And one evening, while we were eating side by side, I even touched his arm, just as I'm touching yours.'

In the half-dark Peter's hand had alighted on Kaeso's thigh, not his arm. The Devil is fond of sinister little jokes of that sort. The believer finds them yet another reason for believing.

Kaeso would have needed more than that to be convinced.

Peter suddenly said to him: 'You won't leave here without being touched by faith. I say it to you as a humble fisherman and a great sinner. That's the gift God has to offer you, because He wants to see you at closer quarters. Jesus also died for those who would like to believe, because that's the first step to loving Him.'

Shortly afterwards Kaeso received a brief note from Marcus junior.

'M. Aponius Saturninus to his brother Kaeso, greetings.

I did indeed receive a goodbye note from our father, in which he revealed his intention of dying like Cato of Utica. The news of his death has reached me along with that of your fight against Pugnax. Friends have also told me that Selene survived. I am not sorry to hear it. I certainly don't approve of your conduct, but what would be the point in reproaching you for it? You will do it better than I could. I simply want to bring home to you a truth which you seem to have overlooked. Our father was not a bad man and he loved us both dearly. I often heard him talk about you with tears of joy and pride, and he brought you up with jealous care. You were his whole life, and he died the day he realized, to his horror, that you did not love him, despite everything he had agreed to put up with for your sake. You had the right to have reservations about the compromises which he endured purely in your interest. You did not have the right to refuse his love contemptuously. A father's love is always worth having. His intentions had always been excellent. You should not expect more of a man than that. I am sorry for you, and I am not withdrawing my affection from you. Thank you for your goodbye letter. Farewell.'

Kaeso wept as though he had heard a cock crow. When Peter asked him, he translated the Latin text into popular Greek. The effort brought on a new fit of crying.

Peter then said to him: 'Jupiter was the father of the gods. Jesus revealed to us that his Father is also the Father of mankind. He's a Father whose actions and intentions are in harmony. You've lost your father, after bemoaning his shortcomings. I shall give you another, who won't disappoint you.'

Kaeso thought long and hard about the idea. Contrary to what might have been reasonably expected, it was his impious elder brother who was well on the way to converting him.

From now on a few victims were taken out of the prison every day. They left putting a good face on things. Waiting is the worst part of the ordeal. The underground chamber in the Tullianum was not being used. The emperor wanted every execution to be public.

Peter was to die on the II of the Ides of October, the festival of the Fontinalia (divine springs), and the tenth anniversary of Nero's accession to the throne.

Kaeso was dispatched on the dawn of the day before the Kalends of October. He had asked for the services of Subrius, and the favour had been off-handedly granted. The tribune was said to be adept with a sword.

The little procession set off in the direction of Aquae Salviae, a field of execution a little to the side of the road to Ostia. Kaeso was accompanied by a certain Savinian, a Syrian bishop whom Peter had sent to found the Church in the Gallic city of Agendicum – later to be called Sens. He kept saying: 'Whatever will happen to my flock in Agendicum?' Kaeso told him that only Jesus was irreplaceable, and he calmed down.

As they were going along the Via Ostiensis, Subrius remarked to Kaeso:

'You seem very cheerful this morning?'

'That's because I am going to find my Father.'

Given the reputation of the late Aponius, Subrius was very surprised at this declaration.

The tribune had two impeccable regulation graves dug: Kaeso complimented him on them. Savinian's head fell, sliced off with a straight, clean cut. Kaeso was almost ashamed, when he thought of the victims of crucifixion. He was being spoiled more than he deserved.

And soon the time of his ordeals was over.

*

Three years later, one morning in summer, Cn. Pompeius Paulus followed the same road as Kaeso.

He had unwisely returned to Rome after the persecution, trusting in his status as citizen and in the lasting quality of Roman law. In so doing he had posed a disagreeable legal problem for Tigellinus. The Prefect did not believe for one moment that the Christians could ever constitute a serious danger to the empire, and in that respect he reflected the general opinion of those who claimed to be in the know. But his attention had been especially drawn to the case of Paul, whose dossier was only too thick. There was, however, no specific criminal law against the Christians, and Paul had been away from the city at the time of the fire. Tigellinus had resigned himself to bringing an ordinary charge of *lèse-majesté*, with the help of false witnesses, who unfortunately looked only too like what they were. Paul had recourse to every procedural device possible, and the trial had given signs of going on for ever. Tigellinus then recalled Seneca's suggestion at the meeting of the Imperial Council, and eventually tried out the expedient. Paul, as a citizen of Jewish birth, had demanded that he be allowed the Jewish dispensation from making sacrifices, but as he could not deny that he was a Christian, judgement had swiftly been found against him. The precedent, duly noted by writers on legal matters, was to put ideas into people's heads later on.

While Nero, in the grip of increasing rapture, was singing in Greece, Paul went to execution at Aquae Salviae. He had really only defended his last case on principle. He was tired of all these fights, which had exhausted his scant store of strength, and he was not sorry that it was all over.

During the years that had passed, he had increasingly had the impression that the struggle between Jesus and the world was an unequal one, for the Lord was really asking too much of fallen human nature. Christianity could not last. It was running counter to the all-too-human course of history and would never be more than a parenthesis. When the gospel had been preached to the whole world, and everyone put in a position to make his or her choice, the end of time would come, and God would condemn a world which had refused to acknowledge him as its Father. But was the universe in which faith was to be on offer to be identified with the Roman empire and the few adjacent nations?

As he walked along beside the Tiber on the Ostia road, Paul mulled these things over in his head. The idea that, for 1,900 years, Christian ideas were to dominate and spread would have seemed to him totally improbable. It was absolutely clear that it would take compulsion to make ordinary people give up exposing children, divorcing freely and committing sodomy, attending pornographic or violent entertainments, worshipping a range of helpful divinities, and exterminating at will any minorities which that cold-blooded monster National Interest designated for public attack. If Paul had been told that 1,900 years later Nero would come back with greater means and greater determination, on a planetary scale, despite the fact that the truth of Jesus had been preached throughout the Earth, he would have replied that this general apostasy probably heralded the end of the world. If he had also been told that new incendiary Neros would play around with the atoms of Epicurus, he would have considered the Apocalypse as just round the corner. But if it had been added that, after more than 2,000 years of subjection and dispersal, the Jews would come back to Israel and, weapons in hand, create an independent state, he would have held it to be more or less certain that the end of time had come. When history goes backwards to that degree, it is usually heading for the exit. But, despite everything, Paul might have been wrong . . .

He stepped, unawares, on Kaeso's grave, which was now overgrown with grass.

Several friends had come with him – Tigellinus, who had reason to believe in the innocence of the Christians, had not bothered to ban them from the city – and were standing about him weeping. Paul said to them: 'Instead of crying, why don't you get on and choose a successor to Peter? I hereby officially announce that I won't be a candidate for the post.' The joke raised a few smiles through the tears.

As Paul became impatient at the slowness with which the perfect rectangle of his grave was being dug out, the centurion said to him:

'You're in a hurry. Got a date?'

'You don't know how right you are. And it'll be the first time too.'

'Who with?'

'A Man.'

Paul was a little ashamed of this unseasonable witticism and added in a very quiet voice: 'I've been waiting too long for this moment.'

Kaeso had stepped gladly out to meet his Father. Paradise is there to fulfil every hope.

By this time the abortive conspiracy of Piso had already, step by step, led to the deaths of a host of ambitious and imprudent men. Nero's timid mistrust had grown worse, and the numbers of people 'in disgrace' had taken on epidemic proportions. Seneca and his wife had cut their wrists, but Nero had ordered the latter to be saved on her death-bed, and she had not had the insolence to try again. Petronius had also cut his wrists, but in his Campanian villa at Cumae. Before he died, as he had left no heir who could be affected, he sent the emperor some beautifully phrased, malicious comments on his novel debauches: Petronius himself had only rarely and reluctantly taken part in them. But he said not a word about Nero's artistic talents, both because they were genuine, and because he had praised them too much in the past. Seneca's brother Gallio had also been sacrificed, as had his other brother Mela, Lucan's father, and Lucan himself, Thrasea, and Lucius, the last of the Silani.

In June of the following year, on the anniversary of the death of his first wife, Octavia, Nero in his turn was murdered. He was the victim of a final aristocratic plot, which the complicity of troops in the provinces and of the Praetorian guard had made inescapable. During his dying moments, when everyone but Sporus had abandoned him, he had continually repeated the words 'What an artist the world is losing in me.' What better proof could there be that his whole life had been inspired and directed by love of art? The Roman *plebs*, whom he had so spoiled, kept an indelible, sympathetic memory of him. For many years those who remembered him with nostalgia came and put flowers on his tomb during the summer, while turbulent pretenders to his identity kept making their appearance. But it was not the ordinary people who wrote history. They confined themselves to the business of living.

The same discreetness which had been the hallmark of Peter's life, his stay in Rome and his martyrdom was to accompany the destiny of his remains, as if the Apostle, now that he was crowned in glory, had playfully exerted his energies on making sure that they could not be found.

Traditionally Peter was supposed to have been martyred in the Circus Vaticanus. He was obviously not buried on the spot, a stone's throw from the north-west wall of a Circus which was in full swing, in pleasure gardens which at that date had not yet been designated as a cemetery. On the other hand it is certain that between 141 and 161 a commemorative monument was raised on that site, for the Romans had the excellent habit of dating the bricks. This leaves us to suppose that Peter's remains must have been brought to the Circus on that occasion. The function of the building was then altered, and the surrounding area gradually changed into a necropolis. It is possible that in 258 the aforementioned remains were hidden in the catacombs of Saint Sebastian, near the Appian Way, when the emperor Valerian confiscated the Christian cemeteries – a measure thought to be responsible for Valerian's death two years later. The emperor Constantine was later to erect the first Vatican basilica, an unforgettably sumptuous building, over the commemorative monument which doubtless sheltered Peter's grave. In the fifth and sixth centuries Rome was plundered five times by barbarian 'Aryan' heretics, who probably left the tomb itself alone. It is, unfortunately, only too certain that in 846 a Mohammedan fleet sailed up the Tiber and pillaged and desecrated the basilica of St Peter, which was not at that time fortified. Only in 1939 did the papacy authorize an examination of the tomb, something which had been constantly refused even before 846. Archaeological research led to the rediscovery of the commemorative monument dating from the years 141-61, but, as could easily have been predicted, the tomb was empty. As a slender consolation, close by were found remains which could have belonged to a second century pope, along with the skeleton of a mouse.

Fortunately the Peter who interests us is alive and well and learning Latin in Heaven.

The Holy Spirit bloweth where It listeth.

THE END

❊ Glossary ❊

ABECEDARII: those learning the letters of the alphabet

ADROGATIO: the full adoption of an independent adult

AEDILE: a class of important Roman officials whose duties included the provision of expensive public entertainments

AGNATIO: consanguinity on the father's side

AGORA: the market-place in a Greek city; also the place of public assembly and hence the assembly of the people itself

ALLIGATIO: the tying up of the vine shoots to a supporting structure

ALLIGATOR: the person whose job it is to tie up the vine shoots

ALTERA CENA: the second course of a meal

AMENTUM: the strap or thong of a javelin or similar weapon by means of which it could be thrown with greater force

ANDABATAE: gladiators whose helmets had no eye-holes, and who therefore had to fight 'blindfold'

ANKULE: see *amentum*

ANNONA: the corn supply, the goddess of the yearly harvest; see also *praefectus annonae*

ARMATURA: armour, equipment, i.e. the weaponry and protective clothing of a gladiator

ARTOCREAS: a meat pie

ARTOLAGANON: a kind of bread or cake, made from flour, wine, milk, oil, lard and pepper

ARTON EPIOUSION: 'daily bread' is the traditional English translation, but *epiousion* literally means 'approaching'; hence Kaeso's difficulty in understanding the phrase.

AS (pl. *asses*): a small copper coin

ATELLAN: a kind of popular, fairly unsubtle Roman farce

ATRIUM: the part of a traditional Roman house which constituted the living and reception room, and had an opening in the roof to admit light and rain-water (which was then collected in the *impluvium*, q.v.)

ATTILI: large fish of the sturgeon family, found particularly in the river Po

AUCTORATIO: a contract by which a free man hired out his services as a gladiator

AUGUR: a diviner of the future

AUGUSTALIS: a member of a college of priests (25 in number) instituted in honour of the emperor Augustus, after his death

AUGUSTIANI: a troop of young men, half of them aristocrats, half from the lower classes, assembled by the emperor Nero as his personal guard; chosen for their looks, they were expected to be sexually available to him

AUREUS (pl. AUREI): a gold coin

AUSPEX (pl. AUSPICES): one who foretells the future from the flight, singing or feeding habits of birds

BALLISTA: a giant military catapult, designed to hurl rocks and other large projectiles at the enemy

BASILIKOI PAIDES: troops of young men, on whom Nero modelled his Augustiani (q.v.), appointed as guards of honour by the rulers of the Greek kingdoms set up after the death of Alexander the Great

BELVEDERE: a summer-house with a pretty view

BESTIARIUS (pl. BESTIARII): one whose job it was to fight with wild beasts in the circus

BIGA (pl. BIGAE): a chariot drawn by two horses

BIREMIS: a galley with two rowers per bench (more traditionally thought of as a galley with two banks of oars)

BISSEXTILE YEAR: the Roman equivalent of a leap year

BULLA: a kind of amulet worn around the neck by children and ceremonially laid aside when they reached maturity

CAESTUS: a form of boxing glove, consisting of a strap of bull's hide studded with lead or iron, wound around the hands and lower arms

CALDARIUM: a room containing warm water for bathing

CANOPICUM: a kind of cake, named after the town of Canopus in Egypt

CANTICA: the songs in a Roman comedy

CARACOLE: an elaborate horse-riding manoeuvre

CARCERES: the starting-gates at a race course

CATILLO: plate licker – the nick-name of a type of large fish

CENA: dinner, a course at dinner

CENA LIBERA: open house

CENTUMVIRI: a bench of judges chosen annually to deal with civil lawsuits, especially those concerning inheritances

CERUSE: white lead, used as a cosmetic

CHILDREN OF SPURIUS: the official designation of illegitimate children

CITHARA: the Greek forerunner of the guitar

CIVIS ROMANUS: a holder of Roman citizenship; as such you were exempt from taxes and enjoyed important legal rights

CLARISSIMA: '*Clarissimus*' was a title given to distinguished public persons: their wives were addressed in the feminine form '*clarissima*', the equivalent of 'Your Excellency'.

CLIENT: In Republican Rome a client was a man dependent on a powerful patron to whom he rendered services and from whom he received protection; under the Empire the relationship degenerated until the clients were merely hangers-on, scrounging for food and money.

CLIVUS: a steep road

COEMPTIO: a form of marriage consisting in a mock sale of the parties to free the wife from certain legal obligations

COERCITIO: the right of a Roman magistrate to take any punitive action he felt necessary in the pursuit of his duties

COLLEGIA: guilds, fraternities, unions

COLONI: tenant farmers

COLUMBARIUM (pl. COLUMBARIA): dovecot, type of funeral monument

CONFARREATIO: a marriage ceremony in which an offering of bread was made in the presence of the *Pontifex maximus* (high priest) and ten witnesses

CONFLAGRATIO: a Stoic concept: at the end of each of a never-ending series of cycles the universe is absorbed into the divine fire, and then restarts

CONSUL: one of the highest officials of the Roman state, chosen annually

CONSUL SUFFECTUS: a consul chosen during the course of the year, to replace one who had died

CONVERSIO: physically means 'turning around'; hence 'change of state', and from this comes the English word 'conversion'

COSTUM: an Oriental aromatic plant, *Costus arabicus*

COTHURNI: high boots worn by actors in tragedy

CROTALA: castanets

CRUSTULUM (pl. CRUSTULA): a type of small cake

CUM MANU: with the husband having legal power over his wife

CURULE MAGISTRACY: The *sella curulis*, an inlaid ivory chair, was the official seat of office of the highest levels of officialdom: hence, a curule magistrate was the holder of one of a number of important posts

CUSTODES: the slaves in charge of the library

CYNIC: The Cynic school of philosophy was interested in the practical side of morality and regarded virtue as the sole basis of happiness, to be sought in freedom from wants and desires

DECEMJUGIS (pl. DECEMJUGES): a chariot drawn by a team of ten horses

DENARIUS (pl. DENARII): a silver coin

DENTEX: a Mediterranean fish mentioned by Roman natural historians but whose type has not been identified

DESULTORES: acrobatic riders who leaped from one horse to another without stopping

DIASPORA: dispersal – the emigration of a people to a number of widely distributed places

DIES COMITIALIS: a day on which the Public Assembly could meet and vote

DIES FASTUS: a day on which the law courts were open for business: therefore, a working day in general

DIES FUNESTUS: a day of public mourning, the anniversary of a national disaster (and therefore a public holiday)

DIES INTERCISUS: a half-holiday (days on which morning and evening were holidays, but the afternoon was not)

DIES NEFASTUS: a day on which no business could be conducted

DIGNITAS: the Roman code of honourable behaviour

DIGRESSIO: in oratory, digression was an acknowledged stylistic feature

DIRIBITORIUM: the building in which votes were counted

DISPENSATOR: a slave acting as steward or treasurer, who dealt with small financial transactions

DIURNA: daily records

DOLCE VITA: high living

DOLIUM (pl. DOLIA): a large storage jar

DOMINE: master (a form of address)

DOMINUS, DOMINA: master, mistress

DORIAN: the last of the Greek-speaking peoples to settle in Greece: associated with the language and culture of the Peloponnese

DRACHMA: a Greek coin

DURA LEX, SED LEX: A hard law, but it's the law

EDITOR: the person responsible for presenting the games

ELECTRUM: amber/a mixed metal resembling amber in colour

EMPORETICA: wrapping paper

ENCOMIUM: a speech in praise of something or someone

ENDROMIDES: coarse woollen wraps which athletes slipped round themselves after exercise

EPHEBE: an adolescent male

EPHEBIA: a club for adolescent males

EPICUREAN: a follower of the philosopher Epicurus, who believed that in life one should rely on the evidence of one's senses and reject all notion of supernatural powers: associated with the pursuit of pleasure

EPIDEICTIC: the oratory of display, such as speeches for delivery at festivals, funeral orations, speeches to honour prominent individuals

EPISCOPI: bishops

EPITYRUM: a dish made of preserved olives

EPULONES: a college of priests who superintended the sacrificed banquets made to the gods

ESSEDARIUS: a gladiator who fights from a chariot

ETHNARCH: governor of a people or province, a title given to the rulers of certain Jewish communities in the Roman period

EUKAIRIA: the doctrine of making one's rational best out of the situations with which chance presents one

EXOPLASIAI: a form of procession, to display the participants in an entertainment

EXORDIUM; the opening section of a speech

FACTIO: a team at the races, and its supporters, who adopted the colours of the team

FALERNIAN: a much-prized wine from Campania in Southern Italy

FAMILIA: household, i.e. all the slaves belonging to one master

FASCES: a bundle of wooden rods, fastened together with a red strap, and enclosing an axe: the symbol of authority carried before certain high officials

FLAMEN (pl. FLAMINIA): a type of priest

FORS FORTUNA: the goddess of Pure Chance

FORTUNA EQUESTRIS: the goddess Fortune of the Cavalry

FORTUNA HUIUSCE DIEI: the goddess of the Fortune of This Day

FORTUNA OBSEQUENS: the goddess of Favourable Fortune

FORTUNA PRIVATA: the goddess of Private Destiny

FORTUNA PUBLICA: the goddess of Public Destiny

FORTUNA RESPICIENS: the goddess of Providence

FORTUNA VIRGINALIS: the goddess of Maiden's Fortune

FORTUNA VIRILIS: the goddess of Male Fortune

FORUM: the Roman equivalent of the Greek *agora* – an open space for markets and for public assembly

FRIGIDARIUM: a room containing cold water for bathing

FRONTES: the two edges at the top and bottom of a papyrus roll

FRUMENTARII: strictly, the military department dealing with the distribution of corn supplies; used as a cover-name for the intelligence department

FUMARIUM: a smoke-chamber for maturing wine

FUNALIS (pl. FUNALES): an extra horse attached to a chariot at the opposite side to the others by a rope

FUNES: ropes

GARUM: a rich fish sauce or flavouring, made from fermented small fish and spices (see *liquamen*); the flavour of much Roman cooking depended on the cook's skill at adding *garum*

GAUSAPA (pl. GAUSAPAE): a shaggy towelling wrap

GENESIS: a horoscope, based on the position of the stars at one's birth

GENETHLIACI: a term for fortune-tellers who calculated the future on the strength of a client's date of birth

GENS (pl. GENTES): a group of families united together by a common name and by certain religious rites

GLOBULUS: a small dumpling or doughnut, rather like the modern Greek *loukou-madhes*

GNOMON: the metal indicator which casts a shadow on a sundial

GOLDEN MEAN: the perfect balance between two extremes

GRAMMARIAN: a person who studies/writes about structure and meaning in language

GRAMMATICUS: a teacher of grammar, and more widely of literature

GRASSATORES: muggers

GREGATIM: in flocks, in swarms, in a crowd

GUSTATIO: the first, light dish of a Roman meal: equivalent to *antipasti* or *hors d'oeuvre*

HALEX: a sauce or flavouring prepared from small fish, the sediment of *garum* (q.v.)

HAMUS: a kind of crescent-shaped cake, so named because of its resemblance to a fish-hook

HARUSPEX (pl. HARUSPICES): someone who foretells the future by examining the entrails of sacrificed animals

HEMICYCLIUM: a semi-circular place equipped with seats

HETAERA: a superior type of prostitute who was expected to have various skills, e.g. musical, in addition to her sexual ones

HIRCIA: large, rough-cut sausages reminiscent of blood-pudding

HYPOCAUST: the central heating system

HYPODORIAN, HYPOLYDIAN: two of the modes, or types of scale, on which Greek music was based

IDES: the 13th day of the month in all months except March, May, July and October, when it was the 15th

IMPERATOR: originally an honorific military title accorded to a successful general: eventually became synonymous with 'emperor'

IMPLUVIUM: the uncovered central space in the *atrium* (q.v.), usually including a rain-water tank

INFAMIA: formal disrepute, leading to loss of civil liberties

INSULA (pl. INSULAE): a tenement building, a shoddily built block of flats

INTER DUOS LUCOS: lit. 'between two groves' – a particular natural feature

IN VINO VERITAS: truth comes out when people are drunk

JUGERUM (pl. JUGERA): a measure of land, 28,800 square feet

KALENDS: the Roman name for the 1st day of the month

KHITON: a Greek tunic

KLEITORIS: the Greek word from which the English 'clitoris' comes

LAGANA: a kind of cake made with flour and oil

LANISTA (pl. LANISTAE): a trainer of gladiators

LARARIUM: the place where the household gods were kept

LARES AND PENATES: the household gods

LATIFUNDIA: a large agricultural estate

LATRUNCULI: lit. brigands: a game like draughts or chess

LECTISTERNIA: an offering in which the images of the gods, lying on pillows, were placed in the streets and all kinds of food set before them

LEIOSTREIA: oysters with smooth shells, regarded as a particular delicacy

LENO: a pimp

LEX PETRONIA: a law regulating the possession and treatment of slaves

LIBATION: a drink offering to the gods

LIBUM (pl. LIBA): a flat cake, made from flour, milk (or oil) and spread with honey

LIBURNA (pl: LIBURNAE): a light, fast sailing vessel

LICTOR: an attendant granted to certain Roman officials as a mark of their status

LIQUAMEN: a fish sauce: from a detailed recipe preserved in a Greek manual of agriculture we know that, strictly, *liquamen* was the fermented fish itself, *garum* the choicest liquid drained from it, and *halex* the dregs

LUCUBRUM: a night-light

LUCUNCULI: a kind of cake fried in oil, rather like a doughnut

LUDUS: games (i.e. public entertainments)

LUDUS MATUTINUS: games held in the morning

LYDIAN: one of the modes, or types of scale, on which Greek music was based

MAJOR ARCHILOCHIANS WITH ALTERNATIVE CATALECTIC IAMBIC SENARII: a very complicated verse form

MALOBATHRUM: an Indian or Syrian plant from which a costly oil was prepared

MAQUIS: rough heathland

MATHEMATICI: those who study mathematics and what were then considered the allied sciences, i.e. astronomy, music, geography, optics, even astrology

MEDITATIO MORTIS: meditation upon death: a Stoic notion, by which man overcame fear of death through contemplation of the idea of it

MENSAE SECUNDAE: second courses

META (pl. METAE): the conical columns set in the ground at each end of the Roman circus, providing the turning-posts and the eventual finishing line

META PRIMA: the first of the two *metae*

META SECUNDA: the second of the two *metae*

MILIARII: very successful charioteers – the name derives from *mille*, meaning a thousand

MINUTAL: a dish of minced meat

MIRMILLO: a kind of gladiator who wore a Gallic helmet, with the image of a fish for a crest; his equipment was heavy-helmet, rectangular shield, left leg-guard, right arm-guard and sword

MISSIO: the releasing of a gladiator from service

MORE FERARUM: in the manner of wild beasts

MORES: manners and customs

MORITURI TE SALUTANT: those who are about to die bid you farewell

MUNERARIUS (pl. MUNERARII): the person who paid for a *munus* (q.v.)

MUNICIPIUM (pl. MUNICIPIA): a town, particularly in Italy, which possessed the right of Roman citizenship but was governed by its own laws

MUNUS (pl. MUNERA): a public show, especially by gladiators

MURENA (pl. MURENAE): a fish of which the ancients were very fond, but which has not been identified

MYRTON: myrtle-berry: a Greek nickname for the clitoris

NARD: an aromatic plant and the balsam derived from it

NARRATIO: the story-telling part of a speech, the part in which the facts of the case are set out

NAUMACHIA: a battle fought at sea or on a lake

NE PLUS ULTRA: the absolute example

NOBILITAS: the Roman upper class

NOMEN: the middle name of the three which every free-born Roman had; the *nomen* distinguished one *gens* (q.v.) from another

NOMENCLATOR: a slave who told his master the names of his visitors

NOMINARII: those capable of reading whole words

NONES: the 5th day in each month, except in March, May, July and October, when it was the 7th

NUMMUS (pl. NUMMI): a coin, usually a small coin

NUNDINA (pl. NUNDINAE): market-day

OCHRE: a yellowish-brown pigment

OCULIFERIUM: lit. an eye-catcher, a window-display

OEGIDA: the inner wood of the larch tree

ONAGER: a wild ass

O TEMPORA! O MORES: What a way people behave nowadays!

PAEDAGOGUS: a slave who took children to school and was in charge of them at home

PAEDOTRIBES: a gymnastics teacher

PAEGNIARII: fencers who fought with buttons at the ends of their foils

PALAESTRA: the wrestling ground

PANEGYRIC: a speech full of praise of someone

PANIS CANDIDUS: white bread of the best quality

PANIS OSTREARIUS: oyster bread, i.e. a type of bread for eating with oysters

PANKRATION: a gymnastic contest which included both wrestling and boxing

PANTHEON: The Pantheon was the great temple of Jupiter, to which all the other known gods were admitted: hence the use of the word to mean 'all the gods'.

PARMA (SCUTAR): small, round shield

PARMULARIUS (pl. PARMULARII): a man armed with a *parma*

PATRES CONSCRIPTI: an honorific title given to members of the Roman senate

PATRONUS: the former master of a freedman or freedwoman

PELLITORY: a plant, *Anacyclus pyrethrum*, the root of which has a pungent flavour and was used for medicinal purposes

PENATES: see *lares and penates*

PERISTYLE: a place lined with columns on the inside

PERLUCIDA: very thin pancakes, so called because they were almost transparent

PERORATIO: the closing section of a speech

PETASUS: the broad-brimmed hat which was part of the distinctive costume of a member of an *ephebia* (q.v.)

PHARISEES: one of the two leading Jewish sects

PHAROS: lighthouse

PHRYGIAN: from Phrygia, a country in Asia Minor

PLACENTA: a type of cake made with honey and cheese

PLATONIC: relating to the Greek idealist philosopher Plato (427–348 B.C.)

PLEBEIAN: belonging to, or typical of, the lowest class of Roman citizen

PLEBS: the lowest class of Roman citizen (after the aristocracy, the senators and the knights)

POPA: the landlord of a tavern

POPINA: a tavern

POPULUS: the ordinary people

PRAEFECTUS ANNONAE: the official in charge of the corn supply

PRAELECTIO: the reading-aloud exercises with which lessons began

PRAENOMEN: the first of a Roman's three names, usually abbreviated when written down

PRAETOR: a magistrate charged with the administration of justice

PRAETOR URBANUS: the magistrate whose particular job it was to deal with the legal affairs of Roman citizens

PRESBYTERI: church elders

PRIMA CENA: first course

PRINCEPS: first, chief or most distinguished person

PROCONSUL: the governor of a Roman province

PROLETARIAN: lower class

PROLUSIO: a preliminary exercise

PROPOMPE: a form of procession, to display the participants in an entertainment

PUBLICANI: tax collectors

PULLATI: those wearing dark clothes, i.e. the ordinary people

PULVINAR: the imperial seat at the games

QUADRIGA (pl. QUADRIGAE): a four-horse chariot

QUAESTOR: a class of Roman official, most of whom dealt with financial affairs

QUINDECIMVIRI: a college of fifteen priests who had charge of the Sibylline books, from which, in times of danger, they had to divine how the peril might be averted

QUINQUENNIUM: a five-year period

QUINQUEREME: a galley with five rowers per bench

RETIARIUS (pl. RETIARII): a gladiator who fought with a net and trident

ROSTRUM (pl. ROSTRA): a stage or platform

RUDIARIUS (pl. RUDIARII): a retired gladiator, one who has been presented with the wooden sword symbolizing honourable discharge

RUDIS: the wooden staff presented to gladiators as a symbol of honourable discharge

SADDUCEES: one of the two leading Jewish sects

SATURNALIA: a festival celebrated in mid-December, in which presents were given, candles lit and slaves allowed to take the roles of master and mistress

SCEPTIC, SCEPTICISM: Scepticism was a school of philosophy founded by Pyrrho of Elis (c. 365–275 B.C.), who inferred from the contradictions presented by the evidence of the senses and the operations of the mind that definite knowledge of the nature of things is unobtainable.

SCUTARIUS (pl. SCUTARII): someone armed wtih an oblong shield

SCUTUM: an oblong shield

SECUTOR (pl. SECUTORES): a light-armed gladiator who fought with the *retiarii* (q.v.)

SELENITE: sulphate of lime in a crystalline form

SELLISTERNIA: religious banquets offered to female deities, whose figures were placed in a seated position

SEPTUAGINT: the Greek version of the Old Testament, made by a group of Palestinian Jews at the request of Ptolemy Philadelphus, one of the Greek kings of Egypt, in the third century B.C.

SESTERCES: small silver coins, each worth four *asses*

SICARII: assassins

SIGMA: the Greek letter Σ

SILPHIUM: a variety of the plant asafoetida

SINE MANU: with the husband having no legal power over his wife

SPARTAN: the Spartans were the great military power of Greece in the fifth century B.C.

SPELT: a species of grain related to wheat

SPINA: a low wall dividing the circus lengthwise, around which was the race-course

SPURIUS: illegitimate

STADION: a Greek furlong, probably about 194 yards: hence used as the name for the Greek running track, which was that length

STAGNUM: a piece of standing water

STOIC, STOICISM: The Stoic school of philosophy was founded at Athens *c.* 315 B.C. by Zeno. The Stoics regarded the world as an organic whole, consisting of an active principle (God) and of that which is acted upon (matter). Stoicism was in the main a doctrine of detachment from, and independence of, the material world.

STOLA: a kind of long female over-garment

STRIGIL: a scraper, made of horn or metal, used by bathers to remove the dirt from their skin

STROPHIUM: a band of cloth worn by females around the breasts, acting as a primitive brassiere

SUDATORIUM (pl. SUDATORIA): the steam-room in a Roman baths: rather like a Turkish bath

SUMAC: a preparation of the dried and chopped leaves and shoots of plants of the genus *Rhus*

SUMMANALIA: a circular cake used in offerings to Summanus, the god of nocturnal lightning

SURMULLET: a species of red mullet

SUPPOSITICIUS: a gladiator who replaced the first to be defeated; Kaeso would thus have had two opponents in quick succession

SYLLABARII: those who had learned to read whole syllables (instead of individual letters)

SYNTHESIS (pl. SYNTHESES): a kind of loose overall worn at meals

TABELLARIUS (pl. TABELLARII): a letter-carrier, courier

TABLINUM: a large room opening for its whole length along the wall of the *atrium* facing the door: screened off by a curtain: sometimes used as a study

TABULARIUM: the Public Records Office

TAEDIUM VITAE: ennui, spiritual weariness with life

TANTALUS: in Greek mythology, he was punished for various sins by being set in the underworld, thirsty and hungry, before food and drink which he could never reach. In another account of his punishment a great stone was suspended over his head, threatening to crush him and thus preventing him from enjoying the banquet

TEPIDARIUM: a lukewarm bathing room

TESSERA (pl. TESSERAE): a token, which could be used to gain entry to somewhere or entitlement to some service

TESSERA HOSPITALIS: a token, usually a small wooden block, which was divided between two friends, so that they might always recognize one another by matching the two halves of the block

THALAMITAE: the rowers in a galley who had the shortest oars (and therefore the least effort and the lowest pay)

THEMA: position of the astrological signs at one's birth (see *genesis*)

THERMOPOLIUM (pl. THERMOPOLIA): a place where warm refreshments were sold, hence, generally, a smart tavern

'THRACIAN', THRAEX: a kind of gladiator, so called because of his Thracian equipment, i.e. helmet, round shield, two leg-guards, right arm-guard and a short sword

THRANITAE: the rowers in a galley who had the longest oars and therefore the most work

THRION: a kind of pancake made with eggs, milk, lard, flour, honey and cheese, wrapped in fig-leaves

THOLIA: a conical hat with a broad brim, to keep off the sun

TIRO (pl. TIRONES): a newly recruited soldier, hence a beginner at anything, e.g. an inexperienced gladiator

TOGA: the long, broad, flowing outer garment worn by Roman citizens in time of peace

TOGA PRAETEXTA: the toga worn by high officials and all free-born children; it had a purple border

TOGA VIRILIS: the toga worn by an adult

TOGATI: those wearing togas, i.e. Roman citizens; tended to indicate the upper classes

TOMUS: a volume, i.e. a flat book, as opposed to the traditional Roman rolled book

TORQUE: a collar or neck-ornament consisting of a twisted band of precious metal, worn especially by the ancient Gauls and Britons

TRIA NOMINA: the standard three names (*praenomen*, *nomen* and *cognomen*) borne by all Roman citizens

TRICLINIUM (pl. TRICLINIA): a couch running round three sides of the table, for lying on during meals

TRIDENT: a three-pronged spear

TRIGA (pl. TRIGAE): a chariot drawn by three horses

TRIREME: a galley with three banks of oars, or three oarsmen per bench

TRIUMVIRI CAPITALES: superintendents of public prisons

TUBILUSTRIUM: the feast of trumpets, held twice a year (23 March and 23 May) to purify the trumpets used at sacrifices

TUNICATI: the common people (because they went around in tunics, without their togas on)

TU QUOQUE FILI: You, too, my son

TYROPATINA: a kind of cheese-cake

TYROTARICHUM: a dish of salt-fish prepared with cheese

UMBILICUS: a rod of wood or bone around which a Roman book was rolled

UNCIAL: the large, rounded, separate letter forms used in early Latin and Greek handwriting

USUS: lit. custom; a year's co-habitation established the relationship as, in practice, a marriage

VAPULATIO: a ritual flogging symbolically administered as an initiation rite for new gladiators

VELITES: light-armed troops

VENATIO (pl. VENATIONES): a hunting spectacle: a killing of wild beasts in the circus, for the entertainment of an audience

VIA (pl. VIAE): road

VIGINTIVIRI: a lower civil court

VIVARIUM (pl. VIVARIA): a cross between a zoo and a wild-life park

VOMITORIUM: a place to be sick, so that you could go on eating

ZEUGITAE: the middle rowers in a trireme (i.e. those between the *thranitae* and the *thalamitae*), so called because they gave the impression of being 'yoked' to the rowers on either side of them